The Chosen Series

MEGANNE

This book is a work of fiction. The names, characters, places, and incidents are products of the author's imagination or have been used fictitiously and are not to be construed as real. Any resemblance to persons, living or dead, actual events, locales, or organizations is entirely coincidental.

Copyright 2020 © Meg Anne

All rights reserved.

You may not copy, distribute, transmit, reproduce, or otherwise make available this publication (or any part of it) in any form, or by any means (including without limitation electronic, digital, optical, mechanical, photocopying, printing, recording, or otherwise), without the prior written permission of the author.

Permission requests can be sent to Meg Anne via email: Meg@MegAnneWrites.com

❀ Created with Vellum

Elysia
Grey Spire
Etillion
Talyria
Vyruul
The Queen's Aerie
Caederan
Endoshan
Emerald Ocean
Kiri's Palace
Tigaera
Daejara
The Mother's Tears
Sylverlands
Sea Of Mist
Keeper's Catacombs
Bael
Holbrooke Estate
Broken Vale
Forest Of Whispers
Ebon Isle
N
NW
NE
W
E
SW
SE
S

MOTHER OF SHADOWS

THE CHOSEN: BOOK I

MEG ANNE

For every girl that still carries a dream in her heart, this one is for you.

CHAPTER 1

Helena stretched a final time before sitting up in the behemoth wooden bed. *Have I already gotten used to this?* She ran her fingers along one of the glossy pillars before smoothing back the luxurious purple satin sheet and throwing her legs over the side. Bare feet met plush carpet, and she padded her way softly to the window; draping a silk robe over creamy shoulders and belting it loosely around her hips.

Peering out the large window she saw crowds of people already beginning to gather for today's festivities. A shiver of anxiety danced down her spine as a quiet knock sounded on the door.

"Enter," she called out distractedly, still taking in the gardens below.

"Good morning, Damaskiri," her maid, Alina, greeted cheerfully. Turning from the window, Helena offered Alina a nervous smile: the title still sounding strange to her ears. "Did you sleep well?"

Helena shook her head as she replied softly, "I was too nervous."

"Well, that's to be expected. I'd be nervous too if it were my life that was about to change so completely," Alina stated matter-of-factly as she opened the wardrobe and began to pull out the number of garments that comprised Helena's festival outfit.

"You'd think I would be used to that by now," Helena muttered with a wry smile.

Alina laughed as she moved efficiently around the room; stopping briefly to ask over her shoulder, "Would you like a bath drawn up, Damaskiri?"

Helena nodded in gratitude. "Yes, please Alina. Thank you."

With a wink, Alina smiled and sashayed into the bathing room.

The weak smile Helena had tried so desperately to keep in place began to falter as soon as the maid had left the room. Worry and doubt, Helena's constant companions in the last few weeks, were starting to creep into Helena's mind yet again. Numbly she folded herself into the soft velvet armchair and looked back toward the window. *How am I ever going to get through this? I can't possibly be who they say I am*, she thought desperately.

Apprehension had her stomach twisting in knots, and her back was stiff with tension. She ran trembling fingers through her chestnut locks while her mind raced through the events that had brought her to this moment. *Had it really only been a matter of weeks?*

HELENA SAT BACK on her heels, placing dirty hands on her knees and eyeing the flowers in front of her. After ensuring no weeds remained, she pushed herself to her feet as clumps of dirt fell softly from her simple blue work dress. She wiped the sweat from her brow and lifted her head to the warm kiss of the afternoon sun. A soft breeze stirred the strands of chestnut hair that had slipped from the knot at her neck. Smiling in contentment, her eyes roamed gently sloping green hills and the wide blue sky that surrounded her garden. Gardening was not easy work, but it was satisfying. It also was a far superior task to staying inside and washing dishes.

The familiar crunch of wheels on gravel had her spinning her head and shielding her eyes to see who was making their way to the little cottage. Recognizing the carriage that bounced and swayed down the path, her smile widened with joy. Helena began sprinting toward it.

The carriage came to a stop seconds before it would have crashed into her.

With breathless laughter, she waved in greeting. "Darrin! You've come back!"

A golden blond head preceded the tall, masculine body that unfolded itself from the confines of the carriage. Laughing green eyes took in the sight before him, and he walked toward his longtime friend with a smile.

Helena drank in the sight of him. She had not seen Darrin since he left to join the elite ranks of the Rasmirin, personal guards of the Damaskiri and her Circle. His sun-kissed skin still held its golden glow, and his emerald eyes had the same mischievous twinkle. He looked larger and more imposing than she remembered though.

"Hellion," he murmured with affection, using the childhood nickname he'd bestowed upon her years ago. She squinted her eyes in mock annoyance. "Been playing in the dirt again?" he continued in his lazy drawl.

She looked down at her dress and saw the smears of dirt in the soft blue fabric. With a helpless shrug, she responded, "What gave it away?"

He reached out a long finger and gently brushed the smudge of dirt her hand must have left across her face. She laughed, slapping his hand away.

"You've grown at least a foot since I saw you last."

She rolled her eyes at the exaggeration. "I was not a wee babe when you left, Darrin. It's only been a few years."

"Things have a way of changing," he said softly, his voice warm and deep.

"Will you tell me about everything? The Palace? The Chosen? The Circle?" she asked with excitement. Helena had always been curious about Tigaera's capital, Elysia, and its inhabitants. She felt worlds away from such wealth and luxury, not to mention the magic—since she was not one of the Chosen and therefore had no magical abilities herself.

He nodded, the warm glow in his eyes fading softly. "Yes, there is much to tell. But first, how is your mother, is she home?"

Helena's smile dimmed and wavered slightly. She tried to look down to hide the pain that lanced through her at the mention of her mother.

"Helena?" he questioned softly, tilting her chin up to meet his gaze.

"Mother passed last winter," she whispered, her voice hoarse with emotion.

"Oh, Helena," he murmured in sympathy, strong arms reaching to pull her to him. "Why didn't you write to me? I would have come."

"I didn't want to interfere with such important work. And there was nothing you could have done, besides." She held him tightly for a moment, accepting the comfort and strength he offered before stepping back, in control of her emotions again.

Darrin studied her a moment longer. "So it's just you then?"

She nodded. "Me and the horses. Anderson comes a few times a week to help fix things around here, and in return, I provide him with whatever extra food I can spare."

Darrin smiled at the mention of his grandfather. "I'm glad he has had you to look after him."

"Of course," she murmured in surprise. "He's family."

He shook his head with a chuckle. "Well, are you going to invite me in or make me stand out here in this blasted heat all day?"

"By all means," she said solemnly, gesturing that he should make his way into the cottage ahead of her.

"After you, Damaskiri," he said softly, earnest green eyes studying her.

She laughed at his game. "So I'm the 'Daughter of Spirit' now?" She shook her head in amusement. "You're setting your aim a little high for me, aren't you Darrin? I can hardly be the Damaskiri, especially seeing as how I don't have an ounce of magic in me."

The Damaskiri was the ruler of the Chosen, in very rare cases a Kiri or 'Mother of Spirit' might come into power, but it had been centuries since the last Kiri ruled. Helena's understanding of the Chosen was spotty at best, but even she knew that only a Damaskiri could call forth Spirit magic and only a Kiri could access all five branches of the Mother's magic equally.

He did not return her smile, nor did he make his way toward the door.

"A Rasmiri soldier never leaves his charge unprotected."

She raised an eyebrow at him and slapped him on the chest. "Maybe you have been in the sun too long, old friend. I believe you might be touched."

He scowled at her. "Just get inside, Hellion."

Confused, but still convinced he was playing one of their old games, she made her way into the cottage.

He followed closely behind her, and into the homey warmth of the cottage. It was too early for a fire to blaze in the hearth, but remnants of her meager lunch were still spread on the table.

"You never were one to pick up after yourself."

She shoved at him and threatened without heat. "If you are insinuating that my home is less than pleasant, I will skin you!"

He held up his hands with a laugh. "Not at all, merely appreciating that some things may never change."

She tossed one of her biscuits at him, aiming for his blond head. He plucked it from the air and devoured it in two bites. Smacking his lips in satisfaction, he asked for another. "Get them yourself, Rasmiri," she gestured to the basket on the table with her head. While he stuffed himself, she walked around the small room picking up discarded oddities in an attempt to tidy for her guest.

With a satisfied sigh, he sat back in the armchair his grandfather had gifted her mother when she first moved into the cottage. He ran his hands over the well-worn wood. She sat across from him on the similarly worn and faded couch, her fingers plucking unconsciously at the fabric. "So how long are you visiting?"

"I'm here on business," he corrected, leaning back in the chair and stretching his long legs out in front of him. She admired the bunch of muscles well displayed by, and encased in, the brown leather of his pants.

"What could the Circle possibly need to send you here for?" She asked, tilting her head inquisitively to the side.

The most recent Damaskiri had died suddenly only a few weeks ago without a new one being selected. The rituals and ceremony surrounding the rise of a new Damaskiri were mysteries to Helena, but she did know that when one came into their power, they would undergo a trial to test their magic. If they passed the trial, they would inherit the realm and claim the title. It was unheard of for a Damaskiri to die before her replacement had been found, which explains how that bit of gossip had managed to find its way to even her small cottage.

Reclining as he was, Darrin's face was covered in shadow. She felt a shiver of unease at the realization. "That's not an easy story to tell, Hellion."

"Perhaps you should start at the beginning then, Darrin," she snapped. She couldn't explain where the change in her emotion was stemming from, but she felt distinctly on edge.

He let out a long breath and seemed to weigh his words carefully before beginning. "Do you remember the stories we heard when we were children, Helena? About how the old masters had re-translated a prophecy?"

"The prophecy about the Mother of Shadows?"

Helena was very familiar with the story, if not the actual words of prophecy. It was foretold that a Kiri would rise, one whose magic would rival that of the First Born, the first of the Chosen. With her acceptance of the throne, the dawn of the Shadow Years would begin. A time when the Chosen would be tested, and those deemed unworthy destroyed.

He nodded. "The masters had discovered that their understanding of the prophecy was flawed. When the Kiri rose, like would call to like, and all of those found wanting would be destroyed."

Helena nodded. "Yes, the purity of her magic would destroy those that chose to corrupt it. The Shadow Years are to give rise to the rebirth of the Chosen; the promise of a new era. How is that flawed?"

"What do you suppose would happen, if the Kiri was corrupted?" he asked the question gently.

She scrunched up her face in thought. "Well, I suppose she would be destroyed too?"

He shook his head as he leaned forward. "Therein lies the flaw. 'Like calls to like,' remember? If she is corrupted, all those who remain pure will be destroyed."

Eyes wide, Helena's mouth turned into a small O of surprise as Darrin continued his tale. "The Circle and the remaining masters gathered that night and declared that when born, the prophesized girl would be taken away from Elysia. She would remain hidden, so as to be uncorrupted by the influence of those that would use her for their own purposes, until she came of age and it was time for her to inherit her throne."

"Imagine if we had known that growing up, Darrin! We would have spent many more afternoons pretending that we were searching for her instead of hidden treasure!" Helena snorted with laughter.

"Helena," he whispered, his voice serious, "It's not a story."

She shivered, suddenly cold; the chill that had found her earlier was now wrapping itself around her heart. "What are you saying?"

He shrugged. "She was hidden, her secret known only to those that sent her away. No one else knew where she was, until now."

The finality of his words stripped her of speech. A few of his earlier comments that she had dismissed as teasing came back to her. *After you, Damaskiri. I am here on business.*

"No," she whispered.

"I see you understand."

"But I have no magic, Darrin. How could I possibly be..." her voice faded.

He moved quickly to kneel in front of her. "I know that you are scared, Helena, but you needn't worry. Events were set into motion from the moment of your birth, and there are those that have planned for this. Your magic was bound so that you may lead a normal life so that it would be guaranteed to be pure. The binding will fade on your twenty-first name day when you come into both the throne and your power. There are people that have made it their life's purpose to protect you. *I* will protect you," he promised fiercely.

She felt as though he was speaking from a world away. "You're teasing me, surely?"

His warm hands wrapped around hers. "Be strong, Helena. Your people need you now, more than ever. We're entering a dark time, *Mira*, and they will need you to lead them. You were born for this."

The term of endearment made her eyes water. "I-I don't want this, Darrin. I'm happy here."

His lips flattened in disappointment. "Don't be a child, Helena."

Her body had begun to tremble. With each word that he said she could hear the faint hammer of a nail slamming the door closed on the life she knew. The ring of truth to what he was saying was too real to ignore, and she had never been one to abide lying. She refused to lie to herself.

"So, what happens now?"

He squeezed her hands in approval. "Now it's time to go home, Damaskiri. It's time to learn about your people and what you will need to do in the days to come."

Memories of stories she had heard as a child came back to her. "Isn't there a festival that's held when the Damaskiri comes into power?"

He nodded.

"Isn't she supposed to undergo some sort of trial of magic, to prove her worthiness before she can claim the title?"

"One of the things you will be prepared for and face upon your return," he assured her.

Struggling to take a deep breath, she looked him straight in the eye. "How long have you known?"

She noted the guilty blush stain his cheeks.

"Darrin," she said firmly, no longer asking.

"Since my tenth name day," he muttered, his voice pained.

Betrayal spiraled through her. She wanted to scream at him: *How could you not tell me? How could you keep this from me?* But she remained silent.

"It was the same day that I was told that I was to spend the rest of my life protecting you. I am to be your Shield, Damaskiri," he said, voice a fierce whisper.

"If I'm the one they speak of in this prophecy, why do you call me Damaskiri? Isn't she," Helena paused to correct herself, the tumble of thoughts racing through her mind making it difficult to focus. "Aren't I," she continued slowly, "fated to be a Kiri?"

"Yes, that is what the Circle believes, but since you have not undergone your trial any title is only honorary at this point. There's no title for 'next in line'," Darrin joked.

Helena didn't smile in response. More of the old stories rose to the surface of her memory. The Damaskiri has her own Circle of protectors. It is comprised of those that have been bound to her since her birth, loyal only to her. They have no mates or families of their own, and those they had prior to entering their service and training they must leave behind so that there will be no ties to bind them to any but her.

The Circle includes the Advisor, the Shield, the Master, the Sword, and the Mate. Each position is for life, if one should die in the midst of their service, a new one will rise to his place, except for the Mate. A Mate is for life, and there is only one.

Her eyes widened at what he had said. He was *her* Shield. Growing up he had been her best friend. Her confidant. He was either the one getting her into trouble or getting her out of it. They had grown up together, and she had never loved one as she loved him. She had always imagined that one day they would have a family of their own. Helena had never known anyone else, and could not imagine sharing her life with anyone other than him… even if they had never taken any steps toward such a relationship.

Noting her expression, Darrin nodded, his green eyes soft with understanding. He knew what she was realizing; it was the thing he had struggled with himself. He swallowed hard and averted his eyes before they could betray him further.

"Do you know the others?" she whispered, her voice sounding strange to her own ears.

He nodded again, still unable to meet her gaze. "All but the—

your," he corrected himself and cleared his throat before repeating more firmly, "your Mate."

She closed her eyes, feeling lost and afraid. "Yes, I remember. There is a ceremony of sorts, is there not? As part of the Festival where the Mate is chosen? They are bound on that day, rather than the day of the Damaskiri's birth, as with the others."

Green eyes searched aqua, seeking something. He saw her fear, and the battle to master it. Her skin had gone even paler than usual. Lips that were usually tilted in laughter were being worried by pearly teeth.

"Helena, I will be with you every step of the journey. You are not alone in this," he whispered his vow to her, begging with his eyes for her to understand. "If it could be any other way… if it could be me," he continued his voice hoarse with emotion.

She hushed him. "No, Darrin. We will not speak of it."

He hung his head, understanding that she was telling him that she did not blame him and that she forgave him. They sat there quietly for a moment, neither so much as moving. He shifted, to look back up at a face that had always been dearer to him than any other. He wanted to promise her so many things, but he remained silent knowing that such promises would only hurt her. It was his duty to shield her from anything that would harm her, including his own desires.

Color had returned to her cheeks, tingeing them a soft pink. She was still biting her lower lip, lost in thought, her brows creased with worry. Her laughing aqua eyes were clouded with the torrent of emotions she was sifting through.

He saw the exact moment that she controlled herself. Her eyes darkened, and the crease between her brows lifted. Her gaze met his, and she asked coolly, "When do we go?"

He sighed and pulled himself upright. "As soon as you gather whatever belongings that you would like to take with you."

She nodded, having anticipated his answer. She stood and made a move toward the back of the cottage where her room sat. "Darrin?"

"Yes, Helena?"

"I don't suppose we have time for me to say goodbye to Anderson?"

He felt his stomach tighten with emotion, and shook his head no.

She nodded, resigned, and walked out of the room.

IN THE WEEKS THAT FOLLOWED, she had constantly been surrounded by people. Darrin was never far, but with all that she had to learn for the Festival, there was no time for the two of them to spend with one another. She was feeling the strain of many sleepless nights. Her emotions were raw, and she felt on edge. There were purple smudges under her eyes, which had not retained their laughing sparkle since arriving at the Palace.

"Damaskiri," Alina called. From the tone of her voice, it was apparent that this was not the first time she had tried to get Helena's attention.

Blinking rapidly, Helena pushed herself back out of the chair. "Yes, coming."

She walked into the bathing room quickly. Alina smiled at her; blonde curls pulled high atop her head, her cheeks flushed from the heat of the water. Helena closed her eyes and took in the heady fragrance of jasmine wafting from the water. The familiar fragrance helped to relax her.

"I remembered that you had mentioned your preference for this scent, Damaskiri. I hope it pleases you."

"Thank you, Alina. I think a nice soak is just what I need before the Festival commences."

"Would you like me to stay and wash your hair?"

Helena shook her head quickly. While it was nice having someone to take care of all the little chores she had always hated, Helena had not and could not get used to the idea of someone bathing her like she was a child.

Alina smiled a final time and walked out of the room.

Letting her robe pool on the floor around her feet, Helena stepped into the warm water and laid back against the cool marble tub. Trying to silence her mind, at least for the moment, she let her eyes close and hummed the old lullaby her mother sang to her as a child. She tried to ignore the pang in her chest at the thought of her mother, who was not actually her birth mother. It was one of the few things that she could not accept. Miriam had raised her, kissed all of her hurts, both real and imaginary. Miriam was her mother, even if it was only the mother of her heart.

Her hands fisted in frustration at her sides in the water, and a wave of longing for her old life washed through her.

After a moment, Helena took a deep breath and told herself firmly it was the last time she would look back. Rolling her neck, she let the water lap at her, willing it to help relax her muscles. Warmth suffused her strained limbs, easing the ache that had built up over the last few weeks. She let out a soft sigh of contentment. The stress ebbed, and she felt the first true sense of calm since arriving in Elysia.

It matters naught what you fear, or that you find yourself wanting. If you were born for this as they say, then you can do whatever is asked of you.

With a final deep breath, Helena stood from the now cool water and stepped from the marble tub. Despite her personal wish to remain safely hidden away in here for the foreseeable future, she knew that the only way to get through this was to meet it head-on. Determined to do so, she began the process of drying her body and hair.

There was a discreet knock on the door.

"Yes?" Helena called, quickly wrapping the towel around her body.

"It is time to get ready, Damaskiri," Alina's melodic voice floated through the door.

Steeling her shoulders and setting her jaw, she opened the door.

It's time.

CHAPTER 2

After an hour of pampering, although she would argue the process of dressing was more akin to torture, she was declared a vision. Alina was beaming with pride at the Oohs and Aahs from other of the Palace servants. Helena blushed under the scrutiny and tried not to drop her eyes to the floor.

'You must learn to control your emotions, Damaskiri,' Timmins had gently admonished. 'One of the royal family would never shy away from any considered lesser than they. Furthermore, they do not waste time with public displays of emotion. To be ruled by your emotions is to be unable to rule justly and impartially. A Damaskiri must be both, and they must remain unyielding. You should never show that another has the power to affect your judgment.'

If there was an etiquette lesson that was deemed most crucial, it had been that one. Her Circle's Advisor had been kind, but very insistent that her years away from the court would be the greatest detriment to her rule.

Conversely, Master Joquil had insisted her complete lack of understanding magic, and her questionable ability to wield it, would see her surely fail. She bit back a smile at the thought of the two older men arguing the point during her first formal meeting with the Circle.

It had been a relief to finally meet the men that would be responsible for her safety, education and overall well-being from now on. She had instantly liked them all.

Timmins held the position of Advisor. He was a tall, well-fit, older man with yellow hair that had begun to fade to white in the last few years. His blue eyes had crinkled with a warm smile when he shook her hand and spoke the vows that would formally bind his life to hers.

'I vow to uphold and obey your beliefs and take them as my own. I will be your voice, spreading your wisdom so that all may know your edicts. I will spend the rest of my days in service to you and your will, until such a time as the Mother reclaims me or the blade of war strikes me.'

Despite his age, she could feel his strength and the power that radiated from him in waves. He reminded her greatly of Anderson, she had thought with an all-too-familiar pang in her heart.

She had turned then to her Master. Joquil had studied her with cool amber eyes beneath thick black brows. He wore his raven hair, lightly flecked with gray, short; his close-cropped beard enhanced the firm set of his jaw. He was also tall, but slender compared to the others. He had spent years training in all aspects of magic and would be the one to teach her how to use her gift. His power had intimidated but also comforted her. He too had taken vows before her:

'I vow to uphold and obey your beliefs and take them as my own. I will be your light, teaching you the ways of the Mother and her Chosen. I will spend the rest of my days in service to you and your will, until such a time as the Mother reclaims me or the blade of war strikes me.'

Next came Darrin, more serious than she had ever seen him, with the candlelight reflecting in his bright green eyes. He had knelt before her, holding her hand tightly in his.

'I vow to uphold and obey your beliefs and take them as my own. I will be your shield, protecting your life and light from any that would seek to destroy it. I will spend the rest of my days in service to you and your will, until such a time as the Mother reclaims me or the blade of war strikes me.'

She saw him swallow and clear his throat before releasing her hand and standing. Her heart had clenched with affection at his promise. He had looked after her since before she could walk, and knowing that he would be by her side now was a constant source of comfort. She could find little to fear, other than worries of her own ineptitude, knowing that he would always be watching out for her.

Finally, she had turned to Kragen, her Sword. The sheer size of him was overwhelming. He was a solid wall of hard, sculpted muscle that towered several heads above the others. Each massive arm had a band of black symbols swirling around it which disappeared up into his shirt. She had made a mental note to ask him what they meant if she survived this whole fiasco. Unlike the others, he had no hair, opting instead for a skin lightly dusted with stubble. He had soft wrinkles near his eyes and mouth, showing that he spent most of his time smiling. Despite his size, she knew she would never have to fear him. If anything, he would tease her mercilessly and become an annoying older brother who always wanted to tell her what to do.

As if following her thoughts, he smirked and stepped away from the wall to move toward her. His voice had been a deep rumble as he unsheathed the weapon at his side and laid it at her feet:

'I vow to uphold and obey your beliefs and take them as my own. I will be your sword, exacting your vengeance and slaying any who would seek to harm you. I will spend the rest of my days in service to you and your will, until such a time as the Mother reclaims me or the blade of war strikes me.'

Mother help those who would seek to harm me, she had thought, imagining Kragen wielding the broadsword as he sheathed it. She had found herself feeling oddly emotional at the promises of these relative strangers, and tried to convey the depth of her feeling in her promise to them.

'I will strive to be true and just, worthy of the gift of service that you have vowed today. I promise to be a light in the dark days to come, using my power to protect and nurture, rather than dominate or destroy. I will be the exemplar of our people acting in their best interests, rather than my own. I further vow that I will never take for

granted your service to me, or what you give up, nor will I forget the gift you are to me. Above all, you are dear to me, and I shall seek to be worthy of your gift.'

Her voice had rung out over the stone walls of the room, and the four men in front of her had not so much as blinked while she spoke. No others had been allowed in the room for the ceremony, and so she was unaware the effect her words had had on them. She improvised slightly when she promised to seek to be worthy of them, straying from the traditional vows of the Damaskiri to her Circle. She understood the sacrifice they had made when they bound their lives to hers, and she wanted them to know that she likewise was bound to them.

Timmins shifted first, his eyes suspiciously shiny. Kragen cleared his throat, and Joquil seemed to lose some of the aloof superiority she noted when she first met him. Darrin alone was unable to contain his smile of approval. She had impressed them with her warmth and sincerity. She was a Damaskiri that they were proud to serve.

Making eye contact with each of them, she lifted the chalice that had been waiting on the table next to her and held it aloft, speaking the final words of the ceremony:

'Blood of my blood these four shall be, my voice, my light, my shield and my sword. I take them unto me, as my own, to cherish and protect as I would myself, until such a time as the Mother reclaims me.'

Each man, in turn, drank from the ceremonial chalice, which had been filled with wine—not blood as she had originally feared. As the ceremony concluded, she looked around the room at them and asked, "So now what?"

Kragen had thrown his head back in laughter, slapping Darrin's back. Darrin had flinched at the contact but chuckled too. Timmins and Joquil wore identical looks of surprise but eventually joined in. Feeling foolish, but knowing that they were not laughing at her, she laughed along with the rest of them.

"Now, Damaskiri, we prepare you." Timmins had smiled.

Coming back to the present, Helena fervently prayed that she would not let them down. Squaring her shoulders again, she forced herself to be still until the servants moved out of the room.

Head high she began her descent into the main wing of the Palace and through the doors that would lead her into the garden and the Festival. The torrent of information that had been forced on her in the last few days was swirling in her mind, and she was desperately trying to remember it all. There was so much she hadn't known, such as the fact that the Festival lasted a full seven days beginning at sunrise on the first day and concluding at sundown on the seventh. Nor had she realized that the selection of her Mate was intrinsically woven into the entire fabric of the Festival.

Helena had anticipated that she would be introduced to her birth parents upon her arrival at the Palace. However, she had been informed that neither her mother nor father had survived her birth. Helena found it difficult to mourn for parents she never knew but was saddened that she truly was without family. Timmins had been vague when informing her that their death was one of the essential elements of the prophecy that had come true, and no one else had deigned to enlighten her as to those other essential elements.

Luckily, this evening's ceremony was strictly a formal beginning of the event. She was only expected to greet the important guests and then, after a few from her Circle spoke, a formal dinner and ball in her honor would begin.

Forcing herself to focus on the present, Helena took in the surroundings of her new home. She had yet to have time to explore properly, but the Palace was comprised of five wings, each representing a branch of magic. The Wings met in the center of the structure but were also connected by walkways between them to symbolize how magic bound everything together. She had been told that each wing was decorated in the style of the branch it depicted. The Earth Wing was styled in neutrals and greens, enchanted to appear as though you were outside. Different rooms reflected different times of day or regions of the realm. Others were magicked to change according to the current time of day or season. It was there that all of the royal guests were kept.

The Water Wing was swathed in blues and grays, rooms enchanted to appear as though submerged, or to have streams flowing through them. Due to Water's ability to soothe, this was predominately where the healers and their families resided.

The Air branch was comprised of soft whites and golden yellows. These rooms were known for their vaulting ceilings and soaring towers. Each room had large outdoor areas connected to them with invisible walls so that when one walked out onto the balcony, they felt as though they were floating. This wing housed many of the Palace's libraries and ceremonial meeting rooms as well as the royal craftsmen and their workshops.

The fourth branch, Fire, was painted in the palest shades of rose to the deepest of reds. Fire was always a representation of passion; however, it was best known for its power to destroy, and as such this branch was where the Rasmirin resided. The rooms were generally stark, but not without beauty. Since the warriors required so much room for training and their barracks, the only times the females of the Palace would use this wing was for one of the annual festivals.

The final wing was for Spirit and was reserved for the Damaskiri and her Circle. Decorated in shades of purple and gold, it was associated with the force that animates and breathes life into all things. As the only one capable of tapping into this power and the strongest of all of the Mother's Chosen, the Damaskiri was the personification of this branch of magic. Helena had found it hard to associate herself with this role, but the unmistakable peace she had found in this wing, compared to all the others, was enough for her not to question it.

She let her fingers brush against a lavender bloom that was spilling down from a planter above as she made her way out to the garden.

She stopped suddenly, forgetting about the parade of people trailing behind her, and tried to take in the beauty that surrounded her. After only a few weeks, Helena was already certain she would never become immune to the splendor of the Palace. Its numerous towers met the sky and disappeared behind clouds, and the creamy marble sparkled in the sun making it appear to glow. It was surrounded on all sides by gardens specializing in the most beautiful flowers and trees from around the realm.

Helena's fingers were twitching with excitement at the idea of one day being able to explore them, and perhaps plant a few of her own favorites, but for now, she would have to settle with the glimpses she could catch as she was escorted by or through them.

Timmins chose that moment to rush to her side. "Is all well, Damaskiri?"

She nodded and gifted him with a small smile. "Yes, I simply couldn't help but enjoy the view. Doesn't it take your breath away?"

Timmins' eyes wandered over the scene before him, and he gave her an indulgent smile, but she could tell it didn't call to him as it did her.

She laughed softly. "It's all right, Timmins, perhaps it is merely in my nature to be impressed by such grandeur."

Eyes twinkling, Timmins replied, "I think you'll find, Damaskiri, that your nature will be the most spectacular beauty of them all."

She beamed at the compliment and held her arm out to him. "Shall we continue on, Advisor?"

He nodded, taking her arm and gently winding it around his own. "Do you remember what we discussed about the welcoming ceremony?"

Helena was slow to respond, "I believe so."

Patiently he repeated himself. "First, you will greet your people. You will wish them the blessings of the Mother and thank them for coming to celebrate your name day. Then you will greet each representative of the royal houses; you will give them the same welcome. Finally, you will present your Circle, and then the males who are of age who wish to declare themselves as prospective mates will step forward and present you with a traditional courtship gift."

She felt herself stiffen at the prospect. *What if no one came forward? Worse, what if none of them appealed to her?*

Helena struggled to quell the panic before it overwhelmed her. Her Circle had only briefly touched upon the process of her Mate's selection, but Timmins had assured her that a Mate had always been found. If Timmins' had noticed her brief hesitation, he did not mention it.

They continued their way through the Palace courtyard and to the platform that had been constructed for the Festival. Helena marveled at the beauty and simplicity of the display. The platform had been erected between a series of ancient trees whose branches were now heavily sprinkled with twinkling lights. In between the two main trees sat a massive throne. The dark wood was polished to a high shine, and its back was comprised of five wooden pillars which twisted up into the trees so as to appear as if the throne was made and anchored by them. The only other decoration was a lovely lavender cushion.

Helena's eyes drifted over the crowd intimidated by the sheer number of people that had traveled to bear witness to the ascension of their new ruler. She picked out a familiar coppery head and smiled.

Gillian, daughter of the previous Damaskiri, had become a fast friend. Helena loved her quick wit and admired how she was all dainty grace and femininity. In sharp contrast to her bright copper curls, Gillian had almost translucent green eyes and fair milky skin. Today she was a vision in an emerald green silk dress that clung to each of her curves.

Helena had initially felt gangly and awkward next to her when they first met, but Gillian had put her instantly at ease, despite being in mourning herself, and had winked conspiratorially, promising to tell her everything about everyone.

Gillian saw Helena and waved cheerfully. Knowing it would be unwise to do the same, Helena simply dipped her head in acknowledgment.

Smoothing down the soft velvet fabric of her own dress, Helena whispered softly, "How do I look?"

Darrin had moved to stand at her left side and overheard her. Leaning down to whisper in her ear, he answered, "You are a vision, *Mira*. Truly."

She smiled up at him and decided that the hour Alina had forced her to get ready was worth it.

"It's time, Damaskiri," Timmins said softly.

Helena ascended the stairs to the platform and made her way to the center. The crowd, which had been chatting excitedly, went quiet for a brief moment and then roared in approval at their first glimpse of their future ruler.

Helena's aqua gown perfectly matched the color of her eyes, which were also emphasized by thick, sooty lashes. The gown left her shoulders and neck bare, displaying a large expanse of her creamy skin. She wore no adornment, save for a simple gold pendant that was symbolic of the Mother. Alina had twisted her long hair atop her head into a riot of loose curls and braids that were anchored by beautiful pearls. As a final touch, Alina had lightly dusted her skin with a golden shimmer; which, under all of the twinkling lights, made her luminous.

Standing in front of her people, and hearing their approval, was the first time Helena had truly let herself believe this was happening.

"Welcome," her voice thundered, and she realized that they must have used magic to project her voice so that she may speak normally, but all could hear.

The crowd instantly settled.

"It is with great honor and privilege that I stand before you today. Thank you for traveling so far to celebrate my name day, and my return home." The crowd cheered loudly at that, and Helena mentally congratulated Timmins.

"May the Mother keep you safe, and bless your days with light and happiness," she continued.

"May the Mother protect you always and grant you her eternal wisdom," they chanted in response.

Helena turned toward the bowers that held the representatives of the royal families for the other six realms.

"Tigaera welcomes its sisters today, and thanks you humbly for gracing us with your presence. May the Mother bless your lands, as she has ours, and keep your days filled with light and happiness."

With those formalities concluded, her Circle moved to stand beside her. One by one they came forward, repeating the vows that they had made to her a few weeks prior. This time, however, she did not repeat her vows to them. When she had asked why Timmins had informed her that it would be a show of weakness of her part to make promises to those that served her. Helena had not understood and was still uncomfortable that she merely sat there while they proclaimed themselves bound to her.

Rising, Kragen and Darrin moved to stand on either side of her. Joquil and Timmins moved to the stairs greeting the eleven males that were making their way toward her to present themselves for consideration.

The crowd seemed to murmur in surprise at one of the suitors. Helena narrowed her eyes and tried to determine who it was that caused the commotion.

As with everything else related to the formal ceremonies during the Festival, Timmins had briefly explained the tradition of gift giving.

'It is a tradition that goes back to the days of the Old Ones, Damaskiri. A suitor must declare his intent with a gift of magic. It is said that while the Festival lasts for seven days, and the suitors will continue to vie for the position during that time, when she receives the gift of her true mate, a Damaskiri will know instantly.'

'How does a man know that he could be the true Mate?' Helena asked.

Timmins leaned back in his chair, pondering the question for a moment, 'Well, it would be naïve to think that all that declare themselves do so without thought of the power such a position holds. However, just as your Circle can be determined from your birth, like will call to like. The Mother creates perfect mates for her Chosen, it is why there is only one, and it is why the Damaskiri has always found hers. It is crucial that a Damaskiri finds that bond before she can truly understand what it means to rule.'

'Not everyone finds their mate though, Timmins.' Helena whispered, thinking of Miriam and those that forsook the potential of finding their mates to serve in a Circle.

'No, not everyone," he had agreed softly, sympathy and

understanding laced into each word. 'But the Damaskiri's magic is much stronger than the Mother's other Chosen; it would only make sense that her Mate's would be too.

'They were made to find each other, Damaskiri. It is said that the strongest and truest power is love…'

Timmins had trailed off then, but his words had left her unsettled for days. The idea of love happening so quickly seemed foreign to her, but then again, she had never been in love. She had pushed it out of her mind and had not thought about it again until today.

He had also insisted that she was to remain seated while they presented their gifts. Helena refused.

'But, Damaskiri, that would suggest that you consider them to be equals. Until your Mate proves himself and is selected, you cannot show such deference.'

'These men will humble themselves before me and their entire realm. I will not subject them to unnecessary displays of power or pride. It is my heart they are trying to claim, Timmins, and if that does not allow them to be my equal, then your ceremony is flawed and will be changed.'

He had stared at her in surprise, admiration glowing in his blue eyes. 'Very well, Damaskiri.'

She stood as the first suitor walked to her throne. His dark eyes widened in surprise, and the crowd's echoing murmurs seemed a dull roar.

She offered him a soft smile, and he closed the distance between them. He went to kneel before her, but she placed her hand on his shoulder and stopped him with a quick shake of her head.

Realizing that she would meet him face to face, as equals, he flushed with pleasure. He was younger than she was but tall. Given the state of his well-worn but sensible clothes, she would guess he came from a trade family, and that his gift of magic had been a surprise to them all.

Swallowing quickly, he uttered the formal declaration, "Damaskiri, may the Mother open your heart to me and allow our souls to find the one they were created for." He said the words with soft earnestness, sweat beading on his brow.

She noticed his hands trembling slightly as he removed the small globe that was concealed in his pocket.

"For you, Damaskiri," he said shoving it into her hands quickly.

Helena looked into the globe and saw that it had been enchanted to contain a miniature ball with the people twirling and dancing within. She held it up to her ear and could hear the soft strains of music. Delighted she studied him with a new appreciation.

"What is your name?"

"Teramos," he replied nervously. "But my friends call me Amos, Damaskiri."

"Thank you, Amos. It is beautiful."

His cheeks flamed with pride, and he quickly shuffled away.

The rest of the suitors were presented without much to distinguish themselves, with the exception of the last two.

She was trying not to fidget when she heard the crowd start to stir again. She felt, rather than saw him come forward. It was as if her body was equally hot and cold at the same time, and she shivered in response. He moved to stand in front of her, and she looked up, and up, to meet his gaze.

His hair was obsidian, smoothed back off his sculpted face. His face was all hard angles, and he had steely gray eyes which stared into hers without a hint as to the emotion behind them. His lips were full and inviting, but with none of the lines around them to suggest he was prone to smiling.

Her eyes continued their perusal, greedily drinking in the golden skin and heavy muscles of the man before her.

"Damaskiri," he murmured, his voice a low growl.

She felt an answering response low in her stomach.

"May the Mother open your heart to me and allow our souls to find the one they were created for," he continued, his gray eyes boring into hers.

At his words, her heart started beating more quickly.

His lips quirked as if he knew the effect he was having on her, and he raised his hand as though to touch her. She heard Darrin and Kragen shift in response and watched him still.

He looked over her shoulder, meeting the gaze of her two warriors. Looking back at her, he then looked down into his hand.

Her eyes followed his and saw a perfect white bloom resting in his palm. She had never seen a more perfect magnolia bloom in her life. The velvety petals were brilliantly white, and the fragrance heady.

"Magnolias are my favorite," she whispered, eyes shyly meeting his.

A dimple flashed in his cheek, and its appearance instantly transformed his face. "I know."

She laughed at his audacity. "How?"

"Would you believe me if I told you I have dreamed about you since I was a wee lad?" he asked, deadpan.

She tilted her head to the side, her laughter making her eyes twinkle. "No."

He shrugged, as though he had expected as much. "I may have bribed someone."

She laughed again in shocked amusement. "I'll bet you did. What is your name?"

"Von, Damaskiri," he replied in the same deep growl.

"Thank you, Von. I shall treasure it, since you did go to so much trouble to ensure I would like it."

He nodded at her, a small smile playing about his sculpted mouth, and with a last glance, he started away.

As he stepped away, she heard the hissing of the crowd. She narrowed her eyes again in disapproval. He must have been the one they were reacting to earlier. She was not pleased that they would feel they had the right to judge anyone who was presenting themselves to be her mate.

She studied the crowd with a frown. The hissing continued, and someone went so far as to throw something in Von's direction.

"ENOUGH!" she shouted, icy anger wrapping itself around her.

Von stopped mid-descent and looked back at her; black brow lifted in surprise.

"How dare you treat one of your brothers this way," she bit out, her voice a whip. "It is not for you to judge or determine the worthiness of another. The Mother and her Vessel are the only ones with the authority to do so. You will treat each other with respect and deference, especially those who humble themselves and their pride as they offer themselves to be *my* Mate."

The crowd was shifting, ashamed and in awe of the woman before them.

"I am to be your Kiri, and my Mate will be my equal; you will not," she paused, eyes singling out the troublemakers, "in *any way*, harm what is mine." Her voice had dropped to a ragged whisper.

With that proclamation, the entire assembly gaped. She had all but declared him as her choice, and she had spent less than three minutes with him.

Shaking with rage, Helena finally realized what she had done. Horrified at the display of anger, so unfamiliar to her, she looked helplessly over her shoulder at Darrin.

He was frowning at Von slightly and looked back toward her, green eyes glowing with some unnamed emotion. She turned her gaze to Timmins and Joquil, certain their reaction would help her gauge how terrible of a mess she had made. She jerked in surprise finding pride shining there instead of the twin expressions of disapproval she'd anticipated.

The final suitor approached her hesitantly, and she felt her lips curl into an amused smile. It was Gillian's twin brother Micha.

"That was some display, Damaskiri," he whispered, with a twist of his own lips.

Helena smiled ruefully into green eyes that were identical to his sister's. "I'm sure I just made quite a mess of things."

He was quick to shake his head. "No, Helena. You just showed your people the depth of strength that resides within you. You established, with a few words, what you expect of them and that you protect what is yours. They love you already."

She rolled her eyes. "So what have you brought me?"

He chuckled at her teasing, and continued lightly, "May the Mother open your heart to me and allow our souls to find the one they were created for."

He then held out a beautifully illuminated book. She accepted it with reverence, gently turning the pages. Each illustration moved, the characters literally coming to life on the page.

"Ooh," she whispered in wonder.

"It is a book of fairy tales. I figured since you grew up so far away from your people and our history, this might be a way for you to learn about your culture." His voice was soft and sincere.

Eyes glittering with tears she met his eyes. "Thank you, Micha, I have never loved anything more." She hugged the book to her chest.

He nodded, smiling in relief and made his way off the stage.

Suddenly, Helena felt exhausted. The weight of all those people staring at her, in addition to the emotions of the afternoon, were starting to bear down on her.

Joquil moved forward and released the crowd to the feast that would start in the tents set up in the gardens. As he spoke lights began to glow in the garden, illuminating the way.

Timmins hurried over to her.

"I'm so sorry," she whispered brokenly, "I don't know what came over me."

He shook his head, "No, Damaskiri, you do not apologize." His voice a soothing murmur.

Kragen placed his large hand on her shoulder. "You are our Damaskiri," he rumbled, "and sometimes that calls for a display of power. You are a natural, Helena."

She blinked up at him in surprise. He had never referred to her by her name before, and the purposeful use of it now could not more clearly reflect his admiration and approval. As she looked at the men around her, she could see that they all approved of her display of temper, and that knowledge brightened her mood considerably.

Darrin wrapped his arm behind her shoulders and squeezed, giving her a gentle hug. He let go just as quickly and took his place at her left.

With a deep breath, she met the eyes of the four men that were becoming so dear to her. "Well, now that we've cleared that up, shall we go eat?"

"I thought you'd never ask," Kragen quipped.

The others laughed and made their way to the main tent for the feast.

CHAPTER 3

Stepping into the tent, Helena paused in delighted awe. Centered in the Air Wing of the Palace, the tent had been erected in its courtyard. Where there should have been fabric walls, there were sweeping views of the six different lands, each scene fading and bleeding into the next. One moment you were viewing a vast ocean with waves crashing against the shore, the next an endless forest with the trees so tall you could not see where they ended. It was a perfect tribute to Tigaera's visitors.

Before any of her Circle could ask what was keeping her, she hurried to catch up with them. At the northern end of the tent, a long table had been decorated in purples and golds, with a countless number of candles ablaze and flowers spilling from their various vases.

Murmuring her approval, Helena took her seat in the center; her chair an echo of the throne she had sat in during the welcome ceremony.

Turning to her right, she asked Darrin, "Did you ever think we would end up at one of the royal feasts?"

His green eyes flashed with humor. "This is hardly my first royal feast, Hellion."

"I wasn't aware they let the Rasmirin attend the feasts. Aren't you lot supposed to be out protecting and defending?" she teased.

Straightening his tunic before looking at her from the corner of his eye, he smiled wryly and admitted, "To be fair, I never said I was an invited guest."

Helena's laughter rang out, causing many of the nearby guests to turn and see what had caught her attention.

Turning back to scan the room before her, Helena continued, "I just can't believe that only days ago I was at home at the cottage and now I'm here." As she looked about the room, her eyes scanned and cataloged the familiar faces.

In front of her and slightly to her left, Micha and Gillian sat and spoke animatedly with a gray-haired man she assumed was their father. Behind them, at another table, Von sat with a contingent of his mercenaries. She noticed the people around him were stealing glances and whispering furiously to their dinner mates.

As if feeling her attention on his, Von glanced up and caught her eye. He nodded and smiled slightly, but it didn't reach his eyes. Instead, his brows were lowered, as if puzzled.

Flustered, Helena looked away, trying to recall the names of the other faces her eyes stopped upon. She noticed Amos speaking to another of the men that had presented themselves to her... *Harris?* she guessed, embarrassed that she had already forgotten so many of their names.

The blond man had been very soft-spoken, and she had trouble hearing what he had said even standing directly before him. *His gift had been the...* she paused, searching her memory, *the bracelet, no... was it the music box?* She shook her head sighing in defeat, eyes now continuing their journey about the room.

Her scan stopped once more, her gaze colliding with a pair of coal eyes staring at her intently from a grizzled face. It was twisted in a scowl, but before she could place it, or discern the expression in those dark, calculating orbs, they were gone.

Suddenly cold, Helena shivered causing Darrin to reach out and touch her arm gently.

"Are you all right, Damaskiri?"

She nodded distractedly. Looking around, Helena could not find whoever had been studying her so closely.

"Maybe you should eat something?" he suggested softly.

Surprised, Helena noticed the food piled high in front of her. "How did that get here?"

Darrin chuckled around his own mouthful of food and simply gestured for her to eat.

SOMETIME DURING DINNER music began to play, but when she searched Helena could not locate any musicians. The center of the tent had been cleared and where tables once stood there was now a massive dance floor in their stead.

As the guest of honor, it was once again up to her to formally open up the evening's festivities. That was why, once her plate vanished without her notice, Darrin led her to the center of the room.

The music stopped, bringing the chatter to a halt as well, all eyes turning toward her and Darrin. After a few beats of silence, the first strains of a song started.

Helena and Darrin bowed to each other and began the first steps of the formal court dance. She was grateful that she remembered to pick up the side of her skirt to avoid any mishaps. The steps became faster, she and Darrin twirling around each other in time with the heavy beat of the drum.

Timmins and Joquil had told her this dance was the embodiment of the Mother's magic, each step representing the interplay of the elements. The solid stomps on the ground depicting Earth, while the gentler motions of the arms acting as Air weaving around them all. The growing speed of the steps, Fire's greedy inferno.

She had stopped them then, to ask whether the sweat dripping down her back was supposed to represent Water.

The two had laughed, recognizing they had perhaps pushed her too hard in their attempts to ensure her perfection of the dance.

Eyes still shining with mirth, Timmins had informed her that the flow of movements into one another was the representation of Water, while she, in the center of it all, represented Spirit.

Now, as the dance was coming to a close, Helena better appreciated the beauty of its movements. The bodies surrounding them on the dance floor were a blur as she continued to spin and weave around Darrin. Her skin was flushed and her head light as blood rushed through her body; her heart racing as it beat in time to the drum. Breathless laughter bubbled up in sheer joy as the dance came to an end.

There was silence in the room again before the crowd erupted in applause and cheers. Still smiling, Helena wrapped her arms around Darrin for a quick hug before stepping back.

Darrin let out a startled gasp as he looked at the floor below them. Everywhere they had stepped during the dance, was now softly glowing. The entire shape a replica of the necklace Helena was wearing.

"Oh," she breathed as she noticed what had caused the crowd to react.

Before she could do more than look back to Darrin, a voice was at her ear asking her to dance. Seeing Micha, her smile grew and as she nodded her assent, she was lost in the sea of bodies now moving around her.

Panting, Helena stepped off of the floor. She had not stopped since her dance with Darrin over an hour ago. She had to turn down Nameless Suitor Number Four's offer so that she could catch her breath.

Fanning herself and leaning her hip against a nearby table, Helena smiled as Gillian made her way over.

"I seem to be lacking the equipment"—Gillian gestured toward her groin—"required to spend time with you at this sort of event."

Helena let out a surprised laugh. "I'm glad you have found a way to persevere despite that handicap."

Gillian smiled conspiratorially. "So are we to be sisters? Micha is quite taken with you."

"I'm not certain how such a sweet man can be related to you," Helena teased with a grin. "Although he is a lot of fun to spend time with."

"You certainly seemed to enjoy your dance together."

"Yes, definitely. A partner who doesn't step all over your feet, or let their hands wander, is much appreciated."

"But wandering hands is the entire point of dancing," Gillian said as she batted her wide, green eyes innocently. "How else are you supposed to know if you'd like to invite the man to your bed?"

Blushing, Helena could only shake her head in mute amusement.

"Seriously, Helena, the physical chemistry is the most important part of any relationship. That's a part of the process you know. You have to try out all your options before you know which one is the perfect," she paused as if savoring the word, "fit."

"I'm pretty certain that is absolutely *not* the point of this process," Helena concluded matter-of-factly.

Gillian simply shrugged and folded her arms across her chest. "Suit yourself, it's your potential lifetime of cold bed sheets. If I were you, there's absolutely no way I'd make *that* mistake! Forever is a long time to be miserable."

"Damaskiri," a gravelly voice she instantly recognized said at her shoulder.

Turning to Von, she offered him a warm smile. "Hello again. Are you enjoying the party?"

Frowning slightly, Von eyed the dancers nearest to him. "This is not generally the sort of entertainment I would seek out, but I suppose it has a certain appeal."

"I bet he lets his hands wander," Gillian muttered below her breath.

Helena blushed fiercely and spoke before Von could address the comment.

"And what sorts of entertainment do you usually seek out?"

It was Von's turn to look uncomfortable. "Erm, quiet ones."

Gillian let out a sharp bark of laughter. "If it's quiet you're doing it wrong, Holbrooke, but I get the feeling you already know that."

"I meant reading, my lady," Von said dryly.

"Hmmm," Gillian murmured, clearly not believing him.

"I love to read," Helena said quickly. "I've spent many nights curled up in front of the fire with a book."

"Mother you are hopeless," Gillian said throwing up her hands in exasperation. "Darling, you are the only one in this conversation actually talking about books."

Confused, Helena looked between the two of them before it registered. Wide-eyed she looked back to Von.

His eyes were narrowed in annoyance as he studied Gillian. He turned back to Helena and his expression instantly softened. "Shall we dance, Damaskiri?"

"Yes, that would be wonderful."

He offered her his hand. She hesitated before finally placing hers in his much larger one, anticipating the bolt of heat that rushed through her at the contact. His hand tightened around hers as he led her to the dance floor.

The music swelled as one song rolled into the next. He wrapped his free arm around her waist, its hand resting warmly against her back as he pulled her closer to him.

As they spun and wove around the other dancers, Helena was only aware of Von's body pressed close to hers. She felt his muscles bunch and shift against hers. Distracted, she missed a step and looked up apologetically.

Ignoring the misstep, Von asked, "Are you enjoying yourself, Damaskiri?"

"Immensely! This is my first ball; I'm pretty overwhelmed by it all. Does it show?" she asked in a rush, excitement making her aqua eyes glow.

"Not at all, Damaskiri," he responded with an ironic smile that was completely lost on her.

"Don't you think, given the circumstances, that you should call me Helena?" she asked thoughtfully.

"Under the circumstances, I absolutely do not think I should call you Helena. There are far too many people around for the familiarity to go unnoticed, and the last thing I need is more rumors. Or the attention of your Sword," he added as if in afterthought.

Hearing her name on his lips, even if not directed at her, lit the fire within her. Without thought, she blurted out, "I look forward to a time when such formalities will not be necessary between us."

Horrified at her boldness, she stared fixedly at his shoulder and began berating herself. *This is not a courtship, Helena. This is politics. Mother's teeth, you have ten other suitors! What is he going to think of you, if you keep throwing yourself at him?*

"As do I," he leaned down to whisper in her ear, "Helena." His lips brushed against her ear softly as his breath caressed her cheek and neck.

She shivered, aqua eyes meeting gray. They stared in growing silence, steps forgotten as they got lost in one another. She jumped when the voice spoke beside them.

"Damaskiri, I believe it is my turn to dance with you," Kragen cut in.

She offered him a smile, before stepping back from Von, eyes still searching his. Wordlessly, he merely nodded and offered her hand to Kragen.

And while his hand had not wandered, she still felt the blaze of its impression against her back as she watched him walk away.

CHAPTER 4

*V*on stared absently at the scene before him. His room was supposed to be comforting as it reflected his home landscape. Unfortunately, it only served to set him on edge. The rocky terrain and mountains were beautiful in an eerie and primal way, but there was no warmth in the vision.

Steel gray eyes shifted from the balcony scene into the interior of the room. On the large four-poster bed the curtains were parted slightly, revealing a sleeping woman. As if feeling his gaze on her, she shifted and stretched.

The sheet fell away from her naked body, long arms stretched above her head pulling her small breasts to attention, the dusky nipples tightening at the subtle change in temperature. Her back arched then, and her eyelids fluttered open.

Von watched the display with disinterest.

"Come back to bed," the woman purred, trying to use her body to tempt him.

When he didn't move, she stood from the bed and walked over to him slowly.

She tossed a head of long black hair off her shoulders, to give him a better view, her hands gliding up her body pausing at her breasts to rub and tease her nipples into rosy points before running them down over her hips.

Eyes half closed she bit her lower lip and bent down toward him, hand reaching between his legs.

He grabbed her wrist tightly before she could make contact with the evidence of his disinterest. "Attempt to touch me again, and I will cut it off," he warned, his voice icy.

She stood quickly in surprise.

"Leave."

He let go of her hand, and she moved to grab her gown from the floor.

With a final heated look over her shoulder, she moved to open the door and left.

Von let out a slow breath and closed his eyes. Not one to generally feel remorse, he was feeling decidedly guilty for accepting her invitation at the feast. He had been so overwhelmed by the intensity of his reaction to the Damaskiri that he had thought to exorcise her from his system with another willing female.

He shifted in his seat uncomfortably, a frown pulling down his lips. She was more beautiful than he had anticipated. Shining chestnut tendrils had fallen from their place in the intricate braids atop her head and down to her shoulders; her laughing aqua eyes, framed with thick black lashes, smiled up at him as they danced. Her slender body had fit against his perfectly, warm under his hands.

He felt his body stir in response to the memory.

Unsettled, his frown deepened.

Even more than her beauty, her spirit had surprised him. He remembered her words as the crowd had recognized him and responded with the usual uproar of disapproval.

'*...you will not, in* any way, *harm what is mine.*' Her eyes had darkened to twin navy pools, her voice a scathing warning. He had never had anyone stand up for or defend him. The thought was laughable; he was the first born of Darius Holbrooke, and the Holbrooke line had been cast out years ago after his grandfather's father had attempted to destroy the Kiri and her Circle.

He had not come to the Festival with the intention of actually claiming, or falling for, the Damaskiri. He had simply hoped to use the time that he was close to her to try to convince her to lift the ban that had been on his family for the last five centuries. His brother needed to see a healer, and none would come to them.

Memories of the broken and twisted limbs and his brother's pained smile as Von had said goodbye did much to dampen his ardor.

Even so, when he had looked into her eyes and spoken the words of intent, he felt as though his own soul had been staring back at him. Never had he felt so vulnerable or connected to anyone. He rubbed the back of his neck with a grimace; it was not a feeling he'd necessarily like to repeat.

The guilt and uncertainty unnerved him. He wasn't certain if the guilt was from forgetting that he was here to help save his family, or if it was from sleeping with a whore after offering himself as a life mate to another.

Scowling he stood and walked toward the balcony, willing the familiar peaks and valleys of Daejara's mountains to ease his tension. Such emotion was foreign to him. He learned a long time ago to rid himself of anything that would weaken him or distract him from his duty. Over the last seven years, he had gained a reputation as the fiercest and most brutal mercenary in Daejara. He and his band had roamed the realm, accepting any task if the money had been good. They had no scruples; they couldn't afford them.

Reminding himself of who he was, and of his purpose, Von felt some of his tension ebb. The reminder, however, didn't keep him from wishing, just for a moment, that he could be the kind of man that would be worthy of such a woman.

SHE HEARD the voices as she rounded the corner and moved toward the meeting that had apparently started without her. Alina had insisted that she dress according to her station, even for a meeting with her Circle, even though she would have to change again for this afternoon's ceremony.

Helena shook her head ruefully, but her smile faded as she heard the men more clearly.

"We cannot allow her to entertain his suit!" Darrin roared.

"Allow her?" Joquil had repeated with a laugh. "It is not for us to *allow* the Damaskiri to do anything. Did you forget your vows already, child?"

"He has a point, Joquil," Timmins soft voice stepped in. "You know who he is, who his *family* are. More importantly, you know what he has done. How can we protect her from evil if she is to bind herself to it?"

"He will not harm her," came Kragen's sure reply.

"It is our duty to protect her," Darrin bit out, "but there are times we will not be there, especially once she completes the binding and he becomes her Mate. She will be destroyed, and in turn, we will all be destroyed."

The men were quiet as his words sunk in.

After a moment, she heard Joquil say, "The Mate is the perfect partner for the Damaskiri. He was made for her, and she for him. They are one. It is not possible that the one she chooses will not be the one that she was destined for. She is to be the most powerful Kiri we have ever seen. All power is two-sided and who better to help her understand the darker side of her nature than such a Mate?"

She heard objections from the others, but Joquil continued, "She has to be able to understand the darkness in order to save us from it. Just because we have kept her safe thus far, does not mean she is prepared for what is to come. The Mother provides for her Chosen; she will not forsake us."

Helena's blood felt like ice. All the lingering joy from last night's festivities and the morning's frivolity faded. She was faced, once again, with the enormity of the burden that was placed on her shoulders. She could not afford to forget it. She pushed the door open and stepped into the Circle's Chamber.

The men were sitting around the table, a fire blazing beside it. Each face was lost in thought. She took note of the worry and concern on Darrin's and Timmins' faces, as well as the absence of both on Joquil's. Kragen alone seemed to be as he always was, she took comfort in that.

They looked up as she entered.

"Good morning, Damaskiri. Did you enjoy your ball last night? It was your first, yes?" Timmins greeted her warmly, all trace of doubt vanished, or at least well hidden.

"Yes, it was lovely," she murmured, pretending that she had not overheard their conversation.

Joquil stood and moved toward her. "We have a very busy day, Damaskiri. We should get started with your final training right away unless there is anything else you all need?" he addressed the other men.

They shook their heads.

Then, if you would excuse us," he asked the others.

They rose and made their way to the door with murmurs of support. Darrin gently touched her shoulder as he walked past.

"Let us review before diving back in, shall we? Tell me, Damaskiri, what do you recall about the five branches?"

Helena mentally shook herself, trying hard to dispel her lingering unease at the Circle's conversation and to project confidence that she didn't feel.

"Well," she began tentatively, "power can manifest in a number of ways, each unique to the user but generally tied to some common element within that branch. Earth, for example, generally provides the Chosen it's gifted with incredible strength, both of body and of mind. Those adept in the Water branch are most commonly healers, and they can influence the sleep or dreams of others."

Joquil nodded and motioned for her to continue.

"Those blessed with an affinity for Air can sometimes control or influence the weather and are almost always known for their speed; while any gifted with Fire can summon and manipulate that element at will."

"And what of Spirit?" he prompted.

"Spirit can only be wielded by a Damaskiri or Kiri. It is the power of self and allows for the manipulation or control of one's mind, including animals. The stronger one is, the more control they can have over another. In some cases, they can also foresee the future."

"And can a Chosen be gifted in multiple branches?"

"Yes, although it is extremely rare to be gifted with more than two branches and even more uncommon for someone to be considered a master of more than one branch. In most cases, a Chosen only has one or two abilities tied to a single branch of magic."

"Do you remember anything else about what happens when there's a dual or multi-gift?"

"The branches influence and work with each other. For example, if someone has both Fire and Air, in theory, they would be able to call forth a storm of Fire."

Joquil was smiling in approval. "Very good, Damaskiri. A Chosen generally does not learn the true potential of their gift until they are of age; in your case, it will remain to be seen how your gifts will work together and what your limitations are. Do you have any questions before we move on?"

"I did have one other question, and I apologize if it's silly—"

"You have been separated from your heritage your entire life, Damaskiri, it only makes sense that you would have questions," he interrupted, dismissing her apology.

She offered him a bright smile in return and continued, "Yes, well, I was curious why no one seems to be using their magic." She paused, trying to explain herself, "Everything, since I arrived here, feels so… well, normal. Are there some kind of rules dictating when magic can be used?" She finished with a shrug, feeling foolish.

It was Joquil's turn to smile. "Ah, I can see how you would think that, Damaskiri. It is not that magic is not being used, it is simply not being used in your presence."

"But, but why?" she asked, eyebrows scrunched in confusion.

"It's out of respect for you. As the future ruler of the Chosen, they did not wish to offend you by blatantly displaying a talent you are unable to use since your own magic remains bound —or was until very recently."

Helena laughed. "But that's ridiculous, isn't the ability to wield magic what it intrinsically means to be one of the Mother's Chosen? It would be as if a musician would not share his songs with his neighbor who could not sing. Just because someone has a gift does not mean they should hide it from one who does not!"

Joquil nodded in agreement. "You are wise to say so, Damaskiri. Your people simply do not wish to insult you. Shall I have Timmins inform them that you wish they stop concealing their magic?"

"Yes, please. I have always been fascinated by the idea of magic since I never had my own. I was looking forward to being surrounded by it when coming here, however, even during my practice with you, it has merely been a lot of talking and no magic."

He laughed at her teasing. "Perhaps we can begin to amend that today. Are you ready to start?"

"As ready as I'll ever be," she sighed.

He smiled sympathetically. "Today I will help induce the meditative state. You were so close to reaching the barrier yesterday that I think a little extra push may help you succeed."

"Have you been holding out on me, Joquil?" Helena lifted a mocking brow.

He shrugged prosaically. "What was the point of wasting good magic when you did not understand what you were doing?"

"I suppose you have a point." Her eyes narrowed playfully as she settled into the large gray armchair which had informally become hers.

Helena sat back in the chair and closed her eyes, beginning to focus on her breathing.

She felt Joquil's hands lightly touch her shoulders, and her breathing became more measured and slow. Her worry and tension faded, and her muscles slackened at the release.

Helena's head fell back against the chair with a contented sigh.

"Stay focused, Damaskiri," Joquil murmured. Helena was certain he was smirking.

She tried to pull her mind back to her, and begin the now-familiar process of seeking the magic within her.

Having one's magic bound was much like attempting to find buried treasure without a map or deciphering a code without a key. If you knew where to look, you could find it, but you could also go in circles for ages and never realize it had been next to you the whole time.

Now that she was used to searching for it, Helena could recognize the wealth of power within her. It felt like a still pool hidden within her very core. In her mind, she could see its black surface patiently waiting for her to dive in and explore its depths.

Under Joquil's patient, albeit smug, guidance she was learning to move closer to its placid shore each day.

There you are, she smiled as she came upon the dark shores within her.

"Call your power to you. Wrap it around yourself, as you would a blanket on a wet night," Master Joquil's low voice called to her as though from a distance.

It seemed as if the pool recognized her presence and was beckoning her, urging her to join it.

Helena moved forward. Each day she was pushing against the invisible barrier between herself and the water, but the closer she got the weaker she felt. Reaching the barrier, Helena felt as though she was straining with her fingertips to brush the edge of the water.

Just a bit further. She wasn't sure if she was attempting to motivate herself or if it was the inky depths before her, or were they one in the same? The thought had her pausing briefly. Mentally shaking herself, she refocused on her task; if she could only get a little closer, she would be touching it.

Bracing herself, she started forward again. Breath labored, Helena could feel her forehead beginning to pound. In her mind, she was now on her knees attempting to crawl to the lapping edge of the water. She could feel herself trembling with the effort.

Fingers were splayed against the wall, pushing so hard she could feel the barrier begin to crack and become malleable. *Yes*, she thought fiercely, *just a little further*. With a final roar, she pushed. The barrier gave way, ripping with a sigh before falling away completely. She pushed herself up and was now standing at the edge.

With a pleasured gasp, she reached out and touched the pool. She tingled from the contact, feeling the source of her power reach out to her, caressing her as it welcomed her.

It was as though she was an empty basin, and her magic was water seeking to fill her to the brim. The tingling turned into pinpricks, and her heart raced.

She heard shouting but did not know where it was coming from. Standing before the pool, she was watching it continue to drain, filling her beyond her capacity. What had initially felt like a pleasant warmth spreading through her limbs was beginning to burn. She cried out in confusion.

Stop, please... it's too much, she thought, limbs shaking and breath coming out in labored gasps. Suddenly, the power began to ebb away, swirling back to its pool.

As she came back to herself, she heard Master Joquil's frantic shouting, and awareness flooded her. Slowly she opened her eyes. When her eyes met his, he gasped and took a few teetering steps back.

She stood slowly, aware of her body in a new way. Each sense was heightened, and it was as if she was learning how to move her body for the first time. She flexed her muscles feeling the new strength within them.

Her eyes flitted to the unlit candles on the wall. Moments later flames leapt from the wicks reaching toward the ceiling.

Joquil, sat quickly, hands firmly gripping the arms of his chair. "Blessed Mother," he whispered in awe.

Helena walked toward the mirror in the corner of the chambers, studying herself in surprise. While the changes were mostly subtle, it was undeniable that her magic had changed her. Gone were the soft remnants of childhood, round apple-shaped cheeks giving way to sculpted cheekbones. Her skin had always had the dewy glow of youth, but now it was as if she was lit from within. Her hair, which had always been notably long, now cascaded down her back in shining waves. The biggest change was her eyes. Aqua eyes were now twinned iridescent prisms, catching and holding the light so that they sparkled.

She held out a hand to the mirror, letting her fingers run over her reflection.

"Are the changes permanent?" she asked curiously. Her eyes flared in surprise at her voice, which sounded like a harmony of voices rather than just one. As she turned her gaze to Joquil, each detail of the room stood out in sharp contrast.

She could detect individual fibers in the fabrics of the cushions and drapes and the flow of the wood grain in the chairs. She could also see with perfect clarity each strand of hair on the Master's head and the multitude of emotions which moved rapidly across the Master's face.

Master Joquil steadied himself before speaking. "I believe so, Damaskiri, however, you can use your magic to dampen the effects, so to speak."

She turned back toward the mirror and blinked slowly. When she opened her eyes, they were aqua again, except for a thin band of iridescent light which remained around her pupils. Her glow had also dimmed, and when she spoke, it sounded like one voice, although still more melodic than usual.

"Will it always feel that way?"

Joquil inclined his head. "I don't believe so, Damaskiri. Think of your body like a starving child. It would slowly die, yes? Well now imagine that you introduce that child to food. The child is starving and desperate, it will shove the food down as quickly as it can, and likely make itself sick in the process. Your body was much the same. When it found its magic, it greedily sucked in as much as it could, and the effects overwhelmed you. With more time, you will learn how to contain how much you take, and it should not affect you so."

Helena nodded in understanding and moved back toward her seat at the table.

"So now that we know I have magic"—her lips twisted in amusement—"how do I pass my trial?"

Joquil smiled with her and leaned forward. "The Damaskiri's trial is a test to gauge her depth and control of her magic. There is not much known about the specifics of the trial other than that it will test the furthest limits of a Damaskiri's power. Given what we have witnessed today that will surely be a substantial feat."

"You could say that."

Joquil chuckled. "You must remember to stay focused and the rest, as they say, will take care of itself."

Overwhelmed, but vastly pleased, Helena sat quietly for a moment. She could feel the waves of her newly discovered power lapping gently within her. With the awareness came the knowledge that she could call its waves to action with the smallest inclination. The pool stirred at the thought.

"Joquil?" she asked too innocently, not ready to face the tasks of the afternoon.

"Yes, Damaskiri?" came the wary response.

"Is there time for us to show the others?" Childlike excitement laced each word.

"I believe we can make time." He couldn't help but smile in response to her reaction and indulge her. "Do you have something in mind, or should I just call for them."

Helena's smile grew, and her eyes twinkled mischievously. "I may…"

He groaned and shook his head, muttering as he left the room. "I am going to regret this, I already know it."

Her laughter followed him out.

Standing quickly, she eyed the room looking for the perfect spot for her little performance. She chose to stand in front of the window, her back toward the door. She took a few deep breaths to help steady her emotions. She drew her magic to her, prepared this time as it flooded her. Before it could overwhelm her, she stopped it.

She heard the masculine voices approaching, and bit back a smile.

"Helena, what's going on?" Darrin asked, concern evident.

"Would you still love me if I never found my power, Darrin?" she asked, her voice small and wavering slightly.

She heard the men shift behind her, their worry and fear palpable at the thought of her failure.

"Perhaps all you need is more time, Damaskiri," came Timmins gentle response.

"No," she said as she started to turn, "I'm afraid that wouldn't help."

As one, each of the men's eyes widened, and their mouths went slack.

She had un-dampened the magic's effect so that they could all witness it in full force.

Kragen was gripping the back of a chair so tightly that it snapped under the pressure.

Her peals of laughter rang throughout the room and seemed to echo with phantom other voices.

Timmins was recovering most quickly, his gasp of surprise turning into an admiring smile.

Darrin was the last to respond, his golden skin pale and clammy.

"You don't like it?" she teased. "Perhaps this is better?"

She closed her eyes and let out a slow breath, feeling her body respond to her requests. Shining chestnut waves became gray gnarls, and supple limbs shriveled with the weight of age.

As one, the men gasped in awe. To cast such an illusion so seamlessly, and without conscious effort, was stunning.

Darrin chuckled, the playfulness of his friend helping him to recover more than anything else could. "No, I can't say I prefer the crone to the goddess, although to be fair both make me right nervous."

Helena shook her head back and forth, releasing the illusion and calling back her magic dampened state.

Kragen whistled. "Gentlemen, I believe we've found our Damaskiri."

"No, Kragen," Joquil said warmly, "we've found our Kiri."

Their cheers were deafening, and all she could do was laugh as they took turns spinning and twirling her about the room.

The days continued to pass in a blur for Helena. It was a continuous cycle of dressing, changing and attending some formal ceremony at which she would smile and pretend to be vastly interested in conversations she couldn't remember, with people whose names she had already forgotten.

There were rare moments that stood apart from the others, but overall it was a tedious process.

She had thought that her greatest challenge would be awakening her magic. However, the real test was learning to control and contain it. It took constant effort for her to keep her power leashed, but oftentimes if she were distracted, it would find a way to sneak out.

At dinner the previous night, she was so engrossed in the storyteller's tale that her visions of the scene had begun to spring to life around him, much to the delight of the Palace guests. The poor man had been so shocked, however, that he had lost his place in the story and was unable to continue.

The day before that, she had been listening to another of Timmins' lectures regarding etiquette, wishing she could be outside feeling the sunshine and breeze on her face instead when a gust of wind whipped through the chamber upsetting all of Timmins' carefully laid documents. She had apologized profusely for the disturbance, embarrassed beyond end that her distraction had caused such havoc.

Now, in a welcome moment of solitude, Helena sat in the flower garden, her anxiety over her upcoming trial and the strain of controlling her magic wearing on her. She was so afraid of letting her Circle down, or humiliating herself further, that it was pure bliss being able to sit quietly and just be.

The last day of the Festival was almost upon her, and in mere hours she would finally face her trial. And then, assuming she succeeded, the final ritual which would bind her to her Mate would take place, concluding the Festival. Her mind sorted through her suitors, affectionately thinking about Amos and Micha, but knowing in her heart that the selection had already been made. She conjured Von's face in her mind, smiling unconsciously as she did.

She let out a heartfelt sigh and closed her eyes, tilting her face toward the sun. Appreciating her heightened sense of smell at the moment, she breathed deeply inhaling the scents of the flowers that surrounded her. In her mind, she was identifying each flower by its fragrance, and appreciating the mundane task immensely.

"Am I interrupting, Damaskiri?" a deep voice asked next to her.

Startled she jumped and twisted to the voice's source, surprised anyone had been able to sneak up on her when she was not actively trying to diminish her senses.

She felt her face flush and her heart begin to race as she stammered, "V-von, what, what are you doing here?"

His lips quirked in an amused smile. "You summoned me, Damaskiri."

"I, I did what?" she asked in surprise, eyes widening in embarrassed realization. With a groan, she closed her eyes and covered them with the palm of her hand.

Von moved to sit beside her, gently taking her hand and peeling it away from her face.

She looked up at him sheepishly.

"It's all right; I didn't mind. I hope I'm not intruding?" he asked again, steel eyes searching hers.

She shook her head. "No, I was just noting the flowers." She felt foolish as she uttered the words. She was supposed to be the most powerful woman her kind had seen in hundreds of years, and she was sitting in a garden daydreaming about a man she had just met a handful of days ago. She must amuse him greatly.

Sneaking a glance at him, she saw his knowing smile. She snapped her eyes shut again.

"It must be hard, having so many demands for your attention when you are used to being only responsible to yourself," he said simply.

Helena nodded, eyes opening to stare at the bright yellow roses in front of her. "Yes, it can be overwhelming. Especially when I'm not sure what I'm supposed to be doing half the time. Stick a shovel in my hands and point me in the direction of a garden and I could happily plod along for the rest of my days. Put me in a ballroom full of people wanting to dance and gossip and, and touch me," she said with an exasperated laugh, "and I am so far out of my element I feel like a floundering fish!"

He let out a surprised bark of laughter.

"I'm sorry," she said softly. "I shouldn't complain, I'm feeling a bit sorry for myself at the moment, which is utterly ridiculous."

He brushed a strand of hair from her cheek and electricity sizzled through her at the contact. "By all means, Damaskiri, I will happily sit here with you and let you unburden yourself."

She tilted her head and studied him, gray eyes shining with amusement and obsidian hair ruffled by the breeze.

He looked more relaxed than she could remember seeing him before. Then again, she had only seen him briefly during the various festivities and had never truly been alone with him until this very moment. Her cheeks flooded with heat at the thought. Timmins would surely give her an earful about the inappropriateness of such a situation when he heard about this. A stubborn voice inside of her questioned: *who's going to tell him?*

She smiled ruefully. "I must seem like a child to you, complaining about not only finding that I have magic, but that I am, in fact, the Mother's chosen Daughter."

He shrugged. "It's one thing to grow up knowing who you are and what you will do with your life, and then quite another having it all turned on its head. I think anyone would struggle with such change."

"And you?" she asked curiously. "Did you know what you would do with your life? Did you know that you would be here, sitting beside me?"

He laughed again, his laugh notably forced. "No. Decidedly not. I knew that I would be a warrior and that I would bring honor to my family on the battlefield. I never imagined that I would be a guest at the royal court fighting for the hand of the Damaskiri. Not my kind of battlefield at all," he finished dryly.

She arched an eyebrow in surprise. "Then why are you here?"

He sighed. "Do you know who I am, Damaskiri? Why those people taunted me during the declaration ceremony?"

She shook her head quickly.

"I am Von Holbrooke, son of Darius Holbrooke," he stared ahead of him, unflinching as he continued, "My ancestors were the ones who declared the blood war on Kiri Celestine Di'Cameron and her Circle. They were responsible for the slaughter of thousands.

"They almost succeeded, but they were eventually defeated and branded as blood traitors. My family line has been banned from Tigaera ever since. None will so much as trade with us, except by coercion, and we live in exile from our people and our birthright.

"I became who I had to be, to help my family survive: ruthless; cunning; a mercenary in every sense of the word. There is no softness in me, Damaskiri. I cannot afford the luxury. So no, I had not planned on ever being one of the declared suitors of a Damaskiri." He glanced down at her quickly, gauging her reaction before continuing, "Life, as you are aware, does not go according to plan. I wanted to bring honor to my family, remind the realms of our power and all that." He snorted dismissively. "Instead, I am ridiculed by those that see themselves as my betters and feared by those who recognize my strength. Yes, I've reminded them of our power, but still, they slight us."

His voice had deepened as he spoke. He had rested his elbows on his knees, hunching forward.

"So, you came here hoping to…" she trailed off, not wanting to finish her sentence, her heart aching at the thought that she was simply a means to an end.

He let out another wary sigh. "I came here to continue my task, Damaskiri. I need to restore my family's name; I need the ban lifted so that my brother can have a proper healer. But nothing goes according to plan," he stated again wryly.

Confusion was etched on her face. Was he saying that that wasn't what he was after anymore? Afraid to ask that question, she asked another, "What's wrong with your brother? Why will a healer not see him?"

"Nial was in an accident when he was younger. It was my fault." Von grimaced at the memory. "He had always been small, but he wanted so badly to be like me. I challenged him, told him to try to ride the new stallion that our father had just won. The stallion was pure temper, not the sort that would allow a rider anywhere near him, but my brother was determined. He vaulted on the stallion's back, and the stallion reared. He couldn't stay on, and he was thrown. The stallion trampled him as he rode away. Nial's legs were damaged beyond repair, they've never grown properly, and he's been confined to his bed ever since. That's no life for a man."

Helena could feel the misery and guilt rolling off Von in waves. *This is why he seeks you.* Despite her bruised ego, she gently touched his back, feeling him stiffen at the contact.

"No matter what happens tomorrow," she said softly, "I will help your brother. He will have a healer, even if I must go myself."

Von looked at her in surprise. "Even after I told you who I am, what my family has done, you would help him?"

She nodded. "I may not understand everything that you've done, nor agree with the decisions you have made, but everyone deserves to be judged on their own actions, not those of their ancestors. You have done what you needed to do to survive and to support your family; there is no shame in that."

He looked at her in wonder. "Is that why you spoke for me?"

Her eyes narrowed at the memory. "I spoke for you because it was the right thing to do, and because you are mine; whether you intended to be or not." Her voice was soft but unyielding. She was reeling from his confessions, his depiction of himself at complete odds with his tale about his brother. Her pride at war with her compassion. She couldn't help but feel like an utter fool for sitting there like a lovesick girl, while he had been strategically plotting, even if it was for a valid, albeit selfish, reason.

He sat unmoving for a moment before reaching his hand toward her. "Helena," he said softly.

She noted the use of her name with surprise.

Grabbing her hand, he continued to meet her gaze intently. "Things do not go according to plan. I told you what brought me here because you asked. It was not my intention to do so, at least not like that, but I would not hide it from you either. You should know who I am."

She remained quiet, uncertain of what he was saying.

He let out a breath and continued, "Helena, your soul calls to mine. I could no more deny that than I could my name. Just because it may not have been my intention at the start of my journey, does not mean that I am not pleased with the result, or that I will not do right by you and our bond."

He nudged her playfully with his shoulder. She bit her lip as she smiled, pleased to hear his admission. "You leave much to be desired in the way of wooing, Von."

He laughed, relief evident in the sound. "I did not realize you desired wooing, Damaskiri."

"Damaskiri I may be, but I am a woman first and foremost, Mate. You would do well to remember that." When she stood and looked at him, it was with iridescent eyes. Her hair danced in the wind, and she turned away from him, but not before watching the grin falter in shock from his face. Her laughter floated behind her as she walked toward the Palace.

He remained on the bench, stunned. He had known that she was whispered to be the most powerful Kiri his people had ever seen, and he thought he had an idea of what that meant. As he watched her hips sway while she walked away from him, he realized that he knew nothing.

AH, that's where she's run off too. Gillian landed softly on a tree branch high above the flowering garden, leaves raining down gently from the contact. *And with him!*

This should prove very enlightening, she thought, jumping down a few branches to better hear their intense conversation.

From her perch in the trees above them, Gillian could overhear Von's story, shocked that he was so blatantly confessing his selfish motivations. Gillian had tried to use every spare opportunity she could to get closer to the young Damaskiri, and she had learned easily enough that the girl was a romantic. Growing up so far removed from court society had not prepared her for the reality and politics of royal courtships. Gillian was certain such a declaration would seriously bruise her tender feelings for her suitor.

Tawny feathers ruffling in the breeze, Gillian leaned forward, unconcerned with looking suspicious. If the two felt her watching them, they gave no indication and would only see a hawk if they did happen to look her way.

Gillian noted the strain around the girl's eyes, but it was not hurt making the aqua orbs glow, it was compassion. *Mother help her, she's falling for it, and for him,* Gillian rolled her eyes in disgust; *she's making this so easy.* Gillian was almost disappointed that the task ahead would not require her to use the true extent of her creative plotting. Almost. The sooner this was settled, the better.

'Your soul calls to mine…' the blood traitor was saying now.

Please! Gillian squawked in amused disbelief. *The warrior wouldn't know the sight of his blackened soul even if he had one, let alone admit that he actually had feelings for the girl.* Green eyes noted the softening of the girl's face at his words, and she winced in sympathy before catching the errant emotion. She could not afford to let herself feel anything for the impostor. She scoffed, *the fool believes him! He is practically doing the job for me.*

With a toss of her head, Gillian spread her wings and took flight, missing the sight of the girl as she stood, or the man's look of amazement as she walked away.

Chapter 6

Helena sat at the ancient sprawling vanity, fingers tapping a mindless tune on its shining surface. Alina was deftly twisting and pinning loose curls atop her head, using magic, instead of pins, to help keep the curls in place. Helena was glad for the shift, the sheer number of pins needed to keep her hair from listing drunkenly to the side of her head made her head ache.

She was wondering idly when she had begun thinking of the Palace as home, and her Circle and Alina as her family. Although it had been little over a month since she had moved here from the sweet cottage and her simple life there, this life, this world, was becoming more real to her than her years at the cottage.

It wasn't the grandeur of her new home, although she loved the soft femininity of her room decorated in its various shades of purple and gold which were both calming and lovely. She especially loved the deep armchair which sat underneath a large window with an unimpeded view of the main garden. And there was definitely something to be said for carpets that were so thick she felt her feet got lost in them. She scrunched her toes into the soft fabric at the thought and smiled, wrapping her lavender shawl more tightly around her shoulders.

Alina noted her mistress's smile, and couldn't help her responding one. "Thinking of someone, Damaskiri?" she teased lightly.

Helena blushed, she hadn't been thinking of Von actually, but at the suggestion, his image blazed brightly in her mind.

Her mind replayed their afternoon in the garden. She knew that she shouldn't be disappointed by his story, and she wasn't really, it was more of a deflation. Her coming back to reality and recognizing that it would be incredibly naïve of her to think all of the suitors had declared themselves because they had dreamed of her since they were children, or heard stories of her beauty and decided they must have her. And really, she chided herself, wouldn't that be worse? To be wanted as an object rather than a person.

Von had stated that he hadn't even anticipated the possibility that he would be selected as the Damaskiri's Mate, he was just trying to help his family. That was honorable in its own right, and she couldn't find it in herself to blame him for it. More than that, he was honest about it. He hadn't tried to hide his reasons for pursuing her behind false claims of emotion and feelings for her.

His honesty gave them a foundation to build from, and that's all you needed to start a relationship she decided. Not that she had been in one before, but surely it would be like any other, built on mutual respect and trust? She hoped that eventually, those would grow into affection and companionship since she had always wanted a marriage full of love and laughter.

She stared wistfully into the mirror trying to imagine Von gazing at her with love or bouncing a child on his knee, but entirely unable to conjure the image. He was too cynical, too… too male, she thought, to be placed in such a domesticated role. It was his maleness, though, that was causing the fluttering low in her stomach.

Well that, and the way his dimple would flash and his gray eyes would light up in surprise when she made him laugh.

Alina's laughter tinkled sweetly. "So that's the way of it?" she asked.

Helena grinned at her ruefully and stuck her tongue out at the girl through the mirror.

"You're very lucky, Damaskiri, to have such a strong Mate. He will be good to you."

Helena smiled at Alina. "You don't believe him to be a traitor then, as the others do?"

She shook her head, lips pursed as she concentrated on pinning the last few curls up. "No, Damaskiri. He's your Mate, which means that he was made for you. You're the most kind and warm lady I've ever met; I cannot imagine the other half of you would not be as passionate." Alina's eyes met Helena's briefly before she continued, "He may be less inclined to show that side of himself, but that does not mean it doesn't exist within him."

Helena was pleased with the thought. "You don't think that if he's the other half of me, he is the darker half?" she asked, repeating her Circle's explanation for the match.

Alina paused, considering. "He might be, Damaskiri, but aren't we all made of both shadows and light? Shadows cannot exist without light though, so you cannot have one and not have the other. Just because he may be that side of you does not make him evil."

"Yes," Helena responded, her smile blooming beautifully across her face, her eyes going soft and dreamy. "I think so too."

Alina chuckled at her mistress's obvious infatuation. "There, all done. You are ready."

Helena glanced into the mirror and studied the reflection that stared back at her. Chestnut curls were piled intricately atop her head with their ends falling softly to her shoulders. Her face was absent of any makeup; the effect should have left her looking fresh and youthful. However, her aqua eyes peered back sharply, the silvery ring around her pupils swirling like a mist of light creating the sense of all-knowing wisdom that belied any innocence. It was a captivating and stunning effect, for all of its simplicity.

There would be no elaborate dress to armor herself with this time. She would wear the traditional attire of the trial: a loose cotton robe, belted with a cord around her hips all in shades of tan.

Standing she turned in a slow circle.

Alina clapped with delight. "I can't think of a lady who has ever looked more beautiful," she whispered in awe, her smile lighting up her entire face.

Helena's lips twisted in a wry smile. "Liar, I see one standing before me."

The girl blushed in pleasure but waved away the compliment.

With a breath that was equal parts sigh and groan, Helena turned toward the door. "I suppose I have to go down there now. Time to get this over with, one way or the other."

Alina reached her hand toward her mistress, tentatively lest Helena should refuse her. Sensing no rebuke, she squeezed her shoulder infusing her gentle warmth and belief. "You will be amazing, Damaskiri. There is no question."

Feeling the soothing magic woven into the words, Helena couldn't help but smile. She was still learning much about magic, and the depths of her own vastly outweighed her maid's, but it was the intention behind the action that allowed Helena to wrap the girl's conviction around her.

With a last smile, albeit strained and lopsided, Helena moved out of the room and fell into formation with her Circle which had been waiting outside.

She could sense the current of their emotions around her, a heady mix of anticipation, confidence, and pride. Her Circle was more sure of her success than she was, but then again, they weren't the ones who had just discovered who they were mere weeks ago.

She felt, rather than saw, Darrin move closer to her. It was an unconscious display of support and protection, and she appreciated the gesture even if he didn't realize he had offered one.

The group took a hallway winding down into the deeper levels of the Spirit Wing where the ceremony chambers were located. Having grown used to the roar of the crowds during the Festival, the relative quiet of their steps was daunting. None but the Circle were allowed into the antechamber of the trial room, and only the Damaskiri was allowed through the gold door at the end of the room.

The decorations were more muted down here, the overall mood more austere and intimidating than warm or comforting. Following a dark purple rug into the antechamber, the group stopped. Helena turned to face her Circle, meeting each man's eyes briefly, attempting to communicate her appreciation for each of them in those few seconds.

There were no rituals to follow at this point, no ceremonial words to say. All that was left was for Helena to take the few remaining steps into the golden room and through the door. She opened her mouth as though to say something, but couldn't find any words. So instead she closed it and shrugged with a small smile. The men smiled encouragingly in return.

Turning from them she took the last few steps on her own and with a deep breath reached for the golden door. It was warm to the touch and surprisingly light for its size. Without a sound, it opened inwards, and she stepped through.

At first, there was only silence and mist; she could not see farther than an arm's length in front of her. Behind her, the door had vanished. She felt the familiar tingle of her magic being called to the surface, even though she had not beckoned it.

As her magic continued to flow, the tingle turned into a burn. She would have thought she was having trouble breathing, but she had not drawn a breath since entering the chamber. In fact, she couldn't feel her heart beating at all. The thought frightened her momentarily, but the drawing of her power had consumed her attention. It was all she could do to focus on keeping herself together.

"Ah, there you are," a voice whispered. It sounded as though someone was standing behind her speaking directly into her ear, but there was no one there.

The hair on her arms and neck rose in response.

"We have been waiting for you," it continued, although now it sounded like multiple voices speaking at once.

Her head began to pound at the intensity and amount of power flowing through her.

"The trial of a Damaskiri forces her to face her innermost self," the voice, singular and distinctly male continued.

"The darkest parts of self and its most hidden fears and desires," another component, discernibly female, took up where it had left off.

"It is your response to these parts of yourself that will reveal both the purity of your magic and your wholeness of self; a true Kiri requires both. The trial begins."

The last echoed around her as the mist swirled and revealed a bed with two bodies moving against one another. Eyes grew round as she realized what she was seeing.

Head thrown back in a carnal growl, Von turned to look at her, never stopping his thrusts. Her body responding to the image, she took a step forward.

A flash of blonde hair caught her eye and Helena looked past Von to see the woman below him. It wasn't her. As her eyes, mirroring her pain and confusion met his, he laughed, the sound a deep growling thunder that swelled throughout the room.

"Come join us, woman, perhaps you will learn something," he purred before giving her a feral grin and looking back to the woman arching up to meet his increasing thrusts.

Betrayal lashed at her like a knife, and she felt her fury wrap around her like an icy blanket. She snarled, and within her, the pool rippled.

Before she could act, the scene in front of her changed. She was now in the halls of the Palace, holding court over her people, every face reflecting their disappointment in her. The people murmured with distrust and unease. She watched her Circle turn their backs on her and walk toward the back of the room. She wanted to call out and run to them, but she was rooted to the spot. She did not know what she had done, only that she had failed miserably; her magic continued to twist and rise its way up and out of the deepest recesses within.

Now she was in the gardens of the Palace, but the sky was dark and the air filled with the acrid smell of smoke. Helena coughed and spun around in confusion, the intensity of the emotions evoked by the previous scenes still swirling within her and only adding to her disorientation.

The towers of the Palace were crumbling, and she could see the remains of fire blazing throughout the courtyard. Where there had once been rows upon rows of the flowers she had loved to get lost in; now there were only charred, almost skeletal, remains standing in their stead. Eyes flicking down, she saw that the ground below her was covered in seared and bloody bodies, or at least what was left of them.

Gasping, she dropped down to help them, and as she turned them over, she began to recognize faces. One after the other: Timmins, Joquil, Alina, Micha, Amos, Darrin… all those that she had come to love.

Body trembling, she stood and looked at her robe, now splattered with blood and ash; the warm liquid dripping down her fingers and onto Darrin's lifeless face. IIis blank eyes staring up at her unseeing. Beside him Micha's head began to turn, the one eye remaining in its socket blinking, while the bloody mouth gurgled as it tried unsuccessfully to speak.

An anguished scream tore through her throat, and an answering bolt of lightning struck a nearby tree, her magic's outward sign of its response to her terror. The still-smoking branches shuddered, unable to withstand the additional assault. With a deafening crack, the tree was rent in two, one half falling toward the pile of bodies below. The unearthly scream continued while her magic's answering storm rolled through the sky, its fury wreaking havoc on what was left of the land.

She knew with complete certainty that she was the one that had slain these people.

Shaking, she tried to move away, but the corpses began to grab her feet, moaning wetly in their attempt to pull her down. In fear, she felt her magic lash out, and the body that had grabbed her exploded, raining warm pieces of flesh upon her. It was Kragen.

"No!" she screamed again, tears falling from her eyes, blinding her. She was completely shaken, overwhelmed by the emotions within her: rage, shame, and anguish vying for her attention and calling her to action.

One by one the images flickered through her mind, Von laughing, remorseless at his betrayal, the backs of the men as they left her, and Darrin's face twisted in the agony of his death.

Sobbing, she fell to her knees. Around her, the wind rose whipping her hair around. Thunder growled in the sky, echoing her own screams.

Within, she felt the depth of her magic swirl through the pool as she pulled it to her, and released it. Her back arched at the intensity of the release and she felt herself come undone.

There was silence, the scene before her replaced again with silvery mist. She felt as though her body had no shape; she merely floated within the mist.

Eventually, the sound of Von's laughter brought her back to herself. Panting, she knelt on the ground; her forehead pressed into her one raised knee. Afraid to open her eyes, lest she sees more bodies or something even more terrible, Helena did not move.

"These events will come to pass, if you do not trust," the voice-of-many whispered.

She jolted to awareness, spine stiffening as though waiting for an assault.

"The eyes can see what the heart knows to be false. If you do not trust in yourself to know the difference, you will be lost," the female voice continued. The ends of her hair fluttered, as though a hand had run through them.

"He is you, and you are he. A betrayal of your bond can only occur if you do not trust," the last words whipped against her.

"A Kiri knows herself, the shadows and the light. To fear the shadow is to betray the light. Recognize the potential for destruction, but do not fear it and it shall not pass." The whisper faded away, leaving her.

Confused and trembling Helena stood. Was she done? How did that test her? She felt as though it had only tormented her. And then she knew.

Her test was to see if she could withstand the worst of herself. She was shown, in the most literal sense, what it would mean if she doubted not only her power, but her bond with her Mate. It all came down to that; it had always been about that. That was why it was such an integral part of the ceremony; he was the other part of her, and she had to fully accept and understand both.

To let that bond unravel would lead to a destruction of her people, the fulfillment of the prophecy so many had tried to circumvent. And in her uncertainty, she would be the source of their downfall. No matter what they would have done with her as a child, the end result would have been the same; it would always have come to the same end.

The door behind her opened. Muscles quaking in protest she turned toward the light filtering through it. She did not know how long she had been in the chamber; her sense of time was utterly gone.

She walked through the door back to the four men that had waited for her. As one they fell to their knees in fear and awe.

"It is done," said the layered voice that had whispered to her in the chamber, her magic's voice.

Helena stood in the doorway, her robe and skin still covered in blood and soot. Her hair tumbled down her back and shoulders in a riot of waves and her eyes iridescent and unfocused, their swirling depths seeming to hypnotize and see straight through to one's soul.

She opened her hand, and the pendant of the Mother dangled from her fingers, the simple knot in the center replaced with an egg-sized stone the same iridescent smoke of her eyes. As the men recognized the Kiri's pendant, Helena's eyes rolled back in her head, and she collapsed.

CHAPTER 7

$\mathcal{V}$on heard the scream, its intensity and pain tearing through his body.

"Helena!" he shouted, coming to attention and reaching for the sword at his hips.

He looked around warily, eyes narrowed and trying to identify the threat. He crossed the room swiftly, feet silent as he made his way to the door.

Sensing nothing, he opened the door and peered outside. A servant was scurrying by with her arms full of fabric. Today's washing, he guessed.

She halted a few steps past him and turned. "Did you need something?"

He shook his head, and she continued down the hallway. After another few moments, he allowed his body to relax. Von could have sworn he'd heard Helena screaming, but if the Damaskiri was in trouble, the entire Palace would be in an uproar.

Releasing his sword, he brought his hand to his jaw and rubbed the day's beard thoughtfully.

Magic had always made him uneasy, his own source of power lending itself predominantly to his skills on the battlefield. He had never been quick to accept things that he did not understand or could not explain. This fit neatly into both categories. He caught a flash of movement out of the corner of his eye and went to grab for the sword again when he realized it was still in his hand.

His body was trembling like a green boy. *Magic,* he thought with a curse. Von knew he would not be able to relax fully until he had personally guaranteed her safety, and not just with his eyes. He was going to make damned sure that she was unharmed, and the Mother help the poor bastards that tried to stop him. Since he was all but the final member of the Circle he decided to go find Helena's guards, and demand to see her. He wanted to hold her. Von's steps faltered as he realized it was not merely want, but a bone-deep need to feel her safely in his arms. He took a shuddering breath to steady himself before resuming his ground-eating strides down the hall. He moved quickly, ignoring the curious stares he was drawing.

As he rounded the last corner, he saw the men he had been searching for walking toward him. They moved tentatively, Timmins and Joquil turning to look behind them often. There was a mix of emotions playing over the men's faces, but concern was most prevalent among them.

Before he could open his mouth to greet them, they shifted in formation and he was able to see the other two. The first thing he noted was the panic etched in Darrin's face. Following the man's gaze, Von's eyes were drawn to the woman being carried in Kragen's arms.

Her limbs dangled lifelessly over his arms, her head lolled back and allowed her hair to all but graze the floor.

In seconds he had reached them, his body on full alert and his senses primed with magic.

"Isn't your job to ensure her protection," he snapped, his voice low and deadly.

Timmins visibly flinched at the waves of danger he felt rolling off Von. He held his hands up and spoke softly, each word carefully measured. "We could not have anticipated this result, nor are we to blame for her collapse."

Not even remotely mollified, Von continued to scowl at the older man.

Darrin moved to speak, taking his eyes off of Helena only briefly, "She entered the door for her trial; hours had passed with nary a sound. When they opened…" he seemed to stumble over his words and Von could tell how the sight had affected him.

Kragen's deep rumble took up the story, "She was covered in blood. Before we could so much as blink she was falling to the floor. From what we can tell, she is unharmed, but the drain on her magic was too much for her."

"She is unharmed, but covered in blood?" Von asked, his lips curling in disbelief and eyes narrowed in censure. "Whose blood is it then?" he demanded, his voice still lethally soft.

"We do not know, my lord," Timmins shrugged helplessly.

"Before she collapsed, she showed us this." Joquil was holding out the pendant, a silver light emanating from the stone.

Von felt his body stiffen at the sight. *So she has passed, why then has she collapsed?* Ignoring his reaction, he continued, "You said you hadn't heard anything, but I could hear her scream from my room." The statement was an accusation.

Timmins shrugged again. "I cannot do much but speculate until she awakens and we speak with her, however, if I had to guess it would seem that the bond the two of you have already begun to cultivate has allowed you to stay connected to her during her trial."

"The books on the Damaskiri trial have always been unfailingly vague. We could not have anticipated that behind those doors she was doing anything other than meditating. We heard nothing," he emphasized.

Von frowned at the old man's words. Had he been connected to her? He knew that he had heard her, and he knew that he had not imagined the pain and terror in her scream.

He looked back at Kragen. "I will take her."

The warrior gazed back at him steadily, before inclining his head in agreement.

"The hell you will!" snapped Darrin, eyes wounded but fierce. "We are her Circle, you sir, have not yet spoken the vows that will bind you to her. You have no right," his voice shook with emotion, "no right to touch her."

"Darrin," Timmins said softly, quiet rebuke in the word.

"The Kiri has already chosen her mate, Shield," Joquil said firmly, his face void of expression. "Even you cannot stand in the way of that."

Von let the men speak, but Darrin would not move from in front of Kragen, and with Helena still limp in his arms Von wouldn't risk hurting her by ramming Darrin out of the way.

"Boy," Von sneered, with thinly veiled disdain, "stand down. You have already failed her once today, do not do so again."

The blond man flinched at the accusation but moved mutely to the side. Kragen stepped forward and set Helena with surprising gentleness into Von's arms.

Von allowed his gaze to sweep over the girl in his arms. Her usually luminous skin was waxy and purplish bruises were in sharp contrast to her eyes. He tried to dispassionately note the blood that covered her, used to seeing such scenes after his own battles. The blood itself did not bother him, it was the sheer amount of it, and that it covered *her*.

He felt a sharp tug in his chest at the sight and immediately snapped his eyes up before he could allow himself to be distracted by his emotions. He turned back the way he had come and started climbing the spiraling stairways as quickly as possible without jarring Helena.

"Joquil," he called over his shoulder, "Perhaps you should do something to ensure we do not draw unwanted attention to ourselves."

The man nodded in agreement, and Von felt the familiar tingle of magic race down his neck as Joquil began warding the passageway. His sensitivity to the use of magic was one of the most helpful skills he had acquired through his years of traveling and warring. It usually meant the difference between the life and death of his men and would signal a potential threat long before one materialized.

Without stopping Von slammed his foot into Helena's door, the door splintering and flying open with a crash.

Within the room, Alina spun around with a sharp cry, her eyes widening in shock at the sight of her mistress in his arms.

"Go grab a healer, quickly. Do not spread tales, and do not come back in this room until I ask for you."

Alina nodded, trembling fingers still pressed against her lips. She rushed quickly from the door, pushing past the four men still standing in the doorway.

Von turned to them, "Guard the door. No one comes in until I say," he said sharply, his voice still deadly soft.

"That goes for all of you," he added with narrowed eyes, sparing a final second to stare at Darrin until the blond man left the room. Joquil followed behind him, gesturing and murmuring under his breath as he sealed the doorway, ensuring privacy for the room's occupants.

Von set Helena down softly on her bed, finally allowing himself to fully catalog her injuries. A warrior by birth and blood, Von was not one to use his powers as anything other than a weapon or perhaps to bring some minor comfort to the otherwise stark living conditions of the road. His grandmother, however, was a noted healer in her time, and she had taught him a few things before her passing.

Closing his eyes, Von called the unfamiliar branch of magic to him, feeling the warmth rush through his fingers. He ran a gentle hand down her body, trying to sense any irregularities within her. He found none.

"What did you do, little one?" he asked her softly, easing himself down beside her.

With no apparent injury, Von could only assume that Timmins had been correct in his assessment that she had pushed her magic to its very limits causing a severe drain of her own vitality.

Not pausing to consider what he was doing, Von reached out to her again, resting his hand firmly on her chest over her heart. Driven by pure instinct he tried to share his own life force with her. He felt the drain immediately, tendons pulling sharply in his neck, and sweat breaking out on his brow.

It wasn't until he felt himself beginning to shake that he pulled away. Letting out a ragged breath he studied her again. The waxen quality of her skin had diminished, and the dark circles under her eyes had faded. She was still too pale, but now, at least, she looked as though she could be sleeping.

He heard her murmur, and his eyes snapped to hers willing them to open. She began to shift restlessly on the bed, a groan escaping her lips as though the movement was too painful.

His lips quirked despite themselves; it looked like his Mate was a warrior in her own way. He understood the fatigue battle could bring and the accompanying sense of frustration at your own body's weakness.

Her eyelids fluttered open, her eyes widening slightly when she saw him watching her.

"Von," she rasped.

"You gave us quite a scare, Kiri," he murmured.

"Kiri," she repeated, pleasure making her eyes glow brightly. "I did it?"

He nodded, returning her smile.

"Why do I feel like I fell from atop the tower then?" She groaned again as she tried to push herself up.

He placed a hand on her shoulder and gently pushed her back down, "I was hoping you'd be able to tell us that. Your Circle says you stepped out of the trial room, showed them your pendant and collapsed."

Her eyebrow furrowed in confusion. "I don't remember that. I, I don't remember much of..." she trailed off, and her eyes widened in horror as it came back to her.

He saw her beginning to panic and immediately began to murmur the nonsensical words one uses to soothe. She calmed quickly but flinched when he went to smooth a strand of hair from her forehead. He noted the reaction but ignored it.

Her eyes flickered up to his, and away again. He could tell she was weighing whether or not to share what had happened, and he knew from experience his patience would do more toward persuading her than any words.

"I saw you," she murmured finally.

He raised an eyebrow in response.

She swallowed and continued, "You were…"

He noted the blush. "I have a feeling I can guess what I was in the middle of. Did it make you nervous, *Mira*?" he teased.

She shook her head, smoky eyes narrowing fiercely. "Not nervous, furious."

He stopped his finger's lazy exploration of her cheek and jaw. "Furious? I've been told I make a woman feel many things during coupling, but that is a first."

Her lips twitched despite herself, and aqua eyes met his. "Perhaps if you had been coupling with *me*, I would have reacted differently."

"Ah." He shifted uncomfortably. "I dare say you would have."

"I didn't like it, Von. The sight of you with another woman…" As she trailed off her eyes searched his, her voice low and tense with emotion when she continued, "You are *mine*, I-I will not share you."

He grabbed her hand in response, ignoring another sharp tug in his chest. "I would not expect you to, Kiri. I would not share you either."

She smiled softly at his words. "I suppose I should warn you that I did not react well… to the sight. I did not realize I was a jealous woman."

He laughed at that, squeezing the small hand in his. "Noted."

Her smile faltered, and she related the other sights that she had seen, her eyes bright with unshed tears.

He felt his own tense response to her words, although how much of it was a fierce protectiveness of the beautiful girl that was lying before him and how much was fear at the possibility of such total destruction at her hands, he could not identify.

"It seems we both have been warned today," he said neutrally.

"Indeed." Looking back up at him and shaking off the final vestiges of her trial she added lightly, "I'm surprised they let you in here all by yourself. I'm not sure if I'm offended or relieved at the lack of people crowding around me in concern." She laughed, belying any possibility that she was offended.

"I did not give them an option," he said flatly.

Her laughter deepened, and she offered him a large smile. "I suppose thanks are in order then."

He shook his head, a small smile playing on his own lips.

"None is necessary, Kiri."

"You did more than just keep them away," she murmured, no trace of doubt in her tone.

He shrugged sheepishly.

"I can feel you," she whispered, tugging on his hand until he met her gaze. "I can feel you inside of me." Her other hand rested on her chest where his had been earlier. "It feels like you reached inside me and left a little part of yourself in my soul."

Her words simultaneously chilled and warmed him.

There was a sense of wonder in her voice. "Can I try?"

He blinked, startled. "I don't know if that's wise, Kiri. Your trial seriously weakened you."

She shrugged off his concern, pushing herself up to face him. Bracing himself, he warily watched her reach for him and rest her hand against his chest. She stared straight into his eyes, and he felt the warm pulse of her magic flow into him. He let out a startled gasp, feeling his own sense of awe.

He could feel her spirit swirling within him sweetly caressing his own as shy and playful as a kitten. He felt her very essence, a heady combination of youthful innocence and pure womanly fire and he knew, with complete certainty, that he would always feel her soul entwined with his own.

She went to move her hand, a satisfied smile on her lips, but he stopped her by placing his own hand over hers.

Slowly, so as not to scare her, he leaned down and brushed his lips against hers. She melted against him with a soft sigh.

Still connected he could feel her reaction to his kiss, his lips moving gently against hers. Her pleasure and curiosity lapping at him like a gentle fire. He felt his own body respond to her eager sweetness, so he pulled away, but not far.

Her eyes opened slowly, and she studied him with eyes now

darkened with desire. Just as he could feel her reaction to the kiss, she had felt his. She knew the effect her desire had on him.

He couldn't help the satisfied smile that lurked on his own lips.

"Mine," she said in a throaty whisper, wonder and desire swirling within iridescent eyes.

He inclined his head, not breaking eye contact.

"Yes, Kiri, and you are mine," responded the Mate, his own voice rich with promise.

He felt a final caress of her spirit within him as she shifted away. *You'll have to show me that again, later.*

He blinked in surprise at her voice in his mind. Before he could ask her what she meant, he heard Darrin pushing the remains of the battle-worn door open, his expression openly defiant.

With a groan, Von moved away from Helena. He pressed a soft kiss to her forehead, still ignoring the dried smears of blood. *It was too much to hope I could keep you to myself,* he thought.

He saw her lips twitch and realized that she could hear his thoughts just as clearly as if he had spoken aloud.

I think it's part of the Mating bond, she offered in response to the unasked question. *I think when you infused your spirit with mine, you showed your acceptance of the bond.*

He shook his head ruefully, his dimple flashing quickly.

He turned his attention back toward the angry man in the doorway.

"Did you not think to tell us that she had recovered," he bit out furiously, as he moved toward her side. "We have been beyond worried."

Von rolled his eyes. "Relax, puppy, she just opened her eyes a few moments ago."

Darrin bristled at the insult; green eyes narrowed in challenge.

"I wouldn't do that, if I were you," Von cautioned, all gentleness vanishing from his stance and expression.

Helena put her hand on Von's arm, and his eyes flickered toward her, warming slightly as they studied her. He nodded, tersely, and walked toward the door, but not without a final scathing glance at her Shield.

As Von left, Helena let her attention return to Darrin.

He stood tense by her side; she could sense the guilt and concern weighing on him.

"You are not to blame for this, Shield. It was not your place to protect."

"It is always my place to protect you, Kiri."

Helena shook her head at his pride. "Do you think so much of yourself, sir, that you could stand between a Kiri and her trial?"

Color stained his cheeks at her admonition. "Hellion," he whispered, his voice conveying all that he was not at liberty to say.

She opened her arms, knowing that he needed the hug more than she did. He moved swiftly, wrapping his arms around her and burying his head in her hair. She felt him breathe deeply a handful of times. With a final shudder, he pulled away, his mask of calm back in place.

He gestured at her torn and bloody robe. "So what did you do to deserve all that?"

It was Helena's turn to shudder.

"That bad?" he asked softly.

"Perhaps you should call the others," she said flatly, ignoring the question and readjusting herself against the mountain of pillows at her back.

He nodded curtly and grabbed the men from the hallway.

As her Circle entered the room, she felt each curious gaze as though the questions were spoken aloud.

"It is not my blood," she told them.

They nodded, but their relief at her admission was palpable.

"The Mother saw fit to warn me what my failure would mean. This is the cost." She gestured at herself. "I cannot fail."

"You did not fail, Kiri," Joquil reminded her.

She offered him a small smile. "Nothing is that simple, Master. My trial is not one to be overcome so quickly."

"But the pendant…" Timmins started in confusion, before stopping himself.

"Perhaps I should clarify. I passed the trial of the Damaskiri. My magic has accepted me, and I was gifted with the pendant of the Kiri.

Now I must face the trial of the Kiri; it is not a trial one can prepare for. It is not the trial written of in your history books, and I cannot rely upon your counsel to see me through this time."

Aqua eyes turned to smoke, and her voice blended with the harmony of many. "The Mother showed me what my failure would mean. I would be the destruction of us all."

The men shivered at the wind that whipped through the chamber at her words, but they stood firm.

The mountain of corpses and acrid smoke filled her mind once more.

"Then you will not fail, Kiri," Kragen said simply, pulling her back from the vision.

Iridescent eyes met his. "Pray you are right, Sword."

"Whatever the Mother sees fit to test you with in the future, you will be prepared, and we will be by your side. You will not face this alone."

She smiled at her Shield. "I hope that I am deserving of your faith in me."

Alina knocked on the door gently. "Kiri, may I allow the healer to check on you now?"

"Am I needed anywhere right now, Timmins?" Helena asked, her desire to curl into a ball and sleep at war with her duty to her people.

"No, you rest now. All that remains is for the Ceremony of Binding, but that can wait, it's just a formality at this point anyway."

Helena felt herself smiling at the thought of Von.

"I'll be outside if you need me."

"Thank you, Darrin, but you should rest as well. It seems it was a hard morning for us all."

"I'll be outside," he repeated.

She rolled her eyes. "Suit yourself."

Alina was followed into the room by Tanya, the Palace's most gifted healer. Tanya exuded competence and unflappable strength. She noted the blood without qualm.

"Are you hurt, Kiri?" she asked gently.

Helena shook her head. "No, merely a bit drained it seems."

She nodded, as though anticipating the answer. "I'll just give you a once over, shall I? And maybe a tonic to help you relax for a bit?"

"That sounds lovely."

Tanya smiled and set warm hands on either side of Helena's head. Her last thought before drifting to sleep was that Tanya's eyes were the exact color of her favorite armchair.

CHAPTER 8

"**W**hy are they all naked?" she squeaked.

Gillian's laugh was a sultry chuckle. "Relax, Helena, they aren't actually naked, much to my endless disappointment. They have that scrap of cloth covering the most interesting bits, see?" She pointed toward the cloth slung low on the candidates' hips that tied off in a flimsy knot on the side.

"But, but why?" she asked again, desperation coloring her voice as she eyed the row of men standing on the dais. Heat flooded her cheeks, and she could not bring herself to lower her eyes past their chins.

The women in the crowd were cheering enthusiastically, calling out the names of their favorites and praying for the fluttering pieces of fabric to get caught in a strong breeze and fall to the floor.

Helena couldn't deny that the sight was a spectacular one, eleven males in their prime were all lined up waiting for her. More specifically, they were waiting for the Ceremony of Binding to begin, at which she would publicly choose her Mate.

"Well, I did warn you that attraction was part of picking a mate," Gillian teased bringing her back to their conversation, "you'll know you've found your mate because of how they respond when you run your hands over their chest—everyone will for that matter."

Helena's eyes went wide at the implication, and she looked at Gillian in panic.

Gillian's enjoyment of her distress was clear. "Relax, Helena; I'm teasing. Tradition dictates that when a Damaskiri rests her hand over the heart of her true mate, her soul will call to his and their heartbeats will sync as the soul is reconnected to its other half."

Helena recalled the other night with Von and the way that she could feel him inside of her ever since. She sent a tentative tug down the invisible tether she felt connecting her to him.

Blazing gray eyes met hers from his spot in the line-up. She couldn't even offer him a shy smile as she looked back toward her feet to avoid the feast of male flesh currently on display.

No one else had realized that the two had inadvertently completed their mating bond while alone in her room, but even if they had, there was no way to escape this final public ritual. Helena was glad that it happened that way, to have to experience that intimacy while thousands of people watched them would have diminished some of the magic in the moment.

Not to mention the reaction to the kiss that had followed. Helena felt her ears turning pink at the memory of that kiss; her toes curling in her shoes. Oh yes, she was thankful that she had been able to avoid that particular spectacle.

"I just don't understand how that requires them to remove all their clothing," Helena said through gritted teeth.

Sighing, Gillian rolled her eyes. "Helena, don't be such a prude. All of the men who are refused tonight will not be lacking sympathy or company for that matter," she added as her green eyes roamed the cheering crowd. "The entire process of finding your mate requires a complete surrendering of self. This is all symbolic"—her hand gestured to the men—"they are standing there to bare their souls to you, to show that they have nothing to hide and that they are willing to sacrifice their pride when needed, in order to best serve the realm. Granted the tradition might be a bit outdated, but the meaning is what matters. Besides, even you cannot deny that it's a little fun."

Helena brought her eyes back to Von. He stood among the others defiantly; his head tossed back—the better to stare down his nose at those standing below him. There was no shame in his stance, just confidence and a bit of impatience, as his arms crossed over his chest.

Helena had to look away. Standing on the other side of Von was Gillian's twin. Micha was built much like his sister, looking almost childish standing next to Von's impressive bulk.

Micha noticed her and winked, his lips twisting up wryly as if to ask *what can you do?* His pale skin was flushed from the attention of the crowd, but he too stood still, awaiting the beginning of this final test.

"If that's what this is all supposed to demonstrate, then why are they the only ones who are naked? Shouldn't I be as well?"

Gillian's horrified reaction was almost comical. "Helena, you are Kiri. The first Kiri in centuries. Of course you aren't going to parade around in the nude." Gillian made a face and seemed to struggle with her words before continuing, "You are the most powerful woman in the world, there is no reason for you to ever debase yourself. These men are seeking to be worthy of you, not the other way around."

Helena frowned at that, Gillian's words sitting uncomfortably. It just didn't make sense, this double standard, if mates were supposed to be two parts of a whole, how could one ever be seen as more than the other? Helena shook her head, causing her chestnut curls to dance. No, she refused to accept that. So long as she was the one being mated, she would never treat these men as less than equals.

Knowing that she still had some time before the sun made its final descent in the sky, Helena looked around for Alina.

The girl was standing off to the side chatting with the healer Tanya. Helena excused herself and started toward the girl.

Seeing her coming, Alina met her halfway.

"Is something amiss, Kiri?" Alina asked.

Helena quickly shook her head and then paused, trying to choose her words with care. "I need you to help me with something, but we don't have much time," she added as she looked back up toward the sky.

Alina was nodding. "Of course, whatever you need, Kiri."

Alina's eyes grew round as Helena explained what she wanted to do.

STANDING off to the side of the dais, Helena was wrapped in a cloak the color of the night's sky. It had a deep hood that was currently pulled low over her face, hiding her from the crowd.

Timmins had stepped to the center of the stage and held up his hands to get the crowd's attention. There were a few last hoots and cheers until finally, as one, the crowd fell silent.

"One of the Chosen's most beloved traditions is the choosing of the Mate. Tonight, our Kiri will make her choice, completing her Circle and formally beginning her reign as our ruler."

Timmins stepped back and swept his arm to the side, revealing Helena to the crowd.

There were low murmurings starting in the crowd as she stepped forward, the cloak parting to reveal the luminous glow of her skin as she moved.

Standing just to the left of the first candidate, Helena's hands trembled only slightly as she lifted the hood and then dropped the cloak.

The crowd was silent before letting out a giant roar of approval. Helena did not stand there naked, as it had first appeared, rather she was wearing a short flesh-colored shift. It hung loosely on her, but due to the un-dampened state of her magic, the glow of her skin emphasized the way the thin material caressed her curves. It emphasized the gentle swell of her hips and the more generous slope of her breasts.

This was the first time the Chosen had seen their Kiri's power unleashed. Her eyes swirled with iridescent fire, and she stood silently before them.

A small rustle of wind brushed her hair up until it seemed to float behind her; she was mesmerizing. The Chosen were entranced.

When she spoke, it was with the melodious voice-of-many, "The

Mother guides and her Chosen bend to her will. It is with her blessing that we are gathered here tonight to celebrate her ultimate gift: the mating bond. Once I join myself to the Mate, the Circle will be complete."

The crowd roared again, chanting for the name of their selected.

Helena turned her back toward the crowd and faced Amos. He could not contain his gasp as he stared at her. His heart was racing when she lightly rested her hand against his chest.

"Be at peace, Amos," she said softly, speaking only so that he could hear her.

Instantly the tempo of his heart steadied enough for him to take a shuddering breath. He blinked and brought dazed eyes back to hers.

"I release you of your promise to me. Your heart and your soul are your own, go forth with the Mother's blessing," Helena spoke more loudly, her voice still enhanced.

Amos nodded and stepped off the stage and back into the crowd.

One by one she continued down the line, each time quietly repeating the same words to the men as they stood before her.

Finally, it was down to Von and Micha. The Chosen were restless, and they shifted and watched to see which of the men would be selected.

Helena stood before Von, her hand steady as she lifted it to rest above his heart, covering the dark whorls of a tattoo that began there before flowing up and over his shoulder.

His skin was on fire under her hand, but his heart continued to beat in time with her own.

His lips were lifted in a small smile.

"Hello, Mate," he said in her mind.

Her answering smile was pure feminine joy. *"Mine."*

She could feel the way his body responded to her claiming. His eyes gazed at hers with a fierce hunger, the gray turning molten with desire.

"Shall we put on a little bit of a show for them?" Helena asked, tilting her head to the side.

Von lifted an eyebrow. *"What kind of show do you have in mind?"* he asked, the voice a seductive purr.

"Not that kind, Mate."

She felt the flickers of his disappointment through their bond.

"Von Holbrooke, do you accept the mating bond?" she asked aloud, her voice magnifying and rippling so that it could be heard across the entire crowd.

"I do," he answered, his deep voice warm and proud.

Closing her eyes, Helena called to the swirling pool within her. Letting her instincts guide her, Helena summoned a small ball of starlight and willed it to grow.

Starting from the place where her hand rested over his chest, the light began to swell and spread. There were delighted gasps from the crowd as they noticed the ball of light that was quickly expanding from where they were connected until there were wrapped in a cocoon of light.

Standing on her tiptoes, Helena pressed a sweet kiss to Von's lips, before falling back on her heels. She felt an answering growl and pressed her lips together to contain the giggle that threatened to spill forth.

Stepping away from him, she looked toward Micha.

He was smiling, but she could see the disappointment in his green eyes.

"Friends?" she asked him softly.

"Of course, Kiri."

Smiling, she repeated the words that formally released him and gave him a quick hug before turning back toward Von who swept her into his arms and spun her around until she was breathless with laughter.

"I have something for you," he declared suddenly, there was a playfulness in his gray eyes she hadn't seen before.

Fascinated, Helena watched while Von produced a crown of magnolia blossoms from behind his back, before unceremoniously placing it on her head.

"What is this for?" she asked, lifting a hand to set it in place.

"You told me you desired wooing, *Mira*. I figured I should probably start now."

"I suppose it's better than nothing, even if it is a little late," she teased, pleasure at his words bubbling up within her.

"I suppose it's a good thing that I can spend the rest of our lives making it up to you."

Helena's heart swelled at the earnestness of his words.

He brushed back a curl from her face, smiling down at her.

She had promises of her own she wanted to offer, but she could not find the words her heart wanted to speak, so instead, she kissed him and hoped that was enough.

CHAPTER 9

"*Von?*"

The whisper would have startled him if it hadn't brought the feeling of warmth and peace he was learning to associate with Helena.

"*Kiri?*"

"*Am I disturbing you?*"

"*Well at the moment I am being lectured by Timmins on the importance of protocol. So, no, definitely not.*"

He felt, rather than heard her amusement. "*Finally, someone else is on the receiving end of one of his speeches.*"

His lips quirked at her irreverence.

"This is no laughing matter, Von. I do not need to remind you what is at stake." Timmins stood in front of him, frowning, his arms crossed over his chest.

"I know the words, Advisor; you need not continue shouting them at me."

"*You're getting me in trouble, Mira. Is there something you need? Preferably something that requires my attendance far away from your Advisor?*"

"*Not at the moment. I seem to be at the mercy of Alina's*"

ministrations once again. I may just go cross-eyed if she asks my opinion on one more piece of ribbon or some such trinket."

"Shall I rescue you? Steal you off to the garden?"

He felt her smile in another rush of warmth. *"I fear that this particular assault is as much your fault as it is mine, Mate. I'd hate to see what she did to me if I interfered or ruined her creation."*

He chuckled softly, earning another of Timmins' frowns.

"Did you really just call on me to say hello?"

There was a pause before she responded, as though she was weighing her words. *"I was just curious if you would still be able to hear me this far away."*

The lie sounded like a discordant note in his mind. *"Are you lying to me, Kiri?"* he teased, curious what she was trying to hide.

"No!" He felt her surprise. *"Okay, so maybe that wasn't the entire truth, although it isn't very gentlemanly of you to call me on it. I was just feeling…"*

Lonely. He had known the answer before she was able to finish her sentence. It seemed their bond came with more than the ability to speak with their minds; it also allowed them to sense one another's emotions and their truthfulness. This revelation was yet another thing for him to consider, especially since it would mean that she could sense his own as well.

Von struggled with his response to her admission. He had never been one to fall for a woman's games, but coming from Helena, the admission was not used to snare, it was simply the truth. That appealed to him.

"You could send for me. I'm sure Alina could use another hand to hold ribbons for her."

"Ha! You really would do anything to escape Timmins. Besides, it's not as if Alina would actually allow someone to see her masterpiece before she was finished anyway. Not even on my orders."

"Really Von, you could at least pretend to pay attention," Timmins snapped.

Feeling like a schoolboy, Von uttered an apology.

"This really is for your benefit you know. You are the one who has to stand up in front of the entire realm this evening."

"I said I was sorry, Timmins," Von's strained voice betraying his irritation.

"Just because she chose you, doesn't mean you deserve her," the older man bit out.

Any vestige of good humor at Helena's mental presence dissipated at those words. Von held himself stiffly, shooting a look of ill-concealed displeasure at Timmins.

"I've killed men for less, Timmins. You may want to choose your words with care."

The man paled but stood his ground. "Even your jaded soul must realize how rare and special a creature she is. She doesn't deserve to be made a fool of in front of her people."

"You think I don't know that? That I would go out of my way to embarrass her? I know the damn words, Timmins." Von stood quickly, his chair crashing to the floor.

"Von?!" Helena's concerned voice rang out in his mind. He ignored her and closed the distance between himself and the older man.

"You think I haven't asked myself what twist of fate made her choose me? Made her soul speak to mine? You think I don't know that I don't deserve her goodness and light after the choices I've made in my life?" His voice a furious whisper. "I will do my part, old man," he finished, stepping away.

"It's not enough to know the words, Von. I had to ensure that you understood them as well. You are binding your soul to hers this evening. More than any other bond, the Mate's vow reunites two pieces of a soul back into one. It is not something that can be done lightly, or without true commitment and intent. You can destroy her if you do not understand the vow that you will make today.

"And I do not merely mean hurt her feelings, or betray her. You can kill her if you do not mean the words you speak tonight. Her destruction is our own. Remember that when you utter those words you know so well, Von."

His temper left as quickly as it came. Von stared at the Advisor, a chill of fear worming its way into him.

The door crashed open, and Helena stood in the doorway, eyes of swirling smoke and chestnut curls flying around her.

"Helena," Timmins said softly.

The Kiri turned her gaze to her Advisor, a growl sounding in her throat. The need to protect her Mate overriding her ability to sense reason.

Von watched Timmins swallow and take a step back.

He understood now what Helena meant when she said that she didn't react well to seeing him with another woman. It was pure instinct that fueled her at this moment.

"Mira," he called to her with his mind. *"He did not truly threaten me. I am fine. Look at me."*

She took a step toward Timmins, lifting her hand as she did.

"Look at me," he ordered.

Eyes of swirling gray met his.

"He hurt what is mine," the multitude of voices snapped.

"You wound my pride if you think the old man could have hurt me, Mira."

She blinked slowly, and her eyebrow furrowed as if confused. Aqua eyes met his.

"But I felt it. I felt your pain."

Timmins watched the silent exchange in surprise but made no move to break the silence.

Von frowned at her comment and spoke aloud for Timmins benefit. "Truly, Kiri, he did nothing more than wound my pride. He was teaching me a lesson, and a valuable one."

Helena met his gaze sheepishly. "I'm sorry for bursting in on you. I'll leave you to your lessons."

"I think, perhaps, we are done now," Timmins murmured ruefully.

"Would you like me to escort you back to your chamber, Kiri?" Von asked neutrally.

As if realizing where she was, and the effect her flight to the chamber must have had on Alina's work, Helena took stock of herself. A few choice profanities rang from her lips.

Von let out a bark of laughter and Timmins raised his eyebrows. Alina chose that moment to round the corner and find her mistress.

"Oh Kiri, what have you done to your hair? We must start all over, and we still have to get you in your gown for the ceremony!"

Pleading aqua eyes met his.

"Come on. I must get to work right away if we're ever going to finish in time."

Shooting him one last look, Helena followed meekly behind her maid.

After a few moments of staring silently at the now empty doorway to the chamber, the two men looked at each other and laughed at the absurdity of the sight.

HELENA STOOD in front of the mirror for what felt like the eightieth time that week. For once, however, she was actually vested in the reflection before her. She stared at the fabric of her gown with something akin to wonder.

"It's perfect, Alina," she said softly, letting the material slip through her fingers.

The gown was stunning in its simplicity. It fit her snugly, molding to her curves from shoulders to hips, and then cascaded like water to the floor. It was a straight line across her neck, baring no skin from the front until she lifted an arm. The sleeves were deceptive, appearing loose and full to the tips of her fingers, and mimicking the fall of material in the skirt of her dress. However, there was a slit from shoulder to wrist, leaving her arms entirely bare.

The material was like liquid smoke, ever-changing and throwing light like a diamond. She twisted to the side, glimpsing the back of the dress, her mouth opening in delight.

All the skin hidden from the front was more than made up for in the deep plunge of the back. She would have felt indecent, had her hair not been a riot of chestnut curls, falling down her back, revealing only glimpses of bare skin as she moved.

Alina had woven a strand of amethysts in her hair, which reflected the light from her dress, and were constantly twinkling in her hair. As a final touch, she fastened the Kiri pendant around her neck, allowing it to rest between her breasts.

The end result was that she appeared to be cloaked in mist, both shrouded behind it and vulnerable to its mercurial nature.

Alina clapped her hands in glee. "You're a vision, Kiri!"

"It's all because of you, Alina, truly."

She shook her head adamantly. "No, Kiri, it takes true beauty to shine through such simplicity."

Helena felt her cheeks warm, her smile shy.

A quick rap on the door had both girls turning toward it.

"I suppose it's time then," Helena murmured.

Alina squeezed her hand in a final display of support and moved to open the door.

Darrin stepped through the doorway. "It's time, Kiri." He stopped, his mouth falling open as he stared at her.

She twirled for him, as she had when they were children. She could see the approval glowing in his eyes as he smiled at her.

"Beautiful," he said simply.

She smiled, pleased, and threaded her arm through his. "I suppose you should walk me down then."

His smile faltered slightly, as though he was only just now realizing he was the one who would be walking her down to present her to the man she would be joining her life with.

He nodded, "I suppose so."

The walk was a short one, only from her room to the chamber where the first of her Circle had sworn their oaths to her. Like with the others of the Circle, the commitment between Mate and Kiri would be done only in front of the Circle. There would be a formal celebration afterwards, but the vows themselves would be spoken with a modicum of privacy, for which Helena was immensely grateful.

Darrin squeezed her arm gently, before leaving her at the door of the Chamber to stand with the rest of the men. Her eyes roamed the room, noting the blazing candles and otherwise barren décor. She smiled at each of her Circle in turn, feeling their pride and approval as they returned her silent greeting. Finally, her eyes fell on Von, who was standing at the window and staring out below, his obsidian hair tied in a queue at the base of his neck.

"Plotting your escape already?" she teased as she admired the fit of his black shirt and leathers.

He tensed at her voice in his mind, but recovered immediately. *"You won't get rid of me that easily, I'm afraid,"* he responded as he turned toward her with a small smile playing about his lips. His eyes widened as he took her in. When they came to meet hers, they were smoky with desire.

Von crossed the distance between them, his hand reaching toward her. Aqua eyes glowed with happiness as she lifted her hand to place it in his. At the display of skin revealed by her false sleeve, Von swallowed quickly. *"You undo me with your beauty, Mira."* Even his mental voice was rough with hunger for her.

Their fingers touched, and she shivered at the wave of warmth it brought. He squeezed her hand to signal he felt it too.

Timmins stepped forward motioning for the two to step into the middle of the room.

She turned to face Von, aqua eyes meeting slate gray. She took a shuddering breath, overwhelmed with the immensity of the moment. It is true, she had bound herself just as tightly to the other four men in her Circle, but this time she was binding her very soul.

She could feel Von's thumbs idly rubbing circles on her hands offering his strength and support.

Timmins spoke, his voice ringing out with authority. "Have you readied and cleansed yourselves for the vows you make to each other today?"

"We have," their voices chorused.

She was pleased at how steady and sure hers sounded, despite the tidal wave of emotion rolling through her.

"Do you understand the importance of the bond you will share?"

"We do."

"And are you prepared to take one another in, to love and safeguard, until the Mother calls you home?"

"We are."

"Then please proceed, and may the Mother watch over and nurture the bond you solidify today." Timmins stepped back, the other men stepping away from the wall and forming a circle around Helena and Von.

Taking her hand, dwarfed by his own, he brought it to his chest to rest over the steady beat of his heart. She felt her own race in response.

Covering her hand with his, he began in his deep growl, "In the name of the Mother, I, Von Holbrooke, bind my life to yours and take you into both my heart and my spirit, to be my Mate. I shall respect and protect you, your beliefs and your people, taking them as my own. I vow to be true to you above all others. I promise to love you wholly and without restraint, in this life and beyond, where we shall meet, remember and love again. From this day forward, my place is at your side, placing your desires and needs before my own, until such a time as the Mother calls us home."

Aqua eyes swirled with smoke as she brought his scarred hand to rest over her heart and pendant. Leaving the hand he had covered on his chest, she covered the hand now resting on hers.

When she spoke, it was with the voice-of-many.

"In the name of the Mother, I, Kiri Helena Solene, accept you as my Mate. I bind my life to yours and take you into both my heart and my spirit. I shall respect you, your beliefs and your people, taking them as my own. I vow to be true to you above all others. I promise to love you wholly and without restraint, in this life and beyond, where we shall meet, remember and love again. From this day forward, you will always have a place by my side. I will hold your life and happiness above all others, including my own, until such a time as the Mother calls us home."

As she finished speaking, the candles flickered and a gentle breeze swirled around them. The wind continued to encircle them, creating an insoluble barrier between them and the Circle. Neither Von nor Helena moved, although their hearts now beat in tandem. She could feel his spirit inside her, much like when he healed her the day before. What had been a whisper of essence was now a firm and solid presence, as familiar to her as her own.

"Mine." Her voice was fierce in his mind.

His lips twitched in amusement. He had never felt stronger or more humbled than he did in that moment surrounded by the full glory of her love for him. He had never understood the emotion before, had not realized that it was what he had been feeling since he first met her. With her spirit infused with his, he knew he would always carry it with him now, like a beacon. She would be his strength and his purpose.

"Always, Mira."

Aqua eyes were bright with tears, as she took a step toward him. Leaning down to meet her, Von sealed their vow with a kiss.

CHAPTER 10

ours had passed since the mating ceremony had concluded, but the revelers had no intention of leaving. Helena found herself stealing glances at her Mate from across the room, the pulse of spirit an unwavering arrow pulling her back to him. It was as simple as a question being formed in her mind, she just had to start wondering where he was and she would know instantly.

She was still unsure of the limitations of this bond between them, in fact, it did not seem that those in her Circle were aware of such a possibility. She had tried to ask Timmins about the bond between a Kiri and her Mate, but he had only murmured a few nonsensical phrases about the two being halves of one whole.

One thing that was becoming clear, even despite any physical distance between them, was that unless she was specifically focused on him, such as when she would speak directly to his mind, his presence would remain a mere imprint. It would be indistinct, like that gentle lapping of waves against the shore or a soft breeze brushing against branches. And while it would give the impression of his general state of mind, it would not provide any detail.

Like now, she could tell without looking at him whether he was actually amused or only pretending to pay attention to his companions (he was pretending) but she did not know what the men were actually saying.

However, this impression of him would sharpen instantly if his own emotions peaked. Flashes of anger or mirth would become currents within her, a wave crashing into her, alerting her to his shifting moods and bringing him to the center of her mind. She was curious if this would become more or less sensitive over time. Would she always feel these subtle shifts in temper, or only be attuned to the sharp blade of anger or jolting tang of fear? Was he just as aware of the same shifts within her?

As if he felt the question, his eyes tangled with hers across the room. And as if in answer he gave her a soft smile, more a slight lifting of his lips at the sides, before turning back to the men in front of him.

Helena felt her own smile in response, and couldn't resist the urge to imagine what it would feel like to walk over to him. Her fingers gently brushing against his when she reached his side. The calluses rough against the tips of her fingers, as she interwove them with his own. She would squeeze gently, just once, as if to say, "I am here."

While her mind wandered, she noticed the slight widening of his eyes and flexing of his fingers, as if he could feel her thoughts being enacted on his body. He turned his head back to her, his eyes narrowing in concentration.

She felt the gentle caress on her palm, almost as if a piece of velvet had brushed against it while simultaneously noting the increasing pressure on her hand. He was squeezing her hand in return!

Helena felt her cheeks warm on their own accord, pleased he had not only been able to actually feel her intentions, but that he wanted to respond in kind. Von's own expression did not shift, except perhaps for the polite smile to warm slightly.

She could now feel a gentle tickling starting in the palm of her hand and working its way down each of her fingers. A phantom finger stroking the length of each one, before starting anew on the next. After all five fingers received a similar ministration, the center of her palm began to tingle. The tingle was constant, like a breath being softly released against it before it was replaced with a very distinct heat.

It took her a moment to place the sensation. It was a kiss! Von was kissing the center of her palm. The tickle returned, but now it was accompanied by a sense of warmth. Wet strokes resuming the exploration along each finger.

Helena felt her cheeks blaze with heat as she realized he was now licking and sucking each of her fingers. There he stood, arms loosely crossed against his wide chest as he leaned against a wall listening to the men continue to joke with one another before him. His head tilted slightly so he could see her clearly. A smirk, proud and male, growing against his will.

"Proud of yourself, Mate?" she asked him, trying to calm the racing beat of her heart.

"Immensely. If that's how you respond to just a thought, imagine what I can do when I'm actually touching you."

She felt his amusement swell within her.

"What?" she questioned warily.

"It will be fun to test what I can do with said thoughts, while I'm touching you as well." With that, he sent her a saucy wink and his smirk became a full-blown grin, complete with wicked promise.

Dazed, Helena blinked a few times, trying to resurface from the sexual fog that now seemed to surround her. The guests around her all begin to shift uncomfortably, the women pulling out fans and the men remarking about whether the temperature seemed to be rising, despite the night sky twinkling above.

As if he could tell her magic had also responded to his seduction, and how those around her were reacting to it, Von threw back his head and let out a bone-deep laugh. The sound rich and warm, wrapped itself around her heart.

Under normal circumstances Von was an imposing figure, towering above most others, all hard lines and arrogance. His sheer size and muscle as much a deterrent to any approach as the ever-present scowl on his face.

But suffused with mirth, Von came alive. The silver eyes which seemed as impenetrable as metal sparkled like molten silver pools. The boyish smile easing the years of hardship and worry from his face.

There was still the coiled strength and promise of violence generating from the muscles that shook with the force of his laughter, but what had once been a wall of stone keeping you out, was now a magnet drawing you in.

Breath catching at the change, all she could do was stare. He was beautiful.

Helena was not a completely naïve farm girl, she had her share of stolen kisses behind the barn with the boys in town, and knew about desire and attraction. But all she thought she knew paled in comparison to the aching throb low in her belly. Nothing she had experienced prepared her for the soul-deep want she was feeling now, as she stared at the laughing man across the room.

VON COULD FEEL the shift in Helena's response to him like a flood of hot water dripping down his body. His laughter slowly subsided, and he brought his eyes back to hers. He started slightly when he noticed the twin aqua pools were now a swirling iridescent storm. Her cheeks were flushed and her chest rose and fell quickly and she struggled to draw in air.

"Mine."

He felt her declaration vibrate within the core of his being. All traces of amusement now completely faded from his face. He took a step toward her before noticing the people around him.

Startled, he looked around, noting the changes in the garden. The dull roar of voices had faded, replaced with the strains of music and the gentle rustle of fabric. Guests were no longer chatting cheerfully in small clusters scattered throughout the room. Instead, they were breaking off into couples focused only on each other. Many were moving deeper into the shadowed areas of the garden, while those closest to Helena didn't seem to concern themselves with the need for privacy. All around, lovers, if only for the night, were paired off, their bodies pressed against each other.

"Mira," his voice rumbled through her.

She was doing this. Her magic, more powerful than anything he had ever encountered, had the ability to influence not just those closest to her, but everyone in attendance.

Poor proper Timmins would be horrified when he was back in possession of his faculties. Currently, his hands were exploring the rather large buttocks of a sharp-tongued healer named Daphne, while his lips trailed kisses along the skin exposed by her dress.

Von allowed himself a chuckle as he made his way to his Mate. That was a memory he would allow himself to dwell on properly later if only as payback for the mind-numbing lectures he had endured over the course of the last week.

"Helena," he whispered as he reached her, his hand brushing back a stray curl that had fallen.

She blinked slowly, aqua eyes searching his. "Von? How did you get over here so quickly? Weren't you just..." she trailed off as she looked around the garden.

"Timmins!" she squeaked in surprise, cheeks flooding with color. It was clear she did not know whether to laugh or hide.

"Von, what did I do?" she questioned, eyes scanning back and forth quickly.

"It would seem your magic responds to the intensity of your emotions. The more intense, the bigger the reaction. Were you thinking about something, darling?" he teased.

Eyes snapped back to his, widening in embarrassment. "How do I uh..." she trailed off.

His hand reached out, fingers gently brushing against her cheek before he leaned over and pressed a soft kiss against her forehead. "I think distance would be a start. A spell of this magnitude is probably best to run its course and wear off on its own."

"But what about"—she gestured helplessly at Timmins—"won't he regret this in the morning?"

Von shrugged. "He might, although he'd be too polite to mention it. Trust me, my love, people are more adept at recovering from a night of unintended loving than you might think. To interrupt them now might cause more embarrassment than letting them wake up in the morning and acknowledge or deny the events of the evening as they will.

"Besides," he continued, "I think to undo what you have set in motion might require a bit more attention than you have at the moment."

Cheeks still tinged with pink, she nodded at him sheepishly. "I think you might be right."

He reached down to take her hand, smiling as he did. "In that case, perhaps it's time we retired for the evening, my love."

An answering smile grew on her face.

THEY STOOD outside the entrance to her room, no visible signs of Von's rage lingering on the door.

She looked up at him shyly, but not without heat, as he opened it and stepped inside, pulling her in after him.

Keeping her close he shut the door behind them and she felt the tingle of magic as he sealed it.

"To ensure our privacy," he said softly, leaning down to brush a soft kiss against her lips. He stepped away from her and walked over to the side of the room to pour them each a glass of wine.

She eyed the door once more, amused that it appeared to be submerged in water. She reached out a finger to brush against the magical barrier, curious if her hand would pass through the substance easily, and surprised to find it was much thicker and less yielding than it appeared.

"Are you sure that's for privacy or is it to prevent my escape?" she mused as she started toward him.

The promise in his heavy-lidded eyes was enough to wipe the teasing smile from her lips.

He offered her the glass goblet full of ruby liquid sparkling like a jewel under the warm glow of the fire. Her hand only trembled slightly as she took it from him and raised it for a quick sip.

He eyed her over the rim of his own glass before taking a longer sip. Her heart was racing under his scrutiny and she quickly set the glass down on the mantle before the trembling in her hands gave her away.

"What were you thinking about before?" he inquired softly.

"Be-before what?" she stammered, the familiar heat flooding her cheeks.

"Before that diverting bit of magic that caused Timmins to behave like a randy stable boy," came the amused response in her mind.

Never good at playing games, Helena responded honestly, "How beautiful you were."

Straightening, Von studied her in surprise. "How beautiful *I* am?"

She nodded. "You looked so at ease, so..." she searched for the word, "alive. It was irresistible."

Setting his own glass down he reached for her. "You that are the beautiful one. Had I known what I would find when I started on this journey, I would have been in much more of a hurry to get to you."

She felt the ring of truth in her heart. *"Truly?"*

"Oh, Helena," he whispered, closing the space between them, "Haven't you realized yet that you were made for me? Had I asked the Mother herself to create a woman to some set specification of perfection in my mind, I could not have come anywhere close to the gift I have found in you. You take my breath away."

She looked down, stunned by the hunger and passion she saw reflected in his molten gray eyes.

Brushing against her softly, his fingers came to rest below her chin and gently lifted until her eyes met his again.

"You are exquisite," he continued in the same soft rumble. "And it's not just your beauty that speaks to me, although when you smile I find it hard not to lean over and kiss you until you forget how to speak." He paused to brush another soft lingering kiss against her mouth.

"And then there's your strength. Your ability to persevere when so many others could never even find the courage to try. But it's your heart that undoes me," he paused again, his voice earnest, "your ability to find compassion for people you have never met, and whom probably do not deserve it. Your unwavering conviction that people are inherently good, even when they've given you no reason to believe in them."

She stopped him then with a kiss, using her lips to convey the nameless emotion that was bursting within her.

He pulled back slightly waiting for her to open her heavy eyes and look at him.

"All that I am, is yours. Regardless of what it is that brought me to you, I am yours. I belong to you, and I will strive to be worthy of you."

"Shh," she whispered soothingly, breathing kisses against his lips. "If I was made for you, then you were made for me. How could you ever see yourself as unworthy? The Mother doesn't make mistakes."

"I-I have not been a good man," came the faltering confession.

Helena merely shrugged. "Do not waste time regretting who you have had to be, Von. You have done what you needed to do, in order to get to me. Now it is my turn to help you carry the burden. You are mine, and I would have no other."

In that moment, he felt a broken piece of his soul fall back into place. "All my life I have been trying to get home, and I have finally found it, in you."

"Von," she whispered brokenly, tears spilling out of aqua eyes.

"Do not cry, my love. I just needed you to know, so that you would have no doubts about me or my intentions."

"I have never had any doubts," the multitude of voices responded. *"I have always known that you were mine."*

"Yes," he breathed before his lips crashed down. No longer gentle, his kisses were brands, each one claiming her as his.

One of his hands wound itself in her curls while the other began to work its way down her back, fingertips teasing the exposed skin.

Helena shivered and pressed herself against him. Impatient, Helena wished that she could feel his skin against hers.

She could feel the change in Von almost immediately, his lips had stopped their assault on hers. "Von?" she asked as she started to kiss along the stubble covered jaw.

She felt the rumbling in his chest before she heard the laughter. "It would seem that you are in a hurry, darling."

Pulling back to look at him, she realized what had him laughing. Her wish had been the only catalyst her magic needed to take action. Their clothes were now piles on the floor below them. Her eyes rounded, she slowly looked up, taking in every glorious inch of him as she did so.

Von's past was etched in every line of his body. Battle-scarred and heavily muscled legs tapered into narrow hips and waist, while his stomach was bricks of muscle stacked atop each other. The deep V between his hips only emphasizing his swelling maleness.

Helena paled at the sight. He was big. Too big. Needing to look away before she panicked, she raised her eyes to his chest, taking in the tattoo that started in its center and wove its way around his right shoulder and arm. The swirling black tattoo was comprised of words, but she was too flustered to make sense of them.

Shaking fingers traced the pattern. He stood still beneath her touch, the rise and fall of his chest the only movement.

"At, at least I didn't completely destroy them," she muttered, daring a glance up at him. His eyes were hooded, but the humor was still on display in the twist of his lips. Blinking she continued, "I really like that dress."

"So do I, I would have greatly enjoyed the opportunity to take my time removing it."

Helena blushed in embarrassment, staring at her toes. "I-I could put it back on," she offered.

"Maybe next time," he responded, before bending to lift her and toss her over his shoulder.

"Von!" she squealed, now face to face with the well-sculpted globes of his buttocks.

He walked toward the bed, each step making her bounce and her hair brush against the back of his thighs.

His warm hand ran up the back of her leg before coming to rest atop the swell of her own backside. He squeezed gently, before giving it a quick swat and tossing her back onto the bed.

The feeling of weightlessness was short-lived before she bounced gently and was splayed beneath him.

Before she could be embarrassed about her own nudity, Von whispered one word.

"Mine," came the low growl.

"Yes," came her heartfelt response.

Placing a knee between her legs on the bed, Von bent down and pressed kisses along the tops of her thighs, before dipping down to run his tongue from the side of her knee up the inside of her thigh.

Helena's legs pressed together on their own volition. Her mind a tumble of thoughts and emotions she was helpless to process.

"Let me taste you," his voice whispered inside her, as he was busy licking and nibbling up her legs.

Swallowing uncertainly, Helena forced her legs to ease back open.

Calloused hands continued the journey his lips had started, touching and spreading her to his liking. Fully kneeling before her on the bed, Von looked up from where his hands were resting on the tops of her hips and straight into her eyes.

"Beautiful," he whispered reverently before he bent down and pressed his lips beneath her belly button. As he continued to kiss back down to the core of her, Helena's hand found its way to his head although she wasn't sure if it was to push him away or hold him in place.

When he finally ran his finger along her seam, she felt the responding tug of their bond inside of her. His fingers began to work her like an instrument, strumming and rubbing as she moved against him. And then his tongue continued what his fingers had started, licking and sucking until she was bucking below him. Gasping for breath, Helena's head tossed on the bed.

"That's it, my love, let go."

That was all it took. One simple command from the deep voice rough with desire and she came undone. There was a loud crash and then the tinkling of falling glass, as all around them the windows and glasses shattered.

Too lost in what had just happened to notice, Helena rode the waves of her orgasm. When she finally came back to herself, Von was sitting back on his heels between her legs staring intently at the floor.

Turning her head to see what he was looking at, Helena finally noticed the broken glass.

"Not again," she moaned, covering her face with her hands.

Von's hand gently circled her wrists before trying to pry her hands from her face. But Helena resisted.

"Look at me," he ordered softly.

Helena shook her head in embarrassment.

"Now, Mate."

She splayed her fingers and looked up at him with bemused eyes.

"Perhaps I should have sealed the entire room?" he murmured.

At that, her shoulders shook with laughter, and she leaned up to wrap her arms around him.

Bringing his mouth to hers, he kissed her gently once, twice. "You are perfect, Helena."

"But I have no control," she pouted.

"I have every intention of ensuring you lose control as often as possible."

"We're going to go through a lot of windows."

"It's a good thing you can use magic to put them back together."

Seeing the gears shift in her mind as she sat up to attempt it, his arm snaked around her and pulled her back to him. "Oh no, you don't. We are in the middle of something or did you already forget?"

Looking over her shoulder she couldn't help but appreciate the sight of Von spread out on her bed.

"I didn't forget," came the soft reply.

"Are you nervous?" he asked gently, fingers running up and down her back soothingly.

Helena shook her head quickly, causing her curls to dance down her back, but he felt the flickers of her nerves as though they were his own.

"What are you afraid of?" he asked, sitting up to better cradle her body against his.

"You're just so large," came the mortified whisper as her eyes dropped to his lap before averting quickly.

He tried not to, he really did, but he laughed.

Twisting in his arms to look at him, her jaw dropped. "That's funny to you?"

"Helena," he gasped, as she scooted, trying to put distance between them. His arms tightened in response, keeping her against him. "Helena, I'm sorry, I didn't mean to laugh. It's just, you have nothing to fear. I promise. By the time we're done you're going to be thankful I'm built exactly as I am."

She raised a brow in disbelief.

"Aren't you the one that said the Mother doesn't make mistakes?"

"I think she may have gotten a little too ambitious when she was working on you," Helena muttered sullenly.

Chuckling Von pressed a kiss to her shoulder. Relenting, Helena laid back down beside him, allowing her own hands to explore the ridges of his body.

"Will you tell me what this means one day," she asked as her fingers explored the whirls of his tattoo.

"Yes, but not now," with that, his lips descended on hers again. It took only moments for the fire to rekindle within her.

Shifting, Von moved so that he was between her legs again. As he felt her stiffen, he whispered, "Look at me."

As she did, he ran his length down her center, twisting his hips to circle her opening. Helena's eyes widened before closing.

"Look at me," he rasped, continuing to tease her entrance.

Helena struggled to keep her eyes open and on him as he began to slowly press into her.

There was no pain, only pleasure, as he filled her. Helena could feel their hearts beating in time, each breath a ragged gasp until he filled her completely. He stayed there, allowing her to get used to the feeling of him within her. Once she began squirming below him, he allowed himself to flex against her.

"Oh," she gasped, eyes rolling back in her head.

She felt his hand run down her chest, pausing to pluck at the hard bud of her nipple, before moving back down to rest on her hip.

"Are you still nervous, Mira?" the deep growl asked.

She could feel that he was at the edge of his control, desperate to make sure she was comfortable before going further.

"More," she purred, arching up into him.

She heard his own answering moan before he pulled back and slid back in.

"Yes," she cried, hands reaching for his as his thrusts picked up speed.

"Helena," he growled.

Iridescent eyes met molten gray, hearts beating in time with each thrust.

Mine. Neither was sure who had uttered the declaration, but with those words, Von buried himself inside her, body shaking with the force of his release, while she wrapped herself around him as she came apart.

He shifted to lay beside her, and she whimpered in protest at the loss. He brushed a soft kiss against her forehead and pulled her close so that her head was resting on his chest.

The soft thundering of his heart became a lullaby that lured her to sleep, but before she drifted off, she felt him stir beneath her.

"What's the matter?" she asked sleepily.

"I was just thinking it was probably a good thing we didn't fix the windows."

CHAPTER 11

Gillian paced restlessly across the floor of her opulent suite; her fingers tapping nervously against her lips as her mind raced. Now that the pair were mated it was time for her to put her plans into motion. It would have been a fool's errand to try to do anything to stop what fate had already decreed to be, so there were no moves she could have made prior to now. Well, other than preparing the ground for the trap she would spring through her friendship with the new Kiri.

Gillian sighed, still lost to the thoughts that tumbled about her mind. It was a shame she actually liked the girl, naïve though she was. Too bad she would stop—could stop—at nothing to destroy her and that blood traitor she was mated to.

As she continued to walk back and forth in front of the massive fireplace, she no longer heard the crackling of the flames. In fact, she was not aware of anything until the mirror hanging on the wall began to fog.

She stopped suddenly, head spinning to look at the swirling mist replacing the glass. Fear and shock at war for dominance within her. The mirror was ancient, its frame a combination of twisting metal and magic. The words of power carved into the metal hidden in the flowing vines and flowers that the metal was shaped into.

Gillian's heart stuttered in her chest, before she dropped to her knees in front of the mirror, eyes cast to the floor in front of her.

"Mistress," she said hoarsely.

"It is time," came the disembodied voice through the mirror.

"Yes, Mistress."

"You know what will happen if you fail me. The impostor cannot be allowed to remain on my throne." The voice wrapped itself around her in an icy caress, each word scraping against her skin like talons; a sharp and deadly tease. Gillian felt her skin break out into gooseflesh as the waves of power rippled around her.

"Of course, Mistress. It will be done."

"You have until the new moon rises," with that the flood of power that had encircled her ebbed. Gillian risked a glance up at the mirror to see that the swirling mist was fading back into her reflection.

Seeing herself again in the mirror she took in her appearance: pupils so wide they almost swallowed the green of her irises, skin bleached of all color, teeth biting down into her colorless lip. Her heart continued to race as she tried to recover from the unexpected visit.

Gillian took a shuddering breath before whispering, "Yes, Mother."

HELENA TILTED her face up to the sky, letting the warm rays of light kiss her skin. Smiling she knelt in the grass, surrounded by the roses and jasmine in bloom beside her. After days, nay weeks, of endless preparation she finally found herself with nothing to claim her time.

Von had left their bed that morning with a whispered brush of his lips against hers and a promise to see her soon. She could still feel the throb of their bond within her, diminished slightly due to their distance, but strong nonetheless. Her own pool of magic seemed to ripple in answer to its steady thrum.

She flushed in pleasure remembering how he had roused her in the middle of the night, his phantom hands exploring her body while his lips worked their way over the peaks of her breasts. He had grinned up at her wolfishly in the moonlight before using his body to keep the promise his magic had made upon her sleep-slackened limbs. She had lost track of the number of times his name broke from her lips as she shattered and clenched around him.

She shook her head quickly before those kinds of thoughts could get her in any more awkward situations. It was bad enough dealing with Alina's knowing grin when she had finally eased herself out of the bed late that morning noting that the shattered glass had all been repaired; and she had yet to run into any of her Circle, sparing her the need to answer for her loss of control at the celebration the night before.

Cringing slightly, she made herself take in the peaceful beauty of the garden. That reckoning would come soon enough, no need to borrow trouble imagining it now. Instead, she wanted to take the time to explore the garden with her heightened senses. She had been careful to keep herself in the magic dampened state ever since her trial, especially when wandering throughout the Palace. No one else seemed to glow with the force of a thousand candles when using their gifts and she was tired of being the cause of stares and whispers.

Glancing around quickly to make sure she was alone, she called to her magic. It came to her like a sigh, the internal well gradually emptying as it was released.

Standing slowly, Helena drank in the changes. Each enhanced sense was in perfect harmony as the garden came to life around her. It was as if time had paused so that she was able to view each moment as it occurred. Each blade of emerald grass shifting in the jasmine-scented breeze, each rustle of the leaves dancing above her and each beat of wings a gentle strum as the bees floated from petal to trembling petal.

The colors were overwhelming in their intensity. The reds, pinks, and purples more vivid and real than any she had ever seen, almost as if she had been viewing the world from muted lenses, never truly understanding what depth and variations existed.

The scents were intoxicating. Closing her eyes, Helena breathed in deeply. She was able to taste the sun and dew-covered petals in the air, while the aroma of wet earth was vying with the fragrant roses for attention. It was all so alive, so much more than her mortal senses had ever been able to comprehend before.

Iridescent eyes caught a slight movement to her right. Spinning to face it, Helena's hand thrust out to the nearby tree to hold her steady. The force of impact caught her off-guard and the tree pulsed once as it came into contact with the full potency of her magic. Between one breath and the next, the tree groaned as it began to expand and grow; its roots snaking deeper into the damp earth while its flowers exploded to life in its branches.

"There you are!" Darrin called in surprise as a bevy of leaves rained down upon him. Noting the riotous curls and swirling depths of her eyes, his hands moved to the sword at his side and he stepped toward her carefully, each snap of grass causing her to flinch.

Realizing that he was reacting to her appearance as if it were a threat, she willed her magic back into the recesses of the pool. Blinking once, twice, she looked up at him with aqua eyes and smiled sheepishly.

"Good morning, Darrin."

Shoulders easing, he moved his hands from his sword and offered her a lopsided smile.

"Timmins sent me to fetch you. Actually, he said, *'Now that the Circle is formed the time is ripe for making plans.'*" Darrin mimicked Timmins voice before smiling conspiratorially.

Helena laughed despite herself, Timmins certainly had a tendency to adopt the lilting tone when he was in full lecture mode, and she could only wonder how much more Timmins had actually said before sending Darrin on his way to find her.

"Not even a day to rest before putting us to work, how very like him," she murmured as she stepped away from the tree to stand beside him.

He gestured to the path ahead indicating that he would follow.

As she stepped toward the path she stole a final glance at the now massive tree in full bloom about three months too early. Worrying her lip between her teeth, she turned back to Darrin.

Matching his steps to hers he asked, "Are you still planning to venture outside of the Capital?"

Helena nodded as she said, "I think it is time to soothe the hurts of the past, don't you?"

Darrin shrugged uncomfortably and spoke slowly, choosing his words with care, "I think that it seems rather soon for you to leave the safety of Elysia, especially since you are still testing the limits of your magic."

"Isn't that what you are for?" she teased.

Wary green eyes met hers. "You know that I would lay down my life to protect yours, Helena. I just know that once we leave these borders, we are welcoming all sorts of new threats that we might be ill-prepared to face. At least without proper planning."

"We're taking a trip to visit my Mate's family and lands, not going on some warring expedition, but your caution is noted Shield. We will make sure that when we leave for the journey we are prepared for all possibilities."

Helena could appreciate his concerns, even as she felt they were unnecessary. While she may be Kiri, she was very much still learning what that meant while he was the one who had been training with the Rasmiri for half his life. More than that, as the Shield it was in his nature to search for potential dangers lurking in every shadow.

The pair continued their way into the Palace. As with many of the common spaces between wings, the floors were polished to a high shine, the wood a glossy mahogany, while the walls were a soft buttery gold. Paintings of all shapes and sizes lined the walls. Helena was unsure who the artists were, but each one told the story of her people. She wished she had more time to stop and study them, but they continued moving swiftly up the spiraling staircase.

As they climbed, Helena noted the lights twinkling above them, not ensconced in any way, but rather floating and moving around freely beneath the massive beams visible in the high ceiling. It was so picturesque here, each window chosen to best reveal Elysia's beauty. She caught glimpses of towering mountains in the distance and shivered with anticipation. Soon she would be traveling through them.

Her life to this point had been sheltered, and she had not traveled much farther than the small town closest to her and Miriam's cottage. A part of her had always hungered for adventure, and now she was in a position to seek it at will. Who knew what waited for her out beyond the snow-capped peaks in the distance? A different kind of chill worked its way down her spine at the thought, and she spared a glance at Darrin. Perhaps she should better heed his warnings.

A small flutter of concern tugged at her through the bond. Helena worked to shake off the lingering sense of disquiet as they reached the threshold of the meeting room. The rest of the Circle were already waiting for them inside; each man standing behind their usual seats around the table. This was Von's first time officially sitting in with them, and she couldn't help the smile that bloomed across her face when she saw him leaning against the mantle.

As usual, his legs were wrapped in his tight leathers; his shirt black and loose, the sleeves rolled up to showcase strong forearms lightly dusted with hair. She admired him, and the way the leather showcased his assets, discreetly for a moment before taking the final step into the room.

His eyes caught her as soon as she appeared in the doorway, a brow raised in silent question.

"All is well," she assured him with a soft smile.

He nodded, returning her smile, and moved to sit beside her as she lowered herself into the seat Kragen pulled out for her. She beamed up at him in thanks before looking expectantly at Timmins.

His voice was warm as he greeted her, "You are glowing this afternoon, Kiri."

She felt rather than saw the smug smile spread across Von's face at Timmins' declaration.

"I'll have you know this glow is the result of me playing with my magic in the gardens," she informed him haughtily.

"Is that what you're telling yourself?" he purred seductively in reply.

Helena stole a glance at him from the corner of her eye, noting that he was staring at Timmins, a small smile playing about his lips.

"That's kind of you to say, I hope you enjoyed the evening's festivities as well."

A slight blush stained Timmins cheeks, as both Kragen and Joquil hid their smiles behind gloved hands. Darrin's sudden coughing sounded suspiciously like laughter, yet no one made any comment.

"Yes, well..." Timmins looked around the table without making eye contact with any of them.

"It was certainly unforgettable," Joquil inserted smoothly.

"Yes," Timmins agreed with relief, "unforgettable."

Helena bit back her own smile. "How wonderful to hear."

Poor, proper Timmins would never hear the end of this, but at least she had turned the topic away from herself.

He fumbled with some papers in front of him before beginning again. "Now, as I see it, with all of the ceremonies and the trial behind us, it is time to shift our attention to the matters of the realm. There have been many --"

Helena cut in, "While I agree that the time for history and politics can no longer be avoided, I prefer to take a more direct path. We will be journeying to Daejara. It is time for us to look to the future and rebuild our alliance with the people we have so grossly neglected."

She felt Von stiffen beside her as the other men traded glances around the table.

"Don't you think it would be more prudent, Kiri, to send someone else on your behalf to start such negotiation?" Timmins murmured carefully.

"Obviously not or that's what I would have suggested," she said mildly.

Von's approval stroked along the length of their bond, yet he remained silent.

"Five hundred years is a long time to go without any sort of communication and simply appear on their doorstep," Darrin attempted.

"Who said anything about simply appearing?" she asked sparing him a glance. "We will notify Daejara's emissaries of our intentions and await our formal invitation from its court. I cannot imagine it will be long in coming, seeing as how their eldest son is now my Mate."

Von let out a humorless bark of laughter. "You flatter me by thinking that my parents are that concerned with my well-being, Kiri. They have all but disowned me due to my years 'running around bloodying my blade for the highest paying arsehole'."

Beneath the mocking words, Helena could feel the pain that admission still caused him; a wound that had never fully healed.

"Then perhaps it is time for them to become reacquainted with their son and his new Mate," snapped the voice-of-many, eyes flashing like diamonds with her ire.

Von studied her carefully from his sprawling position in the chair. His lips raised in wry amusement.

"Perhaps so, Kiri."

She turned her attention back to the other four men. "This is not open for negotiation. The people of Daejara have been left to suffer and fend for themselves for the last five hundred years. There has been no news, no trade, no celebration of the Mother or her gifts in all that time. These people, who have done nothing but have the misfortune to be born on the wrong side of an invisible line, are paying for the mistakes of rulers long since dead. That is unacceptable, and it ends now.

"I do not care how we make it happen," she continued, "but know that this *will* happen. So, let us make the plans that we need to make in order to best prepare ourselves for what we will find when we cross the border. While I am stubborn enough to insist on this meeting, I am not so ignorant as to believe we will be welcomed with open arms by all that we come across."

Kragen was openly smiling at her from his spot at the table. Gone was the girl who had apologized for each question she raised or felt she must ask permission before speaking. In her place sat a woman who was willing to make a stand for what she believed in. Here was a woman he was proud to serve.

Over the years the Mother's power had started to diminish within the ruling families. As the years passed it became more and more diluted in the women who ruled. Few had even passed the trial of the Damaskiri to become crowned true Kiris. Of those, the vast majority had focused on their own comforts rather than on the task of caring for their people. The selfishness and corruption had begun to spread through the courts and their people; a faceless enemy that could not be slain.

Joquil's golden eyes sparkled curiously and he cleared his throat before speaking. "As you wish, Kiri. Perhaps it would be advantageous for Von's men to train the Rasmiri that will come with us? They are familiar with the lands, and opponents, we might find there."

Von shifted in his seat, angling forward as he said, "They are already preparing to do so."

Kragen murmured his approval.

"We will need to plan for more than just ourselves and our guards. I would like to bring some goods we can offer both as gifts and for trade. Perhaps we can see if any merchants or tradesmen would like to accompany us?"

Darrin spoke first. "It is a good idea, but we will need to make sure they are aware of the risks. Let's limit the number we bring with us on this first visit, at least until we can be better assured of our reception."

"Agreed," Helena said with a smile. With that matter of business concluded, at least in her mind, she looked back to her Advisor.

"I will write the formal request and send it this afternoon, Kiri. Once we hear back, we can begin preparations to leave as soon as possible."

"Very well, is that all for now Timmins?" she asked hopefully.

He smiled back indulgently. "We have many nights of travel ahead of us, I suppose my stories can wait for the campfire."

Helena beamed at him.

Chuckling, the men rose to their feet and made their way for the door.

Von reached for her hand as she stood, pulling her toward him.

"I've missed you this morning, Mate."

"Already?" she inquired blandly, trying to hide the way her heart sped up at his declaration.

She felt his amusement at her teasing, but he was solemn as he replied, "Running drills with a bunch of men pales greatly in comparison to waking up next to you."

"Waking up without you did make last night feel a bit like a dream," she admitted shyly.

"I'm sorry I had to leave you," he murmured as he pressed a soft kiss to her waiting lips.

She stepped back with a groan, knowing they didn't have time to finish anything that they started right now.

He chuckled at the distance between them and wove his fingers through hers instead.

"Thank you, for what you are doing for my brother, and for me," he said softly.

Helena tilted her head inquisitively. "I told you he would have a healer, even if it meant I had to go myself."

"Yes, I know, but oftentimes people make promises they have no intentions of keeping."

Helena raised an affronted brow. "Do I strike you as one of those people?"

Von shook his head. "No, you mistake me. I simply meant that I have not had someone I could rely on, outside of my men, in a very long time."

Helena shrugged, trying to find something in the room to focus on instead of the uncomfortable weight settling in her chest at the confession. It was easy to forget that his past was not filled with gentle memories.

He brushed a lingering kiss against her knuckles. "I'm sorry, *Mira*, I did not intend to distress you, merely thank you for your kindness."

She shrugged again, struggling to find her words.

His hand squeezed hers offering silent comfort.

After a moment, she looked back up at him. "Well don't thank me just yet, we don't even know if I'll be able to help your brother, and we have no idea what other events this will set in motion."

"The bravery is not in knowing the outcome, but in being unafraid to try anyway."

To be called brave by this man, this warrior, who had fought so hard and for so long to try to save his people... the emotions overwhelmed her. Instead of trying to reply, she raised trembling fingers to caress his cheek.

Twisting his head, he pressed a tender kiss into the palm of her hand.

Eyes closing at the contact, she savored the feel of his lips against her skin. As her hand lowered, her fingers curled into a loose fist.

"I think I'll save that for later."

His lips quirked in amusement. *"And why's that?"*

"Just to remember what it feels like to have you eating out of the palm of my hand."

Von let out a sharp yelp of laughter: the deep rumbling doing much to ease the ache she had felt at his earlier words. Laughter was the least she could offer to the man who had already brought her such joy. His past may not have many sweet memories, but she would ensure that their future together would be full of them.

CHAPTER 12

s promised Timmins sent the letter to Daejara's court that afternoon. The reply was slow in coming and the Circle was getting restless. In an effort to keep their minds off of the response, Von had suggested that it was time for Helena to get to know his men, especially since they would be traveling together soon.

That was why, two days later, Helena found herself walking out to their training yard, Kragen and Darrin trailing a little ways behind her.

Von had left their room early again this morning to train with his band of mercenaries. Watching the way the men trained together, it was clear that this was more than a group of men that were together for convenience or coin. These were men that had been tested before; that knew how to fight as a single unit. There was brotherhood here, among those others labeled as a bunch of selfish bastards.

Her eyes scanned the yard, quickly dismissing the faces until she pinpointed Von in the center of a ring. Awareness rippled through her at the sight of his shirtless body quietly prowling around his opponent. Sweat was beading and running down his chest and back, creating a path her fingers itched to follow. His dark hair was tied back in a knot, but strands had fallen from it and were sticking to his forehead and neck.

The circling men had no weapons, save the fists that were raised in front of them. Helena eyed his opponent warily. She had seen the man before, oftentimes chatting animatedly with Von, but she did not know his name.

His skin was sun-kissed and his hair a fiery red. It was cut close along the sides but ran in a long braid from his forehead to mid-back. She could not get a good look at his face from her vantage point behind the other men that were loosely surrounding them as they cried out encouragements or curses—depending on who landed a blow.

The red-headed warrior was as massive as Kragen, a mountain of a man with muscles rippling beneath sweat-soaked skin and a tattoo identical to Von's twisting around his chest and arm.

Swallowing nervously, Helena continued making her way toward her mate. She could feel him through the pulsing of their bond but did not reach out with those mental tendrils to offer her own support, afraid to distract him with her presence. She chose instead to stand toward the back of the group of men and watch while she willed her nerves to calm.

The men continued to stalk around each other, every now and then throwing a punch, but they were merely a distraction. The real battle was waging in their eyes, neither man looking away from the other as they scanned for any opening or sign of weakness.

Helena noted the moment that it happened, Von's expression did not change, but his eyes seemed to clear and then sharpen as he flew with inhuman speed at the man in front of him. He landed a series of swift blows and kicks to his sides and neck before swooping low with his leg to knock the giant man to the ground.

The man landed with a resounding thud and laid on his back in the dirt gasping for air.

"You little shit," he growled once he had caught his breath.

Von simply stared down at him with his cocky smirk, legs splayed and hands on his hips.

The men that had gathered to watch them jeered and scattered, but not before many passed coin and insults to each other.

"What are you waiting for? Help me up, fucker," the man growled again.

Laughing, Von reached down offering him a hand. Grasping him by the forearm, Von lifted him easily back to a standing position.

Helena's own lips twitched with amusement as she watched the man grumble and wipe at the dust now coating his back and legs.

Von saw her then, his eyes softening and his smile growing. A gentle breeze rustled the curls hanging down her back and his phantom fingers caressed down her cheek by way of greeting.

Turning his head to see what had caught Von's attention, Helena felt the full force of his gaze before she turned her eyes to meet Von's rival. There was a wicked gleam in his eyes as he sauntered his way over to where she was standing.

The weight of the icy blue gaze kept Helena pinned in place. She felt Kragen and Darrin shift behind her.

Starting at his temple and slashing down to his cheekbone there was a jagged and puckering scar. The scar itself was a pale pink, but the skin around it still an angry red. His sharp nose was crooked from being broken multiple times and his jaw covered by a thick beard, a few shades darker than his hair.

He would have been frightening if it wasn't for the wide grin spread across his face.

"Was there not a healer available to help him with his injuries either?"

She could hear laughter in his amused reply, *"The healers have all offered to help reset and minimize the injuries, but Ronan won't allow it. He feels they are a testament to his foes' inability to kill him."*

"Not his own prowess?"

Von smirked. *"Oh, I'm sure that's the largest part of it."*

"Kiri," Ronan said with a warm smile as he reached for her hand, "I've heard that you have lifted the ban on Daejara."

Helena's hand was lost in his much larger one, the pads of his fingers rough with callouses. She felt her own smile grow. "You've heard correctly."

"I guess that means we'll let Timmins keep his post," Darrin muttered softly enough for only her and Kragen to hear. Kragen's answering laughter was a quiet rumble.

"I could serve you for that alone, but for the happiness that you have brought my brother, I will love you for the rest of my life." He tipped his head and pressed a rough kiss to the back of her hand.

Helena blushed and Von let out a low snarl. "Step away from my mate you silver-tongued sack of shit, or I'll have to knock you on your ass again."

Ronan winked at Helena, but stepped back and turned to address Von, "So territorial, Brother. You must not be assured of your performance in the bedroom if you're worried about something as innocent as a kiss."

Von's eyes flashed and Helena could have sworn she recognized the iridescent shimmer of her own power reflected in his gray eyes. Before she could be certain, it was gone.

Von huffed out a breath. "You have a habit of taking things that aren't yours."

Helena chuckled at the aggrieved tone of his voice. Stepping beside him she placed a sweet kiss on his dirty cheek. "Lucky for you I am not so easily swayed, Mate."

His eyes smoldered as he looked down at her. "That I am."

Cheeks pink now for another reason, Helena changed the subject and asked in a slightly breathy voice, "Brothers?"

"Brothers of the Blade," Ronan offered, at the same time Von said, "Brother of my soul."

"In that case, I must insist you call me Helena."

Something in those ice blue eyes shifted; warmed. "You do me a great honor, Kiri."

She raised a sculpted brow.

"Helena," he amended with a laugh.

She shrugged. "My Mate's family is my family, and I don't believe in such formality amongst friends anyway." Leaning closer, she lowered her voice to a conspiratorial whisper, "Unless, of course, I want to put a certain smart-assed Rasmirin in his place."

"I heard that," Darrin called dryly.

"I meant for you to," Helena replied in a voice dripping with sugary sweetness.

"Does that also apply to certain heartless black-haired bastards?" Kragen asked, eyes crinkled in delight.

Helena nodded. "Most definitely."

"If you want to talk about titles, Mate, we can start with the ones you've given me when you're moaning in our bed," he purred down the bond.

Helena's eyes widened and her blush bloomed a fierce red across her cheeks.

Looking between Von and Helena, Ronan let out a booming laugh that was more of a roar. "Oh, this is going to be fun."

THE GROUP WAS SEATED in the shade of a nearby tree, the morning giving way to the heat of the afternoon. Kragen and Ronan had each spent a few moments assessing each other before they launched into a verbal contest to determine which of them was the bigger badass.

Helena felt like she could easily declare a winner, but had a feeling neither would be willing to accept her choice.

"I appreciate the vote of confidence," Von's voice rumbled.

Helena offered him a small smile. *"I saw how easily you bested him this morning."*

"Neither of us were using weapons or our magic—"

Her mental voice interrupted his. *"Exactly."*

She felt the eye-roll in her mind. *"Ronan is my second in command for a reason, love."*

"Exactly," she repeated for emphasis. *"A commander would never have the respect or loyalty of such a strong warrior unless his own skills were equal or above his men."*

Von shook his head in exasperation, but she could feel the pride her words of belief had caused to radiate out of him.

"Ronan?" Helena asked suddenly.

Four sets of male eyes all turned to look at her. It was a conscious effort not to let herself shrink under the intensity of their combined gaze.

"Yes Kir-Helena?" he asked with a raise of his brow.

"Do you think you could train me?"

The other three men bristled.

"You want *me* to train you?" he asked softly.

Helena nodded. "If it wouldn't be too much trouble."

"Do you mind if I ask why, my lady?"

"Why you instead of one of these lot?" Helena gestured to the disgruntled males around her.

Ronan dipped his head in acknowledgment.

"I don't trust them to—" she stopped as the men sputtered in affronted male pride. Holding up a hand she rolled her eyes, "Let me finish, you bunch of babies. I don't trust the three of them to push me as hard as I would need to be pushed to really learn. I think all three of them would struggle with the idea of putting me in a situation where I might get hurt."

"And I think I would be too hesitant to do anything that might hurt you," she added for Von alone.

He squeezed her hand in answer.

"Hellion," Darrin admonished. "That is what I am for. I am here to protect you, there is no reason you would need to learn to fight."

"But what if something happens to you? What if I am ever in a situation where I am cut off from all of you, would you really want me so handicapped that I could not defend myself?"

"You have your magic," he protested.

"Magic that I can barely control, who knows what would happen?" Her words came faster and were more clearly laced with her growing panic as she continued her list, "Would I be able to even access it in a moment of fear? Or what if I get spent; use too much too fast and cannot withstand a prolonged assault? Or what if—"

It was her turn to be cut-off. "She is right," Von said quietly at her side.

"She should have every possible tool at her disposal, even if we never anticipate a need for her to use it," Kragen agreed.

"It would be my honor to help train you, Helena," Ronan said seriously. "But I think that you should take turns training with all of us.

We have different fighting styles, different strengths. If you really want to have every available tool, then you would benefit from learning all styles. As you said, you never know when a certain maneuver will come in handy."

"I promise not to take it easy on you," Darrin muttered bitterly.

Helena stuck her tongue out in response.

"We will start in the morning. You will come down before the other men begin their drills."

"At least that means I will be waking up with you, instead of to an empty bed."

"Darling, you have no idea what you've just gotten yourself into."

Von at least had the decency to laugh only in her mind.

CHAPTER 13

Training the next morning was a misery. She had known that it would be since the heaviest weapon she'd ever held was a garden rake. Even so, she had thought she was mentally prepared for what to expect, but she had not anticipated the bone-deep weariness that she now felt. Helena's muscles were protesting even as she sat in the steaming hot water.

Ronan had been relentless, he warned her when they began that morning that he was not going to speak to her as his friend or ruler; she was just another recruit and he was now her commander.

He slid his right foot back into the crouching stance he and Von had used in the sparring ring the day before. Motioning for her to imitate him, he had taken one look at her stance and sent her to run laps around the field. After that he had her carry his armor across the field, all the while lifting it up over her head before setting it down to pick it up and do it again.

Through it all, she hadn't complained, just panted and asked if she might stop for a moment to drink some water. She felt Ronan's approval even though he never said anything kind to her. Just continued to push her and complain about her overall lack of strength.

When she'd mistakenly asked when she might train with a weapon or learn some of the movements she had seen the others work through he had laughed at her.

"Little girl, when you are strong enough to hold a weapon correctly, without shaking or dropping it, I will let you train with one. Until then, build up your strength and stamina, now run!"

Even now, hours later soaking in the tub with the oils Tanya had promised would help ease the ache of her muscles, Helena wasn't sure where the certainty had come from that she needed to train.

Seeing the men yesterday, it was as if something that had been at the edge of her vision finally came into focus. Instinct had driven her to ask Ronan to train her, but she knew that it was her magic that had put the idea in her mind. If only she understood why.

"How are you feeling, my love," Von asked softly as he leaned against the doorway, arms folded across his chest.

She gave him a dirty look and slid deeper into the water.

"That well, huh?" he asked kindly, before walking over to her.

He dropped to his knees slowly, grabbing a cloth and some soap before turning that gray gaze upon her.

Helena just watched him above the rim of the water, heart beginning to race at the sight of him fully clothed and on his knees beside her, while she was laying there completely exposed under the water.

As if he could sense her reaction—which of course, he could, she realized—Von smiled softly and shook his head.

"I'm not here for that, not right now anyway." His teeth flashed as he gave her a feral grin. "I don't want to push your muscles any further than they already have been."

He motioned for her to sit forward, and moaning in protest she shifted until her back was facing him. She could feel the tingle of his magic as he ran the now soapy cloth in gentle circles along her back. With each swipe, she could feel some of the pain ease away.

She groaned her thanks and moved to provide him with more access.

Once he was done with the cloth, he swept the wet strands of hair over her shoulder and began to gently rub and press into the muscles of her back and shoulders. His fingers working to help release the tension.

Helena winced as he reached a particularly tight knot between her shoulders, and then whimpered in relief as his skilled hands worked it out.

"How are you feeling now, *Mira*?" he asked softly.

She shifted again in the tub, surprised and relieved to note that the movement barely caused any ache.

Her aqua eyes were thankful when they met his.

Reaching down he scooped her into his arms, disregarding the water that was sloshing onto his clothes, and carried her into their bedroom.

The curtains were closed cutting off the morning sun, and the few candles that were lit guttered out softly as they walked past.

Laying her against the pillows, he crawled in beside her and pulled her back to his chest, curling himself around her.

He pressed a gentle kiss to her forehead. "Rest, *Mira*. I will stay here with you."

"But it's the middle of the morning," she started before a large yawn took over.

Chuckling he snuggled her closer. "Rest now, so that I can reenact all those wonderful things that had your cheeks so pink when I knelt beside you."

Smiling to herself, Helena closed her eyes and wondered how anyone could think Von was heartless.

"Because I was until I found you," he replied down their bond, only to realize she was already asleep.

Von propped himself up on an elbow and watched her sleep. As deep breaths caused her chest to rise and fall softly, he let his fingers trace lazy patterns down her arm, enjoying the feel of her soft skin.

There was no doubt that knowing her had already changed him in numerous and inexplicable ways. He had felt it instantly that first night during the ceremony when their eyes met. There was a moment when everything in him had gone silent and dim before bursting back into sharp focus. As though his soul had recognized itself in hers and came out of hiding to say: *I've been waiting for you. I am here.*

Ever since then, every interaction had only sharpened that awareness. It had disturbed him at first, that connection. It countered every instinct the years of strategy and battle had drilled into him; pulled him toward her light and out of the darkness he'd resided in these past years. He had been helpless to resist it. So, he'd surrendered, to her. To his mate.

He shook his head ruefully, still awed that the Mother saw fit to bless his tarnished soul with such a rare gift. He had been driven for so long with only one goal in mind: punish the self-righteous nobles who saw fit to let thousands of innocents suffer and die. Let their bowels turn to water and their hearts race in fear when they were called to answer for their cruel disregard.

He had been single-minded in that pursuit, willing to sacrifice anything, including himself if it meant that he could save the people he loved. It was that setting aside of pride that brought him to her, he realized. His willingness to beg, if need be, to open the border and get a healer to his brother.

He felt a thousand years old as he brought his eyes back to her beautiful face; the weight of all that death sitting heavy inside him, even while her presence within him continued to soothe the jagged and broken edges he had lived with for so long.

She looked so innocent, so gentle, in her sleep, but he had felt her in those moments when her magic took over. The way that her wrath had been a twin to his own. She was a warrior, every bit as much as he was, although she hadn't realized it yet, or at least not consciously.

A knock sounded gently on the door, startling Von from his thoughts and giving him just enough time to hastily wrap a blanket around his mate before it opened a crack; the warm light of the hallway spilling in behind it.

Alina kept her eyes down as she poked her head in.

"What is it?" Von asked, trying to keep his voice low so as not to wake the woman in his arms.

"There has been news, my lord, from Daejara. The Circle is meeting in the Chambers," she replied, equally as soft.

Von looked to Helena, noting her mouth which had fallen open as she sank deeper into sleep.

"You are going to have to tell them to wait. While I cannot dispute the importance of the conversation they would like to have, their Kiri needs to rest. I do not want to wake her unless I have to."

He noted the small smile playing on Alina's lips as she nodded her head. "Very well, sir. I will inform them that she will be down once she has woken."

With that, she stepped back and closed the door with a whisper of a click. The golden light went with her, leaving the two of them wrapped in shadows.

HELENA WOKE WITH A SIGH, her body feeling heavy and warm. She stretched and rolled toward the center of the bed, meeting little resistance from the limbs that had been quaking with exhaustion before her bath.

Von's scent still lingered on the pillows and she buried her face to drink it in.

As she became more coherent, she sensed a delicate fluttering within the boundaries of her mind. As she focused on the sensation of that flickering presence it came closer, as though it had been politely waiting for her attention before disturbing her.

She reached out a mental hand toward it, beckoning it closer. As it floated to the center of her mind, she felt it expand until it finally released the warm sensual voice she knew so well. The voice resonating in her mind was a mere echo, a diluted version of the deep growl she was used to hearing speak in her mind.

"I hope that you slept well, my love, and that you are feeling better. Word has arrived from Daejara; we will be waiting for you in the

Chamber. There is no need to rush, we will be ready whenever you are."

Surprise warred with delight over the discovery. Yet another facet of the bond had been uncovered. She was curious how he thought to try that bit of magic and how he had achieved that little thought bubble that waited for her so patiently. She sent a gentle tug on the bond to let him know that she was awake.

In response, he sent her what felt like a smile, its warmth causing little ripples of pleasure along their mating bond.

The combination of his voice and presence in her mind, along with his scent surrounding her, gave her a sweet ache low in her belly.

"Missing me already, darling?" came the purr.

She sent him an image of her stretching on the bed.

"Wicked girl," he growled. *"Teasing me so shamelessly when you know I'm surrounded by a bunch of men. What will they say if they notice my reaction to those lovely curves?"*

She giggled at the thought of Timmins or Joquil noticing the evidence of his arousal and took pity on him.

"Thank you for letting me sleep," she replied sweetly.

"Of course, Mira. You needed the rest."

"Will you let the others know that I am on my way and will be there shortly?"

"Already done."

She stood with a small grin, feeling more content than she had since her mother passed away. Her life had become so small before coming to the capital. There was no surprise and very little excitement; just the simple pleasure found in the quiet moments in her garden or sitting before the fire, curled up with a book she had read countless times before.

There had been happiness in that, certainly, but not this sense of completion and purpose. She hadn't realized how lonely she had been, living on her own. She had laughter again, now that she had found her new family, for that's what the Circle had become to her.

Kragen and Darrin were like older brothers, as likely to tease her as to protect her. Timmins the father, providing both caution and comfort for all of them as needed, while Joquil was an uncle that was often away on grand adventures and who would come visit to share stories of the wonders he had witnessed. At least, that's what she assumed they were like, she had never had any of those things before.

And then there was Von…

I'll never be alone again, she thought. Heart full to bursting, Helena dressed quickly, throwing on a simple dress of light purple and braiding her hair.

Her smile was radiant as she stepped swiftly out of the room and toward the men that had become so dear to her.

CHAPTER 14

ounding the corner, Helena saw Gillian standing close to Darrin. Their voices were hushed, so she could not hear what they were saying, but Gillian had her hand resting on his chest and they were both laughing as she stepped closer.

Smiling tentatively, as she did not want to intrude, she offered a small wave before stepping around them.

"Oh, Helena," Gillian called behind her.

Turning toward the pair, Helena raised a quizzical brow.

"We were just discussing the court's impending trip to Daejara. How exciting! You must let me come with you so that you're not bored to death by all those dreary men."

"Being surrounded by a bunch of men sounds exactly like your dream scenario, Gillian dear," Helena replied mildly.

Gillian beamed. "Exactly, so it would be absolutely cold-hearted of you to deny me such a glorious opportunity. Just imagine the potential for wandering off and coming across some delightful male while he's bathing in a stream…" she trailed off and let her eyes wander up and down Darrian as though sizing him up.

"Easy, girl, that one's off limits," Helena replied with a laugh.

Gillian shrugged. "Doesn't mean I can't appreciate the display."

Helena's lips pursed, trying to contain her laughter.

"So, it's settled. I will accompany you as an emissary for Elysia. During our travels, I can keep you company and provide you with much more stimulating conversation than you'd receive otherwise, and once we reach Daejara, I can help rebuild our relationship with their court. You will be glad for the female company. Women are much better at soothing wounded egos than men are."

"She's not wrong on that front, at least" Darrin mumbled.

Helena was still smiling as she said, "Emissary? Promoting yourself again?"

Gillian shrugged. "It makes sense."

Helena shook her head. "If you insist, I won't mind the company."

Gillian clapped her hands in excitement. "Wonderful! I am going to go start packing!"

Standing on her tiptoes, Gillian rested her hands on Darrin's shoulders and kissed him lightly on the cheek before whispering something in his ear.

Darrin's eyes glazed and he stood in place as Gillian rushed off the way Helena had just come.

"Darrin?" Helena called, waving her hand in front of his eyes.

There was no response.

"Darrin," she said more sharply.

Blinking, Darrin straightened and looked at her, the tips of his cheeks and ears turning pink. "Yes, Kiri?"

Shaking her head and rolling her eyes, Helena merely walked into the Chamber muttering as she did, "Men."

The fire crackled merrily in the hearth as a breeze floated through the window; the promise of a storm on the wind.

Helena closed her eyes to take a deeper breath of the rain-scented air. It would be a soaking rain, she decided, heavy but gentle and seeping deep into the earth. Smiling in satisfaction she turned toward the others.

"When do we leave?" she asked no one in particular.

"The Daejarans were humbled by your request, Kiri, but have expressed concern about being able to entertain or house our retinue in the manner we are accustomed."

Helena tried to suppress the roll of her eyes. "*I am hardly accustomed to the manner in which I am currently housed. Assure our hosts that we shall require no special treatment, save a roof over our heads, if possible. We will make do with whatever they can provide and be thankful for that much.*"

"There are some, Kiri, who will not be pleased they will have to settle for less than they feel entitled to," Joquil cautioned.

"Then they are not invited. Only those we trust to be respectful shall travel with us."

The men nodded their understanding.

"So, the question stands, when do we leave?"

Timmins was quiet as he made calculations in his mind. He nodded once to himself as if coming to a conclusion and then addressed the room, "We shall need time to pack and extend the offer to accompany us to the merchants we trust; so that would be three days from now at the earliest, Kiri."

"Make it so, Advisor."

Darrin added quickly, "We will also need to ready the Rasmiri, as your guards they will need to prepare to travel with us as well."

"Doesn't it send the wrong message to our friends in Daejara if we arrive with hundreds of armed soldiers?" Helena asked skeptically.

"You cannot intend to travel without them, Kiri," Darrin replied in exasperation.

Helena shifted to face Von, asking as she did, "How many of your men will travel home with us?"

She noted the warmth that flared in his gray eyes when she said home. "All thirty-six will travel with us."

"If we match that number with Rasmiri, surely seventy-two, plus the Circle and the various merchants will be a safe enough number?"

Darrin scowled at her, "Do you value your own safety so little?"

Helena turned aqua eyes shimmering with flecks of iridescence to him and snapped, "Do you think it wise to overwhelm our host with hundreds of mouths they will be responsible for feeding and housing when it is clear that they already struggle to care for their own? We will bring only those we need and no more."

Darrin stiffened in his chair. "And who gets to decide how many are necessary? Our opinions on the matter are clearly divided."

"I will," Kragen rumbled.

Darrin turned surprised green eyes toward the Sword. "What gives you that right?"

"You are not the only one concerned about her safety, Shield," Kragen replied, the usual humor smoothed from his face. "As her Sword, I will ensure the Kiri's wishes are kept in mind while also being practical about our safety measures. I will consider the Circle's opinions, but I will make the final choice."

"As the Shield, it is my sworn duty to protect her, it is my decision to make!" Darrin snapped, hands pressed on the table as he leaned toward Kragen.

"Enough," snarled Von. "You are a child, Darrin, throwing a tantrum because you have not gotten your way. Your Kiri's wishes are clear, it is not your job to question, but to follow orders."

Darrin stood quickly, chair scraping loudly against the floor before coming to rest a few feet behind him. "Of course, *you* don't see the issue," Darrin sneered. "These are your people; you cannot see past your own bias to acknowledge the potential danger."

Von's voice was laced with barely controlled fury as he replied, "I, better than anyone, can speak to what we will face across the border. Perhaps, if you could set aside your own jealousy you would think to ask for my advice rather than sling insults. Do not question my loyalty or concern for my mate's well-being, you spoiled—"

Helena looked between the two men quickly, determining her mate was the bigger threat.

"Von," Helena cautioned gently through their bond while placing her hand softly over his.

She could feel the muscles clench and unclench beneath hers as he tried to get a hold on his anger.

"Child," he finished with a snarl. Despite the warning of violence laced in his voice, Von had not moved.

Helena was certain that if Darrin had come at him, he would have the man on his back on the floor before anyone could blink. Turning back toward Darrin she watched his nostrils flare and his teeth grind as he tried to rein back his temper.

He couldn't meet her eyes as he said, "Excuse me, Kiri," and strode from the room.

Helena looked around at the other men. "None of you thought to step in?"

Kragen shrugged. "Darrin is hotheaded and quick to speak. It was your Mate's right to defend himself, and you. Besides, it would have been fun to watch him learn his lesson."

Joquil and Timmins shared a knowing look but stayed silent.

Helena shook her head in disbelief. "You are *all* a bunch of children," she muttered, clearly unimpressed with their male logic.

Standing she walked toward the door. "It was only his concern for me that caused this outburst in the first place. Concern you all share, I might add. But I will find him, and I will make it right."

She felt a flicker of temper in her mind. *"Let him lick his own wounds."*

Helena frowned at Von. *"You don't always have to be so quick to goad him."*

Von's eyes widened in surprise. *"Are you taking his side?"*

"No, you buffoon, of course not. He was in the wrong and said things he should not have said, but you pushing his buttons only escalated the situation."

Von's eyes narrowed and he looked away from her and back toward the fire.

Without another word, Helena walked from the room in search of her oldest friend.

SHE FOUND him a while later seated next to a fountain in one of the Water halls. It came as no surprise that he would seek out a place meant to soothe after the heated words in the Chambers.

She followed the blue and green mosaic path toward him, the soft lights flickering against the twinkling tiles like sunlight. She enjoyed the way it made the depiction of the stream seem to move beneath her as she walked.

Darrin was running his fingers through the crystal surface of the water and watching the colorful fish scurry away from the ripples; he did not acknowledge her as she approached.

She sat and studied him before speaking. He was frowning into the water, his shoulders curved into himself as though making himself as small as possible.

"I'm sorry."

"You do not need to apologize for your desire to keep me safe."

He looked up at her hopefully.

"Besides, it is not I that requires an apology; you owe one to him," she added in the same soft voice.

He grimaced and she noted the shame that crossed his face. Reaching out a hand, she gently placed it on his shoulder.

"Helena," he began, her name coming out as a tormented whisper.

Stiffening at the tone, she sat back and waited in silence for him to continue.

His gaze met hers, something she did not recognize shining in the green depths.

"Don't you understand what it does to me? Seeing you with him. That unworthy bastard's hands all over what is mine."

Surprise at his words held her in place.

"It should have been me. We were meant to be together," the words fell out of his mouth in a rush.

"Darrin…" she started, eyes widening in confusion.

He dropped to his knees before her, hands grabbing hers.

"I love you. I have loved you since we were children. My future was always you."

As he stared up at her, she could not find her friend anywhere in those glowing green eyes.

Mute, Helena just stared at him and shook her head in denial.

Taking her silence for agreement, Darrin pushed himself up and pressed his lips against hers.

Wrong, this is wrong, she shouted in her mind, panic clawing through her. As she struggled to break away, he wrapped himself around her; trapping her in the prison of his arms.

He continued to kiss and nip at her lips, as she struggled to break free of his grasp.

"Helena?" her name a question in her mind.

Calloused fingers were trying to work their way down the front of her dress, nails scraping along the delicate skin as she squirmed.

"Helena!"

NO! She screamed in her mind, retreating into herself until she was staring down at the shimmering depths within her.

As if in answer, the magic rose and built until it broke through like a wave.

Darrin was flung from her like a rag doll, flying through the air until he crashed against the wall with a sickening thud.

Then Von was there. Helena had never seen anything like it. If her magic was a wave, Von was a storm. Each blow came faster and with more force than its predecessor; the snap and crack of Darrin's bones a grim harmony.

Von grabbed Darrin by his shirt and lifted him off the ground, holding him pressed against the wall.

"You dare to touch what is mine?" he roared, deadly violence in every word.

Darrin hung limply from his hands, blood dripping from a face that was no longer recognizable.

Von slammed Darrin back into the wall, a small groan coming from swollen lips.

"Enough," Kragen said softly from behind Von.

Von growled in warning, turning to glare at the man over his shoulder.

Helena saw his eyes and pressed her fingers to her lips. Slate gray was now a swirling molten gold.

Her legs shook as she stood and made her way toward him, studiously avoiding looking at the man pressed against the wall.

"Mate," she called to him.

The molten eyes looked toward her but did not see her.

"I am fine."

His lips curled back as he snarled, *"He hurt you. You were afraid. I could feel your fear as if it were my own."*

From a distance, she could hear voices shouting orders to get help, but did not look away. *"Do I look injured to you, Mate?"*

Molten eyes swept down the length of her. Confusion was working its way onto his face, replacing the rage. *"But I felt..."*

"I was scared, but I am safe and unharmed. Let him go now and come to me, my love."

Blinking Von released Darrin, who slid down into a bloody heap at his feet. Gray eyes peered up at her in shock.

Assessing the damage, Von stepped away from Darrin. Remorse and guilt flooded those gray eyes.

With shaking fingers, she reached for him and pulled him to her.

"What have I done?" he whispered hoarsely.

Holding him tightly, she shushed him and pressed herself into his body.

He trembled against her but held tight. *"I—I thought he was hurting you. All I could think was to protect you. I did not mean..."*

Her warrior was afraid of her reaction to what he had done to her friend. Helena was too confused by what Darrin had done to be able to process anything else as they stood there by the fountain.

Tanya rushed into the room, firmly ordering Kragen and Timmins to step back. She ran her hands along Darrin's body and closed her eyes and she began murmuring under her breath.

Helena watched as twisted limbs began to right themselves and as the swelling in his face went down. He was still covered in blood, but he looked like the boy she recognized.

With a groan, Darrin struggled to open his eyes.

Looking around at everyone standing above him, and then at the healer, his brows lowered in confusion, "What happened?"

His voice was a rasp from Von's fingers being wrapped so tightly around his throat.

His green eyes sought hers. "Helena?"

There was something in his expression that stayed the harsh words she wanted to launch at him.

"What is the last thing you remember?" she asked softly instead.

His brow furrowed. "The meeting… yelling at Von… walking out." He lifted scared green eyes back to hers. "How did I get here? What happened?" he repeated, trying to push himself up off of the floor.

Helena felt ice wrap its way down her spine.

Joquil stepped forward quickly and went to his knees beside Darrin. Gesturing for Tanya to move aside, he placed his hands on either side of Darrin's head and closed his eyes.

Darrin's own eyes rolled back in his head, and after a few moments of tense silence, both men opened them at the same time.

Joquil was breathing heavily when he turned to address the group.

"It was a spell."

"What?" Helena breathed in shock.

"It was too finely worked for me to be able to trace it, but imagine a snare, Kiri. A certain set of conditions needed to be met in order for the trap to spring. Once it did, whatever happened next was the result of the spell."

"H-How?" she asked, fear and anger at war within her.

Joquil shook his head. "I would have to know what happened in order to hazard a guess."

Helena blushed fiercely and shook her head in protest. It was one thing to have to live through the confusion of that last few minutes, but to risk further damage to any of them by repeating it… it wasn't a chance she wanted to take.

"Perhaps we should speak privately, Kiri," Joquil offered, sensing her concern.

Helena looked up at Von, who appeared as if he wanted to argue.

Helena nodded and stepped away from him.

As they stepped away from the others, Joquil created a soundproof barrier around them. Instantly the noises surrounding them became muffled. She could no longer hear the gentle lapping of water or the hushed voices of the men across the room.

"What happened, Kiri?" Joquil asked, not unkindly.

"He… he…" Closing her eyes and taking a shuddering breath, Helena started again, "He apologized, and I tried to comfort him. I told him he owed Von an apology, and then when he looked at me it was like he was someone else, I didn't know him anymore." Helena shook her head in frustration. "He told me that he should have been my Mate, that I belonged to him, and then he, then he…" she trailed off.

Joquil nodded in understanding. "Would you say that he was not acting like himself?"

Helena thought back, before nodding. "I couldn't say whether the words or feelings he was proclaiming were really him, but never, in all the years I've known him, have I ever seen him act that aggressively. The man I know would never force himself on me like that."

Joquil's expression was grim as he processed her words. He let out a long sigh.

"It was a sloppy spell, but strong. Whoever cast it effectively seized Darrin's mind, so that once it went into effect he would do and say what they had requested, like a puppet. Fortunately, they are not well-versed in the mating bond and did not understand that Von would respond to your fear."

"Or maybe they did," Helena whispered, eyes widening in horror. "Do you think whoever did this meant for Darrin to go further? Or for Von to kill him for it?"

Joquil merely shrugged, but his lips were pressed into a flat line as he considered her questions. "I could not say, Kiri."

Helena's eyes shot back to where Darrin was still sitting on the floor.

"Does he really not remember?"

"No, it is as he said, Kiri. His last thought before coming to consciousness on the floor was about leaving the Chambers."

"I do not think we should tell him. The shame and humiliation… it would break him," Helena murmured, aqua eyes pleading with his.

"Are you sure, Kiri? It could help us better understand what happened to prevent it in the future."

Helena's hand gripped his. "Please, Master Joquil. Isn't there another way?"

"I will see what I can do without us having to give Darrin back that particular memory."

She squeezed his hand in gratitude. "Thank you."

His eyes shifted away from hers to look about the once peaceful room. Lowering his voice even further he uttered, "One thing is clear: there are enemies in the Palace."

Helena felt the color leach from her skin, aqua eyes scanning every shadow as if they would reveal their secrets.

HOURS LATER, Von and Helena were curled up on their bed listening to the rain fall outside. Her head rested on his chest, his heart's steady beat, combined with the pattering of rain, a peaceful lullaby.

His fingers were brushing through her hair and down her back in quiet apology.

"It was not like going into a battle," he began, his deep voice quiet in its contemplation. "I could see what I was doing, but only as if viewing from very far away. I had no control. Even when I knew it had gone too far, I could not stop myself."

Helena was still against him, afraid to say or do anything to stop the words.

"When I felt your fear through our bond and you could not speak to me, I went insane, *Mira*. My only thought was to get to you and make whomever was hurting you pay with their life. I would have killed him, if you hadn't have stopped me."

"I know," she whispered softly, pressing a kiss to the skin above his heart.

She felt the shudder roll through him.

"I wanted to kill him," he admitted.

Helena sat up and looked down at his face. He was staring at the fire across the room, afraid to meet her gaze.

"Von, look at me," she pleaded softly.

She saw his jaw clench as he turned his eyes up to her, as though afraid of what he would see there.

"I am not afraid of you," she promised as her fingers caressed his cheek.

His eyes closed and he swallowed.

"I think it was my fault," she continued aloud, and his eyes snapped back open.

"Helena—" he began.

She pressed her fingers to his lips. "No, listen, please. I think my magic sent something down the bond. When he was touching me," she paused apologetically as his eyes shuttered at her words, "I turned inward, and it was my magic that responded to my fear. I think through the connection some of that went into you. It would explain why you felt like you were out of control. My magic was fueling your response when I felt like I couldn't protect myself."

Her voice had gotten small as she confessed.

He brushed back the hair from her face. "Helena, I would do it again. I would have done the same thing to any man that touched you. You cannot place this burden on yourself."

Wet eyes looked up at his.

"You are mine. Mine to protect. Mine to touch. Mine to love." With each declaration, he pressed a kiss to her cheek, her forehead and then her lips.

"But your eyes… they were like mine."

He raised a brow in question.

"Not iridescent specifically, but they were swirling and gold."

His other brow lifted in surprise.

He shook his head dismissively. "Perhaps I was enhanced because of the bond like you suggest, but it was my instinct that drove my actions. You are not responsible for what I did today."

Helena frowned but did not speak.

"We are figuring this out together, *Mira*, but perhaps we should speak to Timmins and Joquil about it to see if they can help us better understand."

The worry faded from her eyes at the suggestion and she nodded.

Wanting to leave the fear from this afternoon behind them, she tentatively touched the swirling words on his chest.

"Will you tell me what this means now?"

His mouth tilted up in a grin at her change of subject.

"It's called a Jaka; a Daejaran blessing. Most soldiers get this tattoo once they complete their training and before they go into their first battle. It is given as part of a rite performed by their commander." His hand took hers and pointed out certain words along his chest and arm as he continued, "It asks for the Mother's protection on any field of battle, and for her to take away our fear so that we may only feel the honor of fighting in her name. In a more practical sense, it also helps enhance and hone our power."

Helena's fingers traced the words of the prayer. "So it acts both as a focus and as a shield?"

Von nodded, fingers absentmindedly playing with the ends of her hair as it fell down her back.

"Maybe I should get it as well."

Von's smile was warm as he replied, "You have one session with Ronan and already assume you're done? Or are you simply anticipating walking onto a battlefield sometime soon?"

Helena's answering smile didn't quite reach her eyes.

Von's own eyes softened as he studied her. "Do you sense something coming, *Mira*?"

Helena shrugged. "I don't know."

He pulled her back down to lay on him. "Do not borrow worry until you have to, my love. Whatever comes, we will face it together."

Helena could not fight the shiver that ran through her body at his words. Staring at the rain splattered window, she wasn't certain this storm was the one she was waiting for.

Chapter 15

The next few days moved quickly. The Palace was a study in controlled chaos; everywhere she turned, people rushed down corridors, their arms filled with the supplies that would be traveling with the group going to the Daejaran border.

The lingering sense of unease she had felt ever since Darrin's attack was slowly starting to fade, but she still struggled with the idea of being alone with him. She had, in fact, avoided doing so at all.

While he did not remember exactly what had happened, he also seemed to be keeping his distance from her.

She sighed, knowing that she would have to face him sooner, rather than later.

Taking a final glance in the mirror, she admired Alina's handiwork. She was definitely going to miss the girl while she was away, there was no way she'd be able to replicate the intricate braids that encircled her head.

Helena had decided to forego her usual dresses in favor of more practical traveling attire. Her legs were encased in soft gray leather, her dark boots wrapping up to her knees. Her tunic was a creamy white, held in place by a black leather harness. The tunic was open across the top of her chest, revealing the sparkling pendant hanging just above her breasts.

As a final touch, she wrapped a soft blue cloak around her shoulders. The deep hood hanging down her back would do much to protect against both the sun and any other weather in the days to come.

Helena's hands ran over the curves so prominently displayed by the snugness of the leather. Her lips rose in amusement as she imagined Von's reaction.

As if the thought summoned him, Von chose that moment to walk back into the room.

He stopped short, eyes hungrily raking over her.

"You expect me to be able to ride, while you're wearing that?" he groaned.

"Perhaps not comfortably," she teased.

"You don't play fair, Mate."

Stepping toward him, she placed a swift kiss against his cheek and wove her arm through his. "Will all the Daejarans be riding on wolves?"

Von nodded as they made their way toward the stables. "Yes, the pack trains with the riders so that their instincts meld until they are seamless. A Daejaran never feels truly comfortable riding unless they are on their wolf."

"Will I have a wolf?"

Von quirked a brow at her. "Would you like one?"

"They certainly seem much cuddlier than a horse. Perfect to snuggle into if I want to take a nap, for instance."

Von stopped in place, sputtering, "Helena, you cannot call a Daejaran wolf cuddly! These are beasts renowned for striking fear in the hearts of our enemies before tearing their throats out. They aren't pets! You don't snuggle them for naps!"

Helena's laughter rang through the hallway. "Maybe you don't."

"Helena!" Von protested as she continued without him. "Helena, don't you dare!"

By the time he caught back up with her, she was already in the yard holding out a hand for his wolf to sniff.

"Traitor," Von growled at the smoke-colored animal, the white eyes focusing on Von seemed to laugh.

"Does this beautiful boy have a name?" Helena cooed, still looking at the animal sitting before her.

"Karma," Von muttered dryly, narrowing his eyes at the wolf who was acting more pup than pack leader.

"Hi, Karma. Hi, my sweet boy," Helena continued in her sing-song voice as she gently ran her fingers up Karma's snout, before giving him a few brisk scratches behind his ears.

Von's wolf closed his eyes in pleasure.

Von crossed his arms, annoyed with his wolf and with himself that he was jealous he wasn't the one she was petting.

"Oh hush, Mate, I promise to rub you later."

Von's cock twitched in response.

Helena was laughing when a couple of stable hands approached them.

"Kiri," one with straw-colored hair said nervously, the hands holding his cap twisting it unconsciously.

Helena gave Karma one last scratch before turning her attention to the young men standing a bit away from her.

"Yes?"

"There's something you ought to come see."

Without another word, the boys spun on their heels and ran off back in the direction of a wooden fence.

Helena and Von shared a look before following close behind them.

As they rounded the fence they noticed a group gathered, all murmuring excitedly as they pointed and stared at the small clearing in front of them.

"What is it?" Helena murmured, looking up at Von who had a better view due to his height advantage.

His gray eyes had widened in wonder as his mouth fell open.

Curiosity eating at her, she stepped toward the crowd. Noticing her, they parted to make room for her to pass by.

She stopped in stunned silence when she noticed the creature the others had all been staring at. It was a massive feline. Its fur a glittering white, but what had captured her attention were the impressive black wings that were currently unfurling as it arched its back to stretch its front legs. The wings were capped with glossy black talons that seemed sharp enough to disembowel a man in one fell swipe.

"What is it?" she whispered, in awe.

Hearing her voice, the cat focused glowing turquoise eyes on her.

Her breath caught in her throat; it was beautiful.

Tentatively she stepped closer, offering it her hand as she had done with Von's wolf only moments before. It stalked quietly toward her, twin curls of smoke flaring from its nostrils.

"It's called a Talyrian, Kiri," Joquil said in a low voice behind her.

"They've been thought to be extinct, no one has seen one in thousands of years," Timmins added, his voice trembling slightly.

"They are magical beasts, the sacred mounts of the ancient ones," Joquil continued as if Timmins hadn't spoken.

Helena shot them both a wide-eyed glance over her shoulder. "Where did she come from?"

Timmins shrugged while Joquil shook his head.

"It just showed up this morning, Kiri, and has been snarling at anyone who tries to get too close," Kragen stated in his deep rumble.

The cat nudged her hand with its head, demanding that she pay attention to it.

"Hello, beauty," she murmured, rubbing her hand along its velvety fur.

"It is said that many hunted the Talyrian. Their fur is impenetrable, making their pelts ideal for armor or cloaks."

Helena grimaced at the thought of such beautiful animals being slaughtered.

Those glowing eyes met hers knowingly before dipping in a low bow before her.

Gasps of shock rang out behind her, but she could not look away. Uncertain what the beast was asking, she remained still.

It stood and stamped a front paw into the ground, the earth shaking in response. All around people stumbled to maintain their balance, many eyeing the Talyrian warily and stepping further away.

"I don't understand," Helena said apologetically, as the cat folded down in front of her again.

"I-I think it is asking you to climb onto its back, Kiri," Timmins sputtered, the shock of the moment causing his voice to rise.

"Is that right, beauty? You want to take me for a ride?" she asked as she took a tentative step closer.

The beast snorted and nodded its massive head, smoke again flaring out.

Helena stepped to its side, trying to determine how she was supposed to climb on. The beast dipped lower so that she could easily lift and slide her leg up and over its neck.

Once she was settled it rose swiftly and flapped its leathery wings.

"Helena!" Von called, moving as if to grab her.

The cat snarled at Von, a small stream of fire shooting from its mouth in warning.

Ronan was close enough to wrap his arm around his friend's chest and hold him back.

The cat flexed its wings twice more before its muscles bunched below her and they were launched into the air.

Helena screamed as her stomach flew to her throat, hands digging deep into the silky fur to hold on.

With a few more flaps they were soaring in the air, the people below them tiny indistinguishable specks. The flight was smooth and the Talyrian covered distance very quickly. She stroked the soft neck and leaned forward to speak in its ear, "This is amazing!"

She felt as though she could observe the entire span of Elysia from this vantage point. The sprawling Palace a mere dot among the gardens and forests which glittered like jewels around it. The mountains that had seemed so far just days ago looked as though she could reach out and touch them.

They flew through a cloud, its dew gently coating her skin and bringing her back to awareness.

"We should probably get back before they worry about me," she shouted, her delight at flying through the air at war with her sense of duty.

The Talyrian huffed, those smoking jets curling around her, but it began its decent, flying low over a small stream, its wings brushing along the surface of the water.

Helena glanced at her reflection, noting the flush on her cheeks and wild joy alight in her eyes. She and the Talyrian were similarly colored, the soft grays and crisp whites blending together as if they were one.

Just as quickly as they had taken off, they were back, the Talyrian landing smoothly, shaking out its wings before bringing them back into the sleek body.

Helena slid down its side, turning to stroke its fur in thanks. The cat moved its head, nudging her just hard enough to make her take a few steps to the side to regain balance.

Looking up, she noticed the men running toward her, and the dark gray and black shapes of the wolves. Surrounded by the darkness, the Talyrian shone like starlight.

"May I call you Starshine?" she asked softly, looking directly into the glowing eye.

The Talyrian huffed again, pressing its face into her hand, as it nodded.

"Are you, are you mine?" she asked.

The Talyrian shook out its wings and mane, but huffed once more, as if to say it didn't belong to her, but she belonged to it.

Chuckling, Helena pat it again. "Thank you for the ride, Starshine. I look forward to next time."

The glowing turquoise eyes rolled to look past her at the men now panting behind her.

It swept its wing up and pushed her back, as though to shield her from them.

"These are my friends, Starshine," Helena said cautiously, instinct urging her to distinguish friend from foe.

Von reached for her, needing to touch her and ensure she was really safe.

Starshine's lips curled back revealing her impressive fangs, but Helena spoke quickly, "This is my mate, Von."

At that, the Talyrian twisted its head back to her. Standing beside it, it easily dwarfed her, the tops of its arms well above her head. After studying her for a moment, Starshine lowered her head in a small nod toward Von and then settled herself onto the ground, as if dismissing the group.

Helena could feel the tremble in Von's hand as he pulled her toward him.

"Please never do that again," he whispered fiercely as he folded her in his arms.

"I'm sorry I scared you," she responded, hugging him tightly.

Ronan's arms were crossed, as he grinned at them in amusement. "Haven't seen him almost piss his pants like that since the first time I swung an ax at him."

Von leveled a steely gaze on him, his jaw set.

"What, eighteen years is still too soon?" the red-headed man taunted.

"Shut up, you good for nothing asshole," a sultry female voice said.

Helena turned in Von's arms to better see the tall blonde with spiky hair that had just stepped up to Ronan.

"I should whip you for that," Ronan growled without heat.

She smiled up at him wickedly. "Oh, promises, promises!"

Ronan's smile grew and he leaned down to plant a hot kiss on her lips.

Stepping away from each other, the couple looked back at them smiling smugly.

"I'm Serena," the woman said, stepping toward Helena while offering her hand. "Von's third in command, and this one's" —she tilted her head toward Ronan—"better half."

Helena felt her own smile warm in response, liking this woman already. "Helena," she responded, shaking her hand.

Serena's violet eyes sparkled with mischief. "It's a pleasure to meet you, Kiri."

"Likewise, I didn't know Ronan had a partner."

"He doesn't like to admit to that particular weakness," Serena said mildly, rolling her eyes.

"Never my weakness, always my strength," the large man said affectionately.

Helena was shocked to hear such tenderness out of his mouth until she recalled Von's own confessions.

"You'll have to let me know if the rumors are true," Serena said mischievously.

"Rumors?" Helena asked in confusion.

"If Von's performance in the bedroom really matches his prowess on a battlefield."

Helena blushed fiercely. "I couldn't say."

Serena's light eyebrows rose in surprise. "Oh?"

"I've never seen him on a battlefield, and I'm usually too tired from the night before to see him practice with the others."

Ronan and Von roared with laughter.

"Oh, I like you. We're going to be very good friends," Serena murmured with approval.

As the group gathered, Helena couldn't help but wonder what would happen to Starshine, or why the Talyrian had chosen that moment to reintroduce itself to the world.

She had hoped she would be able to ride the cat while the others mounted on their wolves or horses, but as Kragen had pointed out, the Talyrian was made to fly and there was no way they were going to let her fly in the air while they were hours, if not days, behind her on the ground.

Helena just hoped that she would have an opportunity for another ride among the clouds soon.

Helena heard Gillian's soft drawl and turned toward her. As always, Gillian was the epitome of genteel femininity. Whereas both Serena and Helena had opted for pants and tunics, Gillian was wearing a bright pink gown adorned with small rosebuds along the low scooping neck that showcased her delicate gold necklace its purple stone shining in the sunlight. Her copper curls were swept up in an elegant twist, topped with a wide-brimmed hat that tied off under her chin. The hat was angled to shield both her eyes and bared skin from the sun.

Gillian wasn't quite able to school her face in time, and Helena noted the distaste at her own appearance. Though short-lived, that moment was enough to make her question her own decision to wear the leathers.

Feeling her unease, Von ran his hand along her back, pausing to cup and squeeze her backside and whisper into that space in her mind that had become his, *"You are beautiful, Helena. No wrapping could ever diminish what the Mother has given so freely."*

Pleasure and embarrassment swept through her, but when he kissed her, all she could think of was him.

Serena let out a low whistle causing the couple to break apart.

Chagrinned, Helena turned toward Serena; the tell-tale flush staining her cheeks.

"You shouldn't have let me stop you, Kiri, newly mated to a male like that…" She whistled again. "I'm surprised you two have left your rooms at all."

Before Helena could respond, Timmins called for the group indicating it was time to go.

Von winked and used phantom hands to gently caress her lips, a promise for later, as he started toward Karma.

Helena watched him walk away, struggling to bring her eyes back toward her companion when she asked, "Shall you ride with us, Kiri, or are you going to hole up in that box with the other one?"

Blinking she considered, frowning at the thought of being stuck in a carriage with Gillian rather than out in the fresh air.

"I'd like to ride."

Serena didn't quite contain her look of approval. "Very well, Kiri, let's get you sorted."

The women headed for the pack of wolves that were waiting for riders. The wolves were still, allowing the girls to walk through them as they made their way toward Serena's mount: a light brown she-wolf named Arrow.

Gesturing to a smaller black wolf, Serena said, "That's Shepa. She's a sweet girl, fast and fierce. She will see you safe, Kiri."

Serena checked both mounts before helping Helena mount up.

As soon as Helena was seated there was a bellow back where they had come from.

Startled, Helena looked over her shoulder and saw the Talyrian just as she was stamping her front foot. The ground shook, nearby horses whinnying in fear. The Chosen struggled to remain standing and let out shouts of warning as Starshine reared up to drop down with both front legs.

Oh please. Please don't. Helena prayed as she stared, wide-eyed at the Talyrian.

As if understanding Helena's wish, it leapt into the air instead but shot a quick burst of fire into the air as it roared.

"Mother's tits!" Serena swore. "If I didn't know better, I'd say that cat was jealous you mounted someone else."

Helena's heart clenched, watching the Talyrian fly away. "You heard Kragen, they weren't going to allow me—"

Tilting her head, Serena interrupted, "When are you going to realize that people don't get to tell you what to do anymore?"

Helena's mouth closed as she pondered the question.

Eyes still on the sky, Helena didn't take another easy breath until she saw Starshine circle back. The Talyrian wasn't leaving then, just keeping guard from above; while she was grounded.

Helena was trying, and failing, not to sulk.

"It's not your fault, Shepa," Helena murmured to the wolf as it trotted off behind the rest of the riders.

"I wonder what she'll do the next time you take Von for a ride," Serena mused aloud after a few moments of silence.

Helena's laughter was choked as the image came to life in her mind. Serena gave her a saucy wink and urged Arrow to go faster.

CHAPTER 16

*J*ust before dark, Von's men called a halt for the night, after finding a large forest clearing to set up camp.

Helena tried not to moan as she dismounted, her legs quaking after the exertion of the day.

Joquil had decided that now would be a perfect time for another lesson. Since her trial, he had been urging her to try testing her limits to see what she was capable of when she focused, and not just what her magic was prone to do in response to her emotions.

He was whistling cheerfully as she limped over to him, it was all she could do not to punch him straight in the teeth.

Her lips twitched in amusement as she imagined Ronan's approval at that style of greeting.

"I'm glad to see you are still in good spirits after such a hard day of riding."

Helena narrowed her eyes, shooting imaginary darts at his face.

Joquil chuckled, "Easy, Kiri, I do not have anything extreme in mind tonight. I simply thought it might help you tap into your own powers if you could start to identify others'." His eyes scanned the scattered people, eventually coming to rest on Kragen.

Kragen was making quick work of some tree stumps for the evening's fire.

"Earth," Helena responded automatically.

Joquil rose an eyebrow as a prompt to continue.

"Strength," Helena added, lowering herself to the ground as her legs protested the movement.

"And?"

"Air?" Helena guessed.

"Yes, the speed with which he wields his ax certainly confirms it. What of Von?" Joquil asked.

Helena's eyes scanned the crowd for a glimpse of her obsidian haired Mate, but she had not seen much of him since he left her side that morning.

She thought back as she answered Joquil's question. "He utilizes Air to create shields, he has minor healing abilities from Water, and obviously strength from Earth."

"And what of the Fire branch, Kiri?"

Helena's eyebrows wrinkled in confusion, "I-I'm not sure, Master Joquil. I have not seen…" she trailed off, remembering the feel of his hands, warm against her skin. "He can manipulate his body's temperature."

"Well done, Kiri. The subtleties of the five branches are not always easy to recognize. It's those details, however, that set apart those who have mastered their branch, and those that are simply gifted with one or two skills."

"Furthermore, the ability to combine two branches together…"

Helena's mind wandered as the Master continued his lecture. She hadn't known that Von was using both Fire and Water magic when he was gently working the knots out of her back after Ronan's ruthless practices. She had just assumed the magic of Von's hands was all him, but her Mate had used the soothing heat of Fire combined with the healing properties of Water to completely eliminate the aches in her body. That effortless and subtle use of magic was the trademark of a real master.

Is there anything he isn't skilled at? Helena wondered idly.

"*I'm an abysmal cook,*" came the amused reply.

Helena's eyes were heavy as she rested her head against a tree, Joquil's voice a soft buzz beside her.

"I'm starting to believe that our definitions of abysmal might differ."

"On my honor, Mate, I've only had to prepare meals over a campfire. I rarely have the foresight to pull something off the fire before it blackens on one side, and I have no mind for plants. One shrubbery looks very much the same as any other, which means I'm as likely to poison my meal as season it; much to the dismay of my potions master growing up."

Helena's lips lifted in a sleepy smile as she thought of a young Von at his studies.

"When we get to your home, Mate, I will cook for you. My mother always said I could make a feast with scraps."

"You are my home, Helena. There is no building in any realm that will bring me as much peace at the end of the day, as the feel of you in my arms. I could call a patch of dirt underneath a sea of stars home, so long as I am with you," Von's deep voice was a seductive purr, wrapping her in its warmth.

Helena wasn't aware she had fallen asleep until she felt Von's strong arms lifting her and carrying her to their tent set aside from the rest of the group.

Her eyes opened only briefly, seeing the strong line of his jaw gently shadowed with the day's beard. She pressed her lips against his neck, snuggling closer into him, her last semi-conscious thought sent down their bond, *"You came home."*

"I will always come home, to you," he responded softly, his kiss a whisper against her forehead.

GILLIAN MOVED QUICKLY along the outskirts of the camp, holding her skirt up to avoid brushing against the plants. She didn't have much time to find what she was looking for, that nosy bitch Serena had been keeping an eye on her all night. At least until she wandered off with one of the men from Helena's Circle; the big broody one whose name she could never remember.

Although the sky glittered with stars, very little light was making its way through the treetops. Gillian blinked and reopened her eyes, which now retained the abilities of her hawk form. Few of the Chosen knew of the ability to shift into another form, and Gillian had worked hard to keep that particular talent of hers a secret.

Her eyes scanning the ground could see much more clearly as she worked her way over to the plant she had noticed earlier that evening.

Gillian had thought Helena would be riding with her in the carriage, giving her time to put her plan into action. She had been dismayed this morning to realize her error, once she saw Helena had dressed for riding. Luckily, Gillian was anything if not adaptable, she would simply have to take matters into her own hands.

Reaching the plant, she squatted down quickly. Fingers carefully plucking the heart-shaped leaves, so dark they were almost black. Known as *Bella Morte,* it was a beautiful, but deadly, plant. Used in small amounts by skilled healers it could induce long-term sleep in patients that required excessive treatments. In larger doses, it caused powerful hallucinations that could trap somebody in the prison of their mind. When in bloom, *Bella Morte* had luscious purple blossoms, but many did not attempt growing it in any garden. Just a small scratch from one of the sharp sides of the leaves would be enough to knock out a small child for many hours.

Gillian gathered as many leaves as she could stuff in the small satchel tied around her wrist.

Hearing a branch snap behind her, she spun and stood quickly, hand pressed against her chest as if to contain the heart beating wildly inside it.

"It's not safe out here for a woman alone," a low female voice said.

Serena stepped around the large trunk of a tree, her blonde hair seeming to glow in the darkness.

"Oh, it's you," Gillian said flatly.

"One would think you were trying to sneak off. What with the way you are out here deep in the forest and far away from the safety of the guards. Are you taking a late-night stroll? Meeting someone?" Serena asked mildly. While the words were idle, it was clear from the predatory gaze in those violet eyes that Serena assumed she was up to something.

"Just relieving myself in peace, lady," Gillian lied smoothly.

Serena lifted her brow. "Of course, you were."

"I would appreciate your company on the way back to camp," Gillian said, attempting to win the woman over, "We are, as you said, far from the safety of the group."

"Why did you stray so far, if you were worried about being alone," Serena asked instead, her arms resting on her hips, fingers within easy reach of the weapons strapped there.

"Privacy, lady. It's hardly in my interest to stop somewhere I could be come upon. Not exactly the position I like men to find me in."

Serena snorted in amused disbelief, although she wasn't sure if it was because of the frank admission or if Serena simply found her to be a foolish female.

"After you." Serena gestured back toward the camp.

Gillian nodded stiffly and walked beside her back into the warm light of the campfire.

HELENA WOKE up to the sound of songbirds; it was still early, the sunlight barely peeking through the cracks of the tent.

She assessed her body as she stretched her limbs, pleasantly surprised that all the aches were gone. *Von,* she realized with a smile, twisting to curl into her Mate's warm body.

He was still asleep, chest rising and falling with his deep breaths. Propping herself up on her elbow, Helena rested her head in one hand, while lightly trailing her other over the expanse of skin revealed by the blanket riding low on his waist.

It was rare that she woke before he did, and she reveled in the opportunity to study him at her leisure. He really was beautiful, all those hard angles exuding power even in his sleep. Her eyes flickered up to his face, noting the way his long lashes created crescent-shaped shadows on his cheeks and how those full lips were slightly parted, almost as if they were begging to be kissed.

Helpless to resist the silent request Helena leaned forward. Her hair fell like a curtain around them as she pressed her lips softly against his, her hand continuing its journey down Von's rippling stomach.

She felt him stir against her hand, her fingers meeting velvety smoothness as she continued the caress.

He pressed into her hand, eyes fluttering open to find her smiling knowingly down at him. "This might be my new favorite way to wake up," he declared, his voice rough with sleep.

"If I recall correctly, I promised you a rub," she murmured closing the distance between their lips with another soft kiss; her hand stroking his swelling length.

He let out a low moan of pleasure against her lips as his hips thrust into her hand. His own hand fisting in her hair, holding her mouth pressed to his.

There was a rustling at the flap of their tent followed by a loud cough.

Von's head dropped back to the blanket as he closed his eyes with a groan. "This better be important you bastard!" he growled, the threat of violence in every word.

Ronan's cheerful voice replied, "Indeed it is! The two of you are joining me for a short training session before we head out today. No reason to skip our sessions just because we're traveling."

He opened one gray eye to peer at her. "You don't suppose—"

"That means now, Brother! You have one minute or I'm coming in and carrying your ass out," Ronan shouted.

"The Mother hates me," Von muttered morosely.

Helena couldn't help chuckling, although she felt his disappointment every bit as keenly.

"There's always tonight, Mate," she offered, her voice warm with desire.

He stole a final kiss, his tongue caressing hers before he pulled back with a frustrated growl. He stood, shaking his head and letting out a stream of curses as he began gathering his clothes.

Dressing quickly, they exited the tent before Ronan could make good on his threat. Helena was still braiding her hair as they made their way to a small clearing beside the camp.

Serena offered her a sleepy smile, lifting a small tin cup in salute before taking a deep swallow.

"Tea?" Helena asked hopefully.

Serena nodded and offered the cup to her. Helena took it gratefully. Lifting the steaming cup to her lips, she took a small sip. She closed her eyes in pleasure before taking another deeper gulp and letting out a low moan of approval.

"I thought you only made that sound for me, Mate," Von teased, his voice a sensual purr in her mind.

Helena sputtered, tea flying as she coughed. She spun toward him with wide eyes, her cheeks flaming in embarrassment.

Von threw his head back and laughed. Before she could respond, Serena and Ronan joined in, guessing at what had her looking as though she were ready to throw the cup at her Mate's face.

"Easy now, Kiri. Don't go wasting good tea on a stupid male," Serena's laughter-tinged voice called from behind.

Helena thrust the cup back at Serena and gave Von a narrow-eyed stare that had him attempting to school his grin into a chastised expression.

"See if I let you do any of the things that cause those sounds you like so much now, Mate," Helena growled back through the bond as she stomped to Ronan's side.

"Hey now," Von protested.

Helena looked back at him over her shoulder and smirked.

Von's brow lowered over heated gray eyes. *"You promised."*

"A woman, especially a Kiri, has every right to change her mind."

"I was teasing!"

"Maybe you should have saved your teasing until after I had my tea, Mate," came the haughty reply.

"Technically I did—"

Helena scowled at Von from across the training circle Ronan had corded off.

More laughter was threatening to spill from his lips as he studied the aggrieved woman standing before him. Her face was flushed with color, her aqua eyes sparkling beneath her sooty lashes. She was breathtaking.

"Truce, my love," he said soothingly. *"It seems we are both feeling on edge this morning."*

Helena crossed her arms and pointedly looked away.

"I'm sorry for teasing you, Mira, I promise to make it up to you later."

"How?" she asked, narrowed aqua eyes meeting his.

Von sent her an image of exactly what he planned to do, chuckling to himself when her gaze became unfocused and her scowl slackened.

"All right, you two, enough of that." Ronan grunted, a flush stealing up his own cheeks as he adjusted his pants.

Serena shifted beside him uncomfortably, pulling at her shirt as if seeking a breeze.

Blinking, Helena refocused on her friends. Noticing their reaction, she threw her hands up in the air. "Oh for the love of the Mother!"

Von's shoulders shook with mirth.

She pointed an accusing finger at him. "Don't you start! This is your fault."

"My fault?" he asked with faux innocence.

"You know exactly what you did."

"It would seem to me that Ronan got exactly what he deserved for his wake-up call this morning." Von smiled seeming pleased with himself.

"Apparently, we all have extra energy to burn off this morning," Ronan replied dryly.

"I'm sorry," Helena offered softly, embarrassed that once again her feelings were not only transparent but could so easily manipulate her friends.

Serena grinned. "Don't be, Kiri."

"That's easy for you to say."

Serena wrapped an arm around her shoulder and squeezed, whispering in her ear. "I will teach you some things you can try when you are alone together that will wipe that smug smile right off his face."

"What's all that scheming going on over there?" Von called.

Helena responded with her own smug smile causing Von's brows to lift in surprise.

"If we're all done wasting time," Ronan started, his voice no longer the teasing voice of her friend but the annoyed snap of her commander, "perhaps we can begin our lesson?"

Helena turned her gaze back to Ronan, her body falling into the stance he had taught her during their first session. Legs shoulder width apart, shoulders back, chin up, eyes straight ahead and arms behind her back, each hand grasping the opposite elbow. It was the position all Daejaran trainees assumed when they were at attention. Not only was it a position of respect, it was also one of submission. With their arms in that position they were unable to draw a weapon or defend themselves, or at least in the case of the recruits. Any fully trained warrior would be able to cause massive damage even without their weapons, but it was a symbolic position as much as anything.

"Very good, Kiri," Ronan murmured before continuing, "today we will practice shielding. Are you familiar with how to cast a shield?"

Helena shook her head.

"Shielding most commonly comes from the branch of Air. Most warriors create an impenetrable barrier that they wrap around themselves for protection. However, those that are not gifted in that branch have learned how to use their other talents in a similar fashion. Those with Earth may reinforce their skin with its strength, making it all but impossible for a weapon to penetrate. Those with Fire may make their skin so hot it can melt any weapon or burn any who touch it."

Helena listened, fascinated.

"It is one thing to be able to form a shield and another to be able to fight while maintaining one. Serena, help me demonstrate."

Serena stepped in front of him, violet eyes shining as she called her power to the surface.

There was not a visible shift in the air, but Helena could feel the shift in the air as it thickened and reformed around Serena. It was not a bubble as Helena had assumed, but a skin-tight layer that moved as she did.

"May I?" Helena asked, lifting a hand.

Serena nodded while Ronan and Von watched in silence.

Moving toward her, Helena pressed her hand against her friend's arm, feeling a slight resistance before her hand settled on warm skin.

"How can I still touch you?" Helena asked curiously.

"My magic recognized you as a friend."

"Shields can work in a variety of ways, Kiri, it depends on the talents of the Chosen that has called it. Serena is gifted with Air and Fire. Her shield is both barrier and transformative. It will keep magic and weapon from breaking through, at least so long as her magic can sustain the shield, but it will also adapt to the threat."

"How is that possible?"

"Fire is known for its transformative properties. It not only burns, it makes the elements shift between their various forms. When I weave it into my shield, it adds an additional layer of protection. Here, it will be easier to show you than explain. Try summoning a ball of Water and throwing it at me."

Helena raised a dubious brow but called her magic to her. She felt the cooling rush of Water as it rose to the surface. Concentrating, she willed the Water to begin filling the palm of her hand. She let it go when the Water was the size of a melon swirling and spinning in her hand.

Lifting iridescent eyes, she drew back her arm and willed the ball of Water toward Serena's chest.

The Water sizzled turning to steam as soon as it made contact with the shield. Serena grunted and took a startled step back, her hand lifted to rub at her chest.

Ronan placed a concerned hand on her shoulder.

Shaking her head in surprise, Serena looked up at them with wide eyes. "Usually I do not feel much of an impact through my shield, but your magic felt like a full-grown Talyrian running straight into me. I was not expecting it."

Helena grimaced. "I'm sorry, I hope I didn't hurt you."

"Nonsense, Kiri. It is I who was unprepared. You have reminded me that even in practice I cannot lower my guard."

Serena bowed her head in thanks before offering her usual sassy smirk. "Perhaps you should help the men learn that lesson as well."

Seeing the playful light in her friend's eye, Helena's own smile grew in response.

"What?" Ronan asked as Von shouted, "Wait!"

It was too late, calling twin balls of Water to each hand, she flung the magic out to both men, aiming for their heads.

The unexpected assault had both men sputtering and dripping. Ronan shook off, his long braid causing droplets to fly and shimmer in the morning sun.

Von stalked toward her, a low snarl lifting his upper lip.

Helena's laughter froze as she shifted her body bracing for his attack.

One moment he was across the clearing, the next he was standing directly before her. Helena hadn't even blinked, but Von had cleared the distance in an instant.

Before she could ask how he managed it, his arms were wrapped around her pressing his drenched clothing into her.

She squirmed in his arms, but his hands moved faster than she could track them to begin tickling her sides.

"No fair!" she cried between bursts of laughter.

"Keep squirming against me like that and I'm throwing you over my shoulder and carrying you back to our tent, no matter what Ronan threatens," he whispered hotly in her ear.

Helena felt the stirring low in her belly at the words. Still, his hands continued their assault.

"Shield," his voice commanded in her head.

Trying to focus, Helena called her power to her once more. She tried to weave Fire and air to make a shield like Serena's, but it felt unwieldy and she could not make it take shape.

"Focus," Ronan called.

"I am!" Helena panted, still twisting in Von's arms.

"It should feel natural, Kiri. You should not have to force it into being, merely call it to you," Serena offered.

"If he would just. Be. STILL!" Helena emphasized each word before shouting the last, Von freezing in place around her.

She watched his eyes move comically side to side before looking up at her in approval.

"Well, that's one way to do it," he drawled.

Serena had her hand clasped over her mouth to hide her smile. Ronan shook his head smirking at the pair.

"Release me, darling?" Von's sweet words in sharp contrast to the molten heat in his eyes. Helena's heart fluttered in her chest.

Be free, she thought, pulling her magic back toward her. Von's limbs lowered until he was standing relaxed before her again.

"And again!" Ronan shouted, giving her no time to prepare.

Von dipped low, aiming for her knees.

Twirling, Helena sidestepped him and called her magic to her. Instead of trying to force it she merely shouted into the swirling depths of her power: *shield!* As Von reached her, she felt her magic snapping into place, Von making contact only briefly before flying away from her and landing on his back in the dirt.

She felt the impact through their bond, her own breathing a bit strained as a result.

Gasping, Helena rushed over to him and knelt at his side. "I'm so sorry! Are you okay?"

Von struggled to sit, bemused eyes meeting hers. "Next time, Mate, Ronan gets to be your target."

The group exchanged amused glances before laughing.

"I think that's enough for today. With the day's ride still ahead of us, I'm not sure we can withstand too much more of your abuse, Kiri," Ronan said with the laughter still sparkling in his blue eyes.

The teasing tone of his voice removed the sting of his words. She still had much to learn about controlling her magic, and even more still about its limits, but each day she could feel that simmering pool inside her becoming more responsive to her will. She just hoped that she would be ready when it mattered.

CHAPTER 17

The group was scattered around the campfire, it had been another long day of travel and many had already sought out their tents to get some rest. The Circle, along with Helena and some of Von's men remained.

Von's arm was snaked around Helena's waist as her head rested on his shoulder. She stared into the center of the fire, watching it dance in the gentle breeze. Next to her, Kragen sat, his legs stretched out in front of him as he leaned back against a tree. Darrin was beside him, arms crossed over his chest. Serena and Ronan were seated to his right both sharpening their blades in companionable silence. Across from Helena, Joquil and Timmins were chatting softly, voices indecipherable over the flicker of the flames.

The scenery had started to change that afternoon, shifting from the gently sloping hills into the harsher jagged peaks of the mountains. The air was already feeling cooler and smelled more of pine than the heady scent of flowers that had been following them from the Capital. It was peaceful there, around the fire, but Helena could not escape the feeling that something was waiting for them.

A shiver raced down her spine causing Von's arm to flex and pull her closer.

She felt the ripple of a question within her mind and offered him a small smile in response.

A rustle caused the group to shift as they sought out the source. From the back of the camp, Gillian stepped out from her tent and walked over to the group, pulling the sides of her dark cloak tighter around her.

"I'm exhausted but I can't sleep." She pouted as she stepped over Kragen's legs and folded herself into the space next to Darrin.

Darrin shifted over to accommodate her, but she scooted closer, her body following his.

"It's cold out tonight," she murmured, pressing against him.

Darrin eyed her warily but wrapped his arm around her shoulder to offer her his body heat.

"What are you all doing out here?" she asked, her voice loud after the silence.

"Just enjoying the evening," Helena responded in a more subdued tone.

"Are you just sitting here in silence?" she asked almost accusingly as she looked around at them.

"Would you like a story?" Timmins offered before anyone else could speak.

It wasn't clear how Gillian felt about the suggestion, her face obscured by the shadows.

"You did promise me some stories, Timmins," Helena offered when Gillian didn't respond.

"In the tradition of the campfire, I suppose I shall make it a good one," Timmins said with a laugh.

"If by good, you mean bloody, by all means," Ronan chimed in with his deep growl, setting his ax down and resting his elbows on his knees.

Timmins offered a dark smile and took a moment to settle himself, eyeing each of them before clearing his throat and beginning.

"Many generations ago, long after the Mother had found her Mate and given birth to the Chosen, a prophet arose foretelling the fall of the Chosen. As the Mother's children, the Chosen ignored the warnings of the prophet and as the years passed the warnings were forgotten."

"Time went on and the Mother's gifts began to weaken, fewer of the Chosen were able to access more than one of her branches. Of those, few, if any, ever learned to Master their branch. And still, the Chosen flourished—"

"So much for the prophecy," Gillian snorted as she interrupted Timmins' recounting.

Timmins raised a brow, waiting for her silence before he continued. "And so it was, years turning to centuries. There were some that had not forgotten the words uttered by the prophet, those that had continued to pass the warning through the generations, knowing the day would come when it could no longer remain unheeded.

"Finally, the day had come when the first of the prophets' signs came to be: a Daughter of Spirit would be born on the longest day of the year. This girl would be marked by the Mother, bearing her sign on her flesh."

Helena's spine stiffened, the hand that was interwoven with Von's going slick with sweat.

"It can't be me they're speaking of," Helena sent the worried thought to Von, *"They got the prophecy wrong. I wasn't born in the summer, and I don't bear any mark of the Mother."*

Phantom hands brushed the hair off of her face while his warm hand squeezed hers reassuringly.

Unaware of the silent exchange, Timmins spoke on, "This Damaskiri's Circle would never be complete as she would not find her Mate. Feeling betrayed by the Mother she would seek to grow her power. Eventually, she would learn how to twist the Mother's most sacred branch of magic, and thereby corrupt it completely."

"How—" Helena began, but Timmins silenced her by holding up his hand.

"The Chosen were unaware of this corruption and continued to serve their Lady faithfully. By that time, the second of the prophecy's signs came to be: A Mother of Spirit would be born, and she would grow to be more powerful than any in living memory, her power more akin to the First Born, the original Chosen. She would be born to an Ungifted, identified again by the Mother's mark upon her flesh. She would rise once the ultimate corruption had occurred."

Despite her attempts to tell herself it was just a silly story, panic rose in Helena's chest, her hand clamping down and squeezing Von's as she fought to breathe.

"Once this Kiri came into her power, she would become the ultimate vessel of the Mother. Her purpose to seek out the corruption that continued to spread across the land. She would use her gifts, like calling to like, so that she may identify the unworthy and destroy them."

Timmins paused and Helena felt herself shaking in Von's embrace.

Gillian yawned loudly. "A tale that has been told to every Chosen child so they would jump at shadows. Everyone knows no Kiri has ever been born of an Ungifted."

The family that she had never met… was is possible it was because they had never existed? Had Miriam really been her birth mother, never realizing who her daughter was destined to be? The questions whirled in Helena's mind, her heart continuing to race as she struggled to make sense of the story.

"I had heard," Helena stopped to lick her lips, mouth suddenly dry, "that it was possible for this Kiri herself to be corrupted, that she could give rise to the Shadow Years?" The last word a question.

Timmins tilted his head quizzically, studying Helena across the fire. The flames casting eerie shadows across his usually kind face.

"And what have you heard of the Shadow Years, Kiri?" Timmins asked.

"Only that it would be a dark time when the Chosen were tested, and that if the Kiri was corrupted, she would destroy those that had remained true to the Mother's gifts."

"I suppose that is one way of looking at it," Timmins murmured.

The men shifted around her, the rustling of clothes blending into the crackling of the flames.

"The Shadow Years refer to the rise of the Shadows, although no one has seen a Shadow for thousands of years," Joquil offered.

"I've only ever heard whispers about the Shadows," Ronan said, his voice somber.

"What's a Shadow?" Von asked, Helena's thoughts echoing his question.

"A Shadow is the remnant of a Chosen."

"A remnant?" Helena asked, still confused.

"When a Mother or Daughter of Spirit is corrupted, they use their ties to the Spirit branch to enslave the Chosen. Over time the souls of the Chosen are consumed by the one controlling them, burning out all that they are until they are mere shadows of themselves. Even after their souls have been expended, a Damaskiri can continue to control the Shadow, creating a mindless husk that thinks or feels nothing other than what it is told to."

Ice ran through Helena's veins. This was what they feared she would do? Create an army of soulless warriors? Why put her in power at all if that was what she was capable of?

Helena's thoughts continued to churn as she retreated into herself, no longer listening to the voices that continued to speak around her. Nothing was making sense. How was she supposed to be the girl they spoke of in the prophecy? Was the prophecy even real, or was it just a story told to scare children as Gillian had suggested?

"Hush, Mira, your thoughts are so loud I can hear them as if you were shouting them into my ear. It is just a story, you and I both know in your heart you could never misuse your power so completely."

"But—"

"Hush. I know your heart better than my own, and it is pure. You are filled with light, Helena. I am the half of you that was created in darkness. You never need to doubt yourself in that regard."

He stopped her protest with a gentle kiss. "Come," he said aloud, his deep voice warm and comforting, "let's get away from the others and spend some time under the stars."

Appreciating the attempt at a distraction, Helena willingly stood, waving a half-hearted goodnight at the others as she followed quietly behind Von.

"Do you think that Talyrian of yours would allow a second rider?"

Helena stopped, considering. "I'm not sure. She's certainly big enough to carry another."

"Call for her and let us see if she will take us for a ride amongst the stars."

Helena let out the low warbling whistle that had become her call to Starshine. Within moments the burst of brightness in the dark sky streaked down, landing nimbly before them. With a great huff, she shook out her mane and gently pressed her face into her mistress.

Helena stroked the velvety fur lovingly. "Would you take us for a ride Starshine?"

The great beast turned its glowing eyes toward her Mate, snorting loudly.

"Please, Starshine. For me?" Helena begged sweetly.

The Talyrian studied her for a long time, Helena certain that she would take off and deny the request. Finally, she folded her front legs, bowing low.

"Thank you," Helena whispered, as she wrapped her arms around the wide neck and hugged her affectionately. "I promise to spend extra time brushing you tomorrow!"

Small jets of smoke shot out as if to reiterate her annoyance at the request.

"Okay." Helena chuckled "And give you a special treat."

The Talyrian flapped its wings, suddenly impatient to be off.

"All right my beautiful girl, let's go."

With that Helena quickly mounted, pulling Von up behind her. Wrapping his arms around her waist he pressed against her, his lips leaving a trail of fire along her neck as he placed gentle kisses against the bared skin. Suddenly, the Talyrian flapped its massive wings twice more before launching them into the air.

Von let out a startled cry, unprepared for the takeoff. Helena laughed as his arms squeezed her tightly, the sound a joyful tinkling that followed them into the night.

THEY FLEW AMONGST THE STARS, the weightlessness of flight doing much to alleviate the anxiety she had been feeling these last few days. Feeling Von pressed against her back didn't hurt either. They hadn't been properly alone since leaving the Palace, and she had missed those quiet moments with him.

"I can feel you thinking. What could possibly be distracting you from such a view, *Mira*?" Von asked in his soft rumble.

"I was just thinking about how this is our first time away from everyone in days."

"I would say that's a reasonable distraction," he murmured before biting down gently on the back of her neck.

She shivered in his arms, the heat of his mouth more noticeable with the cool breeze washing over them.

"Perhaps we should take advantage of it," he whispered in her mind as he continued to nibble and lick the skin he could reach.

"I think you might be right," she responded, her voice breathless even through the bond.

Helena nudged Starshine and the Talyrian started her descent.

Soon they were landing in a small clearing in the forest. The ground was dappled with moonlight and there was the soft burbling of a stream in the distance. The night was cool, but Helena felt nothing but heat as Von pulled her against him.

Starshine's eyes glowed in the darkness, and she let out a soft huff before padding away from the couple.

"It's like she knows what we intend," Von murmured with a chuckle.

"She's smart. I have no doubt she does," Helena agreed before adding, "She won't stray far though."

Looking at her, he brushed his fingers gently down the side of her face. She pressed into the caress, her eyes closing as she did.

"You look beautiful bathed in moonlight, Mate. I think it should be all you ever wear, at least when we're alone."

His voice was a harsh rasp that moved along her skin, phantom hands plucking at the bindings of her gear as they undressed her.

"Which one of us is in a hurry now," she teased, remembering their first night when her magic had done the work for her.

"Don't mistake me, Helena. I have every intention of taking my time enjoying you tonight. I'm just ready to get started."

No longer in a mood for teasing, Helena's eyes opened to meet his, the hunger shining in their depths a twin to his own.

They stayed there, holding each other under the watchful gaze of the stars for a heartbeat before his lips were on hers.

The kiss started gently, but it wasn't long until he was groaning low in his throat and deepening it. Helena responded in kind, her mouth parting under his as his tongue slid in to taste her. As they kissed, Von's hands, both real and phantom, continued their exploration of her body. She could feel garments slacken before falling to the ground, and then the gentle breeze swept against pleasure-heated skin.

His hands were gentle as they traced a path along her back, although the skin was rough from his time wielding his sword. She felt them settle at her hips before following her curves back up and resting just below her breasts.

"Please," she begged, her lips still tangled with his own.

His fingers teased the soft globes, gently running back and forth on the undersides before splaying beneath them and lifting her breasts a bit higher. She could feel them grow heavy in response, aching for the feel of him.

He pulled back from her, studying her body, now bared, before him. His thumbs lifted to brush against the tips of her breasts, turning her nipples into tight buds before lowering and taking one into his mouth. His fingers continued to pluck and tease at the other as he pulled back to blow softly on the wet tip.

Helena let out a low moan, her head falling back. She could feel her braid brush against her skin, the sensation an additional tease that had her gripping Von's shoulders.

Von's answering growl was pure male satisfaction as he dropped to his knees before her, his mouth continuing to kiss and lick down her belly.

Helena licked her swollen lips before biting down on the bottom one. Her hands stroking Von's hair as she watched him lick up the skin between her hip and thigh. Her heart was racing, and she was struggling to catch her breath.

Von's hands slid around her hips and grabbed her ass, pulling her into him as he licked up the center of her. Helena gasped, pleasure shooting through her as he lapped at the small bundle of nerves. She felt Von's hand slide down the back of her leg, coaxing it to bend so that he could lift it to rest on his shoulder. She teetered, but he steadied her without stopping his assault.

Watching his head work between her legs was quickly pushing her over the edge. She could feel those phantom hands playing with her breasts while his real one teased and circled her entrance. Helena's hips were rocking into him, begging him to fill her. Her cries becoming wild as he finally relented and slid two fingers inside her.

Around them, wind began to whip through the tree, its intensity growing with hers.

"Von!" she cried, his name a plea.

"Yes," he ordered, *"come for me."*

Helena shattered, her muscles clenching around his fingers while he greedily sucked on her bud.

The wind died down as quickly as it had appeared, but all around them leaves began to fall from the trees.

Von looked up at Helena, his gray eyes molten as he gave her one last lazy lick. He chuckled, lips still against her when she struggled to keep her eyes open.

"Oh no, you don't. I'm nowhere near done with you yet," he said in her mind, her limbs going liquid at the promise.

Still kneeling before her, he pulled her down to him. Without releasing her, he quickly laid out her clothes to create a makeshift bed and then laid her down while getting rid of his.

She lifted a hand to his face, pulling his lips to hers.

"I love you," she whispered before their lips touched.

"And I you," he replied as he slid into her fully.

Helena moaned and arched into him, her body stretching to accommodate his length.

"Now let me show you how much," he purred as he began to thrust.

"We're going to be here awhile," she finally said, her voice panting in his mind.

"Oh, Mate. You have no idea." His laugh was wicked as her nails scraped down his back.

Their cries were lost among the trees as he proved how much he loved her there beneath the stars. Again, and again. And again.

CHAPTER 18

Helena fought to keep her eyes open as Shepa moved beneath her; the steady rhythm of the wolf's easy lope lulling her to sleep. She had barely slept last night due to Von and her not making it back to camp much before dawn, not that she was complaining.

Blinking rapidly, she struggled to focus on the scenery around her, before she embarrassed herself by falling sideways off her mount. While they were not quite at the Daejaran border, they were only a handful of days away and were finally starting to move into the more inhabited parts of the borderlands.

Around them the effects of the ban were evident. The people were poor, their small houses in disrepair and their children running around in scraps of cloth that looked as though they'd barely make it through another washing.

Her heart tugged in her chest as the little ones stared at the procession with acute distrust in their eyes. That they were so young and still had that kind of reaction spoke volumes to the quality of the interactions to which they were accustomed.

Ahead of her Von let out a sharp yell, holding up his fist in the air. As one the group slowed to a full stop. She let her concern flow through the bond.

He twisted in his saddle to meet her eyes, ordering as he did, *"Find Kragen or Darrin. Do not leave their side."*

Before she could respond with how she felt about that particular order, he was off, Ronan and Serena following close behind.

She let out a low growl, annoyed at being left out. Sighing she looked around at the grim-faced men encircling her; eyes scanning for the familiar faces of her Circle. They were not far, only a couple men away in fact.

She motioned for them to come join her and watched as they wove their way over to her on their horses. Kragen's bulk would be much better suited to the fierceness of a Daejaran wolf, she thought errantly.

"Kiri?" he asked, his voice low.

She shrugged as she responded, "I'm not sure what's going on, Von told me to stay with you."

His jovial face became serious, brows lowering over vigilant eyes.

Darrin moved so that he was in front of her, his shoulders stiff and his lips set in a harsh line.

The horses and wolves were snorting impatiently, but otherwise, it was quiet. The clear blue sky had filled with dark gray clouds as they had progressed throughout the day, the dark sky now adding to the ominous undercurrent surrounding them.

They waited for what felt like an hour, but it could not have been more than half that before Von, and his small party returned to the group. None were smiling.

"What is it?" she asked, while she attempted to decipher the emotions she felt flickering through their bond.

He looked at her, uncertainty shining in his gray eyes before he finally said, *"A warning."*

She sat up straighter on her mount, eyes widening in disbelief.

"A warning for us?" she asked aloud for the benefit of the men around her. "Who would want to leave us a warning, and how would they even know we would be coming through here?"

The soldiers began murmuring and shifting around her, their unease palpable. There was a soft click, and Gillian descended from the carriage.

"What's going on?" she demanded, her eyes narrowed as she took in the scene.

"The town has been leveled, the buildings burnt and the bodies …" Von's face seemed to pale, and he swallowed thickly before continuing, "what remains of the bodies has been left for us to find."

Helena felt her stomach twist; it must be terribly gruesome for her Mate to be so affected by the sight of a few dead bodies. She felt his gratitude as she sent a wave of her strength to him.

"What did the bodies look like?" Timmins asked sharply.

Serena opened her mouth to respond before quickly closing it again, her face tinged with green. Quickly she dismounted and rushed away from the group before heaving into a nearby bush.

Concern gave way to outright fear as she watched her friend continue to be sick at what she had seen. From the corner of her eye, she saw Gillian play with the small gem hanging from her necklace, her own face worried as she stared at Serena.

"They were shriveled as if they had been sucked dry. Their skin was bleached of color, except for the eyes which were pure black. All had their mouths gaping open, stuck in a scream that will never end," Ronan finally said, shuddering at the recollection.

The murmurings grew in strength at the news.

"How do we know it was a warning?" Helena asked, her voice strained.

"The bodies were lined up beside the road. If they weren't a warning for us, they were certainly a message to someone."

"What could do something like that?" Helena asked. At the silence she turned toward Timmins and Joquil, "What could do that?" she demanded again, her voice blending into the harmony of many.

Timmins' eyes were troubled, but he shook his head mutely.

"I do not know, Kiri, but I will send a message to the Capital and have our scholars search through the records to see what they uncover."

"Do it at once."

With a clipped nod Joquil set off back toward the cart that carried his supplies.

Helena's unease and fear were reflected in the lightning flashing in the sky.

"We will stop here for the day," she ordered.

"Helena," Darrin protested.

Unleashing the full force of her swirling gaze at him, she snapped, "That was not a request."

He flinched at the harsh edge of fury in her voice and nodded meekly, "Yes, Kiri."

Turning back toward Von and Ronan she added, "Gather as many men who are willing, we will ride back to the bodies and give them a proper burial. They have suffered enough; it is time to return them to the Mother."

Ronan opened his mouth, but Von stopped him with a shake of his head. He could feel her determination and anger vibrating through him. She would not be denied.

Swiftly dismounting from her wolf, she let out that low warbling whistle.

Starshine circled the group once before landing a bit away. Helena made her way over to the Talyrian, comforted by the thought of such a beast in the face of potential danger.

"Mate?" Von asked, concern laced in the word.

"This is something I need to do," she responded without looking at him.

"Let me do this for you. Spare yourself this burden, Mira."

"No. These are my people; I was unable to protect them once. I will not hide from my duties to them now."

"Helena," he said once more, the voice in her mind a gentle plea.

In response she mounted Starshine, using the pressure of her thighs to convey her readiness to move.

They were in the air between one heartbeat and the next, flying over the procession and straight toward the devastation that awaited them.

BILE ROSE in her throat as she noted the seemingly endless row of bodies. Each had been placed with precision, by height. The smallest of the bodies so offensive she could not bear to look at them.

Over the rise, she could make out the Rasmirin soldiers coming to assist with the burial, but she could not wait.

Starshine landed softly, smoke curling up from her nostrils as the glowing eye studied her mistress. Helena placed a palm on the velvety neck, before stepping away.

I need to dig a grave, she thought; debating her options. Each one of these people deserved their own grave, but as there were none left to tell the stories of their lives or remember them, she would settle for one mass grave. The thought of any of these people not being with their loved ones was unbearable. At least this way any that had been family or lovers could at least go to their final rest together.

Helena eyed the scorched earth dispassionately, looking only for the best place to dig. Her eyes finally settled on a patch of land at the base of a mountain. There was a small stream burbling to its side, the weak sunlight glittering off of it prettily.

Taking a deep breath, Helena dove into the depth of her magic, calling it to her. She felt the comforting strength of Earth and the gentle play of Air before her magic went to work. The ground before her shuddered, she heard the startled cries in the distance and felt Von's own shout within the recesses of her mind. She ignored them all, continuing to focus.

Dirt rose before her, rising in a funnel that spun and twisted as it gathered speed. She looked to her left, and the twisting earth followed, moving up out of the ground. She let out a soft breath, and the dust settled into a giant mound of dark earth leaving a chasm where it had once been.

That much done, she stepped toward the tiniest body, her eyes blurred as she saw the streaks of dirt and tears that remained on the hollowed-out face. While the body was practically weightless, still she trembled as she carried it over to the hole. She lowered herself carefully down and leaned forward calling her magic toward her once more.

"Rest now, little one. The Mother will keep you safe," she whispered as she pressed her lips to the cool forehead.

The little girl was gently lowered into the grave on a cloud of Helena's magic. Once her body was settled, Helena rose and went back to the row of remaining bodies to continue.

Seeing her resolve, the men started at the other end, each picking up one of the fallen and carrying them to the side of the grave. When Helena would reach them with another of the children in her arms, she would call the wind that would carry the bodies down to the bottom.

"Why doesn't she just move them all that way?" a wary voice asked.

"Because this shouldn't be easy," she spat, her voice strained with the effort such continued use of magic cost her. The reservoir of strength was there, but it was still an untrained muscle, shaking with exertion.

"These people did not die easy, and it is not for us to do what is merely convenient because we do not want to be faced with such a reality. This is the least we can do."

The men straightened, her words humbling them.

Von placed a warm hand on her shoulder offering comfort and support. "Rest now, my love. Give us the opportunity to pay our respects as you have yours. We have the need for this as much as you do."

She blinked at him, iridescent eyes shifting to aqua as she did.

Nodding, she stepped back, allowing the men to finish moving the bodies into their final resting place. Once they were done, they turned to her.

Calling back the wind, the mound of dirt swirled and danced in the air, falling as gently as rain until it filled the hole completely.

Ignoring their stares, she moved to kneel again. She pulled the small dagger out of its sheath and cut the base of her finger.

The Circle all let out surprised shouts, but Helena pushed her now bleeding hand into the earth, her heart speaking the words she could not utter.

Mother, protect this place. Make it a testimony of your love for your children. Let no one disturb the rest of those that were so violently taken from this land. Please, let them rest gently.

This was no time for harsh words, although the need for vengeance was also loud in her heart. There had been enough anger and violence here; now it was time for peace.

When she finally rose, the clouds had cleared, and the sun was setting behind the peaks of the mountain. When she looked down, she was startled to see a burst of color. What had been a dark patch of earth was now a riot of flowers all in full bloom, each seeming to glow with a gentle light.

There were awed gasps as she stepped away, her knees shaking so badly that she stumbled. Von was there, his strong arms catching her and pulling her to him.

She blinked up at him, dark purple smudges looking like bruises under sunken eyes. The magic had cost her. The queen had handled the assault of her people, but now the woman needed to make sense of the tragedy. Her eyes were filled with tears, and her shoulders shook when he pulled her head into his neck.

"It's okay my love. I'm so proud of you for being so strong. Cry as long as you need. I've got you. I will be your strength now."

With that, he lifted her in his arms and carried his crying mate away from the equally wet eyes of her soldiers.

THE NEXT FEW days were more of the same. Each new town had more bodies awaiting them by the side of the road. Every time, the procession would halt, waiting while Helena buried them. With each corpse that she carried, her cheeks became gaunter and her eyes more haunted. The physical toll her magic demanded finally became too much for her to continue. That was when Starshine took over. The Talyrian flew low over the row of bodies, spouting her flames until the dead would turn to ash and drift away on the gentle breeze.

The Circle was beyond concerned. Helena had retreated into herself, becoming more silent and withdrawn as the days passed. Von could feel the strain Helena had put on herself and tried to reinforce it with his own power just to keep her standing, but even he was at the point where he felt drained.

"We need to rest," he declared to the Circle.

The men nodded their agreement, but Helena opened her mouth in protest.

"Enough, Kiri. Your people are exhausted, let them rest for awhile and regain their strength." He knew that she would not consider her own need for rest, which was why he guilted her into considering the fate of the others.

She closed her mouth and eyed the group, her eyes filling with concern as she saw how haggard they had become. "Fine."

The Circle let out a collective sigh.

"She needs to eat," Darrin said in a voice only Von could hear. "She is wasting away before us."

Von's lips were a flat line as he nodded. "She is punishing herself."

"Punishing herself?" Darrin sputtered, "But why?"

"She feels guilty that so many have died and she was helpless to stop it," Serena said softly as she joined them.

"What could she have possibly done?" Darrin asked, his voice rising with the question.

"It does not need to make logical sense, Shield. She is reacting with her heart which rarely follows such rules," Serena stated, her blond brow rising as if daring him to challenge her assessment.

"She's not doing anyone any good by not taking care of herself," he finally muttered.

"On that, we agree," Von said darkly.

He could feel his Mate's pain, each day it gnawed at him through their bond; a dull ache he could not ease. Despite understanding the cause of her distress, he had no idea how to help relieve it. Back at home, when he would get twisted up in his own feelings of guilt over his brother, he would resort to training to try to sweat it out of his system. It did not necessarily solve the cause of his guilt, but it helped dull the edge enough that he could focus on other things. Perhaps that could work for Helena as well, not that she was in any shape to wield a weapon.

He studied her snuggled into the side of her Talyrian whose wing was protectively curled around her. For now, he would let her sleep, but while she slept, he would speak with Ronan about his plan. Once she woke he would bully her into eating, certain her annoyance at his pestering would at least do something to put some color back in her cheeks.

SHE WOKE WITH A START, struggling to rise, her heart pounding in her chest. As she sat the top of her head smacked the underside of Starshine's membranous wing. The Talyrian huffed in annoyance, twisting its head to glare at her.

"Sorry," she murmured, scooting out from under its protection.

Starshine continued to stare at her until Helena began running her fingers through the silky fur of her mane.

Letting out a deep rumble that was more like the scattering of rocks down a mountain than a purr, the giant cat finally closed its eyes.

She felt his presence before she saw him. She closed her own eyes, breathing in his scent as he drew near.

His hand caressed the length of her back, and she felt herself arching into it.

"How are you feeling, my love?" he asked in his deep growl.

She looked up at him, the weight of the last few days still in her eyes. "Better."

He lifted a dubious brow.

"I can feel them"—she rubbed at her chest—"all those lives taken before their time. They're a weight in my heart. I can't just forget about it."

"No one is telling you to forget about them, Helena," Von chided sternly, as he wrapped her in his strong arms. "But you have to take care of yourself. You won't do them any good pushing yourself so far that you are too weak to care for them, or avenge them."

His words stirred something in her, and some of that weight shifted allowing her to take her first deep breath in days. It was still there, that weight in her chest, still pressing her to *do* something, but it was less insistent. She knew he was right; she was no good to anybody in her current state.

Her stomach growled loudly, and she covered it with her hands, cheeks flaming as she looked at Von.

He threw back his head and laughed. "Ronan will be so disappointed to know I won't need his help anymore."

Confused, she furrowed her brows and asked, "What?"

He shook his head, his laughter enveloping her with its warmth through their bond. "Nevermind, Mate," he said, kissing her forehead. "Let's find something for you to eat."

They rejoined the group around the fire, Helena thankfully accepting a bowl of some sort of vegetable soup.

The men gently teased her as she ate, relaxing when she would snap at them and return their taunts with her own. It was a far cry from the easy banter they usually shared, but it was a start, and for now, that was enough.

Gillian watched the group from a distance, fingers still mindlessly stroking her necklace before she stepped back into the forest and blended into the darkness.

CHAPTER 19

They started again early the next morning. Von would have preferred that they rest for another full day, but Helena refused. She had to admit the evening of rest and a good meal had done much to ease the bruised look from her eyes. Feeling his attention on her, she met his gaze, sending him a warm smile.

It began with a sound, or rather, a lack of sound. Birds had been chirping animatedly as they hopped from tree to tree alongside the caravan but were now strangely absent.

Disoriented, Helena glanced around, noting the unease that rippled through the procession. Both Darrin and Kragen maneuvered their animals in closer to Helena's, creating a barricade around her.

Next was the smell. The air, still heavy with morning dew was quickly being overcome with the overpowering and acrid scent of smoke. The wolves began growling low in their throats, their eyes swiveling wildly as they attempted to locate the source of the fire.

Then came the screams. There was a moment of stillness, a deep breath waiting to be exhaled before everything came alive with motion. It would have been pure chaos, if not for the utter precision with which it was executed.

Von's chin lifted toward the sky as his mouth fell open, his war cry filled with promise. Her heart was in her throat as she watched her

Mate prepare for battle. There was no time to do anything more than send a plea down the bond for him to stay safe before she offered a quick prayer to the Mother asking for the same.

Von's men, all mounted on their wolves, led the charge over the hill. Helena's Circle stayed close to her, faces set in harsh lines as they followed close behind. A few of the Rasmirin stayed back to protect the merchants and their carts, but the rest were closing in on the Circle.

The sky was black with smoke, the small houses all alight. Everywhere people were screaming and trying to flee the burning buildings.

Who's attacking? Helena wondered, eyes scanning the scene below her, desperate to try to make sense of the situation. Were these the men that had been leaving the brutalized bodies as a warning for them? Would they be too late again?

Then she saw them. They were creatures of one's darkest nightmares; things from a tale children would spread to horrify and torment each other. They had been human, once. Their limbs skeletal, the gray flesh stretched taut over bone. The awkward jerking movements of the bodies reminiscent of a marionette attempting to dance.

The creatures were hairless, faces gaunt, but it was their eyes that had her screaming. Where life had once shone, there were now milky white pits run through with shimmering black lines. Their mouths were almost as bad. The lips were flaking and peeled back to reveal teeth blackened with rot. They didn't close their mouths, the jaws hanging open to emit an endless wet gurgle.

Helena felt her stomach twist with revulsion, everything about these bodies grated against her with their sense of wrongness. It was then she noticed, one of the things reaching elongated fingers toward a child too terrified to do more than hold onto its stuffed toy while it sobbed for its mother.

I cannot lose another one, she thought, not even aware she was already moving.

"Kiri!" the men shouted behind her, but it was too late, she was flying down the hill in a race to save the child.

She grabbed the girl, pulling her up onto Shepa and using her body as a shield, leaving the bony fingers clutching air.

The little body trembled in her arms as Helena's eyes frantically searched for a safe place to hide her so that she could get back to her men and help save the rest of the villagers. There were some villagers loading up carts with people and fleeing. Helena gave the child to one of the women, their wide eyes showing white as they took in the scene around them.

"Keep her safe!" Helena shouted, spurring the wolf back to the burning buildings.

There was a scream of rage, and Helena saw Starshine shoot from the sky straight toward a group of the creatures. Fire poured from the Talyrian's mouth while her claws tore at their bodies. Still, the creatures moved, immune to the pain.

Mother's teeth, what unholy creatures are these?

All around her, wolves tore into creatures who continued to fight with one or more missing limbs. They didn't bleed so much as drip a thick oily substance that shimmered slightly before evaporating. In a blur of fur and fang, Karma lunged at one of the monstrosities. The wolf's teeth shining wetly before closing around its throat and tearing head from jerking body. Karma let out a savage snarl as it dropped the head from his teeth, letting it bounce and roll before turning back into the fray.

Helena's initial reaction was concern that Von had been separated from his wolf, before the realization that Karma had discovered how to stop the creatures had her shouting wildly, "Their heads! You've got to remove their heads!"

She continued screaming at the top of her lungs, also using her magic to enhance her voice and carry the message across the battlefield. She felt the fresh surge of adrenaline throughout the crowd as her people attacked with renewed vigor.

The Circle were still working their way back toward her, Joquil's lips moving frantically as he called down shields of protection while also blasting the monsters back to give the men time to work through them. Timmins fought beside Kragen, the latter towering over everyone and smiling maniacally as he made quick work of the skeletal bodies in front of him. His massive swords were glowing with the molten heat of Fire. When they made contact with one of the creatures they would cut through their limbs like soft butter. It was clear, Kragen was in his element, his laughter when another body fell causing Helena to shudder, but her eyes continued their scan.

Darrin's teeth bared as he used his sword to hack and cleave at the bodies before him. His green eyes met hers, and she could feel his frustration with her. His sole duty was to protect her, and she had taken that from him when she ran thoughtlessly straight into the battle to save the child. She shrugged apologetically, his head dipping in acknowledgment as he focused back on the creatures coming toward him. The entire interaction took less than a second. The rest of her men accounted for, Helena turned her attention toward the pull of her bond to lead her toward her Mate.

As she moved forward, she saw Ronan and Serena fighting as one. Their backs were toward each other, their gift of Air making their axes swing faster than her eye could follow. Their blades had grown slick with the creature's black substance, but they were relentless as they continued to behead them. Helena's eyes narrowed as one of the creatures reached its hand toward Serena's arm, but her shield sizzled at the contact. The creature jerked back, giving Ronan enough time to swing his ax down and sever the head from the body.

A sudden searing pain knocked Helena from her mount. She stood and looked down trying to identify the source of her injury, but found none. She looked back up, her braid whipping through the air with the speed of the movement when she realized it had been Von who took the blow. That the pain had been strong enough for her to feel through their bond had her gaze hazing with red. She stumbled slightly as it continued to throb within her, but she used their connection to pull the pain to her so that it could not distract or weaken her Mate.

Helena tried to control her flare of panic when she saw four more of the beings close in on him. She gripped Shepa's fur, using it to help pull her back astride the wolf's back. Angling herself toward Von, she pushed with her power to reach him. Spurred by her will, Shepa leapt into the air and flew into the chest of one of the creatures, knocking it down before ripping its throat out. There was no screech of pain, just a wet gurgle while its limbs continued to flail.

Molten gold eyes met hers. There was no time for words, Helena dismounted and dove into the swirling pool of her magic; a controlled plunge straight to the bottom before pulling up and unleashing the power around her. The sky came alive. Bolts of lightning were bright scars among the black clouds, while thunder roared so loudly the few remaining trees shook from its intensity.

Von let out an approving growl, turning his focus back to the other three still moving toward him. He stood still letting them come closer with each jerking step. Once they were within range, he blinked away. That was the only word Helena could think of for the move she had first noticed when they were practicing her shielding with Ronan.

One moment Von was standing beside her, the creatures an arm's length away, the next he was facing them his teeth bared in a feral grin from over fifty paces away. The creatures twisted in confusion, searching for their prey. Von struck. Instead of his sword, a rope of Fire was snaking in his hand. He pulled back an arm before lashing it forward and wrapping the flame around one of the beings and pulling it to the ground. Once on the ground, Karma dove forward and finished it.

Helena was tired of being an observer. It was time to end this. *Now* she urged.

Fire rained from the storm her magic had created in the sky. The glowing red embers turning to ash if they touched anything but the creatures. When an ember would hit one of those skeletal bodies, it would erupt into a pillar of Fire before consuming them completely.

Just like that, it was over.

Helena could feel the heat of her Fire still pulsing under her skin. Rage caused her body to shake, and she snarled when she felt a hand touch her shoulder.

Darrin stepped back, his face leached of color.

"Kiri," a voice called softly. She turned to the voice, her teeth still bared and her eyes swirling with iridescent fire.

Von stood before her; eyes gray once more.

Her heart continued to race, fueled by the rage she could not seem to contain.

"She pulled too much power too quickly if she releases it she could kill us all," Joquil murmured to the others, his voice laced with fear.

"If you don't have anything helpful to say, get the fuck away from her," Von growled without looking away from Helena.

"Helena," Von called to her through their bond.

She was still staring at him unblinkingly.

"Mira," the deep voice begged.

She shuddered, trying to focus on the images that flickered through her mind: Von holding her close as they danced; Von kissing her after her trial; Von's eyes devouring her in her mating dress.

With a gasp she came back to herself, knees shaking so hard she started to fall.

Von's arm shot out to grab her, cradling her as she dropped to the ground.

His warm hands brushed the hair that had fallen out of her braid back from her face as she began emptying the contents of her stomach on the smoking remains of a creature.

Von's hand gently ran along her back, her stomach continuing to heave even after it was empty.

"You don't have to all stand around watching me humiliate myself," she rasped.

"They need to see that you are okay, Kiri," Serena said from behind her.

Her arms shook as she tried to push herself back into a sitting position.

Von eased her back until she was sitting beside him.

The Circle along with Ronan and Serena surrounded them, each looking grimmer and more battle-worn than the last. All were coated in ash, their sweat leaving dark smears along their skin. None appeared injured, save a few tears in their clothes, which could have been scratches that have already healed.

The rest of the Rasmirin were helping the villagers put out the remaining fires while the Daejarans tended to their wolves.

"Starshine?" Helena asked, eyes scanning the sky for the streak of white.

The Talyrian prowled over to its mistress, dropping down to lay beside her. Helena rested her head against its side, brushing trembling fingers over the soft fur.

"What were those things?" she asked wearily.

"Those, Kiri, were Shadows," Joquil said, his voice graver than she had ever heard.

She looked from face to face, trying to gauge how bad this news was.

All shifted uncomfortably, seeming troubled.

Helena recalled their conversation from the campfire and gasped, horrified. "You mean those things were Chosen?"

Timmins and Joquil nodded grimly.

"That's awful," Helena whispered. Another piece of the story clicked into place and had her asking, "But who was controlling them? I thought only one who was gifted with spirit was able to create a Shadow."

Von picked up the question for her, "I thought with Rowena's death that no other damaskiris remained."

"Could there be another out there?" Helena asked.

Timmins shrugged; worry making him look years older.

The group eyed each other, all with more questions than answers.

Around them what was left of the blackened bodies smoked, while ash flew through the red and black sky. Had she been paying attention, Helena would have recognized this scene from her trial. Instead, her brows were frowning in concern as the question tumbled through her mind, *was there another like her out there?*

The group had been exhausted after the battle, none wanting to go farther that day. It was not so much that they were too tired to move on, but that they were afraid of what they might find when they got there. That did not mean, however, that there was not work to be done.

After the storm had cleared, and Helena's strength had returned enough for her to move about on her own, Kragen insisted that the Circle have a meeting. At Helena's request, both Ronan and Serena joined in. As Von's next in command they were fast becoming an extension of her own Circle, and she trusted them just as much as she did the others.

They met in Joquil's tent, the space cramped with the excess of people. Helena sat resting between Von's thighs; his arms wrapped tight around her waist. They were waiting for Serena, and for the moment, Helena had her ear pressed against his chest. She was listening to the beat of his heart which was still beating in time with hers.

Despite the gravity of the day, she couldn't help the smile that appeared at the reminder of their connection.

"Mine."

"Yours," he agreed, a hand lifting to caress her cheek before pressing her head a bit closer to his heart.

It still surprised her, how gentle her Mate could be with her. He exuded a raw fierceness and was more likely to scowl than smile when around the others. Despite that outward display, with her, there was an ever-present tenderness. She could feel it lapping at her through their bond, sometimes warm with his love and other times burning white hot with his need for her.

She had just turned in his arms and pressed a gentle kiss above his tattoo when Serena rushed in offering an apology for the delay.

"Sorry everyone, I had to go back and grab what I wanted to show you from where I kept it in our tent."

"Is this what you found on the bodies?" Joquil asked eagerly, sitting forward in his chair.

Serena nodded, holding the object out for his inspection. Within her palm, there were several small gems. They were a dark purple, almost black, and dull. Joquil kept one of the gems and passed the others around.

Helena held one in her hand, holding it up to the light for a better look. No matter how she twisted the gem, it did not shine when it hit the light. Rather it seems to reject it, as though it was pushing the beams away so that it could stay shrouded in shadows.

Laying the gem flat in her palm, she was startled at the feeling of revulsion that spread through her. There was a malevolence within the gem, something that recognized her and was promising nothing but harm.

She quickly shoved it into Von's hand; eyes narrowed as she tried to shake off the feeling of unease holding the gem had caused. Von lifted a brow in question, but she didn't know what to say.

Facing the others, she asked, "Do we know what these are?"

Serena shook her head. "No clue. We didn't notice them when we first checked the bodies, but by the time we found the third one, we figured they must mean something. Each stone was sewn into the hem of a shirt or tied off in a leather cord they wore around their wrists or neck. Most of the leather and fabric had burned away, so the stones came loose, but there were a couple that still had them intact."

"How many of these did you find?" Kragen asked.

"Not many, considering the size of the horde. Only about fifteen."

Joquil's frown was severe as he studied the pearl sized gem.

"Joquil, is something the matter?" she asked softly, the others all turning to study the Master.

"I do not know, Kiri. I feel as though I have seen a stone like this before, but I cannot recall where. Another reason to search through the records it would seem."

"I will help you," Timmins offered.

Joquil offered him an appreciative smile. "More eyes would be helpful, thank you. I feel certain we will find the answer to how the Shadows came to be in that village today if we can find out more about these gems."

"Did you have anything else to report?" Kragen asked Serena and Ronan.

The two shook their heads and stepped back to allow space for Darrin to enter the center of the tent.

"I think we need to discuss the carelessness with which Helena acted today."

"I'm right here, Darrin. There's no need to speak of me as though I'm a child."

"Then perhaps you should stop acting like one," he snapped.

Helena's back went straight as she narrowed her eyes at him. "Excuse me? Would you like to say that again, Shield?"

"I think you heard me the first time, Kiri." He was primed for this fight, his frustration from the battle rising to the surface now that she was safe.

"He is concerned for you, Mate. As your Shield should be. You scared him today riding headfirst into danger without any thought to your safety. You left them behind scrambling to try to reach you."

Helena's tried not to let her face show her surprise at the admonishment. Von always took her side. *"You left me behind,"* she accused instead.

"It is a habit for me as the Daejaran commander to take the lead in battle. I am used to defending those I care for, not fighting beside them."

"You fight with Serena and Ronan," she pointed out.

"That is different, Mira. They have trained as long as I to be warriors. I met them in the training ring when we were all mere babes. With you, Helena…" his voice seemed to sigh and linger on her name, *"you are the purest soul I have ever known. I will do anything in my power to protect that. It's not that I don't believe you can hold your own; I just do not want you to become tainted by the realities of the battlefield. There is no place for you in that sea of death."*

"It would seem you have a lot to learn, Mate. My place is at your side. We are stronger together, did you not feel that today? The way that our power was enhanced when we fought side by side?"

"I did. My power feels different since we were Mated, deeper somehow. Almost as though there is more for me to access than before."

"Like how you can teleport from place to place now?"

She felt his chuckle in her mind. *"Yes, that has been a useful new skill. It surprised me the first time it happened. I merely had to think about where I wanted to be, and I appeared there. I cannot go far distances, only within the range of what my eyes can see."*

"I've been calling it blinking."

"Blinking?"

"Yes, in the time it takes to blink you manage to appear in a new spot."

He let out a surprised laugh at her explanation. The group, having become used to these bouts of silent communication between them, were studying them expectantly.

Only Darrin continued to glower at her. "Are we interrupting?" he asked dryly.

Helena met his glare with one of her own. "You shouldn't be so quick to speak, Darrin. Von was taking your side."

Surprise flashed across his face momentarily before he schooled his features back into a mask of haughty superiority.

"You do realize, Shield, that I'm the one in charge here? You don't get to lecture me for being naughty."

"You seem to be the only one here, Kiri, forgetting what we vowed to you. We are here to protect you, with our lives if need be. How can I do that when you throw yourself in the heart of a battle against an enemy we know almost nothing about?"

Finally chastened, Helena's shoulders drooped, and she sighed heavily. "I did not mean to be thoughtless; I just could not stand the thought of burying one more child. When I saw the Shadow reaching for her, I just…" she trailed off, heart heavy again with the weight of the bodies she had given back to the Mother.

"And how do you think we would feel, Helena, if the next body we place in the ground is yours?" Kragen asked. The rebuke from him came like a slap compared to the ribbing she was used to from Darrin.

The rest of the men were silent, the words filling the tent as silent tears dripped from her cheeks.

"I will be more careful next time," she said weakly.

"That is all that we ask, Hellion," Darrin said, his voice gentle, before turning and leaving the tent.

Von hugged her to his chest. *"Do not cry, my love. It is only their love for you that makes them speak so harshly."*

Helena nodded, too overcome with emotion for words, spoken or otherwise.

AFTER SPEAKING WITH THE CIRCLE, Helena made rounds throughout the camp, stopping to check on the wounded; of which there were blessedly few. She also offered small words of comfort to the villagers that remained. They had all been effusive with their thanks, overwhelming Helena with their gratitude. Most no longer had homes, but many had at least walked away with their lives. They had been lucky.

There was something about the attack that was niggling in the corner of her mind. She couldn't quite put her finger on it just yet, but it was almost as if they had won too easily. Like it had been a test of sorts, to feel out their strength before the real strike came. Helena was the first to admit she was not an experienced warrior, but even to her it had seemed too convenient that they came upon those Shadows at precisely the right moment, when for days they had always been far too late.

Her thoughts had taken over, and she was standing still staring into nothing when Gillian found her.

"How are you feeling, Kiri?" Gillian asked softly.

Helena jumped, the words snapping her out of her reverie.

"Oh, I'm sorry, Kiri!" Gillian apologized profusely, placing a hand on her shoulder to steady her, "I did not mean to startle you."

Helena offered a wan smile that didn't quite meet her eyes. It was hard to participate in idle conversation with the events of the day weighing so heavily on her mind.

"It's not your fault, Gil, I should know better than to let my thoughts wander like that. Did you need something?" she asked as she studied her friend.

As always Gillian was the perfect portrait of a lady, her hair pulled back into a riot of curls and her purple dress pristine, the same color as the stone in her necklace, hugging her curves shamelessly before draping more demurely as it fell toward the ground.

"Not especially, Kiri. I mostly wanted to check and see how you were. You've been so concerned with the others, and it didn't seem like anyone had thought to look in on you."

"That's sweet of you. I'm fine, all things considered. A bit tired, if I'm being honest."

Gillian smiled kindly. "That's to be expected, of course. I've never seen magic like yours, Kiri. When you called that Fire from the sky," Gillian paused as a shiver coursed through her body. "It was terrifying. I'm certainly glad to be on your side."

Helena felt the twin of that shiver in her own limbs. Gillian wasn't the only one who had been frightened by the intensity of her magic. In those final moments of battle, Helena had not been herself, had not even been aware of what she was doing; only that she needed to protect her people.

No, if she was being honest, she hadn't been thinking of her people at all. She had only been thinking of Von. It was her desire to protect him that had her taking that deep dive into the depths of her magic and channeling her rage into the storm that had been its result. She hadn't known Fire would rain from the sky with such deadly abandon. How had it known to only harm the Shadows?

The question had been plaguing her for hours, but she was too afraid to voice it to any of the Circle. Too ashamed to admit that so much of her power was still a reflection of instinct rather than intent.

"Kiri?" Gillian called.

Helena blinked and looked at the girl, smiling apologetically, "Sorry, I don't mean to keep doing that."

Gillian squeezed her shoulder affectionately, "No need to apologize. Let's talk about something a bit more cheerful to get your mind off of things for a while!"

Helena tried not to frown at the suggestion. What she really wanted was to be alone with Von for a while, the warmth of his body against hers blocking out everything but him.

"How are things going with Von?" Gillian asked impishly, as though she had plucked the name straight from Helena's thoughts.

She tried to fight the blush that rose to her cheeks at the question. The truth was things with Von were better than she ever could have imagined they would be. Never had she imagined such a connection was possible with another person. Mates were something only the Chosen were gifted with finding, and having grown up thinking she was Ungifted; it was never an option open for her to consider. Not since she had been a little girl prone to flights of fancy anyway.

Even then, her dreams of finding a Mate were woefully inadequate compared to the truth of the bond. The overwhelming intensity and completeness when he was buried inside her, their bodies as connected as their minds. Being able to feel his response when she touched him, knowing exactly what caused him to lose control and spend himself inside her… the thought trailed off, and she found herself once again staring off into space, Gillian smirking knowingly beside her.

"Ah yes, a much more pleasant thought, I can see."

Helena shrugged. "He is wonderful," she said simply. "He is brave, and so strong, in every sense of the word, but he can also be quite tender when he wants to be. I never imagined there could be so perfect a man, or at least perfect for me."

"I wouldn't say he was perfect, Kiri," Gillian said, doubt coloring her words.

That caught Helena's attention, and her focus zeroed in on the girl beside her. "What do you mean?"

"Well," she started hesitantly before her brows lowered with a frown and she shook her head. "Never mind, Kiri, it doesn't matter. All has ended well."

Gillian had started to walk back toward the camp, but Helena's hand shot out and stopped her, turning her back to face her.

"No, Gillian, tell me what you mean." There was no request in her words, only demand.

The playful teasing from before was gone entirely. "Please, Kiri. It's better if you do not know. It will only hurt you."

"Tell. Me." Helena's teeth were gritted; she could feel her magic waking inside her, responding to the uncertainty and need to protect coiling within. Whatever rumor Gillian had to share, Helena knew it was tied to Von's colorful past. He had more than admitted he was not proud of who he had been before he met her. She couldn't believe they would still be so foolish to whisper such insults after all he had done to protect them. She wanted to hear what others were still saying so that she could put an end to it once and for all.

"Kiri." The word was a whimper.

"Now!" Helena shouted, lightning flashing in the sky as thunder growled in the distance.

"*Helena?*" the concerned voice asked in her mind, feeling her loss of control.

"It's just, one of the girls at the Palace. She had mentioned…"

Gillian seemed to pale as she watched Helena transform as her magic took over. Those swirling eyes pinning the girl in place.

Helena did not speak, her silence a clear instruction.

"The girl had mentioned how Von singled her out to pleasure him. The night of your ball. She had been bragging about how she had ridden one of the Damaskiri's stallions because she was more of a woman than you, despite all you stood to inherit."

Helena saw red. There was a sharp pain in her hands as her fingers, no not fingers, claws, punctured the flesh of her palm. Where her nails had once been jet black claws, very similar to the Talyrian's, now jutted out of her fingers. Helena let out a low hiss as visions of Von smirking while thrusting into another woman surfaced in her mind. The images from the trial were coming true. The wind howled, and around her a tempest raged, her hurt and anger fueling the storm.

"Helena!" Von shouted, running from their camp to her side. Seconds behind him the rest of the Circle followed.

She turned to face him, her lips curled in a snarl. "I warned you, Mate. I warned you that I would not share." Despite the chaos of the storm, her words were low, guttural.

"Leave us!" she snapped at the Circle as they approached. They paused, considering defying her order, but finally relented, slowly stepping away as they returned to the camp.

"Not you!" she added as Gillian attempted to slink away. "Tell him the story you were so eager to share with me."

"I wouldn't say eager is quite—" Gillian hedged before Helena cut her off.

"No more games, girl."

Von looked between the women, eyes wide. She could feel his confusion snaking through their bond; his desperation to connect with her. She closed him out, not wanting him to feel what Gillian's words had done to her. Not wanting him to feel the doubt that was taking root in her heart; a part of her still trying to protect him.

Gillian repeated her story, frightened green eyes studying Helena's claws before moving to stare at the ground. The rain pelting her had turned her elegant hairstyle into a sopping mess.

Von stiffened, his face losing all of its color.

"Tell me she's lying, Mate, and I will remove this memory from her mind so that she may never repeat such filth again," the Kiri ordered, no hint of Helena in the voice infused with many.

Von hesitated, and in that moment, she felt the flicker of shame.

The emotion was like a whip across her heart; she felt both its lash and the resulting sting.

"Tell me," she begged, her voice, once again her own, thick with emotion.

"Helena, I love you…" he started, his hand reaching out toward her in a pleading motion.

Her eyes swam with tears, and she could no longer make out his face through the blur. That lying traitorous face. The face that had become more beloved to her than any other.

"I warned you," she whimpered, face crumpling as her tears began to fall.

"It was before—" he tried, but she shook her head holding up her clawless hand for him to stop. There was nothing he could say at this moment that would make anything better. That one moment of hesitation costing him more than he may ever realize.

He was clutching at his chest as if he could feel her heart breaking. At least one of them could; she had gone numb. Her falling tears the only visible sign of her pain, inside there was only a lonely howl within a vast emptiness.

"You took another as your lover after you declared yourself to me. You know, as I do that as soon as you uttered the words, our souls recognized each other. You were mine from that moment. How dare you stand there and try to tell me it had happened before we were Mated. How. Dare. You!"

Von stood before her, his head bowed in shame, and his eyes clenched shut in pain. Still, he clutched at his heart while the storm raged around him, drops of water running down his face like tears.

"Leave me," she whispered.

His eyes opened at that, surprise shining in the gray depths. *"Helena…"* echoed within her mind, but it was faint, as though he was shouting it from a distance. Silently she continued to build the wall that would close him off from her mind, not wanting to share that intimacy with him when she was feeling so shattered. Not wanting him to know how much power he held over her by seeing the damage his carelessness had caused.

"I cannot look at you right now. Leave. Take some men and go on without us. We will meet up with you at your parents' home in a few days' time."

He dropped his head once more, shoulders sagging. He did not try to speak again, merely turned and walked away, each step looking heavier than the last.

Despite her words, Helena watched him. Her heart protesting the distance between them, while a small voice within her was begging for her to relent. With her eyes focused on her Mate, Helena didn't notice the small smile of satisfaction curling Gillian's lips.

CHAPTER 21

*V*on sat with his head in his hands, his third cup of Ronan's home brew almost empty. He couldn't get the image of Helena's face out of his mind. How that small flicker of hope was still shining in her eyes when Gillian had repeated her story; and the moment it died.

Shame was too small a word for what he felt right now. Loathing was little better. One stupid moment brought on by a lifetime of bad decisions; all of which were made in response to years of being found unworthy, could be his undoing. Von slammed his fist on the table, causing the wood to crack under the force. The blow wasn't enough to temper his pain, so he let out a roar and flung his arm out causing his cup to fly across the tent.

He stood quickly, his chair falling behind him. He had made one choice that he regretted as soon as he made it, and now he was left on the brink of losing all that he had come to love. There was his brother, and his men, but those relationships were tainted by a sense of duty. Only Helena had ever loved him freely, without ever demanding anything from him in return; besides his faithfulness.

His chest rose and fell with labored breaths; the need to dull his pain a siren's call. He knew he had failed her; knew with a bone-deep certainty she might never forgive him. It didn't matter that they had only just met at the time, she was right, he had felt something shift in him in that moment. It had scared him. He was there to finish a job, period. It should have been no different than any of the other jobs he had taken in the last decade. Granted, this was a task he had given to himself, and for once it didn't involve bloodshed, but regardless of that, he had planned to see it through.

Von's head throbbed, alerting him that he was nowhere near drunk enough for this line of thinking. Moving to where his cup had fallen, the thoughts continued. When he had come to Elysia, he doubted he'd even make it across the border, but years had a way of making people forget the threat that was supposed to exist, and it was easy to bribe a guard to allow his men through the pass. His only goal had been to lift the ban and find help for his brother. He never anticipated he might actually be the Damaskiri's Mate. He had never allowed himself to imagine any sort of future for himself at all, save clearing his family's name.

Von pressed calloused fingers against his eyes. His thoughts were splintering, and it was becoming more difficult to focus; the brew was starting to create a pleasant fog in his mind.

He felt like a coward as he hid in his tent, but he couldn't leave her. No matter what she asked; his heart felt like it was being pulled from his chest at the thought. Instead, he had decided to get completely shit-faced while he waited for her to calm down.

He knew he didn't deserve her forgiveness, but he was not above begging. He had once planned to humble himself just to become one of her suitors, knowing the Chosen would taunt him as soon as they heard his name; but that had been no real hardship to bear. He didn't give a Shadow's shriveled cock about their opinion of him. But for a chance at her forgiveness... for that he would walk, no he'd crawl, naked through the streets of Daejara. Nodding emphatically for good measure, he crouched down before the cup, swaying slightly.

Recovering his balance, he checked the cup for dirt. Blowing on it and shaking it twice for good measure; the silent tirade continued in his mind. His pride, the one thing that had got him through years of neglect and battles, had no place here now. Not when Helena's trust in him was on the line. He would do what he must, even if it required debasing himself completely.

Von had just stood and was reaching to refill his glass when Serena walked through the tent. His eyes were blurry enough that he squinted to try to see her more clearly.

"What are you doing here?" he demanded, the cup slipping through his fingers and rolling back across the floor. His eyes followed its progress across the floor, but he made no move to recover it. Instead, he narrowed his eyes and stared at it as if he could will it back to him.

"Let me get that for you," she said dryly after they stood there in silence for a few moments. Stepping around him, she reached down and picked it up.

Von blinked trying to keep her in focus as her image began to swim in front of him.

Serena turned and crossed the short distance to where Ronan's small cask sat, her back facing Von.

"What are you doing here?" he asked again his voice sounding decidedly petulant.

"We could hear you roaring from across the camp. Everyone is talking about what happened. About how Helena has thrown you out of the camp…" She looked over her shoulder at him briefly as she continued to fill his cup. "I came to check on you." Once she had finished, she faced him again and offered him a cup now brimming with the pale red liquid.

Von snatched it from her hand, the liquid sloshing over the rim as he took a greedy gulp. He scowled as he looked into his cup. "Ronan is losing his touch, each cup's bitt'r than th'last," he slurred.

Von smacked his lips together, surprised to find them feeling numb. "Fuck maybe not," he groaned as his legs gave out and he sat down hard on the floor. "I haven't been this drunk since… since…" he trailed off, staring at Serena in confusion.

"Are there two f'you?" he asked, his words blending together.

Serena laughed, one hand coming up to rest just above her necklace. "You are that indeed, Commander. Are you feeling better at least?"

Von stared at her stupidly. He didn't know if he was feeling better, he couldn't really feel much of anything as he sat there. He felt like there was something important he had been thinking about; something that he needed to do, but he just couldn't make sense of anything with the fog thick in his mind.

"Here now, drink up, you'll feel better after a good rest."

"Now ther'sa good 'dea." Each word was harder to pronounce than the one before, but Von held up his cup, staring at it with one eye to make sure it made it the full way to its destination. Slurping down the last of the bitter liquid, he wiped his mouth with the back of his hand.

Serena peered down at him with amused green eyes.

Wait. There was a single moment of clarity that broke through the fog before Von slumped over; unconscious. Serena didn't have green eyes.

GILLIAN STARED down at Von's motionless body with a sneer.

"Pathetic," she sneered, "letting a woman get you worked up enough to leave yourself so defenseless, and you call yourself a warrior."

She shook her head, not accustomed to the lightness of such short hair. She ran a hand along the back of her head, the silky fine strands sticking up in its wake.

Mother would be so proud if she could see all that she had accomplished in just a few days. Rowena had never believed her daughter would be capable of pulling off such a glorious deception, but it had been easy really. It just required a few well-aimed suggestions, offered when they would be most effective.

For Helena it had been simple, the girl was too naïve to do anything other than take a story or person at face value. Everyone had seen that she had been worn down for days. The constant barrage of death had taken its toll on her physically and mentally. Delivering her message right after the battle, when any possible defense was completely gone, was priceless if she did say so herself.

Gillian set about the room, clearing up any sign of her presence there.

Von had been a little trickier to manage. Luckily the *Bella Morte* in his brew had worked out. She had a plan B, but it was much less elegant. Her fingers caressed the ax hanging from her hips. Less elegant, but just as effective.

For a man with such a notoriously strong will, he had been surprisingly easy to manipulate. Both times. Then again, today it was Helena that had delivered the fatal blow. Gillian had merely set events into motion.

The first time though… Gillian sighed wistfully. It had been fun to ride him, his powerful body leaving its imprint on her for days after. All it took was a few whispered words as she slipped something into his drink and he had taken the bait gratefully. She wondered idly if anyone had ever found the body of the serving girl whose appearance she had borrowed.

It wasn't like she could be certain Von had really gone through with the deed unless she was there to see it through, and it was essential his guilt be real when she presented Helena with his indiscretion. And she certainly couldn't do it as herself! No, stealing that woman's form had been the only option, and it wouldn't have gone well at all if she showed up while Gillian laid her trap. Not at all. Sometimes death really was the only option.

Too bad her mother wanted this one alive. He would have made a fun plaything. Unfortunately, orders were orders, and she didn't dare break one. Not with Micha's life on the line.

Gillian looked around the room, scanning for anything she may have overlooked. She needed to move quickly. She could not risk the Circle, or even the real Serena, finding her. Seeing nothing out of place, she moved back toward the body now sprawled on the ground. She ran her hand through his hair gripping it tight and yanking his head back. She wet her lips as she watched that luscious mouth fall open.

What the hell, Mother will never know if I had a taste before completing my mission.

Gillian licked up the side of his face, his sweat salty and tasting of guilt. *Delicious*, she thought before pressing her mouth to his and biting his lower lip until she drew blood. She lapped it up and smiled, heady with the sense of accomplishment.

"Let's go home, lover. Mother is waiting for you." Her voice was a sensual purr, completely at odds with the pointed nails that raked roughly down his chest. Drops of blood beaded until they pooled into a crimson feast, which she quickly bent to devour. Using some of her power she closed the scratches. No one must know she stopped to take a sip. Mother would be furious.

Gillian's hand lifted to her necklace, the purple stone beginning to glow faintly against her fingers. Her other hand still woven through Von's hair. One moment they were there, and the next they were gone.

CHAPTER 22

Helena's heart felt like it was splintering. Not a metaphorical breaking, but a physical tearing apart. It was a tightness in her chest that caused her breaths to come out in shallow gasps. She felt lost; her anchor cut away, leaving her at the mercy of a storm-fueled sea. Even her skin didn't feel as though it fit right. It was clammy, as though a part of her essence was leaking through a casing that could no longer contain her.

Blind to her surroundings, she paced the length of their room. Helena's mind raced as it combed over every moment since the first when his hand had brushed hers, and an unknown part of her came into being. Flipping through the memories, she searched for some sign of his betrayal; any small moment she might have missed because she was too busy falling in love with him to see him clearly.

Even as the thoughts crossed her mind, she dismissed them. It wasn't as simple as falling in love. She had found her Mate. Her soul's other half. The part of her that she hadn't realized was missing until she felt what it was to be whole. As much as one can lie to themselves, one cannot ignore the magnitude of such a moment; the feeling of utter completeness when you are reunited with the person that carries the other piece of you.

It came as no surprise that Von had a history, he had warned her of it often enough. He went so far as to tell her the night they were formally mated that he hadn't been a good man. It wasn't his past that had its claws tearing at her heart right now. Never mind the other lover, she had been fleeting. Someone he had used while trying to deny the bond that had already taken root inside of him. Although a small part of her still itched to test some of the new powers she had discovered, perhaps rake those lovely claws right down the bitch's face. She could feel a flicker of Fire in her, but it was sluggish, calling to her from far away.

Helena squeezed her eyes shut, her head pounding in time with her heartbeat.

No, the part she kept replaying was the feel of his guilt in her mind. The confession of his heart, when his words proclaimed innocence. Even in knowing she would be able to feel the deceit through their bond, his first impulse was still to explain it away. Since knowing him, her every instinct had been to protect him. Could that be what caused his hesitation? Had he been trying to protect her feelings from a mistake that was made in a moment of weakness? Or was he merely trying to protect himself?

She struggled to clear her thoughts, the pulsing in her temples overwhelming her with the pain. Opening her eyes, she winced at the brightness of the room. Her mind was telling her that she had overreacted, telling him to go ahead without her. Her heart told her that she should run after him and throw herself into his arms.

Not even a few hours later and she already felt his absence. Rather, she couldn't feel him at all. It was the first time since waking up after facing her trial that his essence wasn't hovering at the edge of her awareness. She felt its lack pressing against her, wanting her to collapse into its void. Even her soul wanted to chase after its Mate and beg his forgiveness for doubting what it knew to be true. Her trial had warned her this test would come, and she had failed.

Helena sighed. She had been foolish listening to Gillian's story. She had just been so tired from the battle and so heart-sore after days of burials, she wasn't thinking clearly. Not to mention her surprise when Von didn't immediately shut Gillian down with one of his scathing dismissals. Instead, he had hesitated, his face losing some of its healthy glow, and their bond throbbing with his shame.

Noticing a flash of white, Helena turned to face the trunk she had been using as a side table next to their bedding. The Magnolia.

The ghost of a smile flit across her lips. She remembered Von's teasing words when presenting her with the gift. She had made a point to ask Alina to pack it with her things, wanting to keep close the physical reminder of the moment she first met her Mate.

With that thought, a piece of her settled back into place. It was an answer to a question. Even when Von thought he was just playing a part, he had cared enough to give her something personal. Simple compared to some of the other courtship gifts, yes, but so much more memorable for its specific meaning to her. A music box or book spelled to tell stories were lovely trinkets, but they were gifts that could be given to anyone, and therefore meaningless. Von had taken the time to give her something she would find special, proving that even before he met her, when he had no reason to, he had cared about her.

Von regretted his decision to bed the other woman, and though it had happened before they made any promises to one another, he had done so after presenting himself to her. Feeling as he did now, that act still ate at him, a small splinter that he couldn't quite remove. His guilt stemmed from that; it was not a desire to lie to her, but rather his regret that he couldn't deny Gillian's claims.

Helena had no doubt of Von's love for her. She felt it in every look and every phantom caress he sent through their bond. She took a deep breath, finding it a little easier this time as the tightness in her chest had started to ease. She wasn't pleased with what he had done, but she wouldn't punish him for it. Much. Especially when the punishment seemed to hurt her just as much as it did him.

The headache continued to pulse but seemed to be fading. She decided to go find Starshine and see if the Talyrian could catch up to Von's party. They couldn't have gotten too far, even if they had left immediately.

Holding open the flap of the tent, she let out the soft whistle that had become her call for the Talyrian. She waited, eyes scanning the horizon until the ball of white appeared and streaked through the sky toward her.

"Take me to him," she requested softly, projecting an image of Von to Starshine as she did so.

Those turquoise eyes seemed to roll, but she lowered until Helena could mount easily. Between one breath and the next, they were in the air and already too far for Helena to see her Circle calling after her.

THE SKY WAS dark when they made it back to the camp. The first thing she noticed as Starshine landed was Timmins pacing before the campfire, his hands tugging at his hair.

Kragen was leaning against a tree, sharpening his ax. Darrin and Joquil sat around the fire and stared into its flame. At her appearance, all four stood and faced her.

Timmins had opened his mouth to launch into what was sure to be a tirade, but Helena stopped him with a glance.

Her face was tear-streaked, her aqua eyes blinking furiously as they filled again.

"Helena?" Darrin asked softly, hands outstretched as if to catch her.

She took a trembling step toward them, her whole body shaking.

"He's gone," she whispered.

"What?" Ronan asked sharply, just reaching the group, Serena close on his heels.

Helena swallowed before turning to him. "Von is gone. I—I can't feel him anymore. Starshine and I rode for hours, and then circled back to double check, but he's not out there."

Her hand was clutching at her chest, trying to ease the ache.

Ronan snapped out orders, but she couldn't make sense of them. He couldn't have gotten too far; it had only been a few hours since she had sent him away. She knew he would have continued on their path toward his parents' home, it was only another two days ride from here, but even still she and Starshine had searched, the circles increasing with each pass.

When they had gotten closer to the border, and she still couldn't reach him through their bond she had started to worry. As the hours went by and the sun faded from the sky worry had given way to fear. Von was gone, without a trace, or at least too far for her to be able to sense him through their bond. Unless her asking him to leave had done something to their bond.

She was trying to recall if she had felt something in her shift when she had stopped him from coming toward her and telling him she needed time. His face had been frozen in shock, his pain at her words a twin to her own, but that had been it. She would have felt it, wouldn't she, if she had broken their bond?

"Helena?" Darrin called, shaking her slightly.

She blinked up at him. "Yes?"

"How long has he been gone?"

She shook her head. "I don't—I don't know. We had—there was… I told him to leave." Her face crumpled, and she couldn't stop the tears as they flowed from her eyes.

"Shh, *Mira*, we will find him. Tell me what happened." The order was gentle, his hands soothing as they rubbed up and down her arms.

Helena hiccupped as she tried to control the tears. Around her the others were quiet, waiting for her story.

So she began, haltingly, telling them everything that Gillian had said about Von seeking the girl out and sleeping with her after declaring himself at the ceremony. The men exchanged surprised looks but asked her to continue.

She told them how she had sent him on ahead, asking him to give her some time to process what she had heard before she had to speak with him.

"So he could have only been gone for a couple of hours at most, but he wouldn't have left, Kiri. Not even if you had ordered him to, he would have come to one of us and stayed out of your way until you cooled off, knowing you would come for him," Serena stated.

Ronan nodded. "Nor would he have left without Karma." Ronan gestured at the wolf pacing restlessly among the others.

Helena felt foolish, of course Von wouldn't have left Karma. She should have checked immediately once she realized he wasn't within range.

"So if he didn't leave, where is he?" Helena asked, silently adding, *and why can't I feel him anymore?*

Ronan and Serena shared a look.

"What?" Helena snapped, looking between them.

"Where's Gillian?" Serena asked, her violet eyes seeming to glow.

Helena's back stiffened. "Gillian? I don't know; I haven't seen her since this afternoon."

"I caught her out in the forest, our first night out. There was something about the girl that wasn't sitting right, so I wanted to keep an eye on her. I saw her keep stealing glances at me, so I made a show of going off with Ronan and then circled back to watch her. Almost immediately she snuck out of camp and hurried through the forest. I came upon her crouching over something, but couldn't see what it was in the darkness."

"Why are you just telling us this now?" Kragen demanded.

Serena shrugged. "We didn't have proof of anything, just my feelings. I didn't want to come between the Kiri and her friend unless I had good reason."

"Wait a moment," Joquil's voice interrupted, causing the group to look at him. "Didn't Gillian have a necklace with a purple stone?"

She saw Darrin's eyes widen in recognition. "Yes, I don't think she was ever without it. It was very similar to those gems you found on the Shadows."

Joquil's face was grim. "I think I know how Von disappeared, Kiri."

"How?" she asked sharply.

"Gillian had a Kaelpas, as did those Shadows."

"I thought the knowledge of how to make those died centuries ago," Timmins whispered in awe.

"What's a Kaelpas?" Helena asked, her voice strained as she pronounced the unfamiliar word. She could feel her magic, usually a calm pool, bubbling inside of her.

"It's a very rare, very powerful bit of magic. Completely

untraceable unless you carry one of the spelled gems. They work like beacons. Let's say you and I both have one, Kiri," Joquil explained, "I would be able to teleport to you, wherever you were because your Kaelpas would guide me to you. I could also travel to a destination I had been to before, even if there was no one with a Kaelpas in the vicinity. It takes powerful magic to create a Kaelpas; it requires mastery in three of the branches: Earth, Air, and Fire."

"They also take the entire cycle of a moon to charge. The farther you travel or, the more people you try to transport with a single Kaelpas the faster is it extinguished," Timmins added.

"So what you're saying is that Gillian brought those things, those Shadows, to us before. It was how they knew where to strike so that we would find the bodies."

"It certainly supports our theory that their presence was a test of our forces," Ronan murmured.

"And how Von could vanish without a trace," Serena concluded.

Helena could no longer hear them, her blood roaring in her ears. Gone. Her Mate was gone. Not just gone, taken.

She flexed her fingers, the rise of magic causing them to tingle. The tingle quickly turned to a burn as her fury continued to feed on her reservoir of strength.

There was no rational thought, just a word on an endless loop in her mind. Taken.

Her magic continued to build, a tidal wave getting ready to crash. She was losing herself to the swell of magic within her.

When she looked back at her Circle, and Von's most trusted warriors, her eyes were swirling iridescent pools, flashes of lightning in their depths. Thunder filled with the promise of her retribution echoed in the sky.

"Helena?" Darrin asked, eyes wide.

As she leveled her eyes on him, he paled. There was no sign of the woman they knew in those eyes.

"We will find him," the Kiri said, her voice a harsh harmony of many, her words an edict that would not allow disobedience. "And when we find her, we will repay her hospitality. For every new mark on his skin or scar on his heart, she will pay with her blood." The last word came out as a snarl. The wind tore through the trees, growing in intensity as she spoke.

"As you command, Kiri," the Circle said as one.

She knew nothing but endless glittering rage. She had warned them; no one would harm what was hers. She would show them what happens when they disobeyed. One way or another she would find her Mate. Like calls to like—they would not be able to keep him from her indefinitely. And when she found him, his captors and any that tried to stand in her way would pay.

With their lives.

THE CHOSEN: BOOK 2
REIGN OF ASH
MEG ANNE

For the men in my life that taught me distance don't mean $#!+
Real love endures zip codes, time zones and lifetimes.
Grandpa, Dad, and Gabe you are the proof.

PROLOGUE

illian could feel the weight of her mistress's stare and allowed her eyes to dart up to the woman on the throne. She had many titles, but Gillian knew her best as mother. At least, she had. Once.

There was nothing left of the mother Gillian had once known in the woman sitting above her. In truth, it felt like there was a chasm that separated the once kind, if only mildly affectionate woman who raised her from this aloof and cold-hearted queen. Now instead of mother, she was simply referred to as Mistress by Gillian and Rowena by those too stupid to know what was good for them. Or those that had a death wish.

As the last Damaskiri, she was both Helena's predecessor and a woman believed dead by the people she once ruled. She was a Queen in hiding, biding her time until she could strike against her enemies and reclaim her rightful place amongst the Chosen.

Rowena leaned back slowly, her eyes never drifting from the red-haired girl kneeling before her. Sitting as she was, she was the personification of queenly grace, her posture perfect and unflinching. She was stunning in a cold and frightening way. Her face was currently schooled into an expressionless mask; her ice-blue gaze glacial as she stared. Her colorless blonde hair was pulled up into an elaborate mess of braids and surrounded by the glittering and twisting spikes of metal that comprised her crown. A fitted black satin dress encased her lithe body, the severity of its color only enhancing the luminosity of her skin.

Rowena tilted her head to the side, the movement deliberate and calculating, a predator assessing its prey. The silence lengthened and became uncomfortable until Gillian finally shifted nervously, her skirts rustling as they moved against the ground. There was a metallic tinkling as Rowena's fingers tapped a steady beat on the dark arm of her throne.

Gillian's green eyes widened, noting the sharp-clawed tips of the rings which adorned each of the slender fingers on mother's right hand. She forced herself to look away, shifting her focus back to the stone floor.

After another long moment of strained silence, Gillian bowed her head lower, allowing a waterfall of copper curls to spill over her shoulder and obscure her face. The protection from Rowena's scrutiny was welcomed, even if only imagined. That icy gaze missed nothing.

"The prisoner?" Rowena finally asked, her voice as expressionless as her face and as weighted as her stare.

Gillian felt her shoulders stiffen as she relayed the latest report. "Still under the effects of the *Bella Morte*, Mistress."

"You were careless in your dosage." It was both a statement and judgment, the words leaving absolutely no room for doubt; she would be punished for her transgression.

She swallowed thickly. Her mistress's punishments were unfailingly harsh and varied. One thing Gillian had come to expect was that she would never see it coming.

"I do not believe he is lost to the dreaming, Mistress." Gillian winced, hearing the quavering in her voice.

"You do not *believe*?" The question was a harsh crack.

Gillian found herself grinding her teeth before she could respond.

"He is not showing any side effects besides the hallucinations," she amended.

"Other than remaining in a drugged stupor since his arrival," Rowena contradicted caustically.

"Yes, Mistress. It is as you say," Gillian meekly agreed.

"You had better hope that he wakes, and soon. For your brother's sake, if not your own. Micha's remaining days on this earth are a direct result of your success…" She paused for one endless moment before adding contemptuously, "Or your failure." The words were savage but measured, the threat delivered as matter-of-factly as one might discuss the weather.

Fear scratched down her spine and Gillian could feel her body break into a sweat, despite the chill in the room. Before she could respond further she was dismissed, Rowena standing and exiting from one of the doors in the back of the cavernous room.

Gillian did not move immediately, not trusting her limbs to support her or that her mother would not be back. While she waited, she let her eyes bounce from the arched windows and soaring ceilings back to the throne of twisting metal sitting in the center of the dais.

Once it was clear Rowena would not be returning, Gillian stood and made her way to the door. Her legs trembled as she exited the room but she made it to the safety of the corridor before slumping against the stone wall. Her eyes fluttered closed as her heart raced and a thought tinged with desperation raced through her.

One moment. I just need one moment.

Gillian struggled to calm her heartbeat. Eventually, she peeled herself off of the wall and took a final, shuddering breath as she continued her journey to the prisoner.

He would wake; she would see to it. She would bring his mind back to his body even if it required her to take him to the brink of death to do so. There was no room for failure. Micha's life depended on it. No matter how much she enjoyed her plaything, Micha's life was worth infinitely more to her than stolen moments in a prison cell.

One way or the other, it was time for Von to wake up.

CHAPTER 1

Helena sat beside the fountain, a picture of quiet devastation. She could no longer see her reflection rippling in the water's pristine surface. She also couldn't remember the last time she moved, or even hazard a guess as to how long she'd been sitting there. Despite her statue-like stillness, the serenity was only an illusion. Every night since Von's capture she had sought out a place where she could be alone to search for some sense of their bond, some spark that would help guide her to him. And just as it had been every night since she started her search, there was only a vast and endless darkness.

Helena flinched violently as a warm hand brushed against her icy shoulder. She spun around, teeth bared in a feral snarl until she recognized the green eyes studying her with concern.

"You forgot your cloak again," Darrin murmured gently, offering her the deep purple garment lined with sable fur.

"Oh, thank you," she rasped, her voice raw with disuse.

Her stiff fingers tried to take the cloak but could not bend enough to grasp it before Darrin let go. It fell clumsily to the floor. She sat unmoving; her eyes, which tracked its progress to the ground, were the only sign she was aware of what had happened.

"Here, let me," he offered finally when she made no move to pick it up. He lifted and deftly wrapped the warm fabric around her shoulders.

Helena shivered as its warmth seeped into her skin.

"What time is it?" she asked, her words coming slowly as she struggled to come back to the present.

"It's getting late, and you missed the evening meal. Again." His voice held none of the gentle rebuke she was used to hearing. In its absence, there was only worry.

She had not been taking very good care of herself and it showed. Her aqua eyes, usually shining with light, were bruised and dull. She had missed more meals than she ate and had gotten little, if any, sleep. The sleep she had managed to get had been fraught with nightmares, which only added to the haunted look in her eyes. The lack of food and quality sleep, combined with a headache which had only grown in intensity since Von's disappearance, left her looking decidedly haggard.

Von would be so disappointed in her if he saw her walking through the corridors of his home like a ghost of the woman he loved. She could almost hear his deep growl echoing in her mind: *"What do you think you're doing, Mate? That body belongs to me; take better care of it."*

The wave of longing that slammed through her at even that paltry imitation of him had tears blurring her eyes. She swallowed the emotion back down and gave herself a mental shake. She could not go on like this for much longer; both her body and her heart would give out on her soon. If not for her own sake, she could at least try to take better care of herself for him. She had vowed to find him and destroy his captors after all. She could hardly make good on the promise to avenge him if she was too weak to do more than sit there and scowl menacingly. The mental image caused a barely discernible smile to flit across her lips before quickly fading.

Helena blinked back the last of the tears and really looked at Darrin for the first time. "Do you think there's something left for me to eat?"

Relief flooded his face at the request. "Yes, Kiri. I believe we can scrounge something up for you."

She nodded once and stood, ready to follow him back into the manor. They had reached the Holbrooke Estate only a day after discovering Gillian's betrayal. Helena winced as she remembered her first meal with Von's family.

THE CIRCLE SAT around a massive oak table that was colored and pitted with age. The room was bright, lit both by the fire roaring beside them, and by soft balls of light which floated above them. Helena had been given a place of honor at the head of the table, although the sneers Von's father, Darius, wore whenever she caught him looking at her did much to undermine the display of hospitality. Margo, Von's mother, was much kinder. She had welcomed the group with warm hugs and wept silently when she had learnt what had become of her eldest son. Von's younger brother Nial had not been feeling well and was unable to come and greet the group, although he had sent his apologies for his absence and promised to meet with them soon.

Helena had moved through the introductions numbly, allowing Timmins to explain what had happened. All of the fury and promises of vengeance had burned out of her, leaving only a fragile shell in its place. Well, that was not strictly true; her wrath continued to simmer along the surface of her magic, but it was leashed by the lack of a target. Without it to fuel her, she was left with little to buffer her against the storm of emotions raging within. Guilt. Fear. Sorrow. All were relentless as they continued to crash against the inner barriers of her mind.

She couldn't recall much of the short tour they were given as Margo led them to their rooms. Despite being at the base of a mountain the manor was warm. It had wide halls and vaulted ceilings that created a sense of openness and flow from room to room. There were also large windows in every room so that the beauty of Daejara was incorporated throughout their home. It often seemed as though they were sitting outside, although the fact that they were sheltered from the biting winds was certainly a welcome reprieve.

The dining hall sat to the east of the home, overlooking the view of the massive cliffs and sparkling blue ocean below. Helena had never seen the sea before, but there was something about the roar of the crashing waves that called to her. Perhaps, if she could get away from the prying eyes of the Circle, she would take Starshine out over the water to get a better look.

Thinking of Starshine had her remembering her last night with Von under the stars. The feeling of his warm hands running along the length of her back. The scrape of his teeth as he ran them over the cords of muscle in her neck before biting down gently, and then licking his way back to her ear to trail sweet kisses down to her lips.

She felt her lower lip quiver at the memory. Her desire for her Mate was quickly overshadowed by her grief at his absence, and at the way things had been left between them. It was her fault he had been taken. If she had not been so stupid and believed Gillian's lies... if she had not trusted the harlot in the first place... if only she could tell Von how sorry she was, and how much she loved him.

The sniffling brought her out of her memories. She looked around the table with wide eyes, shock quickly replaced by mortification as she watched each person sob. Serena had her head buried in Ronan's neck, while the warrior hastily wiped at his eyes. Darrin had his head bowed over his plate, shoulders shaking with tears. Timmins was blowing his nose while Joquil dabbed at his dripping eyes. Margo and Darius clung to each other, their cries echoing loudly in the spacious room.

Kragen's eyes were dry but despondent, anguish cutting deep lines in his usually smiling face. "I much prefer the days you would have us seeking out dark corners to fumble beneath a maid's skirts to this, Kiri," he muttered.

Helena blinked and let out a startled bark of laughter. That was all it took to break the spell; the men and women parroted Kragen's sentiment as their tears were swiftly replaced with watery laughter.

"You and I both, Sword." While her smile didn't quite reach her eyes, the gentle teasing had worked. She was no longer drowning in her misery and was able to get through the evening without further incident.

"PERHAPS I WILL ACTUALLY MAKE it through a meal without embarrassing myself," she murmured, heartened by the fact she would be eating in relative solitude.

Darrin chuckled beside her. "No one blames you, Helena."

She sighed. "No, I know that... it would just be nice to have my feelings be a little less," she paused searching for the right word, "contagious."

He placed his hand lightly on her shoulder. "One would only have to look at your eyes to know what you were feeling."

She blinked up at him before smiling sadly. "I haven't been doing a very good job of being a leader these past weeks, have I? I've been too busy wallowing."

Darrin made a dismissive sound, not bothering to answer.

Helena squared her shoulders and said with forced determination, "Well, no more of that. It's time I got back to my training. Will you let Ronan know I would like to work with him in the morning? And tell Joquil I'd like to continue with our lessons as well."

Darrin's eyes widened in surprise before he nodded quickly. "Of course."

I really must be pathetic these days if that was enough to shock him, she thought dejectedly.

"Oh," she added aloud, "and I would like to set aside some time to see Nial. He was the entire reason for this trip, at least originally. I would like to see what I can do to help him."

"Are you sure you're strong enough for something like that?" Darrin's question mirrored her own concerns.

Helena shrugged as they rounded the corner and walked into the kitchen. "Honestly, I have no idea, but until I see what I'm dealing with, it's too hard to say one way or the other."

Helena had met Nial only briefly. She had taken one look at his dark hair and those familiar gray eyes and practically put down roots in the floor. The similarity between him and his brother had been enough to have her heart lodge in her throat. She had stood there like a slack-jawed fool, staring at him with hopeful longing. It had taken a few moments for her to recover enough to stumble through an apology, her cheeks a blazing pink. Nial had kindly waved it off, smiling as he adjusted the soft blue blanket in his lap.

Once her heartbeat had returned to its normal pace, she realized there were a number of subtle differences between the brothers. To start, Nial's voice lacked Von's deep growl and his gray eyes were more a stormy gray-blue than silver. Helena had also noticed that his wavy dark hair was much shorter than Von's. Even so, it hurt to look at him, the visual reminder of what she had lost was more than she could bear, and she had limited her interactions with him. Yet another reason she had avoided so many meals. *Coward. No more hiding, Helena,* she chided herself. *Von deserves better than this.*

Darrin moved across the room, opening a chilled cabinet to gather the leftovers from the evening meal. She watched him open up various containers before selecting one that appeared to be full of a vegetable stew and another full of a fluffy white substance.

"Potatoes," Darrin said in answer to her lifted brow.

Helena's stomach growled as the smell of the food hit her nose.

Darrin laughed loudly, his eyes crinkling with mirth as he said, "Well, I guess I don't need to ask if that sounds good to you."

She stuck out her tongue in response as he quickly dished out large portions of each.

"Can you manage reheating these?" He gestured toward her hands. "I'm not certain where anything is in here or I would offer to do it myself."

Helena nodded and stepped over to him, her fingers running over the smooth surface of the large wooden counter as she did. Grasping the dish, she closed her eyes and called the smallest tendril of magic to her. She felt the heat of Fire quickly rush to the surface, and found herself making soothing noises to gentle the rush. She released her magic entirely once the spicy steam was wafting up to her face.

Darrin let out a low whistle. "Such a convenient talent."

Helena nodded in agreement, accepting the spoon he was holding out to her. She dug in greedily and immediately let out a startled yelp as her eyes began to water. Her hand was pressed over her mouth while she blinked back tears.

Darrin howled with laughter beside her. "All right, perhaps it's not as convenient as I thought if you make it too hot to eat."

She glared at him. "You're lucky I'm too hungry to dump this on you."

He held up two hands and stepped back. "Merely an observation, Kiri."

She rolled her eyes. "Standing on formality will not protect you, Shield."

He lifted a shoulder while his smile grew. "You can't blame me for trying, Hellion."

She winked at him, before taking another spoonful of the stew and making a show of blowing on it. His laughter died down and he stood across from her, watching her silently.

She lifted her brow. "What?" she asked, her mouth full of stew and the word coming out garbled.

He just shook his head, a small smile playing about his lip. "It's just nice to see you looking happy, Helena."

She swallowed and looked down into her bowl before speaking. "I miss him, Darrin."

"I know," he said gravely.

She shook her head slowly. "No, I don't think you do." Her aqua eyes blazed brightly as they met his before continuing, "I feel as though a piece of me is missing. It's not something as obvious as a limb, but I feel just as crippled. Nothing feels right without him here. I'm so lost..." She trailed off, averting her gaze as she did, her voice thick with emotion.

"We will find him, Helena. Do not lose hope."

He watched a small tremor work its way through her body, her fingers gripping the spoon in her hand more tightly. When she looked back up, there were hints of the swirling iridescence in her eyes and her voice resonated as though spoken in harmony. "I haven't and I won't."

Darrin nodded, his shoulders relaxing at the small appearance of her power. "Good. Now eat up."

Helena made a face but continued to work her way through the meal until it was mostly gone. Taking the bowl from her, he made quick work of rinsing it out and setting it to dry with the others.

"Feeling better?" he asked, his voice too inquisitive to be casual.

She nodded, smiling ruefully. "Yes, mother."

Darrin laughed, and pulled her into him, hugging her tightly. "We are going to get through this; you'll see." The words were soft as he rested his cheek atop her head.

"I know," she said just as softly, her words muffled by his chest. She clung to him as they stood in silence, willing his promises to come true.

CHAPTER 2

"*H*arder, Helena," Ronan boomed as she swung the heavy training stick into the dummy.

"I'm swinging it as hard as I can, asshole," she panted as she lifted it again, her muscles screaming in protest. They had begun their workout with the dawn, and hours later she was well past the point of tolerating the Acting Commander's instruction.

"My granny could hit that sack of feathers harder than you," he taunted.

She growled low in her throat before swinging the stick for all she was worth. The dummy exploded with a satisfying thwack; gray and white feathers rained down upon them.

"Satisfied?" she asked, smiling up at him as she dropped her weapon to the ground.

"Now now, there's no need to whip your cock out and start waving it around. It's highly unladylike."

"Whipping my—" Helena sputtered.

Ronan's shoulders were shaking with laughter as he watched her face turn pink with indignation. "I'm just teasing you, Kiri."

"I would be happy to get the measuring stick out if you'd like. In fact, that sounds like a great idea. We can have all your men line up and drop their pants right here," Serena purred as she pulled feathers out of his braid.

"The Mother's tits you will!" Ronan growled before pressing a swift kiss against her smiling lips and muttering, "Minx."

Helena merely shook her head as she watched the couple; yearning for Von flared swift and hot through her at the sight of their easy embrace.

"Tough morning?" Serena asked lightly, violet eyes studying her friend with concern.

Helena grunted.

Blonde brows lifted in amusement as Serena replied, "Oh, I see."

Ronan's hand ran down Serena's back to curl around her waist. "That's enough for today. We lost a lot of progress in the last couple of weeks, but we should be able to make up for it quickly, so long as you continue to take care of yourself."

Her cheeks flamed at the gentle reprimand, but she nodded, still struggling to catch her breath.

"Just you two this morning?" Serena inquired, as her eyes scanned the small courtyard they had used for their practice.

Ronan nodded, the morning sun glinting against his scar and causing it to stand out in sharp relief against his cheek. "We wanted to test her limits today. It has been awhile since our last session, so I needed to establish her baseline and determine where we need to focus in order to rebuild her strength and stamina."

Helena whimpered when she realized she would not have Von to help ease the ache from her muscles this time. Her heart constricted painfully in her chest. Everything had become a constant reminder of his absence. Feeling the weight of their twin stares upon her, she straightened her shoulders and stood with her hands on her hips, attempting to convey a haughty confidence she did not entirely feel.

"Are you sure you still want to meet with Nial this morning?"

Helena nodded once.

"We can push it back. I'm sure he'll—" Serena ventured but was cut off.

"No, I've waited far too long as it is. I should have met with him by now. I just… wasn't ready."

Ronan leaned down and kissed Serena's forehead. "I will leave you two ladies to your morning. Helena," he turned to look at her sternly, "do not push yourself so hard that you cannot practice tomorrow. That's an order."

He turned and strode away before he could see the ball of Water she had manifested in the palm of her hand. Serena could hardly suppress her giggles as Helena let it fly straight into the back of Ronan's head. The large man stopped and turned slowly, his brows lowered menacingly over ice-blue eyes.

Helena bit down on her lip as she fought back her own laughter.

Ronan lifted a finger and pointed it at her face. "You," he said deliberately, "are very lucky."

Helena raised both brows in surprise. "And why's that?"

"If I wasn't so damn happy to hear you laughing again, I'd make you pay for that bit of cheekiness. As it stands, I'm just glad to have my friend back." He blew her a kiss and continued with his leisurely stroll to the manor.

Serena wrapped her arm around Helena. "For what it's worth, so am I."

Helena rested her head on her friend's shoulder, saying in a voice tinged with sadness. "I'm trying."

"We know, dearest," Serena replied matter-of-factly, giving her a tight squeeze before leaning down to sniff her delicately. "Perhaps you should bathe before we go up to meet the youngest Holbrooke. The poor lad has suffered enough already; he doesn't need to be assaulted by your ripe stench."

Helena sputtered with laughter as she shoved Serena, who landed on the ground in an undignified heap.

Serena was a picture of astonishment as she gaped up at Helena. "All right, I deserved that," she said between breathless bouts of laughter.

Helena wore a self-satisfied smile as she offered Serena a hand to help her stand. "Yes. Yes, you did."

Bathed and changed into a dove gray gown, Helena met Serena in her suite's sitting area as she quickly braided her damp hair. Her rooms were large and airy, and much lovelier than Helena had anticipated given Von's description of life in Daejara after the ban.

The focal point of the room was a hearth that was as tall as she was on the western side, the wall surrounding it comprised of large gray stones. The rest of the room was painted a soft lilac where it was not covered by colorful tapestries. The floor consisted of long, dark wooden planks that peeked out beneath the various plush rugs that littered the room.

Also within the room was a massive four-poster bed, its golden coverings matching the heavy curtains currently pulled back from the floor-to-ceiling windows that opened onto a balcony overlooking the sea. The strategically placed furniture was made from the same dark wood as the floor and included a large bookcase, writing desk, and vanity. There were a few chairs and one low bench set up beside a glass table where Serena currently sat sipping tea.

Helena did a quick twirl, and asked dryly, "Do I pass inspection, Commander?"

Serena laughed at her use of the Daejaran title and offered a mocking nod. "You'll do, warrior."

Helena rolled her eyes, chuckling. She could not deny that her practice with Ronan had done much to ease some of the weight she had been carrying within her. It had felt good to whack that training dummy, imagining Gillian's smug smile on its face as she did. She had found release in running and pushing herself until she was ready to collapse. At the very least, it had given her something to *do*. She was so tired of feeling impotent. It had also given her something to focus on and allowed her to finally block the flurry of thoughts running on a never-ending loop inside her mind. For that alone, she was almost giddy about continuing her training tomorrow. Although, she was certain her muscles would be arguing with that sentiment come the morning.

There was a soft knock at the door before a flaxen head peered around the side. "Are you ready for me to take you up, Kiri?" Effie, the maid, asked in her sweet voice.

Effie looked deceptively young, probably because she was such a tiny thing. Her proportions were more doll-like than those of a woman well into her twenties. Her long blonde curls fell down her back and framed an elfish face with wide sky-blue eyes and long sooty lashes. She had a smattering of freckles across a slightly upturned nose and perfectly pouty lips that were almost always smiling. Helena had liked her instantly.

"Yes, thank you, Effie," she said with a smile that actually reached her aqua eyes.

Effie blushed and bobbed a quick curtsey before stepping back into the hallway.

"She's not used to people taking notice of her," Serena commented under her breath as she placed her empty cup on the table and stood to walk toward the door.

"I'm familiar with the feeling," Helena responded wryly.

Serena snickered. "I'm sure you are."

The stares and whispers had been almost constant since crossing the border, although people were finally polite enough not to blatantly comment on the shimmering iridescent rings around her pupils. Kragen had enjoyed a good laugh the first time Helena threatened to break the finger of the next person that tried to poke her in the eye. By the seventh, he was offering to do it for her.

"Everyone is just curious about their new Kiri," Serena offered as they exited her room.

"Lucky me," Helena muttered, her words dripping with sarcasm.

Serena snorted. "At least they ceased asking you to perform bits of magic for them."

"Because *that* went well," Helena retorted, ears burning as she recalled her failed attempt to make a teddy bear dance for a young boy in one of the villages.

All she had meant to do was make it twirl about a little. Instead, the thing had exploded leaving stuffing and bits of fur floating in its wake.

The boy had burst into tears and hid in his mother's skirts. His mother had been kind, but Helena was mortified. Kragen and Ronan had teased her ruthlessly for days after.

She still couldn't seem to find the level of control required to use her magic in the simplest of ways. At least, not consistently. The harder she tried, the more unwieldy it became. Lately, it felt more like she was trying to wrestle with a wild beast rather than simply coax a small wave of magic.

Large magic was no issue, or it hadn't been so far. Helena had a growing suspicion that Von's kidnapping was playing some part in her struggle for control. When she'd broached the topic with Joquil, he'd brushed away her concerns stating that there was no record of a Mate's proximity having any effect on a Kiri's magic.

Effie escorted them expeditiously through the halls until they reached a quiet corner in the northeastern part of the manor. Helena could hear waves crashing in the distance as Effie gave the large wooden door a perfunctory knock.

"Come in," a deep male voice called from inside.

Effie opened the door, standing aside to let the ladies enter before her. Once they passed through the doorway, she made a small curtsey and shut the door, leaving the ladies alone with Nial.

Helena was prepared this time, steeling herself against the despair that threatened to wash through her at the sight of Von's brother. There was a boyish charm to him and intelligence shone brightly in those familiar gray-blue eyes. He flashed her a broad grin, his eyes crinkling with good humor.

"Hello again, Kiri," he said by way of welcome.

Helena made her way toward his overladen table. It was littered with open books and parchment and looked ready to collapse at the hint of a stiff breeze. She eyed the open window warily as she approached him.

"Forgive me for not standing," he quipped.

She rolled her eyes, her lips quirking despite herself. "Ever the comedian, I see. And call me Helena, please, we are family now, after all," she murmured warmly. Noting the ink stains on his fingers and the pages filled with lines of precise notes, she added, "I'm not interrupting your studies, am I?"

He was quick to shake his head. "Not at all." As he turned to address Serena, who was standing just behind her, his eyes opened wide and his nostrils flared.

Helena's eyebrows furrowed as she looked from Nial to Serena. Serena's face had drained of color, her eyes unblinking as she stared at the man seated before her, mesmerized. Helena coughed discreetly, causing both of them to blink rapidly and straighten.

Nial held out his hand to Serena. "I don't believe we've met. I'm Nial."

"Serena," the warrior said in the softest voice Helena had ever heard her use.

She placed her hand in his, jumping when he leaned down to kiss the back of it. As soon as he let her go, she stepped hurriedly back, her cheeks and chest splotched with pink and her violet eyes glazed.

Curious at her reaction, Helena asked, "You two have never met? I thought you and Ronan had known Von since you were children."

Serena gave a start at the mention of her lover's name. She blinked and shook her head, dragging her eyes from Nial back to Helena. "No, Kiri, neither Ronan nor I have had reason to visit the Holbrooke home before now. We always stayed in the barracks, or visited our own families, when Von would make his infrequent trips home."

"More's the pity," Nial said in a low, honey-coated voice.

Serena blushed, her eyes darting to the floor.

Helena froze. The tone of his voice so like his brothers in that moment, she felt her own cheeks flush. Letting out a jagged breath, she refocused, reminding herself that she had a job to do.

Interesting, Helena thought, studying the two. If she didn't know better, she would say that Serena was as infatuated with Nial as he obviously was with her. Helena knew she was wholly committed to Ronan though, so it didn't quite add up. *Something is definitely going on here*, Helena decided, determining to get to the bottom of it. Eventually.

"I'm sure Von explained in his letters to you why I wanted to visit..." Helena interjected, trying to get their conversation back on track.

Nial nodded, his eyes continuing to examine the tall blonde beside her as he asked, "Do you really think you'll be able to help me?"

Helena shrugged. "I certainly hope so." She didn't think now was the appropriate time to mention that she had never attempted something of this magnitude before.

Nial moved his hands from the table to his sides and pushed himself back. Helena noted the wheels attached to his chair with surprise.

"What a clever idea!"

Nial grinned up at her. "I may not be able to do many of the things my brother can, but at least this way I don't need to be completely dependent upon the help of others to get about."

Helena was more than a little impressed as she returned his smile. "You came up with this?"

"I did."

"Brilliant!" she exclaimed, eyeing Nial with more interest.

"Just because my body has limitations, does not mean that my mind does," he joked.

"I never thought for a moment that it did," Helena said sincerely.

Nial offered her another warm smile before wheeling himself over to his bed. She was just about to offer to help him when he placed both palms on the bed and pushed himself up, twisting in the air to land with a soft plop.

Helena blinked, trying to cover her astonishment. She really shouldn't be so shocked; he had obviously learned how to do much on his own, especially if those muscles flexing and bunching as he maneuvered his chair were any indication. This man did not seem at all like the crippled brother Von had described to her so long ago.

"I suppose you'll need to see the legs," Nial asked tightly, lifting one of his dark brows.

Helena's expression softened. "Yes, seeing the extent of your injuries would best allow me to understand how to undo the damage."

He nodded, his lips twisting into a frown as he warned, "It's not a pleasant sight, Kiri."

She shrugged. "I'm not easily frightened."

As he worked his pants down his legs, she lifted the blanket that had fallen to the floor and held it up to offer him a modicum of privacy. She heard the gentle rustling of fabric before he let out a low grunt.

"I'm ready."

Helena set the blanket onto the vacated chair and tried to keep her face in a calm mask as she took in the twisted limbs. She heard Serena gasp behind her, Nial's ears turning red at the sound. His shoulders were stiff and his lips flat as she reached out a cool hand to run down the length of the leg. He grimaced, flinching at the contact.

"You can feel that?" she asked neutrally.

He bit down on his lip and nodded. "Yes. My legs are quite sensitive actually."

"That's a good sign. The nerves cannot have been completely damaged. That should assist with the healing," Helena offered as she continued her inspection.

That's probably the only good sign, she thought while trying to keep her expression neutral.

His legs had been broken in multiple places; the skin was discolored and thick with scars from where his bones had pierced his skin when they broke. It was clear that the bones had never been properly reset. Both kneecaps appeared as though they had been completely shattered. His limbs were utterly mangled, only marginally resembling the shape they were supposed to be.

How could someone ever survive this kind of pain?

Her aqua eyes glittered as she looked back up at Nial's face. There was a new level of admiration and respect in them. This was a man who had looked adversity straight in the eye and didn't back down an inch. He could teach her a thing or two in that regard.

Nial was staring straight ahead, bracing himself for what he was sure would be bad news.

"It might take me a few tries. I am still learning, but if you don't mind… I would like to try," she said softly, her hand coming to rest over his closed fist.

He looked up at her in surprise. "Really?"

She nodded, her smile soft.

"Yes." He cleared his throat. "I am more than willing."

Helena moved to sit beside him, apologizing with her eyes when the movement made him wince. Nial's anticipation of further pain gave her a moment of pause and her hands trembled slightly in her lap. His eyes were clenched shut and he was breathing quickly through his nose. Her instinct had always seemed to guide her before; she sincerely hoped it wouldn't let her down now. She didn't think her heart could stand the disappointment of another failure, let alone witnessing devastation in those blue-gray eyes.

Mother guide me, she fervently prayed as she placed her hands on either side of his left leg. Helena took a deep breath to begin the process of centering herself before diving into the pool of her magic. As always, her magic was waiting for her; its smooth surface rippling in greeting as she began to draw it into herself. She used it first to enhance her senses, allowing her eyes to see through his skin and into the muscles and bones beneath. Brushing her fingers down the length of his leg, she moved slowly, allowing her fingers to act as magnets that guided the bones back into place. She continued to move them, each wiggle an attempt to untangle the muscles that had knotted around the broken bones. As she moved, she also pushed her magic into his body, shielding him from the agony such adjustments would cause.

Helena lost track of time, working down his leg a number of times before switching to the other. She could feel her own body start to shake, her magic draining her even more quickly than usual given the way she had failed to take care of herself.

There was a hand on her shoulder and she heard Serena's voice calling from a distance, "That's enough for today, Kiri."

Ignoring the voice, Helena continued to knit the bones back together, her fingers moving as though they were placing pieces of a puzzle.

"Helena," her friend finally snapped, shaking her.

She blinked, trying to refocus on the physical world, her hold on her magic slipping until it settled back into her inner reservoir. Still blinking, she looked into Nial's awed face.

"Did I do it?" she asked, her voice hoarse.

Tears filled his eyes as he threw himself on her, wrapping her in his grateful embrace.

Startled, she looked over his head at Serena, who had tears streaming down her cheeks. She untangled herself gingerly, not wanting to jostle him. When she looked down at his legs, she let out her own awestruck gasp. Where two grotesque imitations of human limbs had lain previously, there were now two perfectly sculpted legs. The skin was soft and responsive beneath her fingers, his toes twitching as she ran a finger down the arch of his foot.

"Can you try to bend it?" she asked, her voice still a gentle rasp.

Nial's face twisted in concentration as he tried to repair the link between his mind and the muscles he had not used for almost twenty years. Before long, both knees were bent and his feet were flat on the bed.

Serena cheered as he swept his legs over the side of the bed, Helena moving to offer assistance as he attempted to stand. He swayed slightly, trying to adjust to the feeling of standing again. When he straightened to his full height, he was almost as tall as Von. Helena wrapped her arm around his waist, helping him take his first teetering steps since he was a child, her own eyes filled with tears.

"How do you feel?" Serena asked, her eyes bright with yet more unshed tears.

"A little weak," Nial admitted.

Helena helped him sit back down. "That's to be expected. While the muscles have healed, it will likely take time for you to regain full strength in them."

"You can train with Helena in the mornings. While she learns how to use weapons, you can work on building up your own strength again," Serena offered.

Nial's smile was blinding as he looked up at her. "Thank you,

Helena, from the bottom of my heart thank you. I will never be able to thank you enough for what you have done for me."

Helena rolled her eyes at his dramatics but was grinning as he continued effusively, "You have given me something I long ago stopped believing was possible. Not only that, but in my wildest dreams, I never imagined that there was a possibility I would recover completely. You've truly gifted me with a second chance at life."

"It seems to me you were doing just fine, even without the use of your legs, Nial."

Nial's eyes seemed to glow as his stare moved to Serena. "There are certain things a man needs full use of his body for, at least if he wishes to do them properly."

For the second time ever, at least to Helena's knowledge, Serena blushed. Although this time, as Serena looked away she was biting back a smile.

CHAPTER 3

Helena curled up in an armchair; her body and mind were so fatigued she could do little more than sit there while she half-listened to the men speaking around her. Things had been progressing, at least on the trade front. The merchants she'd brought with her from Elysia had made the connections necessary to establish new trade lines and set up shops in the central market. As for the rest of them, their new mission was less about diplomacy and more about rescue.

They had gathered in the library to discuss their next steps, but Helena couldn't find the energy to participate in the conversation. Her Circle had been relentless as they chased down leads that might take them to Von. Time and time again they returned empty-handed. The problem was that there was simply no trace of Gillian or Von; they had literally vanished from the camp, leaving no trail for the others to follow.

Kragen and Ronan had taken charge of the Holbrooke's garrison, sending riders off in every direction to see if anyone had seen them, but Helena knew it was futile. After learning of the Kaelpas stones and how they could instantaneously transport one or more people across the realm, she knew it wouldn't be as simple as searching a nearby town. No, this would require smoking the she-rat out of her hidey hole.

If only there was someone that could at least point us in the right direction, she thought desperately.

"What if we send for Micha?" Kragen suggested in his deep rumble.

Helena's ears perked up at the question. "You think he might know where his sister went?" she asked from her chair.

The men spun toward her, seeming to have forgotten she had been sitting there.

"It's a possibility worth considering, Kiri. They are twins and share a linked history. It seems unlikely they would have many secrets between them," Kragen responded.

Helena chewed on her bottom lip, thinking about the playful man who had been one of her first friends in the Capital, as well as one of her suitors. "Could he have been part of it?" she asked no one in particular.

"I highly doubt Gillian was acting alone, although I'm not certain Micha is involved," Timmins answered thoughtfully.

"At the very least, he should be informed of his sister's actions. His reaction to the information could be highly illuminating. If his friendship with Helena is genuine, perhaps he would be willing to help us locate his sister," Darrin added.

"You mean turn against her," Helena clarified dryly, her tone indicating the likelihood of that possibility.

"I don't hear you coming up with any ideas," he muttered darkly as his arms crossed his chest.

She lifted a brow at his insolence but left the comment unchallenged. There was a creak as the door to the library opened, Effie stepping in with a tray loaded with fruit, cheese and a selection of dried meats.

"I thought you all might like a snack," she said by way of explanation, setting the tray upon the table.

"Thank you, Effie. It was very kind of you to think of us," Helena said, making no move toward the food. The others all stepped eagerly to the table, loading up plates with their treats until the tray was almost bare.

"Would you like me to make you a plate, Kiri?" Effie asked, her voice a gentle chastisement for the men who had not thought to leave anything for Helena. For all that she tried to remain unobtrusive, the girl's pointed words brought the men to a halt.

Helena's eyes twinkled with laughter as they paused in their eating to look comically from their plates to her empty hands. Darrin's ears turned bright red and he quickly offered his plate to her. Kragen, Helena noted, merely shoved another piece of cheese into his mouth and winked.

"Nice try," she said sarcastically, rolling her eyes at Darrin before looking back at the maid and shaking her head. "Thank you, Effie, but I'm fine."

"You missed the afternoon meal while you were with Lord Nial," she countered. Again, while delicately delivered, her reproach was a direct hit.

Helena laughed. "I much prefer when you are focused on the others."

The girl's lips pursed with laughter, but she knew she had made her point and felt no need to comment further.

Helena let out a deep sigh, relenting. "Fine, a little something to eat would be most welcome."

"How is it that she can boss you around, but we cannot?" Darrin asked in annoyed disbelief, watching Helena accept her plate.

"Because I like her more than you," Helena teased.

Effie blushed at the compliment and moved to start clearing off the table.

Kragen cuffed Darrin on the back of his head. "Rein in your pride, Shield. It doesn't matter who gives her food, just be happy she's eating and stop asking stupid questions."

"Especially when she spent most of the day channeling a great deal of power," Joquil added sagely, as he crunched neatly on a cracker.

Helena shook her head as she bit into a piece of cheese, its tangy flavor making her stomach growl in approval. Effie smirked at the sound.

"Are you certain you aren't gifted with Spirit, Effie? It seems like you are a bit of a mind reader," Helena joked before taking another small bite.

Effie shook her head, blonde curls dancing as she did. "No, Kiri, simply observant. I am ungifted, but I grew up listening to my gran tell me stories about the Masters of Prophecy."

The girl's words unlocked a memory in Helena's mind. She looked up at Timmins, her brows furrowing as she recalled his story about her prophecy. "Timmins, that night around the campfire you said that the prophesied one would be born to an ungifted woman and would be marked with the sign of the Mother—"

"That's not the way my gran told it," Effie interjected, Helena's attention making her more confident than usual.

"What do you mean?" Timmins asked looking sharply at the maid. Helena could see that he did not appreciate being told by a mere slip of a girl that he had gotten his facts wrong.

Effie's eyes rounded as she turned toward the Advisor. "I didn't mean…"

Timmins waved her off. "What did your gran say?" His question was more demand than inquiry.

"Well… Gran always said that there was much the Chosen had forgotten about the Mother and her Mate and that… that the prophecy regarding the Mother of Shadows was a warning," the girl finished tentatively.

All four men were looking at her unblinkingly, Effie's shoulders rolling in as she tried to make herself smaller under the joint scrutiny. She turned beseeching blue eyes to Helena, looking ready to bolt.

Helena's face was filled with understanding as she encouraged in a soft voice, "Please continue, Effie."

Swallowing audibly, the girl tried to muster her courage before beginning again. "Well, the prophecy *was* about two queens marked by the Mother, but it never referred to a physical marking. They would be twins of her gift, but not of her power. The first of them would be known as the Corruptor, the one who would be filled with resentment at what the Mother did not give her. She would corrupt her gift to gain greater ability. The second would be known as the Vessel, the one blessed to be a true recipient of the Mother's power. Upon learning of the Vessel, the Corruptor would seek to destroy her, seeing her as the ultimate sign of the Mother's rejection. With each act, her corruption would pull her further away from the Mother's gift, meaning that she will never be able to truly comprehend the full price of her actions."

Effie licked her lips, her quavering voice gaining strength as she continued, "The Vessel, responding to the threat, would stop at nothing to protect those she safeguarded. But her power would be raw, still untested, and if left unbound it would be her and the Chosen's undoing. The Mother's gift always comes with a price and that price demands balance; just as the Mother had her Mate so too would the Vessel. He would carry the other half of her soul, holding a part of her power within himself as it would be too much for her to contain on her own. If for any reason, the bond never fully matured between the Vessel and her Mate, the Vessel would undergo the Fracturing, so called because her mind would shatter and she would be lost to the madness of her magic. Once Fractured she would unleash the full extent of the Mother's power on the Chosen without knowledge or understanding of what she did. She would become a Mother of Shadows, as much a slave to her magic as all those that served her."

There was no sound in the library as the girl finished her retelling, save Helena's shallow gasps of breath. Out of everything she had just heard, the reason for the Corruptor's betrayal stood out in sharp relief; she hadn't found her Mate. Sensing Helena's panic before the suitors had declared themselves, Timmins had assured her that a Mate had always been found.

Had he lied?

She turned her bewildered aqua eyes to Timmins who appeared to shrink under the unasked question. Embarrassment colored his cheeks and he sheepishly shrugged his shoulders. He knew what had caught her attention and felt guilty for having been found out. Helena scowled at the realization.

What other little white lies had he fed her in the name of keeping her calm?

Joquil spoke before she could give voice to the accusation. "But we checked; when Helena was born she had the Mother's star on the base of her skull…" Joquil trailed off.

Timmins tore his eyes from her and picked up the question where Joquil left off. "If the prophecy does not refer to a physical marking, then how are we to know who it refers to?"

"By the bonding of the Vessel to her Mate," Effie said, seeming surprised that they did not know this. "While Chosen can find their mates, such a bond is nowhere near as strong as that of a Kiri and her Mate, and even that connection pales in comparison to the bond that the Vessel will forge with her Mate. They will know true fusion, their powers feeding and growing with one another until they achieve a total binding, their souls forever entwined and strengthened by the other. Neither will die so long as the other still breathes. They will take their final breaths together, returning to the Mother as one. That is, of course, if they complete the binding. If the bond is rejected, or simply does not achieve its completion, both will be at the mercy of the Fracturing."

The words of the explanation crashed into Helena as their true meaning crystalized and began to shriek within her mind.

"The Trial of the Kiri," she whispered, blanching.

If what the girl said was true, her and Von's separation was more serious than any of them realized.

"If what you say is true," Timmins' question mirroring Helena's thoughts, "why is there no mention of this in any of the histories that have been passed down from Circle to Circle?"

Effie shrugged. "I was simply telling you the story that my gran told me when I was young. She always said that no one knew what the prophecy really meant, or when it would come into being. So long as a Damaskiri never allowed herself to be fully corrupted, there would never be a reason for the Vessel to rise. Everything would be contingent upon that final choice."

"So what of the Corruptor, how are we to know who the prophecy speaks of without the marks to rely on?" Darrin interjected.

Effie raised a brow and pressed her lips together, as though trying to hide a smile, before stating, "I am not sure, but I suppose it would be obvious, given the prophecy's warning of her betrayal."

Darrin scowled at her logic and turned away from the group while the men shared disturbed glances. Eventually, Kragen's deep voice asked, "Is your gran still here, child?"

Effie shook her head. "No, sir. Gran left a few years ago to live with her friends in the Baelian Forest."

Kragen brows rose in surprise. "She went to Bael? Do the tribes still live amongst the jungle beasts there?"

"I do not know, sir. I've never been. She did leave me instructions on how to reach her, if I ever had need to. Should I..." she looked around before finishing her question, "Should I try to reach her?"

"I think it would be very wise for us to speak with this gran of yours, and perhaps with those friends of hers as well, especially if they are who I am starting to believe they might be," Joquil answered.

"And what of Micha?" Darrin asked, facing the group again.

"Send for him," Kragen said. "He could still be useful in determining where his sister is hiding. In the meantime, Effie, you will write to your gran and see if we might be able to visit her."

Effie nodded moving to do so at once. Before she reached the door, she stopped, pausing in front of Helena. "I'm sorry, Kiri. I did not know my words would upset you so."

Helena reached out a hand and placed it gently on the girl's arm. "There's no reason to apologize, Effie. You might have very well given us a piece of the puzzle we so desperately needed."

Smiling with relief, she fled from the room. Helena looked up at her Circle after the door closed.

"This changes everything," Joquil declared.

"This changes nothing," Helena countered.

"How can you possibly say that?" Darrin challenged, his green eyes narrowing.

She lifted a hand to silence him. "Our mission has not changed. Finding Von is still our priority. It is perhaps even more crucial now than before because if her story is true... well, you heard her. If we are not able to complete our binding, it would be the end of us all."

The men were grim as they stared at her. Closing her eyes, she begged, *Please, dear Mother, please let me find him in time.*

I$_T$ WAS LATE when Effie opened the door to Helena's room. She noted the hearth and the fire that had turned to smoldering embers with a flicker of concern. Using that as an excuse, she stepped inside, turning to close the heavy door with a soft click. That complete, she let herself take a few more tentative steps, scanning the dim room as she did. Still, she did not see Helena.

Effie had just opened her mouth to call out her name when she noticed the figure half hidden behind the heavy curtains. Helena was staring out the window, the moon illuminating her with its blue glow, her eyes unblinking as they stared out into the night.

"Is everything all right, Kiri?" Effie asked in a whisper-soft voice.

Helena turned her head slowly, eyes blinking owlishly as she tried to place the girl's face. It took a moment for clarity to arrive.

She smiled sheepishly, her eyes sad as she asked, "Have you ever had a night where you had to stay awake to greet the dawn?" She turned her face back toward the sky as she continued, "A night where you could no longer be certain about the promise of a rising sun?" Helena sighed before adding even more quietly, "A night that felt so long and you felt so helpless, that you actually needed the safety of the sunlight, just to help you believe that all was not lost?"

Despite the grief etched in every word, her voice was hollow, as though she was consciously trying to keep her emotions at bay.

The maid's lips turned down in an empathetic frown as she processed the questions. "I don't know if I have ever quite felt that hopeless, Kiri, but I've never lost someone who I cared about in the way that you have. For what it's worth, I'm sure that wherever he is, Von's out there looking up at the sky wishing he was here with you too."

Helena's answering smile was wistful.

"Are you sure there isn't anything I can get you?" the girl asked, desperate to wipe the despondency out of those aqua eyes. She had only known the Kiri a short time, but it was impossible not to feel her own heart breaking, just a little, as she watched her fight to hold onto her hope as another day passed without word of her Mate.

Helena shook her head. "No, thank you. I'm just going to stay here and stargaze awhile longer. It was sweet of you to come up and check on me, Effie."

The girl nodded, still frowning as she walked out of the dim room.

HELENA FELT a little of the tension ebb when she heard the door click shut. The mask she had been wearing these last couple of days was hard to maintain. She had stopped her nightly vigils by the fountain and had ensured that she made it to every meal on time. She had even made a conscious effort to get to know Von's family. Helena was trying, she really was, but the empty space in her mind where Von's voice used to be was cutting more deeply each day.

She had never felt this kind of loneliness before, not even after her mother had passed away. There had been a time when she had been little and Miriam had traveled to a neighboring village to help a new mother with the birth of her first child. Helena had been distraught, too young to understand why her mother was leaving her. It had been the first time they had ever been separated and she had been inconsolable, crying for hours after Miriam left.

Once the sun had gone down, Helena had gotten it into her head that she was going to go find her. Anderson caught her running down the dirt road just as the sun had set in the sky. After asking where she thought she was going, Anderson had sat her on his knee and solemnly pointed at the sky.

"Do you see that star, little bug?" he asked.

Helena had wiped dirt-smeared hands across her wet cheeks and nodded slowly as she continued to sniffle.

"That's the Mother's star. You can see it from wherever you are in Tigaera. Do you know what that means?"

Helena shook her head, her tears slowing as curiosity took over.

"That means that the Great Mother is watchin' over your Mama right now. So you don't need to feel lonely, little bug. So long as the Great Mother has her in her sights, your Mama ain't far at all. She'll be tuckin' you in right and proper again soon, but for now, you'll keep old Anderson company until she gets home. Is that okay with you?" he asked in that same grave tone, peering into her tear-stained face with his kind green eyes.

Helena sniffed back the last of the tears. "Doesn't Darrin take care of you, Papa Anderson?"

Anderson winked at her and ruffled his hand through her tangled curls. "You keep tellin' him that, little bug. You just keep on tellin' him that."

Helena covered her mouth as she giggled into her small hand.

"There now, there's my girl. I missed that pretty smile."

Helena grinned up at him, beaming with the full glory of her newly gap-toothed grin.

"When you smile at me like that, little bug, you're like my own personal ball of sunshine."

Helena threw her arms around his neck and squeezed with all the strength in her six-year-old body, tears long forgotten.

Anderson stood with her slight weight in his arms, pretending to stagger as he groaned with mock strain. "My little bug has been growing again. Pretty soon you'll be a real lady and you won't want to come hear my stories anymore."

"Don't be silly, Papa! You have the best stories," Helena assured him as he started walking toward his small cottage. "Will you tell me the one about the lost Kiri?"

"Again?" Anderson asked, feigning surprise.

"Please Papa Anderson!" she begged. "It's my favorite!"

He pretended to consider it, thick gray brows furrowing. "Well, all right, if you insist little bug. Can you help me remember how it starts?"

Helena enthusiastically began to recount the story as Anderson carried her back inside, his low voice eventually joining in with hers.

It was not lost on Helena that the story she had so loved to hear when she had been younger had ended up being about her. But as with many things looked upon with age-wizened eyes, she no longer felt the same when recalling that story. There was no flutter of delight when thinking about where the lost Kiri could be, nor about the idea of the Mother's star.

As much as she wished that the Mother was watching over Von, she knew that he wasn't out there staring up at a star in the night sky thinking of her doing the same. No, Helena was certain that wherever Von was he was definitely not looking at stars. If he was, she would be able to feel him instead of the bottomless silence that had taken up residence inside her, taken up residence in the space that had been his and his alone.

Wherever he was, if Von had been able to contact her he would have done so by now, which meant that something must be preventing him from doing so. If that was the case, Helena was going to need a not so small miracle in order to find him.

So she stood there, head pressed against the cool stone as she stared out into the night sky, praying that the Mother would grant her another day and another chance at finding some answers.

CHAPTER 4

The mist swirled around him, making it impossible to discern anything past the stretch of his arm. Sometimes he would hear voices calling him, but when he tried to chase after them, all he would find was more of the dense fog.

Von continued to wander aimlessly, searching for something that would help him escape this place. He had lost all track of time and had no recollection of how he got here.

The only thing that had been constant was the overwhelming feeling that he was forgetting something. It was as though he had lost something and desperately needed to find it, but he didn't know what that something was and the harder he tried to recall what it was, the more confused he became. His thoughts and memories were slipping away like grains of sand slipping through his fingers. All he knew was the swirling fog.

"Von!" a childlike voice called from somewhere within the mist.

He spun, gray eyes scanning the horizon for the source of the voice.

"Come catch me!" the voice taunted, seeming to come from further away.

Von took a few tentative steps forward, startled when the mist parted to reveal a grassy knoll that hinted at familiarity. He blinked a few times, his eyes squinting against the harsh light of the sun which shone down from a cloudless blue sky.

"Betcha can't reach me before I get to the stables!" the small boy called to him over his shoulder as he ran down the hill toward a sprawling manor home. He had a mop of dark hair that was blown back as his arms and legs pumped furiously.

He was not aware of making a conscious decision to chase after the boy before he was already running; his legs felt much shorter than they had only moments before. Von looked down, surprise flaring brightly before fading almost immediately. Gone were legs that were thickly corded with muscle and his hands were no longer calloused or battle-scarred. He was no longer a man in a man's body, but a boy merely on the cusp of manhood.

There was no time to wonder at the change, the urgency to catch the boy spurred him into action. Even stunted, Von's legs made easy work of the distance between them, and he was upon the boy within a few heartbeats. The stormy eyes grew wide when they noted how close he had gotten. The boy's tongue darted out, his eyes narrowed in concentration as he pushed with all he had to try to clear the remaining distance between himself and the wooden stables only a few lengths away.

Despite the unfamiliar pang in his chest at the sight of the boy, Von felt no mercy and easily overcame him, hand slapping against the wood in clear victory. The boy skidded to a stop a hairsbreadth before he would have crashed into the side of the stables. He was scowling in disappointment, face flushed from the exertion.

Now that they were closer, Von could study the boy more carefully. He was no more than seven and small with dark hair that was thick with waves. His blue-gray eyes were so large that they seemed to take up the entirety of his face and were currently staring up at him with something akin to worship shining in their depths. Before Von had a chance to say anything, the boy's lips twisted back in a disappointed grimace, "I almost had you that time!"

His hand moved on its own accord, ruffling the mop of hair as an unfamiliar voice said, "You'll catch me one day, Squirt."

Von took a mental pause, trying to catalogue the differences in his voice. It was not so much unfamiliar as long forgotten. It was still his voice, but lacking the deep inflection and growl that had developed over the years. It was warm, unburdened, and still ringing with the innocence of one more boy than man.

His hand started to shake, and a sense of foreboding shot through him as the core part of himself, the part that was still Von, the man, realized what he was seeing.

"Nial," he said in a strangled voice.

The boy looked up at him from the side of his eye, tongue slipping back out as though weighing his next words.

"Nial!" he shouted, wrapping the boy in a bone-crushing hug.

"Get off me," his brother grunted, trying, unsuccessfully, to push away from his brother's uncommon display of affection, even though it secretly made him warm with happiness to receive the attention.

"Let's go look at the new horse father brought home!" Nial declared, already making a move in that direction.

Von's hand lurched out and caught the back of his brother's shirt, pulling him up short. "No!"

Dark brows lowered over bright eyes. "Stop treating me like a baby. I can ride just as well as you can!"

Terror raced through Von at the words. His own lips had mouthed them as his brother spoke. He had witnessed this scene before; he had not only witnessed it, he had lived through and barely survived it. Perhaps this was his chance to do it over, to change the outcome and save his brother from a lifetime of agony.

Nial struggled against Von's hold, finally slipping from the tight grip by wriggling his way out of the rough-spun shirt.

"Nial!" Von shouted as the boy hurried away from him and rounded the corner into the stables.

The stable boys were nowhere to be found, likely off having a quick lunch before returning to their afternoon chores.

Despite his speed, Von did not make it into the stables in time. His brother had already thrown himself atop the black stallion, too excited to notice the eyes that swirled with madness at his unwelcome presence.

"Nial," Von said, his voice trembling with fear despite trying to speak calmly. "Get down from there. If you want to ride, we'll get the pony ready for you."

His brother's cheeks flushed with wounded pride. "I'm too big for the pony! 'Sides I'm an excellent rider, you told me so yourself!"

"Yes, Squirt, you are an excellent rider, but that horse has no love for any rider. He's not ready for *you*." Von's voice broke on the last word, cracking with his anxiety as he tried to coax his brother from the horse.

"He lets you ride him," the voice was small, the words petulant.

Von nodded slowly, daring to step closer to the horse as he said, "Yes, but just barely. The beast fought me every step of the way. Let's get you down from there and I will let you ride Kismet."

Kismet was Von's new wolf and he had refused, until now, to let his brother get anywhere near him.

He could see the debate warring in his brother's eyes but knew he had lost when the small shoulders straightened with determination. "I can do this, Von. You just watch," and with that, the boy kicked into the stallion's sides.

The horse reared, snorting angrily before kicking open the fence in front of him and tearing off out of the stables.

Von saw his brother's eyes widen in panic; his small mouth opened on a soundless scream as he held on for all he was worth. Von's fingers scrambled clumsily as they tried to grasp the reigns, but it was too late. The stallion was enraged and using his anger to fuel his speed.

Before he could mount and chase after his brother, he heard the screams.

Running at full speed, his heart pounding somewhere in the vicinity of his throat, Von rounded the corner just in time to watch his brother go flying from the back of the horse. He looked like a ragdoll, his limbs flailing bonelessly until he crumpled into a heap dangerously close to the stallion's hooves.

Nial cried out, one of his arms and both of his legs bent at awkward angles.

Von swallowed back his fear, charging forward to try to get to his brother before the horse noticed him. He felt like he was running against water, each step harder and slower than the last. He knew what was going to happen and he was desperate to try to stop it from happening again.

He opened his mouth to shout his brother's name as the stallion reared again. Nial's eyes were showing white as they rounded with fear. He was motionless as a stain began to grow in his tan trousers.

A tear rolled down his young face, shame and fear colliding as the seconds slowed to hours. An entire lifetime passed in those handful of seconds. Nial's frightened eyes found his brother's, the panic tearing into him like a brand as he reached his one good arm out helplessly.

He wouldn't reach him in time. He would fail.

The stallion's hooves came down, and with a sickening crack and a scream, his brother fell back to the ground, unconscious. Von reached his side only moments later, the stallion running toward the forest and away from the small human that had set him off.

The sight of blood and bone jutting out from his brother's twisted limbs had Von bending over and retching. His whole body cramping as his stomach emptied again and again. As he knelt there beside his brother's broken body, the mist began to swirl and overtake him.

It was then he knew with certainty where he had been trapped all this time. The Mother was finally punishing him for his sins.

He was in hell.

CHAPTER 5

Helena wiped the sweat from her brow, appreciating the cool breeze that licked at her hot skin.

Kragen had joined her training this morning and Ronan pulled no punches as he set them against one another. Serena had kept her promise and was working with Nial a short distance away. Ronan spent the better part of the morning throwing the two confused glances when he thought no one was looking. Helena didn't blame him; she was just as busy trying to decipher the shy smiles on their faces. Her attention moved back to Nial, wondering how he was still standing when her own muscles were limp with fatigue.

She was hoping no one noticed that the tree she was leaning against was all that was keeping her upright; the last thing she wanted was for the men to cluck at her like oversized mother hens. Luckily, the others were too busy trying to pretend they weren't staring at each other to give her any notice. It was nice, not being the center of attention for once. Helena was more than happy to use her rediscovered invisibility to watch the rest of them.

Nial was red-faced and panting as he struggled through the stretches meant to build the strength in his legs.

Perhaps it is only his desire to impress his trainer that had him pushing himself so hard, she mused.

He caught her gaze and lifted a questioning brow.

So much for being invisible, she thought with a chagrined shrug.

He shook his head at her, his lips quirking with his own smile as he refocused on the woman barking orders at him. He blew Serena a kiss and said something that had her blushing but was far too soft for Helena to hear from her spot beneath the tree.

An unexpected ring of steel met her ears and had her shifting her own focus back to the others.

Twisting slightly, she watched Ronan and Kragen attack each other, or at least it appeared to be an attack, although she was still fairly certain they were only practicing. Kragen and Ronan were both dual wielding axes, the weapons spinning and flying through the air as they reinforced the moves with their magic. Both were exceptional warriors, but Ronan was hacking away at Kragen like a man possessed. The latter was clearly on the defensive as he ducked away from the deadly metal.

Helena tried to bite back an amused smile as she realized Ronan's performance was for the benefit of the lithe blonde across the clearing. Her friend had obviously grown tired of being ignored by his lover.

The men had removed their shirts and sweat was already dripping down their bare chests. The purely female part of her appreciated the swell and flex of their impressive muscles, but the tired trainee was only interested in how much longer it would be before they were done showing off and she would be dismissed.

She plucked at the shirt sticking to her skin, wishing it wouldn't have been inappropriate for her to remove it as well. Helena snorted as she imagined the reaction that move would get her, especially if her Mate had been there to witness it. She could almost hear his voice purring down the bond, *"If you're in such a hurry to get naked for me, Mate, I don't mind an audience."* Helena fanned at her face, hot now for a different reason.

Serena and Nial joined her, jolting her out of her wistful daydream. Before she could say anything, Serena let out a low whistle. "The only thing that gets me hotter than watching a man work his weapon, is watching a sweaty, half-naked one."

The frank sexual appraisal in her voice had Nial's shoulders stiffening and his usual easygoing smile vanishing. Sensing his discomfort at her words, Serena's eyes scanned his face before clouding over. Frowning, she looked away and remained silent.

"There is something impressive about watching someone who is a master of their craft," Helena added neutrally.

Nial relaxed at her words, but refused to meet her gaze, focusing instead on the warriors in front of him.

Helena let out a little huff, annoyed that male egos were such fragile things, even as she felt a flicker of sympathy for his obvious desire to prove to Serena that he was as much of a man as the others.

"Kiri!" Joquil's voice rang out as he entered their practice area.

"Over here, Joquil!" she called, pushing off of the tree and automatically bracing herself for bad news. He had never sought her out during one of her practice sessions before. She could only imagine that his doing so now was an indication of something urgent.

"Micha has arrived, my lady." Joquil's face and voice remained impassive, but Helena heard a low grunt as the two men behind her ceased their sparring.

"It would appear that practice is over for today," Serena commented lightly.

Helena nodded distractedly, her anxiety at what the meeting would reveal causing shivers to race down her neck and arms. In response, the wind whipped through the trees causing leaves to rain down upon them.

Joquil's expression did not change as he brushed a few leaves from his head and shoulders. Helena couldn't help but appreciate that he was as unflappable as ever, his steadfastness doing much to ease her nerves.

"Where would you like to meet him, Kiri?" Joquil asked patiently.

Helena thought for a moment, before declaring, "Have him meet me by the fountain in an hour. I will wash up and change." There were grumbling protests behind her, but Helena ignored them. "Will you have Effie set up a small picnic for us? Micha was my friend before all of this occurred. I would like to maintain that pretense, if it even is a pretense, to prevent us from giving away our hand sooner than strictly necessary."

Joquil nodded, approval warm in his amber eyes as he said, "It shall be as you say." With that, he turned and walked unhurriedly back the way he came.

Helena sighed as Micha's laughing green eyes swam into her mind. For as much as she wanted answers, there was a part of her that was greatly dreading this encounter. She didn't want her memories of him tainted by finding out he was involved in his sister's scheme.

Serena rubbed her back soothingly before smacking her soundly on her butt. "Move it, Kiri."

Helena stuck out her tongue, chuckling as she made her way back into the manor. Kragen fell into step beside her, his silent strength bolstering her courage. No matter what the meeting revealed, she would not be facing it alone.

On impulse, she wrapped her arms around his sweaty torso and squeezed. Shock at the unexpected embrace had him standing still until he recovered and lifted her into his own bone-crushing hug. He pressed a sloppy kiss to her forehead, his laughter vibrating in his chest when she squealed and started wiping the slobber off on his equally sweaty shoulder.

"Unhand me you brute!" she crowed, her laughter ringing down the halls.

Curious faces peered around corners and stuck out of doorways to see what had the usually reserved Kiri making such a racket.

At the end of the hallway, Margo and Effie stood, watching the scene unfolding before them. Margo had her hand pressed against her lips, eyes shining brightly with her mirth. Effie's eyes were wide and her mouth had fallen open in shock as she watched the tattooed warrior start to tickle her. Evidently, they were not expecting to see such a playful side from their new ruler and her Sword. Especially not after she had done little more than mope about their home the last few weeks. It was clear they did not know how to react to the sight.

"Traitors!" she cried at them, realizing her error when the color drained from their faces. These were the people that had been declared traitors and suffered for centuries because of it. Thinking quickly to try to recover the jovial atmosphere she shouted, breathless with her laughter, "If you won't punish Sir Sweats-a-Lot, I guess I will!"

The crowd had grown in size, although Kragen had not stopped or slowed as he walked down the corridors leading to her rooms. She could feel their collective intake of breath as they waited to see what she would do.

She called her magic forth, feeling it ripple in its excitement to be set free. Around her she could feel her curls waving in the air, lifted in a wind only they could feel. Her skin was pulsing with the flood of her magic rushing to the surface, and she could see she was starting to emit a soft glow as it grew in power.

Deciding to pay him back in kind, she planted her hands on the sides of his ribs, the only place her hands could really reach given the way his arms were banded about her. Calling Fire, Air and Water, she shot her magic into the surface of his skin.

He froze, eyes snapping wide in surprise as her magic took over. He let her go with a yelp, squirming while his hands tried to slap away the playful balls of electricity that were moving across his body.

All around them gasps of delight rang out.

She was using tiny sparks of lightning to tickle him. There were no painful shocks, only the warm buzz of energy causing his muscles to spasm as he tried to twist away from their relentless assault.

"You are a cruel mistress," he tried to pout while laughing.

Taking pity on him, she pulled her magic back. At least, she tried to. Some of the magic did flow back into her, while other sparks shot out landing in the crowd.

Suddenly the gasps of delight were turning into shocked chuckles. Some were wiping tears of laughter from their eyes as others wriggled and twisted under the dance of her magic. It had no mercy as it sought its own form of revenge, moving from victim to helpless victim, tickling and tormenting, until one by one the sparkling balls of light reunited with her.

Whispers broke out as they stared at her in her un-dampened form, her magic, simmering just below the surface, still making her glow.

Her eyes were shining iridescent pools as she spoke in a voice that echoed in harmony with itself. "Serves you right for standing there laughing at me."

They could tell by her smile that she was not offended. Any that had not already fallen in love with her because of her devotion to Von and his people, or how she had healed Nial, did so then and there.

HELENA WAS STILL SNICKERING when she made her way back to the fountain, and to Micha. Effie could barely suppress her reaction to the display of Helena's magic and had been caught staring at her in awe three times before Helena finally dismissed the girl so that she could finish dressing in peace. She could hear the whispers and giggles as she passed people in the halls, a small smile tugging at her lips in response.

It had been a good morning. Unexpected, but much needed. There was a lightness within her that left her feeling almost buoyant after so many nights of being weighted down with a growing sense of helplessness.

It felt good to laugh, to let go of her fear just long enough to relax with her friends. She knew it would be fleeting. The feeling would likely dissipate completely by the time she finished with Micha, but it was even more precious and necessary because of that. No matter what happened, she could not afford to let go of her ability to laugh.

Laughter was a symptom of hope. Without the presence of one, there was generally a lack of the other. Losing it would mean that Gillian had won, and she could not bear to give her that kind of power. Not with so much at stake.

With renewed purpose, Helena entered the small garden. Micha was standing with his back to the entrance, his hands clasped behind his back. She watched his fingers fidget, the only indication of his nerves.

"Mother's blessings to you, Micha," she said softly.

He spun, a smile blooming across his face in greeting. He threw open his arms already stepping toward her.

If he's an actor, he's a very good one, a warning voice murmured in her mind. Helena's smile felt forced as she walked into his embrace.

He pulled her close and she caught a whiff of the spicy cinnamon scent she had grown to associate with him. The familiarity had her muscles relaxing enough to return his hug.

Micha stepped back, his hands warm against the sides of her arms. "I must say, I was shocked when I received your summons, but it will be nice to see my sister again. Where is she by the way?" he asked, his smile still firmly in place as his eyes looked past her in search of his twin.

Helena felt her eyes narrow in suspicion but kept her voice even as she said, "She's out at the moment, so I'm afraid she won't be joining us for lunch today. You aren't too disappointed that you're stuck with just me for company, are you?"

Micha's laugh was warm. "Not even remotely, Kiri. Although, I find it hard to believe any in your Circle, especially your Mate, would willingly let you go anywhere by yourself."

Helena's answering laugh was genuine, his observation was not far off the mark, and she knew that Darrin, Kragen, Ronan and Serena were all tucked just out of sight. The only reason Timmins and Joquil had not joined in was because they were busy pouring over the tomes that had arrived early that morning from the Palace archives. They were searching for anything that would corroborate Effie's retelling of the prophecy.

She pretended to pout, laughter still evident in her voice as she said, "I'm not completely helpless, thank you very much."

Micha let go of her arms completely and stepped back. "I did not mean to imply that you were. I still fondly remember the way you handled the crowd during your welcoming ceremony."

Helena's smile grew as she remembered her instinctive reaction to defend Von only moments after meeting him. "Yes," she said wryly, "I suppose that was fairly memorable."

Micha laughed at her. "Just a bit."

Helena motioned for Micha to take a seat at the table Effie had set up for them. "Would you like to eat?"

Micha rubbed his flat stomach as he gave her a wide grin. "You have no idea how much I'm looking forward to a real meal. As exciting as travel is, there's little you can do to make camp food edible."

Helena's smile turned sympathetic. "You aren't wrong, my friend."

They each took a spot at the small wrought-iron table. There were two plates, a pitcher of deep red juice and two crystal goblets waiting for them. Her stomach twisted in protest, nerves making it hard to appreciate the food on her plate.

"Kiri—" Micha started.

"Helena, please," she corrected automatically, cutting off whatever he was about to ask.

He smiled up at her, before turning his attention back to his plate. "Helena, as much as I love a good holiday, and as flattered as I am that you summoned me, not to mention that you are seeing fit to personally entertain me, I can't pretend to understand why it is you felt the need to bring me here."

Helena waited for him to take a bite before responding, "To be frank, Micha, it concerns your sister."

He dropped his fork, his face draining of color as he worked to swallow his mouthful. "Gillian? What's wrong with her?" he finally asked in a voice full of concern.

Helena's lips pursed as she tried to work through her phrasing. Truth be told, she was completely winging it. "It's not so much that something is wrong *with* her..." she trailed off. *Although being a traitorous, backstabbing bitch is certainly an unbecoming quality in a friend,* she silently seethed.

"Helena," her name was a plea for information.

Helena filled her glass with the juice, taking a quick sip before she tried again. "Gillian has betrayed us," she said simply.

"Betrayed you?" he gaped, his voice a hoarse croak. The tips of his cheeks and ears turned a bright shade of pink. "Now see here —"

"No, you see here!" she snapped, her hand clenched around the goblet causing it to crack as her nails lengthened into sharp black claws. Bright red drops seeped through the fissures in the crystal looking like drops of blood as they splattered on the table.

Micha blanched at the sight.

"Your *sister*," she hissed, "has abducted my Mate."

Micha's lips opened and closed as he tried, and failed, to respond. He looked like a gaping fish, and Helena found herself holding back inappropriate laughter at the thought.

"And you brought me here as a hostage? To try to get her to trade him for me?"

Helena blinked in surprise. Truly the thought hadn't even crossed her mind but hearing him suggest it now she definitely saw the appeal.

"No," she said after a few heartbeats.

Micha wiped at the sweat on his brow, the food sitting forgotten before them.

"Then—then you mean to kill me?" he asked, his voice now a high-pitched whine.

Helena's brows came together as she stared at him in shock.

"Kill you?" she sputtered, equal parts offended and shocked. "Who in the Mother's name do you think I am, Micha? Did you *do* something requiring your execution?" Her words had taken on a feral quality, her voice dangerously soft.

His eyes flicked down to the sharp claws that were raking across the top of the table before he stammered, "N-n-no, Kiri."

"Then what reason could I possibly have to kill you?" she asked as she tilted her head inquisitively to the side. "Perhaps you had better stop giving me ideas, Micha, and let me explain."

He nodded mutely, his cheeks and ears the only color remaining on his terrified face.

"I want to know where she's taken him. You are the closest person to her. Tell me, Micha, why would your sister be so foolish as to declare war on me in this way? What could possibly motivate such idiotic behavior? She has to know I will find her, and when I do…" she trailed off, letting his imagination fill in the blanks.

She didn't think it possible, but he became even paler. She could see his pulse flicker beneath the thin skin of his neck, his eyes fluttering as though he was fighting to remain conscious.

He swallowed and licked his lips. "I don't know, Kiri, I swear! I cannot believe she would come up with such a scheme on her own."

"What would cause her to do so?"

He shook his head. "I—I'm not sure."

Helena slumped back in her chair, the claws retracting back beneath her skin. His terror was too genuine to be an act. He had no idea of his sister's schemes or her whereabouts.

"Can you not hazard any guess where she might be hiding?" she finally asked, her voice returning to its normal tone.

Sensing the change in her, Micha relaxed a bit in his seat.

She could see the sweat stains under his arms and felt herself frowning in sympathy. She hadn't intended to get quite so carried away, although it had felt damned good giving into her anger now that it had a target. If only momentarily and not the right one.

"If I had to guess, Kiri. I would say perhaps she has returned to our mother's land. She was born in the mountains of Vyruul. It's fairly isolated, almost impossible to find unless you have been there before. She would feel safe there, if she was trying to hide."

Excitement prickled beneath her skin. Finally, a direction.

"You will take us there." It was not a question.

Micha nodded. "Yes, you have to believe me, Kiri. I want to help. I want to find her, whatever caused her to do this, it cannot be good. She needs me, I am certain of it."

"I cannot promise you any leniency when it comes to her, Micha. Do not ask me to." The words were fierce.

He swallowed again. "I know, Kiri. But please, will you at least let me talk to her when we find her? Before you..." He struggled to continue his sentence.

"Condemn her?" Helena offered ruthlessly.

Micha blinked and nodded, fully curling into himself as the realization that his sister was a dead woman sank in.

"I am not without mercy, Micha," she said taking pity on him. "But she took what's mine. She pretended to be my friend while plotting against me and leading an army of abominations to our camp. She was the cause of countless, meaningless deaths. *Children's* deaths, Micha. She cannot be allowed to go unpunished, no matter the reason for her actions."

His green eyes widened with horror at the recounting of his sister's crimes. It was bad enough that she had taken Von, but he had no idea that her treachery had run so deep. When he spoke again his voice was deep with conviction.

"I will help you find her, Helena. And when we do, I will not interfere when you pronounce her sentence. She has earned her punishment; I only ask to speak with her before any sentence is carried out."

Helena nodded; it was a small enough request, and not one she felt inclined to deny him.

Her Circle peeled away from the shadows in which they were hiding. It was Darrin who spoke first. "When do we leave, Kiri?"

Helena shook her head. "We don't, at least, not right away. We are not prepared for what we might find when we get there. You"—she turned to Ronan—"will work with him"—she gestured toward Micha who started at the appearance of her men. "Come up with our strategy for when we arrive, as well as various contingency plans. We will not underestimate her again."

Ronan nodded.

She turned her attention back toward Kragen and Darrin. "You two will work with Effie. We should have a response from her gran soon. We will go to Bael as planned and meet with the Masters of Prophecy. I am sure there is much they will be able to tell us that could help with our plans for Vyruul."

Again the men only nodded. Her eyes found Serena's smiling face. Helena could feel the approval radiating from her in waves.

"Now, if you all will excuse me," Helena stood and let out the low whistle that would summon her Talyrian. She had been itching to get away from the manor for a while now. She could not imagine a better time to go for a ride.

Starshine was there within moments, as if she had already

anticipated her mistress's need of her. She flapped her majestic gray wings as she landed, the earth trembling slightly as her massive paws met the ground.

Helena's hands were already buried in the velvety white fur at her neck as she leaned in to whisper in the beast's ear, "Take me away from here, Starshine. I want to chase the stars with you for a while."

The Talyrian let out a soft roar of approval, small wisps of smoke flaring from her nostrils as she bent low enough for Helena to mount her.

Helena eyed her friends with amusement. Her Circle had grown accustomed to the sight of Starshine and were not as terrified of her as they had once been. Starshine was still fiercely possessive of her though, and the Talyrian did not hesitate to stake her claim by shooting jets of flame at whoever dared approach Helena without her permission. Von was really the only person that Starshine seemed to tolerate without question, likely because Helena had declared him as her Mate, a position the Talyrian understood.

Micha, on the other hand, had never seen a Talyrian and could not stop blinking as he stared at the massive white feline and her leathery gray wings tipped with deadly talons. He looked like he was about to piss himself, and Helena felt a small flicker of pity at all that she had made him endure in such a short period of time.

With a small wave, she pressed her legs into the Talyrian's sides and was almost immediately flung into the air. Helena wrapped her arms more tightly around Starshine's neck as they soared toward the sparkling blue of the sea. Her laughter bubbled up as the feeling of joy that always seemed to accompany flying overtook her. For the second time that day she felt real stirrings of hope.

I will find you, my love. Wait for me; I am coming. She shot the words down the yawning emptiness of their bond, knowing in her heart that even if he could not hear the words, a part of him would know she had not given up her search.

CHAPTER 6

Gillian stood outside the door, her heart continuing to race within the confines of her chest. It was not that she dreaded what she would find when she entered. At least, not in the sense that she would be surrounded by human filth or have to observe evidence of sadistic torture as one would in most dungeons.

In fact, dungeon was a rather misleading term. Von was being kept in a cell that was decorated as lavishly as any of the guest suites on the upper floors. The only distinctions being that he was tied to the bed and there was only one spelled entrance into the room, the door behind which Gillian currently cowered.

No, bearing witness to the cruelties of being a prisoner was not what held her steps. As it was, she rather enjoyed blood play under the right circumstances. What had her heart fluttering like a captive bird was the possibility that he would be awake, especially if he remembered how she had manipulated both him and his Mate. Conscious and coherent were two words she did not want to have to use when describing her prisoner.

She knew she was no match for Von's strength or temper once he woke. Even had she been able to shift into a form that would give her a chance to overpower him, his magic still vastly surpassed her own. And that was assuming she was at her full power... which she was not.

Every new shape pushed at the limitations of her magic and she wasn't sure how many more she could add to her repertoire. Humans were by far the biggest drain on her magic. Triply so if it was a specific person she was shifting into. There were just too many minutiae to replicate if she didn't want to be exposed as an imposter.

She had only ever attempted a human shift a handful of times prior to Von's capture, hating the sense of hangover that the heavy use of magic caused once she shifted back. Here she was weeks later, and she was still feeling sluggish after her latest attempt.

Since she could not rely on her magic to protect her, her only hope was that she would be there when the first vestiges of the drug wore off. That would be the only way she and her mother would have enough time to act. They would have to work quickly in those initial moments before he regained his full abilities if they wished to retain the upper hand.

Rowena had not seen fit to enlighten Gillian regarding her grand plans for Von, although Gillian anticipated he was to be her finest conquest yet. She did not envy him the title. Being the focus of Rowena's attention was daunting, to say the least. Gillian would be happy enough if she could just fade into the ether of her mother's mind never to be thought of again. Unfortunately, she knew the likelihood of that was less than slim. Her mother enjoyed her playthings too much to give one up so easily.

Helping her mother had seemed simple enough when she was first approached with the plan. Granted, she had been overcome with shock at the time, having just learned that her mother was still alive after weeks of mourning her death. There were no words that could adequately depict the degree of stupefaction she had felt when her mother had first spoken to her through the mirror.

One night just as she had blown out the last of the candles to go to sleep, she heard an icy voice whispering her name. Gillian had thought she was imagining things until she saw the figure cloaked in thick fog take shape in her mirror. When Rowena had told her what she needed to do in order to keep herself and her brother alive, she had not hesitated to acquiesce. Frankly, she hadn't been capable of doing more than nod her head in mute agreement let alone consider the option of refusal.

It was all theoretical at first. She would befriend the new Damaskiri until her trial had been completed and her Circle finalized. Then she would need to separate the young Queen from her Mate and bring him to her mother in Vyruul. *Easy.*

Gillian knew she was clever enough to outwit any opponent, but those kinds of tricks only worked so long as your prey did not expect you to strike. Once they were alerted to the threat, they would be much harder to trap.

She had never stopped to consider what would happen *after,* let alone what it would feel like to have to look her prey in the eye each day as she wove her snare more tightly.

Helena had been a definite complication. Under other circumstances, Gillian was certain they would have been friends. There had been moments when she forgot what she was supposed to be doing and simply enjoyed spending time with the new Kiri. One visit from her mother had sorted her out quickly enough. The image of what she intended to do to Micha, and not only do but make Gillian participate in, had her running for a basket to empty her stomach. She could not afford friends, not with her twin's life on the line. Instead, she had stopped thinking of Helena as a person and started thinking of her as a means to an end.

It had been much easier after that. Each step of her mother's plan moved forward flawlessly. Although, witnessing the results of the Shadows' attacks had been difficult. She had not anticipated the sheer number of deaths she would be responsible for simply by leading the Shadows to Helena.

Her stomach clenched in protest as she thought about the rows upon rows of bodies they had discovered in the days leading up to her final betrayal.

Her mother's army was vast. She hadn't even bothered to send her strongest generals to test the strength of the Kiri's party knowing her victory was already assured without their participation. She had been a cat playing with a mouse: teasing and distracting her with a paw so that she would not see the teeth until they had already snapped closed around her. Gillian could hardly bear to be around the Shadows. Their empty white eyes with the black lines snaking through them and their mindless devotion to their mistress made her shudder with revulsion each time she was near one.

Gillian blinked, coming back to the present. She could not afford to be distracted. Not now, when time was so crucial. Bracing herself, she took one last breath before laying her hand against the solid oak door.

There was a soft hum as the wood beneath her hand grew so cold it burned momentarily as the magic in the wood tested her identity. After ensuring she was allowed to proceed, it silently swung open. The lights in the corridor flickered once in response to the release of air from the cell. There was no sound, no hint as to what she would find once she stepped past the spelled boundaries of the threshold.

"Mother's tits, Gillian. You've come this far," she whispered to herself, finally gathering the courage to step forward.

Even though the room was only dimly lit, having no natural light with which to brighten the golden walls, she could see every detail of him clearly. Her eyes scanned Von's prone form, starting from the bottom of the bed.

He still radiated strength, despite being bound and in a drugged sleep. He was naked, body splayed spread-eagle; each limb tethered to a post by a length of enchanted rope. His wrists and ankles were an angry red where the cords had rubbed his skin raw in his stupor. The thick stubble covering his sharp jaw was a testament to the amount of time he had been unconscious.

She moved closer to the bed, reaching out a hand to run it along the length of his body. His skin was warm to the touch and he felt like velvet covered steel, soft but unyielding. She trailed her fingers up, lingering to appreciate the way his manhood lay heavy against his thick thigh. It was impressive even though it was as dormant as he was. The only benefit of this particular prisoner, at least in her opinion, was being able to enjoy the feast he made for her eyes.

She let her nails scrape against the muscles of his stomach and up over the tattoo that covered most of his chest and shoulder until it came to rest by his neck.

His eyes were moving furiously beneath waxy purple lids.

Still lost to the dreams then, she concluded with relief. There was no chance he would wake while still under the hold of the *Bella Morte*.

Emboldened by the discovery, she leaned forward, allowing her breasts to graze against his chest and rubbing herself against his silky heat.

"It seems as though our play time is not over just yet, lover. Are you ready to have some fun?" she rasped before biting down on the cords of muscle between his neck and shoulder.

Gillian looked up beneath thick lashes to check his face. There was no change and his body remained slack beneath her, not flinching or responding to her attack. Satisfied, she licked up the side of his neck, the musky taste of his sweat arousing her.

She eyed his thick cock and licked her lips. "I wish I could take you for a ride, handsome, but it's no fun when you can't play." With a languid sigh she lifted her head once more, pausing to brush her lips against his. As she pulled back, she bit down and pulled his bottom lip out until she drew blood.

The sight of the deep ruby liquid rolling down his jaw caused her heart to pick up speed. Gillian lapped it quickly, enjoying the coarse feel of his stubble against her tongue.

"Do you think there is power hidden in the blood?" she whispered against his mouth, her eyes closed as she savored the metallic taste of him. "My mother believes that our power is entwined with our very essence, but I have read that our blood contains some of that power as well. Shall we test that theory?"

Gillian lifted up and tilted her head to the side as she studied him. "Perhaps not," she sighed. She couldn't chance her mother finding out.

She stepped back, but not before licking at his mouth a final time. It was time to begin her vigil. She moved away from the bed and sat down in a thickly padded chair. She wasn't sure what she was watching for exactly. She had never witnessed one so far gone to the *Bella Morte*, but she was certain she would be able to discern whether he was waking or fading if any change did occur. Letting out another sigh, she settled back into the chair and braced herself for the wait.

VON WAS SURROUNDED BY MIST. Voices taunted him from its depths.

One voice, in particular, caused him to bare his teeth in feral rage. It whispered to him of blood and power; it grated against his senses with an overwhelming sense of wrongness. This was not a voice he wanted in his mind.

There was another voice, however, a gentle one that would call to him from across a great distance. Sometimes he thought he could hear its owner sobbing softly, and he would be overcome with the need to find and protect it. No matter how hard he searched, he could not find the source of the voice. The harder he tried to hold onto it, the quicker it would fade.

The gentle voice would generally come to him after a particularly bad memory. It would find him in the moments just after the vision would fade when he would be gasping for breath, his body coated in sweat as though he had been finishing one of Ronan's workouts. Its sweetness would help calm him down, providing a balm for his ravaged soul and giving him something to focus on other than the pain radiating within him.

The memories were no longer always factual depictions of events in his past. They were twisting, becoming more brutal with each experience. No matter what he had actually done in those moments, within the mist he was his worst self. A man ridden by guilt and anger, no longer capable of mercy or kindness. The worst of the visions were when he was merely a helpless observer. In those, he was able to do nothing but watch the most horrific events unfold one after the other without end.

Here in the mist, he had no true sense of time, but each vision felt like it took less time to come than its predecessor. Each one left him more disoriented and battered than the last. At least until the voice that was more than a voice came, wrapping itself around the fragmented pieces of his mind and pulling him back together, back to his true self.

Von knelt there, hands trembling and heart furiously beating. He was not certain how much longer he could withstand these attacks. If he had some way to fight back, an enemy that he could pursue, he might stand a chance. But how can you fight that which you cannot see? These were assaults on his mind and there was little he could do against them. He feared for the time when the voice would no longer reach him, when it would not be there to piece him back together. That's when he would be lost entirely, his sense of self shattering under the strain and leaving him completely broken.

As if summoned, the mist began to swirl and pulse with light.

"No," Von moaned, attempting to brace himself for what it would reveal.

As the mist began to roll back, he saw an aqua-eyed woman staring at him in horror.

"Helena," he gasped with a pain so fierce he felt tears stinging his eyes as it burned through him.

Nothing had prepared him for this. Despite all of its cruel tricks, this was the first time the mist had allowed him to see anything of his Mate. He stretched his hand toward her.

All of his longing for her was quickly replaced with fear as an arm wrapped around her waist and pulled her back. Those beautiful eyes rounding as a scarred hand held a knife to that delicate throat.

"Helena," he roared, fear turning to wrath within him.

Von tried to go to her, but his body was held fast with invisible ropes. He could not move. His struggles grew increasingly frantic as the knife pressed deeper into her luminous skin. He saw drops of red begin to bead and let out a roar of grief so filled with his fury the hand holding the knife slipped. The blade swept up piercing his Mate's lip.

He felt the resulting sting on his own mouth. Von pressed his hand to his lip and noted the smear of blood with surprise. The pain gave him something to focus on and with a final tug, he pulled himself upright. The arm banded about Helena disappeared. She now stood before him, whole and untouched.

"*Mira*," he groaned, taking a few fumbling steps toward her before collapsing to his knees and wrapping his arms around her.

He felt her hands sink into his hair, comforting him.

"My love," he whispered against her, closing his eyes and breathing in the scent of her. Von waited, anchoring himself in her presence, knowing that when he opened his eyes again she would be gone.

He was right.

It was the mist's most diabolical trick yet. It gave him the thing he longed for above all others, only to taunt him with her nearness before proving how quickly it could snatch her away. She would never be his so long as he was trapped here, and the mist would ensure he never again forgot what he was missing.

From the recesses of the mist, Von heard the echoes of the voice. *"I will find you, my love. Wait for me; I am coming."*

He curled into a ball, letting the words wrap around him and surround him with their strength. He found himself mouthing the words as they echoed before fading completely.

Once he could hear it no more, he let out a harsh breath, begging as he did, "Please, do not leave me here."

CHAPTER 7

ews from Effie's gran arrived by way of the woman appearing on the Holbrooke's doorstep.

Eyeing her now, Helena could not imagine this woman being anyone's grandmother; she was tall and slender, her skin unmarked by age. She had light brown hair that was pulled back off her face to fall in long graceful waves down her back. Her eyes were a deep midnight blue and were the only hint as to the years to which she had borne witness. Those midnight eyes were now pinning her in place with their focus.

"Kiri," the woman said in her rich voice as she dipped into a low bow.

Before Helena could respond, Effie rounded the corner at a dead run. "Gran!" she cried, sprinting into her arms.

"Hello child," she murmured, holding the waifish girl tightly. Laughter twinkled in her ancient eyes as she stepped back to examine her granddaughter. "The Mother has certainly graced you with her blessings."

Effie blushed at the compliment and batted her grandmother's prodding hands away. "No more so than you, Gran."

Darrin had been observing the exchange with barely contained amusement. Midnight eyes turned to him as he snickered at the comment.

"You disagree, Shield?" she asked in a deceptively soft voice.

The smile fled from his lips. "Not at all, my lady."

She snorted with derision. "Please, call me Miranda. I am not yours, nor have I ever been anyone's, *lady*." The way she spat the last word conveyed a sense of disgust at the thought.

"Miranda," Helena obliged before Darrin could embarrass himself further, stretching out a hand to the other woman. "It is a pleasure to make your acquaintance. Effie has spoken very highly of you."

"And you as well, Kiri."

The rest of the Circle were scattered behind her. Both Timmins and Joquil eyed Miranda warily, distrust evident in their rigid stances. Kragen wore his trademark smirk as he walked toward the woman and lifted her off the floor in one of his bear hugs.

"Oh my," she gasped, her cheeks flooding with color when he set her down with a saucy wink. "Watch yourself, Sword. I don't care what vows you made, you don't get to my age without breaking a few rules, if you know what I mean."

It was Kragen's turn to blush, and Ronan let out loud barking laughs at the sight of his colored cheeks.

Ronan sketched a quick bow to Miranda, smiling as he straightened. "I would hug you as well, lady, but I'm afraid I am spoken for and do not trust myself to behave around a woman as beautiful as you."

"Horse shit," the older woman cackled, pleased despite the crass words.

Unfazed, his smug smile grew and he winked.

"Seriously? Can no one keep their hormones in check these days?" Helena asked dryly.

"I can," Joquil offered from behind her.

Timmins, she noted, remained silent, and she couldn't help but laugh as the image of him lifting the serving woman's skirts came to mind. From the slightly glazed look in his soft blue eyes, she could tell he was lost in the same memory.

Helena shook her head ruefully. These men might be bound to her, but it was clear they took their liberties where and when they wished. She could not find it in herself to begrudge them the chance to find some happiness in companionship, even if it was fleeting.

Her thoughts then turned to Von, imagining how he would react to the woman standing before them. She was sure he would be as charmed as the rest of the men, offering silky compliments and flattering her shamelessly, knowing it would make Helena laugh.

All the while, he would be murmuring wicked promises to her through their bond. *"No one could surpass your beauty, Mira. Know that as soon as we are done here, I am taking you upstairs where I can undress you under the soft glow of the moon. Then, I am going to bury myself deep within you."*

Oh yes, she knew *exactly* how her Mate would behave, and she missed his roguish teasing fiercely.

"As much as I enjoy flirting with handsome men, I seem to recall there was a matter of some urgency that led my granddaughter to summon me."

Helena brought herself back to the present, embarrassed at how easily she had been distracted by thoughts of her Mate, but Timmins was already speaking.

"Your granddaughter shared a story with us that she heard from you," he started.

Miranda was nodding. "About the Corruptor and the Vessel."

"Yes, well, I have searched every record I could find regarding the Mother of Shadows prophecy and I cannot find any translation which supports your rendition."

Miranda simply peered at him, as if this were not news to her. "And why would you when it was never written down?"

Timmins bristled. "How can we verify the integrity of your retelling if we do not have a record of it in the Archives?"

Miranda raised a brow, studying Timmins as she looked down her nose. "There is much, Advisor," his title sounding like a taunt as she continued, "that was never written down. It is not the Mother's way to provide all of her Chosen with information they could potentially misuse in their failed attempts to understand it."

Timmins looked ready to explode at the insult hidden within her words.

Joquil pressed a steadying hand to his chest and asked, "And how would you know this if there is no record?"

"I did not say there was no record, merely that it was not written down. The Mother chooses her historians with care and tasks them with passing down her wisdom to those deemed capable of possessing it."

"The Masters of Prophecy," Helena murmured.

Miranda nodded again, approval radiating warmly from her midnight eyes as she said, "That is one of the many names the group has been given throughout the years. They are also known as the Keepers."

A grim sort of tension filled the room. The men had just been presented with yet another fact they did not know, on a topic they'd spent most of their lives assuming they were the experts in. Miranda's declarations were so matter-of-fact that it left little room for doubt. She was certain about the matter at hand, almost to the extent that it surprised her when what she said wasn't common knowledge for the rest of them as well. *Almost.* Miranda was certainly savoring having the upper hand.

Helena's lips twisted into a wry smile; in a way it was like meeting a female version of Timmins. While Joquil was the one entitled Master, it had always been Timmins who they turned to in their search for knowledge. He enjoyed problem-solving and sharing obscure, long-forgotten pieces of information with others. His recall for small bits of arcana was unparalleled, at least under usual circumstances; it was part of what made him such an excellent Advisor. It must be driving him absolutely mad to not be the one with all of the answers for once.

"You do not have to simply take my word for it, Kiri. You and your Circle can come speak with the Keepers yourselves. They have been expecting you."

All traces of humor were forgotten as everyone turned wide eyes back toward Miranda. It was true that they had already anticipated the need to travel through the Baelian Forest to meet with Miranda, but it was another thing entirely to feel as though it were predestined. The magnitude of the statement rendered them all speechless.

"May I come too, Gran?" Effie asked with thinly veiled excitement, seemingly unaware of the frisson of apprehension among the rest of them as her enthusiasm broke through the silence.

Miranda stroked Effie's cheek. "Of course child, so long as the Kiri doesn't object."

Effie turned her earnest blue eyes toward Helena, who immediately smiled and nodded her approval. Beaming, Effie wrapped her in a tight hug. "Thank you, Kiri!"

"When are the Keepers expecting us?" Joquil asked coolly.

"As soon as we can get there. Troubling times are ahead, Master, and there is much that needs to be said if your Kiri has any hope of defeating the Corruptor without losing herself to the Fracturing."

The men of her Circle scowled at the implication that she would fail without this meeting. It stung their pride to hear Miranda assume that they would not be enough to protect her from any foe.

"It is your belief the Keepers can help better prepare us?" Timmins questioned.

Miranda nodded once, her eyes scanning the group. "We have been waiting centuries for the opportunity to do so. Just as you have a destiny, so too, do we."

We. There was a pregnant pause as they processed her use of the word. It was the first time she had referred to herself as one of the Keepers, although given all that she had alluded to it was not much of a revelation.

"Why not simply tell us now and be done with it?" Darrin snapped.

"That is not the way of things, Shield. There is a time and a place for such conversations. All will be revealed as the Mother wills," she paused then, closing her eyes and inhaling deeply. When her eyes reopened, a brilliant blue light sparkled in the midnight depths. "There is still time, for now."

"We have already been preparing for this journey for the last several days. We should be ready to leave come morning. Does that suit you, Keeper?" Helena inquired formally.

Miranda smiled as she inclined her head in a small bow. "Yes, Mother of Spirit. Tomorrow will be soon enough. Tonight, I would like to spend time with my granddaughter."

"Of course. Please rest and enjoy yourselves. We shall be off at first light."

The men recognized the dismissal and dispersed. There was still much to be done before they started on another journey. Despite the old woman's warnings about what lay ahead of them, Helena felt only a rush of excitement at the possibility that she was moving closer to finding her Mate. Von was being used as a pawn in another's game, but Helena would find him and repay that foolishness tenfold. No one took her Mate from her and survived the insult.

Outside the wind howled as it whipped through the trees. Shutters slammed against the windows as lightning flared brightly in the sky. Helena's aqua eyes were wild and shimmering with translucence while her smile showed more fang than tooth. She may not yet know precisely where he was, but she was certain that she was about to start the next leg of the journey that would lead her back to him.

MICHA AND NIAL were both waiting for her outside her door. She lifted an eyebrow in surprise to see both men prowling in the corridor beside her room.

Pausing mid-step she asked dryly, "Is there something I can help you with?"

Their heads snapped toward her at the words and both men spoke at once. "I am coming with you when you leave for Bael," insisted Nial, while Micha begged, "Do not forget your promise to me, Helena."

Both brows lifted until they nearly touched her hairline. "If you feel that strongly about it, gentlemen, I will not stop you. I am sure we will have need of the additional manpower. Just know that if you slow us down or interfere with our plans, I will not hesitate to leave you alongside the road. The condition I will leave you in, however, will depend entirely on how much you annoy me in the process. Do I make myself clear?"

She watched relief brighten Nial's stormy eyes, while determination continued to shine through Micha's soft green ones. Each man felt he had something to prove, and while she could guess as to what that might be, she was curious to watch it play out.

"We leave with the dawn. Pack only what you need. I do not know how long we will be gone, and I cannot promise this is where we will return."

They nodded their understanding and each hastened off in a separate direction.

She shook her head at their dramatic interception. The real reason she had agreed to their coming along was that she had her own feelings of intuition that they had a part to play in the days to come. She just wondered if their schemes would align with her own.

CHAPTER 8

Helena finished tightening the strap of her belt with a frustrated huff. She hadn't slept well and was feeling decidedly grumpy as a result. Her eyes were scratchy and the muscles in her back and neck felt knotted. It was not an ideal way to start a journey, but her dreams had kept her tossing and turning into the first hours of the morning. Even now the sky was more black than pink, the sun just starting to peek up from its hiding place beyond the sea.

Helena could not recall her dreams in any real detail. She could only grasp at the wispy memories, a certain color or feeling all she could hold onto until even that much had slipped away. The one thing that hadn't faded entirely was the soul-deep terror she had felt when her eyes would snap open and her heart would pound between bouts of dreaming. Her dreams had been some kind of warning; she was sure of it.

It was infuriating that the Mother would find it important enough to send her the warning, and then not see fit to let her hold onto it. Did everything need to be cloaked in such mystery? Just once, it would be really nice to have something neatly packaged and handed to her with explicit instructions on what to do with it. That would certainly be a welcome change of pace, given all that had transpired since Darrin had come to the cottage so many months ago. Apparently, the Mother disagreed.

She was still muttering darkly under her breath when Darrin approached her. "Are you ready to go, Helena?"

"Mother's tits!" she snarled as the leather strap snapped against her skin, his voice startling her despite its softness.

Darrin lifted both hands defensively and stepped back.

Kragen placed his hand on the younger man's shoulder. "Perhaps we should get the Kiri some strong black tea before we start. It might do much to brighten her mood."

Unamused, Helena bared her teeth at the men. Feeling more feline than human at the moment, she felt a low growl start in her throat and wasn't at all surprised to see Starshine quietly stalking toward the trio.

Kragen laughed at the display of temper, entirely unimpressed since he knew she had no intention of acting on it.

Helena scowled. It was rare for her to be in such a mood, but her growing sense of unease due to the dreams she could not recall, and the lack of sleep said dreams had caused, were taking a toll.

Serena made her way over to join the growing group. She wrapped a comforting arm around her friend and said in a low voice, "Here now, Kiri. Perhaps you would like to ride Starshine this morning? That always seems to help refresh you."

"So she can fall out of the sky when she falls asleep? Look at her; she's barely awake as it is," Darrin retorted with some heat.

Serena spun toward Darrin, levelling him with a cool stare. She blinked her violet eyes once, twice, and then dismissed him entirely by turning her back to him. Helena's lips quirked up despite themselves and Serena's own lips lifted at the sight.

The thought of riding Starshine was tempting, but she knew how her Circle felt about her being too far out of their sight. She wouldn't allow anyone except Von to ride the Talyrian with her, so her compromise was to ride Karma, Von's Daejaran wolf, beside the others instead. She had her own wolf, Shepa, but since Von's disappearance, both Helena and Karma had found solace in spending time with their human's other favorite companion.

Starshine nudged her mistress with her massive head, the turquoise eyes studying her carefully. Helena buried her fingers in the thick white mane and had just rested her forehead against Starshine's snout when a barely audible gasp had her lifting her head back up to track the owner. Miranda stood near the manor; the hand pressed against her lips did little to cover the growing smile on the Keeper's face.

Helena's brows furrowed as her tired brain tried to decipher Miranda's reaction to the Talyrian.

Miranda moved quickly toward the small group.

Starshine's reaction was instantaneous. She growled, a deep rumbling sound, and shot a jet of flame at the woman's feet.

Miranda jumped back, her mouth agape, but she recovered quickly. "I see you have found your rider."

Starshine's massive head dipped in the semblance of a nod.

Helena looked between the two, her look of shock mirrored on her friends' faces. "Have you two already met?" she finally asked.

Miranda nodded. "Oh yes, the Keepers have always been familiar with the Talyrian pride."

Timmins, unfortunately, chose that moment to join them. It seemed he was destined to be outshone by the Keeper. He had overheard Miranda's last comment and was already scowling when she asked, "What do you know of the Talyrians?"

Helena shrugged, not in the mood for a history lesson. She was far too exhausted for that. "I know that they are very possessive and quite fierce. They can cause the earth to quake, shoot fire, fly, and have no trouble expressing their opinion despite their inability to talk." Despite feeling irritable, Helena was smiling as she spoke.

Starshine's gaze was tracking her closely as she turned to face Miranda.

"Your Starshine is more special than you know. A Talyrian will only choose a rider that can match them in power. To try to form a bond with one of lesser power would destroy the rider." Miranda's voice was mild as she shared her information.

Helena could feel her heart begin to race erratically. She sent a startled glance to Timmins, whose own eyes were focused with a single-minded intensity on the Keeper.

"Starshine is the Queen of the Talyrians. Just as the Chosen have a matriarchal society, so too do the Talyrians. She is the most powerful Talyrian in the pride. It says much that she came to you, Kiri. Especially when her ancestors retreated many centuries ago because there were no Chosen who could match them in power."

Helena's entire body stiffened. "I'm sorry." She blinked a few times trying to clear her mind. "What exactly are you saying?"

"With the Mother's power becoming so diluted in the Chosen, the Talyrians could no longer risk linking themselves to their riders. The link between a Talyrian and its rider requires the rider to be able to withstand the additional flood of power. If the rider is not strong enough they would become overwhelmed by the power flowing through their bodies and their minds would shatter."

"Like the Fracturing?" Helena asked in a soft voice.

Miranda's head tilted as she paused, considering. "In a way, I suppose it is similar. The Fracturing is a loss of self that causes a Kiri's power to overtake her body. She is still alive, but she is no longer herself with unique thoughts or desires, merely a receptacle for her power. What happens to a Talyrian rider is more of a slow death. When they are not strong enough to contain and channel the additional power, it eventually burns up everything within them, leaving nothing in its wake that can continue to animate the body and so they die."

Helena was floored. She turned toward Starshine and stared in horrified awe.

Miranda continued, "As a Mother of Spirit you can access all five branches of the Mother's magic: Earth, Air, Fire, Water, and Spirit. Talyrians also possess all five branches, although their ability to wield it is obviously in a different capacity." She paused in consideration for a moment before asking a bit incredulously, "Have you never heard the story of the first Talyrian?"

Timmins scoffed, looking deeply aggrieved. "Obviously not, Oh Wise One, but perhaps you would indulge us, humble simpletons, a little while longer."

Miranda's midnight eyes flashed with annoyance, but she ignored him. Looking back to Helena she said, "I will save that story for another time. For now, it should be enough to know that a Talyrian is a creature of Spirit. Whereas a Kiri has the potential to control or influence with their gift, a Talyrian can link to their rider and share their abilities. My granddaughter told me that when you are angry, you grow claws similar to Starshine's?"

Helena merely nodded while Darrin added in a shaking voice, "And when she's in the midst of one of her tantrums she's also prone to starting storms, but that is hardly a Talyrian ability. It is not like she begins to breathe fire or sprouts wings and start flapping around."

"At least not literal fire," Kragen muttered.

"She has been known to call it from the sky though," Serena interjected, just as softly.

Helena rolled her eyes but remained quiet.

Miranda was deeply amused. "Her power remains her own. How she influences the elements and people around her can manifest in many ways, but this is something unique to her and Starshine. There are some Chosen that can take on the forms of others, but never their actual powers. When Helena channels Starshine through their link, she's taking on actual qualities of her Talyrian. Perhaps she will one day grow wings and learn to fly, but I have never seen nor heard of such a thing happening before."

"I have heard of some Kiris that were able to control animals, is that something—"

Miranda cut Timmins off. "Do you really think the Queen of the Talyrians is going to allow anyone to control her? What woman, let alone queen, would ever be okay with someone else telling them what to do? What she *agrees* to do is a result of her own will and her trust in her rider's decisions. Make no mistake; she is very much in control of her own actions."

Timmins' face was bright red; his lips flattened with annoyance. Miranda's own lips twitched with mirth. She took far too much enjoyment putting him in his place.

Helena was done merely being a silent participant in this

conversation. "You said that I can take on the characteristics of Starshine. Do you mean that I will be able to turn into a Talyrian? Like a shifter?"

Miranda shrugged. "It is possible you could shift into a Talyrian if that were your gift, but you would not *be* a Talyrian. I find it highly unlikely that this link would allow you to become a hybrid version of Starshine and yourself, Kiri. However, those claws of yours are certainly for more than pretty decoration. You and Starshine are both very powerful; who is to say what you will learn to do now that you are linked. I almost feel sorry for the one who causes you to find out."

Helena shivered at that. Starshine pressed against her, those turquoise eyes assessing her. Helena stroked the velvety fur until she felt the deep rumbling reverberate through her hand. *I always knew you were special, beautiful girl, but I never anticipated you were a Queen.*

Starshine huffed, little wisps of smoke flaring from the great cat's snout.

Helena chuckled, *You're right, I should have known better. Anyone as majestic and as used to getting her way as you must certainly be a Queen.*

Timmins cleared his throat; he was pale now, but desperately trying to retain his position of authority as a member of her Circle. She offered him a gentle smile, empathizing with his consternation.

"It seems we still have much to learn," he said in a stilted attempt at compromise.

Miranda lifted a sculpted brow. "The Mother's Chosen should always be open to learning. It is their mistaken belief in their own excellence that gets them into trouble."

Timmins looked ready to launch himself at the Keeper. Serena and Kragen were trying, unsuccessfully, to muffle their laughter.

"Time to head out you lazy layabouts," Ronan shouted from a short distance away.

Thankful for the distraction, Timmins hurried off without another word.

Helena shrugged apologetically as Miranda shook her head. "You think for one tasked with being a pillar of knowledge, he would be more open to learning."

Serena lost it completely and was snorting with her mirth.

Helena was little better off. "I... I think he is simply not used to being the one without answers," she finally offered.

Miranda huffed. "His pride is wounded, the foolish male. I will try to treat him more delicately so as not to offend one of your Circle."

"Please don't put me in the middle of it, I beg of you," Helena insisted, still chuckling despite herself. She wasn't sure what "more delicately" looked like, but she had a feeling it would continue to rub her Advisor the wrong way.

"Hmm," Miranda replied, her gaze narrowed as she watched Timmins' retreating back.

Feeling significantly better than she had when starting her morning, Helena gave Starshine one last rub between the ears before starting toward Karma. At least there would be no shortage of entertainment on this leg of their journey. It would be a welcome distraction from what awaited them at the end.

IT TURNS out that entertaining was the absolute last word Helena would use to describe this particular journey. Despite being a smaller close-knit group of friends, the overall mood and energy of the group could only be described as cautious apprehension. There was a palpable underlying tension and little, if any, playful banter between them. In its place, there was only a strained silence that was broken intermittently by half-hearted attempts at conversation.

It wasn't just Von's missing presence that had them on edge either. Traveling again only served as a reminder of what they had unexpectedly stumbled upon the last time. They had been woefully unprepared to come face to face with the remnants of the Shadows' savage attacks, and it was impossible to forget the sight of those bodies lined up alongside the road. Especially the tiny ones. The knowledge of what could be waiting for them kept them ever vigilant. It was exhausting.

The worst part of being constantly alert, at least in Helena's opinion, was that nothing ever seemed to actually happen to warrant that level of focus. They were jumping at every crack of a branch, but so far there had been nothing more threatening to face than their own idling tempers. Perhaps that was threatening enough.

The days were long and the bitter winds of Daejara were swiftly replaced with a thick wall of humid air as they moved into Bael. Bael was a tropical region, the trees thick with ropey vines and the air heavy with the buzz of colorful insects.

Where Daejara was a pristine and untouched beauty, Bael glittered like a jewel and seemed to be in a constant state of shimmering motion. There were explosions of color and life everywhere she looked. If it wasn't for the heat that had her shirt sticking to her skin as soon as she stepped out of her tent, Helena thought she might quite enjoy it here.

Miranda and Timmins had started bickering as soon as they stopped for the night to set up camp. She had refused to tell him how much farther it was until they were to meet up with the rest of the Keepers. To be fair, it was not merely that she had refused, rather she had shrugged with a slight smile and stated cryptically, "We will know once we've arrived."

As amusing as she found their disagreements, she wasn't much up for refereeing another one at the moment, so she had peeled away from the group and called Starshine to her for a quick exploration of the jungle around them.

When Helena had heard they would be traveling through the Baelian Forest, she had anticipated a traditional forest. One filled with dappled light filtering down through thick branches and dark green leaves, with crisp air scented by the clean smell of pine. Instead, she had been caught completely unawares by the bright bursts of flowers that ranged back as far as her eyes could see.

The only thing that seemed to live up to her expectations was a sky primarily concealed by the unseen tops of the trees that towered above her. Even so, she didn't have a name for the massive trees with their waxy green leaves that were as large as she was.

Helena's steps had slowed. She was distracted by visions of the vibrant blooms growing alongside the rest of her favorites in the Palace gardens. It was a peaceful image that captivated her with remembered smells and feelings. Her fingers itched to find the seeds that would make it a reality.

Starshine snorted beside her, the small wisps of smoke seeming to hang in the heavy air. Her wings were pulled in close to prevent them from brushing against the foliage. It was clear the Talyrian was on edge. Helena had assumed that it was because there was a sense of confinement underneath the trees when you were used to soaring in the sky. Starshine shook out her mane and let out a soft huff that emphasized her desire to be elsewhere.

Sighing, Helena was about to give in. As she turned to fully face the Talyrian and tell her it was time to head back, she caught a flash of movement from the corner of her eye.

The shadows between the trees had rippled. Startled, she froze, going completely motionless for a series of thumping heartbeats. Curiosity ate at her, causing her to slowly turn her head back toward the trees.

There was nothing there.

Letting out a breath she wasn't aware she was holding, her shoulders started to relax.

Before she could move, she saw the shadows flicker, flaring infinitesimally brighter before fading back into their normal shade of black. Now certain there was something there,

Helena called her magic to her, using it to enhance her senses. Sounds that had been too low for human hearing were suddenly clanging loudly in her ears and the rich scent of damp earth flooded her nose. Each color was so bright it was almost painful in its intensity, but she was able to dilute the effect by focusing intently on the ground.

Nestled between two trees was a patch of darkness that seemed to pulse and grow, feeding itself with the surrounding shadows as it began to take shape. Its form was barely discernable and its edges were blurred, dangling vines momentarily visible around it until they were consumed again by the inky darkness. She felt her mouth grow dry as a distinctly feline shape emerged. It was still cloaked in shadow, but its outline was unmistakable.

There was another ripple and suddenly the darkness came lunging at them.

Helena cried out, too stunned to react.

Starshine roared and sprang forward to meet the massive shape that was now hurtling toward them. Helena tried to form her magic into a ball of fire, but could not. Frantic, Helena tried again, she could feel the pool inside her slosh, but there was no answering surge. Her eyes widened as she watched Starshine swipe her massive paw at the now-visible cat.

The beast was large, although nowhere near the size of the Talyrian. It was a soft gray with lavender stripes running through its fur. It snarled, saliva dripping from its gleaming fangs that were easily the width of her wrist. Its fur bristled as it crouched in preparation for another attack.

Starshine bellowed, jets of fire shooting from her mouth aimed in the direction of the striped beast. It dodged the attack, barely, and let out an angry roar.

Helena was shaking. She could not stand there and do nothing. She pulled at her magic, trying to shift it from her senses into one of the other branches. A small ball of light began to build in her hand and thunder softly growled in the sky.

Her heart raced. She let out a grunt as she tried to make the lightning expand in her hand, but it flickered out.

"No!" she shouted desperately.

Starshine's large turquoise eye turned toward her at her cry. Sensing its opportunity, the cat prepared to lunge again, now having a clear shot at Starshine's exposed neck.

Fury built and something snapped within her. Helena could feel her magic rise up and overtake her. The claws pushed out of her fingers and her toes, and her muscles were bunching as she launched herself at the beast. She struck it on the side, knocking it down before those dripping fangs could reach her Talyrian.

Starshine bellowed, pacing behind her. The Talyrian wanted to strike, to defend her mistress, but could not attack without hitting her, so she paced and snarled, her wings flapping uselessly at her sides.

Helena's claws raked at the now-exposed belly of the beast. She could feel the warm blood coating her fingers, but she did not stop. She had turned completely feral. Helena was still snarling and digging into the now dead corpse when arms like steel wrapped around her waist.

"Be easy, Kiri. You have done well."

She was thrashing and snapping in the arms, the voice unrecognizable in her current state. Her claws pierced through the skin of the one holding her.

An angry male voice hissed, "Mother's tits, Helena! Sheath those thrice-damned things! I'm not here to hurt you." The arms about her tightened as bit-off fragments of cursing continued.

Starshine was snarling, crouching low as she approached Helena. Her iridescent gaze met the turquoise one and something began to settle inside her.

She took a few shuddering breaths and slumped in Ronan's arms.

She was surprised he was the one holding her, instead of Darrin or Kragen, but then again he was a fearless warrior in his own right. He probably hadn't stopped to think and had simply done what he felt necessary once he saw her.

The claws receded and she was in her normal state once more. She gasped for breath, her heart still racing with adrenaline after the attack. She pushed weakly at the arms holding her; they released her slowly ensuring that she could stand on her own before dropping her completely. Helena lifted her eyes to his.

Ronan's scar was pulled more harshly than usual as his lips were tipped in a frown. His ice-blue eyes shone with worry. She could feel them on her as he searched her face for the answer to a question he had not asked.

She took a deep breath, inhaling the metallic tang of blood. Her brows knit together and she wiped at her nose. Ruby red liquid smeared on her fingers. It was hers. The beast's blood was a silvery purple that matched its matted fur. Helena held out her trembling hand to Ronan, wordless.

He tore at his shirt, a piece tearing away so that he could wipe at her face.

"Here, Kiri, allow me. Are you hurt anywhere else?" he asked in the soft voice one reserves for use when speaking with the gravely injured or a frightened child.

She did an internal check of her body and met his eyes as she shook her head in the negative.

Ronan nodded and then pulled her to him for a bone-crushing hug. "I was terrified for you, little one. What would Von do to me if something happened to you while he was away and unable to protect you himself?" The question rhetorical.

Warm tears filled her eyes. "I'm sorry," she rasped, not certain what she was apologizing for other than causing him concern.

Ronan stepped back, clearing his throat. "You have no concern for your own safety. You should have run; the Talyrian could have handled the caebris on its own."

Her brows furrowed at the unfamiliar term he had used to name the beast. She turned her head to look down at it, but he grabbed her chin and firmly shook his head no. She swallowed, her stomach rolling.

No longer satisfied with the distance, Starshine nudged her with her head.

Helena automatically began to stroke the velvety fur. "Thank you, beauty, for acting when I could not."

Ronan stilled at that. "What do you mean you couldn't?"

"I-I tried to use my magic and it wouldn't come," she stuttered, shrinking slightly under his harsh scrutiny.

Ronan's frown deepened.

She didn't like saying it aloud any more than he liked hearing her say it. Miranda had warned them this was an eventuality the longer she and Von were parted. The sluggishness of her magic, combined with the blood dripping from her nose when she had sustained no attack, were clear signs that the bond was straining.

"Say nothing to the others of this," she ordered, forcing herself to assume the role of Kiri once more.

He moved to protest, and she shot him a narrowed-eyed glare. He muttered to himself before nodding once and saying, "Fine, Kiri, but you will not be without an escort again."

Starshine protested the insult by shooting a small spout of flame at his feet.

Ronan let out a startled shout and jumped to the side. "I meant no insult, lady," he said hurriedly as he addressed the Talyrian. "I just want to assure that your mistress is well protected."

Starshine lifted her paw as though to swat at him.

Sensing all he had done was insult her further, Ronan looked at Helena for intervention. Amused, despite the corpse leaking blood on the ground behind her, Helena simply shrugged. Ronan gave her a glare of his own.

"Why weren't you carrying a weapon?" he snapped instead.

It was her turn to look sheepish. "I assumed between my magic and Starshine I would be fine. We hadn't seen anything to indicate..." she trailed off.

"Why do we bother training, Helena, if you fail to use those skills when you need them?"

"I wouldn't say I failed, Ronan. I did kill the caebris after all."

His arms were crossed against his chest, as he considered her words. "So you did, but at what cost?" he asked, referring to her still-dripping nose.

Helena scowled and Ronan shook his head, ready to let the fight go, as the words had stemmed from his concern for her rather than any real disapproval.

"Help me find him, Ronan," she pleaded softly. "Before it gets worse."

Ronan's nod was stiff, worry evident in every line of his body. "Let's get you cleaned up and back to the others."

Helena sighed, she was not looking forward to that conversation at all.

CHAPTER 9

onan's answer to her run-in with the caebris had been more training. The morning after the attack he had woken her by lifting her from her pallet and throwing her into the icy stream.

She had stood spluttering, shivering, and shooting daggers at him with aqua eyes swiftly shifting into iridescence.

In response, he tossed his sword at her feet and uttered two completely serious words, "Beat me." There was an unspoken message that followed, whispering to her in his rasping growl, *and I will stop.*

He pushed her past every physical limit she thought she had, daily. He woke her up before the dawn and had her running drills with at least one of the others but sometimes two. If one of the Circle was unavailable to be her partner for the day, he would unleash himself on her, holding none of his ferocity back.

Helena was ready to murder him. There was only so much of his taunting she could take. She didn't care that his stubborn brutality had paid off and that she had already far surpassed any accomplishments she had previously bragged about. After a few weeks under his determined tutelage, she could now best most of them in both hand to hand and armed combat more often than not.

Except Ronan; that smug bastard continued to beat her, howling with laughter each time he landed a blow or knocked her on her ass.

She remembered the day she had first watched him training with Von, and how he had been the one laying on his back in the dirt cursing at Von to help him stand. Her desire to be the one to put him there, even just once, was what drove her to keep standing long after she wanted to curl into a ball and whimper.

Helena had not asked him for mercy, not once. She knew what drove him to push her so hard was his fear of what could happen to her if her magic ever failed her completely. She could see the concern burning in the back of his icy blue eyes when his calloused hand would reach down to pull her back to her feet. Not that she would allow him to help her up.

Her stubbornness was more than a match for his. If she was being honest with herself, it was because she was just as shaken as he was. The possibility of being in a situation without magic to defend herself, or the others, disturbed her deeply. It had only been a handful of months at most, and already calling her magic to her had become as instinctual as breathing.

That was not to say she always had control of it, or even that she was always successful. There were still far more mishaps than she would willingly admit to, but the urge to reach for it was ever present. It was an essential part of her now.

And so they trained, both single-minded in their focus to make her as fierce a warrior as any Daejaran he had trained. The fact that she could already beat both Darrin and Kragen had left her thinking that there was something seriously lacking in the Rasmiri training plan if two of their best could be so easily outmatched, but she would never say so aloud.

"And again," Ronan snapped, his fiery red hair pulled into a tight knot on the top of his head. Sweaty strands were sticking to his cheeks and neck, looking like trails of blood in the glittering morning light.

Helena wiped at the sweat on her brow, her gaze severe as she moved into position. Her magic was rippling inside her, urging her to pay attention to it like a cat purring at her feet. It was hard to deny that part of herself, but the unspoken rule between them was that there would be no magic during their sessions. The whole purpose of her training was to ensure she would not falter if there came a time that her magic was unresponsive, so she ignored the urge to let it wrap itself around her and instead focused on finding an opportunity to strike.

She circled him slowly, eyeing him as a predator assessing its next meal. She quickly weighed and discarded each potential move, already anticipating how he would counter it before her strike would land.

He tossed his ax from hand to hand, shifting his weight between each foot; his coiled energy not allowing him to stand still.

Helena forced herself to be aware of the sounds in the early morning air: the low hum of the insects beginning to wake with the warmth of the sun and the soft caw of the birds that sought their breakfast. The jungle was alive around her, but her focus noted it only as a static image. She was aware of it, but only as a means of determining how it could help or hinder her. The rest of her mind was zeroed in on the opponent in front of her.

Her opportunity presented itself when Ronan had started to twist his body to keep her in front of him. Her move was immediate; there was little, if any, forethought before she swept her leg out and knocked his feet out from under him.

He had been expecting her to strike with her weapon, not with her legs, and fell with a muffled grunt. He was already using his momentum to spring back up, but she landed on top of him before he could get his feet beneath him.

She knew that his sheer bulk could work against her so speed would be her asset. She twisted her body around his so that she moved from his chest to his back, wrapping her arms around his neck to cut off the flow of air as she did. She increased the intensity of her hold as he struggled to dislodge her.

Her legs were iron bands around his torso, one of his arms also caught in the hold. He continued to squirm, but eventually tapped at her leg as the hold on his neck became too much for him. She released him immediately, the surge of victory sweet.

Before she could say anything, he pulled her to him and lifted her in an elated hug.

"Uh, Ronan, I don't think you usually hug your trainees when they beat you," she pointed out chuckling.

"Shut up, Hellion," he murmured gruffly, using the childhood nickname he had picked up from Darrin.

The Circle had decided it was a very fitting name for their Kiri and had taken to using it whenever they were exasperated with her. Needless to say, they were now using it quite often.

Ronan held her tightly, squeezing her in his arms. "Well done, Helena, truly. There are few seasoned warriors that can get past me. That you were able to do so after just a few weeks is incredible."

She bristled with pleasure at his words; the compliment doing much to ease the frustration his weeks of taunting had caused.

"You know what this means, don't you?" he asked as he stepped back from her, still holding onto her arms.

"Again?" Helena asked, trying not to wince at the thought.

Ronan laughed and shook his head. "That's not what I was going to say, although we should definitely test if you can repeat your success. No, Kiri, I was going to say that now that you have proven you can beat not only your team but also your Commander, you have earned the right to wear your Jaka."

Helena went completely still at his words, her eyes going wide at the declaration. She had thought in passing once about asking for a Jaka, the idea of inking her flesh with words of strength and protection a comforting one, but to hear that she had officially earned the right to bear that symbol had tears quickly filling her eyes.

She tried to blink them back, but Ronan spotted them.

His smile was warm as he wiped one of her tears away. "He would be so proud of you. You realize that, don't you?" Ronan's voice was gentle and warm.

She sniffed back tears as she nodded, the words causing a ball of emotion to lodge at the base of her throat.

His fingers wove into the tangle of her hair and pulled her back into his chest as tears blurred her vision. "He would fight me for the honor of being the one to mark you, declaring it his right as your Mate, although as the one who trained you tradition dictates that it should come from me."

Helena laughed at that. Von would absolutely balk at the idea of anyone else touching her so intimately, let alone permanently marking her. He would most definitely pull rank and declare that as *his* Commander, the ritual of the Jaka was his to perform, not Ronan's. Despite the fact that no such rule existed and he would be completely making it up.

She pulled out of the comforting embrace and wiped at the wetness on her cheeks with a chagrined sigh. "I'm not usually so weepy."

Ronan offered her a crooked grin. "That's what every woman says when she's caught crying."

Helena rolled her eyes. "I can knock you on your ass again if you're going to insist on turning into a massive asshole."

He laughed at the brazen declaration. "You can try, sweetheart," he taunted.

Helena pretended to consider it, before pronouncing in her most carefully neutral voice, "I think that I've wounded your male ego enough for one day."

His knowing grin made her smile despite herself.

He nudged her with his shoulder. "I meant what I said. You did well."

She beamed, the sweat, dirt, and achy muscles long forgotten as they leisurely made their way back toward the camp.

"So when do I get my tattoo? Do I get to pick where it goes?" she asked, recalling that both Ronan and Von had their Jakas over their hearts and down their right arms, although she had not noticed the same markings on Serena.

"It is your choice. Most go for the traditional placement," he rested his hand on his chest to indicate his own markings, "but many of the women prefer their back or arms." Ronan shrugged as if the placement did not matter. "We place it over the chest because it is closest to our heart. Thus the words rest above the most vulnerable part of ourselves. But it is merely symbolic. The location does not make the words any more powerful."

Helena considered it, trying to imagine her skin marked with the dark ink. She could not imagine herself with the symbols swirling along her collarbone and over her shoulder, no matter how hard she tried. She liked what Ronan had said about having the words rest above her heart though, which had her asking eagerly, "Can I put it on my ribs? Just under my chest? That way it will still be close to my heart."

Ronan's smile widened. "As you wish, Kiri, although I should warn you that is one of the most painful places to be marked."

Helena shrugged, not overly concerned with his assessment. Pain, she had realized, was subjective. There were jagged edges in her soul where none had ever existed before losing Von. She was already living with the agony of that loss scraping and tearing at her very core every day. She highly doubted the handful of hours someone poked at her flesh would even register. Nothing could possibly compare to the all-consuming ache of losing the most vital part of yourself.

VON WAS LOST in the mist, his nerves frayed and over-exposed. As soon as the mist would begin to fade, he'd break into a sweat and start shaking, terrified about facing the fresh hell it would torture him with.

He had watched the most horrific and painful parts of his life replay, sometimes in slow motion, on a continuous loop. His brother's accident. His father's shame when he declared himself a mercenary. Ronan almost dying, his face slashed in half and blood covering his unconscious body. Other soldiers whose names he did not speak but would never allow himself to forget. Men who had died due to his arrogance and the sheer stupidity of decisions he had made because of it. Battle after bloody battle, and all of the bodies of the innocents that accompanied them.

Then there were the other visions. The ones that hadn't happened but still could. Those hallucinations almost exclusively involved Helena, her aqua eyes beseeching him to save her and then condemning him when he could not. Over and over again he had watched her get beaten, raped, or torn apart by one type of savage monster after another. Every time these visions assaulted him, he damn near pulled his arms out of their sockets trying to get free of the invisible chains that held him in place. It was driving him insane watching the nameless and faceless beings torment her.

With every failure, he felt his grip on sanity slip a bit more.

He swallowed, his throat still raw from the last bout of screaming. His lips were cracked and bleeding from biting down on them in his struggles, his body sore and bruised from pulling so hard against his restraints. There were also wounds he could not account for, deep red welts along his wrists and ankles. Their presence did not seem to make any sense as he had never seen any bindings. But then, what of being trapped in this misty place made actual sense? Who could even say what was real or not here?

There was a chattering of voices in the distance that seemed to be growing closer. It was not one of the voices he recognized, or associated, with the visions.

Von laid curled into himself, his aching body protesting each movement as he forced himself to try to move into a sitting position. Everything within him objected to the weakness his position conveyed, and yet there was nothing he could do to protect himself against the relentless assaults.

Even so, he refused to meet the next bout of torture while lying down like a child. Until they actually broke him, he would continue forcing himself to stand up and face it head-on.

He could not guess how long it had been since the last vision, but he knew since he was mostly coherent that the next round was nearly upon him. The voices which seemed to be beside him now confirmed it. Despite their nearness and volume, he could not make sense of the words, only the underlying urgency.

Something was happening. Von struggled to focus, trying to force his brain to comprehend the sounds around him. He pulled himself toward them, staggering to his feet. He was rewarded with the word "vessel" but alone the word meant nothing to him.

There were two distinct voices now, one of which was clearly angry. He could feel the emotion more than hear it. In fact, that voice was not raised at all. It was more of a harsh whisper he strained to hear. Von could sense the anger of the speaker through the tendrils of ice it wound around him. It was a cold so fierce it burned white hot. The effect caused the hair on the back of his neck and arms to lift in warning. This kind of anger was something best avoided.

The other voice was a soft, protesting keen.

This must be some reprimand, he decided. Someone must have failed and the keening voice was trying to get out of a punishment. At least, that was the sense he got, given the way the other voice seemed to cut off and speak over the other.

Was it him? Had he failed and this person was taking the blame for it? He certainly felt like a failure.

Von couldn't understand what the mist was trying to accomplish this time. He felt no personal connection to these voices, only confusion. Although, he was still warily anticipating the emotional blow that was sure to follow. It always did.

Up ahead a dazzling light flared through a crack in the midst.

Von squinted, shielding his eyes from the unexpected brightness. *What in the Mother's name is happening?*

The beacon of light was new to him, as well. There would be illumination during one of the visions, and there was always an eternal glow in the mist, but not the harsh yellow light which was currently blinding him.

He stumbled toward it, his body in agony at the movement. The light grew brighter the closer he moved toward it, and something was whispering frantically in the back of his mind for him to remain in the safety of the mist.

Von laughed harshly at the thought, *the safety of the mist.* What kind of warrior was he, if he was content to remain in the arms of his captors, even the invisible ones?

The light was becoming painful in its intensity; its harsh glow beginning to make his eyes burn. He squeezed them closed to gain some relief but did not stop moving. This was no gentle sunshine; he felt no warmth the closer and brighter it became.

His curiosity was eating at him. Von was certain this was some trick of the mist and he was eager to uncover its deception. If nothing else, the end of the vision would allow the soft, lilting voice to find him once more and soothe the ache the vision would surely leave behind. With a final push, he stepped into the blinding center of the beacon and forced his eyes wide open with a ragged gasp.

ROWENA PACED at the foot of the prisoner's bed. Her anger was making the room turn cold, as ice began to coat the surface of the walls. Gillian shivered and tried to cover her reaction by rising to her feet. It had been four weeks since she had last promised her mother that Von would wake. Four weeks with absolutely nothing to show for it.

She had sat in the room with him so long she had begun to feel like she was the real prisoner. Resentment ate away at her insides; *why should she be trapped so? They had the bait, why did it matter if he was conscious or not? At least this way he was not a threat to them.* The thoughts, though they bolstered her courage, would never be voiced. She knew better than to question her mother.

"Wake him," she hissed.

"Mother, I—" Gillian started to protest.

The use of the word caused Rowena's lips to twist with distaste before her face settled back into its expressionless visage.

"Now," she ordered. For all that the word was whispered, it cracked like a whip.

Gillian shrugged helplessly, conscious not to repeat her slip as she said, "The drug has him in its hold, Mistress. There's nothing I can give him to counteract it while he is unconscious."

"You had better hope, girl, that he wakes. My patience with you is waning. I gave you until the turn of the moon, and you have failed to meet your deadline. Does your brother's life mean so little to you?"

Gillian's heart constricted in her chest. *No, not Micha. Not after everything she had already gone through to protect him.* "Please, Mistress. Give me another day. I will—"

"You have one hour, or I will crate you up and send you off to the

Vessel myself. Let her have her way with you for all the grief you have caused her. I am sure she has many plans for what she would like to do to you, *Daughter*, if given the chance. It matters not to me. I will still have my prisoner, even if you are too incompetent to follow the simplest of requests."

Each word landed like a blow. The fact that this was the first time that Rowena had called her daughter since appearing to her in the mirror cut her more deeply than the rest.

Gillian's back stiffened. She lifted her chin and met her mother's emotionless gaze, feigning a confidence she did not feel. Despite the words "she wouldn't" which repeated in her mind, her mother certainly *would* cart her up and ship her out. She would just enact her own punishment first. Rowena was not one to give someone else the pleasure of hurting someone for her. She was sadistic in that regard and needed to see the effects her brand of brutality could cause. That meant that despite her threat, before she made a gift of Gillian for Helena, Rowena would make certain that Gillian suffered, likely by slaughtering Micha.

Before she could respond there was a sound like crackling leaves that had her twirling to stare at the bed. Von's gray eyes shone unseeing up at the canopy above his bed before blinking rapidly. She was too stunned to move. Only moments before he had been catatonic, the same state he had been in since his arrival in Vyruul.

Von turned his head, his eyes landing on her and narrowing. In that moment she was not sure who she was more afraid of, her mother or the madman whose eyes glowed with the promise of a slow and painful death.

She had thought, given how long he had been under, that he would be more disoriented when he awoke. It was clear, however, that Von was keenly aware of his situation, if perhaps not all of the details.

Gillian was frozen in place, so startled by the unanticipated change of events that she could not react. This was her greatest fear come to life, save Micha being slain at the hands of their mother. At least he was safely away for the moment. That she even had the ability to feel relief at that realization only underscored how unmoored she had become by Von's very conscious presence.

"You," he growled, his voice no less terrifying despite its harsh rasp.

Gray eyes swiftly became a molten, shining gold. With a powerful tug that should have been impossible given the amount of time he'd been incapacitated, Von pulled at the bindings holding him to the bed. The entire bed lurched with the movement.

Gillian distantly noted the blood that dripped down his wrists, the force of the impact against his restraints having caused his skin to split. Suddenly, everything went black and she felt herself falling.

CHAPTER 10

*H*elena was sitting with the other women listening to them share stories about their various conquests. She couldn't help but appreciate the idle chatter after the morning's grueling workout.

She allowed her gaze to wander over each of the women, lingering momentarily on Serena's face. The blonde was staring off in the direction of the men. Helena let her eyes follow Serena's path, expecting to find Ronan, and only mildly startled to find Nial instead.

The two of them had been dancing around each other for weeks now. They were overly polite and courteous, both often studying the other before quickly looking away to try to avoid being caught doing so.

Helena's eyebrow rose. *When are those two going to admit that they are interested in each other?* Her next thought followed in quick succession. *Poor Ronan.*

She could not imagine her proud friend taking the news graciously. His warrior instincts would demand retribution, or at the very least, the right to fight for his woman. He wouldn't simply allow her to waltz off with a new lover. His pride would never recover from the insult, not to mention his heart. There was little doubt that he loved her with every part of himself; to lose her would be a devastating blow.

Helena sighed. She was borrowing trouble worrying about something that may never come to pass and she already had more than enough to focus on without adding to the list preemptively. Helena allowed her aqua eyes to fall back onto her friend's face.

Serena was frowning now, clearly trying to puzzle something out. As if feeling Helena's eyes on her, Serena's gaze met hers and she turned a bright pink. Blushing was becoming a habit for her where Nial was concerned. She squirreled that thought away for now, determined to tease her friend about it properly another time.

The women had grown silent around her, and it was obvious someone had asked her a question she had missed.

Helena blinked, clearing her mind of the errant thoughts in order to focus properly on the conversation. Miranda was regarding her curiously, one of her sculpted eyebrows lifted as if waiting for a response. Effie was smiling brightly, sitting on a log beside her gran with her legs tucked up beneath her simple red dress.

"Apologies, Keeper, my mind seems to have wandered. What were you saying?"

Miranda's smile was warm as she repeated her question, "No need to apologize, Kiri. I was just wondering if you had any luck with your training. I know that you've been working with the fierce one." Her head gestured toward Ronan who had his arms crossed and was glowering at Timmins. "But what of your powers? Are you still struggling to control them?"

Helena tried not to scowl. She had finally made progress after weeks of effort with Ronan, and instead of being able to enjoy the accomplishment for a few hours, she had to answer for the fact that her magic was more like a prepubescent teenager than a prophesied ruler.

She opened her mouth to respond when a voice answered for her.

"Our Kiri has never been one to lord her talents in front of others. She hates showoffs," Darrin's quietly amused voice responded as he took a seat next to her.

Helena smirked at him, remembering all of the times growing up when she had told him she wouldn't be his friend anymore if he always insisted on showing off. Mostly she had been annoyed he had been able to do so many more things that she had, and it was her way of trying to level the playing field. Not that it ever worked for very long.

Miranda's midnight eyes were shrewd as she pointed out, "I never said anything about showing off, I was asking about control."

"Some days are better than others," Helena responded dryly, refusing to elaborate.

If Miranda was startled by the shortness of her tone, her face did not betray it.

Micha was the one to respond, which surprised everyone. He had barely spoken more than a handful of times since they had left the Holbrooke estate. Taking her words before they had left to heart, he had blended unobtrusively into the background and had chosen to remain silent and watchful during their trek.

"That is true for all of the Chosen, Kiri," he mumbled, stepping closer to the group.

She smiled thankfully at him, appreciating the show of support.

Miranda harrumphed, annoyed that she had not gotten a straightforward answer, but seemed resolved to let it go. Helena couldn't help but wonder why she was so concerned about it in the first place. *It was really none of her business, was it?* The thought troubled Helena.

As if to underscore her unease at the line of questioning, there was a low buzzing just under the surface of her skin. She rubbed her arms without conscious thought.

"Are you all having a party without me?" Kragen asked in his booming voice.

Helena rolled her eyes. "I would hardly call a bunch of women sitting around in the dirt a party, but to each their own, Sword."

There were murmurs of protest at her words, Serena feigning wounded pride as she shouted, "Hey!"

"That simply means you aren't doing it correctly, Kiri. I find that a group of women in the dirt can be quite an enjoyable time," Kragen smirked.

"You would," she retorted, trying to hide the smile his words had triggered.

"I second that." Ronan laughed, wrapping his arm around Serena, who gave him a tight smile.

"And I," Darrin chimed in.

"Because you would know," Helena sniped sarcastically turning to Darrin. "Tell me, Shield, when was the last time you had a group of women playing with you in the dirt?"

Darrin turned pink but answered gamely, "I seem to remember a time, Hellion, when you —"

"And that's enough of that story!" she said quickly, knowing exactly what he was about to share and wanting nothing to do with it. Helena frowned and began rubbing her arms in earnest, the harsh buzz beneath her skin growing painful.

"Cold, Kiri?" Nial asked softly from behind her.

She tried not to flinch at his voice, but she had not heard his approach. Helena shook her head but did not respond.

Timmins and Joquil were the last to join the circle, joining in on the cacophony of happy and relaxed voices that surrounded her.

She was smiling softly, enjoying the comradery, even as she shifted in her seat uncomfortably. Her behavior was starting to draw some concerned looks from the others, but no one mentioned it.

"The last time we sat around like this Timmins was telling us one of his stories," Joquil reflected.

"When isn't Timmins boring us with one of his stories?" Kragen asked and then quickly ducked as a rock came hurtling toward his head.

"Har har har, you jackass," Timmins said dryly.

Helena laughed despite herself.

"I believe it's Miranda's turn to tell us a story," Ronan called out loudly as he pulled Serena into his lap.

Nial frowned before wiping his face of all expression.

"Oh yes!" clapped Effie. "Please Gran, you promised to tell the story of the first mate. It's one of my favorites!"

"I thought it was the Talyrians?" Kragen asked Darrin in a carrying whisper.

Miranda looked around the group sprawled about the clearing. The stars were just starting to appear in the sky as the sun began its descent. "I suppose it is the time of day made for storytelling," she said finally.

There was rustling as everyone settled in, making themselves comfortable. For her part, Helena was struggling to simply stay present with the people around her. Her skin felt as though she was being prickled with thousands of electrified needles. Fairly certain she was experiencing another side effect of the separation from Von, Helena didn't want the others to realize what was happening.

She bit down hard on the inside of her cheek, trying to use the pain as a distraction. It worked. She focused on it, grinding her teeth slowly back and forth to increase the pressure. The buzzing only receded slightly, but it was enough to allow her to hear Miranda's lilting words.

"When the Mother first walked among the world she had created; she did so alone. As a being comprised of energy and intent, she was nothing like the two and four-legged, or even the finned creatures she had made. Thus, while she was surrounded by the beauty of her creation, she was never truly part of it. She spent many centuries with the beings she had molded from her power, infusing bits of herself into them so that they could continue to evolve as the years passed. This is how the Talyrians, Draconians, and even the Macabruls came into being."

Kragen nudged Darrin. "I told you it was about the Talyrians!" His over-enthusiastic exclamation caused the rest of them to snicker.

Miranda's midnight eyes glowed with warmth as she continued, "Eventually the first humans were made, and the Mother felt more drawn to these beings than any of the others. She was still too powerful and *other* for their simple minds to comprehend, but she studied them anyway. She was convinced they were the answer to her loneliness, if only she could find a way to bond with them. Despite infusing them with greater parts of her essence than ever before, it quickly became clear to her that the only way the humans would be capable of interacting with her would be for her to make herself more like them. These humans became the first Chosen. They were beings with raw and undiluted power, capable of magic we have not seen for millennia. Even still, the Mother's power was too vast for them."

Helena struggled to pay attention, but the buzzing returned in full force. Her ears were ringing and each word Miranda spoke sounded as if it was coming from far away. She bit down until the metallic taste of her blood was coating her tongue and tears were filling her eyes.

In the distance, Starshine roared.

Miranda's storytelling halted, and the others shifted nervously in their seats. Kragen and Ronan both stood, hands unsheathing their weapons. Starshine's roar had been a call to battle: one they were answering.

No one seemed to be looking at Helena, although in their own way, each person around her was seeking to protect her. If only they knew that their so-called enemy was not one they would actually be able to fight.

Helena's eyes lost focus, so she squeezed them shut. Within her, there was a sharp snap and she felt the bond that ranged between her and Von, the one that had been nothing but an endless chasm of silence for so long, pull taut. There was another roar, but this one was solely in her mind and it was a voice she had secretly feared she'd never hear again.

Von.

When her eyes snapped back open, they were not a shining blue but swirling iridescent mist. Her teeth were bared in a feral snarl, her nails growing and curling into deadly black claws. She heard shouting around her and let out a low warning growl. All of her attention was turned inwards. Where there had once been nothing, she could feel a growing rage.

"*Von?*" she asked frantically.

There was no answer.

Helena tried not to panic. She didn't want to know why she could only feel his emotions. All that mattered was making sure the bond did not go silent again. She honed in, flooding the tether between them full of her magic, pulling every last drop from the pool within her and sending it toward the howling wrath. If he was surrounded by enemies, she would make damn sure they could not hurt him again.

There was a loud crack of lightning, roaring thunder, and the sharp scent of burning wood. More screams called to her and she hissed. It was a final warning.

She felt as though she was using their bond like a rope, climbing and pulling herself toward him.

Helena knew the moment she found him. There was a shiver of awareness that ran along her skin, although she was only passingly aware of her physical body. Helena was wholly focused on the thin barrier that was separating his mind from hers.

She sent her love for him to press against the barrier. It was a request for entry, the equivalent of a lover's gentle caress. She would not force her way into his mind, to do so would be the worst sort of invasion. If he was still in there, she would give him a chance to grant his permission before breaking the barrier.

The barrier rippled in answer before fading completely. She was in.

Helena had a sense of being surrounded by mist before a room came into sharp focus. She could still feel her actual body, crouched on the jungle floor, from a world away. At the same time, she could also feel restraints biting into her, no—Von's wrists.

Their individual consciousness' were blending, and she could feel his jumbled thoughts like a rush of water washing over her. There were no complete sentences, only assorted words and phrases: *the voice, stay in the light, Helena...*

Upon hearing her name, she called to him, *"I'm here!"*

There was a surge of confusion that was quickly replaced by fury. Von's head turned. Helena was seeing through his eyes. Gillian was standing above them, her already milky skin deathly pale and her mossy green eyes showing white.

"You!" Helena shouted although it came out in Von's harsh rasp. They pulled against the restraints, the entire bed jerking beneath them as the wood gave way under the force of their joint strength.

With a roar, they were free and lunging toward Gillian. Her green eyes went white with snaking black lines moving beneath the surface. That was when Helena became aware of the other woman in the room.

Rowena watched Von break free and acted swiftly. She sent her power into Gillian's body. The girl was too senseless to move to defend herself. Rowena shuddered as she pulled the essence into herself, feeding off of the girl's power and bolstering her own strength.

Her lips curled in an almost sexual smile. The extra flood of power was always heady.

She threw out an arm as Von launched himself at Gillian and Gillian's body lurched like a marionette before collapsing to the floor. She had not drawn enough to turn the girl into one of her Shadows. That would require a complete drain of power, and she still had plans for the girl before she could allow that to happen.

Von stopped short, now crouching on the bed. His hands fisted around the restraints at his ankles and pulled. The supple leather broke cleanly in two. He faced her, eyes a glowing molten gold.

Rowena smiled wickedly. "So glad you are back amongst the living, Mate. I was growing weary waiting for you to wake. Now the games can really begin."

She lashed out quickly sending her twisted Spirit magic toward him.

Von's eyes narrowed and he snarled before speaking in a voice that had the smile fall from her face. "You do not know who you play with, woman, or you would not be so eager." His low rasp had transformed into a melodious and richly layered voice that she had heard only once before.

Rowena's bolt of magic bounced off Von with no more effect than a feather.

His head had dropped down to assess the smooth skin of his chest before his lips curled with amusement and those molten eyes lifted to stare up at her through his lashes.

"My turn," the voice-of-many purred as Fire erupted from Von's hands.

With no choice but to retreat, Rowena snapped the purple stone from its resting place in her ring and vanished.

"Helena!"

"Kiri, come back to us!"

The voices were tugging at her, but she resisted their pull a bit longer. For all that she was in Von's body, it was clear he was not conscious of her presence. She could feel him there, but he was diminished. Whatever had him in its grasp had not let go entirely.

Helena sent her awareness through his body, seeking out the source of the corruption. She found traces of it throughout him, like gray smudges marring the shining brilliance of his soul.

Her magic was beginning to wane, the extent of power required to submerge herself within him more than she had ever used before. With what little she could still use, she wiped at the smudges until they were gone.

His body shuddered and took a ragged gasp when the last of them disappeared. His eyes were heavy; the urge to sleep and let his body finish repairing naturally was overriding her ability to keep it awake.

She could not hold onto him for much longer. Recalling a trick that Von had used once before, she whispered to him, knowing the words would be waiting for him once he woke. *"We are coming, my love. It will not be long before you are in my arms again. I love you."*

With those words, she felt herself snap back into her own body, the chamber he had been in momentarily superimposed over the jungle clearing. Her eyes swam in and out of focus before she fell over in an unconscious heap.

CHAPTER 11

When Helena came to, she was dizzy and disoriented, her body feeling more than a little battered. The air was thick with the acrid smell of smoke, causing her to wheeze painfully. Blurred faces were hovering over her, but even blinking she could not call them into focus.

"Helena," a frantic Darrin called. She felt him take her hand in his and even that small shift had her groaning.

She turned her face toward the direction of his voice, but the movement caused stars to explode behind her eyelids. She tried to open her eyes but quickly closed them again. Something was wrong with her eyes. Helena tried re-opening them, but instead of seeing faces or bodies, she could only make out swirling colors. Where Darrin should have been there was a flicker of deep forest green.

Earth, she realized. She was seeing his gift. *How is that possible?*

Helena allowed her eyes to roam and was able to catalog where each of her friends were, without being able to discern any of their physical features. Her Circle seemed to glow more brightly than the others since their gifts were threaded liberally with a soft shimmering lavender she recognized as her own.

I must be dreaming, she decided, although the overwhelming pain shooting through her body contradicted that possibility.

She felt a cool hand brush her matted hair off of her face. Helena whimpered, the touch was gentle and yet it still grated. Helena opened her mouth to try to speak but was shushed by the owner of the hand. She assumed it was Miranda who was currently trying to pump her full of healing vitality. Rather than dull the ache, the power seemed to make everything come into sharper focus. It was as if her mind had wrapped her in some sort of protective fog to alleviate the pain, but Miranda's magic was stripping it away and forcing her to endure the full extent of her injuries.

"You need to let it go now, Kiri. You're still trying to use your power and it is fighting you. Release it. There you go sweet child," the kind voice murmured, punctuating each order with another soothing sweep of her hand.

Helena didn't feel like she was using any magic, she felt entirely depleted in all honesty, but she went through the mental process anyway. She visualized pulling the tendrils of her magic back into her and then letting them flow back into her inner pool. Usually rippling and shining, it felt muddied and almost completely empty.

Fear had her gasping, but strong hands held her down.

"Be still, Helena. Please," the strong voice was begging with no small amount of desperation.

Kragen. She had scared him. *What have I done?* All Helena could recall were those moments she had been joined with Von. None of the corresponding moments her physical body experienced were available to her.

"Wha—" she croaked in a terrible rasp.

"We're not entirely sure, Kiri," Timmins murmured from close by, anticipating her question. She detected a subtle quiver of concern in his voice.

"What he means to say is that your power fucking exploded," Serena interjected, not one to mince words. Despite their crassness, her words were spoken in a very subdued tone. If Serena was subdued, then it must be *bad*.

Helena blinked a few more times before her vision finally began to clear, her friends' faces taking shape around her. Ronan stood back with Effie cowering in his arms. She was obviously terrified. Micha was white-faced and solemn, standing a little to the side of them. Nial was crouched beside Serena, not touching her, but obviously trying to bolster her with his silent support. The Circle were all touching her in some way, their hands pressed against various parts of her body. Helena let her gaze wander further, eyes trying to catalog and make sense of what she was seeing.

There was smoke everywhere. Trees to the side of the clearing were burning and the sky was a deep, angry black. In the swirling mass of clouds above them lightning flared brightly before an answering crack of thunder rolled in the distance. Helena blanched, *did I do this?*

From the clouds, small gray flecks were floating to the ground. It was clear that it wasn't rain. *What is that?*

She squinted, trying to make sense of the objects. Her eyes widened and she croaked, "Ash."

The sky was raining ash down upon them. Peering closer she could see a dusting of the gray soot coating them all.

"For her reign shall be one of ash," Miranda intoned.

Beside her Timmins and Joquil stiffened, exchanging furtive glances before turning back toward her.

"Welcome back, Helena," Miranda continued as if she had not been quoting words of prophecy mere seconds before.

A question must have been apparent in her eyes because Darrin was quick to supply an answer, his voice filled with giddy disbelief, "Your eyes went all misty, like they do when you access your power, but this was different. You weren't in control; it was like it overtook you. You were growling and muttering things under your breath. A storm began to rage around us, the lightning hitting a few of the trees and cracking them in half. Then you smiled vacantly, not really seeing any of us, before saying 'My turn.' That was when fire began to fall from the sky. It didn't seem like there was any way we could avoid the flames, but not one of us was harmed. Finally, everything died down and you collapsed. When you woke your eyes were still swirling with that rainbow mist, but they are blue again now."

Helena was dumbstruck by his recounting and beyond horrified to see the consequences. She had thought her magic was only being used where Von's body was, but apparently she had pulled so much that it was unleashed around her body as well. The thought of that much power and destruction was more than she could process.

Helena swallowed, her throat raw. "I saw," she paused to drag in a ragged breath. "Von." It was all she was able to say before her voice failed her.

Nial let out an audible gasp, while Ronan and Serena asked in unison, "Where?"

"How is that possible?" Effie whispered to no one in particular.

"Was Gillian with him?" Micha demanded, bracing himself as if for a blow.

Helena closed her eyes and dipped her chin in the semblance of a nod.

The man dropped his head and his shoulders slumped. He had been hoping that despite the story of his sister's betrayal she had been innocent. Hearing she had been with Von was as good as declaring a notice of execution.

"Can you still feel him?" Miranda asked with calm authority from her place at Helena's head.

Helena allowed herself a moment to seek out the thread that connected them. She plucked at it tentatively, weak with relief when she felt the solid presence at the other end. There was no answering thrum down the bond to indicate that he was conscious yet, but he was alive, and she could feel him again. It was more than she'd even thought possible after the last few months.

"Y-yes," she rasped.

Nial's eyes closed at the news before he slouched against the smoking remains of a tree behind him. He jumped forward with a startled yelp and rubbed his back.

"Hot," he said by way of explanation, his cheeks pinkening with embarrassment. Kragen snickered and even Timmins let out a few amused chuckles before covering them up with a polite bout of coughing.

The moment of levity allowed the group to relax, notwithstanding the fact that Helena was still lying in the dirt looking very much the worse for wear. Her complexion had taken on a waxy sheen and there were large purple smudges below each of her eyes. Her cheeks were hollow, her lips cracked and bleeding, while her overall appearance was emaciated and frail. Helena's magic had used her body to fuel its rage leaving her as little more than a shell in its wake.

Despite her ravaged body, Helena's mind was alert and sharp. It was a frustrating contrast. Knowing that Von was alive was pushing at her to get up and keep going, but she could barely lift her hand without it shaking badly.

"You need to rest," Miranda insisted firmly as if sensing her internal battle of wills.

"Keepers," Helena countered.

"We aren't far now. I am sure they will come to us given the state of things here. Besides, you are clearly not fit for travel at present."

Helena scowled, or she tried to, as any movement at all left her wincing.

Serena stood. "Here, let me make up a tent for you."

"I'll help," Effie offered, following close behind.

They had only intended to stop here for a quick break and meal. Their plan was to continue on a bit further before resting for the evening, so no formal camp had been set up. Apparently, plans had changed and they would now remain here for the foreseeable future. As much as she wanted to rush off, Helena couldn't deny that sleep sounded wonderful. It was all she could do to keep her eyes open. They started to drift closed but an errant thought had them flying back open.

"Starshine?" she demanded.

"Your Talyrian set off once the storm started in earnest. We think that she sensed the threat and went to keep watch. We have not seen her since," Joquil supplied in his usual matter-of-fact manner.

Helena frowned at the news, hoping she was all right. That was Helena's last coherent thought before the world went dark.

VON COULDN'T PLACE his finger on what was different, only that
something was. The mist wasn't gone completely, but it was greatly
diminished. He was reclining in a field he didn't recognize, beneath a
clear blue sky. There were no discernable landmarks nearby and he had
not heard any voices since waking. All the pain and fear were gone, in
fact, it was actually peaceful.

Von stretched and rose to his feet, deciding to explore. For the first
time since finding himself in this place, he was curious as to what he
might find. The walk was a pleasant one, the breeze keeping him cool
despite the presence of the sun. He had no clear destination in mind,
but he did feel a strong pull to continue following a stream he had
come across.

After some time, although he could not say how long, Von saw a
garden materialize on the horizon. This he recognized. Picking up his
pace, Von hurried toward it. It was the Kiri's garden from the Palace in
Elysia. A smile tugged at the corner of his lips as he remembered the
day Helena had unknowingly summoned him here.

He had been in the middle of a conversation with Ronan. They had
been discussing their men's rotation schedule which they had decided
was necessary given the Chosen's hostile response to their presence at
the Palace. Ronan had been listing off the pairs when Von had felt a
sharp tug in his chest. He'd looked down, certain that someone had a
hold of him but saw nothing. Then there'd been a tickling at the edge
of his consciousness. A feeling that he was needed somewhere. Then,
like now, he had followed that intuition until he found Helena sitting
on a bench in the garden. Her eyes had been closed and she had been
smiling, her rosy cheeks giving him a pretty good idea of what she'd
been thinking about.

Von blinked. As if the memory summoned her, Helena was sitting
at a fountain he had not noticed. Her fingers were trailing along the
surface of the water and her eyes were downcast as they watched the
ripples.

Von swallowed thickly, *Mother she's beautiful.*

Her dark hair was pulled up off her neck, but strands had gotten
loose and were falling about her face in soft curls. Her body, which he

had always appreciated for its curves, was wrapped in a lilac dress that revealed more than it concealed.

Here's a vision I don't mind being lost in, Von thought with a leer.

He saw her freeze, her eyes lifting from the water before her body turned to face him. The aqua orbs widened when they saw him standing there. To his shock, they filled with the sheen of tears before she launched herself at him. He stumbled back slightly, his arms wrapping around her to hold her tightly against him.

"*Mira?*" he asked. "What's wrong my love?"

"You're gone," she whimpered, her voice sounding small and lost.

Von chuckled at that. "I'm right here, Mate."

"You're not real," she mumbled dejectedly, sniffling into his chest.

Von ran his hand along her back, enjoying the way she felt in his arms. Feeling inspired, he let his hands roam lower and squeezed appreciatively. His hips pressed into her and he lowered his mouth to whisper into her ear, "That feels pretty real to me, Mate."

A shiver raced down her body and she pulled back to meet his gaze. "I must be missing you even more than usual if my dreams have taken this kind of turn," she murmured. Her eyes had gone soft and thoughtful, but they were no longer wet with tears.

"Your dreams? Sweetheart, I'm pretty sure you're visiting mine." Von laughed, letting his eyes run down her body and appreciating the swell of her breasts revealed by the low-cut dress.

He watched her brows furrow thoughtfully, her nose scrunching up as she considered what he said. He pressed a kiss to her nose, tilting her chin so that her eyes met his again.

"Why does it matter whose dream it is, so long as we are together?"

Her eyes sparkled mischievously at the thought before she broke out into a large grin. "I suppose you're right."

"Do you mind saying that again?" he asked, pretending to clean out his ear. "I'm not certain I heard you correctly."

Helena laughed and slapped his chest playfully. "You were lucky I admitted it at all."

"I suppose that's true. Can we take advantage of our good fortune now?" he asked, lips hovering above hers.

"If you don't, I may have to tell everyone about how you've lost your skill at seduction," she said a bit breathlessly.

Von snorted. "As if anyone would ever believe that. You should aim for a more realistic threat next time."

Helena shrugged before closing the space between them and kissing him. Von groaned low in his throat and pulled her closer. She tasted amazing. His hands moved up her body until they were framing her face and his fingers were woven into her hair. Cradling her head between his hands, he adjusted its angle so that he could kiss her more deeply. He felt her pulse fluttering wildly against his hands as he did.

She bit his lip and then licked it sweetly before running her tongue along his; her hands roaming across his chest and pulling at his shirt until it came loose. Von pulled back somewhat, chuckling at her whimpered protest as he lifted the piece of cloth up and off.

"Why the hurry, love? Not that I'm complaining mind you," he asked with a grin, breathing hard as he stepped back to her.

"I'm not sure how long we have, and I don't want to wake up and not have felt you inside me again," she panted, running her hands along the now exposed skin.

Her words left him reeling. This must be his dream indeed if his sweet but somewhat shy mate was speaking so. Not a man to take one of the Mother's rare gifts for granted, he grabbed her about the waist and lifted her until her legs were wrapped around him.

"By all means, Mate, do not let it be said that I denied you."

She was giggling and flushed until he pressed his hips into her center and continued with the gentle rocking motions. Her eyes widened and then closed, her head lolling back as she pressed down into him.

"Like that do you?"

"I've missed this," she murmured. "The way that your body fits mine so perfectly. How with just one touch from you I feel like I'm on fire."

Von felt his head empty; the thought of teasing her and prolonging their time together disappearing completely as he sank to his knees on the grass. He maneuvered their bodies until he was on his back and she was straddled above him. Helena settled against him, causing him to harden even more.

"Take what you need, lady," he whispered hoarsely.

Her eyes were shining as she moved to free him from his leathers. "I need you," she professed.

"I am yours."

"Mine," she growled in affirmation, her eyes beginning to swirl before she closed them and captured his lips.

He was thrusting helplessly into her hand as she began to work it up and down. Von moaned when she stopped until he felt her shift and start to slide her hot center along his length.

"Helena," he groaned.

She slid down him in one long thrust. Von's hands were clenched on her hips, holding her down while he enjoyed the sensation of being buried completely inside her. *Finally*. It was like coming home. Her breath hitched as she began moving above him, his own breath coming out in shallow pants as he matched her thrust for thrust, driving into her.

She increased the pace until her inner muscles began to spasm around him. Helena threw her head back yelling his name. Von came right behind her, pulling her down so he could kiss her as he emptied himself inside her.

They laid there, wrapped around each other under the sun's warm rays, slowly coming back to themselves. She went to lift herself off him but Von protested, tightening his hold on her.

"Not yet."

Helena laughed and peppered kisses over his face. She lifted herself up slightly until she was resting her weight on his chest and looking down at him. Her fingers traced over his eyebrow and nose before moving down to his lips. He caught them in his teeth, biting down gently.

"I miss you," she whispered brokenly.

He released her fingers with a gentle kiss before replying, "Not nearly as much as I miss you, Mate."

His gray eyes met hers solemnly and in their shared silence, she could feel all that he had endured since they had parted, knowing he was experiencing the same. They were wholly connected, hearts and minds completely in sync despite the time they had spent apart.

"I'm sorry—" she started, her voice thick with emotion, but he placed a finger against her lips and shook his head.

"You never need to apologize to me. Not for that. It was I who had wronged you, my love. More than that, I had many opportunities to come clean about what had happened—"

Now it was she who cut him off, "No, Von, please don't. It was Gillian's fault. She's the one who bewitched you. Without her trickery, you never would have done anything to apologize for in the first place."

Von gave her a lopsided smile, moving to place a curl behind her ear. "You have a kind heart, Helena, but I am not blameless here. Her magic ensnared me, yes, but it was not as if I was without memory of the incident. It was my pride that kept me from telling you what I had done. When you spoke of your trial and what you had witnessed, that was a warning for both of us. I should have told you then, but it was easier to let myself believe you'd never find out..." he trailed off.

There was a longer silence, their eyes saying what they could not. Helena kissed him, a sign of her forgiveness and love. With that kiss, another broken part of him settled back into place.

She pulled back, swirling aqua eyes meeting his as she declared fiercely, "I am coming for you. I *will* find you."

"I know you will, my love. I will be ready," he promised as he kissed her again, and pulled her back into his arms.

Helena settled against his chest, listening to the familiar thump of his heart. She smiled and pressed her lips against his skin, right over his heart. Their hearts were still beating in time, as they had been since speaking the words that bonded them to one another. It was a small detail but it brought great comfort.

No matter the physical distance between them, they would always be one. She closed her eyes, still smiling softly. Eventually, they both began breathing deeply, lost once again to their individual dreams.

HELENA WOKE UP SMILING. Despite the chaos that had ensued earlier that day she was more at peace than she had been in months. She no longer felt any pain from her power's earlier outburst, which was a welcome and pleasant surprise.

She shifted slightly, disrupting the soft furs that were wrapped around her. While there was no pain, her body did ache, but in a familiar and enjoyable way.

"Von," she whispered in hushed awe, pressing her fingers to her lips which felt swollen and slightly bruised. It may have been a dream, but in her heart, she knew it had been real.

"Mate," came the faint but fierce reply.

Helena's closed her eyes as her shoulders began to shake, a lone tear snaking its way down her cheek.

She'd done it.

When she had connected with him and removed those stains, she must have gotten rid of whatever had prevented them from reaching each other through the bond. It was still a strain, neither of them at full strength, but it was a start. At the very least they should be able to communicate and that was enough, for now.

In the quiet darkness of her tent, Helena began whispering words of thanks over and over.

"Mother if you are listening, thank you."

iranda had been right. The morning after her little tantrum, as Ronan had started referring to it, the Keepers sent word that they were on their way. That was it. Keepers were notoriously cryptic, so no one was surprised that they had not provided an estimated date for their arrival.

Helena snorted derisively and rolled her eyes when Timmins relayed the message, but secretly, she was relieved not to be traveling for a while. Her body had yet to fully recover from the power-storm even days later.

She wasn't the only one still feeling lingering effects from the storm. While the sight of the damage she had caused left her wincing with remorse each time she witnessed it, her friends looked at her in much the same way. She couldn't blame them; her body had been slow to recover. Each one of her companions had taken it upon themselves to care for her and as such, she'd had an almost constant parade of visitors.

This morning, Effie had arrived with an apple for her to snack on, and then Miranda strode in no more than two minutes later with a soft blanket for Helena to wrap herself in. Less than five minutes after that, Kragen appeared and made a snarky comment about how terrible Helena looked and forced everyone out so that she could rest. On and on it went, each of her friends trying, in the ways they best knew how, to ensure she got well. It was sweet of them, really, but Helena was starting to wish they would just leave her alone.

If it weren't for the worry that burned brightly in each of their eyes when they looked at her, Helena would have ordered them away by now. Instead, with each demand, she merely bit her tongue and relented. She was fortunate to be surrounded by those that loved her. There were many others that could not say the same.

As they had every few moments since she woke up, her thoughts spun back to Von. Helena sent an idle caress along their bond; it was a gesture so filled with tenderness it was as though she had run her fingers through his hair while he slept.

There was no answer, nor had she expected one, but she could feel his steady presence at the other end. The feel of him within her was enough to keep her satisfied. From what she had experienced when joined with him, his mind and body had been in a condition similar to the one she was currently in: utterly battered. Unfortunately for her Mate, he did not have the benefit of well-meaning friends to care for him. Rather, Von was at the mercy of the enemies that surrounded him.

The thought of Gillian and that blonde woman had Helena's lip lifting in an unconscious snarl. She knew without having to be told that the woman with emotionless blue eyes was the one Effie referred to as the Corruptor. She had felt the perversion of magic when the woman struck out at Gillian.

The memory caused Helena to shudder with revulsion. What she had felt while in Von's body was nothing like the warmth she associated with her own power. Her magic felt familiar, almost like she was greeting an old friend or beloved pet when she called it to her. In comparison, the wrongness of the other woman's magic had grated against her senses like razor sharp nails sliding along glass.

All that she had learned from Joquil about the rare Spirit magic indicated that the wielder must employ restraint at all times. Helena had her own handful of mortifying reminders of what could happen when overwhelmed by emotion to help reinforce that particular lesson. Spirit magic took many forms, as did every branch of the Mother's power. However, it was the only branch that had the potential to control someone completely. In its basest form, it was the ability to influence another with your will and when used, it should be a mere coaxing, not a full-on assault.

As the ultimate representation of the Mother's own power, Spirit magic was revered. It was why those that had the ability to weld it became Kiri, or Damaskiri if they did not pass their trial. In either case, they were the Mother's representatives amongst the Chosen. To twist such a sacred gift... it was utter blasphemy and beyond reprehensible.

Helena's eyes were beginning to burn with iridescence when she heard a tentative scratching at the entrance to her tent. Serena peered around the flap and raised her eyebrow in silent question when she saw Helena's furious expression. Helena forced herself to shake off the rage that had started to swell within her and focus on the woman before her. "Yes?" she asked, her voice sounding mostly calm.

"They have arrived, Kiri," Serena replied formally.

The use of her title was a code. Helena had come to realize that her Circle and those closest to her would use it as a sign of caution when surrounded by potential enemies. That Serena did so now while referring to the Keepers gave her a moment of pause.

Weren't these people coming to help them?

Helena nodded, to indicate that the warning had been received, and pushed herself out of her chair. The blanket Miranda had brought her earlier fell to the floor. Helena eyed it for a moment before deciding it wasn't worth the effort. As it was, it was a struggle just to keep her legs from buckling as she took slow, measured steps toward the tent's opening.

Serena reached out to offer her support, but Helena shook her head. She already knew that she looked awful, but no one else needed to see that her weakness was more than skin deep. Her power flowed into her at the thought, a gentle reminder to never refer to herself as weak. The flood of magic helped calm her quaking limbs, and when she left the tent, she did so gracefully. More importantly, she did it on her own.

The light that filtered through the trees was a weak and watery green. The effect of it was startling. Each of her friends looked more than a little sick. Helena would have laughed at the thought, except that their expressions were all schooled into hard lines. That alone was enough to stay her reaction, but it was the sight of Effie's sweet face completely devoid of her usual smile, that had Helena faltering slightly. Even Miranda, who was a Keeper herself, was facing the three hooded figures solemnly.

Helena could not make out any facial features under the blood-red hoods. They were each tall and slender, standing shoulder to shoulder, as they faced her friends.

The Circle was more scattered, effectively providing a thick barrier between Helena and the Keepers. Ronan and Kragen were standing the closest, each of their thickly muscled arms crossed over their chests. Ronan was scowling, but Kragen was expressionless. Behind them, and slightly to the left, Darrin stood with his hands at his sides, his twitching fingers the only sign of his unease. Effie was at his side, her own small hand moving to curl around his and stop the outward sign of distress. Helena was thankful for her small gesture of support, as she continued to take in the scene in front of her.

Joquil was to the far right of the clearing, his body leaning casually against a tree. Micha was at his side mirroring the posture. Timmins was beside Miranda, standing at the far left of the group, his brows lowered in displeasure. Nial was in the back, Serena having moved to stand next to him after leaving Helena's tent.

It was an odd sight, certainly less welcoming than she had expected, given Miranda's association with the group. Schooling her features to conceal the thoughts that were whirling through her mind, Helena made her way to the front. Kragen and Ronan shifted to make a space for her between them. The not-so-subtle drop of their hands to rest beside the hilts of their axes had her lips lifting in a bemused smile.

Before Helena could settle upon the appropriate greeting the Keepers swept into low bows, the ruby-red fabric of their cloaks brushing the dirt floor.

"*Kiri*," they rumbled in unison, their voices echoing spectrally in her mind. Helena stiffened at the sound. This was the first time she had heard a voice in her head that wasn't Von's and she wasn't sure how to feel about it.

The shifting of her friends underscored their own disquiet.

Helena weighed the option of bowing in return but Miranda caught her attention, the older woman having stepped forward to stand beside her. She cut her chin to the side, a discrete but emphatic no. It looked like she would not be returning their bow after all.

"Keepers," Helena said with more bravado than she was feeling, "thank you for joining us."

The figure in the center moved forward. Long skeletal fingers appeared from the bottom of its sleeves to lift the hood back to reveal its face. There was a startled gasp behind her, but it was the only sound in the entirety of the clearing. Even the animals had decided to make themselves scarce for this particular meeting.

Helena couldn't blame them. The Keepers were terrifying. There was no other word for the beings that stood before her. The other two followed the lead of the first and removed their hoods. She swallowed thickly, silently wishing they would put them back on.

Their faces were gaunt, hairless, and a white so pale, she could make out the pulsing of purple veins beneath the thin skin. Their eyes were pits of black and their mouths were stitched shut, thick black cords woven in a crisscrossing pattern along the length of them. The only distinguishing marks between them were the swirling tattoos that covered almost every visible inch of skin. The markings were a deep navy blue, but as Helena stared at them, they seemed to shift and move in a serpentine fashion.

Without conscious thought, Helena decided the only way to get through this encounter was to brazen it out. "It would seem that Miranda got the looks in the family."

Behind her Kragen and Ronan snickered with appreciation, while she saw Timmins close his eyes in dismay. Miranda's own lips curled in an approving smile.

"Kiri, may I introduce you to the Triumvirate," she said by way of introduction. "These are the oldest of the Keepers, those who have sworn their loyalty to the realm and have shaken off all vestiges of their past lives in order to lead and offer guidance without any of the bias of mortality."

"One could argue that it is mortality that allows for the most valuable of guidance," Helena murmured.

"*Our Kiri is wise*," the voices hissed in her mind. It was hard to discern any type of emotion, but Helena could have sworn she sensed amusement.

"You will have to forgive my ignorance," Helena replied. "I had not realized the head of the Keepers would be gracing us with their presence."

"Nor had I, Kiri, or I would have better prepared you," Miranda said drolly. There was a hint of censure in her voice, as though she was not pleased by the appearance of the Triumvirate.

The figure in the center tilted his head to the side as though examining her. "*Perhaps it is us who should ask your forgiveness. We were merely curious to see whom the Vessel would be, after carrying the prophecy for so many years. We could not miss an opportunity to meet the woman who is responsible for the fate of the Chosen.*"

"No pressure," Ronan muttered.

Helena raised an eyebrow. "I hope that I have not disappointed you after such a long wait."

"*You are more than we allowed ourselves to hope for,*" the voices echoed.

Helena shivered at their response, not feeling overly comforted despite the words.

"Seeing as we are all aware of the prophecy, how is it you think to help us?" Timmins asked. It was the most outright disrespectful she had ever heard her Advisor and Helena turned toward him in surprise.

The Keepers' faces turned toward him in unison. "*You know of the Mother of Shadows, of what will befall the Chosen if the Vessel becomes corrupted, but you know nothing of the Corruptor. Nor what it will take to defeat her. We merely offer information… and a choice.*"

"A choice?" Helena repeated, her eyes snapping to the central figure.

There was a slight dip of its head. "*There is always a choice, Kiri.*"

"Convenient," she bit out, her stomach twisting inside of her.

"*Our words will be for you alone, Kiri, if you wish to hear them.*"

Helena swallowed back her fear and stepped toward them. "Very well."

As she spoke, all three lifted their hands toward her.

"Helena!" Darrin cried out in warning.

"Kiri!" the others' voices echoed, the whistle of blades being drawn sounding behind her.

The black pits where their eyes used to be began to glow scarlet. Helena could not look away, drawn to what she saw within the fiery depths.

As one, the Triumvirate touched her. Helena heard someone scream and had the distant thought that it might be her. There wasn't enough time for her to consider the notion further because she was already falling.

CHAPTER 13

*V*on was stretched out on the bed, bonds firmly back in place. His eyes were closed, feigning sleep. He didn't want to let on that the effects of the drug had already worn off. It was a game he'd been playing since that little red-haired bitch dosed him again. Every day since he'd broken free she had been force feeding him healing brews liberally dosed with a sedative that knocked him back into unconsciousness almost immediately.

Once he finally came to he would pretend to be asleep, while Gillian and the blonde one plotted and schemed in hushed whispers over his bed. The women were careful never to reveal any specifics, but Von knew that eventually, they would divulge something useful. Until then, he would bide his time gathering strength and seemingly inconsequential information. One never knew what could be important later on, and he had every intention of paying their hospitality back in kind.

The warrior in him began to assess his enemy's strategy. *What reason would they have to keep me docile but not completely out of commission?*

The answer came to Von almost instantly; the demented bitches wanted to make Von one of their puppets. For him to have the most value, he needed to be in peak condition, but they couldn't risk him fighting back. Thus the drugs. They wanted Von at full-strength and firmly under the blonde's control, but the only way that would ever happen is if he was unconscious when she made her move. *They are biding their time as well,* Von mused.

Von let his thoughts continue to wander, knowing the answer he sought was lingering at the fringes of his mind. As a Commander of his own men, he was well-versed with this kind of strategizing: weighing and evaluating an enemy's strengths and weaknesses, looking to strike when it would have the biggest impact... this was his bread and butter. He was absolutely confident he'd be able to discern their plot, and then do everything in his power to undermine it.

It can't just be my health they are waiting on, he decided. While it was true that the *Bella Morte* had delayed their plans considerably, keeping his mind trapped in the misty place while sapping his body of strength, there had to be at least one other piece out of place. When the answer came this time, it was like a gentle caress: *Helena.* They were waiting for Helena.

Von hoped his lips hadn't twitched with the smile he suppressed at the thought of her. His Mate's visit left quite an impression on his jailors. They had spoken of little else in the days since. Unfortunately, the entire reason he was still strapped to this bed was because of the state he was in after her visit.

Once her spirit left him, his body had collapsed into an exhausted sleep, leaving him vulnerable to his captors. The women had made their move, acting quickly since they knew there was no way they could control him if he was fully conscious and gaining his strength back.

Luckily for him, they hadn't realized that Helena had been able to reestablish their bond, if they were even aware the bond existed in the first place. His connection to her provided an added level of consciousness and protection. So while he was lost to the darkness of the sedative, there was an untouchable part of his mind working to peel back the fog encasing it. This allowed him a few hours of hard-won clarity each day.

Clarity he fully intended to use to whatever advantage he could manage.

It had taken him awhile, at first, to brush off the webs clouding his mind, but each day it was easier. The combination of Gillian's healing brews, plus Helena's reservoir of power was doing much to speed the process. He should have been able to do it on his own regardless, his power more than enough to combat the effects of such a drug, but the *Bella Morte* had done considerable harm. His own power was perpetually drained due to the constant work required to repair the damage. In his current state, there simply was not enough left over to fight off anything else. This meant that as badly as he wanted to communicate with Helena, he hadn't been able to do more than seek her glowing warmth at the other end of their bond.

Von tried to push back the wave of frustration that threatened to overwhelm him. Patience was not one of his virtues. He was a man of action. One that liked to weigh his odds, decide on a course, and then act swiftly. The fact that he was literally chained to a bed while his woman was about to battle her way through their enemy's forces, without him, did not sit well with his warrior's heart.

Although, the part of him that recognized his Mate as a warrior fiercer than even himself allowed Von to quiet the need to act. He might be stuck here, but he was not entirely useless. He still had a part to play.

A sense of peace washed over him. Helena was coming for him, even now she was preparing to do so. Von settled back into the bed, trying not to rattle the magically reinforced chains as he did. He would continue to collect information and once he was able; he would pass it on to Helena to help her prepare her strike. He would use this time wisely.

Thinking back to Gillian and the other woman, Von was slightly taken aback to learn their plan revolved around attempting to control him and then use him against Helena. What a bunch of fucking idiots. It was growing increasingly clear to him that they had no idea who was coming for them. How these women could continue to underestimate their opponent, especially after the little fire show she had demonstrated for them last time, was surprising. Perhaps they simply didn't realize how much power truly simmered beneath such a sweet-looking face.

Von allowed himself a mental shrug, let them continue to underestimate her. It would only make his Mate's job that much easier.

He must have made a sound because he heard a rustling that grew louder with proximity.

"Awake so soon, dearest?" Gillian asked in a saccharine voice.

Von knew it was pointless to try to deny it. Opening his eyes, he stared up at her with blatant malice. His gray eyes had darkened to the point that they were almost black.

"Oooh," she cooed, batting her green eyes, "someone is feeling fierce today. The tonics must be working."

It was all he could do not to bare his teeth at her. Instead, dark brows lowered over glowering eyes.

"Come now, precious," Gillian chided, her cheerful bedside manner making him want to stab her in the eye. "I'm helping you feel better. No need to be so rude."

Von had no need for words as he stared up at the female leaning over him. The promise of a slow and painful death was glittering in his eyes for all to see. He might even enjoy her death more if he got to watch it happen, rather than keep the promise himself. Von's amusement grew as he began to imagine all the ways his Mate would repay Gillian for this. He was already grinning by the time he began to picture Helena cocking back her arm to slam her fist into the other girl's throat.

The redhead tried to blink back the apprehension that clouded her eyes once he began chuckling. Gillian cleared her throat uncomfortably.

It was the first time she had been alone with him in this room since he had woken up. There had always been at least one or two other guards with her, if not the blonde woman as well. Apparently, he really was waking up more quickly than usual. He'd have to be more careful not to alert them, or he might lose the moments of awareness he'd been fighting so hard for.

Von refused to back down, staring up at the woman unblinkingly. Let her be uncomfortable, the stupid cow. She was a pathetic excuse of a woman, allowing herself to be manipulated and used by another. She was probably too stupid to realize that she wasn't going to be alive at the end of this. There was no way the other one would let her live once she had accomplished her goal. Assuming, of course, that Helena didn't handle the problem first.

Von was smirking as he mentally hurled insults at her, berating her for being stupid, weak, and ugly, among a litany of other shortcomings. The more childish and petty the insult, the wider his smile grew.

"Yes, well." Gillian's pale skin flushed as she pulled out the bottle of healing tonic.

He eyed the soft blue liquid balefully, not ready to fall back into oblivion just yet. "She is coming for you," he taunted, his voice a harsh rasp.

Gillian stiffened, the hand holding the bottle spasming at his words.

"When she finds you she will *destroy* you," he vowed, his voice dipping deeper with each word. "There is no version of this where you do not pay with your life, Gillian. It is foolish of you to cower here thinking you are safe behind these walls. No walls could ever protect you from her wrath. Aren't you supposed to be smarter than that? You were always so quick to point out how much cleverer you were than everyone else in the Palace, but I guess those were just more empty words. No one with any actual capacity for intelligence would remain a sitting duck while death itself came for them."

"Death comes for us all eventually," she responded primly, her voice brittle and strained.

"Yes, and if we are lucky, it will be gentle. Yours will not be."

Gillian swallowed, visibly shaken. "I liked you better unconscious," she finally snapped.

He gave her a grin that was too feral to appear anything but threatening. "I will like you better when my Mate has finished draining the life from your body."

Gillian lashed out with Air, using it to cut off the supply of oxygen in his lungs.

He tried to counter, willing Air to keep the organs inflated, but he was just too depleted. He felt his lungs seize and his mouth opened on a gasp.

Gillian poured the minty liquid down his throat, causing him to sputter.

He tried to spit it back out at her, but his body had reflexively taken great gulps of air once she cut off her attack. She had won this round, getting him to take the sedative, but she had not come out unscathed. Von could see the way his words twisted around her, ensnaring her with their promises. She was petrified.

Good, he thought smugly, eyes already drifting shut, *she should be*. That was his last coherent thought before darkness came for him.

CHAPTER 14

The feeling of falling was disorientating since she wasn't actually moving at all. There was a part of Helena that could still sense her body standing in the clearing with her friends, and another that felt as though she was tumbling down a deep hole. Her conscious mind was being pulled into another reality while her body stayed in the physical world.

Helena took a moment to get her bearings once the whirling motion settled and she could reestablish the feeling of being still. A small gasp left her mouth as she identified her surroundings. The Triumvirate had pulled her into the chamber from her trial. She glanced down quickly and noticed she was no longer dressed in her traveling clothes, but was now wearing her simple tan trial gown instead. Confused, she spun in a slow circle, searching for anything that would give her an idea of why she was here.

There was no sign of the Triumvirate, so she was alone, at least for the moment. Without their guidance, she was uncertain what, exactly, she was supposed to do. The last time she was in this chamber, the room swirled with mist and her trial had begun. Helena hesitated for a moment, wondering if something similar would occur again. It did not. She had the feeling that the trio was testing her, and would not be remotely surprised to learn that they were playing an elaborate game.

Growing annoyed, she let out a huff of breath and decided to investigate the chamber.

Once she lifted her foot to step forward, the chamber came to life around her. Gone were the smooth stone walls and in their place was a sprawling hillside that stretched out as far as she could see. Helena blinked and shaded her eyes; the bright sunlight blinding in its intensity after the relative darkness of the room. The scene was familiar but she was having difficulty placing it, as if it was a place she had been once long ago. There were no landmarks that she recognized, although there did seem to be some type of building far in the distance.

Left with no other option but to walk toward it, she did so tentatively. The scene rippled and changed, growing progressively more dark and stormy with each forward step she took. Helena couldn't stop her little jump when the sky began to crackle with lightning and growl with thunder. The ominous backdrop was further intensified by the presence of roiling purple clouds in a starless navy sky.

She squinted up at the sky as she felt the first few drops fall from above. As the wetness met her skin, she was surprised to find it warm rather than icy. Touching her fingers to her face, she felt the thick liquid smear across her cheek. The fingers she pulled away were stained a deep red. It was not rain that fell from the sky but blood. Helena felt her stomach lurch in response to the realization but managed to keep walking, certain that whatever it was she was supposed to see would only be revealed if she continued with her search.

As she began to crest the hill, the blood-rain began to fall in earnest. Her hair was hanging limply where it was not already stuck to her face and neck. The plain garment she wore had turned crimson and was clinging to her damp skin. Helena wiped at her face once more, trying to keep the blood from dripping into her eyes and noticed that her fingers had curled into black claws. A deep sense of foreboding had her moving more cautiously, knowing that her claws only appeared when she felt threatened. That was when she saw the first of the bodies.

She was forcing herself to walk quickly now, trying hard not to linger and search the faces of the dead. It was an impossible feat. Each step showed her another person she recognized. Helena swallowed hard, trying to breathe through her mouth as the stench of decay caused her stomach to roll.

Death was everywhere.

Helena was stumbling now, trying to scale a growing mound of bodies. A sea of familiar faces stared up at her, their eyes accusing in their vacancy. This was her fault they seemed to shout at her. She took another step and felt something roll and crack beneath her feet. Falling, she threw her arms out, trying to catch her balance. Her hand made contact with something soft and warm.

"No," she moaned, already knowing what she would see when she moved her hand.

It was the final scene of her trial. The bodies of her friends twisted and broken beneath her feet. The sky thick with smoke and still raining both blood and fire. It was a slaughter.

Helena's breath caught in her throat, her eyes starting to sting due to the smoke. It was becoming too much for her.

"Why are you showing me this?" she shouted angrily, feeling her power build in response to her distress.

The Triumvirate's spectral voices greeted her then, speaking separately and all at once:

"Chosen One."

"Vessel."

"Mother of Spirit."

"You have a choice before you."

"Loyalty or love?"

"Mercy or vengeance?"

"Life or death?"

"The path you choose will decide our fate."

"The fate of all the Chosen."

The voices were indistinguishable, each picking up where the other ended, sometimes harmonizing in one richly layered voice.

"What will you choose?"

"You cannot choose both."

"Your choice will be our salvation."

"Or our demise."

She could feel the brush of air against her ear as if the next words were being whispered straight into them by invisible lips.

"Know this: you require balance."

"A tether to this world."

"One to hold your soul in place."

"The tether is fragile."

"Stretched too far and ready to snap."

Helena was shaking as they spoke, the words reverberating so that she could feel them with her entire body. They were deadly soft but crystal clear.

"Without the tether, you will fracture."

"Eternally lost to the darkness."

"No way to return."

"The choice will be made for you."

"You will damn us all."

"See the cost of your choice."

Helena shuddered as the bodies that had been still beneath her began to writhe and moan in misery. "You show me only one path!" she cried, as desperate for clarity as for the end of the vision. She was not sure how much longer she could stomach the sight of her friends' decaying bodies. "What is the other future?"

"Unknown," the trio hissed, the word echoing around her.

"What is the point then? You show me this but speak to me in riddles. You're no help at all!" she roared.

Her magic was swelling within her, responding to her strained nerves and emotions, yet trapped in her body as it had no focus for its release. She could see the sparks begin to form and leap on her skin, her body a conduit for the magic that was rising to dangerous levels.

The scene around her began to fade. As it did, Helena's eyes looked up and noticed a small figure staring at her from one of the windows in the tower above her. She was too far away to make out the features but could not mistake the pale blonde hair that seemed to shine like starlight in the darkness. She felt her resolve strengthen. She may not have answers, but perhaps she had a focus after all.

THE FEELING of returning to her body was overwhelming. Her skin felt tight and itchy as if stretched too thin over a frame it no longer fit. She could only assume it was because of the growing tide of magic welling within her. The sparks that she witnessed in the vision were present here, her friends shouting out and trying to reach her once it was clear she was back among them.

Her entire body began to shake with the force of her restrained magic. It needed an outlet, but she knew that if she let it go, she could easily destroy everyone around her. Helena bit down on her lip, immediately tasting blood as she tried, unsuccessfully, to concentrate enough to ground her power. It was not enough; she simply didn't have the control required to manage that much power. That was when she felt her knees buckle, her body starting to tumble to the ground.

With a roar, Ronan reached her, pulling her shaking body into his and taking the brunt of the fall. Her power snaked across his skin everywhere that it made contact with his. He grit his teeth against the assault of magic.

There was hardly time to see what was happening in the chaos around her. Miranda was hurling obscenities at the now-empty place the Triumvirate had been standing. Effie was snarling and muttering under her breath, tugging against the arm Darrin had banded about her waist. He was barely holding her back from launching herself at her grandmother. Kragen, Serena, Nial, and Micha all had weapons drawn and were forming a tight circle around Ronan and Helena. Timmins and Joquil were chanting something from just outside the formation, their hands beginning to glow with the combined force of whatever power they were calling forth.

It was Ronan's terse words that brought her back to herself.

"Ground it damn you."

Helena was panting with the effort to push her magic back into her reservoir. It was fighting her, like a cornered animal that wanted to defend itself. She was pleading with it, begging it to calm down, but it would not listen. Her power had a mind of its own.

Ronan could sense what was going to happen before she did.

Helena looked at him with pleading iridescent eyes.

"Do it," he snapped harshly before shouting to the others, "Get down!"

Around her the others all dropped, not questioning the order.

Helena threw her head back and screamed, her power tearing up out of her body and launching itself into the sky in one solid beam of purple light. The beam began to arc and spiral until it finally burst and fell back in millions of sparkling pieces to the earth. It was both beautiful and terrifying. Unsure of what would happen once those fragments of power made contact, Helena held her breath. Her body was still trembling from the torrent of power, but she could feel what still lingered flowing back into the pool.

The first of the glowing motes touched the top of a charred tree. Helena sucked in a breath when the branches were illuminated with that same purple light. Almost immediately the tree began to swell and grow, small green leaves unfurling and then turning to luscious blooms. All around her, everywhere her magic made contact, it was the same. It would seem that her desire not to harm had her magic sending pure vitality into the land she had damaged so badly only days earlier.

She watched in mute amazement as the land came back to life around her. The places her magic did not touch were quickly concealed by vibrant green leaves that were growing to abnormally large sizes. She had thought the flowers in Bael were big before, but they were nothing compared to the melon-sized blooms that were popping up now.

Ronan slowly lifted his body off of hers, moving more quickly once it was clear that there was no danger. His look of surprise was so comical that Helena snickered and then began to laugh in earnest. He turned to her as if questioning her sanity, which only made her laugh harder.

Realizing that she was laughing at him, he scowled at her and snapped, "Overcompensating much?"

Helena had tears streaming down her face from laughing so hard. Her stomach was sore from the force of it. It wasn't that there was anything funny about what had happened, but the sheer absurdity of a warrior staring up at a flower like it was about to sprout fangs and attack had her snorting with hilarity.

Ronan let her fall to the dirt, feigning disgust while barely concealing his own relieved smile as he watched his Kiri rolling around on the ground.

One by one, her friends slowly walked to stand around her, their faces shining with varying degrees of wonder and concern. As they took in the land around them, and her unharmed body, they relaxed until they too joined in.

CHAPTER 15

*N*ight had fallen on their camp. Gone were the joyous sounds of laughter and in its place was a strained silence. It was time for answers.

Miranda cleared her throat while the men in Helena's Circle all glowered at her. It was evident they all believed that the Triumvirate's visit had been some sort of trap. Even her granddaughter seemed uncertain as she looked over at her with wide blue eyes.

Darrin remained at Effie's side, the violence of her earlier reaction had caught him off-guard. He kept looking at her like he wasn't entirely sure what to do with her. His puzzled expression had Helena biting back a smile. A man who seemed confused about a woman was always quality entertainment.

As for herself, Helena wasn't sure what to believe about the Keepers or their parlor tricks. She had not sensed any malicious intent from them, although there was much to be desired about the way they delivered their messages, not to mention their overall countenance. The thought of those stitched lips and glowing eyes had her suppressing a shudder.

Kragen caught the movement and wrapped a protective arm around her shoulder.

She smiled up at him, appreciating the gesture of support.

"Did you know?" Timmins finally demanded, barely able to restrain his fury. His face was flushed and his blue eyes were narrowed as he waited for Miranda to answer.

The woman opened her mouth, ready to flay the skin from his bones with her words, when she caught the expressions on their faces. She sighed, seeming to age before them. Her shoulders drooped, and she clasped her hands in her lap. Miranda's eyes met hers.

"I had, and still have, no reason to believe that they had any intention other than assistance." Both her eyes and her voice were imploring Helena to believe her.

She did.

Helena nodded once. "Nor do I."

There was rustling as the men turned annoyed glances in her direction. Apparently, they didn't want her to be the one talking right now. *Well, they could just go right ahead and stuff it.*

Her temper flared. She was the Kiri, Mother bless it, and she would do whatever she damn well pleased. If they didn't like it, nothing was stopping them from leaving. Except for the vows they had made.

The memory of the night they had made those promises to her, and she to them, had her swallowing her own harsh words. These were her protectors; it was their duty to worry and care for her.

Sensing her shifting mood, the men tried to look appropriately chastened. Only Nial and Serena seemed to be looking at her with any amount of lingering amusement.

Rolling her eyes, Helena continued, "I do not deny that their methods were questionable, but it is the only way they were able to communicate."

"Don't make excuses for their behavior, Kiri," Joquil admonished. It was rare that he would speak against her. Even more rare for him to have such deep lines of worry bracketing his lips.

"I'm not making any excuses, merely stating facts," she replied calmly. "There is much we do not know about the Keepers, that is true. However, they did show me, once again, what is at stake if I make the wrong choice. They also left me with a warning."

"What did they say?" Miranda asked cautiously.

Timmins scowled at her and the older woman responded by sticking out her tongue.

Helena shook her head and smiled. The way those two bickered was like watching two children resort to hair pulling because they were uncertain of how to show their affection.

"I think they were warning me of the Fracturing, letting me know that if I do not find Von soon, I will not have a choice to make at all."

Their words floated through her mind, no less disturbing the second time.

'Without the tether, you will fracture.'

'Eternally lost to the darkness.'

'No way to return.'

'The choice will be made for you.'

'You will damn us all.'

"What will the choice cost?" Effie asked in a small, subdued voice.

Helena looked at her with haunted eyes, not needing to use any words to convey her answer. The girl's shudder was indication enough that she understood. Vividly.

"So the course is clear. We make for Vyruul and find Von," Ronan declared.

"You say that as if it will be easy," Miranda scoffed. "The journey from Bael to Vyruul is a long one, or have you already forgotten?"

"Perhaps if we hadn't been wasting time in this Mother-forsaken jungle we could have been well on our way by now," Timmins snapped.

Miranda leveled her gaze at him, a sharp edge in her voice as she responded, "If I recall correctly, you are one of the ones that helped make the choice to come here. Furthermore," she continued, raising her voice to speak over his sputtering protests, "we all decided to stay when our Kiri's health demanded rest."

Helena tried not to squirm at the mention of her title; she wanted no part of their feud.

"We all wanted to see if we could learn anything further about the prophecy," Joquil said neutrally, studying his hands with interest.

"And none of us would risk Helena's health," Serena added while the others nodded their agreement.

"It would not be a far journey by Talyrian," Helena said lightly as if her words would not have the impact of a verbal explosion.

"Absolutely not!" Kragen and Ronan yelled in unison while Darrin shouted, "I forbid it!"

She raised an eyebrow, daring them all to try to stop her.

"And what is your plan once you get there?" Micha asked softly.

As one they turned to look at him. Helena noted the color staining his cheeks and almost felt sorry for him.

"What do you mean?" Serena asked.

"Well you do not simply arrive and politely request Gillian hand over your Mate and expect that to work, do you? She will be expecting you, planning for your arrival. You need some plan if you expect to get what you seek."

Now Helena's cheeks burned. It was not that she had forgotten what would be waiting for her once she got there, but the pure logic of his comment left her feeling foolish.

"What would you suggest?" she challenged, trying to regain some semblance of authority.

Micha looked startled, surprised that she would ask him such a question. From the looks Darrin and Ronan shot her, they were as well.

Helena shrugged. "You know your sister and the lay of the land better than anyone here; what would you suggest we do?"

His eyes shuttered as he thought through a list of potential scenarios. When he met her gaze again, he seemed slightly defeated. "It is clear I do not know my sister as well as I thought I did. I never imagined her capable of something such as this. However, she is very clever. I would expect a trap. She will have prepared for every possibility and have planned accordingly. You will need to do something unexpected."

"A distraction," Kragen mused.

"Yes, exactly." Micha nodded. "Gillian's biggest weakness is that she does not anticipate anyone to be as clever as her. She will think your first move is your only move. She will not expect a diversion."

Helena could sense the wheels beginning to turn in her warriors' minds. She was glad for that. It would take their collective energy to come up with something good enough to trick the sneaky bitch.

"Use me," she said suddenly.

"What?" Timmins snapped.

Darrin snarled, "Excuse me?"

Kragen and Ronan just looked at her with lowered brows, displeasure at her statement obvious. Joquil and the others remained calmly quiet, waiting for her to elaborate.

"Use me as your distraction. They will not expect me to come on my own. I will offer myself up in exchange for Von. While I keep her busy, you can sneak in and go to work on their forces."

"That seems too simple." Darrin frowned. "And I do not like the idea of you meekly offering yourself up like a calf to slaughter. You shouldn't go into the enemy's camp on your own."

"Who said anything about meekly?" Helena responded with a terrifying smile.

"Hellion…" Darrin trailed off, his green eyes scanning hers as he asked, "What are you planning, wicked girl?" Years of understanding passed between them and even he could not stop the smile that grew as he began to anticipate her reply.

Her answering smile was smug as she asked, "What kind of damage do you think a Talyrian could do?"

"Kiri! You will be a flying target," Joquil protested.

"You must not think much of my shielding abilities if you think that is the case."

She saw the considering looks on the others faces.

Turning back to Micha she asked, "Do you think it could work?"

He tilted his head, playing out the scenario in his mind before nodding slowly. His green eyes were sad as he said, "I do. She does not know what a Talyrian can do, so she would not know how to plan for it. You will cause enough chaos that she will be quick to surrender and hear you out, leaving the field open for your men to move in."

Ronan and Kragen were nodding along. "It's certainly a start."

The group gathered closer as they began to brainstorm in earnest.

Miranda remained seated and was looking at her thoughtfully. Finally, her eyes met Helena's and she murmured in a voice so low Helena was certain the others couldn't hear, "And her reign will be of ash."

"That's the second time you've said that," Helena commented in a low voice, moving to stand next to the older woman.

"I do not believe it will be the last," she retorted.

Helena shivered as the woman's words wrapped around her, the scenes from the Keepers' vision fresh in her mind.

"Let's hope that is not the case," Helena whispered, her face ashen.

"From your lips to the Mother's ears," Miranda replied, just as softly.

CHAPTER 16

Days were passing quickly as the group made their way to Vyruul. Despite the number of miles that had been reduced between them, the distance Helena felt between her and her Mate didn't seem to lessen. She was still keenly aware of his absence beside, as well as within, her. Although she couldn't decide what she missed more: the feel of his body pressed against hers or that deep growling voice calling her *Mate* within the recesses of her mind.

Their bond was intact, something she checked compulsively multiple times a day. Whenever she plucked at the mental tether that bound them, she was always able to feel his flickering presence along its length; however, they had not had any meaningful contact since she had found him in her dreams. Helena was sure that it was because of his captors, although she could only guess as to what they were doing to him that interfered with his ability to access his magic. Everything she pictured only caused her fury to grow.

Helena's rage had become a living thing always simmering just below the surface. These days a thought was enough to make it boil over and send her spiraling into the darkest recesses of her mind. Whether it was because they finally had a plan, or that they were mere days away from finding him, she couldn't say. In either case, her need for vengeance had become all-consuming.

She had withdrawn from her Circle, choosing to visualize all the ways that she would repay Gillian's treachery instead of making idle conversation. For a girl that had grown up in a quiet cottage, it would seem that Helena had quite the sadistic imagination. She was fairly certain this was not a discovery her mother would be proud of, although there was no question Von would approve. The thought had her lips curling in a feral smile.

Ronan picked that moment to turn to her. Whatever he saw on her face gave him pause, but after a moment he maneuvered his wolf toward her. "Kiri," he said by way of greeting.

She lifted a brow at the formality. "Bastard," she returned, the word thick with warmth and gentle teasing despite the iciness of her eyes. It was Von's preferred greeting for his oldest friend, and Helena had used it intentionally, knowing Ronan would pick up on the sentimentality of its usage rather than any perceived insult.

As predicted, a smile stretched across his scarred face. "It would seem you are feeling more yourself, lady."

"As opposed to what, exactly?" she asked mildly.

"Your body has regained the weight it lost during our time in the jungle and there are no longer shadows beneath your eyes."

"Oh," she said, shifting in her saddle so that her cloak draped around her more loosely.

She was only a little surprised to find that he had been paying attention that closely, but it still rankled that he felt the need to comment on her weight at all. His answering grin was all teeth.

The smugness of the expression had Helena rolling her eyes. "I suppose you'd like a cookie for your expert observation skills?"

"Not if you made them," he countered.

Helena sputtered. "I will have you know I make delicious cookies, thank you very much. You would be damned lucky if I ever offered to share them with the likes of you."

"I don't think Von would let you share your *cookies* with anyone but him," Ronan retorted dryly.

The subtle emphasis on the word had Helena studying him more closely. The satisfied look in his eyes took away all of the indignation she was feeling.

"You're provoking me on purpose," she accused.

"It worked," he said simply.

"Why?" she pressed.

"Because there has been a weight to your thoughts that doesn't belong there. I have noticed it often the last few days, and its presence disturbs me. You are sunshine, Helena. There is no place for darkness in those eyes."

His words had the effect of a pail of water being dumped atop her head. They were a frank assessment, but no less effective for it.

Helena sat there, her mouth opening and closing like a gaping fish while she processed what he had said. That he had actually cared enough to intervene. Not even Darrin had nerve enough to call her out on her temper.

"Thank you," she said softly, humbled by this man and his words.

It had stunned her that he knew her well enough to know what she needed, even better than she did. And not only that but also by the way he always seemed to look after her, even when it had never been his responsibility to do so. There were those in her Circle, bound to her by life vows, who paid less attention to her subtle shifts in mood. It spoke deeply of his commitment to Von, and to her.

They shared a look that said more than either of them could verbalize. The moment hung between them, stretching until Ronan finally ended it by clearing his throat gruffly, "If you had wanted to postpone getting your Jaka because you were too scared of a little needle, you could have said so. I don't think you needed to stage a tantrum to get out of it. That was a little much, even for you."

Understanding was shining in her aqua eyes as she sneered playfully. "Please, I bet you cried when you got yours, you big baby."

Ronan laughed, a deep guffaw that had the others turning in their seats to stare back at them curiously. "Ah, Hellion, that's more like it."

She grimaced at his use of her nickname but smiled all the same. "Does this mean that I still get my Jaka?"

Ronan nodded. "Whenever you are ready, Helena, it would be my honor."

"Tonight?" she asked, suddenly eager to bear the mark of protection.

He lifted a brow but nodded his agreement. "Sure. Usually, it takes a couple of days to get the ceremony organized—"

"No," she cut him off. "No ceremony. Just us." There was no hidden meaning in the words; she simply did not want to be bared for so long in front of the others.

"Serena is more than capable of doing it, if you'd rather," Ronan offered, his ears suddenly red.

Helena laughed, amused that her friend was having a bout of modesty at her expense. "No, you are my Commander, are you not? It should be you."

He was pleased to hear her words, although it took a while for the color to fade from his face. "As you wish," he said finally.

They rode beside each other in companionable silence until finally breaking for camp that evening. As she dismounted Karma, Helena was pleased to realize that she had not thought of torture or blood once that afternoon.

HELENA FOLDED the simple gown she had selected, tossing it in her knapsack once she was done. Serena and Effie had helped her modify the garment so that she could undo the ties over her shoulder and peel the fabric down instead of having to remove it entirely. Serena also helped her fashion a cloth that tied around her chest so that she could retain some modesty while Ronan tattooed her. She had appreciated their help, and the sound of their soft voices as they had gossiped and laughed together that afternoon. It had given her mind something to focus on.

She was alone now, however, and the silence was overwhelming.

Needing to distract herself until it was time to meet up with Ronan, Helena decided to bathe in the secluded glen not far from the campsite.

While she had asked Ronan to forego the official ceremony, Helena liked the idea of cleansing herself in preparation for her Jaka. It was a sacred mark of the Mother, and receiving it while coated in sweat and dirt was highly unappealing.

Checking to make sure she was not forgetting anything, Helena allowed her eyes to scan her tent before she finally nodded and stepped out.

A cool breeze greeted her and had her shivering slightly. The weather had started to turn in the last few days, the humidity of the jungle yielding to the cooler temperatures of the north. Helena had never been to Vyruul, but what she had heard about the mountainous region had her anticipating jagged peaks reaching toward the sky from a sea of ice. And if the last few days were any indication, the temperature would only continue to drop as they moved deeper into Vyruul. They were a day or two away from the border, and none of them were quite sure what to expect once they arrived.

Shaking off the thoughts of what may or may not be waiting for her in Vyruul, Helena let out the low whistle that called Starshine to her side. After a few moments of silence, the sound of beating wings filled the sky. She looked up, smiling when she saw the Talyrian flying toward her.

Starshine landed with a soft huff, smoke flaring out from her nose, her turquoise eyes luminous.

"Hi girl," Helena said softly, lifting her hand to brush the velvety snout in greeting.

A deep rumble started in the Talyrian's chest, causing the ground to tremble slightly.

Helena snickered as she began to scratch behind the large cat's ear. "Feel good?"

Starshine closed her eyes in response and began to purr louder.

After a few moments of indulging Starshine, Helena gave her a final pat and asked, "Keep me company for a while?"

Starshine huffed her assent and nudged Helena with her massive head, pushing her in the direction of the pool.

She stumbled slightly and laughed over her shoulder. "In a hurry all of a sudden?"

The Talyrian didn't justify the question with a response, which only amused her further.

"So what have you been up to, lady?" she asked aloud, not expecting a response but enjoying the playful banter regardless.

A turquoise eye rolled toward her and then away as a small jet of flame lit up the darkening sky.

"Killing things?" she guessed, only half joking.

Starshine snorted.

"Hunt, kill, same difference," Helena amended, laughing at the absurdity of carrying on a one-sided conversation.

Starshine shook her head, seeming to disagree with Helena's assessment. The silvery mane shone brightly as she did.

"Did you have a Mr. Starshine to keep you company? A he-cat to help you pounce on unsuspecting bunnies? Or to pounce on you?" she teased while mimicking a cat pounce.

Starshine stopped her slow prowl and just looked at Helena without blinking. The Talyrian queen was clearly not impressed with Helena's pouncing skills.

"I'm sorry, were you the one pouncing on him?" Helena asked deadpan, blinking up with wide innocent eyes at Starshine. The Talyrian stared steadily back, unmoving. "Were you off pouncing with multiple Mr. Starshines?" she pressed, enjoying herself entirely too much as she barely held back her laughter.

The Talyrian seemed to sigh, resigned to her mistress's baiting, and let out another deep huff before she started walking again. A large plume of smoke curled up in the air and was floating behind her as she moved through the trees.

Helena waited a moment and then started after her. "What, too personal?"

Starshine let out a low growl, which only caused Helena to break out into happy peals of laughter. "It's not like you don't make your opinions clear about *my* mate. I only thought it fair to inquire about your own…" Helena trailed off searching for the right word, "companion."

She had finally caught back up to Starshine who paused only long enough to lift her giant paw and swat at Helena. The duo had just reached the small clearing beside the shallow pool when the sound of splashing greeted them.

Starshine's teeth bared in a warning growl, while Helena reached for the hunting knife she had strapped to her thigh. They took a cautious step forward, all amusement fleeing in the wake of a potential threat.

The sound of a girl's high-pitched giggle had her freezing in place. Two more steps confirmed what her ears had already recognized. It was Effie, splashing in the water. Helena felt her shoulders relax and was just about to call out a greeting when another person came into view.

Darrin.

"Well isn't that a surprise," she murmured to her feline friend, not sure what to think about the couple currently splashing around in the water.

Starshine moved her head in the semblance of a nod.

"I guess you aren't the only one that goes off to pounce with a tom," Helena mused.

Starshine growled softly, but there was no temper in the sound.

A pang in her chest kept Helena from announcing her presence. She didn't want to interrupt them and rob them of the moment they were having. Effie's face was flushed with color, as she laughed and tried to run away from Darrin who was pursuing her. Her blonde hair was hanging down her back in a golden stream, her blue gown clinging to her curves in a way that Darrin was helpless to ignore. She watched the way his eyes trailed down Effie's body before reluctantly dragging back up to her face, his own eyes bright with predatory interest.

With a lunge, Darrin wrapped his arms around Effie's waist and pulled her down into the water. She popped up, sputtering and pushing her wet hair out of her eyes. As she rose, she was face to face with Darrin, barely any space between them. Their laughter slowly died as they stared at each other as if finally seeing each other for the first time. The smile fell from her face, and Helena could see Effie's chest frantically rising and falling with her shallow breaths. Darrin stared down at her, his green eyes intense as he lifted a hand to brush stray drops of water from her cheek.

Helena felt her breath hitch, suddenly uncomfortable with bearing witness to such an intimate moment.

"Come on, girl," she said under her breath, nudging Starshine as she started walking away from the couple in the water. "Let's go down a bit further."

Her movements felt leaden as she walked, and Helena told herself firmly it was just the long journey and not jealousy that weighed each step down. Too bad she wasn't buying it.

It wasn't a longing for Darrin that made her heart heavy, but the simple fact that she wasn't the one experiencing that stolen moment of sweetness with her Mate, that she had experienced so few stolen moments with him before he was taken from her. She could feel the ripple of magic that rose in response to her anger at the reminder.

The sudden tidal wave of emotion caused her face to flush as her thoughts turned again to the red-headed girl who was responsible for her current lack of moments.

Gillian, Helena snarled softly.

Sensing her rapidly diminishing mood, Starshine headbutted Helena to pull her attention away from her thoughts. Unfortunately, the move had the unintended side effect of sending Helena flying into the water, arms flailing wildly.

At least, she thought it was unintended.

When she popped back up out of the icy water, Starshine sat at the banks, licking her paw while her tail twitched behind her. If she didn't know better, she would have sworn the Talyrian was laughing at her.

CHAPTER 17

Helena braided her hair as she made her way back toward the camp. Starshine prowled behind her until the others came into view and then let out a soft sound that could have been a farewell, before she moved into the shadows.

Her dress was still damp from having fallen into the water, despite Helena having called some Fire to help dry it off. She moved toward Ronan who was seated beside the campfire, staring off in the direction of Serena and Nial. Seeing the two heads bowed closely together while they whispered animatedly had Helena sighing heavily.

She said nothing as she moved beside the red-haired warrior. His hair was unbound and hanging in thick red waves down his back. Helena had the completely improper thought of running her fingers through it to see if it was as soft as it looked. She stroked her own hair instead, pouting slightly when she realized Ronan's hair was probably softer than hers. The inane thought made her chuckle.

Ronan turned slightly in his seat and lifted his eyes to her. He gave her a smile that didn't quite reach his eyes and turned back toward Serena.

"I've lost her," he said in a rough voice.

"But she hasn't—" Helena started, almost horrified at the thought.

Ronan glared at her, offended on Serena's behalf. "No, she hasn't said or done anything so final. But it only takes a look to see what is between them."

Helena studied the blonde, whose cheeks were flushed and violet eyes were shining under the warm glow of the fire. Although, it was more likely that the dark-haired man with stormy eyes was responsible for her friend's happy blush.

Turning to Ronan, she watched as his eyes devoured the woman who had been his lover and partner for most of their adult lives. You don't have that kind of relationship with someone and not learn every nuanced expression on their face. He obviously saw something when he looked at her that made it clear she was falling for the other man. Then again, Helena had known immediately that there had been something between them.

"Will you not fight for her?" Helena asked quietly, no judgment or censure in the question, only curiosity.

He smiled up at her wryly. "If I thought there was a chance, do you think I'd be sitting over here watching that?" There was a bitter edge to his words that cut deep.

"I suppose not," she replied, smiling as she imagined him throwing Serena over his shoulder to carry her off and remind to whom she belonged.

"One cannot fight what's between them. I've seen the mating bond falling into place before. I recognize the symptoms," Ronan's voice was low and thick with the emotions he struggled to hide.

"Mating bond?" she repeated stunned, turning to study the couple more carefully. "You think they are mates?"

Ronan laughed without humor. "What else would snatch her from me so easily? I've loved her since we were kids, and she has loved me. There's never been another for either of us, until she met him. Now she barely remembers that I exist."

Helena heard the way he struggled not to choke on the words; the admission was costing him dearly. She placed a hand on his shoulder, squeezing slightly as she offered silent comfort. They stood there quietly, and Helena saw the moment that resignation wrapped itself around him like a mantle.

He lowered his head and took a shuddering breath, staring into the flame for one, two, heartbeats before slowly coming to his feet. When he turned to her, his glittering blue eyes were lost.

"Is there no hope then?" she asked, her own heart breaking for her friend.

A side of Ronan's lip curled up as he considered the question. "As long as the Mother watches over us, there is always hope. But I will not make her choose, Helena. Not to assuage my pride. Not when the Mother pulls her to another."

Helena wrapped her arms around him, giving him a quick and fierce hug. When she pulled away, they both pretended not to notice the tears still shining on the other's cheeks.

"Come, you have a job to do," she said firmly, making the words an order that would help him refocus.

Ronan nodded, a true smile growing as he looked down at her. "My needles are yours, Kiri."

"You don't have to look quite so gleeful at the thought of making me bleed," she muttered, his chuckle following her into the tent.

HELENA STRETCHED out on the faded green blanket that Ronan had laid out for her.

"Get comfortable, we'll be here awhile," he ordered, turning to set up his supplies while she got into position.

She maneuvered herself so that she was laying on her side, her head cradled in the vee of her arm.

Turning toward her, Ronan's eyes scanned her with professional assessment. "Over the ribs and heart?"

After a steadying breath, she affirmed, "Yes."

He nodded and moved to sit beside her. As he shifted away from the makeshift table he'd set up she noticed that the liquid in the small glass dish was white not black. Seeing the questioning look in her eyes, he said, "I thought something subtler would suit you better. Besides, I already told you, you are sunshine. Your mark should shine as you do."

"And will it?" she asked surprised.

"I added some powder to the ink that should give it a metallic hue once it heals."

Pleasure filled her at his words.

Noting her reaction, he grinned smugly. "You are my Kiri, not just another warrior in the ranks. You deserve a mark as unique as you are."

She smiled up at him, eager to see what it would look like. "So what are you waiting for?"

He shook his head and rolled his eyes, moving into position with his hands hovering just over her skin. She could feel the heat rolling off of him and closed her eyes to concentrate on her breathing.

"Ready?" he asked softly.

She gave a terse nod and grit her teeth.

The first prick of the needle caused her to flinch. The second and third came in rapid succession until each was lost in the other, becoming a string of scratching fire that worked its way along her skin. She felt sweat break out all over her body in response to the pain, but she laid as still as possible, thinking only of breathing in and out.

"You are faring better than Von did," Ronan said after a while.

Her eyes flew open at that. "I am?"

Ronan nodded, biting down on his lip as he focused intently on the placement of the needles. He sat back and wiped at her skin before dipping his needle back into the ink and moving back over her.

She tried to ignore the sight of the smeared blood on the cloth he absentmindedly placed back on the table.

"He was cursing the entire time. If I recall correctly, he was so creative with his insults that our Commander was blushing and finally threatened to beat him bloody if he didn't shut his mouth."

Helena smiled at the thought, imagining the abuse Von hurled at those around him. Ronan adjusted her positioning slightly so that she was more on her back than her side, starting to work his way toward the center of her chest. She took in a sharp breath; the pain was more intense there.

"I offered to hold his hand," Ronan said quickly, to distract her.

She blinked at that, too startled to laugh. "And did he take you up on your offer?"

"What do you think?" he asked, raising a brow.

"Which body part did he threaten to remove if you tried?" she responded.

Ronan just stared at her, letting her arrive at her own conclusion.

"And did Serena have anything to say about that?" she asked, before wincing at her use of Serena's name. She looked up at him apologetically.

He shrugged and his smile, when he looked down at her to respond, held only a hint of sadness. "She informed Von that if he went anywhere near my cock, she would rip his off and shove it down his throat."

Helena tried not to laugh, but a snicker escaped anyway.

"I guess it's a good thing you did not end up holding his hand then."

"No, not his hand, just him."

"Excuse me?" she asked incredulously.

Ronan nodded. "Oh yes, I had to hold him down. He was squirming so badly it was nigh impossible for our Commander to continue."

Helena was having trouble imagining her Mate in that depiction. She gave Ronan a questioning look, doubting him momentarily.

"Ask him about it yourself, once we get him back. He won't be able to lie to you."

She shook her head in amazement. "I suppose I'll have to."

They grew quiet for a while as he continued his steady pace.

"Will you tell me what they mean? The symbols," she clarified when he did not begin speaking right away.

"Each one on its own means something different, but when they are woven together, they become a blessing, enchanting you with the Mother's protection. This one," he said indicating the symbol he was currently outlining over the center of her ribs, "is the symbol of the Mother herself. It is always placed closest to the heart, since we owe our existence in this world to Her. She is at the center of everything, and so too is her mark." He finished a complex swirl and sat back to gesture to the looping symbol that linked with it before flowing into others along her ribs. "This one is strength and that one balance. And these here are for accuracy, agility and speed."

Helena nodded her understanding.

"We're almost done," he said quietly, noticing her expression as he moved to fill in the Mother's symbol.

"I'm fine," she panted as the needle stabbed at her. Ronan raised a brow, calling her on the lie. Rolling her eyes, she bit down on her lip and nodded for him to continue, feeling light-headed as the sound of her heartbeat pounded in her ears.

"Individually, the symbols do not *do* anything, but when they are combined like this, they become a sort of enhancement, infusing your power with their abilities."

"I don't feel any different," she murmured, trying to focus on his words and not the pain.

"That's because I'm not finished yet," he retorted.

"Perhaps you should hurry up," she said with mock sweetness.

"Would you like me to do this right or quickly?" he taunted.

"Why not both?" she asked seriously, her hopeful look dropping at his expression. "Just don't mark me with anything offensive," Helena said finally, a bit resigned.

At his silence, she lifted her head to study his face again. "You didn't mark me with anything offensive did you?"

He scowled down at her. "No, Hellion. Nothing disrespectful. But it is customary to incorporate something personal into the Jaka, as well as something that reflects its bearer."

"Isn't that what you did with the ink?"

He shrugged. "In part, I suppose."

She hesitated before asking, "What symbols did you add to represent us then?"

"For you, I added the symbol of life, since you are the Mother's Vessel," he murmured as he gestured toward something that looked like flowering vines wrapping around the symbol of the Mother.

"And yours?" she asked, trying to lift her head to see what he was doing.

He scowled at her and pushed her back down. "Settle down, or I'll call one of the men in here to hold you down."

She made a rude gesture to show him what she thought of that suggestion.

Ronan shook his head as he laughed, still not answering the question.

"Hey! I'm waiting," she reminded him.

"Patience," he murmured, refusing to answer.

Just when she was about to push him, he sat back and nodded. "Just one last thing and we'll be done."

He set his tools down and cleaned her throbbing skin with a cool cloth, wiping away the excess ink and blood. Once she was clean, he rested his hand above the Mother's mark and bowed his head. She watched his eyes flutter closed and he said something hushed she could not understand.

Once he was done speaking she felt a tingling rush work its way through her body. The colors in the tent had grown muted as it became dark outside. However, they were now blazing brightly.

Helena blinked, trying to get her eyes to adjust. She turned toward Ronan, who was looking at her with something akin to wonder, his mouth hanging open in a way that frightened her.

"What?" she asked, startled to hear her voice come out in the richly layered way she associated with her magic.

He blinked a few times. "Your eyes," he said hoarsely.

She reached for a mirror he had set to the side and pulled it to her face. Staring back at her were twin pools of swirling iridescence. That was nothing new. Unexpected, but not new. It would seem the Jaka had called her magic forth.

Curious to see what her tattoo would look like with her enhanced vision, she moved the mirror down to see her Jaka for the first time. Her skin was red with irritation, which only made the shimmering mark stand out in sharper contrast. Helena's breath left her in a whoosh. It was beautiful.

The twirling lines seemed to sparkle like a cloud of diamond dust along her skin, catching and pulling the light to the symbols now inked into its surface. She studied the Mother's mark first, which looked like two hands cradling something between them. Her own mark, twisted around it like a vine with flowers in various stages of bloom. Helena followed the vines, moving the mirror as she did, noting the symbols he had already indicated and picking out a few others. She opened her mouth to ask him about them when realization dawned. He had included a symbol for each of her Circle.

"Ronan," she whispered awestruck, as she peered more closely.

There was Darrin and Kragen, the runic shapes representing a shield and sword hidden along a snaking piece of vine from her own symbol. A little beside them, also hidden in the vines were the symbols of knowledge and power, Timmins and Joquil respectively. Von's mark left her speechless. Her fingers fluttered above it, aching to touch it. At first glance, it was nothing special, but upon deeper inspection, it was a spiral of stars that worked itself around the vine and ending just below her heart. It was the symbol for completion blended with the symbol for the soul.

"It's perfect," she breathed, trying to push down the emotion that threatened to spill over. She'd had enough of tears, and this was not a moment for them.

Before she set the mirror down, she caught one final symbol, barely visible to her at the base of her ribcage. It was the very tip of the tattoo, a trio of arcing lines that connected into a tight knot.

"Loyalty," Ronan supplied in a subdued tone.

Her throat too tight for words, Helena reached out and grasped his hand firmly in hers. She squeezed it tightly before letting go and turning to him.

"Thank you."

Ronan bowed his head. As he did, she felt a small ripple in her mind. It was not the feeling she associated with her connection to Von, but it was familiar all the same. Focusing on that sensation, Helena quickly realized what it was.

Her glowing eyes studied the man standing before her. She was experiencing Ronan's feelings.

As she turned deeper into herself, she found that there were five new threads in total, one for Ronan and one each for the rest of her Circle. The tether connecting her and Von was unchanged although it now seemed to pulse with increased awareness. The other strands were vibrant and steady within her, and it was not difficult to identify which strand represented who.

She reached for the one that felt like Ronan and waited. There was no reaction from the man standing before her, although she was able to focus more clearly on what he was feeling. His sense of pride at her happiness with the tattoo warmed her.

Smiling, she focused on the others. Helena felt flickers of awareness, but not an actual connection. Whatever Ronan had done when he'd incorporated himself and her Circle into the tattoo had deepened her empathetic connection to each of them, but it was not the two-way bond that stretched between her and her Mate.

Helena wondered how long it would take for the others to realize what had happened.

CHAPTER 18

Gillian paced back and forth between two of the pillars in the throne room. Her mother had summoned her and she had no clue what to expect. Things with Von were progressing, albeit more slowly than her mother would have liked. The dose of the healing brew that she had been giving him each day was no longer necessary, although she continued to use it as an excuse to keep him sedated.

Stupid male with his stupid eyes, she thought darkly. He was the one who was chained, not her. What did she have to fear from him, really? The memory of their last interaction rose in answer. *Right.*

She shuddered and began biting at the soft flesh beside her thumbnail. There was something about that cold silver gaze that made her edgy. She much preferred when he couldn't look at her. Perhaps Rowena would be willing to consider blindfolding him so that she could avoid it even in his waking hours. Gillian did not go out of her way to ask for favors from her mother, but this one might be worth it. If for no other reason than to escape the sinister promise lurking in those eyes.

The soft click of a door shutting halted her steps and had her spinning to face the throne where Rowena now sat. Being seated did nothing to diminish the icy power that radiated out of her.

Gillian clasped her trembling hands together and was glad for the folds of her dress that concealed them.

"M-mistress," she said by way of greeting, hating herself for the nerves that made her stutter. Once she had finished her approach and stood before Rowena, she genuflected and nervously lifted her eyes up to assess her mother's mood.

Rowena stared down at her without moving, her face an expressionless mask. Only the slight tightening of her mouth alluded to her temper. "The bitch queen moves with her band of rogues to surprise us. Even now they approach our border. How can that little fool really believe that anything she does would go unseen in my lands?"

"Her underestimation works in our favor," Gillian pointed out, blanching when her mother narrowed her eyes. The question had been rhetorical and she had not be given permission to speak. Lowering her gaze, Gillian bowed her head apologetically.

After a long moment of silence, her mother continued, "We will be ready for her with a little surprise of our own. It's time to ready the prisoner."

Gillian lifted her eyes, unsure what her mother meant.

Seeing the question on her daughter's face, Rowena rolled her eyes with exasperation. "Must I do everything myself? Bring him to me so that I may begin drawing from him."

Understanding dawned, and Gillian clenched her hands into tighter fists, her nails cutting into the soft skin of her palms. "Of course, Mother. It will be done."

"See that you do not waste time."

Gillian nodded to show that she had heard her and swiftly made her way out of the room. She had mixed feelings about her mother's twisted use of power. There was something about it that grated against her and left her unsettled for days after witnessing it. While she was no great fan of Von's, other than using his body for her amusement, a part of her could not stomach the thought of him as one of her mother's puppets. To see such strength cowed... it was a shame.

Shaking her head to clear it of the unwanted sympathy, she steeled herself for what lay ahead and made her way to Von's room so that her mother could begin the process that would turn him into a Shadow.

"KIRI," Timmins said in a respectfully subdued tone from the entrance to her tent.

Helena looked up from the map Micha had sketched for her and idly asked, "Why is it we never seem to stay anywhere that has actual walls. These lands have inns don't they?"

The side of Timmins' mouth curled up in an amused smile. That question had become a familiar refrain as the climate continued to drop the closer they came to the heart of the Vyruul mountainside.

"You know it is not safe to announce our presence here."

Helena's answering smile acknowledged his words of caution, while the shiver that ran down her spine reinforced them. The truth was, something knew they were here already. Helena had never felt anything like the bone-deep certainty that she was being watched; she had been tense and on high alert for days.

Sighing, she turned to face him fully. "What did you need, Timmins?"

Her Advisor looked at her carefully before speaking again, "We are less than a day's ride from the keep, according to Micha."

Helena nodded, her indication that he should continue.

"We will need to select our base camp and begin preparations for the attack."

She raised her eyebrow at that. "What do you mean begin? Preparations started days ago."

"I just meant..." Timmins trailed off and looked at her with concern etched in his expression. His usual confident demeanor was nowhere to be found as he noticeably deflated before her.

Helena could feel his worry tugging at her from the depths of their Jaka-enhanced connection, but she didn't need it to know something was weighing on him. She could see him struggling to find the words he needed, so she did not press him and remained quiet as she waited for him to continue.

"Helena, I—I do not have a good feeling about what awaits us. You said yourself there was another woman in the room when you joined with Von. Gillian is not the only one we will face and I highly doubt she was the mastermind behind kidnapping Von. We need time to better plan and prepare for the true enemy—"

The change in Helena was instantaneous as she cut him off, "One enemy or thousands; the plan does not change. They took what is *mine*," the word came out in a snarl that echoed in the voice of her magic, "and now they must pay." Her hair flew up around her, rippling in a non-existent breeze while her eyes twinkled with iridescence. It was not Helena talking; it was the Vessel.

Timmins stared at her with wide eyes.

"Do you doubt my ability, Advisor?" she asked in a deadly soft croon.

"No, Kiri," he replied, his voice even and his answer immediate.

She waited a beat before speaking again, letting him feel the weight of her power fill the room. "You do bring up a good point, though. One I had already been thinking on, in fact. We cannot prepare for something that is unknown."

"Kiri?" he asked, his tone wary as if anticipating what she was about to say.

The smile that curved her lips was filled with bloodthirsty promise. "I think it's time we do some spying of our own."

HELENA ROLLED her eyes as her men fussed around her. They had moved her away from the campsite and into a large snow-covered clearing, so that if she lost control again, her magic would not destroy anything of value. If she did not agree, at least in part, with their assessment that this experiment could yield potentially dangerous results, she would have already begun the mental descent that would take her to the threshold of Von's mind.

Since being marked by Ronan, she had felt more centered and in control of her power than she had since Von disappeared. She had also been feeling increased flickers of awareness along their mating bond as they closed in on where he was being kept. The result was that Helena was stronger than she had ever been, and she was ready to test her power.

"Are you sure about this, Helena?" Darrin whispered, crouching beside her.

She pressed her palm to his stubbled cheek and offered him a reassuring smile, aqua eyes staring into green as she said, "I need to do this, Darrin. He needs to know that we are close so he will be ready when we come for him. Not to mention the fact that we would greatly benefit from any information he has gathered. I know that I can reach him," she finished fiercely, her voice was strengthened by her conviction.

"You may need to do it, but I don't need to like it," he muttered darkly.

Helena couldn't contain the chuckle that escaped at his petulance. "Were you hoping to talk me out of it?"

The stubborn set of his jaw was answer enough.

"And how, exactly, did you think you were going to stop me?"

Darrin shrugged and looked away as he said, "I would have found a way."

"Mmm," she murmured, the disbelief in her tone evident. Helena called her power to her, feeling it readily respond. "Look at me," she demanded in the multitude of voices.

Surprised at the change, his eyes snapped back to hers.

"I am the Mother's Vessel. I do not need protection. It is those who seek to oppose me that require protection from *me*."

"I am your Shield," he protested in an angry whisper. "It is my duty to protect and defend. You are too important to our people to be so careless with your life."

"It is because of our people that I cannot afford to hide behind you. I am their leader, Shield. Let me lead." There was no room for argument and he knew it. Helena could almost see the frustration rolling off him in waves as he stood and argued anyway.

"And I am your Shield!" he shouted. "Let me fucking protect you! Mother's tits, Helena."

Infusing her voice with her power she stood slowly. "Do not forget to whom you speak, Shield. You made a vow to be in service to me and my will. Obey it."

"I made a vow to protect you from those who would seek to destroy you. I *am* staying true to my vow, you stubborn ass!"

The sky cracked in half as a bolt of lightning and the answering growl of thunder lit up the sky. In the distance, Starshine roared, sensing her mistress's temper and seeing it as a call to battle, one that she was clearly eager to answer.

"Kiri," a soft voice called.

Helena whirled around, hands balled into fists.

Effie stood just off to the side, her trembling hands held up in the position of surrender. "He means no harm, Kiri. He is just worried about you. We all are."

The rest of her Circle flanked Effie, unwilling to step in the middle of this particular argument. From the set of their jaws and crossed arms, Helena could tell that they were not necessarily on her side.

Seeing the wary way Effie and the others waited for her reaction was sobering. Helena took a shuddering breath, trying to reign in the temper that still rose too quickly to the surface. "I know." She turned to face Darrin again and said more softly, "I know."

"It is not just the Chosen who need you," he said softly. "I need you, too."

Her eyes softened, and she looked from Darrin to Effie. "But Von needs me more. Don't you understand yet? Without him, I will cease to be me. This has to end, Darrin, for all of our sakes," her voice carried despite the gentle way she said the words. She watched as the fight left him, his shoulders drooping as he released a deep breath.

"Then I will stand guard while you do what needs to be done." With those words, Darrin turned on his heel and stomped off.

Helena's eyes still shimmered with iridescence as she turned back toward the others. The added level of awareness her Jaka granted pulsed as she met the steady gaze of each. If she were to close her eyes, she would be able to identify who was standing where simply through that connection. Each man had their own unique sensation, some combination of their power and personality, that was unmistakable. And now, when amplified by the intensity of their emotion, it was a force she couldn't ignore if she tried.

The feel of them was overwhelming, especially since her own emotions were riding high. It should be too much for any one person to bear, all of these conflicting feelings swirling through her: Darrin's receding anger, Kragen's steady strength, Timmins' gentle concern, and even Joquil's quiet displeasure. But she didn't have a choice. As the Kiri's Circle, these men were bound to her. They had placed their lives in her hands, and she was responsible for their well-being. That included dealing with mercurial moods.

Something shifted within her, settling into place. She was their ruler and the decisions she made would affect them all. While that meant she owed it to them to listen and take their opinions into consideration, it also meant that it was ultimately up to her to trust herself to make the right decision. They needed her to lead, to make the choices that they could not. So she would.

Sensing the shift in Helena, Serena stepped forward. "We will all stand guard," she said softly. The others nodded their agreement before moving away to stand in a loose circle around her.

Nial was the only one who hesitated, walking toward her and placing a hand on her shoulder. "I know that I have made no formal vows to you, Helena, but I still serve. It is my brother you are bound to, which makes you family. If you have need of me, for anything, my help is yours."

"Nial—" she whispered.

"I serve, Kiri," he said firmly, before squeezing her shoulder and backing away.

Those not in her Circle traded looks with each other before kneeling. Effie, Miranda, Micha, Nial, Serena, and Ronan each bowing their heads in a formal show of respect. Her Circle, seeing the others and sensing the importance of the moment, also dropped to their knees. Helena opened her mouth to protest, feeling overwhelmed at the sight of her friends submitting to her in this way.

"We serve," they said, their voices booming across the clearing.

"You guys," she whispered, her fingers pressing into her lips to stave off the emotion that was threatening to overpower her. She needed to focus now and could not afford to let go of the righteous anger that had been guiding her until now.

Ronan's eyes met hers first, his smirk full of male arrogance as he said, "I never swore loyalty to Von; hopefully he won't be too butthurt when he finds out about this."

Snickers met the comment and Helena felt her lips twitch as she said dryly, "I won't tell him if you don't."

With a wink, Ronan stood, and the others followed. "What do you need us to do?"

Amusement fled as quickly as it had come. "Be ready," she said, her power making her hair dance and eyes glow, "this visit may not go unnoticed."

CHAPTER 19

*V*on woke with a start. Something was coming and his instincts were screaming for him to prepare. He shifted in the bed, arms and legs still bound with magic-enhanced chains. Von snarled and pulled, feeling the chains go taut instead of give. Growling with frustration, he worked himself into a sitting position and stared in the direction of the door.

He could feel his heart racing, but instead of panicking he felt himself slip into the intense focus that always preceded a battle. Even chained he would put up a fight. Von's eyes took in every detail of the room, searching for something that he could use while also cataloguing potential threats. During his assessment, he felt a gentle tug along his bond with Helena. It was the strongest the bond had felt since being trapped here.

The tug came again, more insistent this time. Von hesitated, torn between staying vigilant and wanting to follow the pull. Was this what had awoken him? The possibility gave him pause. Maybe it was not a threat after all.

Focusing on their bond, he tentatively asked, *"Mira?"*

The answering voice was not the sweet, slightly husky voice he associated with his mate. It was raw power that responded, *"Mate."*

Von snapped to attention, his own magic rising to the surface in response to Helena's. This was not to be a moment shared between lovers then, but a Kiri calling upon one in her Circle. There was a part of him that mourned the fact, wishing to feel her body move beneath his again, even if only in their shared dreams. However, the part of himself that belonged to her could not deny the call to battle he heard in her voice.

From his place on the bed, Von grinned. There was no joy in the expression, only a feral hunger as he answered, *"Kiri."*

"We have need of your services, Mate."

He appreciated the double meaning of the words and could not help the sexual purr that laced his voice as he asked, *"I am always ready to service you, Mira. But perhaps you could specify what it is you require?"*

Von felt her amusement and the punch of arousal his words evoked. He closed his eyes as he felt the gentle pull of fingers through his hair followed by a sharp tug and the sting of a bite along the corded muscles of his neck.

"Focus, Mate."

"Apologies, Lady. What do you need?" Von willed his body to obey as he waited for her to reply.

"Information. We are close, perhaps only a day away. Can you tell us anything about where you are being kept?"

"Very little, unfortunately. I have not left this room, at least as far as I am aware," he replied apologetically.

There was no censure in her voice when she asked, *"What of your captors?"*

"The blonde is the one calling the shots. There's no question about it. She only visited me the one time you were present, but it is clear that she has something on Gillian. As to what that is I couldn't hazard a guess. I also couldn't say which of the Mother's branches she's been gifted with. I have never felt it's like."

"Corrupted," Helena rumbled, still using the harmonious voice that indicated she was channeling her power.

Von considered the word and nodded. *"Yes, that is what I feel. She has twisted her magic; it makes her... unpredictable."*

He could feel her sigh, disappointed that they had so little to go on. Not wanting to let her down, he offered, *"Gillian still visits me daily. She is usually only here long enough to drug me, but perhaps there's a way for me to get past her."*

There was a pause while Helena thought over his offer. Finally, she said, *"Not alone, and certainly not while bound. It is not safe for you to wander through the castle on your own. Especially since we do not know enough about the enemies you could encounter. No, Mate. Stay put. I have another idea, someone else who might be able to tell us about the blonde."* Helena paused again and then added, *"Just because you cannot escape, does not mean you should have to remain chained."*

Von felt a surge of molten power rush through him and then all four chains snapped. He pulled his arms down, his muscles protesting and welcoming the movement in equal measure.

"While I truly appreciate the freedom, Mira, could we not have started with that part?" he snarked.

"Apologies, Mate. I did not think to try intentionally using my power in this way," came the chagrined reply.

"I was only teasing, Mira. There's no need to apologize. And were you referring to using your power through our bond again?" he asked while rubbing the tender skin at his wrists.

More magic filled him, soothing and alleviating the pain in both his wrists and ankles as she said, *"Yes, exactly. It feels like I am trying to send something as vast as the ocean through a hole the size of a pin. There's just too much power to funnel in that way, especially if my intention is not to destroy. Instead, it is safer and easier to tap into our bond and have my power reinforce your own. Then it's as simple as thinking of your body as an extension of mine. I just need to picture what I want it to do, and it responds. Honestly, it's still foreign and a bit awkward, like I am trying to put on a pair of trousers that were made to fit someone else. But it's getting easier."*

Von laughed at her analogy, and asked, *"Do you think you could make that connection with someone else? Use your Spirit magic to influence their actions from a distance?"*

There was a pause before she spoke again, *"I'm not sure. It's possible, I suppose, but I think it would be hard without having the kind of bond that you and I share. It would likely not work in the same way."*

"You would have to use force," he clarified, following her train of thought.

"Yes, I think so. Generally, when my magic influences other's, it is tied to the intensity of my emotions. I am sad and so others cry—"

"Or you are thinking of me and suddenly everyone has need of a dark room," Von teased.

"Sometimes they don't even wait for the room," Helena replied dryly, *"but yes. It is my emotion and power that drives them to act, but the actions they take remain their own. To manipulate their will to the point that I am forcing them to behave in a specific way... that is something else entirely. Add distance to that equation, and it only becomes more unlikely. It is our bond that allows me to tap into your power at all, and even still the distance between us interfered in my ability to reach you until now."*

"Not just distance, but two meddling bitches who kept me trapped within the mist. You could not reach me because I was lost; the part of me that is my essential self was locked within the furthest depths of my mind," Von said darkly, as the familiar burn of anger flared within him.

"Yes," she agreed sadly, *"you were lost, but I could still feel you. I just didn't know how to find you or even where to even look. Our bond is a tether; it connects us even beyond something such as space. When you are close enough, it acts as a compass; an instinctual pull that will unerringly lead me to you. If we are too far, it is simply a psychic link. A way to remain in contact and know if you are safe. I think, had you not been taken so far away, even trapped in the mist, I would have been able to reach you. We were too far apart; our bond was stretched to its limit."*

There was something in her voice, something she was not saying, that had him tensing on the bed. The torture, being unable to save her and forced to watch while she was torn apart... his visions had not been just meaningless nightmares. They had been a side effect. A warning.

"The tether was breaking," he said with a feeling of horror so great he could hardly process it.

"I-I think so."

The thought of losing their connection, of losing *her,* was too much to even contemplate. He could not imagine a future, a life, without her in it. *"I would have died there, had you not found a way back to me,"* he concluded with certainty, the image of his broken body curled around itself coming back to him. *"Had the tether snapped and I lost you, Helena, I would have ceased to exist. There is no place for me in a world without you."*

"Stop, please," she begged, and Von could feel the tears she was fighting back choking his own throat. *"I cannot bear the thought of it. I have already seen what happens if the tether breaks. If something had happened to you, Von... something worse than you merely being kept from me. If the day came where I could no longer feel even a hint of you within me... I would have torched the earth in my despair. What was left of my soul would have died with you, and everything that makes me who I am would be gone. Except my power, which would remain, unchecked."*

"Your trial," he remembered, haunted by the memory of her covered in blood in her bed as she told him what she had seen.

Helena did not need to confirm his words. Instead she said, *"You keep me grounded and whole. My power is too great for me to contain on my own. As my Mate, you are the balance. If I lose you, Von, there is nothing that will stop me from destroying everything and everyone."*

"Mother of Shadows."

"That would only be the beginning. By the time I finished, nothing would remain," she gently corrected.

"So you will not lose me," he declared. He could feel her struggling to contain her emotions and did the only thing he could to comfort her. *"No need to be so dramatic, Mate. You could simply settle for telling me that you love me, like other wives do."*

Von felt her incredulity and the wave of astonished mirth that came in response to his words. *"And what do you know about other wives, Mate?"* she asked in a dangerous purr before adding more to herself, *"Besides, you started it."*

Von was grinning despite her revelations. All he knew, was now that her voice was once again in his mind, he felt more whole than he had since first waking from the nightmare he'd been trapped in. They had shared moments, but nothing close to the true strength of their bond. He had felt its lack more than he had realized.

"I have missed this, Mira."

"As have I, Mate." There was a sadness that tinged her words and he wanted nothing more than to take her into his arms and hold her.

"Soon," he promised fiercely.

"Aye, but first we deal with the bitches who thought to come between us."

The promise of violence in her voice excited him more than it should have. He loved that his woman was as much of a warrior as he was, that he did not have to apologize for, or hide, that part of himself from her.

"Aye," he agreed, echoing her words as a cruel smile curved his lips. *"I look forward to bearing witness to your justice, lady."*

"Not as much as I look forward to giving it," she crooned. He could feel her sigh as she said a bit wistfully, *"I must leave you now, I need to conserve my power for what lies ahead."*

He bit back the whimper of protest at her words.

"I cannot do much about you being physically alone... not yet. But know that you are not alone. I am here if you have need of me. Don't forget to make it appear as though you are still bound when she comes for you."

A whisper-soft caress stroked the length of his body and he felt her pull away from him. When he tried to follow, protesting the growing distance, her voice swelled in his mind, *"I am still here, my love."*

He flushed, embarrassed at the need for her that clawed at him. Hearing her in his mind again, and feeling her steady presence, was a balm to his soul. He had been lost to the mist for so long; he had forgotten what being whole felt like.

Not that he was whole, not yet. He wouldn't be until there was not even a breath separating him from his Mate, but it was a start.

Instead of responding, he settled back into the bed and waited, knowing it would not be long before he would be whole again.

CHAPTER 20

Rowena watched her daughter's retreating back from her place on the throne. Her patience had long since worn thin. It was time to play the aggressor once again and force the imposter to come out of hiding. There were whispers that she was finally drawing near, but Rowena had been on high alert ever since the girl's mate first came to stay in the castle. So while she skulked about in the forest, believing that she would be the one to start this war, what she didn't realize was that Rowena was already ten steps ahead of her. It had been her intention, after all, to initiate this exact scenario. Now that the time for action drew near, however, Rowena found that she was no longer willing to wait for the other woman to make the next move.

Her fingers tapped restlessly on the wooden arm of her throne as she waited for her daughter to return with their prisoner. It was insulting that she should have to wait at all but Rowena forced herself to remain calm. No good would come from her losing her temper now, and these things take time.

Minutes ticked away and Rowena shifted restlessly in her chair wondering what was taking her daughter so long. That girl was getting more useless with each passing day. Soon the threat of her brother's life would not be enough to ensure her willing compliance, but that was a problem she could easily deal with just as soon as she handled the imposter.

The silence around her grew as she waited, but Rowena didn't mind silence. After spending years in the Palace surrounded by sycophants and the incessant chatter of voices she almost appreciated it. Once she was back on the throne, she would have her fill of company again. For now, the remoteness of her family's home suited her just fine. If nothing else, it allowed her to build up the army of Shadows that had become so useful these past few months. The mindless beings with super-human strength were very effective at quelling protests and rebellion.

Rowena's lips curled into a smile at the thought.

She felt a ripple along the current of her power, followed by a stinging lash, much like a whip, against the edge of her awareness. The pulse of power caused Rowena to freeze in place. *Was it possible that the little bitch had found a way to sneak in after all? No,* Rowena realized, *her arrival would have much more fanfare than that.*

Precautions had been taken to ensure that their prisoner would not be in any state to access or use his own power. Even so, Rowena placed sensors in his room so she or her guards would be able to act quickly in the event he got free. The power flare she felt was one of the sensors going off. Since it was tied to her own strength, the release of power instantly alerted her wherever she was. She was more than a little intrigued that it would go off now after so much time had passed. Just when she was about to put the next step of her plan into action.

It was also too much of a coincidence for her to ignore.

Rowena rose swiftly and crossed the room. Apparently, it was time for her to engage in a more direct manner with their prisoner.

GILLIAN STOOD outside of the door, hesitating only for a moment before pressing her hand to its cool wooden surface and stepping inside. Von's eyes snapped to her, tracking her movements like a predator assessing prey. She swallowed, uncomfortable with the comparison. She did not appreciate feeling hunted when he was the one in chains. Relieved to see that much, at least, had not changed, Gillian braved a few steps closer to the bed.

She eyed him dispassionately, only mildly disappointed that he was no longer naked. As much as she had appreciated the visual feast, her mother had ordered that she dress him after dosing him a few nights ago in "preparation" and she was not about to force the issue. Gillian wasn't sure how giving him skin-tight leather pants and a fitted white tunic did much to prepare him for anything. If she had to guess, it was more her mother's way of removing the distraction of his heavily muscled body, since a naked Von was hard to ignore. *Mother knows she had enough trouble ignoring that temptation herself.*

Mouth suddenly dry, Gillian licked her lips and cleared her throat.

"Meal time already?" he drawled insolently.

Gillian shook her head, "You have indulged in our hospitality for long enough, Holbrooke. It's time for you to get to work paying your debt." She knew it was the wrong thing to say as soon as the words left her lips.

Silver eyes glittered with malice. "Let me loose and I'll begin repaying you for your hospitality right now."

Gillian forced herself to let out a shaky laugh and roll her eyes in a show of haughty amusement. "Oh, Von, always so quick to threaten violence. I was merely teasing. Let us start again, shall we? No more secluded meals in your room. Now that you are well, you will be joining me upstairs."

She waited for a reaction to her announcement, but he did not so much as flinch.

Taking a steadying breath, she tried again. "You are coming with me," she announced with false bravado.

The smile that stretched across his face showed how easily he saw through her. Lifting a mocking brow, he asked, "Who's going to make me?"

"I am," said a voice just behind her.

CHAPTER 21

Helena could feel the tendrils of her magic melding back into her reservoir of power. She took a deep breath, the weight that had been lodged in her chest for months no longer present after finally being able to speak with Von through their bond again. There had been so much she wanted to say, things she could feel that he wanted to say to her as well, but it had not been the right time. They would have time for such things once she was able to hold him in her arms again.

Feeling a dripping wetness at her nose, she lifted a hand and wiped at it. Seeing the smear of red against the stark paleness of her skin gave her pause. It would seem that even despite her power's increasing strength, and the renewed connection between her and Von, the side effects of the Fracturing had not diminished.

As she refocused on the world around her, Helena's eyes found Ronan's across the clearing. He was frowning darkly, having tracked the movement of her hand across her face, but said nothing. Her eyes met his steadily, and she offered a helpless shrug. There was nothing she could do about it, save rescue her mate, which they were already in the middle of doing. What good was there in calling attention to the urgency with which they needed to act, when everyone was already moving as quickly as possible?

Ronan shook his head, his brows lowered over glittering blue eyes. Helena could tell that he understood her predicament, but it was clear that he was not happy about it all the same.

Perhaps it was because she was still attuned to Ronan after their years together, or maybe it was simply her position at his side, but Serena sensed the shift in his attention and turned to face him. Her blonde brow was lifted in question as her eyes scanned his face. When he did not acknowledge her, she followed his brooding stare to where Helena was sitting. Seeing that her friend was back among them, Serena quickly stood and closed the distance between them.

"Did you learn anything, Kiri?" she asked in a hushed voice once she'd reached her side.

Helena met her friend's gaze, noting the concern mixed with eager anticipation in her violet eyes. With a rueful shake of her head, she was forced to admit, "No."

Disappointment quickly replaced anticipation in her friend's eyes. Serena worked quickly to hide her reaction, but it was too late.

Helena pushed away her own sense of frustration, knowing that even though they were no better off than when she started, at least in terms of gathering information, she still had come out of the meeting with a plan. Just because Von was unable to tell her about where he was being held, didn't mean that there wasn't one among them that could.

Serena opened her mouth to ask a question, but Helena beat her to it by shouting, "Micha!"

The young man ran forward, startled to hear his name. "Yes, Kiri?" he asked tentatively, as if uncertain that she had really called for him.

"I have a couple of questions and am hoping that you can help me, Micha," Helena stated in a more subdued tone. "Are you aware of a blonde woman that might be working with your sister?"

Micha's face scrunched up as he replied, "No, Kiri. No friends that I am aware of. The only blonde I have ever seen Gillian spend any meaningful amount of time with was our mother, before she rejoined the Great Mother, of course."

Helena frowned at the news, having been hopeful he would have been able to finally solve that mystery for her. She sighed before mentally shifting gears and asking, "But you are familiar with where your sister is staying?"

"Well yes, Kiri, of course. If my sister is staying in Vyruul, then she is most certainly at my mother's estate. It was where my mother was raised, and where we would go to visit her family when my mother was tired of our antics and wanted us out of the way for a while."

"So you grew up there?" she asked intently.

"Yes, Kiri," he confirmed, "more or less. The Palace was our home while my mother ruled, but I am well-versed in the layout of the estate, if that is what you are asking."

"Tell me, Micha, if a prisoner was being kept there, where would that be in relation to the entrance?"

Micha looked at her with confusion, not because of her question; it was clear she was asking where Von was being kept. He was confused because he had never had any need for a room that would be used in such a capacity.

After a moment of contemplative silence, Micha green eyes brightened and he said, "My mother had a series of rooms that only she could enter. The doors were spelled with a lock that would only open under her touch. If I had to guess, I would assume that Von was being kept in such a room. They were several floors underground, far away from any of the living quarters. I believe she used them as storage. We were not allowed down there, of course, so it is hard for me to say exactly. But you know how it is when you tell a child they are not allowed to do something. It becomes their personal mission."

Micha was grinning with the memories the words called to the surface of his mind.

Helena chuckled, no stranger to such childish antics. She and Darrin had been much the same when they were younger. They were always quick to devise a plan that would surely land them on the business end of a belt, or at the very least, one that resulted in a stern lecture. Either from her mother, Anderson, or if they were in serious hot water, both.

She shook her head, pushing away the memories so that she could focus on the matter at hand, although an amused smile lingered in her aqua eyes.

"I must admit, it would have been too good to be true, if we could have simply snuck in and rescued him without garnering their attention. So, I'm not surprised to hear that we will need to find a way to get them to open the door for us. But I think I have a plan that will help with that," Helena could not entirely keep the excitement out of her voice.

There was a lot at stake but the thought of pulling one over on Gillian, after all that she had put them through, was heady. It would be especially rewarding to fool her using one of her own tricks.

The men in her Circle, having noticed her conversation with Micha, had already moved to encircle her.

"I am going to walk through the front doors as an invited guest."

Kragen raised an eyebrow, while Timmins and Joquil exchanged confused glances. As always, it was Darrin that spoke first. "And how in the Mother's name do you plan on getting them to do that? Are you actually planning on waltzing up to the front door and knocking?"

"Well, yes." Helena's face was serious, but there was an unmistakable twinkle in her eyes, while she awaited the men's reaction.

They were dumbfounded and had nothing to say in response to that. In fact, the Circle could not seem to find any words to say at all.

"Allow me to point out, if you don't mind," Ronan started carefully, "that seems like the quickest way to find yourself trapped in a room of your own. How exactly do you plan on avoiding capture, or is that part of your plan as well?"

It was hard not to laugh. Helena could tell that the men wanted to shake her and were barely restraining themselves from doing so. Feeling the need to put them out of their misery, Helena let them in on her plan. Her full plan.

"Gillian is not the only one with the ability to alter her appearance. You have seen me do so a handful of times, although I've never tried to fully shift into another person."

Realization dawned on their faces as she continued, "There is perhaps only one person who could very easily walk up to the door and be let in without being thrown into some dungeon."

"You are going to transform into me," Micha whispered in amazement.

"Yes," Helena confirmed.

"That is absolutely absurd," Darrin snarled.

Helena shrugged. "Is it? She has no reason to question his appearance there, since he has knowledge of the estate's existence. In fact, it would be more surprising if Micha didn't go looking for his sister upon hearing of her disappearance. It would be the first place to look if he was trying to find his sister."

Kragen was nodding his agreement while Darrin continued to frown in annoyance.

"It is not easy to assume the identity of somebody else. Especially not when you're trying to fool someone who knows them best. It is not merely enough to look like Micha, you will need to be able to adopt his mannerisms and knowledge as well," Joquil pointed out in a carefully neutral voice. The men could not argue with her reasoning, but that did not mean that her plan was entirely without holes.

Helena nodded. "Yes, there is much that I will have to learn in order to pull this off. Even though I should only need to be Micha for a short time if all goes well."

"When it comes to war, darling, you can never assume that anything is going to go well," Ronan said dryly as he crossed his arms over his broad chest.

"That's what you're here for," Helena said with a smile before turning her aqua gaze back to Micha's stunned face.

He looked like he wanted to protest but could not find a good enough reason to argue. His shoulders drooped and he sighed before asking, "What is it that you want to know?"

"I think the real question is, what do I need to know?" Helena countered. "You are the only one who can tell me what Gillian is going to expect from me. You are her twin, after all."

Micha nodded grimly. "Yes, I suppose you're right. If you will grant me a little bit of time, I can better anticipate what information you may need."

Helena nodded her consent as Timmins said, "You should not go far, Micha. If our Kiri is to learn your mannerisms, she will need to be able to observe you."

"I've always wanted to train a monkey," Kragen said, grinning widely before looking at Micha and adding, "Dance, monkey, dance."

Micha scowled and snapped, "I'm not your fucking monkey. I'm only here to try to save my sister. It would serve you well to remember that, Sword."

Kragen's smile vanished as quickly as it appeared and his eyes glittered with menace as he replied, "Did you not just make your own vow of allegiance? She is still your Kiri, regardless of your sister's actions. Your loyalty is owed to her, regardless of who you share blood with. You're still alive because you serve a purpose, monkey. But everyone's purpose runs out eventually. Perhaps it would serve you better to remember that."

The two men stared at each other while Ronan and Darren stepped closer to where Kragen was standing with his hands balling into fists at his sides. Knowing that he would not survive a fight against any of them, let alone all of them, Micha simply walked away.

"I did not think the child had it in him," Ronan muttered once he was settled out of hearing.

"Every man finds his balls eventually," Serena stated calmly, not even flinching when five sets of male eyes landed on her.

"That may very well be true," Helena said, wiping tears of laughter from her eyes, "but I do not think they appreciate you pointing it out."

"No more than you would enjoy me commenting on the size of your tits," Ronan confirmed.

"I did not comment on the size, merely pointed out that he found his," Serena said mulishly.

Helena's smile grew as she said, "True enough." Turning to Ronan she added, "And you only mention my tits because Von isn't here to repay you for doing so."

"Allow me," Darrin said, slamming his fist into Ronan's arm with considerable force.

Ronan grunted, rubbing his arm as he said, "Make sure to remind me to pay you back for that."

Helena threw back her head and laughed, so grateful for the friends that were around her. There was too much at risk for them to give in to the emotions that were always riding a killing edge. These moments of mirth were as essential to their continued sanity as breathing.

"As much as I'd love to continue with this conversation," she said finally, "I think we should probably eat. It may be a few days before we have anything resembling a real meal again."

"It's your turn to cook," Darrin pointed out.

Helena frowned playfully. "But I'm the Kiri... doesn't that get me out of chores?"

"It didn't when you were seven, and it sure as shit doesn't now, Hellion," Darrin replied with a warm smile.

She rolled her eyes as she stood, bumping him with her hip as she passed. "Then get out of my way."

Dipping into a mocking bow, Darrin called to her retreating back. "As you will, Kiri."

CHAPTER 22

"I am."

The cold voice caused Gillian to jump violently and spin toward the open doorway.

Gillian's mouth opened and closed helplessly, as if she wanted to say something about the unexpected appearance, but one narrow-eyed glare from the woman in the doorway kept her silent. It was obvious that the blonde had decided to change the plan without informing Gillian. Von tucked that information away for later examination while trying to see what he could learn through a quick study of his newest visitor.

He was not moved by her beauty, although there were some that might be. He much preferred laughing aqua eyes and cheeks that always seemed to be tinged with a sweet blush when he was near, to this woman's coldness. There was something about the set of her lips that was too cruel. While the angles of her face and body were too harsh to inspire anything other than a strong desire to put as much distance between oneself and her as possible.

This was an adversary that required he tread carefully, not a woman that could be won over with soft words.

The woman in question clearly fancied herself some sort of monarch; a crown of dark metal sat atop her almost colorless hair. The black stones which ringed it seemed to suck in the light rather than reflect it. It was an object that should have inspired respect but fell woefully short. The effect of the crown was such that it appeared a gash across the top of her head standing out in harsh contrast rather than any form of glittering adornment. She was trying too hard to be a symbol of power and strength, and the crown seemed to mock, rather than reinforce, her authority.

Von, sensing that his disinterest would garner a reaction nothing else could, asked in a bland voice, "And you are?"

His disrespect proved effective. He watched the woman flinch and press her lips together, her cheeks flooding with color as she snapped, "The rightful ruler of the Chosen and your new Mistress."

"Mmm," he murmured, "then we appear to have a problem. I've already made a lifetime vow of service to another woman. And maybe no one had the heart to tell you, but you seem to be confused. I happen to have it on good authority that our Kiri is a beautiful and vibrant woman in her prime, not some dried-up corpse."

The blonde's icy eyes were shooting daggers at him. Von also noted the way her metal-tipped fingers dug so hard into her fleshy palms they drew blood.

Deciding to press his advantage and taunt her further, he added, "Couldn't find a man with the balls to bed you so you decided to steal hers? Here's the thing, sweetheart, you might have me tied down, but you still can't make me fuck you."

Gillian went pale at his words, cringing when the blonde snapped in a voice so filled with ice-cold fury that the walls began to twinkle with frost. "You arrogant—"

"Asshole? Bastard? Twice-forsaken son of a whore?" Von merrily supplied, grinning widely while staring her down with hard gray eyes. He couldn't help it; he was enjoying himself. There was something about sizing up a new opponent that made him feel alive. He might be her prisoner, but by the time he was done with her, he would make this woman beg for mercy.

Her eyes widened and her nostrils flared. Von had a moment of self-preservation and sent a thought to Helena. *"Darling, now might be an excellent time to join me."*

The blonde lifted her hand, blood dripping down her palm and onto the floor as she said in a voice lacking inflection, "I should have realized you would want to skip the foreplay." Her ice-blue eyes drained of all color before turning completely black and she began rapidly muttering under her breath.

Her words were unintelligible and Von was just getting ready to goad her further when he felt the first slam against his mental barriers.

The blow was so unexpected he curled into himself. It was like receiving a blow to the lungs, and it knocked the breath from him momentarily. Bile rose in his throat at the feel of her trying to peel back the layer of his mind that protected his deepest thoughts. His skin turned clammy as he grit his teeth and focused on repelling the invasion.

Von noticed the moment that the blonde realized something was wrong. She frowned deeply, her black eyes lightening to blue as she stepped closer to the bed. She hadn't anticipated his being able to resist her attack. Not that Von felt like he had resisted much of anything.

She must have seen something in his eyes because a wicked smile bloomed across her face. Curling her bleeding hand back into a fist, she allowed her blood to drip onto his leg as she began chanting with renewed effort.

"Helena!" he shouted desperately down the bond, his body arching up off the bed as his vision began to fade. He had no clue what she was doing, but it felt as though he was being flayed alive, his mind and body left bare for her to pluck and prod to her liking.

THE PAN DROPPED from Helena's fingers as electricity hummed painfully over her skin. She could hear Von calling for her along the length of their bond, but the corrupted power she could feel clawing at him kept her from being able to form words. It was as though she was under attack as well.

"Helena!" Effie shouted, trying to move to her side.

"Kiri!" a multitude of male voices exclaimed at the same time.

Helena was unable to do or say anything. She could feel herself being pulled back to Von. It was not a conscious choice, more like her power's instinctive response to the attack. The transition from campsite to the stone room was both instantaneous and disorienting. Helena could feel her physical body collapsing to the ground near the fire but she was also aware of a much larger body reclining on a bed beneath her.

There was no mistaking where she was; her magic had pulled her back into Von's body. A sweet numbness filled their joint body as they pushed up off the bed, no longer retaining the illusion of being chained.

"We've got to stop meeting like this," she purred in the voice of her magic, as Von's eyes made the shift from steel to molten gold.

The blonde's eyes widened and her smug smile fell from her face. "You!" she snarled, lurching away from Von's body. Turning toward Gillian, who was watching the scene unfolding before her with horror, she shouted, "Don't just stand there you little fool!"

"Mother!" she whimpered, as Helena threw out an arm and ribbons of Fire wrapped themselves around the frightened redhead.

Helena felt a moment of shock as she processed the word. *How is that even possible?* Batting the thought away to deal with later, she kept her attention on Gillian. The blonde backed out of the room, eyes never leaving them.

Von's lip curled in a sinister smile, enjoying Gillian's mewls of pain as the Fire began to singe skin and cloth alike.

With a frustrated growl, the blonde stepped into the hall. "If your final act is to buy me time, so be it, at least your death will be more useful than you ever were!"

"Help me! Please, Mother!" Gillian sobbed as the blonde fled.

Helena protested the retreat, knowing the true threat was currently escaping and wanting to pursue her. She looked back to the cowering girl, an annoying sliver of sympathy worming its way into her heart, despite everything she had done. No one should have to face such betrayal from a loved one. Especially a mother.

"Give me one reason I should spare you," Helena demanded in the harmony of voices; Von's approval radiating along their joint consciousness at her words.

"I-I," she stuttered, crying out as the bands of Fire drew tighter. Tears filled the eyes that were so like her brothers, suspended from her eyelashes like drops of rain caught on a branch. "Mercy! Please, Helena. I was only protecting Micha."

Helena loosened her hold on the Fire, startled by Gillian's words.

"She does not deserve mercy," Von snarled.

"We cannot kill her, my love. Not yet. We will need her if my plan is to work," Helena cautioned.

"You think that blonde bitch will let her live after this? She does not care what happens to her daughter. She all but left her for us to finish off."

"It doesn't matter, we cannot risk it. She might be our only chance. Gillian lives."

Von's growl of frustration escaped and caused Gillian to flinch.

"Just because she must live, does not mean she needs to be conscious." Drawing back his arm, Von let his fist slam into her jaw.

Gillian's head snapped and she crumpled to the floor.

Helena looked on in amusement. She might feel sorry for the girl, but it didn't mean she hadn't deserved it. Not after what she had done. A sense of disorientation grew and Helena had a vision of the campsite superimposed on the small room. A wave of nausea hit her causing Von to stumble.

Von took a tentative step toward the door, knowing this might be his only chance at escape. Helena tried to refocus on him and the room, but could feel herself being pulled back.

"Be careful!" she warned, her voice thin along their bond. Her magic was fading, having been pushed too far already.

Already Von's eyes had returned to the usual gray. She could feel a gentle caress along the bond, and his concern for her.

"Do not worry about me. Just stay safe until I get to you."

With a final fervent *"I love you"* their connection was severed, neither certain who had sent the thought.

PULLING his focus back to the present, Von's eyes scanned the room. Gillian was out cold; she was not going to be an issue. Stepping into the hall, he checked for signs of others. There was nothing. Balls of Fire flickered from glass orbs which floated every few steps along the otherwise dim corridor. There was a muted fabric, that had once been a vibrant red, running the length of the hall. It was clear this was not an area that received much attention.

Letting his instinct guide him, Von shielded and took off at a run. Reaching a corner, he slowed, peering around the dank stone wall before continuing. After several more turns he reached a dead end.

Von slammed his fist into the wall. Earth infused the blow causing the wall to tremble under the force, small bits of dust raining down from hole he'd left behind.

"Leaving so soon?" a cloyingly sweet voice called.

Von spun, his lips pulling back as he bared his teeth like a cornered animal ready to strike. The blonde was standing there surrounded by a small army of Shadows awaiting her command. Von lost count at seventeen and knew, without a doubt, that he was completely and utterly fucked.

Feigning indifference, Von shrugged and allowed his body to relax. "With a hostess like you, you can't blame me."

The blonde tilted her head, studying the change with interest. "Do my Shadows not concern you?"

Von's answering smile was pure arrogance as he replied, "Woman, I've single-handedly destroyed entire cities. What's a handful of mindless corpses?"

With a quick move, Von threw out a wave of his power, but it was significantly weaker than it should have been, harmlessly sparking when it came into contact with her shield. Apparently, Helena wasn't the only one who was drained. Von did not allow his expression to alter, despite the failed attack.

Looking entirely too gleeful, she simpered, "Why don't you be a good little boy and get down on your knees? There's no reason to lose a warrior as strong as you to such foolishness."

"There's only one woman I will ever kneel for, and you are not even fit to speak her name."

The amusement fled from the woman's face and she scowled, "You dare speak to me that way?"

Von's arms crossed against his chest as he defiantly lifted his chin. "I just did. Do you need me to repeat myself?"

Rowena threw out an arm and Von heard a sickening crack. Looking down he noticed a finger hanging crookedly at the wrong angle. His own shields were no match for whatever power she was wielding.

His shoulders began shaking with laughter and his eyes met hers. "Is that all you have bitch queen? It's going to take more than that to bring me down." The laughter died down and he said in a voice filled with venom, "I. Will. Not. Kneel."

"Yes, you will," she ground out, eyes narrowed into slits, as another wave of magic hit his body. There was another crack and Von was falling.

Looking down he noticed the bone in his shin sticking out of his leg. There was another loud crack and the world around him began to dim. As his hands slammed into the stone floor, he felt the sticky warmth of his blood. The last clear thought he had before everything went black was *If I get through this, I will need Nial to make me one of his chairs.*

CHAPTER 23

Helena came back to her body in a rush of sensation. The colors of the forest seemed too bright to be real, while the sound of her friends' voices felt like they were being screamed directly into her ear. With a wince, she covered her ears and ducked her head in between her legs to try to drown out some of the intensity.

Miranda was the first to notice she had returned to them. She placed a warm hand on Helena's shoulder and was holding out an embroidered linen kerchief when Helena was finally able to meet her gaze.

Confused, Helena raised an eyebrow.

Miranda gestured toward her face and pressed the cloth into her hand. Understanding dawned; she was bleeding again.

"I thought these side effects would have abated somewhat now that we are closer to one another," she muttered wiping at her nose.

"Physical distance is only part of the problem. The Fracturing is a result of the bond being significantly weakened to the point it is entirely severed. You and your Mate have not had a chance to properly reinforce the bond, although you have been able to keep it stable enough through the strength of your connection," Miranda explained, while motioning for Helena to keep the kerchief when she tried to hand it back.

"I just thought..." Helena trailed off, staring into the blood-spattered cloth.

"Thought what, Kiri?" Miranda prodded gently, her voice filled with warmth and understanding.

"It just seemed like things were starting to get better. We have reestablished our mental connection, for the most part. At the very least I've been able to feel flickers of him, if not connect with him outright. I was even able to find him once through our dreams. And now the Jaka has also seemed to further reinforce the bond." Helena listed off each of the things as she thought of them, seeming a bit lost to learn that they weren't enough to prevent the side effects of the separation.

Miranda took Helena's hand in her own, forcing her to look up before saying, "Those things are definitely helping. They are, perhaps, the reason that the side effects are progressing so slowly. But think of it like filling a dish that has a hole at the bottom. There's only so long the dish will remain full before it starts to drain again. Your connection to your Mate is the same. Until you two are together again, you will keep wasting energy trying to keep the bond whole. It is an impossible task."

Helena frowned. "So the mood swings, the physical tolls and effects, not to mention my power's ability to overwhelm me... those will all continue until we are reunited?"

"Yes, Kiri, if it does not worsen in the meantime," she said a bit apologetically.

"Lovely," Helena murmured as she tried to stand. Stumbling, Helena fell into the older woman. Miranda caught her with a muffled grunt. Flushing she said softly, "Apologies, Keeper."

"None are necessary, Kiri," Miranda replied as Joquil and Kragen rushed over to them.

"Are you all right, Hellion?" Kragen asked in his deep rumble.

Helena nodded wanly. "Yes, fine. It seems like I can only project my consciousness for so long until my body protests and pulls me back."

Joquil studied her with serious amber eyes. "Your soul is determined to reattach to its other half, which is why you feel the pull to reconnect to Von so strongly, but your physical body cannot stay empty for long without beginning to break down."

It was similar to what Miranda had said, but Helena still found the words surprising. "Is that what I'm doing? Sending my soul to his body?"

Joquil nodded. "You would not be able to call your power to you and use it through him otherwise. It is one thing to share a mental link, to speak to one another and be aware of each other's emotions. It is something else entirely to fuse your power."

Helena looked at Miranda for confirmation, but the woman only shrugged. It hadn't been a lack of power that pulled her back then, but her body's need for her soul. That certainly explained why her body felt so weak, despite the deep pool of her magic still rippling within her.

Distracted by the realization, Helena did not hear Micha's approach.

"Kiri?" he asked.

As her eyes focused on his, she felt her rage begin to spiral. Memories of what had happened, and what she had heard, while connected to Von had her curling her hand into the material of his shirt. Overhead, the sky began to darken and let out a warning crack of lightning.

"How, by all that is holy, is your mother still alive?" she asked in a guttural snarl, her teeth bared as she leaned into him until her nose almost touched his.

Micha's green eyes widened with a mix of shock and fear. "W-what do you mean, Kiri? My mother di-died." His Adam's apple bobbed as he swallowed back his panic.

"No, Micha, she did not. Your mother is very much alive. She is the one behind Von's capture." Aqua eyes bore into his, daring him to protest, but the confusion in his expression could not be faked. Letting him go, she watched as he stumbled before regaining his footing.

Having overheard the encounter, the rest of her Circle had already joined them.

"How can she still be alive, Timmins?" Helena demanded.

Timmins expression was dark as he admitted, "I do not know, Kiri."

Joquil spoke from beside her, "Traditionally, a new Damaskiri does not rise until the current ruler dies. I did not even know it was possible for one to come into her power while the other still lived. She must have employed powerful magic indeed to fool us."

"You don't say," Helena snapped.

"At least we know who we are facing now," Miranda said prosaically. "It will help with strategizing, yes?"

Helena looked back at Micha who had completely retreated into himself before saying slowly, "I would not count on much of anything when it comes to the Corruptor." Speaking quickly Helena filled them in on what had happened when she was with Von.

After she finished, the only sounds in the camp were the crackles and snaps of the fire and the distant roll of thunder.

Taking a fortifying breath, Helena said, "The plan does not change, but the timetable must be pushed forward. We cannot leave Von with her any longer. She has already tried to turn him once. Now that she knows she cannot, there's no reason for her to leave him unharmed."

Nial was the first to respond, his voice hesitant, "I want to save my brother as much as you do, Helena... but shouldn't we be fully prepared before rushing into this battle?"

"We've already discussed this," Helena said flatly, meeting each of their eyes in turn. Her friends' expressions were grim but accepting.

A feeling like a spark of fire in her hand had her yelping and shaking her hand in surprise. Seeing nothing wrong with her hand, she sent her focus deep, ignoring the startled shouts of her friends. Before she could do more than establish Von was alive, pain lanced up each of her legs, causing her to fall toward the ground. Hands reached out to grab and steady her, but Helena saw nothing but glittering black rage.

The sky cracked in half with a blinding bolt of lightning, while thunder shook the earth.

"That bitch!" Helena roared. Pushing her friends off of her, she ran toward a larger clearing, shouting, "Starshine!"

It took only a moment before Starshine's brilliant white fur gleamed against the darkness of Helena's storm as the Talyrian shot twin flames from her snout. She landed quickly, causing the ground to tremble in response. Helena was already moving to mount her but was brought up short.

"Helena! You can't mean to go right now. She'll be expecting you," Darrin shouted, before releasing her arm.

Spinning around, she pushed him back and said with deadly fury, "Try to stop me again."

Startled, he froze in place.

Helena looked at the rest of them, daring them to so much as move. "Rally the troops, I will find you once I have him. This ends now."

"Kiri!" Ronan shouted. Helena's narrowed eyes did not faze the warrior who only said, "Bring him back to us."

With a nod, Helena climbed onto Starshine's back. She pressed her heels into the Talyrian and without so much as a backward glance, they took off toward the sky and the man that meant more to her than breathing.

CHAPTER 24

Helena stood at the edge of the forest, staring out at the twinkling white land that was sprawled out before her. The massive black structure was half-hidden in the snow-covered mountains and seemed to have been carved out of the rock that surrounded it. Its many twisting spires were reaching up through the mist and into the inky sky.

It had taken the rest of the day and most of the night to reach the castle. Above her, the sky was just beginning to fade from black to a deep navy. The sun had yet to make an appearance over the horizon but stars had already begun to slowly wink out. A few of the stalwart sentinels remained, ready to stand witness to the battle to come.

"It's not very welcoming is it?" Helena asked.

Beside her, Starshine let out a huff of agreement, her breath turning to curling wisps of steam in the frigid air.

Despite the large number of windows, not a single light was ablaze in any of them. "If I didn't know better, I wouldn't even believe there were people in there," Helena mused aloud, more from an effort to avoid thinking about what lay ahead, rather than any need to voice the thought.

The cold was overwhelming and her cloak did little to stave off the chill. Helena called some Fire to her, using it to warm both the garment and herself.

"I suppose this is where you leave me," Helena said once she was warm, turning to fully face the Talyrian queen.

Starshine's ears flattened, a clear indication of her disapproval.

"I'm sorry, beautiful, but I can't pretend to be Micha with you following me around. It's going to be hard enough to pull this off as it is."

Starshine huffed again, her annoyance unmistakable. The large feline sat back on her haunches and pulled her wings tightly into her body, refusing to leave. Helena sighed and rolled her eyes but did not force the issue. It would have been a waste of words. Instead, she chose to use the time wisely and begin her transformation into Micha. Unsure of any official way to do so, she simply let her instinct act as a guide.

Helena closed her eyes and called forth an image of Micha as she had last seen him: mussed russet hair framing a pale and slightly freckled face, mossy green eyes and long lashes that went blonde at the tips, and rumpled but well-made clothes that hung off of a tall and lean frame. Once the image was clear in her mind, she willed her body to duplicate it, taking the time to carefully focus on the specific features and characteristics that made up the man.

At first, nothing seemed to happen, but then she could start to feel her bones and muscles lengthen and stretch. Looking down, she noticed that her curves had disappeared, although there was a new bulge that had her blushing and quickly averting her gaze. It may technically be her body, but there was something that didn't feel right about showing too much interest in that particular detail. Lifting a hand, Helena noted that her fingers were no longer slender with oval-shaped nails in desperate need of filing. Rather, she had the thick blunted fingers of a man.

"Weird," Helena murmured, startled to hear the deeper timbre of her voice.

With a small chuckle and a shake of her head, Helena made to move back to Starshine. Before she could take her first step toward the

Talyrian, Starshine let out a long, threatening growl that forced her to take a few stumbling steps back instead.

"Starshine it's me. It's me, girl," she said holding up her hands.

The great cat went silent, tilting its head until those luminous turquoise eyes could better study her. After a tense moment, the Talyrian moved her head forward, sniffing the air between them and letting out a confused whine. Starshine could sense her mistress but did not recognize her through the glamour.

Not wanting to frighten or provoke her, Helena held out a hand for Starshine to sniff. The Talyrian bared her teeth in silent warning but pressed her muzzle into Helena's hand. As the moments passed, her hand grew warm from the humid puffs of air coming from the Talyrian's nose. Helena ran her other hand over the velvety fur, feeling tense muscles begin to relax as Starshine confirmed that the familiar scent was coming from the wrong person.

A soft buzzing filled the quiet space between them. Helena's body tingled as the feeling washed over her. Once it passed, Starshine let out an approving sound and pressed her head into Helena's hip.

She raised a brow, about to tease the Talyrian for her odd behavior, when she realized what had just happened. Suddenly worried that Starshine had somehow managed to undo the disguise she had so carefully crafted, Helena quickly scanned herself. She was pleased, and more than a little relieved, to see that she still appeared to be Micha. Whatever the feline had done, it had only affected her ability to see Helena's true form, not interfered with Helena's glamour.

Helena was intrigued by this new display of magic. She had not realized that the Talyrian had powers outside of flight and fire, which she had always seen as being natural abilities versus magical ones. That said, no one could look at a Talyrian and not know that they were magical beings. Or be a little in awe of their overwhelming majesty.

Shaking her head ruefully, she gave Starshine another rub. "What other secrets are you still hiding from me? Hmmm?"

Starshine just closed her eyes, rumbling in pleasure at the caress. Helena let out an amused snort. "It's a wonder I even bother talking to you at all. Not like you will answer me."

A slit of turquoise appeared, and Starshine shot Helena a glance that negated the comment. The Talyrian had no trouble communicating if one counted expressions and body language as forms of communication. Helena allowed herself a final moment of amusement, enjoying the quiet moment with Starshine before the smile started to fall from her face and her eyes moved back to the castle before them.

Setting her shoulders, Helena took a deep breath. "It's time."

HELENA MADE her way to the door, the howling wind making her cloak snap behind her. Walking in another person's body had been odd, at first, but the little time she had spent in Von's helped her quickly adapt.

This was absolute insanity. The others had known it, as had she, but there really was no other play available to them. The only way they were getting inside this castle without a full-on siege, which there was no guarantee they would win, was sneaking in. But without any real understanding of what they were walking into, it would be easier to enter as a welcomed guest rather than trying to remain hidden within the shadows.

That didn't make it any less stupid. She was literally standing on her enemy's doorstep about to ask them to let her in. Insane didn't begin to cover it.

Offering a quick prayer to the Mother and sending a rush of love and longing to Von through the bond, Helena forced herself to push everything from her mind. Gripping the icy metal of the knocker, she lifted it and slammed it back down and onto the heavy wooden door.

There was a groan and a shudder as the sound of the knock reverberated in the room beyond the door. There was no answer. Helena had known, due to the utter stillness, that there were few people inhabiting the massive structure. She shouldn't have been surprised that there wasn't someone waiting for her at the door. But she was.

Lifting her hand to knock again she flinched a little when there was a creak and the door slid back just enough for a familiar green eye to stare at her through the crack. The green eye widened as recognition dawned and the door pulled back further to reveal Gillian's thunderstruck expression.

"Micha!" she gasped. Joy filled her eyes but was immediately replaced by horror. "What are you doing here? You shouldn't be here. It's not safe!" she said, furtively glancing around as if checking that they were, in fact, alone.

Rage and revulsion churned in her belly, and Helena had to force her expression into something more appropriate. Thankful she had spent the journey with Starshine planning for this moment and thinking about what she would say, Helena focused on the ruse and finally uttered the words that she committed to memory.

"Sister, is that any way to welcome your brother home?" Helena asked, using one of Micha's most troubled expressions. "I've been so worried about you. Rumors have been flying around the Palace since your disappearance. I hadn't given them any credence, knowing you couldn't have pulled off what they had been accusing you of. I mean, what reason could you possibly have for abducting Helena's mate?" Helena paused, letting some of the brotherly concern fade from her voice and replacing it with the annoyed tone she had heard so often from Darrin when he thought she was being stupid. "When you didn't return and put the rumors to rest, I realized that you were, in fact, absolutely irresponsible enough to kidnap Von. What I don't understand is why? What reason could you possibly have to be so stupid?"

Gillian's face had turned a bright red and she was clenching her teeth so hard, Helena could hear the grinding from where she stood. With another quick check over her shoulder, Gillian turned back and spat, "I did it for you! To protect you, you ungrateful ass!"

Helena allowed her eyes to widen, trying to convey shocked disbelief. "Me? How does stealing the Mate, help me? She had already soul-bonded with him; it's not like I had a chance at filling the position."

"No! Not to open up a spot for you," Gillian sputtered. "To save *you*. Mother threatened—"

"Mother? Mother is dead, how could she be a threat to me?

"Mother is alive," Gillian hissed.

"I-I don't understand."

Gillian swallowed, her earlier fear at seeing Micha returning. "Mother faked her death. I-I helped her. But I had to Micha!" she protested, seeing the anger Helena wasn't quick enough to hide.

"Had to? Why?" Helena asked, trying to sound confused instead of enraged.

"She threatened to kill you if I didn't. She was tired of hearing about the prophecy, of the whispers that she was not a true Kiri as she had no Mate of her own. That another, more powerful than any we had seen, would replace her. It drove her mad, Micha. She snapped."

Helena shook her head. "So why didn't you tell me? I could have helped you, Gillian. You're my twin, you know I would do anything for you. We could have worked together to stop her."

Gillian reached out and grasped her brother's hand in her own. "And I would do anything for you. Micha, I was trying to protect you."

"I know," Helena forced herself to say softly.

Tears filled Gillian's eyes and she threw herself at Helena, holding the woman disguised as her brother as if her own life depended on it.

Helena swallowed back the bile and endured the embrace as long as possible before pushing Gillian back and asking earnestly, "Don't you see? This has gotten out of hand. You have to release Von before things go any further. I can help you."

Gillian was openly crying now. "It's too late," she whispered.

The bottom dropped out of Helena's stomach, and her knees almost buckled at the words. "What do you mean? What happened?"

Gillian shook her head, red pieces of hair falling from her braid. "I'm not sure, only that Mother no longer needs to keep Von alive. She has been…" Gillian trailed off looking sick.

"Has been what?" Helena snapped, barely restraining herself from shaking Gillian.

"Torturing him," Gillian whispered, her eyes still dripping with tears.

"Is she with him now?"

Gillian shook her head again. "No. She finally stopped about an hour ago. I think she got bored once he passed out. He's locked up in his room again."

"Take me to him. We've got to get him out of here."

"Micha, you don't understand. If she catches us, we're dead."

Helena could feel the rage burn through her as she snapped, "What good is our life if he dies? Do know what Helena will do if that happens? We will be on borrowed time as it is."

"We already are," Gillian admitted, sniffling back some tears.

"So wouldn't you rather your last acts on this earth be selfless ones? What are you going to say for yourself when you face the Great Mother and have to answer for your crimes?" Helena asked, infusing her words with tendrils of her compulsion magic.

Gillian's eyes seemed to glaze, Helena could tell that the thought had taken hold. Worry filled the girl's green eyes as she asked, "You don't think She would forgive me for my actions when they were to save you?"

The question gave Helena pause. Despite every disgusting thing this woman had done, she truly believed she had been saving someone she loved. Helena couldn't fault her for that, although she despised her for what she had done in the name of that misplaced belief.

"It is not for me to say," she said finally, "but I do know, that the more we can do now to repair the damage, the better it will go for us all."

Gillian chewed on her lower lip, before nodding finally. "All right, Micha, if you are sure. But I do not think we will be able to get him out of here alone. Not without our Mother finding out."

"Leave that part to me. Just take me to him," Helena said firmly.

Nodding again, Gillian motioned for her to finally step inside. "Stay close," she whispered, as she pushed the heavy wooden door closed.

Helena nodded once to indicate that she understood. She walked quickly, adrenaline causing her heart to race as she followed the red-headed woman deeper into the darkness.

TIME CRAWLED as they made their way to the room where Von was being kept. Helena could feel the stiffness in her tense muscles, but could not seem to make herself relax. She kept waiting to run into someone, or for Gillian to realize that she was an imposter, but neither happened.

The twisting halls were completely empty and eerily silent. Helena followed closely behind Gillian, noting the general state of disuse throughout the castle. The rugs were faded and threadbare and the stone walls pitted and chipped. Where pictures had once hung, there were now squares of dust framing discolored stone. With each twist of the halls, it only grew more dank and dark, the flickering lights barely illuminating anything.

Helena tried to track the number of turns they had made, knowing she would need to move quickly once she had Von, but it was starting to feel more like a labyrinth than a castle. Not only that, but her mind was filled with images of finally getting her revenge on the red-haired schemer. The woman had been responsible for some of the worst pain she had ever endured, and she was finally going to be able to return the favor.

The thought filled her with a grim giddiness that would have horrified her, had it been anyone else. But this was the woman that had taken Von, had been the impetus of every terrible thing he'd endured since. There was no punishment too great for that crime.

Realizing she was losing focus, Helena forced herself to think only of how many turns they had made since reaching this floor: seven. *Where was everyone?* Helena wondered again, *it wasn't just Gillian and her mother holed up here, was it?* She was just about to ask when Gillian stopped suddenly in front of a large wooden door.

She turned to face Helena fully and asked in a hushed whisper, "Are you sure about this? It's not too late for you to leave before Mother sees you."

"Open the door, Gillian," she demanded.

Helena could no longer remain patient, knowing that her Mate was only separated from her by a piece of wood and the woman that was quite literally standing between them. She could feel him now, had felt him as soon as she had stepped into that dark and empty castle. As they'd made their way down the winding halls to this part of the castle, the feeling had only grown in intensity. Helena had known that he was seriously hurt, which only frayed the already worn edges of her patience. But after Gillian confirmed he had been tortured; her need to see him could no longer be contained. It had become a living thing: wild and thrashing within her.

Gillian was clearly terrified. Helena didn't blame her; she should be. The girl's hand shook as she lifted it and pressed it against the door.

Helena could feel a tremor of magic as the door's spell recognized Gillian and swung open. She made a move to step over the threshold, but Helena caught her arm, pulling her back. "Gillian, wait."

Confusion colored her face, and Helena studied it for a moment considering her next move. Now that the door was open, Gillian no longer served a purpose. The wait was over.

"Micha?" she asked in a quavering voice, sensing something was amiss.

"I'm not Micha," Helena said flatly, allowing the glamour to fade.

Gillian's eyes widened as Helena was revealed and she moaned in horror, "No! Oh no! What have I done?"

"Something useful, for once. Thanks for the idea, by the way," Helena said with a fierce smile, gesturing to her body.

Gillian struggled to break free from Helena's grasp, but it only served to make Helena tighten her hold, using the power of Earth to make her grip unbreakable. As she bore down on the fragile bones of Gillian's wrist, she also allowed the sharp tips of her deadly black claws to appear, their razor-sharp points biting into tender flesh until pinpricks of blood appeared. Gillian went limp, deflating as she said, "She's going to kill you."

Helena leaned close, her aqua eyes glittering with promise. "Not if I get to her first. But that's not your problem, Gillian dear. You should be much more concerned with what I'm going to do to *you*."

Gillian swallowed, fear making her eyes large and her face pale. She still seemed too stricken to do more than stand there, waiting for Helena's to act.

Not wanting to disappoint her, Helena called on her power, letting all of the rage and pain her separation to Von had caused feed it.

"Helena," Gillian implored, "please…"

Helena's iridescent eyes narrowed, and her hair flew around her as though wind was blowing around them. "I warned you, but you didn't listen. No one harms what is mine."

She let the magic go and Gillian flew back from the force of the blow, her head slamming back into the stone wall. She crumpled to the floor, blood beginning to flow freely from the impact. Gillian struggled to sit up, attempting to use her magic to stem the blood, but Helena was faster, already moving closer with another swirling ball of pulsing light in the palm of her hand.

Left with no choice, Gillian lashed out, redirecting her magic into an attack. A blue-white orb shot through the air, but Helena easily intercepted it. Her own power vastly outmatched Gillian's and she was able to absorb the bolt of magic without injury.

"Now now, play nice," Helena sing-songed.

Gillian grit her teeth, blood staining them red. She called another swirling ball of magic and tried again, but Helena easily swatted it away, laughing when it hit the door, causing it to burst into thousands of jagged splinters. Helena was thankful for the shield she'd placed around herself, as she brushed the small flecks of wood off of her shoulder before looking back at Gillian. Her chest was rising and falling rapidly as she fought against the Air Helena was using to hold her in place.

Helena could almost read the girl's thoughts through the emotion that raced across her face. There was a flash of calculation in Gillian's green eyes as if she was weighing her options. It was obvious that she was sizing up her adversary and had just realized that this was not the naïve, powerless, girl she had met in Elysia. There was no way she could beat the woman standing over her. No way to beat the Vessel.

With the realization, all remaining fight left Gillian.

"Finish it," she said bitterly, turning to spit a mouthful of blood onto the floor.

Helena tilted her head, studying the broken woman. The layered voice of her power seemingly devoid of emotion as she asked, "Where's the fun in that? We were only just getting started." She called twin balls of power into her hands. One flickered and danced like a living flame, while the other swirled like a miniature tornado. "What shall it be, Gillian dear? Should I purify your blackened soul with Fire or steal the very life from your lungs with Air?"

"Stop playing with me and finish it!" she shouted, staring up at her with shining green eyes.

"Why not both?" Helena crooned, ignoring the demand.

Her brows lowered menacingly over iridescent eyes that had flickers of lightning in their depths. She fed the orbs of power until they swelled in her hands, becoming more erratic in their movements. Once they were as large as her head, she stopped, pinning Gillian with her gaze. There was no need for words as she released the Air storm.

Gillian swallowed back a cry, slamming her eyes shut and muttering frantically under her breath.

"Mother forgive me," she whispered before Helena's magic stole the air from her lungs, causing her to sputter and choke. Her eyes began to bulge as she gasped for breath.

The girl's words finally sunk in, and Helena faltered as other, more cryptic, words rose unbidden:

'You have a choice before you.'

'Loyalty or love?'

'Mercy or vengeance?

'Life or death?'

Was this the choice the Keepers had alluded to? All three options could apply to this moment, she supposed. Choosing mercy and life over vengeance and death... Spending time meting out revenge under the guise of loyalty, while just beyond that door her love still suffered. Could the ramifications of this choice really lead to the slaughter in her vision?

Helena shuddered at the memory of the carnage. It didn't seem possible, and yet...

Another whimper brought her focus back to Gillian. Helena could feel the shift in her magic. Her hair settled back around her shoulders while the ball of Fire snuffed out.

When she'd arrived, Helena had every intention of making the woman pay for her actions with her life. Now that the moment had arrived, Helena realized that death would be too easy for Gillian. There was no punishment there.

"No, I don't think so," Helena said finally.

"Wh-what?" Gillian stuttered, her eyes flying open in shocked disbelief.

"Death is a kindness you do not deserve. You need to answer for what you have done."

Any magic Helena used right now would have killed the girl. She was too amped up and fueled by rage for it not to. Thinking of Von, a dark smile grew across her face.

"Helena," Gillian whimpered, seeing the threat of violence that still remained in her eyes.

"Just because I'm not going to kill you, Gillian, doesn't mean I'm going to just let you go." With that, Helena closed the distance between them, pulled back her arm and slammed her fist straight into Gillian's nose. There was a wet crunch and blood sprayed everywhere as the girl's head flew back, slamming into the wall again. Helena couldn't help but think that Ronan would approve.

By the time Gillian's head hit the floor, she was unconscious.

The need for revenge made it hard to step away but her need for Von was stronger. As she stood, a flicker of color caught her eye. Gillian was still wearing her necklace; the one that held the Kaelpas stone she'd used to help the Shadows find them and to take Von away.

Helena grasped it and yanked. The chain snapped and swung haphazardly from Helena's hand. "Perhaps you still had some use after all."

Stuffing the broken necklace into her pocket, Helena quickly rose and ran into the room.

CHAPTER 25

*H*elena did not know what to expect when she stepped across the threshold and so there was no way for her to prepare for the onslaught of emotions that rose at the sight of Von, bloody and battered on the bed. Not that knowing would have made any difference.

She was frozen in the doorway as her brain struggled to process each of the conflicting emotions… Anger at his mistreatment… Fear that she would not have time to heal him and also escape… Joy at the mere sight of him alive, at all. And love. More than anything, she felt a love so great it outshined all else.

Her eyes settled on his face completely blocking out his broken body for the moment. Matted strands of hair were stuck to pale golden skin. Dried blood was crusted everywhere while fresh blood was still trickling out of his mouth and nose. His bottom lip was split and swollen, as were his eyes, those beautiful eyes she was desperate to see. They were so bruised and swollen, she could hardly recognize them as eyes. It looked as though someone had used his face as a punching bag, for hours.

Rushing to his side, she pressed her hand to his face, pushing back blood and sweat-soaked strands, until her hand was resting against his neck. Beneath her fingers, his skin burned hot and she could feel the feeble, yet steady, throb of his pulse. Letting out a shuddering breath, she leaned down and pressed her lips against his, tasting the salt of her tears mingle with his blood as she did.

"Von," she whispered, her lips still touching his. *"I am here,"* she added when he did not stir. There was a flutter as his eyes shifted beneath their lids, but still they did not open.

"Mira?" he rasped along their bond, his psychic voice filled with pain.

"I need you to try to wake up, Mate."

She pulled back slightly, hoping to catch a glimpse of gray. She watched as he struggled to open his eyes, but they only cracked open before immediately closing again.

Moving her hand to rest above his heart, she closed her eyes and used her senses to assess his injuries. Her eyes snapped back open as a tidal wave of nausea caused her to gag.

"That bitch!" she seethed once she had recovered enough to speak.

Rowena had not only tortured Von, she had used what magic she possessed to "heal" the wounds. It was clear the woman possessed none of Water's soothing magic. This was Fire and Earth fused into a cruel imitation of healing. Instead of using magic to repair the damage she had caused, she used it to lock it in and override the body's natural instinct to heal. No wonder Von could not break through to consciousness; his body was stuck in perpetual agony and his brain was trying to protect him in the only way it could.

Helena could feel the seconds slipping away. She needed to get him out of here now, but in his current state he was in no condition to be moved. To heal him fully would require more time and magic than she could spare since she could not risk being weakened or caught unaware. That left her the choice of doing just enough to get him mobile and stave off the pain. She would have to finish healing him once they were safely away.

She gave him another quick kiss, saying as she did, *"Try to stay with me; this may hurt."*

There was a vibration along the bond that she took to be acknowledgement before she let herself slip into the healing trance she'd last used with his brother. Allowing her magic to guide her, she reset bone and repaired tissue, doing only enough to help him walk and stop any bleeding. All of the bruising would have to remain. She moved quickly, using none of the care and finesse she had with Nial. There simply wasn't time.

Helena knew when she was finished because a harsh hiss greeted her ears.

"Mother's Tits, Helena. I've known Daejaran wolves with a gentler touch than you."

When she opened her eyes, Von was smiling up at her, albeit crookedly. His gray eyes had lost enough of the swelling that they could open, and they were currently shining with an emotion too vast to name.

It was the most beautiful thing she had ever seen.

"You're lucky I love you. It could have been much worse," she muttered, settling for flippancy to keep herself from breaking down into gut-wrenching sobs.

He grimaced at the thought, and pushed himself up into a seated position, groaning a little with the movement. Helena couldn't keep herself from staring. He may still be covered in bruises and blood, but she was a starving woman and he was her feast.

Sensing her eyes on him, he looked at her from under thick lashes. "Darling, as much as I'd love to oblige you, I don't think there's time for that."

She blushed and made a face. That hadn't been her intention. Not really. It was just, he was here. He was alive. She reached out and touched his cheek, heart too full for words.

He pressed his face into her hand before brushing his lips against its center. They stayed there for a moment, enjoying the feeling of being with each other again, and knowing that the time for words would come later.

"Can you walk?" she asked, even though she knew that he could.

"Aye," he affirmed as he stood. He teetered a little, and she moved to quickly support his weight as he adjusted.

"Hold on to me," she murmured.

"Always, *Mira*. I'm just a little unsteady," he said gruffly, pressing his lips to the top of her head. She could feel him breathe her in, his ribs expanding under her hand.

Her heart contracted at the tender words, but before he could say anything else that would cause her to risk spending time they didn't have in this prison cell, she said quickly, "Then I think it's time we get you home."

"*Mira*, I told you, as long as I'm with you, I'm already home."

Her breath hitched, tears thick in her throat.

Von lifted a hand and caressed her cheek, turning her face up toward his. Leaning down, he pressed a kiss full of promise against her lips. Helena felt her knees go a bit weak when he finally pulled back and winked at her. With that he grasped her hand in his and pulled her toward the door.

THEY MOVED QUICKLY, hands still intertwined as they made their way through the halls back toward the exit. Von had snickered when he saw Gillian's inert body, approval radiating off him in waves. Helena had thought he might have been disappointed that she hadn't killed her outright, but he'd made no mention of it. He'd just brushed his lips against her knuckles and gestured for her to lead the way.

The halls were still empty, but there was something about the lack of security that caused her to move more cautiously. They were using Air to conceal the sound of their footsteps and would pause before making any turns, using their enhanced senses to check whether it was clear. The longer they went without seeing anyone, the more concerned she became. It seemed absolutely impossible to her that the woman who had orchestrated this whole scheme hadn't planned for this exact scenario.

"*Where are the others?*" Von asked suddenly across their bond.

"*If you're referring to Rowena's people, I am wondering the same thing myself,*" she replied, guessing that he might be thinking along the same lines.

"No, I meant ours. How many fighters do we have? What is our plan?" Von asked the questions one after another, his years as a Commander making him eager to hear the strategy.

Helena didn't bother to meet his gaze, choosing instead to scan for signs of Rowena's men as she listed, *"The rest of the Circle, Ronan, Serena, your brother, Micha, along with a couple of others I do not think you know. They were making their way to the castle when I left them. They should be here soon, if they aren't already."*

Von stopped short, halting her own forward movement.

"You came here alone?" he asked in a voice filled with quiet thunder. *"And you plan on attacking with only two handfuls of men? Are you out of your mind?"*

Helena felt her hackles rise, and turned to face him with a frown. *"Are you really complaining about the manner in which I just rescued you, Mate? Do you doubt my ability? Or my judgment?"* She wasn't sure which part offended her most.

His brows lowered over darkening gray eyes. *"Helena, you have to know how foolish that was. What if she captured you as well? What are the rest of us supposed to do if something happened to you? How in the Mother's name are we supposed to defeat her with such a small force? You cannot think to win this fight so hamstrung."*

"I got to you, didn't I?"

Exasperation filled her at his words; she was not some helpless farm girl anymore. She was the Mother's Vessel, the strongest in history, if the prophecy was to be believed. If she wasn't capable of a rescue mission, then there wasn't much hope for her abilities at all.

"Do you have any idea what your absence has been doing to me?" she continued a bit desperately. *"The toll that each day of our separation took on me? I've been coming apart, Von. I couldn't wait any longer, not when I could feel you again. Not when she was hurting you and I could finally do something about it!"* Her words were hurried, reinforced with all of the emotion she'd had to bury the last few months in order to simply function.

Von's expression softened, and his lifted his free hand to caress her cheek. *"Mira—"* he started but she cut him off.

"You have to know that if there had been a better option available, I would have used it. I would have done anything to get you free of this place. But this was the only way. No one else would have been able to get past her defenses without bloodshed."

"I wouldn't say you did either, Mate," he teased, his frustration with the choices she'd made in his absence evaporating with her words.

He might be a Commander, but she was Kiri. Her will was law, and he lived to serve.

They exchanged tight, feral smiles. *"No, I suppose not. But better one deserving bitch than any of our men."*

A heartbeat passed and he squeezed her hand, indicating he was ready to continue. As she made to move forward, he stopped her again. *"Wait. Did you say my* brother *is with you?"*

This time Helena had no trouble meeting his eyes. Her smile shone with radiance as she nodded and said simply, *"I did."*

"You healed him," he said with no small bit of wonder.

"I did," she repeated.

She watched her strong warrior blink in stunned silence. When he spoke again, his voice was thick with emotion, *"Thank you, Helena. I cannot tell you what this means to me, to my family."*

"Hush, my love," she murmured, pressing her fingers to his lips as though he had spoken aloud. *"Nial has already thanked me more than enough. Healing him was my promise to you. I never intended to do otherwise."* She contemplated telling him that Serena would likely be thanking her in the near future, as well, but figured it was not the right time for that bombshell.

Happiness and awe made his eyes shine like silver. He shook his head, laughing a little. *"Of course you did. You have proven time and again that you are capable of performing miracles and showing compassion and mercy where others would, or could, not. You are the true miracle, my miracle."*

She rolled her eyes at his proclamation, but smiled despite herself. *"Worship and adore me later, Mate. We have an escape to finish."*

His smile was wolfish as he replied, *"Oh, I have every intention of making that my first priority once we are safely away.* " Before she could respond he repeated his earlier question. *"So what's the plan?"*

Helena filled him in as they made their way carefully down the last hall. There was only one more turn until they reached the receiving room. Just as they were about to take the steps that would put them out in the open, they heard the soft rustling of footsteps.

A lot of footsteps.

Exchanging glances, they froze, pressing their bodies into the wall. Even with his injuries, Von used his body to block hers, so that anyone who discovered them would see him first. There was a loud shout, and Helena panicked, certain that they had finally been spotted as the sound of footsteps grew louder. Von's hand squeezed hers, each of them bracing for an attack.

It never came.

Helena peered over his shoulder, tentatively stepping away from the wall. Something was wrong. Something was very, very wrong. A searing pain in her side had her gasping. Von spun toward her, reaching out to hold her as she slumped against the wall.

"Helena? Mira, what's wrong?"

"My—my Jaka," she gasped.

His eyes widened at her words, yet another unexpected discovery he did not have time to fully process. As she closed her eyes, trying to ride out the waves of pain, she was able to see the threads that tied her to the men in her Circle. Each flashed brilliantly, flickering and pulsing with light. Focusing on a strand that flared brilliantly once before dimming to a dull gray, Helena's eyes snapped back open.

"Ronan!" she shouted, no longer concerned with being overheard.

Von's eyes bore into hers as he snapped to attention. "What about Ronan?"

"He's in trouble. They all are."

"How bad?" Von asked, every inch the warrior.

"As bad as it gets."

She could see Von scanning, anticipating the distance between them and the door, as she moved her hands off of her throbbing side. The movement caused her to run her hand over the small lump in her pocket. The Kaelpas. Pulling it out, she held the gleaming purple stone up for Von to see.

He glanced down at it and then back at her. "Do you know how to use that thing?"

"Has that ever once stopped me?" she retorted as they pressed themselves together.

Closing her eyes, she took a shuddering breath and pictured the clearing she had been in with Starshine only an hour before. There was a small pop and then nothing. The spot where the couple once stood was now completely empty.

CHAPTER 26

$\mathcal{M}$icha stepped away from the others who were busy strapping the last of the weapons to their bodies. Serena's violet eyes caught the movement and froze him in place until she nodded once and refocused on her task.

This was where he left them. While they moved into place around the castle, he would go inside and try to reason with his mother. Perhaps if she and Gillian could hear him out, they would let go of this ludicrous idea to retake the throne. Although, Micha wasn't sure how happy Gillian would be to see him after Helena's trick, or that she'd even be alive to see him at all.

Micha frowned, not fond of any of the scenarios that awaited him. He was no fool and he was well aware that the likelihood of his success was slim, but if there was even the possibility he could end this without further lives being lost, he had to try. The others had only agreed to let him go off on his own because they hoped he would act as a further distraction for his mother, thereby giving Helena much-needed time to escape with Von and the rest of them an opportunity to get into place unannounced. Diversion or peacekeeper, Micha had a role to play, and he would see it through.

That didn't mean he had to like it.

He was not like the others. The differences between them were

463

glaringly obvious. Men and women alike, they all seemed eager at the promise of violence, whereas Micha shied away. He was not a fighter. Battle, and the resulting death, did not appeal to him in any capacity. He'd much rather hole up and get lost in a good book, a peaceful pastime he'd spent most of his life enjoying. Micha desperately wished he could leave the heroics to the others and go home to his library. But his place was with his family and his family was here. He needed to try to save them despite his vehement wish otherwise.

What had surprised Micha the most, was how easily Helena stepped into the role of warrior. It was not her need to protect the ones she loved that shocked him. That had been abundantly clear since she first set foot on the stage during her welcoming ceremony. It was how she did not cringe, or so much as flinch, at the thought of harming another. For one so nurturing and compassionate, she'd quickly embraced war and violence as a necessity. Helena had a warrior's soul and a mother's love, as deadly a combination as he'd ever seen. Micha was just glad he was on her side.

When he'd first met her, she had been so sweet. A lost little lamb in need of love and protection. He'd been enchanted at the first sight of those luminous aqua eyes. More than a part of him had hoped that she might choose him.

Now he could see that he'd never even stood a chance. A woman like her deserved a man that could fight by her side without a second thought. A man who could see her thirst for blood and revel in her prowess on the battlefield, not one who would fear her when she stood surrounded by the bodies she had slain. She needed a man that understood and loved all the facets of her soul: the dark as well as the light. He was not that man; he had never been and never could be. It would not stop him from serving her though.

Micha took a steadying breath, letting his eyes briefly rest on the others and offering a quick prayer to the Mother that they would still be standing when the day was done. He may not be able to join them on this killing field, but he could fight in his own way.

Without a word, he turned and started toward the place that had once been his home.

RONAN WATCHED Micha's retreating back, the calm that always preceded battle overtaking him.

Serena stepped up to his side. "Do you think he'll succeed?"

"Not a chance," Ronan said with derision.

"What about us?" she asked softly.

Ronan slanted a glance at her, uncertain which *us* she was referring to. "That's harder to say," he answered neutrally.

Serena let out a deep sigh. "I was afraid you'd say that. We've faced battles with worse odds and made it out relatively unscathed. At least we've got Helena on our side. That should help even the odds a little."

Well that answers that question, he thought without bitterness. "Indeed it will," he agreed.

"Ronan—I," she started hesitantly.

So they were going to have this conversation after all. "Serena, how long have we known each other?" he asked, wanting to make this easier for both of them.

Her eyes were warm as she replied, "It feels like our whole lives."

He nodded, returning her smile. "And in all of those years, have I ever given you any indication that I want anything other than your happiness?"

She blinked furiously and shook her head, silky blond strands flying wildly about her head.

Ronan gave her a sad smile, lifting his hand to gently brush a rogue tear off her cheek. "Then if we make it through this, know that you have my blessing to follow your heart, wherever it leads you. Not that you need it."

Serena pressed her hand over his, holding it against her cheek when he would have pulled away. "You know that I will always love you?"

He winked, pushing down the small pang her words caused. "And you know I will kill him if he hurts you. Being Von's brother won't save him."

Serena's laugh burst out and she threw her arms around his neck, holding him tightly. Ronan held her, his eyes closing as he savored the moment, knowing it was the last time she'd be in his arms.

There was a soft cough, and the two stepped away from one another. Nial stood there looking apologetic and determined in equal measure. "They are ready," he said, tipping his head to indicate the others.

Ronan nodded, squeezing Serena's shoulder a last time before walking toward Nial. He stopped when he was alongside him, the other man stiffening slightly. Ronan dipped his chin until his eyes were level with Nial's, forcing the other man to meet his icy gaze.

"Treat her well, or you will deal with me. I don't care who you are puppy, if you hurt her, I will destroy you."

Nial swallowed, but did not flinch as he responded, "I am glad that she has you to look after her, but you will never need to worry about her with me."

Ronan narrowed his eyes, slapping his hand on Nial's shoulder, causing his knees to buckle under the force. "I'll be the judge of that." Ronan walked away, sucking in a harsh breath and letting his mind empty of everything but the fight ahead as he let it out.

Kragen studied the barren scene, not liking how little coverage there was for their approach.

"What are you thinking?" Darrin asked.

"No matter what we do, we'll be completely visible against the white of the snow. If she has any guards, they'll spot us at once," Kragen grumbled.

Darrin contemplated the castle, eyebrows furrowing as he tried to think of a solution. His eyes cleared and he turned to Kragen with some excitement, snapping his fingers as he did. "What if we were able to make it harder for them to see?"

Kragen lifted a brow, unimpressed with the words. "What do you think I'm trying to figure out over here? Which gift basket to send them?"

Darrin scowled. "No, asshole. What if we combine our powers to create a fog. One that would obscure the land between us and the castle enough to mask our approach."

He lifted his brows as he considered the suggestion. "It could definitely work, although it could hinder us as well."

The blond man shrugged. "We wouldn't need to see until we reached the castle, would we?"

"Not unless someone was able to sneak up on us through the same fog," Ronan interjected, having just reached them.

Kragen nodded. "My thoughts exactly. What say you Joquil? Is there a way to control the fog, so that we could release it once we've cleared the land?"

Joquil's amber eyes assessed the landscape. "Perhaps. It will take the combined efforts of many of us to create that kind of weather. It could weaken us."

"I have read about entire armies using such a strategy in the past. They had a dedicated force purely focused on controlling the weather. That amount of power definitely takes a toll," Timmins warned, having just joined them.

The men eyed each other carefully. They were not lacking for power, any one of them more powerful than a handful of other Chosen, but the idea of weakening themselves when they were uncertain what exactly they'd be facing was unappealing.

"Even still. It may be our best option," Kragen rumbled.

Ronan nodded his agreement while Serena pointed out, "We can always rely on our physical skills. We do train without our magic for a reason."

Joquil scratched his chin. "To create the type of fog you're speaking of will require the use of four of the five branches: Water to create the moisture, Fire to turn it to mist, Air to disperse it, and Earth to ground it and keep it from simply floating off."

Nial cleared his throat, his face reddening as he said, "I am a master of all four branches."

"What are you proposing?" Timmins asked.

"I can make the elements work in harmony, while the rest of you are on the move. I—" he let out a soft chuckle, "I am the weakest fighter by far, I don't think any of us would deny it. I simply do not possess the same level of skill as the rest of you. But this I can do, and would do, gladly."

The Circle digested the words. "It could work," Joquil said, echoing Kragen's earlier words.

"It will require more power than you alone possess," Miranda said, placing her hand on Nial's shoulder, "but I can assist you."

Timmins' blue eyes widened in surprise as he turned to the Keeper. She felt the weight of his stare and shrugged prosaically. "What? I am hardly rushing head-first into a melee. I have my power to offer as well, and I will do so. From here," she added with a smirk.

Timmins shook his head, while Kragen grinned. "So we have our ranged team in place."

Effie stood quietly to the side, looking small surrounded by the others. Tilting her chin up, she squared her shoulders and declared, "I will go with the rest of you."

Darrin spun to her in surprise, opening his mouth to protest, but Effie kept talking, "I have been training with Helena when she works with Kragen and Ronan and have demonstrated some skill with the staff. I may have no power to offer, but I will fight in the way that I can. Just as the others are. I did not come with you all to sit on the sidelines and watch. I came to help."

Kragen placed his hand on her shoulder, squeezing in approval. Darrin looked like he had swallowed a lemon, but he did not argue.

"All right, little warrior," Ronan said. "I will create a shield for you, it should protect you from most blows. If they get through it though, you run. No one will think less of you for staying alive."

Effie frowned. "I'm not a coward."

Ronan and Kragen turned to her with twin scowls.

Ronan snapped, "Did you hear me say that you were? If you are going to be a part of the fighting force, when your Commander gives an order you obey it, or you don't fight. Going rogue in the midst of battle could lead to death. Yours or your cil'virga."

Effie flushed and ducked her head. "Sorry," she squeaked.

Ronan tilted her chin up. "No need to apologize, little warrior."

She grinned, posture relaxing as Ronan stepped back.

The group quieted, their eyes looking around as they mentally readied themselves. Ronan assessed his cil'virga, the Daejaran term for an elite military team. There was much to be desired in the way of their size, none of them expecting that this is where they would end up when they set out for Bael and the Keepers. They had gone in search of information, and at the time, it had made sense to have a smaller force for ease and speed while traveling. But the things that had been assets when they started could very well be what crippled them now; they may have started off on a rescue mission, but they were now heading into battle.

Luckily the men and women surrounding him were some of the Chosen's strongest and they were only facing off against one red-headed girl and her mother… And a potential army of Shadows.

Ronan sighed. He'd faced off against worse enemies with less.

"Let's go," he said finally.

THE FOG WAS thick and completely blocked out the sky as they crept closer to the castle. It had an eerie effect, seeming to envelope them completely in a world of white. Ronan lost sight of all but those right next to him. As always Serena was at his right side, her silvery blonde hair now twisted in tight braids. Kragen took up the spot on the left, the spot that would have been his if they'd been following Von.

It was odd; he hadn't lead anyone into battle in years. Not since Von had been promoted to Commander and again when he broke from the military entirely to create his mercenary band. Von had always been the one to lead; he had been born for it.

Ronan had no desire to lead. He was much more familiar with following orders than taking them, but that didn't mean he couldn't pick up the mantle with ease. There wasn't much Ronan wouldn't do to save the man that was the brother of his soul.

Seeing the black stone of the gate, he held up a fist. The others halted around him. He waited until he could hear the sound of footsteps fall silent around him before he opened his hand toward the sky, releasing the flare that would let Nial and Miranda know it was time to let go of the fog. It moved lazily, floating away from him in wisps until he could start to make out all of the others. Before long there was a cool breeze and the fog lifted completely.

Ronan let out a whispered "Fuck" when he saw what they had walked into.

Spinning in a slow circle, he lost count of the Shadows that had surrounded them. The hunched and mottled gray bodies were completely still as they stared with dead white eyes, the black lines snaking through them all that was moving.

"To me!" he shouted. The others reacted immediately, moving in tight and turning so that their backs were toward each other as they faced their enemy.

There was a heartbeat of silence, each army assessing the other, until Ronan let out a fierce battle cry.

Then there was nothing but chaos.

Fire blasted out of his hand in an arc, setting four of the Shadows in front of him on fire. The rest of the Shadows moved inhumanly fast, the first of them jumping toward Serena. She swung her sword once he was airborne, the Fire and Earth enhanced weapon aiming true. There was a garbled groan and then a thump as the ghastly head flew from the body, covering them in its thick black ichor.

Ronan quickly lost track of the others as he began swinging his flaming axes, cutting heads from bodies with each swing. He kept moving, knowing if they caught him, they would take him down. With each turn he'd catch a glimpse of one of the others. Kragen, taking on multiple Shadows at once, ducking and spinning so fast they could not touch him. Darrin running and sliding beneath a grasping hand so that he came up behind a Shadow, slitting its throat so cleanly, the head teetered drunkenly on its neck before tumbling to the ground. Effie was expertly swinging her staff, stunning the Shadows with her blows while Serena worked to finish the kill. Even Timmins and Joquil had a swath of bodies around them. Joquil was weaving powerful Water magic, freezing the Shadows in place and allowing Timmins to swing his mace into their frozen heads making them shatter into small gray shards.

Around them, bodies continued to fall, but there was no end to the waves of mindless, soulless creatures. Ronan's hands were growing slick with the black blood, his grasp on his ax slipping. It was a minute movement, but it changed the angle just enough that his blow did not land at the neck but instead bit into the shoulder.

The Shadow grinned at him as it launched itself at him. Ronan swung again, but the missed blow allowed another Shadow to reach him. He felt the nails and teeth scrape against him, piercing his shield.

Ronan grunted, pain flaring hot in his side as the poisonous blood made contact with his skin.

Then Serena was there, making quick work of the Shadow at his side so that he could dispatch the one before him. There was barely enough time for a hurried "Thanks" before more filled in the empty space.

Ronan couldn't miss the look in Serena's eyes as she braced for the next attack. It was impossible to say whether they had been fighting for hours or minutes, but the Shadows were relentless, and she wasn't sure how much longer they'd be able to hold them off.

There was a whimpered cry, and Ronan spun, seeing Effie go down under two of the brutes. Before he could move to assist her, Darrin was there, tackling them and knocking them to the ground. They were stunned just long enough for him to finish the kills. Effie blinked up at him with wide-eyed amazement. Darrin offered her a smug grin, before helping her stand and quickly dispatching three more.

Ronan lifted his eyes, seeing Nial and Miranda in the distance, using blasts of power to distract some of the Shadows. They were so focused on the ones in front of them, they did not notice the handful that had crept up behind them.

"Nial!" he shouted, using Air to reinforce the word so he would be able to hear it.

Nial spun but went down under the combined attack. Serena had also spun at the word, and was already flying back across the field to his aid. Trying to buy her time, Ronan let out another blast of Fire, in an attempt to clear a path for her. It worked, at least long enough for her to get past them and start to make her way up the hill.

Unfortunately, the Shadows closest to him, now on fire, were still coming at him, trying to grasp him with their smoldering hands. Ronan continued his deadly dance, but there were too many, and his cil'virga was spread too thin. Kragen was trying to work his way back to him, but couldn't cover the distance in time. He knew he was in trouble when the searing heat of fire crept up his back.

The pain was fierce and immediate, but Ronan only shouted, "It will take more than that to stop me!" and spun around, axes slashing into the ring of bodies around him, severing limbs and knocking them down as he did. But the damage was done.

The remaining Shadows smelled his blood and began flocking toward him, grasping and pulling at him until he stumbled, falling beneath the writhing mass of bodies.

CHAPTER 27

Micha let himself into the castle, making his way down the familiar halls unimpeded. Despite spending most of his formative years here, the place felt foreign. If not in appearance, certainly in tone. What had once been a warm, welcoming home, richly decorated in vibrant fabrics and colors, was now dark and distinctly oppressive. Not a single fire burned in any of the large hearths, and Micha shivered at the chill that permeated through the thick stone walls.

His senses were screaming at him to get out, that this was not a safe place, but he forced himself to continue on. He was slowly working his way toward the back of the castle, toward the room his mother had often referred to as its center of power. Micha remembered loving the sound of that when he was young, as if the castle was alive and powerful, just like him. When he'd asked how she knew which room held the power, his mother had simply responded that there were certain places where the Great Mother was more present and if you were lucky you might find one. She told him it meant that they were very blessed indeed to have such a place in their own home. Given the recent turn of events, it seemed likely he would find her there.

Micha continued to wander, ghosts of childhood memories haunting him with each step. He rounded a corner and stopped dead.

"Gillian?" he whispered, staring in horror at the bloodied face of his twin.

Gillian had been taking stumbling steps toward him, using the wall to keep herself upright. Deep purple bruises anchored bloodshot eyes that were all but swollen closed.

At the sound of her name, her eyes shot up wild with panic as she shrieked, "What are you still doing here? Changed your mind and come back to finish the job?" Her voice was completely distorted due to her injuries.

He frowned at her words and took a few steps toward her, holding up his hands in a placating way when she flinched. "Illy, it's me."

Tears filled her eyes at the nickname, and she collapsed to the floor. "I-Ika," she stammered.

Micha moved forward, going to his knees before her. "It's okay, I'm here now," he murmured soothingly, wrapping his arms around her and pressing her gently into his chest. He couldn't bear to see her suffering this way. Even though he'd been disappointed when he'd heard what she had been up to these past months, he couldn't bring himself to stay mad at her. This was his twin and he would love her regardless.

Gillian sobbed as he held her, whimpering over and over, "What have I done?"

"Shhh, Illy. It's all right. Everything will be all right," he promised.

"How can you say that?" she hiccupped. "The world is quite literally going to shit."

Micha chuckled at her words. "It just looks bad at the moment. You'll see, we will get through this together."

"How touching," an icy voice sneered from behind him.

The twins froze, moving away from each other and looking up at their mother. She stood just behind them, arms crossed with lips set in a severe frown. She looked impossibly young, as if the years had been going in reverse, erasing all of the smile lines that were once etched into her beautiful face.

Micha met her gaze and tensed. There was no recognition in her eyes. Nothing to indicate that she was pleased to see her son. This was not the woman he remembered. She was a cold, inhuman shell.

"Mother," Micha said formally, helping his sister stand. "It is good to see you well," he lied.

Rowena snorted. "I can't say the same."

He flinched as if he'd been struck, mouth falling open in shock. *Who was this imposter? This woman couldn't have actually given birth to him.*

Rowena turned coolly assessing eyes to Gillian, noting her injuries and stating, "It's a pity she didn't do me a favor and just kill you while she had the chance."

Gillian stiffened under his arm, chin trembling as she fought against further tears.

Micha opened his mouth to protest his mother's harsh words, but she lifted a hand before he could speak, cutting off his air supply and causing him to choke.

"That's quite enough out of you, traitor," she snapped, lifting her fisted hand higher and causing Micha's feet to scramble for purchase as he began to rise off of the floor.

"Mother please!" Gillian cried. "I've done everything you asked. You promised to spare him!"

"I have no use for a blood traitor. He led my enemy straight to me. As if that wasn't bad enough, you, my sorry excuse for a daughter, not only invite her in, you let her take the only leverage I had and walk back out! I've never seen a more worthless pair," Rowena spat, her voice filled with venom.

Micha's face was red as he struggled against the invisible hands that held him. Rowena's eyes flashed with malice and she clenched her fist tighter before jerking it quickly to the right. A loud crack echoed off the stone walls as the bones in Micha's neck shattered and his body fell lifelessly to the floor.

"Micha!" Gillian wailed, staring aghast at her brother's crumpled form. Body shaking, Gillian moved to launch herself at her mother, calling what little bit of power she could to her hands.

Rowena laughed darkly. "Oh child, as if *you* could ever stand against *me*."

Gillian howled in rage.

Narrowing her eyes, Rowena lifted both her hands, palms facing Gillian. Black ropes of her insidious power snaked out, causing Gillian's eyes to widen in horrified recognition. She'd seen this spell before.

"No!" she shouted desperately, turning to run.

Rowena only laughed harder. Her power wrapped around Gillian, snaking into her still-screaming mouth. Gillian's green eyes turned milky white, black lines slowly forming within them, as her flailing limbs went still. Rowena did not stop, letting the full force of her power continue to seep into Gillian's body.

Gillian's long limbs twisted, her body shrinking into itself as her skin turned a dull sickly gray. In opposition, Rowena seemed to swell. Her skin luminous with the power she was absorbing as she fed from her daughter's soul.

When she was done, her daughter no longer stood before her. In her place was Rowena's newest Shadow.

Rowena beamed at her creation, "Perhaps now you won't have so much trouble following directions." With that, Rowena began walking, stepping over her son's corpse without pause.

Behind her, Gillian's soulless body followed with slow, ambling steps.

CHAPTER 28

When they arrived in the clearing, Helena staggered, bracing a hand against the rough bark of a tree to steady her while she gagged. She felt as though her body had tried to turn itself inside out. Von was beside her, looking much the same as she felt, although he'd at least managed to remain upright.

He ran his hand along the length of her spine, the touch soothing, until she was clear-headed enough to stand on her own.

"Better?"

Her lips twisted in a grimace. "Definitely not my preferred method of travel, despite the convenience."

He chuckled and looked around. There was a thick fog rolling into the trees, blocking their view of the castle and surrounding them in a sparkling mist. Von paled at the sight, his eyes widening and darting over to her. Helena was quick to press her lips to his, letting the warmth of her body against his remind him that she was real and that this was not another of his horrific dreams.

Von rested his forehead against hers, sucking in a shaky breath. *"It would seem I am not as recovered as I'd hoped,"* he admitted, smoky gray eyes staring into hers.

"You will be," she promised as they straightened.

There was a searing pain in her side; the Jaka, reminding her that they needed to hurry. She moved away from her mate, although not far, shielding her eyes and using her power to help her see through the fog.

"What do you see?" he asked softly.

Helena shook her head, not having spotted anything of note, when her eyes finally found them. She let out a horrified gasp; the army of Shadows before her seemed endless as they swarmed her friends. Her eyes jumped from one to another, counting heads as she searched for one of fiery red. He wasn't there.

Panic began to claw at her, but she pushed it down, focusing instead on the psychic thread that told her he was there. She turned her head, thinking perhaps he'd been cut off from the others, when she saw a flash of red hidden beneath a mass of squirming limbs. They'd taken him down, she realized. Anger flared incandescent, causing her power to simmer and call her to the battle.

Before she could join them, she needed to find the rest of her friends. That was still only five. *Where were the others?*

Her gaze continued to scan the field, noting the snapping jaws of the wolves as they too took down Rowena's monstrosities, but only stopping her frantic search once she spotted the last of her friends. Nial was beside Miranda, colorful orbs flying from their hands and into a wall of approaching Shadows. Serena was just about to reach them, her ax alight with fire as her mouth opened on a war-cry that had the others ducking. She let go of her weapon. It flew in tight circles, until it made contact and neatly lopped off the head of the nearest Shadow, before returning to her open hand.

Helena's rage grew with each passing second. These were her people, the ones she'd vowed to protect. She could not let them continue to fight alone. Especially not when they were so clearly outnumbered.

She spun to Von, her voice urgent, "I need to go."

"Not without me," he countered, thick arms crossed over his broad chest.

Helena eyed him. He was barely pieced together, but there was no way he'd willingly stand back while the others were under attack; it went against everything he believed in. Helena should know; it was the same for her.

"I don't have time to argue with you about all the reasons why that's a bad idea. Please stay safe, my love. I just got you back." She leaned up and pressed a kiss, hot and fierce, against his lips before taking a few steps back.

His eyes smoldered, love and desire swirling in their depths. "You as well, Mate."

She nodded and let out the low whistle that would bring Starshine to her.

When she spoke again, her eyes had begun to swirl with iridescent fire, and her voice was thick with power. "Your brother is to the west; it looks like he could use you. I will clear the field."

Von looked up as dark roiling clouds began to amass in the early morning sky before nodding and taking off in the direction she had indicated, using his power to cover the distance via a series of blinks. Helena watched him go, hating that he was entering a battle when he was already weakened. She would just have to ensure it was a short one.

Determination filled her as her Talyrian came into view. Starshine had barely landed when Helena launched herself onto her back.

"Fly, girl," she shouted, drawing her power, every churning drop, to the surface.

Starshine took two running steps and flung them into the air, gaining height quickly. Once airborne, they were surrounded by heavy black clouds and Starshine streaked through them like a falling star. Thunder growled and lightning cracked as the pair approached the place where her friends were fighting.

Helena let out an inarticulate cry which caused the others to look up in raw panic. Their reassurance at the sight of her was palpable, their cheers turning to battle cries that spurred them to fight with renewed vigor. Holding out her hands, now glowing with her power, she let out one savage word.

"Burn!"

Starshine roared, letting out a pure beam of fire that caused an entire row of Shadows to turn to ash. Helena threw her hands up, releasing her power into the clouds. Her hair flew behind her, the ends looking like living flame as they floated on the air. There was another roll of thunder as fiery comets began to streak through the storming sky.

The world was on fire.

Everywhere she turned, Shadows were alight. Helena channeled her power to create shields for each of her friends, using her connection through the Jaka to help isolate where they were, and using proximity to locate the others. She did the same for herself and Starshine, allowing them to fly unscathed through the sky.

Catching Kragen's eye, Helena pointed to where Ronan had fallen. Her Sword made his way over, easily dispatching the few lingering Shadows, until he was able to pull Ronan up. The man was covered in thick black blood, and it seemed he'd acquired several new injuries that would scar.

Helena watched as long as she could, waiting to ensure he was all right before refocusing on the fight. She finally moved on, once he'd pulled his weapon out of a dead body and swung it into another Shadow.

They continued circling the field as Helena's power fueled the firestorm. The air was thick with ash, floating up from the charred bodies and spiraling into the air. It was getting hard to see clearly, but it looked like they were finally making a dent in Rowena's army. Helena could sense someone watching her. The hair on the back of her neck lifted as she risked a glance toward the castle. That was when she saw her.

It was the scene from the Keepers' warning, but not. A blonde woman was standing on a balcony, but she was not alone. Unlike her vision, she was flanked by six others and they were nothing like the hairless, skeletal creatures fighting below. These beings still appeared mostly human, having only the same white eyes shot through with black that indicated they were some form of Shadow. All of them were clearly male, except one.

Helena gasped, recognition shooting through her at the red-haired female at Rowena's side. The bitch queen had turned her own daughter into a monster, taking her soul and feeding on her power until there was nothing left but an abomination. Disgust caused her stomach to roll and Helena launched a ball of Fire toward the balcony.

Rowena's lips curled in amusement as her own mouth opened. Two things happened at once: a large creak, like the sound of a gate being lowered, echoed over the field just as Helena's fireball froze and began to plummet. The glittering ball smashed into the stone of the balcony, missing its mark entirely. Starshine shot jets of fire at Rowena, but they hit an invisible barrier and turned to smoke. Helena fumed while Rowena laughed.

It was then that the second thing Rowena had done became apparent. Row after row of shadows made their way through a now open gate and onto the killing field; their mindless bodies stumbling over the corpses of the fallen. There were not mere hundreds of new Shadows, there were thousands of the creatures marching toward her friends.

Comprehension dawned. This was where everyone had gone, why she hadn't seen a single person when she made her way to the castle. All of the people that should have been needed to keep a castle such as this running, all of the villagers that would have helped work the land and feed them; Rowena had turned every single one of them into one of her Shadows.

It was no wonder she had not bothered them these last months, she has been building her army. With every Shadow Rowena created, she also added to her own power, not just her fighting force.

Helena looked at where her friends were still fighting, clearly losing ground under the new assault. They'd been making progress, had almost completely eliminated all the Shadows that remained, but they would not be able to fend off a couple thousand more. Each one of them was already showing signs of fatigue. She watched as Darrin slipped, his weapon lopping off an arm instead of the creature's head. The Shadow did not stop, slashing at Darrin with its remaining hand, causing thin ribbons of blood to appear.

They were outmatched.

Her stomach dropped, she alone would not be enough to save them. There were just too many, and if Rowena added her power to the fight, she could destroy them all. Helena needed to get them out. Now.

Sensing her need, Starshine dove, eradicating the entire front line of the Shadows with a long torrent of flame. It was enough of a break for her to be able to shout to the others, "Back! Get back!"

Helena watched as her friends ran, Effie stumbling and falling to her hands and knees. Darrin was already beside her, lifting her into his arms and running. Timmins and Joquil continued to fend off the remaining Shadows that were closest, keeping an open path for Kragen and Ronan to run through. Once together, the four men followed after the other two.

She fed the storm, fire flying through the sky until there was a wall of flame between her people and Rowena's army. It should be enough to buy them the time they needed to escape. Starshine made one last turn, ready to head back, when a blast of power hit her.

Helena and Starshine let out twin shrieks of rage at the impact that rocked Helena so hard she was almost hanging off the side. Starshine righted, allowing Helena to climb back into place, but her wing had been damaged and each flap of her great wings was an obvious struggle. The blast of power must have obliterated the shield that had been protecting the Talyrian.

Releasing some of the Fire she was still channeling, Helena pressed her hand into Starshine's fur, assessing the injury and pouring Water's healing magic into her. Bone and flesh knit itself back together, allowing Starshine to continue flying them to safety.

They landed and Helena slid off, running toward the others. They were all there, some in better shape than others, but all alive. There was no time to explain what she intended.

"Go!" She screamed to Starshine, who let out a roar and took to the sky.

"Everyone grab onto each other!" she barked the orders, trusting they would follow without question.

Von moved to stand beside her, wrapping his arm around her waist, his eyes never straying from his brother. Helena hastily scanned her

Mate, checking for new injuries, but while he was covered in foul black ichor, there were none. She allowed herself a brief instant of relief before shifting her focus.

Ronan was at her other side, his hand clasping and squeezing hers. The others pulled in. Serena and Nial holding each other, while Darrin still carried Effie. Timmins had hauled Miranda to him, and Joquil and Kragen filled in the spaces between them. Even Karma and the rest of the bloodied, battle-worn Daejaran wolves drew close, sensing the urgency in her order.

"Where's Micha?" she asked, just now realizing his red head was not among them.

Ronan frowned and shook his head. There wasn't time for Helena to feel more than a pang at the news, the need to get away overriding every other emotion. She pulled the small purple stone once more from her pocket.

"Helena," Von said tersely, "are you sure that's possible?"

She wasn't. Knowing that the stones worked off charge, and not knowing how much remained, she could only hope. Safe; they needed to get somewhere safe. Her mind scrambled to think of a place she could transport them.

"Hold on!" she shouted, squeezing her eyes shut and focusing on the image of a campsite they'd had near the border. Helena used every last vestige of power that remained to reinforce her intention as the world went black.

CHAPTER 29

Several days had passed since they had made it back to the Palace. Their injuries had been relatively minor. Surprisingly, Ronan suffered the worst out of all of them, if you discounted Von.

Helena couldn't help the small snort of laughter that escaped at his reaction when she'd healed him.

Unable to distinguish between new and old injuries, or perhaps it was because she was simply too tired to try, Helena had flooded his body with her healing magic. When Ronan had looked in the mirror he'd scowled darkly and shouted, "Put it back!"

Her magic had repaired *all* the damage, meaning that the scar that had bisected his face for so long was gone. The rest of them had been greatly amused to see the amount of female attention he was now receiving, but it only annoyed Ronan further; a testament to the fierce reputation he'd worked so hard to foster having vanished along with the marks of battles fought and won.

"I hope that smile is for me, Mate," Von whispered in her ear, large hands kneading into the muscles of her back.

"Mmm," she murmured, eyes closing. "All of my smiles are for you."

He nipped at her ear playfully before moving to stand before her.

Helena looked up into eyes that were anything but playful, her cheeks flooding with color as his desire rolled over her. The air between them was charged as Von held out a hand, helping her out of her chair and pulling her into his arms.

They had spent the past few nights tangled together, whispering until the sky began to lighten, not wanting to close their eyes and find that being together again was a dream. It had been a time of tenderness, letting bodies and hearts heal from their separation, their need to simply hear and touch each other surpassing any other physical need. But no longer. Her Mate's intention was clear.

He dropped his head to kiss the fingers grasping his, looking up at her through thick black lashes and grinning wickedly. "It's time for bed, Mate."

Helena felt her mouth go dry, only capable of nodding. Von led her to their bed, stopping to pull back the thick purple blanket before facing her again. He let his fingers trace the edges of her dress, dipping them into the valley between her breasts briefly, before continuing his exploration.

She could feel her breath hitch, the gentle caresses at complete odds with the hunger she could see in his eyes. The same hunger she was feeling. Von lifted his other hand, both grasping the thin cotton before rending it in two.

Helena looked down, shocked. Large aqua eyes looked back into his. "I liked that dress!"

Von chuckled. "I'll get you a new one. We're now even for the time you ruined the one I liked."

He peeled the dress away, his hands continuing their exploration of her body. His touched faltered when he caught the subtle shimmer of her Jaka in the soft light. He was silent as he traced the tattoo along her side, his touch sending flickers of electricity throughout her body. His thumb brushed the underside of her breast as he followed the swirling marks that represented their bond.

"I'd be lying if I said it didn't bring me great pride to see you wearing the mark of my people." Von's low growl was as sensual as his touch. His eyes were molten silver as they bore into hers. "But I hate that you were marked by another."

Helena tried to bite back her smile. "I knew you would say that."

A corner of Von's mouth curled as he purred, "Did you now?"

She tilted her head to the side as she teased, "I would have to be an utter fool not to." He chuckled at that, his eyes dropping to her lips as she continued, "But even you cannot deny that you are more than adequately represented in the mark."

His eyes filled with pleasure as they swept over the Jaka again. "Aye."

The possessive pleasure she heard in the word also reverberated through their bond and she felt her lips tip in delight. This was her Mate. The man who, with only a look, had her soul cry out *'Mine.'*

Von knew the instant her mood shifted from amusement to arousal, his nostrils flaring as his eyes darkened in response. He bent to kiss her, pressing his body against hers until there was not even a sliver of space between them. The kiss was a fierce claiming, his mouth and tongue moving against hers in an erotic prelude to what their bodies would do.

Helena shivered at the contact, feeling her nipples contract into tight points while heat flooded her core.

He pulled back to rest his forehead against hers, chest rising and falling with his harsh breaths. *"I do not think I can be gentle,"* he warned her, cherishing the added intimacy of speaking to her through their bond.

"Then don't be," she responded, wrapping her arms around his neck and pushing up onto her toes. Her fingers threaded through his silky black hair as she kissed him with all of the pent-up desire she'd been feeling.

Von's hands gripped at her hips, fingers digging in deeply as he took a step back and sat down hard on the bed, pulling her body on top of his.

Helena straddled his lap, rubbing herself against the straining bulge beneath his pants. "I need you," she whispered hotly against his lips, biting and sucking on them as he ran his hands along the sides of her body.

Von growled low in his throat, twisting so that Helena fell onto her back and he was kneeling between her spread legs. He moved his hands up her thighs, stretching her wider.

"Please," she whispered, wanting the feeling of completion that would come when he slid into her.

He let his fingers slip through the slickness at her center, smiling at the harsh gasp and lift of her hips the movement caused. His eyes bore into hers when he slipped a finger inside of her.

"Is this what you want?"

Helena shook her head from side to side. "N-no," she moaned.

"No?" he asked, lifting a dark brow, his fingers stilling inside her.

"M-more," she panted, pressing down around the finger that was curling inside her.

Von slid another finger in, working her slowly as his other hand released the binding of his pants. "Better?" he asked in a carnal rumble.

"No," she whimpered, eying the flesh now exposed and hanging thick and heavy between his legs.

Von grinned, tracking her eyes. "Feeling greedy, Mate?"

Helena nodded, her tongue darting out to wet her lips. "Very."

His eyes darkened at the sight of her tongue and he let out a low grunt. Von pulled his fingers slowly out of her, rubbing her wetness into the small bundle of nerves and causing her to groan. He removed his pants and returned to her, grasping her around the knees and pulling her toward where he was standing. He used his power to create the phantom hands that continued to run over her body as he took his thick length into his hand and ran it along her center.

"Is this what you want?" he asked again, his voice harsh with need.

"Yes," she moaned, trying to press the tip of him deeper inside her.

"Good," he growled, slamming into her in one long thrust while his fingers, real and phantom, rubbed and plucked at her.

"Von!" she cried, arching off the bed and coming apart around him.

"Mine," he snarled, bending over to capture her lips with his.

He began pushing into her, thrusting hard and fast. Her heart raced in time with his, each of them reveling in the feeling of being joined again.

Helena met him thrust for thrust, nails digging into his back as she held him. She could feel him all around her: his smell, his body, his love. It was overwhelming. Her need began to spiral again.

Sensing it, Von bit down on the skin between her neck and shoulder, hips driving faster. Helena broke, crying out his name. He followed, stealing her cries with his lips as he emptied himself inside her.

They lay there, wrapped around each other, hearts still pounding and bodies slick with sweat.

"Now I'm home," he whispered.

Her heart was too full for words, so she held him tighter, not letting him move away from the cocoon of her body. She let her hand continue to run up and down his back, tugging on the strands of hair that had grown long while he was away.

He chuckled and looked down at her. "Enjoying yourself?"

"Aye," she responded, hands now squeezing the firm muscles of his butt.

His smile fell and his eyes glittered. "Keep it up."

The sexual warning had languid muscles tensing with desire. "Like this?" she whispered, hands cupping the heavy weight of him.

Von flexed into her, hard once more.

"Already?" she teased.

He gave her a look, equal parts adoration and arousal. "Always. I will always be ready for you, *Mira*. To remind you that you belong to me," he whispered, taking her lower lip between his teeth and running his tongue along the length of it.

"Mmm," she murmured in approval.

"Besides, Mate, we have barely begun to make up for the time we lost."

She smiled, fingers running up his back and into his hair. "If you insist."

"I do," he said fiercely, his body reinforcing the promise of his words.

Helena's eyes rolled back, feeling whole once again as a broken part of her soul finally fell back in place.

CHAPTER 30

Helena woke up slowly, enjoying the feeling of being curled around Von. He ran his hands over her hair, pressing his lips into the top of her head. "Good morning, Mate."

"Morning, my love," she whispered, snuggling deeper into him.

"Timmins has already sent word. The Circle is meeting to discuss the formal steps of declaring war against the traitor Rowena."

Helena scowled, annoyed that the bitch had found a way to sour her morning already.

"We cannot put it off much longer, *Mira*," Von said with soft understanding. "Her army is vast already. We need to call on our allies if we are to have any hope of defeating her."

She pressed her face into his neck and muttered inaudibly.

"What was that?" he laughed, pulling away to see her face.

"I know," she sighed, rolling her eyes and sitting up.

Von's gaze darkened as he took in the sight of her naked body, his hands moving to trace over the sparkling swirls of her Jaka. He replaced his fingers with his lips, pressing a lingering kiss over the central mark between her ribs before looking up at her with hopeful eyes.

She slapped his hand away with a breathless laugh. "You're the one that said we had to go."

He frowned, looking like a child that had been denied his favorite toy. "What's five more minutes? We're late already."

Helena smirked. "Only five minutes?"

Von grinned lasciviously and made to move on top of her when a knock sounded on the door.

They each let out annoyed sighs and pulled the discarded remnants of clothing up to quickly dress. Helena laughed when she found the torn dress she'd worn the night before, Von winking as she used her magic to repair the damage.

Alina popped her head in, her smile radiant as she took in her mistress slapping away the hands of her Mate. "They are calling for you, Kiri," she announced once she caught their attention, trying not to laugh at Helena's flustered expression.

"We're on our way," Helena informed her maid.

With a quick nod, Alina disappeared back through the door.

Once they were both dressed, and appeared mostly unrumpled, Von grasped Helena's hand in his and led her down toward the Circle's Chambers.

THE MEN WERE MILLING around the hallway, chatting in quiet but jovial voices when they rounded the corner. Helena smiled when she saw that Ronan had been invited to join them. Still an unofficial member of the Circle, he had more than proven that he deserved a place as one of her trusted advisors. Helena had briefly contemplated asking if he would consider being the leader of the Rasmiri, but his loyalty to Von and the people of Daejara had held her back. Perhaps it was something she and Von could discuss later.

A sense of peace greeted her at the sight of the ones she had come to love; safe and whole at home. There had been a moment, when Helena had considered unleashing everything she had at Rowena, but the energy required for such an attack would have left the rest of them vulnerable. She'd had to choose between eliminating her enemy and protecting thousands of nameless others, or saving the lives of the ones she'd already sworn to protect and letting Rowena go. It had not been an easy choice, but she'd made it gladly.

Seeing them here, now, laughing and joking with one another, only reinforced that she'd made the right choice. They would deal with Rowena together.

Kragen saw her first, lifting an arm to wave. "There they are! We were about to draw straws to see which of us was going to have to haul you two lovebirds out of bed."

From the glower on Darrin's face, Helena could already tell who had drawn the short straw.

"Lucky for all of you, none of you were foolish enough to try," Von drawled as he punched Ronan on the arm by way of greeting.

Ronan frowned and rubbed his shoulder. "What was that for? I wasn't the one that was going to interrupt you..." He trailed off, smirking smugly as he added, "This time."

Von grinned. "That would have earned you a punch in the balls instead."

Ronan gave Von a skeptical sidelong glance as he protectively placed his hands in front of his crotch; years of friendship and familiarity causing him to doubt such a blow wasn't about to be delivered anyway.

Noting the stance, Von snickered. "At ease, bastard. I was only paying you back for touching my Mate."

Ronan looked confused for a moment, trying to ascertain when he'd inappropriately touched Helena, before his knitted brows lifted and he laughed with understanding.

"It was beautifully done," Von added in a more subdued tone, referring to the Jaka he'd so lovingly traced earlier that morning. "I could not have done better myself."

The red-haired warrior shrugged in a show of dismissal, but Helena noted the way his cheeks tinged red at the compliment.

"It was also incredibly useful," Helena added, offering her own appreciative smile.

The two men made murmurs of agreement, although Von's lips

twitched with laughter as he threatened, "Don't think that means you can do it again."

Ronan winked at Helena. "Only if the lady asks me to."

"Dream on," Von sneered, punching his friend again.

Ronan's shoulders shook with laughter and Helena shook her head in amusement at their antics before kissing Von's cheek and stepping past them toward the others. "Shall we get started?"

The men nodded and followed her as she made her way into the familiar room.

A black lacquered box sat unopened in the middle of the table shining in the soft glow of the firelight.

"What's this?" she asked with delighted surprise as she stepped into the room. "A present? It's not my name day."

She stepped toward it quickly, filled with giddy anticipation. Her hands eagerly reached for the lid, lifting a cream piece of parchment. It had been sealed with a deep purple wax; a knot of thorns its emblem.

Helena looked up from the box and back toward her Circle. The smile began to fade from her face as she took in the expressions of confusion and unease. The same feelings grated against her mind's inner barrier through her connection to each of them.

Her blood turned to ice and her brows knit together.

"Helena," Joquil cautioned.

Her aqua eyes were transitioning to iridescent as she scanned the box for any lingering sense of magic, something that would indicate who it was from or what was inside it. There was nothing.

Using a nail to peel back the seal, Helena unfolded the small piece of parchment. Two words were scrawled in a feminine hand: *Your move.*

The note fell from Helena's trembling fingers. Kragen moved quickly to snatch it before it hit the ground. She struggled to open the box's latch until it finally came free with a soft click.

"Helena!" Von shouted, realizing who the package was from after reading the words over Kragen's shoulder. Her name also reverberated within her mind as he reinforced the cry through their bond.

He blinked, crossing the distance between them with his power, but he was still too late. Helena had already opened the box.

Her face drained of all color and her mouth opened on a keening wail that amplified the men's fear tenfold. The Circle closed in around her.

Von looked into the box and felt his stomach lurch. He made a move to grab Helena when her knees buckled and she fell to the floor. He caught her and fell with her so that they both knelt on the floor. He tried to comfort her by tucking her into his body.

"No," she sobbed, seeming to gasp for air.

All traces of the happiness she'd felt just moments ago completely vanished and were replaced by bone-deep terror. V

on tried again to wrap his arms around his shaking Mate, but she pushed him off.

On her hands and knees she panted, struggling to breathe.

Darrin peered into the box before staggering back. Horror and revulsion stole across his handsome face. He heaved and barely made it to the window before becoming violently ill.

"Breathe. Breathe, my love," Von murmured, stroking her back and adding through their bond, *"Please, Mira. You've got to try."*

Helena took a deep shuddering breath, her entire body shaking.

Von winced as he felt her nails crack and break as she scraped them along the ground. He watched as she grasped and crumpled the forgotten piece of parchment that Kragen had let slip through his fingers, blood smearing along its creamy surface. Watched as she slowly sat back on her heels, threw her head back, and screamed.

The scream shattered every piece of glass in the Palace, and echoed through the grounds and beyond. Birds scattered from their perches in the trees, taking flight in an attempt to flee the pain and rage that created that sound.

In her fist, the note began to smoke and caught fire. It burned quickly until all that remained was a smoldering pile of ash. The men paled as they took in the sight of her. Her hair flew around her like flame and her eyes glowed with swirling light as she stared past them, unseeing, and snarled the words that were both promise and verdict.

"My turn."

THE CHOSEN: BOOK 3

CROWN OF EMBERS

MEG ANNE

CHAPTER 1

"That traitorous bitch!" Helena seethed as she slammed her hands onto the top of the worn wooden table. "If it's a war she wants, I'll damn well give her one!"

Von rested his hand on top of hers, working his fingers beneath her palm in an attempt to pry it off the now smoking wood. His sharp hiss of pain caught her attention.

In surprise, Helena looked down and noticed the imprint of her hand where it had been seared into the wood. Her temper was flaring out of control, ping-ponging between grief and anger and causing her magic to react. Bolstered by Von's presence, it was more potent than ever and did not require her conscious thought before flaring to life. Her power was taking cues from her emotions; a dangerous, and potentially deadly, combination.

Balling her hands into fists, she stepped back from the table and continued her restless pacing. "She mur-murd—" Helena choked on the word, unable to say it out loud, to let it be real. Murdered. Rowena had *murdered* him. Anderson. The man who had loved and protected her for as long as she could remember. Every hurt—small, imaginary, or otherwise—garnered the same loving attention and care.

And now he was dead. All because of her and how much his death would hurt her. She hadn't seen it coming, hadn't even thought of needing to protect him. She'd failed him.

Bile rose up as the image of his face bloomed in her mind: mouth frozen open in an eternal scream, two gaping red holes where kind green eyes had once been. Like a rubber band, Helena snapped back from tears into anger. Spinning to face the men standing around her she growled, "I will destroy her."

"We," Von corrected, moving into her line of sight, "*we* will destroy her. Together."

Iridescent eyes collided with molten gray and she could feel him willing her to step back from the murderous edge on which she was teetering. Helena was trembling as her emotions raged within her; her heart was pounding, beating erratically like a bird trying to escape its cage.

She was not the only one affected. Around her, the Circle shifted restlessly, the intensity of her rage seeping into them. Kragen was the first to lose control, slamming his fist into the wall with a roar. Ronan wrapped an arm around him and pulled him back, whispering harshly into his ear. Kragen gnashed his teeth, and with a nod from Von, Ronan pulled him from the Chambers. Helena stared at the hole Kragen's fist had left in the otherwise unblemished stone.

"We need to be rational, Kiri," Joquil said in a low voice.

Sparkling iridescent eyes flew to where he was standing beside Timmins. Joquil straightened under her scrutiny, but did not back down from her withering gaze.

"Fuck rational," she snarled dangerously.

Joquil swallowed back his response when he saw her thunderous expression. Before he could try again, his warm amber eyes began to show flickers of iridescence. A dark smile curled his lips and he purred in a voice filled with malice, "Shall I bring you her head, Kiri?"

Timmins gave a start at the words which were so out of character for the Master. He looked with growing horror between Joquil and Helena. When his eyes met hers, his posture relaxed and the same eerie smile grew on his face.

"Out!" bellowed Von.

Timmins and Joquil blinked, their eyes returning to normal. Without delay, the two men rushed for the door and away from the woman whose power threatened to overtake them.

"Helena," Von said in a low, measured voice, trying to pull her attention back to him.

Her eyes went to his as Darrin cried out, "Don't you dare tell me to leave the only person who understands what I've lost."

Von growled, irritation flickering in his gray eyes. As one, Helena and Von pinned Darrin with their gazes.

Darrin was the picture of grief, his bright green eyes bleak and red-rimmed. "That man raised me, and that evil bitch just sent me his head," he fumed. "Perhaps you should be the one to leave! Let me grieve with the only person who is capable of feeling the same loss that is tearing me apart."

"Shield, get. The. Fuck. Out!" Von roared.

Instead of moving toward the door, Darrin stalked toward Von. "Make me."

"Wrong answer." Von slammed his palm out, shoving Darrin with all of his considerable strength. Darrin flew back, falling into the table before crashing to the floor. Von grabbed Darrin by the front of his shirt and lifted him up, pushing him out the doorway before kicking the door shut.

There was a crash as Darrin slammed his fist into the door, causing it to shake. Still staring at the door Von replied almost conversationally, "You might be grieving, puppy, and I'm sorry for that, but not even the Mother will save you if you come back into this room."

There was no response. Von, the only one able to resist the seductive pull of her magic, slowly turned back to face his Mate.

"*Mira*," he said, brushing his fingers along her tear-stained cheek.

Her lips pulled back in a silent snarl, but she did not speak.

"Helena," he tried again. When she still did not respond, he demanded, "Mate." The order echoed along the length of their bond, startling her out of her fury.

Helena glanced around the room, surprised to see it was empty. "Where did everyone go?" she asked, her voice hoarse.

"I asked them to leave," he said with a wry twist to his lips.

She blinked up at him, confused, before asking warily, "What did I do?"

He wrapped her in a hug, pressing a kiss to her forehead. "It doesn't matter."

"Von…"

"Shhh," he murmured.

"Don't shush me," she protested weakly.

He just held her tighter, asking softly, "Are you all right?"

Taking a deep, shuddering breath, she admitted baldly, "No."

Von held her, giving her the time and space she needed before she could speak further.

"She killed him, Von. He was…" Helena trailed off, unable to think of a way to describe everything Anderson had been to her. "Family," she said finally. "Anderson was my family, and he never did anything in his life to deserve what she did to him." Helena's voice faded toward the end, the threat of tears making it hard for her to speak.

"We will put an end to Rowena. Trust me; no one wants that more than I do, Helena. But we need to be smart. She did this, knowing it would provoke you. She wants you to strike while you are unprepared to face her. You saw her army; we need far greater numbers if we are going to face that again."

Helena nodded. "I know, but—"

Von's voice was warm but firm as he interjected, "Do not mistake preparation for a sign of weakness. She landed a great blow today, but this is just one battle of what will surely be many. You will be the one still standing at the end of this. Let us call on our allies and gather our forces. Then we will face her, on our terms and when we are the ones with the upper hand."

His words made sense, and yet they grated. "You speak like you've done this before," she muttered petulantly.

"Maybe once or twice," he affirmed.

There was comfort in knowing she would not be facing this alone. "I want to give him a proper burial," she said suddenly.

"Whatever you want, *Mira*."

"Can you bury just a," she grimaced, "head?"

"You are the Kiri, you can do whatever you damn well please."

"Except rush into battle," she countered.

"Except put your life in danger," he amended.

The small smile that rose in response to his words did not last long, her pain outweighing all other emotion. "I don't know what to do," she confessed in a small voice, her head still tucked into his chest.

Von's hand moved comfortingly over her back, "Tonight you grieve the man you have lost. Tomorrow we will celebrate his life and then we can worry about the rest."

"Okay," she agreed, lower lip trembling as her emotions bubbled up again. She sobbed until her tears ran dry and the sky went dark. Von held her the entire time.

"Will you tell me about him?" he asked once she started to pull back from him.

The pain in her aqua eyes shot through him but she was smiling softly as she said, "Yes."

HELENA WAS CURLED up in her favorite cushioned chair, a blanket draped over her lap as she stared silently across the room. A soft snore had her eyes moving to her Mate and a tired smile rose at the sight of him. Von was splayed across the settee beside her, entirely too large and masculine for the dainty piece of furniture. He couldn't help but radiate strength and presence, even when he was all but unconscious.

Von had urged her to come to bed with him hours ago, but she could not quiet her mind enough to drift to sleep. Finally he'd relented, seeing that she needed time to process her loss now that the initial wave of grief had passed. That didn't mean he'd gone far. She'd rolled her eyes when he'd stretched out muttering under his breath about furniture that was too small, while trying, unsuccessfully, to make himself comfortable. Her heart had swelled a little, appreciating how he was giving her space while also letting her know that he was there for her.

As his grumbling gave way to deep, steady breathing, she had thanked the Great Mother once again that it was not his head she had found in that box. There was no question in Helena's mind about whether or not she would have survived that particular loss. If the last few months were any indication, *no one* would have survived that reaction, especially since she'd nearly come undone by mere separation.

Not that it made her heart hurt any less for having lost Anderson. A numbness had settled over her since she left the Chambers cradled in Von's arms. It allowed her to spend the twilight hours lovingly flipping through long-forgotten memories of the man that helped raise her. While there were still a few tears, they were silent, quietly slipping through her swollen eyes as she allowed herself to relive their time together. Helena was also accompanied by the steady ache of grief, but the memories were more bittersweet than painful: a tender bruise being accidentally brushed instead of a dagger twisting through her heart.

She knew that this was not a pain that would quietly fade. Its ache would always remain to some degree. It was the kind of pain that would rear up unexpectedly, as strong and fierce as if it had just happened, in the days and years to come.

Helena couldn't believe that he was gone, that he would never know her children. Never meet the man who held the other half of her soul. Never again hold her in his stooped embrace as he pressed paper-dry lips to her forehead and wished her goodnight. So many moments had been stolen from them, but there was one that she would miss more than any other: the sound of his gruff voice uttering her name with exasperation, even as his eyes twinkled with pleasure, whenever she tried to take care of him.

She let out a low, sad sigh. Anderson's loss would stay with her, but she would not let it change the woman he'd helped shape. He'd already made her promise as much just over a year ago.

The memory of that day surged forth, unbidden. The details that sprang up surprised her with their intensity. It was not a time she cared to dwell on. She had not let herself think of it at all since it had passed. Helena had considered it the darkest time of her life until Gillian's betrayal had shown her just what kind of darkness truly existed in the world, and in her.

Yet, as the recollection of that afternoon swirled into focus within her mind, Helena realized that perhaps what she most needed right now was to remember the words that had provided comfort and a glimmer of hope when she had been lost in darkness.

HELENA SCOWLED at the bright cerulean sky, irritated that the world did not see fit to mirror her mourning with storm clouds and icy rain. There was something about a cheerful spring day that did not feel appropriate for a funeral. Especially not when it was her mother's. Her shoulders sagged at the reminder. Even as she brushed and braided her hair, readying herself for the day, she had not wanted to think about what awaited her outside her small cottage.

Moving to the large wooden armoire that held both hers and her mother's clothes, Helena wilted further. *How in the Great Mother's name were you supposed to select the outfit you wore to bury someone you loved?*

Ignoring the wet blur that rapidly filled her eyes, Helena randomly selected and pulled out a dress, deciding that choosing would be an impossible task. Whatever she chose would end up being remembered as what she wore to her mother's funeral. The only way to avoid it would be if she just attended the funeral naked.

The irreverent thought made her lips twitch. Her mother had always been pragmatic, and she probably wouldn't have bat an eye, noting that it was exactly what Helena had worn the first time they'd met anyway. Helena pushed the silly thought away. It was an amusing diversion, but certainly not the way she wanted to go say goodbye to her mother.

Glancing down at the soft purple fabric clenched in her hands, Helena went still. She'd grabbed her mother's dress; the one she saved for special occasions and holidays. Helena had always thought her mother looked as beautiful as a Kiri when she wore it, with her chocolate brown hair falling in contrasting waves against the vibrant fabric. She stroked trembling fingers along its length, smoothing out the wrinkles she'd caused.

Closing her eyes, Helena pulled the dress to her nose and inhaled deeply. The faint scent of roses still clung to the material. She stood breathing in the familiar and comforting scent of her mother's favorite perfume for a few silent seconds. With a pang, she forced herself to lower the dress. If she didn't hurry, she would miss the entire ceremony. Spurred into action, Helena let out a shuddering breath and quickly pulled the dress over her head, letting it fall loosely around her. When she opened her eyes, a soft gasp left her lips.

While she lacked some of her mother's more generous curves, and her hair was several shades lighter, wearing that dress it was as though her mother was standing before her. Helena traced her reflection on the cool glass, not noticing that her aqua eyes were red-rimmed and watery or that her eyelashes were dark spikes from a night spent crying. Her nose was bright red and her face puffy, but all of those details faded. As she gazed into the mirror, all she could see were her mother's eyes.

A sob bubbled up but Helena pushed it back. *How can she be gone, when she's staring back at me?* A sharp knock had her jumping and stepping back. With a final, lingering glance at the mirror, Helena left the small bedroom and went to open the door.

Looking grimmer than she had ever seen him, Anderson stood waiting for her. He had combed and parted his white hair, and made sure to wash and press his best clothes. His gnarled hands were spinning his faded work hat in a distracted manner while he waited for her to answer. At the sight of her in the doorway, his hands faltered, and his mouth fell open before a wide grin stretched across his face.

"Well, look at you. If you ain't the spitting image of your mother…" his words trailed off at her flinch. Understanding filled his green eyes and he pulled her into a bear hug. "No need to be sad, little bug. Your mama may have returned to the Great Mother, but just because she's not here with you and me, doesn't mean she's gone. She's just watching you from above now. Besides, Old Anderson here has it on good authority that your mama wouldn't want you to be sad.

Not when she is at peace without a single care in the world. Don't give her a reason to linger here, worrying about you."

Helena made a face at his words. They were soothing, but she was feeling selfish and in no mood to be understanding.

Anderson chuckled at her dubious expression. "It's just like when you were little, 'member? Your mama went away, but she ain't gone forever. You'll be with her again one day. In the meantime, Old Anderson will keep you company."

Tears filled her throat, but Helena fought them back. She squeezed Anderson as hard as she dared, trying to ignore how frail he felt in her embrace. Frail was not a word she wanted to associate with the man who always seemed larger than life.

His voice was gruff as he asked, "Would you do this old man the honor of accompanying him to say his goodbyes to the daughter of his heart?"

Warmth spread through her at his words. She had always thought of Anderson as her grandfather, and hearing that he had considered them part of his family as well made her feel less alone. Shared grief somehow seemed easier to face.

Her heart too full for words, Helena merely nodded and wove her arm through his. With a soft click, the door shut behind her and they made their slow way to the large oak tree that divided their two properties. It was, or had been, her mother's favorite place to come and relax after a particularly grueling day. Helena could think of no better place for her to be now. Anderson had hired some men from town to dig the grave and take care of the details. All that was left to do was say a proper goodbye.

As they cleared the last rise, tears began to fall from her eyes in earnest. It was not the sight of the tree, but the beautifully carved wooden bench that Anderson had crafted and placed there.

"Somewhere for you to sit when you come to visit her," he'd said gently, as he watched her reaction to his gift.

She squeezed his hand, trying to suffuse her thanks into the action.

He gestured toward the bench. "Go on now; go say your words. I'll give you two some time alone before I come and join you."

Nodding, Helena stepped away and swiftly crossed the distance. Once she reached the bench, she lovingly traced the words Anderson had carved into its sun-warmed wood: *So too, shall I love.* It was her mother's favorite expression. One she had uttered often when reminding Helena that the Mother loved all her Chosen equally, and it was up to them to do the same. It had become a personal motto that embodied the kind of life Miriam wanted to lead, and the kind of person she hoped her daughter would become: selfless, loving, compassionate.

It was too much. Helena broke down, sobs causing her shoulders to shake. Her knees gave out, and she collapsed on the bench, wrapping her arms around the back of it as though through it she could actually hug her mother. In reality, it was all that was keeping her upright.

After a few moments, Anderson was there, pulling her up and wiping the tears that were still streaming down her face. He didn't say anything, just settled himself down next to her and held her as she allowed her tears to wash away the pain of her loss.

Helena hiccupped as her tears finally subsided.

"Feeling better, little bug?"

She wiped at her nose, not surprised when Anderson held out a faded piece of cloth. "A little," she admitted, after she cleaned up her face.

"There's nothing harder than having to say goodbye to someone you love," he said somberly.

Helena stayed quiet, knowing that he was referring to his wife, whom Helena had never met.

"I wish I had the words to take away your pain, Helena, but there is nothing anyone can say to soften that blow. The body may be gone, but never the spirit. Never the memories. Hold those close when you miss her most and she will never truly leave you."

Helena swallowed and nodded, the use of her given name adding weight to his words.

"She was so proud of the woman you've become. That is how you honor her, bug. You hear me? You stay true to yourself and you will never let her down."

She nodded again, this time taking a shaky breath to try to combat the threat of fresh tears. "Yes," she rasped.

Anderson nodded, as if it was settled, and then pulled her back so that her head fell onto his shoulder.

"What about the ceremony?" she asked.

Anderson shrugged. "Fancy words aren't going to change anything. You just let your heart speak for you. That is more than good enough."

"Okay," she whispered, settling back into him. That, at least, Helena knew she could do.

As they quietly said goodbye to one who had been an essential part of their world for so long, they sat like two puzzle pieces learning how to fit together now that the piece that had held them together was lost.

As the memory faded, the soft light of dawn began to streak the sky with pale shades of pink. Thus began a day for goodbye but also remembrance. Helena had shed enough tears. It was time to remember what Anderson had taught her and celebrate his legacy; to honor his life with her memories and to be the woman he had helped raise. Perhaps she no longer had Anderson, but she would always have his words.

It would have to be enough.

CHAPTER 2

The men of Helena's Circle surrounded her. Darrin's fingers had gone white from tightly grasping her right hand, while Von was a steady presence at her left side. Kragen, Joquil and Timmins stood just behind them. The others had also come to pay their respects to the man their Kiri had loved. They may not have known him, but they still grieved his loss because of the effect it had on the woman they served.

Ronan's ice-blue gaze caught hers from across the courtyard as he looked up from the small garden. Helena had spent the early hours of the morning planting it in Anderson's honor. She'd done so using a combination of actual gardening and her power to help the cascade of flowers grow outside of their normal season. Ronan did not smile, but his gaze radiated warmth and support.

A bit away from him, Serena and Nial wore matching somber expressions, their fingers interlaced as they waited for Helena to speak. Miranda and Effie, along with Alina and the rest of the household staff, all filled in the space behind her friends. A few people from neighboring villages had also made the trip, traveling throughout the night to pay their respects to the new Kiri's loved one. Helena was not sure who had spread the word, but she could only assume Timmins played a part.

It was a large group, much larger than Anderson had probably ever expected, given that he had spent the whole of his life tucked away on his small piece of land. She hoped, despite so few of the people that came to pay their respects actually knowing the man, it was clear that he had been deeply loved.

The weather was mild, only a few fluffy clouds moving through the clear sky while a soft breeze made the leaves dance on their branches. It was a beautiful day, but this time Helena was not nearly as bothered by the realization. She wanted Anderson to have peace and gentleness now, when it was clear that his passing had been anything but.

"It's time, my love." Von's voice was gentle as it filled her mind.

Helena gave a barely discernable nod to indicate that she heard him. She knew that the others were waiting for her to say something. There were formal words that needed to be spoken. Words which were supposed to help speed Anderson's journey back to the Great Mother, but Helena was not going to say those words today. Instead, she would follow Anderson's advice and allow her heart to speak for her. It seemed important not to stand on formality; not for the man who had taught her how to see dragons in the clouds and find the best worms in the dirt.

"The Mother brings people into our lives for a number of reasons. Some are sent to challenge us, some to love and shape us. For me, Anderson was all of those things." Helena's voice was steady, although a bit thicker than usual. "Those of us that knew him would agree on that point. You could not help but be a better person for his guidance. He was patient and fair, and knew how to talk you into doing just about anything whether you originally intended to or not. I can't count the number of times he talked me into doing chores by simply making me believe we were playing a game."

She broke off as a few in the crowd chuckled appreciatively. Beside her, Darrin let out his own watery laugh, having experienced the exact same thing himself.

"But as with all of her Chosen, the Mother only lets us borrow them for a while before calling them back home to her. Anderson has been called home. In my heart I do not believe it was time for him to go. Then again, I don't think I could ever truly believe it was time, not today and not twenty years from now. None of us wish to say goodbye to someone who has been a fixture throughout our life."

Murmurs of agreement met her words. Helena let the silence grow, forcing herself to take a deep breath. As she fought to remain present and not get lost in her emotions, a bright flash of orange caught her eye. A giant butterfly, easily the size of her fist, fluttered delicately above the newly planted flowers, hovering for a second before coming to rest on a large purple bloom. *Anderson.*

Helena could not say what brought the thought, so certain and absolute, to her mind, but she knew it to be true. This was his way of showing her that he had not truly left her after all. The words he had spoken came to her again, *"just because she's not here with you and me doesn't mean that she's gone."* Neither was he.

Feeling stronger, she allowed herself a small smile as the butterfly flitted back up into the sky before becoming an orange speck that faded completely.

"No one is ever truly gone. Not so long as you remember the lessons they have taught you during your time together. I choose to focus on that, the time we had, instead of the time we have lost. Anger and hatred can make the world a cold and dark place. But even in the darkness, there is always the chance for light, for hope. We are that hope. It is our choices, the ones we are faced with every day, that will bring color into the world or leave it in darkness. I choose to bring light. I will not let Anderson's death be the foothold that allows darkness to overtake Tigaera." Her voice had changed during her speech, and the gentle wind picked up speed causing her hair to lift and flow around her shoulders. The murmurs grew louder as her power began to transform her.

"Rowena thought to cripple me with her blow, and that cannot go unanswered. She sought to weaken me, but she has only made me stronger. Rowena clings to darkness, using fear and isolation to take down her enemies. But there is something she has forgotten. I am not alone." Von's love swelled within her, and she thought she heard a firm *never* whisper through her, but she was still speaking and could not be sure. "Tigaera has many allies; allies we will call on now. More than that, nothing can remain hidden in the light. No matter where she goes, Rowena cannot escape the combined force of Elysia. She. Will. Not. Win."

Helena's words were a promise that reverberated throughout the crowd. There was a period of stunned silence as those gathered realized what she had said; what very few in the crowd had actually known. Rowena was alive and this man's death had been a declaration of war.

A few hesitant claps sounded before the entirety of the crowd erupted into cheers.

"For the light!"

"For our Kiri!"

"For Elysia!"

There was more to say, more to do, but for now Helena was done. With a formal nod, she spun from the crowd and began to take slow, measured steps back toward the Palace.

"I did not realize that his funeral would become a war rally," Darrin said mildly.

"Neither did I," she replied tartly.

"Do you think this is what he would have wanted? For his death to be used as a call to battle?"

Helena's brows lowered over sparkling eyes. "I think Anderson would have wanted us to remember who he raised us to be. I do not have the luxury of mourning by closing myself away from my responsibilities, Darrin. Anderson knew who I was, who I was destined to be. He would expect me to be nothing less."

Darrin's shoulders fell. "I know."

She placed her hand on his shoulder, forcing him to stop and meet her gaze. "I wish that I could undo this. That I had the power to call a spirit back to its body, or that I could have at least protected him from *her*," Helena all but snarled as she spat out the word.

"You could not have known where Rowena would strike," Darrin reminded her. She heard his forgiveness and knew that he did not blame her, but Helena was not ready to absolve herself. If she had not been the Vessel, the one prophesied to bring down the Corruptor, Rowena would never have had reason to kill Anderson. His death had been unnecessary, but she would not, could not, allow it to be meaningless.

Darrin saw her thoughts in her eyes and nodded his understanding. Changing the subject, he added, "Thank you for speaking today, for being strong when I could not. He was all the family I had left. Losing him…" Darrin trailed off, letting out a harsh breath.

She took his hand in hers, squeezing hard. "You still have family, Darrin."

He smiled appreciatively, although his eyes were still dull with grief.

"We will honor his memory the way he taught us," she said firmly, her eyes finding a small orange speck darting through the sky just above them.

Shaking off the weight of his pain, Darrin straightened and met her gaze head on. "Where do we start?"

Helena's smile was warm, and slightly fierce, as she replied, "We live."

"THAT WAS SOME SPEECH TODAY," Von murmured as he stroked Helena's hair. They were curled up in bed, her head resting on his shoulder as she stared into the dancing flames of their fire.

Her smile was wry as she replied, "It wasn't exactly what I had pictured, but I suppose that's what happens when you improvise."

His chuckle vibrated beneath her cheek. "Perhaps the words were not exactly what you intended, but that does not make them any less true."

Helena sighed. Word had already spread far and wide about her declaration that morning. Missives had begun pouring in from every corner of Elysia. Some offered support while others minced no words indicating their displeasure with their Kiri for throwing them headlong into a war they were sure they could not win. How anyone could get all of that out of a ten minute, impromptu speech was beyond her, but she would deal with it. The one thing that remained clear was that they needed to rally their allies, and fast.

Rowena would not wait long before striking again. She would continue to chip away at Helena, in increasingly inventive and twisted ways, until she finally provoked the Kiri into action. Helena wanted to be ready so that they could make their move on her own terms. Right now Rowena had the upper hand, she had already amassed an army, had been doing so for the better part of a year right under everyone's nose. Helena was starting from scratch. Sort of. At least she was Kiri. That had to count for something. Helena did not feel comforted by the reminder.

Sensing her wandering thoughts, Von brushed a finger beneath her chin and pulled her face up toward him. His gray eyes assessed her face, a small frown forming at what he saw. He pressed a kiss between her eyebrows, trying to smooth the crease that had taken up residence there.

"Timmins has already sent out the call. Tigaera's allies are on their way."

"It will not be enough to only call on those we know to be loyal. If we are going to defeat her, we will need to seek out those that have not yet chosen a side."

It was Von's turn to look worried. "You seek the aid of the tribes?"

Helena nodded.

Von straightened, his eyes widening with surprise as he asked, "How do you expect to find, let alone entice, them?"

"By any means necessary," she said grimly. "I cannot afford to let Rowena get to them first."

Von let out a low whistle.

Helena's concern colored her voice. "I know that I do not have much to show for myself, let alone enough to give them a reason to align their fate with mine—"

Von cut her off, "Helena, within your first handful of weeks as Kiri, you lifted the ban on Daejara that had been in place for thousands of years— something no one else bothered to even attempt. Then, with the assistance of less than a dozen people, you saved all of the Chosen."

She rolled her eyes. "I would hardly equate rescuing you to saving an entire race of people."

"Helena," he said firmly, his tone brooking no argument, "you know as well as I do what would have happened if the Fracturing occurred. It would have been the destruction of the Chosen. Rescuing me was your only option."

Her lips twisted in amusement, even as his words pushed back the wave of doubt that had been threatening to drown her. "You sure think highly of yourself, Mate."

It was his turn to grin. "Not of myself, of you. You have already faced insurmountable odds."

"Just barely…"

"You are capable of more than you know."

She sighed, struggling to sit up, but he held her tight.

"Helena, you are only just beginning to understand your power. Imagine what you can do now that we are together; now that our power is once again feeding off and strengthening the other's. Do not doubt yourself, my love. The fate of the Chosen may rest on your shoulders, but it is not a burden you bear alone. You have already proven yourself to be a formidable enemy. Rowena was not prepared for you. That is what causes her to lash out. She seeks to use your compassion against you, seeing your greatest strength as a weakness she can exploit. Your silence will only enrage and confuse her."

"She will not stop until she gets what she wants," Helena said quietly.

"I know."

"More will die."

Von tightened his arms around her. "I know."

Her voice was small as she whispered, "I do not think that I can say goodbye to anyone else that I love."

As much as he wished he could tell her she wouldn't have to, Von refused to lie. Instead, he pressed another kiss to her forehead and held on to her.

CHAPTER 3

"More than half of the Daejaran forces have refused to come."

Helena's head whipped to face Timmins so fast her hair lashed her face.

Before she could speak, Von snapped, "What?"

Timmins shrugged apologetically, holding a piece of parchment up for Von to see. "According to my letter from the newly appointed ambassador, there are those that feel—" he paused searching for a politically correct phrase.

Ronan interjected, sparing Timmins the indignity of failing to find a tactful response. "Tigaera ignored Daejara for centuries. There are many that cannot be bothered to care about the fate of the Chosen here, when none could find it within themselves to spare that same concern for them."

Helena frowned, but did not speak. When phrased that way, she could not fault their logic.

Von scowled darkly. "Ungrateful, small-minded—"

She placed a hand on his arm, cutting him off with a rueful shake of her head. "What of the others?" she asked Timmins.

He lowered the stack of papers clutched in his hand and met her gaze with a pained expression. "Many have replied, but they are not sending the forces we've requested. They wish to meet with you before committing."

"They do not believe me," she clarified, her voice hollow.

Timmins winced. "They find it hard to imagine the army you've described, having never experienced anything like Shadows themselves."

"The fools," Kragen snarled.

"They have forgotten what it means to serve," Von muttered.

"Can we blame them?" Joquil asked. They all turned toward him, varying degrees of surprise on their faces as he continued, "They are not the only ones who have forgotten. The Chosen have known nothing but peace, unless they are familiar with the stories of their ancestors. The kind of war you are describing… it is the stuff of legends, not reality. They do not understand that kind of power as they hold barely a sliver of it themselves." Joquil shrugged as he concluded, "You are asking them to imagine something they cannot begin to comprehend."

"So we show them; we make them believe," Darrin said, crossing his arms.

Joquil lifted a brow. "You think it will be that easy?"

Darrin gestured toward Helena. "You doubt her?"

"Never!" he snapped, offended by the implication.

Helena rolled her eyes at their childish bickering before asking, "Timmins, how many are coming?"

He cleared his throat. "Two representatives per realm."

Her jaw dropped. "Per realm? Out of all of the hundreds of territories and villages, only four are sending representatives?"

Timmins nodded, causing the rest of the men to begin shouting in outrage. Helena's eyes met Von's; it was as she had feared. They could not expect others to follow her blindly, not with the lives of so many at stake. She would have to convince them and find the tribes; those long forgotten or ignored by the Chosen.

Von dipped his head, indicating she should share her plan with the rest of the Circle.

"We will need Miranda," she stated.

Timmins' brows flew up in surprise. "What do we need the Keeper for?"

"If the Chosen have forgotten who they are, it is time they remember. Who better to help them than a Keeper?" she countered.

Timmins frowned but said nothing.

"We will hold a banquet in two days' time."

"Kiri, they will not be here by then," he protested.

Helena ignored him. "Miranda will be our esteemed guest, as well as our entertainment. After dinner we will call upon her to share tales of the Chosen's past. All will be invited, even though many will be unable to make the journey in time. We will need to *persuade*," she emphasized the word, "every bard we can to be in attendance so that they may pass her stories on to those that cannot make it."

"You think to sway them with stories?" Darrin asked, disbelief heavy in his voice.

Helena shook her head. "When the representatives of the realms are all present, I will meet with them and show them what we are up against. When they return home, they will be greeted by the Keeper's tales which will reinforce what they learned from me. I anticipate it will make a very convincing argument."

"Once they are swayed, others will fall in line," Ronan murmured.

"You will spread fear," Timmins cautioned.

"Not fear, truth," Helena corrected. "We cannot ignore this threat. Ignorance is not a luxury we can afford. To remain ignorant will see us all killed."

It was clear her Advisor did not like the plan, mainly because of its reliance upon a woman he could hardly tolerate.

Von squeezed her hand, urging her to continue.

"After they leave, the rest of us will need to be ready to travel."

Kragen groaned. "No more tents, Kiri. I beg of you."

She chuckled despite herself, "I am weary of the road as well, Sword. This time, we will employ faster methods." Her stomach rolled at the thought of the Kaelpas stone, but a little discomfort was well worth the time that could be saved with the purple stones.

"Do we even know how to recharge the stones?" Darrin asked, following her line of thought.

Joquil nodded. "I was able to find the spell in the archives."

"After looking it over, I think I might have found a shortcut," Helena added, referring to the amount of time required to charge the Kaelpas stones.

"Okay, so say we have an unlimited supply of stones. That doesn't help with traveling to places you've never been," Darrin reminded her.

Helena was sorely tempted to stick her tongue out at him but checked the impulse. "We will start by traveling to places that we *have* been, seeking out others that can get us close to where we need to be as we search for allies."

Her intention became clear, the men going still around her. Joquil looked stricken, his face bleaching of all color. Helena was about to ask him what was wrong when Ronan burst out, "You cannot be serious."

"Helena, no. We are not willingly seeking out the Triumvirate. Or calling on the lost tribes. That is a suicide mission. They are called the Forsaken for a reason. They have no allegiance to the Chosen!" Timmins sputtered.

She did not back down, shrugging as she said, "They are gifted, which means they have been blessed by the Mother; that makes them Her children. So what if their power is different than ours? We cannot be blind enough to believe that we win this fight on our own."

There was more that he wanted to say, but Timmins bit back the words.

Beside her Von remained quiet, letting the others come to realize the value of her plan. He understood their fear and had already had time to process his own. "It's a brilliant strategy," he said quietly. Despite its lack of volume, his voice carried.

"Rowena will not see it coming," Ronan said slowly.

"You are assuming that the Forsaken will agree," Timmins started.

Darrin picked up the argument, "They have no reason to side with us."

"They have just as much to lose if Rowena wins," Joquil pointed out.

Helena sat back, arms crossed while the men continued to debate. Around and around they went, until finally Von interjected, "No one has dared to approach them before."

"Because no one knows where to find them," Darrin snapped. "Or do you not know what the word lost means?"

Von glared at him but ignored the barb. "The Chosen have long been afraid of powers that we do not understand. Do you not think that the appearance of a Talyrian is a sign that it is time to get over that fear?"

The other men faltered, not understanding.

"The Talyrian pride is considered one of the lost tribes, according to the archives," Helena informed them, clasping her hands in front of her on the table.

"Been doing some light reading?" Ronan queried with an amused lift of his brow. Helena's lips raised in a small smile.

Joquil sat back, amber eyes glowing brightly as the meaning of her words took root in his mind.

Timmins mouth fell open. "You think the appearance of Starshine is a sign that the others might also be willing to come forth? And not just the Talyrians but the rest of the Forsaken?"

"The old man finally figured it out," Von snarked along the bond. *"You would think for one that spent his life face down in a book he would have arrived at the point more quickly."*

Helena snickered. *"It's not like you realized the Talyrians were one of the lost tribes either."*

She could feel his shrug as he said, *"But I am the Mate, not the Advisor. My qualification for the position is not reliant upon my ability to retain useless pieces of information found in old books."*

"I didn't realize that you had any qualifications..." Her teasing smile faltered as his silver eyes blazed.

"Oh, Helena. I think you'll find that I am more than qualified." The voice that whispered through her mind was all seductive purr and

it caused a bright blush to bloom on her cheeks. Von chuckled, his point made.

Ronan's eye caught Helena's and she blushed harder at her friend's knowing smile. *How had Von distracted her so easily?* With everything else going on, it was indeed a testament to his *qualifications* that he could pull her thoughts from the matter at hand. The rest of the Circle was looking at her, waiting for her to elaborate now that they were on the same page.

"If we cannot convince the Chosen to join us, we will need to recruit other allies. Where else should we look, if not the tribes? It only takes a few people to commit before others willingly join. What's the expression?" Helena paused, trying to recall it before snapping her fingers. "Wisdom of the crowd! And what better way to inspire confidence than with the aid of the Talyrians?"

A collective sigh went around the room. She had a point. None of them could deny the awe the first sight of Starshine had stirred.

"So first we try to convince the Chosen, then we seek to do the impossible and find the lost tribes," Timmins concluded warily.

"What else is new?" Ronan asked with a grin. "Pretty much everything we've accomplished up to this point should have been impossible."

"Exactly. It's just another Moonsday for us," Kragen quipped.

Helena laughed, relieved to see the others following suit. No one said her plan would be easy, but at least they had one. Helena's smile wobbled as a thought took root in her mind, *but so does Rowena.*

CHAPTER 4

*H*elena grew increasingly restless as the hours slowly passed. It was the morning of the banquet and guests had begun to pour into the Palace immediately following her announcement. All were eager to take part in the first formal event hosted by their Kiri since her trial many months ago.

Von didn't need their bond to determine that his Mate was on edge. "Helena," he called, trying to pull her attention back to him.

She blinked, turning away from their window and toward where he was standing just behind her. "Yes?"

He chuckled and shook his head. "This was your idea, *Mira*. Why are you so nervous?"

She wrinkled her nose. "Just because it was my idea, doesn't mean I'm not allowed to be terrified of the outcome."

Von threw her a skeptical glance. "You're eager to face Rowena one-on-one but afraid of your people's reaction to free food and entertainment?"

Helena threw her hands up in exasperation. "It's not the party I'm worried about! It's the backlash from the stories. It's the realms' response to learning about the depths of Rowena's corruption and what that means for the Chosen. It's the fact that everything hinges on garnering the help of people that were shunned by the Chosen for centuries."

He placed his finger to her lips to stop the torrent of words that were spilling forth with increasing frequency. "Shhh," he murmured.

She frowned, not appreciating being silenced. *That only works if I let it,"* she reminded him via the bond.

He smirked and responded in kind, *"It wasn't you I was silencing, darling. It was your unfounded fears."*

"Unfounded! Von—"

"Shhh," he said again, his gray eyes growing serious. "There is no reason for you to borrow trouble, Helena. Worry about the things you can control. Take them as they come. You have enough to deal with, without worrying about things that have not even gone wrong yet."

Helena pouted, she wasn't sure if she was more annoyed that he had shushed her, twice, or that he had a point. She let out a breath and her shoulders fell, a small bit of tension ebbing away.

"I'm just feeling a little stressed," she muttered.

Von's eyes strayed meaningfully toward their bed. He knew exactly what they could do to let off some steam. Seeing the distracted expression on Helena's face, any thought of getting her in bed fled. Well if that was off the table, there was one other surefire way to help her work it off. "You haven't trained with Ronan since we've returned. Let's go down and join the others for his workout."

She looked up at him appraisingly, her words measured as she said, "I suppose it would help kill some time."

He smiled indulgently, purposely taunting her. "You keep bragging about how you've bested all the men of the Circle, but there's still one you've yet to take down."

Her eyes glowed at his challenge. "Do you really want me to beat you in front of your men?"

"I would love to see you try," he laughed, clearly unconcerned.

Her grin turned feral. Without another word she turned toward the door, making her way to the training field, not needing to look to know that he was following close behind.

IF RONAN WAS SURPRISED to see his friends stalking toward him, he did not let on. He nodded by way of greeting, continuing his demonstration without missing a beat. The others were not so unaffected by the sight of the Kiri and her Mate.

Von and Helena moved to the back of the group; their long, easy strides in perfect time with the other's. It was a large, sprawling mix of people comprised predominately of the Rasmiri and Daejaran forces. Also in attendance were Kragen, Darrin, Serena, Nial and Effie. A couple of months ago, Helena would not have expected the small, flaxen-haired girl to pick up a weapon. After watching her more than hold her own against an unrelenting swarm of Shadows, Effie's desire to train only made sense. No one could afford to be caught unaware.

Ronan pulled one of the warriors forward. "Watch closely to see how versatile this block is," he called to the crowd, moving himself into a defensive stance. With laser-like focus, he indicated the warrior should attack.

The dark-skinned man launched himself at Ronan without question, using a series of moves that on anyone else would have rendered their opponent unconscious. But Ronan was not any opponent. Red hair glinting like fire in the sun, he lunged, neatly dodging the other man's flying fists to spin and land his own blow. Now behind his student, Ronan used his hands and knee to knock the man down before acting out a killing blow. Only mildly chagrinned, the man picked himself up off the ground and moved back into formation.

"What did you see?" Ronan asked.

"Demetrius attempted an obvious attack that you saw coming from miles away," someone shouted with derision.

There were a few chuckles but Ronan merely scowled until the murmuring faded back to silence.

"His body position telegraphed where he was moving first, which allowed you to counter the movement and side-step the attack," Nial answered smoothly.

"Exactly. Had I not known what to look for, a shift of weight in the feet, the slight lifting of his right arm, I would have missed it and my opponent would have been successful. However, since I knew exactly what to look for, I was able to use his momentum against him, using it to disable him quickly and efficiently. Now, break off into pairs and practice. Each blow landed by the attacker means two laps for the defender!"

There were a few groans, but the men and women were eager to get to practice. Soon the sounds of grunts and punches filled the air around them.

"Shall we?" Von whispered in her ear. Helena's grin was more than answer enough.

Stepping apart they moved into position facing each other, each pulling their hair up into tight knots.

"Pretty," Helena called, allowing herself a moment to appreciate the stark male beauty of her Mate. His obsidian hair, pulled back from his face only enhanced the brilliance of his gray eyes and the sharp angles of his cheeks and nose. There really wasn't anything 'pretty' about him. He was too much of a warrior to be anything but lethal, but when she looked at him, Helena only noticed the seductive curve of his lips and the ways his muscles bunched and shifted as he removed his shirt. She licked her lips, helpless to ignore her primal response to him.

Von winked at her, knowing by the tell-tale blush on her cheeks where her thoughts had wandered.

For those that had stopped to watch the Couple, there was no doubt this was more than mere sparring practice. It was understood that they would not use their power to enhance their combat. This was a full-fledged test of physical skill and strategy. Those in the Circle had already moved in, eager to see them in action.

"It looks like they want a show," Von teased, a small smile on his lips.

"Oh, they'll get one," Helena promised smugly, not hesitating before she attacked.

Von countered the move easily, laughing as he blocked two more rapid-fire blows. *"Is that all you've got?"* he taunted.

"Not even close," she assured him, ducking low and using her

momentum to knock him off-balance. He recovered quickly, which kept him from falling completely.

The crowd continued to grow around them, people beginning to cheer for their champion, but Von and Helena blocked out the distraction, focusing solely on each other. Their bodies became a blur as they moved, each attack and counterattack so perfectly in sync with the other, that their movements appeared choreographed. It was a dance, but a potentially dangerous one.

He had to give her credit. Helena was a masterful fighter, using her size and speed to easily duck and weave around him. His years of experience were all that kept her from easily defeating him.

Von wiped sweat from his brow. "Tired yet?"

"You wish!" Helena took two running steps toward him, launching herself in the air so that her legs wrapped around his neck. Helena rotated in the air, her legs' hold on him causing him to twist and flip with her in the air before pulling him to the ground. She landed on both feet. Von was not so lucky.

The crowd went crazy as Von landed hard on his back, the air flying out of him in a loud whoosh. He was momentarily stunned and not entirely sure how he ended up in the dirt. Helena was still standing, looking down at him with her hands resting on her hips.

"Don't look so proud of yourself," he grit out, reaching out a hand and grasping her around the ankle. One firm tug was all it took to pull her down beside him. She landed on her ass with an undignified grunt.

Von laughed, easing himself up into a sitting position. "Truce?" he asked.

Helena gave him a considering look, the competitive part of her wanting to continue until he admitted that she'd beat him. She took a deep breath. "I suppose it wouldn't look very good if we showed up to the banquet completely covered in bruises. It probably wouldn't hurt to stop while there are still places that have not yet started to swell."

His chuckle was cut off by a groan as he got to his feet. "Mother's tits!"

Helena laughed. He may never admit that she'd won, but the damage she'd caused was more than enough for her ego.

"I'm glad I'm not the only one that sees stars after a sparring match with our Kiri," Ronan boomed, slapping Von hard on the shoulder.

Von grunted, giving Ronan a baleful look. "No need to look so giddy."

Ronan shrugged. "Can't help it brother. The last couple of months I was the one ass to ground. It's a nice change to still be standing at the end of practice."

Helena giggled causing both men to scowl at her. "If I recall correctly, it was only the last couple of weeks of practice when I was able to knock you on your ass consistently."

"Now's not the time to be cute, *Mira*. My pride is wounded enough as it is. No one has defeated me in hand-to-hand combat in ages." Von groaned again as he discovered a new bruise.

"Perhaps you should start training with Serena and Nial," Ronan said. "It never hurts to cover the basics."

Helena laughed harder when Von lashed out, striking Ronan hard enough that he stumbled. "Well played," she said, giving Von a soft kiss on the cheek.

He brushed a stray piece of hair away from her forehead and pressed a quick kiss to her lips. *"It is worth every ache to see you smiling at me like that again."*

The look in his eyes seared through her, but they moved apart as the rest of the Circle joined them.

Nial stepped over to his brother. "I can't lie; it gives me great joy to see I'm not the only Holbrooke that can be bested by a woman."

Serena elbowed him sharply in the ribs. "Nial and I would be more than glad to put you through your paces," Serena teased, grinning at Von's dark look before adding to Helena in a softer voice, "nice job."

Helena returned the smile. "It was a close one."

"As it should be," Kragen said, holding up his fist for her to bump with her own.

Helena touched her fist to his and raised a brow asking, "How do you figure?"

Effie made a dismissive sound, answering for him, "The Mate is supposed to be a perfect match for the Vessel. It would hardly do for either of them to be weaker than the other."

"Well when you put it that way," Helena said.

The others chuckled, happy to have things feeling normal again.

"I guess that's all the time we have for practice today."

Following Ronan's gaze, Helena watched Timmins approach their group.

"Seems you are right," she said to Ronan with a sigh.

"Did you really want to continue rolling around in the dirt?" Darrin asked.

She gave him a cheeky smile, before looking at Von. "With the right incentive, rolling around in the dirt can be quite a bit of fun."

"Aye." Von grinned, his eyes going silver.

Darrin made a puking sound. "I'm sorry I even said anything."

The others laughed, Effie taking Darrin's hand in hers with a shy smile. His expression changed, softening as he looked down at her.

Timmins made a small sound, pulling their attention back to him. "The first of the delegates has arrived," he informed them.

That was all it took for Helena's smile to fall and the easy comradery of the morning to fade. It was time for her to be Kiri once more.

CHAPTER 5

$\mathcal{E}$verywhere she looked there was an exquisite exhibition of magic with each Branch represented in stunning detail. Massive hearths set in each of the walls were blazing with Fire of every color. The flickering flames were coordinated throughout the room to add to the overall atmosphere. Toward the front, where guests were greeting each other, the flames were the brightest. As you moved back into the room, the flames turned deep violet and flanked a dance floor that was currently empty.

Spheres of swirling lights were floating throughout the room, shifting colors to match the nearest hearth. Also drifting throughout the room were trays of various delicacies that never went empty. Soft strains of music pulsed throughout the hall, but the swell of voices nearly drowned it out as people laughed and chatted happily.

Those details alone were stunning, coming together to create an atmosphere of festivity that was absolutely unparalleled, but even they paled in comparison to the true centerpiece of the room.

The back wall was gone, replaced by a massive waterfall surrounded by lush plants and flowers. It stretched high above the natural ceiling, which had been made to appear like the night sky. At its base was a deep pool, illuminated by both the blue flames from the nearby hearths as well as submerged balls of light. A few guests splashed in the pool, surrounded by a transparent rainbow mist caused by the churning water. Simply put, the hall had been transformed into an oasis.

Helena let out a small gasp of pleasure, unable to remain unaffected by the beauty before her. It was lavish, a complete study in excess, but it was also a celebration of the power that flowed through each of the Chosen. For that reason, it was glorious.

Feeling the weight of thousands of eyes focused on her, Helena began to fidget, suddenly self-conscious. Before she could try to duck out of sight, the hall erupted into loud cheers of welcome.

Alina had been right, as usual. The hour spent dressing and primping had not only been worth it, but necessary. Tonight, Alina insisted that the Kiri needed to exude power. To that end, she had selected a dress of deep aubergine, the dark purple color a perfect contrast for her eyes. The bodice was snug from shoulders to hips before flaring out and falling in waves to the floor. It was the only color she wore.

Every other sparkling detail served to emphasize the purity of her power. The stitching was a metallic silver that glittered where it was caught by the light. Alina had curled her hair and then pinned it up using small stones that created a similar effect. Not to be outdone, her Kiri pendant seemed to radiate its own inner light, twinkling where it rested just above her breasts. To further enhance the effect and tie everything together, Alina had dusted her skin with a sparkling gold powder. From head to toe, Helena was aglow.

Still uncomfortable under the weight of such scrutiny, Helena forced herself to smile and prayed that it didn't look like a grimace. With another roar of approval, the Chosen began to celebrate in earnest. The party could officially begin now that their Kiri had arrived.

Von's quiet chuckle had her eyeing him. *"You look radiant, Mira. Nothing to worry about on that front."*

Helena smirked; apparently her prayer had been rerouted from the

Mother and sent through the bond. Either way, the reassurance was welcome. *"You look all right, too."*

His only response to her teasing words was a sardonic lift of his brow. Helena tried to bite back her grin but failed miserably.

Von looked absolutely sinful. He'd been dressed to matched, his formal pants and coat a fitted black material doing nothing to disguise the bulk of his muscles. His shirt was the same deep purple as her dress, with the top-most button undone in a classic act of defiance.

He'd also allowed Alina's brother Aemond, Von's personal valet, to talk him into a shave and haircut. The difference was astonishing. The thick black locks that had hung in loose waves past his shoulders had been chopped so that the ends now barely touched his neck. It was still long enough for pieces to fall down into his eyes, but Aemond had styled it in a way that kept it back. The sharp angles of his nose and jaw were more defined without the thick strands of hair obscuring them. His gray eyes appeared bigger and more luminous. Even his lips seemed fuller. He still had the savage aura of a man forged in battle, but where he had once been nothing but warrior, he was now clearly royalty. Helena had had trouble keeping her eyes, and hands, off him ever since.

"You're staring again, darling," he teased.

"It's not very polite of you to point it out. Not when you can feel my reaction to you and there's nothing I can do about it." Helena wasn't entirely sure she kept the pout out of her mental voice.

His eyes went molten. *"They've all seen you, there's no reason we can't escape to a dark room somewhere and help you get more... comfortable."*

Helena was sorely tempted. It felt like it had been ages since she'd lost herself in her Mate's body. He saw the answer in her eyes and some of the heat left his own. Using his phantom fingers, he brushed a finger along her cheek and over her lips. *"Later then."*

"Definitely," she agreed. Forcing herself to look away, she scanned the room again.

Seeing her friends laughing and having a good time helped her relax. Even after all they had been through, they did not get bogged down by what was ahead of them and still knew how to make the most of the small moments of pleasure they were granted.

Kragen and Ronan were talking animatedly beside one of the many bars, each man holding a sloshing mug of amber liquid. Not too far away, Serena and Nial sat, heads bowed toward one another as they shared a plate of food. Even from where she stood some distance away, Helena had no trouble noting the happy blush that stained her friend's cheeks as she laughingly accepted a piece of food that Nial held up to her lips.

Looking toward one of the many open doorways that led out to a balcony, Helena caught sight of Effie's blonde curls. She was looking longingly at the dance floor, while Darrin stared longingly down at her. A small smile played on Helena's lips as she watched the couple that still pretended nothing was between them. Seeing his chance, Darrin tenderly clasped her hand in his as he leaned down to press his lips against her fingers before gesturing toward the dance floor. With an excited squeal, Effie pulled him after her, their joint laughter lost in the dull roar of the crowd.

Still smiling, she let her eyes wander some more until they eventually landed on Miranda, who looked stunning in a dress of crimson. The Keeper's expression was solemn. Curious, Helena followed her gaze to where Miranda's granddaughter spun in Darrin's arms. Sensing her, Miranda caught her eye. The older woman smiled slightly, dipping her head in greeting, but her midnight eyes were unreadable. Before Helena could ponder further, Miranda turned and made her way deeper into the room.

Deciding to let it go for now, Helena's eyes finished their circuit of the hall. The only two of the Circle missing from the jubilant crowd were her Advisor and Master. They were in the Chambers awaiting the arrival of the last delegates. Timmins was going to summon her as soon as they arrived so that the real meeting could begin. But until then, there was no reason she and Von could not enjoy themselves as well.

"I like the way you think," he growled, close to her ear.

"You just enjoy any opportunity that allows you to rub up against me," Helena muttered dryly.

"You say that like it's a bad thing."

She grinned at him and pulled him toward the dance floor. The sea of bodies parted, granting them access to the now crowded space beside the waterfall. The music was fast and pulsing. All around them, partygoers turned into swirls of color as they danced in time to the music. Helena and Von joined in, bodies moving as one. Helena closed her eyes, focusing only on the music. There was no conscious thought, no intent, simply a fusion with the pulsating beat. The weight and sadness of the past few days began to fade with each twist of her body. It was a cleansing. The anger, frustration, and heartache were all washed away.

Opening her eyes, Helena faltered slightly as she met Von's burning gaze. He looked ravenous. She bit her bottom lip, feeling shy and overexposed. He reached for her, running his warm hands along the sides of her body until he grasped her hips and pulled her against him.

She could feel him, warm and solid against her, completely attuned to his desire raging through their bond. It felt like there were words he wanted to say bubbling up within him, but all he managed to get out was a single drawn out word before he slammed his lips down on hers in front of everyone.

"Mine."

Everything faded except for him. Weaving her fingers through his feather-soft hair, she tugged at the strands as she kissed him with all of the pent-up passion that had been pushed aside given the recent turn of events.

They were completely unaware of everything around them, until a sudden roar of water and thousands of small explosions caused them to step apart. Hearts pounding and eyes wide they glanced around. Small gasps of amazement met their ears as colorful bursts of light bloomed across the sky. Von snickered, already realizing what had happened. Helena blushed fiercely, and muttered a fervent curse as understanding dawned. Once again, her power had responded to the intensity of her emotions. At least this time her guests remained unscathed.

In response to the added intensity of the rushing water, the rainbow mist pressed in, growing thicker. Helena lifted bemused eyes back to Von, expecting to find his silvery gaze shining with amusement. Instead she was shocked to see Von looking stricken. His skin had gone pale and his eyes were wide with terror, the black of his pupils almost entirely swallowing up the gray.

Not wanting to draw attention, she shouted down the bond, *"Von!"*

He didn't respond.

Helena reached out a trembling hand, firmly grasping him about the arm and slightly digging her fingers in. *"Mate!"* she shouted again, using her power and his title to reinforce the call.

That grabbed his attention. Von blinked rapidly and took a deep gasping breath, as if he had been drowning and just finally caught a breath of air. Helena studied him with no small amount of concern. *"What just happened?"*

Von looked at her, embarrassment and shame causing his cheeks to pinken. He glanced at the people around them before interlacing his fingers with hers and pulling her to a more secluded spot against one of the walls.

"I got lost," he said, his voice sounding strained even along the bond. It cost him, deeply, to admit it.

"Lost?"

"In the mist."

And suddenly she understood. Months of hellish hallucinations still had their claws in him. Her hand tightened around his, squeezing hard to remind him that he was safe. *"What can I do?"*

He shook his head, smiling wryly. "Nothing, *Mira*. No need to worry."

She gave him a look; it was far too late for that. Anything that caused him to react that way pretty much ensured she was going to worry.

Von pressed a swift kiss to her lips, effectively ending the conversation. He didn't want to talk about it. Not here, not now, and possibly not ever. She let out a frustrated sigh, but before she could press the issue, a flash of color caught her attention. Turning slightly, she noticed Timmins standing in the main entryway staring at her. Following her gaze, Von noted the appearance of her Advisor. "Looks like it's time for the real party to start."

Helena frowned, brows furrowing as she replied, "You and I have very different definitions about what constitutes a party."

Von's deep laugh eased a little of the tightness in her chest.

"Let's get this over with," she huffed.

A LONE MAN pressed the heavy door open and moved into the darkness of the room. His footsteps were silent. After years spent staying out of view, he'd perfected the art of moving without making a sound.

He'd also learned to never assume silence was an indication of solitude. Out of habit, he glanced around to verify that he was, in fact, alone. Confident that he was, he made his way to the corner and pulled a sheet from the mirror it had concealed. Dust filled the air as the sheet fell to the floor. His eyes blurred and the need to sneeze was overwhelming, but he resisted any reaction. For his Queen, there was nothing he couldn't endure.

Remaining unseen by the Circle for years required a willingness to reside in darkness; to live and walk amongst those long forgotten by the glittering excess of the Palace dwellers. All in all, this room was a notable upgrade from his usual residence.

"You're late."

Eyes wide, he found himself staring into the cool blue gaze of his Queen. He dropped to his knees, bowing his head as he knelt before the swirling figure in the mirror. "Apologies, my Queen."

"I will not tolerate mistakes, not even from you."

He remained silent, knowing from experience that was the only correct response.

"Have they arrived?"

"Yes, my Queen. The impostor has already left the party to meet with them. The Keeper hid her exit by calling everyone to the stage to listen to her lies."

Even through the mirror, he could feel Rowena's icy rage. "Then it's time. You know what to do; the Circle must be broken."

"Yes, my Queen," he replied, risking a look upwards, but she was already gone.

CHAPTER 6

The air was thick with tension. Everywhere Helena looked someone was staring back at her, although their reasoning for doing so clearly varied. Some were wary, others curious, and some openly hostile. At least the expressions reflected in their eyes gave Helena some insight into how she should proceed. Thankfully some of the staring eyes were friendly.

She remembered a few faces from her naming ceremony, but most of the representatives were strangers. Also in the room were the rest of her Circle and Ronan. Helena hadn't been comfortable with the thought of leaving him out of the conversation when he'd become such an integral part of their team.

Each of the realms in attendance—Etillion, Endoshan, Sylverland and Caederan—had two delegates present. That meant that Helena and her Circle were outnumbered, but only just. There was very little she knew about their realms, other than a few salient facts Timmins had drilled into her mind over the last couple of days.

Etillion and Endoshan were northern lands that shared a border with Tigaera. There was no love lost between them, despite their shared ancestry. The realm had once been united, but sibling rivalry had caused it to split in half a few hundred years ago. Their delegates, pointedly ignoring each other, were distinguished by the burnished golden color of their eyes and lilting way they spoke.

The two with curious gazes wore robes of forest green. The silver tree embroidered on their chests made it obvious they were the Etillion representatives. The female was thin with an open face that seemed prone to smiles. She had short brown hair that swung just past her pointed chin. Beside her was her male counterpart. His brown hair was thick and curly, hanging in waves down his back. He was tall, but slender, appearing more scholar than warrior. Perhaps that would be a point in Helena's favor.

Helena was not surprised that the delegates from Endoshan were in sharp contrast to their neighbors. Instead of robes, they were swathed with silks of the deepest black. The thick bands that were wrapped around them served as sheathes and usually bristled with weaponry. There was no doubt these were warriors. Both of the men were bearded but had shaved heads. They were two that had no trouble hiding their annoyance at her summons.

Standing just behind them were the two men from Sylverland. Their home was located just to the south of Tigaera and was best known for its series of lakes. The water was so pristine, it was commonly believed to be infused with liquid silver, creating its notable hue and thus its name. Its inhabitants, the Sylvanese, were distinguished by their pale blonde hair and silver eyes. The two before her were adorned in various shades of blue, their attire comprised of thick, expensive fabrics. These were men of means who were more familiar with a life of luxury than war. Something about the way the two men stood beside each other alluded to a familiarity that surpassed mere friendship. Helena couldn't put her finger on what exactly it was, but she couldn't help but be reminded of the way Nial and Serena positioned themselves when the other was near.

Last were the pair from Caederan, a realm that was situated between Daejara, which was to its south, and Talyria, which was to the north. Not knowing much about them, Helena found herself sharing the same wary expression they wore. The female looked familiar, with black curls framing a round face with interesting reddish-brown eyes. She was short, shorter than any other person in the room, and plump. The combination served to make her appear all the more curvaceously feminine. Standing next to her was a man of similar build. Rather than appearing feminine he exuded brute strength. The width of his chest and arms, and the scars that covered him, were warnings to tread carefully in his presence. His beard was long and braided, small bells woven into the thick strands. They both wore colors of the sunset, deep oranges and reds that complimented their dark hair and complexions.

Helena forced herself to meet each of their gazes. Despite the nerves that had her stomach twisting inside of her, she exuded confidence and control. She was their Kiri, chosen by the Mother as her Vessel; she would not back down.

"Greetings brothers and sisters," she said formally.

Kragen and Ronan's faces darkened like twin storm clouds when no one returned her greeting. She caught their eyes and allowed herself a small smile. Their stances relaxed, but Kragen crossed his arms, ensuring that everyone got an eyeful of his impressive strength. As far as warnings went, it was subtle, but effective.

"Mother's blessings, Kiri," the woman from Caederan said in a sweet, high-pitched voice.

"To you as well," Helena replied, letting some warmth infuse her voice. "Thank you all for traveling here under such short notice. I—"

"Why *have* you called us here?" one of the men from Endoshan demanded. His lips were pulled down in a severe frown and his golden eyes flashed with something that felt like disdain.

Helena could feel Von bristle behind her, not appreciating the way the delegate dared to address her. *"Relax."* She sent the thought along the bond while lifting an amused brow at the man who'd spoken. "If you'd let me finish, I was just getting to that part."

The delegates from Etillion snickered, enjoying the fact that they'd just witnessed a rival being summarily dismissed. The man scowled and gestured with his hand that she should continue.

"Oh thank you, if you insist," Helena said with mock graciousness, unable to keep the comment contained. She was fairly certain her Circle could feel her mental eye roll. *Who does this guy think he is?* Apparently, the thought had been transmitted, because Von answered.

"I believe he is the Endoshan heir."

"More like a royal jackass."

Von's laugh rumbled through the room, startling the delegates and causing them to look around uneasily. The Endoshan heir's frown deepened. He did not appreciate being the butt of some unknown joke.

"The Corruptor has risen," she said finally, using the title from the prophecy to ensure they knew of whom, and what, she spoke. The comment was the equivalent of lighting a match before tossing it into a barrel of oil. There was a shocked hiss, the sounds of gasps echoing throughout the room, before eight different voices rose into a roaring cacophony.

"That is impossible!" the heir countered.

"You would believe that," the female Etillion snapped, her eyes wide and frightened as her skin was leeched of all its color. Her companion placed a comforting hand on her shoulder, and the two shared a long silent look before turning back toward Helena.

"How do you know this?" the taller of the Sylvanese men asked, his voice deep and melodious.

"She captured my Mate."

Eight pairs of eyes turned to Von, using his presence to silently contradict her statement.

"I got him back," Helena stated dryly. "In the process, I was introduced to her army…" she paused, ensuring she had their complete attention before adding, "of Shadows."

The room erupted once more. The Caederan woman shrieked and the man she was with reached for a weapon that was not there. The Endoshans and Sylvanese had similarly violent reactions. Only the Etillions remained calm, their golden eyes serious as they processed her words.

"So the prophecy is true. The Corruptor seeks to eradicate the Chosen."

The words were spoken so softly it took Helena a moment to realize who had uttered them. She finally nodded to the man from Etillion. "Yes."

"That would make you the Vessel?"

Helena nodded again.

"That. Is. Impossible!" the Endoshan heir seethed.

She studied him, her head tilting as she did. "Why are you so determined to believe that? Will it keep you or your people safe if you deny it?"

His partner stopped him with a hand on his arm before he could respond further. While his mouth remained closed, it did nothing to stop the rapid rise and fall of his chest or the fiery anger that burned in his eyes.

Knowing that the only way to maintain control of the room was by remaining calm, Helena met and held the gazes of each delegate before speaking further. Once all murmurings had ceased she said matter-of-factly, "Rowena is real, whether you want to believe it or not. The threat she poses cannot be ignored. It is not merely my court she stands against; it is the entirety of the Chosen. Nothing is sacred to her. She did not hesitate to damn her own child by turning her into an abomination. The other she murdered in cold blood."

Their shock was palpable.

"Ro-Rowena? B-but she is dead..." the Caederan female stuttered, her hand clenching the arm of the man standing next to her.

"She faked her own death," Timmins said gently, not wanting to upset the woman further.

Her eyes moved from him back to Helena. "You are sure?"

"Unequivocally."

The woman's eyes shuttered. "Then we are doomed."

Von snarled behind Helena. "Will you give up before you fight? Do you think so little of the one blessed by the Mother or are your people simply not worth fighting for?"

"Shut your traitorous mouth, Daejaran," the Endoshan heir hissed. Fury and power rose within Helena. How dare he speak to her Mate that way. There was a surge of wind that caused the shutters to fly open. Nearest to the window, the Caederan woman squeaked and jumped away.

This time it was Von that reached through the bond. *"Let it go, Mira. You cannot combat centuries of prejudice in a single night."* There was a tenderness in his voice that conveyed how much it meant to him that she wanted to try.

"The man is rude and ignorant. I am growing increasingly alarmed by the thought of him overseeing or leading any realm."

"As am I," Von murmured.

"Please, Tinka meant no offense," the Caederan man said, mistakenly believing the surge of power was in response to his companion. He held out a hand as if that would prevent further insult, "but we know nothing of the Vessel's power. What you are asking—"

"I did not realize a Kiri had to prove herself. Did I not pass the Mother's trial already?"

The question was met with uncomfortable silence, many of the delegates dropping their eyes or glancing around at the others uneasily.

"I'm not here to perform parlor tricks for you," Helena snapped, her eyes flashing iridescent. Ronan let his eyes slowly travel from Helena to where the window now gaped open; she bit back a smile as he winked.

"We are not asking for them," the Sylvanese man interjected, "but do you not think we deserve to know more about the woman who is asking us to put our lives, and the lives of those we love, on the line?"

"That is the case whether you choose to believe me or not. Your realms have been allied with Tigaera for centuries. We've been blessed that they have been years filled with peace and prosperity. But now we are on the cusp of war and you want to abandon us to face our greatest threat alone?" Helena's words were harsh, but she refused to hold back. She had already lost people she loved, would likely lose others, she didn't have time to dance around egos or fear.

The words struck home. Helena could tell by the way their shoulders slumped and they looked to their partners. She was almost afraid to hope, was actually holding her breath, when the first of them spoke again.

"Etillion will stand with Tigaera," the pair said in unison. "We do not require proof. Your words and request alone are more than enough. We are allies as you say. It is our duty to stand for the Chosen and to protect our people."

Helena forced herself to release her breath slowly. "Thank you."

The others were not so quick to make promises of support. The silence swelled until finally, the Caederans, still looking peaky, stepped forward. "If things are as you say, then there is no choice. Caederan will stand with Tigaera."

"This is not a decision we can make for Sylverland. We will take your words back to our people and discuss the best course of action."

Helena wanted to shout at their short sightedness, but she forced herself to keep from reacting. The Circle was feeling less diplomatic. All around the room, anger and disapproving stares were leveled on the two men in blue.

"I'm glad I've never given the lot of you cause to look at me like that," Helena said to Von.

"To be fair, there have been moments of extreme exasperation, but you have more sense than to do or say anything stupid enough to make us."

His response made her smile slightly, even as she turned to the men from Endoshan and saw their answer reflected in their eyes.

"They still do not believe me," she said a bit dejectedly.

"They are too arrogant by half."

The heir opened his mouth, likely to formalize his refusal, but no words escaped. Instead, a large, thundering boom shook the room. Dust and debris fell to the floor as the room continued to shake.

"Mother's tits!" Kragen swore as a piece of wall fell and smacked his head.

Just as quickly as it started the room stilled. Looking around, Helena asked, "Is everyone all right?" There were soft murmurs of assent.

The overwhelming scent of smoke began to permeate the room through the open window. Taking a step toward it to see what was happening, Helena went cold as the first of the terrified screams reached her ears.

They were under attack.

CHAPTER 7

Helena flew through the halls, the sound of her thundering footsteps echoing loudly. Kragen and Ronan were barking orders at the Rasmiri guards. Darrin and Von were close by, neither man wanting her to barge into a situation they knew precious little about. Timmins and Joquil had helped arm the delegates so that no one was unprepared for whatever they were about to face. Helena had the feeling it wasn't going to be that simple. Knowing Rowena, nothing would prepare them for whatever trap she had set.

"How did they get in?" Helena snapped, the voice of her power amplifying the fury she was feeling.

"It's too soon to say, Kiri," Timmins responded.

"I want you to find out who is responsible for this, and I want you to bring them to me. Alive," she ordered. Timmins nodded.

"The rest of you, with me," she shouted as they rounded the last corner before stepping into a world of chaos.

It was impossible to forget the horror of the Shadows, but seeing them here, in her home, was devastating. They swarmed like ants, their gray skeletal bodies relentlessly pursuing the guests that had only moments before been laughing and dancing. There were already hundreds of corpses littering the floor as a small contingent of Shadows cut a path through the partygoers.

There was little time to process what was happening. Helena could only just make out Miranda helping frantic guests escape the slaughter. Serena and Effie were already covered in blood, both fighting as best they could in their formal clothes to provide cover and distraction for Miranda. Nial and the few Rasmiri already present were holding their own but could not seem to bring down the Shadows. No one had been prepared. Not for a fight in the heart of the Palace, and certainly not for facing off against the Shadows.

Gasps of shock sounded behind her as the delegates came face to face with the nightmare few believed to be real. She heard a few uttered prayers to the Mother before one of the Sylvanese asked, "What do we do?"

"Help get the others out of here," Helena ordered, seeing from the horrified faces of the Etillions and Caederans that they would not be much help on the battlefield. With quick nods they moved away, helping pull people off the ground and supporting them as they limped, or dragging them when they couldn't manage that, into the hallway they had just left.

"But how do we stop them?" the Sylvanese man asked. His pointed demand for clarification was laced with steel; he had no intention of sitting out this fight.

"Magically, they are immune to everything but Fire. Barring that, nothing short of removing the heads will keep them down," Von informed him.

There were a few answering war cries as blurred figures rushed into the mass of bodies. Helena was startled; it was a blur of black and blue. The Endoshans had decided to fight after all.

Around her, the Circle was braced for battle. Grim faces and weapons emanating with power were only waiting for her final command before adding themselves to the fray. Helena was at a loss; no one saw this coming. They should have; *she* should have, but she had mistakenly believed they would be safe.

Sensing her struggle, Von spoke for her, easily stepping into the role of Commander, "Draw them away from the guests. Work together, no one should be facing one of these dickless corpses on their own."

"Should be easy enough to do. I only count ten," Darrin called, surprise coloring his voice.

"Pity, that doesn't leave any for you to kill," Kragen grinned as he lunged into the fray, his weapon flying as he began to swing for their necks. Darrin was right behind him, not about to be left behind.

Only ten had done this? Helena felt sick. Rowena was toying with her, showing her how easily she could sneak in and wreak havoc; how little effort it took to destroy her people. Helena called on her power, feeling it rise to the surface, eager to eliminate those that dared to invade her home. Just as she was about to lash out, she hesitated, not wanting any of her Fire to harm one of the innocents still making their way out of the room. There were simply too many moving bodies between her and the Shadows.

"There, to the left," Von shouted, pointing to a figure standing slightly apart from the others.

Helena's stomach knotted with revulsion as she saw the figure Von had indicated. It was a Shadow, marked with the same snaking black lines writhing in its eyes and rotting gray flesh as the others. But while they could do little more than mindlessly attack, this one still retained the ability to call on its power. Helena flashed back to Vyruul, riding on Starshine and seeing Rowena standing on a balcony flanked by six figures. This creature was one of her generals.

As if he could feel her eyes on him, he twisted in a slow, serpentine fashion. He tilted his head as he observed her before letting his mouth fall open in the sinister imitation of a grin. "Kiri," he rasped.

Helena was stunned to hear him speak, although given his use of power it probably shouldn't have been so unexpected. Before she could recover, he launched a liquid green orb in her direction.

Snapping to attention, she reinforced her personal shield as she dodged it and let her own ball of Fire fly. Where the general's orb made contact, the floor began to smoke and dissolve. *Acid*, she realized with growing horror. Just as Rowena had twisted her magic, so too had her general. Instead of the pure form of Water, this monster was able to conjure acid. No wonder Rowena only felt the need to send ten Shadows; the sheer amount of destruction he could cause with just a single ball of his acid made him a one-man killing machine.

Letting the others deal with the handful of Shadows that were still standing, Helena focused solely on him. Around her wind began to whip past, thunder growling in the sky as a storm of power began to rage. The sounds of battle were quickly drowned out by the roar of thunder. The Chosen began to scream in earnest, not realizing it was Helena who was feeding the storm. Bodies pressed against one another, frantic to escape the fury they felt building in the room.

The general continued to smile as he lazily lobbed ball after ball of acid at Helena. He was not threatened by her display of power. Maybe he needed a little more convincing. Fire had been Helena's go-to since she'd inherited her power, its scorching heat and ability to destroy a perfect complement to the extreme emotions that usually fed into it. But with the amount of people in the room, she didn't feel confident she'd be able to control it completely, even with Von's return.

Helena felt a feral smile of her own begin to grow. She couldn't burn, but she could bury. Channeling the energy of the storm, Helena funneled its power through her body to blast the raised dais on which Rowena's general was standing. There was a loud crack as the wood splintered and rocked before it came crashing down. The general snarled in outrage as he lost his balance, collapsing with the wood. Helena wasn't finished; she needed to keep him out of the fight long enough to give her Circle an advantage.

The power of the lightning continued to crackle along her skin and pulse in her blood. She released it into the ground again, feeling the earth shake from the force. Try as he might, the general could not stand back up. He was too off-balance from the quaking beneath his feet.

The earthquake was the distraction her people needed. They were down to just a few remaining Shadows. Darrin slammed his shield into a Shadow, stunning it long enough that Kragen's sword was able to swing true. Ronan and Serena had another cornered. It was still coming after them even though one of its arms and most of its left leg had been removed. In a move only possible due to the years of experience between them, Serena swung her blade up while Ronan swung his ax around. The Shadow did not know which blow to dodge. Serena's blade, reinforced with her power, rent the Shadow in half, while Ronan's ax made easy work of his head. It crashed to the ground with a sickening thud and dark spurts of blood.

Since the general was still struggling to get free of the rubble, Helena released her hold on the lightning, allowing the room to settle. Von was beside her, swinging a flaming sword to dispatch the only one still standing. The air sizzled where the flames made contact with its rotting skin. With a final, gurgling cry, the last of the Shadows fell.

The general broke free from the wood, bellowing as he watched his final man fall. He glanced around as the Circle and their allies closed in. Ronan was spinning his ax in his hand, while Von and Helena held swirling orbs of power in their palms. The Sylvanese were bouncing on their feet and the two Endoshans wiping foul black ichor from their curved blades. Every one of them staring intently at the vile creature.

He tried to find an escape route but there was none; members of her Circle had every possible exit blocked. Finally, he let out a laugh that sounded like the crackle of leaves. Raising both emaciated arms into the air, he threw back his head and let his tainted power arc out of him. Ronan charged, looking to tackle the general, but the horrified gasps of the others had him spinning around.

Where the massive waterfall had once burbled there was now a rush of acid-green water burning a path through everything it touched. Helena's mouth fell open. There was no time to think, she had to act. Diving deep into the pool of her power she cast a shield that surrounded her people just before the acid could make contact. It hit the invisible barrier and Helena screamed. She could feel the searing burn of acid as if it was touching her skin.

Von growled in rage, feeling Helena's pain as if it was his own. The rest of her Circle roared, desperate to protect and defend their Kiri. There was nothing they could do against such power and they lacked the time necessary to coordinate the complex blend of power required to diffuse the acidfall.

Acting on instinct, Helena connected to the heart of her power. Her hair flew up around her, and her pupils contracted, disappearing completely beneath the iridescence of her eyes. The men that comprised her Circle transformed, turning into pulsing pillars of light. Von shone the brightest, the depth of their bond strengthening any power he held on his own.

She plucked at each glimmering strand of their power, now illuminated by her un-dampened state, and wove them with her own substantial thread. With her power now liberally reinforced by her Circle, Helena called on Earth. There was a thunderous groan and then the world shook violently as a massive sinkhole began to grow where the waterfall had once stood. The roiling mass of acid began to slide into the gaping hole.

Pushing more of her power into the earth, thick brown mud bubbled up, entirely replacing the dance floor. The mud, heavy with liquid, began to pour into the sinkhole, covering and eventually containing, the acid.

The startled shouts of the delegates pulled Helena back. Banking some of her power and releasing her hold on the others who had started to look a bit pale, Helena turned once more to the general.

He was gone.

CHAPTER 8

Helena screamed in outrage. It was a feral, inarticulate sound that had the others wincing and covering their ears. There was an answering roar in the distance as Starshine and the Daejaran pack added their voices to the chorus. Seething, she spun, needing something, anything, to unleash on.

"Mira," Von called, feeling the desperation building within her.

It was too late; she was too far gone for reason. She was balanced on a knife's edge, the sheer intensity of her power combined with all of the emotional extremes of the last few days pulling her toward violence. She hadn't been this out of control since under the effects of the Fracturing. That it was happening now, within the presence of her Mate, was terrifying.

"We have to stop her before she brings the rest of the place down and kills us all!" Darrin shouted.

"Is that your way of helping?" Ronan snapped.

"This cannot be the Mother's blessing. This is her curse!" Tinka wailed. The Caederan woman looked a child standing next to the warrior. Her entire body was trembling as her companion wrapped his arm around her and murmured softly.

Serena, disheveled and covered in sticky black ichor, gave the woman a disgusted glance. "Get them out of here!" she ordered. It was unclear who she was speaking to, but Effie, the most used to taking orders among them, reacted first.

"Here now," she said, her sweet voice entirely unexpected after the horrors of the past few minutes.

Tinka flinched when Effie held a hand out to her, and Darrin's green eyes went flinty.

"You either go with her, or you can go with me," he snapped.

"Let's go, Tink," the Caederan man said in his deep voice, eyeing Darrin warily.

"But Khouman—" she whispered, fear still thick in her high-pitched voice.

"None of that, Tinka. This is our Kiri. You cannot doubt the Mother's choice when she just saved all of us."

With a slow nod and an apologetic glance, the Caederans carefully made their way out of the still smoking ruins of the room.

"That goes for all of you!" Darrin boomed when the other six stayed behind. There were a few uttered curses and protests as the rest of the delegates fell into line behind Effie. Darrin stepped back.

"There, that was much more helpful," Ronan murmured.

"Is everything a joke to you?" he asked, irritation giving his voice an edge.

"Puppy, the day I stop taking the piss out of you is the day I die. Life's too short to be a miserable bastard."

"What's that supposed to mean?" he bristled, chest expanding as he took a step toward Ronan.

Kragen moved quickly, grabbing Darrin by the back of his shirt. "There now, let's not go and do something stupid while we're still in the middle of dealing with our first crisis."

"You may want to consider calming the fuck down. We already have one out of control person on our hands. Let's not add you to the list." Ronan sounded downright reasonable as he spoke. If it wasn't for the way his worried eyes kept moving to stare at Helena, he would have seemed almost chipper.

Darrin struggled to break free of Kragen's grip, his cheeks and ears turning bright red with his embarrassment.

"Do you promise to behave?" Kragen asked.

"Yes," Darrin bit out.

Kragen released him and Darrin stumbled forward. Straightening, he looked to Von, "Help her, damn it. You're her Mate, use that bond of yours and fucking do something."

Von lifted a dark brow, having mostly ignored the other men until now. "What exactly did you think I was over here trying to do? Egg her on?"

Joquil stepped forward, "She needs a way to safely release the power. She pulled too much and has started to lose control of it."

Looking around Von tried to find something that she wouldn't utterly destroy. As it was the room was almost completely done for, but the structure was still sound. If it collapsed it wouldn't just be the people inside the room that were lost. Short of getting her out of the Palace entirely, Von was at a loss.

Darrin's words came back to him. *Use that bond of yours.*

An idea sparked. Von turned back toward the fuming woman who held his blackened heart in the palm of her currently clawed hand. If ever there was a reason to risk annihilation… The thought drew out, loosely forming into a plan. The land could not handle the brunt of her power, but he could.

Years of battle allowed him to remain calm, despite his growing concern. Placing a hand on either side of her face, Von called her again, infusing his voice with every ounce of love and wonder he'd experienced since he first met her. *"Helena."* Her name was a prayer, reverently uttered and full of unspoken hope.

Power exploded through him as her shimmering eyes focused on his, unable to ignore his plea. Von's back arched from the force of it, everything she had been holding onto slamming into him. Her power was an inferno, burning him from the inside out. Gritting his teeth, he pressed his forehead to hers. He began to pant, his eyes turning molten silver as their joint power filled him.

"Vessel," he rumbled down their bond, his voice echoing with the harmonious voice-of-many generally associated with Helena's power.

Helena blinked. *"Mate?"* The word was a question, as if she was not entirely sure who was speaking.

Her power was intoxicating. Von had never felt anything like its seductive pull and could easily understand how it could take over completely. As it continued to flow into him, Helena's eyes began to return to normal, although flickers of iridescence remained.

Unable to contain all of this power on his own, Von's hands began to tremble. *"I need you to take it back now, Mira. Not all at once; just a little at a time."*

Her eyes widened as she realized what was happening. Refocusing, she placed a hand over his racing heart. Helena closed her eyes, drawing the power back into herself and through her, back into the room. Von braced himself, half-expecting what was left of the room to come crashing down around them. But instead of destruction, Helena chose transformation.

He could still feel her need for violence, her power throbbed with it, but it was not all-consuming. Her priorities had shifted, righting themselves as the part of her that was compassion and light came back into control. At least for now.

THE ROOM WAS SUFFOCATING. Helena felt as if each one of the souls of the fallen was trapped and screaming at her to release them. Peace; they all needed peace. It was too soon to feel this much grief and loss again. *When will I get a break from burying people that I love?*

Von's heart continued its steady, if rapid, beat against the palm of her hand. It grounded her, giving her something tangible to focus on. He was holding onto her excess power, but he would not be able to contain it for much longer. She needed to release it as quickly as possible.

There were too many bodies for her to individually carry them, as she had done for the villages they'd come across during their trek to Daejara. Not to mention the fact that simply sifting the earth to make graves was far too delicate a task when she had so much power requiring immediate release. That didn't mean she wouldn't honor them.

Helena refused to allow this room to be a haunted, feared place. She would not allow it to be a blight for her or her people. The Palace had been erected as a testament to the power and glory of the Chosen. It would continue to serve that purpose, albeit in a new way. With that determination in mind, Helena's power flowed into the room.

The others looked on in rapt fascination as all around them objects began to lift up off the ground before flying through the air. It was happening faster than any of them could track. The room that had started off the evening as a lush, glittering oasis and then quickly descended into chaos and carnage, was amidst yet another transformation. The mounds of smoking dirt and piles of bodies disappeared. In their place, trees and flowers bloomed. Helena was creating a forest right in the heart of the Palace.

Let their blood bring new life. One for every one lost, Helena thought, not feeling the tears as they fell from her eyes. She had probably only met a small handful of the dead, but that was not the point. None would be forgotten. Even though she could not tell you each of their names, the trees could. If one was to place their hand upon the bark of the tree, they would hear the name of the one they represented whispered amongst its leaves.

By the time she was done they were surrounded with life. The trees ranged in size and age, each reflective of the one whose name they now carried. A gentle breeze tickled the leaves, making them dance on their branches. Helena tipped her face up, enjoying the sparkling night sky, even though they were on the bottom floor of the Palace. At least there could be beauty in magic, as well as destruction.

"It is a beautiful memorial, Kiri," Timmins said in a hushed tone.

Overwhelmed by the events of the day, Helena could only nod. She let her eyes wander around the forest. While she was pleased with the result, it didn't lessen the pain of losing so many of those she was supposed to protect.

Guilt ate at her. She had known, on some level, this would happen. There had been a moment in Vyruul when Rowena had taunted her from the balcony. She'd had a choice, go for Rowena or get her Circle out. She'd chosen to save the people she knew, the ones that had grown to mean more to her than all others. In doing so, she'd put every single one of the remaining Chosen at risk. These deaths were on her.

The Keepers had warned her about this. Their words haunting her as she stood in this place made from the bodies of the dead:

'The path you choose will decide our fate.'

'The fate of all the Chosen.'

A shudder racked her body. One thing was becoming increasingly clear. There might be peace for the dead, but until Rowena was stopped, Helena would have none.

CHAPTER 9

It was either very late or very early. Either way, Helena couldn't sleep. Every time her eyes fell closed, the piles of bodies were there to greet her. The weight of all that death, and knowing that she was the reason for it… that she was asking people to willingly place themselves in situations that guaranteed even more of it, was too much for her to handle.

"Helena, you are not the only ruler to ever be faced with this," Von murmured, using his thumb to gently free the lip she had been unconsciously biting. She looked up and the devastation in her eyes nearly undid him. She was in pain; he could feel it resonating through him. It was the kind of pain that gnawed at your soul until it incapacitated you completely.

"Darling, you have to be kinder to yourself," he said, moving to pull her into his arms.

"It's my fault."

"No more than it is mine."

"They are my people, my responsibility—"

"Is it my fault every time one of my men dies in battle?" Von cut in.

"Well, no, but—"

"Do you blame or look at me differently because I have had to kill men in battle?"

"Of course not!" she protested, twisting to stare at him.

"Then why are you doing it to yourself?"

The question threw her. Her brows furrowed as she tried to find an answer.

Von gently stroked her face, running his calloused fingers lovingly over her skin. "You cannot keep holding yourself to a higher standard. It will cripple you. As a leader you need to make decisions. Those decisions will protect some, and they will lead to the deaths of others. Your people follow you by choice. They know what awaits them on the battlefield, and *they fight anyway*. Do not be so arrogant as to think you can control every outcome. Not only do you rob your people of their heroics, but you place such a burden on yourself. You need to be able to be decisive and defend your decision no matter the outcome. If it does not go the way you intended, you learn from it, and from your enemies, and then you *move on*. You have to, because there will always be another battle or decision waiting for you."

Helena sat a bit dumbfounded, his words a balm for the raw edges of her soul. Von was not one for long speeches or declarations, but her warrior had known with only a look exactly what kinds of thoughts were tormenting her and he'd just slain them all.

"I love you," she said simply, wrapping her arms around him and snuggling close.

"And I you," he whispered against the top of her head. "You should try to rest now. There will not be much opportunity for it in the days to come."

"I don't think I'll ever sleep again," she sighed.

"Yes, you will. And you will laugh, and make love," he punctuated that with a squeeze that made her squirm, "and you will be happy again. I promise you, *Mira*."

"When did you get so smart?"

Von chuckled, "It's just experience. There are moments in life that always stay with us, they may give us purpose or direction, but they do not determine the entire course of our lives. The only thing that determines that are the choices we make each and every day. Think about it. I may have never met you if I hadn't decided to ignore the ban and plead for the case of Daejara and my brother."

"I don't believe that," Helena murmured sleepily. "The Mother would have found a way to bring us together."

"Likely so," he agreed, not wanting to dwell on the thought of a life spent never knowing the woman curled up in his arms. "I'm just saying, each choice we make opens up new opportunities. Nothing is definite except that our lives are comprised of millions of choices."

"Mmm," she murmured, her body going lax against his.

"Sleep now, my love. I will keep watch."

Von settled in, content to hold his mate in his arms while she slept. After months spent without the simple luxury of being beside her, there was nowhere else he'd rather be.

THE LIGHT KNOCKS on the door startled him, and Von jumped before looking down to ensure that Helena still slept soundly.

"Enter," he called softly, his fingers playing with the soft ends of hair that ran down Helena's back. Other than a few whimpers, Helena had remained asleep. Each time she'd started to grow restless, he'd press his lips against her forehead and whisper that all was well. Upon hearing his voice, she would immediately settle. Even in her sleep she needed reassurance that he was still with her.

If he was surprised to see Nial standing in the doorway, Von did not show it. "Brother," he said, his tone no less warm despite its low volume. He still couldn't quite believe that his brother was healthy and whole once more. Seeing him walking, let alone fighting, took his breath away every time he saw it.

"How is she doing?" Nial asked, concern shining in his stormy blue-gray eyes.

"She is stronger than she gives herself credit for, she will be fine."

"It cannot be easy."

"No, but she will manage. What brings you?" Von asked.

"They were worried," he said, meaning the Circle, "but none felt comfortable interrupting you two."

"And they sent you?" Von asked, amused.

"They figured I was least likely to be harmed, given that you are fondest of me."

Von chuckled. "They do not know me very well. You more than any of the others, save perhaps Ronan, should know better than to interrupt us when we are alone."

"That's what I said."

The brothers laughed.

The easy smile started to fade from Nial's face as he sobered, remembering what else he had come to share. "The delegates have already started their journey's home." At Von's lifted brow Nial continued, "They were eager to get back to their people and warn them about what was coming."

Von nodded, it only made sense. "They are not the only ones with such a trip ahead of them."

"Do you know when we leave?" Nial asked.

"Tomorrow."

"And where do we head?"

Von hesitated, it was not that he didn't trust his brother, but there was still the matter of how Rowena was able to get her people inside unbeknownst to the rest of them. If there was a spy on the loose, he did not feel comfortable giving away any information that could be used against them, not even under the protection of sight or audio shields.

Nial sensed his train of thought and said, "It doesn't matter, I will tell the others to pack for all possible scenarios. Can you tell me how long we'll be gone?"

Von shrugged. "As long as it takes."

Nial sighed, nodding as if that was what he had expected. He laughed suddenly, "Did you ever think that not just one, but two Holbrookes would be part of the force fighting *for* a Kiri?"

As a son of the realm that still bore the scars of a centuries-long ban, established due to a rebellion led by his ancestors, the thought hadn't even been a possibility.

"I cannot say that I did," Von confessed with a wry smile.

"It suits you."

"What does?" Von asked, not following his brother's train of thought.

"Happiness. I have not seen you like this since before..." Nial trailed off, not wanting to say the words that had always brought such pain in their wake.

"Since before your accident."

Nial nodded.

Von took a deep breath, trying to steady himself as the old ghosts came back to haunt him. "Watching your future stripped away from you in a heartbeat was unbearable for me. I would not accept that one with such passion for life could be content to remain locked away in his rooms."

"I would not be here without you," Nial admitted, the depth of love he had for his brother embedded in the words.

"Nor I," Von said with a rueful smile.

That made his brother grin. "You're welcome then!" With another soft laugh, Nial started to step back toward the door.

"It suits you as well," Von called after him.

Grinning over his shoulder, Nial replied, "I never believed happiness like this was in the cards for me. But here we are, two Holbrookes, both mated and preparing to defend the world. Sounds pretty perfect, if you ask me."

"Getting a little ahead of yourself, aren't you?" Von asked, referring to Serena. "Last I checked, you two haven't taken the vows."

"A mere formality. It's only a matter of time, brother. We Holbrookes are irresistible."

Von shook his head, seeing the little boy his brother had once been in the man's shining eyes. "Good night, brother."

"Night!" Nial whispered, softly shutting the door behind him.

Adventure, love, and purpose; it was all Nial had ever wanted, and because of the amazing woman in his arms, now they both had it. Von would never be able to thank her for the gift she'd given him. Running his fingers along her hair again, Von had to admit, it was more than he had ever allowed himself to hope for. They might be on the brink of the bloodiest war in history, but he was still the happiest he'd ever been in his life. That alone was worth fighting, and dying, for. More than worth it.

Whatever he had to do to protect the woman he loved, he'd do without question. He'd been a harbinger of death and destruction before, and had done it for infinitely less noble reasons. Von would gladly step into that role again if it would spare Helena the heartache of experiencing it herself.

Let their enemies come. He'd be waiting.

CHAPTER 10

When Helena woke, she felt more rested than she had in weeks. It was surprising, all things considered, but welcome. True to his word, Von hadn't left her side until she'd woken up to the sound of birdsong. The steady thump of his heart had been the perfect lullaby.

All of the insecurity and doubt he'd kept away started to bubble up within her again in his absence. There was much to do, and so little time. *How am I supposed to know if I am focusing on the right things?*

As if he could feel her troubled thoughts, Von sent a lingering caress along their bond. There were no words; he must have been talking to one of the others, but the phantom touch was reinforced with his message from last night. Blocking out the niggling doubts, she took two slow breaths and made her way to the clothes Alina had laid out sometime the night before. The fact that the woman had the foresight to do so, even after the chaos, was impressive.

She dressed quickly, lacing up the travel leathers and soft cotton tunic with practiced fingers. Her thoughts began to wander again as she moved to lace her boots. She couldn't help but think about what lay ahead of them. Nothing was straightforward. Not their direction, and certainly not her plans.

Originally, she'd thought that a visit to the Triumvirate was in order, seeking their knowledge of potential futures to help inform and guide their movements. But if last night's events were any indication, there was no time to spare. They needed allies now, which certainly pushed the timeline up. They would have to proceed blindly, but that was all right. It was no more than she'd had to do for most of her life anyway. So, they would head toward the lost tribes first.

Helena fought back a shudder at the thought. There was nothing specific that she was afraid of, although the hushed stories whispered about them in every corner of Tigaera certainly didn't endear them to her. But stories were stories. At most there was perhaps a sliver of truth to be found there. She could not imagine that the Forsaken would deny their aid after learning of Rowena's army. Then again, many would call her a fool. It was hard to say what, exactly, would happen when they reached out to those who so many had routinely ignored.

She wanted to sigh but pushed back the impulse. It was too easy to imagine defeat. Not wanting to give the possibility any more power, Helena decided to only consider a more positive alternative. If they could get all of the lost tribes to join them, they'd have a force that would vastly outnumber Rowena's.

Smoothing her hands along the supple leather, she ensured everything was in order before standing and snatching her deep amber cloak from its resting place on the chair. She was already moving when she twisted it around her shoulders. Leaving her room, with all of its comforts, was easier than she would have imagined. Her future, and that of all the Chosen, was waiting for her to determine its outcome.

Helena took the stairs at a run, eager to be outside amidst her friends. Already she could hear the hum of their voices, along with the flickers of their power. She smiled, enjoying their connection. It reminded her that no matter what they discovered, they'd do so together. She might be the one to make the hardest decisions but they would help her face the consequences, whatever they may be. There was a certain peace in that.

When a small voice in her mind warned her that she might also have to say goodbye to them, Helena immediately silenced it. It was too painful to contemplate, no matter how true it might be.

Moving quickly through the colorful halls of the Palace, Helena forced herself to meet the gazes and match the hopeful smiles of the Chosen. The closer she got to the stables, the more desperately hopeful the gazes she encountered. She was their Kiri; they believed she would protect them. Helena would not give them any reason to doubt their beliefs, even though she doubted herself.

Stepping out of the last hallway and into the brilliant sunlight, Helena took a deep breath, filling her lungs with the sweetness of the morning. Last evening had been filled with death and bloodshed, but the morning still greeted her all the same. The simple truth of it rocked her. Life went on, and so would she. *Hadn't Von said the same?*

As if her thoughts had conjured the man, Von's smoky eyes caught hers from across the field. His hand was buried in the thick fur of his wolf Karma as he checked to make sure that all of the necessities were properly stored. They would not be making this trip on wolf-back, or even Talyrian back for that matter. As promised, Helena had worked with Joquil to find a way to escalate the creation of Kaelpas stones.

They took a notoriously long time to charge, but given the strength of Helena's power, combined with her control of all five Branches of the Mother's power, she was able to imbue the small purple stones with enough strength that she could circumvent the full timeline. Not only circumvent, but entirely replace. Helena had spent the better part of a morning making dozens of the stones. She would likely spend countless more keeping them charged in the days to come. Especially given that they were the primary means of transportation for the foreseeable future.

That did not, as Darrin had pointed out, get them past the need to have a guide to help them reach unknown locations. They were limited to traveling only to those places in which at least one amongst them had already been. Luckily, they had a Keeper in their ranks.

Miranda had traveled much of Elysia in her time as a Keeper. It was because of her, that they were even able to travel directly into the lands of one of the forgotten realms. Their first stop would be the Ebon Isle. It was notorious for its storms, which were caused due to the massive maelstrom always present just off its coast. That was also how its people inherited their affinity for water and air. They were said to be created from the storm's fury itself, the ability to channel its power innate in each of them.

Helena could not help but feel a kinship with the people who could command the sky and sea. She only hoped they felt that same connection. Their power would do much to strengthen their forces.

She crossed the distance between her and her Mate quickly. Heat and approval flared hot in his eyes as he took her in, and she could feel his desire for her throb through their bond. Her lips twisted, of course he would think now was an appropriate time for such intimacy.

"There is never not a good time," he countered, his own lips twisting in a sensual grin.

"Yes there is. Like right now, when we are mere minutes away from entering an unknown land to try to garner the aid of its people who do not recognize the Kiri as the Mother's Vessel."

He frowned. *"Well, when you go and put it that way…"*

"What other way is there to put it, Mate? I only speak the truth." Her eyes were bright with mirth.

"I cannot help it if I hunger for you. I've only just gotten you back. Would you deny your Mate his pleasure at the sight of you? Especially when for a time you were only a vision he imagined during the worst of his nightmares?"

Helena's smile fell completely. *"Never."* Her mental voice shook a bit as she delivered the promise, but his smile was understanding as he responded.

"There is much time we need to make up for, my love. But we will have the rest of our lives together to do so. For now, we will focus on ensuring that such a future exists. Then we can ignore the rest of the world and lose ourselves in each other."

Her stomach tightened at the sexual promise in his words, even as she mourned the fact that such luxuries would have to be on hold for the foreseeable future. *"And how long do you think the world would let us ignore it?"*

"I don't give a fuck what the world wants. After this business with

Rowena concludes, Mate, you and I have some things to take care of. Far away from here."

The smile that she gave him was radiant. *"I can't wait."*

His eyes were molten as he replied, *"Nor I."*

She shook her head, pushing away thoughts of uninterrupted time with her Mate, and all that would entail, to focus on the growing number of people standing in front of her. *How in the name of the Great Mother am I supposed to travel with all of these people without Rowena knowing exactly where we are?* It was going to be impossible. A full army would also put their potential allies on edge. Helena sighed, already knowing that her Circle was going to be very unhappy with her newest request.

Kragen sidled up, seeing the calculating look in her eyes. "What are you thinking?"

"That we cannot travel with these numbers."

He frowned, deep brackets etching themselves in his face. "We cannot be unprotected."

Sighing again she agreed, "I know."

"What do you propose?"

"Dividing our numbers."

Helena could see that he wanted to argue, and what it cost him to push back that instinctive response.

Darrin had no such trouble. "Do you truly wish to make it that easy for her to murder you then?"

She shot him a dirty look. "Yes. That's exactly what I have in mind."

Darrin scowled, not appreciating her sarcasm.

"What do you have in mind, *Mira*?" Von asked in a carefully neutral voice.

"A series of go-betweens. Soldiers that make the initial jump with us, to become familiar with the surroundings, before coming back to the bulk of the force here. That way, if we come upon Rowena or any of her army, our reinforcements will not be far behind. We could have several of them, that way the majority of the army could appear almost instantly."

The men considered her words carefully. "If we scheduled regular check-ins we could help them become familiar with the landscape and any new locations. It would mitigate the distance the rest of the army would need to travel to meet up with us," Von said.

Kragen mulled the suggestion over. "It could work."

Darrin frowned, as usual. "I do not like the idea of us being unprepared."

"I cannot show up on their doorsteps with an entire army at my back. It would be as good as declaring an outright war. They are not our enemies, and we do not want to give them the impression that we believe them to be," Helena countered.

"I know, but I still don't like it."

"Fair enough, but we will all be there to protect her," Von reminded him.

Helena quickly agreed, "Yes, of course. The full Circle, Ronan, Serena, Nial, and Miranda." At Darrin's deepening scowl, she added, "Effie, of course is welcome if she'd like to come with us."

"And the Talyrian?" Ronan asked, having been listening the entire time.

"Obviously," Helena agreed.

"What of the wolves? And a handful of other guards."

When Helena hesitated, Von said, "It would be odd for a Kiri to travel without at least some of the Rasmiri in attendance."

"And for the Daejaran Commander to be without his men," Ronan pointed out.

Exasperated, Helena rolled her eyes. "How many men are you suggesting?"

The two men commented without thought.

"Twenty," Von said.

"At least forty," Ronan stated.

They shared a glance, their lips lifting in amusement.

"Forty?! The entire point is *not* to seem like we are marching on them," Helena nearly shouted.

"Anything less may indicate weakness."

Helena threw up her hands. "Are you all unable to defend me then?

Or yourselves? How weak I must seem, to require so many men to protect me!"

"When has that ever been the point?" Ronan asked, his eyes glacial.

"It's not about protection. It is about appearances, Kiri. These are the men that follow you. You must be a force to be reckoned with, not someone they can easily dismiss."

The sky turned black and wind whipped through the air. "Let them try," she said, her voice harmonious and filled with the threat of violence as her eye shone with iridescence.

Darrin paled and swallowed audibly. "Hellion."

Helena blinked, and the storm instantly subsided. "Forty then. No more. And that number includes the Circle and the other's I've mentioned."

"Forty plus mounts."

Helena crossed her arms, but she didn't argue further. The Daejaran pack was fierce and would make traveling once they arrived much easier. "Fine," she agreed.

The men of her Circle nodded. "I will select the Rasmiri who will join us," Darrin announced.

Helena's spared a glance for Ronan and Von. "Which of you will select the men from Daejara?"

Von smirked. "For all that he pretends to be in charge, I am their Commander. That said, I would not question anyone that Ronan put forth as an appropriate guard."

Ronan's eyes seemed to glow with the compliment, but he said nothing.

"Choose wisely," Helena said, before turning her back on both of them.

"Of course, Kiri," Ronan murmured.

"We will get through this," Von promised, sensing the swelling tide of anxiety in her.

"So you say."

"Helena." Her name was both question and protest.

"I do not want to lose more good men and women. I hate that I

place so many in danger."

"You cannot control that."

Thunder growled and shook the sky. Helena watched her Mate glance up before adding ruefully, *"If any of us could control the future, I would put every last gold piece on you. But, Helena, you cannot. These men and women serve because it is their wish. They believe in this cause, in Elysia, as much as you do. You are their hope."*

Helena shuddered. *"And that is why I fear."*

"Because you are wise and compassionate. Do you think Rowena mourns the loss of her Shadows?"

"Only in as much as it affects her own power."

"Exactly. And that *is why you will win. You put the needs of others before yourself. Your compassion is your greatest strength."*

She wanted to argue further, but his words swelled within her, giving her hope. With one last breath, Helena turned back toward Von and the Chosen that were already moving into place behind him. *"Let us hope you are right, Mate."*

CHAPTER 11

$\mathcal{E}$yeing Miranda, Helena broke off from the others and approached the older woman. "Keeper?"

Turning midnight eyes on her, Miranda responded, "Kiri."

"Thank you for your assistance," she started awkwardly.

"Why do I get the impression you didn't come over to review our itinerary?"

Helena sighed. "Because I didn't."

"What's on your mind, Kiri?" Miranda asked, not unkindly.

"Last night…" Helena trailed off, uncertain of what exactly she was trying to say.

Nothing if not patient, the Keeper waited for her to continue.

"There was a moment where it felt like I was still under the effects of the Fracturing," Helena confessed, confusion and fear making her voice small. "How is that possible?"

Miranda laid a hand upon her arm. "Your Mate has returned, but the bond is not fully complete and so your power continues to overwhelm you."

Helena's brows furrowed. She could vaguely remember Effie referencing something similar when she'd spoken of the prophecy so many months ago, but the meaning of the words had been forgotten.

Seeing the question on her face, Miranda elaborated, "The Vessel is a conduit of the Mother's own power. The depth of it surpasses comprehension and it is too much for anyone to hold on their own. Your Mate helps reinforce the barriers within you that contain and hold that power in check. He is the tether that binds you to the world, to your innermost self. And it is the bond between you that allows you to maintain control over your power instead of being overtaken by it. With the bond incomplete there are..." she paused, searching for the right word, "cracks, that allow the power to leak out."

"How—why—" Helena broke off as frustration ate at her. After everything, she still was not free from the effects of the Fracturing, although the bulk of the side effects had been thwarted simply by Von's presence. But what the Keeper was saying could not be denied.

Von had already proven in the last handful of days that he was the only one who could help her rein in her power. He'd done it once when she'd been lost inside her grief over discovering Anderson's mutilated remains, and then again just last night when he'd taken the full force of her power inside himself for her to draw back out at a more manageable level. *What happens when even he cannot withstand the next explosion of power?*

Fear snaked up her spine, causing her to shiver despite the mild weather. This was the absolute last thing she wanted to have to worry about with the looming threat of Rowena's next ambush.

The Keeper shrugged. "I cannot begin to understand the intricacies of your bond, Helena. I can only offer the answer to the first question you posed. Once the bond is fully accepted, you will control your power absolutely."

"But I have accepted it!" she burst out. "Our souls recognized each other. We spoke the vows. I can feel him, even now, in the depths of my mind. What's left for me to do?"

Miranda's eyes were as apologetic as her words. "I am sorry, Kiri. Truly. I wish I could tell you."

"Helena? Is everything all right?"

She found him without needing to search. Von was staring at her, dark brows lowered over concerned gray eyes; his lips were set in a deep frown.

Offering a small smile, she replied, *"Everything is fine. Just more cryptic warnings from the Keeper."*

He crossed his arms, expression dubious. *"What aren't you telling me?"*

Helena made a face, annoyed that he could sense the omission, even as it underscored her point. How could their bond possibly be incomplete when they were so in tune with one another?

"Keeper?" Helena asked softly, eyes still focused on her Mate.

"Yes, Kiri," Miranda responded warily, as if already knowing what Helena was about to ask.

"How much longer do I have before I lose control completely?"

The silence expanded between them until Helena finally twisted back toward her. The woman's face was pale, her eyes wide and unseeing. When she spoke, her voice sounded from far away.

"The mist stalks its prey, unwilling to release its hold. It sinks its claws in deeper with every swipe. You must find where its hold is deepest and reclaim the final piece. If you fail, all will be lost. The sky will glow red with flame, the air will fill with ash, and the Mother's Tears will run with blood." Miranda blinked, her eyes coming back into focus as she swayed where she stood.

Helena grasped her, keeping Miranda upright as they shared a look of mute horror. Both women were stricken by the prophecy she'd just shared. Helena swallowed, throat suddenly dry. Once again, she was presented with the warning from her trial, albeit from a new avenue. The words were meant to be enigmatic, but Helena knew enough to make out the gist of their meaning. A part of Von was still being held hostage by the mist. Helena frowned, silently berating herself. The warning signs had been there all along, she just hadn't understood them. A vision of Von, ashen and wide eyed when he saw the mist surrounding them in Vyruul, filled her mind, while his broken words from the night before echoed back like an eerie soundtrack: *'I got lost.'*

She had already searched him, had pulled out every lingering piece of the *Bellamorte* she'd found, but she must have missed one. In doing so, it seemed that she'd inadvertently kept them from being able to complete the bond. Aqua eyes moved back to her Mate, running over his body as if it would reveal the part of him that was still under silent attack. Helena knew it wouldn't be that simple. If it had been obvious, she'd have already dealt with it.

Von met her gaze, his own eyes clouding as he tried to decipher her troubled expression. Before he could inquire, Timmins broke through the moment with a bellowed, "Kiri! It is time!"

Blinking, Helena and Miranda shared a final look of trepidation. Helena sighed and pushed the Keeper's warning aside to refocus on the task at hand. She would have to address the issue, and soon, but for now her attention was required elsewhere.

Reaching for Helena with a trembling hand, her nails digging in where they made contact with Helena's arms, Miranda whispered, "You cannot fail."

The unspoken message behind the Keeper's words was clear. Von's life was not the only one at stake if she failed. But when hadn't that been the case since she'd ascended? This was just another thing for her to add to her increasingly long list of impossible things to do.

MIRANDA, looking for all the world like nothing had just happened, stepped forward with a Kaelpas stone glittering in her outstretched palm. "Are you ready, Kiri?"

Helena nodded, scooting in closer to the older woman. She would be making the initial jump with her Circle and their friends, along with one designated runner who would be coming straight back to collect the next group. With each new group, a new runner would step in so that no one person had to make the leap more than twice, which would also leave almost a handful of people remaining in Tigaera that already knew how to reach the others if necessary.

Von moved into position beside her, weaving his fingers through hers. She squeezed once, enjoying the way his warmth tingled up her arm, before reaching out her other hand to rest it on Miranda's shoulder. There was a bump at her hip, and Helena twisted, chuckling when she saw Starshine's turquoise eyes balefully glaring at her.

"I'm sorry, girl. I know you'd rather fly."

There was an annoyed huff and a small bit of smoke curled in the air. Helena bit her lip, not entirely sure how the Talyrian would react to travel via Kaelpas stone, but the wolves had made the jump from Vyruul last time. She could only hope it wouldn't affect Starshine too badly.

There was another feline grunt, but Starshine pressed herself against Helena. The rumbling purr she felt everywhere they connected made her grin. Starshine wasn't happy about their means of travel, but she still enjoyed being near her mistress. Helena definitely reciprocated both sentiments; her stomach was already knotting in anticipation of using the stone.

"Brace yourselves," Miranda murmured. Helena thought the Keeper sounded a little too amused for her liking, but the feeling of being squeezed through space made any further thoughts impossible.

When the ground steadied, Helena grasped her knees and took several gasping breaths. "Will it ever stop being terrible?" she panted.

There were a few grunts of agreement from beside her, where the others were in more or less the same state. Von and Miranda alone appeared mostly unaffected. Helena shot him an annoyed glance. It wasn't fair that she had to suffer while he still looked entirely unruffled.

Feeling her ire, he grinned at her and shrugged.

"Bastard. You could at least pretend," she said without heat.

He coughed half-heartedly. *"Better?"*

Helena rolled her eyes, amused despite herself. Finally able to stand, and breathe, she pushed herself upright. As she took in their surroundings, her mouth fell open in awe. They were poised on the edge of a dock that was surrounded on all sides by angry waves. There must have been a shield keeping the worst of the water from touching them or the dock, although her hair was entirely at the mercy of the wind and had already ripped free of her neat braid.

The feeling of being suspended in the middle of the sea was intimidating, but it paled in comparison to the mass of churning wind and water rising up and towering above them. She'd heard that the

Ebon Isle was known for its storms. Now that she was face-to-face with one she certainly understood why, although that didn't make the greeting-by-cyclone any less surprising. The tempest twisted on top of the inky sea, dancing with the edges of the maelstrom. It was surreal to watch wind and water mate in the sky, while just beside it there was a massive whirlpool that seemed to drop all the way to the center of the world. The juxtaposition was hard to comprehend.

A grumpy roar had Helena pulling her gaze from the storm to her Talyrian. Starshine shook out her wings, pacing along the edges of the dock and whining. Eyeing the sky, Helena imagined that the Talyrian was not overly fond of the torrential downpour. One-by-one the Circle moved toward her, and together they made their way carefully to the place where the dock met the land.

Lightning split the sky and Helena swore she could feel an answering throb within her. Nothing was natural about this storm, and her power was humming with the need to answer its call.

Darrin eyed the sky, his frown deepening as the storm seemed to worsen. "I can't say I'm impressed with what I've seen of the mysterious Ebon Isle," he muttered.

Ronan bumped his shoulder. "Unmanned by a little rain?"

"A little rain? Are you blind?"

Ronan chuckled. "Let us hope the Storm Forged are feeling hospitable."

Darrin grimaced at the thought of having to spend the night in the rain. The others laughed. Effie took pity on him, and put her small hand in his, offering silent comfort.

Timmins had just smoothed away his own grin when he asked, "Should we start making for the keep?"

"It would be best to wait for the others to arrive," Kragen said, but after a quick look back at the dock, he saw that they already had. Letting out a low whistle he shook his head. "It's almost worth feeling like a wrung-out tunic for the convenience of that kind of travel."

"Almost," Helena emphasized dryly.

Von was considerate enough not to laugh out loud, but she snarled at him anyway due to the flickers of mirth shooting along their bond.

The group made their way toward a stone keep sitting precariously atop a hill of rocks. The keep had obviously been crafted with magic. There was no other way it would have been able to withstand the assault of the water, or the crumbling bed of rocks it rested upon.

They must have been quite a sight, trudging through the wind and rain, with the Daejaran pack loping beside them and one very annoyed Talyrian prowling at their side. Miranda walked just beside Helena and Von, being the one that had the connections to the Storm Forged and the only one who had been to the isle before. Unfortunately, there had not been time to send word they'd be coming, nor did Helena or the Circle feel comfortable announcing their plans.

"Halt!" a disembodied voice rang out. The storm grew in intensity, the howl of the wind eclipsed only by a crack of thunder.

They came to a sudden and complete stop, their eyes warily searching for the speaker.

A man separated himself from the wall of rock he'd used for camouflage. His face was as hard as the stone behind him. With only a quick glance, Helena could tell this was not a regular Chosen. He was tall, very tall. She had to crane her neck back to meet his eyes. His skin was a dusky blue while his hair was the color of the sea during a storm. The power of the storm raged in his eyes, which were a deep, glowing sapphire. Now she understood why the people of Ebon Isle were referred to as the Storm Forged.

"Mother's blessings to you!" Miranda called, stepping forward.

The man glowered at her, lifting his twisted driftwood staff threateningly in his hand.

"We seek an audience with the Stormbringer," Miranda continued.

"And you are?" the man asked, the thunder in his voice echoing in the sky.

"The Keeper Miranda Ikusimón. I am joined by the Mother's Vessel and her Circle."

If the man was impressed by her answer, or her companions, he did not show it.

Helena could feel the men of her Circle growing impatient behind her. None of them were used to being the ones on the defensive.

"We seek his aid!" Timmins added from his place just behind Miranda. The Keeper scowled, not appreciating his assistance.

That caused a reaction. The man threw his head back and laughed. "And why would the Stormbringer wish to ally himself with the likes of you, Chosen." He bit off the word, slinging it at them like an insult. "The Mother has no place here. The Storm Forged do not recognize her divinity."

"You may not recognize the Mother, but that does not mean she has abandoned you. I can feel her in the air even now. The threads of your power tie you to her whether you wish it or not." Helena did not need to shout for her words to carry. The air itself amplified and carried them on its currents.

The man was impressed by her manipulation of his power. He was the one behind the storm and had not anticipated one in their ranks being powerful enough to do so. The wind began to die down as the man considered the group before him.

"If you prove yourself untrustworthy, you will taste the wrath of the Storm Forged. There will be no mercy."

Starshine growled menacingly in response to the thinly veiled threat being aimed at her mistress. The man, finally noticing the Talyrian, seemed to lose a bit of haughtiness. He blinked a few times, not convinced he was seeing things correctly.

"Then it is a good thing we do not seek to harm," Helena countered.

The man nodded and the storm died completely. In the distance, the cyclone continued to make its way across the horizon but the clouds cleared, and the sun began to shine.

"Welcome to Ebon Isle, Mother of Spirit," the man said when Helena made it to his side.

"Thank you for agreeing to speak with us, Stormbringer," she replied, making no move to hide her smile when his eyes widened at her use of his title. He had thought to hide it awhile longer and had not anticipated being found out before he was ready.

A moment of stunned silence passed and he laughed again. "Well met, lady. I should expect nothing less from the Mother's Vessel. Nor from one with the power to command a Talyrian."

A deep growl emanated from Starshine and Helena's smile turned feral. "You don't know much of the Talyrians nor their queen if you think I have any control over her."

From where she stood, Helena watched his throat bob as her words sank in. He looked unnerved as he hazarded another glance at Starshine who was now openly snarling at him. In an attempt to divert further insult he said hurriedly, "Please, make yourselves comfortable in my home. You are the welcome guests of Anduin Stormbringer."

For now. The unspoken words echoed loudly in her mind, reminding her that his extension of friendship was tentative at best, and that they would need to proceed with extreme caution.

Helena smiled her thanks, looking back to convey the need for continued caution with the others. There were a few nods, the warning received, before she turned back to face the man with glowing eyes.

Without another word, Helena and her people followed Anduin as he led them up the hill and into his keep.

CHAPTER 12

The keep was a celebration of the sea and sky, or perhaps it was simply a reflection of the people who lived on the Ebon Isle. Decorated in every shade of blue and green, it felt as though she was moving through the water while the air teased her skin. Helena found it thrilling; her power was eager to come out and play with the magic she could feel surrounding her.

Curious stares met them as they filed one at a time into the massive hall. It was a circular room; the entirety of it comprised of windows, save for where it connected to the hallway they just exited. The room was filled with the Storm Forged. They had the same glowing eyes as their leader, although the shades were every variation of the sea. Some had skin or hair the color of sea foam, others appeared as though they had been painted the deepest shade of indigo. It was both startling and breathtaking. The Storm Forged were every bit as fierce and lovely as the cyclone making its way across the horizon.

Von took his place beside her, his steady gaze reinforcing her calm. Joquil, who had been even more reticent than usual, moved to stand at her other side. Surprised to see him there instead of Darrin or Ronan, she gave him a curious look. His amber eyes were wild, as if he was having a strong emotional reaction that he was trying unsuccessfully to contain.

She placed a hand on his arm, not wanting to voice her concern in the midst of strangers. Joquil continued to meet her gaze, silently conveying a message she did not understand. With a final searching glance, Helena dropped her hand. She would need to make time to speak with him as soon as they were done here.

Ronan and Nial stood beside Von with Serena not far behind them. Darrin and Kragen were behind Helena, Effie almost hidden between them. Timmins stood next to Miranda, both a bit ahead and apart from the rest of the Chosen. It was the traditional spot of the Advisor, or rather, the one who would speak for the group. Not that Helena had any intention of letting someone speak for her. She was mostly just amused by the continued posturing between them. Both of them were trying to take the lead, and neither wanted to concede ground.

The rest of their force had been tasked with finding a place for the wolves, after which they were sent to the barracks to find rooms and rest for the evening. Once the storm had cleared, Starshine had taken to the sky, intent on exploring this new territory.

Knowing that there were none in this room incapable of protecting themselves, Helena released her stranglehold on her power, finally allowing it to rise to the surface as it had been clamoring to do since they'd first set foot on the Isle.

"You have come a great distance to seek an audience, Kiri," Anduin said, his voice booming throughout the room. "Especially given that the Chosen have no love of those they call the Forsaken." The silence that followed his words was heavy as the Storm Forged waited for her to tell them what required her to seek out their aid.

"I have. It is time for the Chosen to remember who and what they are. That includes the Storm Forged."

There were a few outraged hisses; none in this room wanted to be compared to the pampered children of the Mother.

"We have a common enemy, Stormbringer."

He took a seat, moving like liquid as he slid into it, greatly amused by her words. "And who would dare make an enemy of me?"

"The Corruptor," Miranda supplied, once again using the title from the prophecy known to all of Elysia's inhabitants.

His smile fell and his sapphire eyes blazed. "You came all this way to tell me bedtime stories? I have to say, I'm disappointed." If it weren't for the way the Stormbringer's fingers gripped the arms of his chair, Helena would have believed him unaffected.

"I would not waste my time with so foolish a reason, Stormbringer."

He waved away her words, eyes seeking out his court as he replied, "The Corruptor is no more than a boogeyman. A myth."

"She has already amassed an army of Shadows."

Anduin's laugh was incredulous, but Helena thought she detected a note of hysteria. Whispers rose around them like the shrieking of the wind.

"The only thing Anduin will respect is power, Helena. You have to show him that you are a bigger threat to him and his people than she is." Von sent her the thought, having already assessed the opponent before them.

"I do not wish to anger him..."

"Trust me, Mira. Show him who you are."

With that, Helena allowed her magic to run free. Her eyes sparkled with iridescence and her hair fell in long waves down her back before lifting in a breeze no one else could feel. When she spoke again, her voice was layered and harmonious. "Stormbringer."

Anduin sat up in his chair, startled by the change in the woman before him.

"How did you obtain your title?"

He tilted his head, not expecting the question. "There is no other that can match my power." There was no arrogance in the answer; he was stating a fact.

"Let us strike a bargain, Stormbringer."

Intrigued he leaned forward. "What kind of bargain?"

"A test of our power, mine against yours. If I best you, you will ally your people to my cause. If I do not, my people and I will leave here without any ill will or further request."

The Storm Forged broke into surprised laughter. None of the

Chosen reacted; this was not a game to them. They knew Helena was deadly serious.

Seeing that she was not kidding, Anduin's eyes glowed more brightly. "What you speak of is not done lightly, Kiri. The only time a reigning Stormbringer will fight is to defend their title when a challenge has been placed on the throne. It is a fight to the death. If you were to defeat me, you would obtain the title." His words clearly conveyed how unlikely such an outcome would be.

"So be it."

Tension swelled as her words were whispered and repeated throughout the room.

"You seek to challenge me?" he scoffed. "Do you even know what you ask?"

"Do we have a bargain?" she countered, not wanting to admit that she had absolutely no idea what the hell she was doing. Instinct and Von's words were all that guided her.

The smile on his face was predatory. "We do, Mother of Spirit. But not tonight. If we are to do this, we will follow as tradition mandates. It will be a true challenge."

Helena nodded her assent. Excited whispers filled the room.

Rising from his seat, Anduin addressed his people. "A challenger has stepped forward. Tomorrow Aegaeon's Challenge will commence. Tonight we will feast!"

Cheers erupted around the room, but they were bloodthirsty and frightening. Whatever Aegaeon's Challenge entailed, it would not be easy. Sensing their dismissal, at least until the feast, Helena and her Circle made their way out of the hall and back toward the suite of rooms that had been set aside for them.

"How was that for power?" Helena asked, her heart racing in her chest. *Mother's tits, what have I just gotten myself into?*

"I don't think it's exactly what I had in mind," came the uncertain reply.

Helena spun, causing the others to halt in surprise. "Perhaps you could be a bit more specific next time, Mate!"

Von looked chagrined, which caused Ronan to snicker. Soon Kragen and Serena joined in, the others following suit not long after.

"You think this is funny? All right wise guy, you are in charge of discovering what the hell I just signed up for, and then figuring out how I avoid getting us all killed tomorrow."

Ronan nodded, but his eyes were still full of laughter.

"Only you would be laughing at the threat of execution," she muttered.

He shook his head. "You misunderstand, Hellion. It's just amusing to see that no matter the situation, some things never change."

She waved him off, too worried to appreciate his levity. "It doesn't matter. See what you can find out."

Still chuckling, he nodded and made for the barracks.

As SOON AS the door shut behind them and an auditory shield was placed around the room, Helena spun on her Master. "Joquil!" she shouted, causing him to flinch.

His amber eyes lifted from the floor, seeming to shine from the shadow of the alcove he was perched in. Swallowing he asked, "Yes, Kiri?"

"Did you know?"

He paled. "Yes," he admitted, bowing his head.

"And you didn't think to warn me?"

"Kiri, I—"

Von moved beside her, scowling while he crossed his arms. Even Timmins looked uneasy as he eyed her Master.

Joquil cleared his throat, unaccustomed to, and uncomfortable with, the attention. "I did extensive research into the lost tribes during my —" he paused for a long moment, seeming to be at a loss for words, "training. I was curious about their magical abilities, and how they differed from those of the Chosen."

"Wolfshit," Von said, not buying it. Joquil gave him an assessing glance but did not have a chance to comment before Timmins spoke up.

"Where did you even find any information about the tribes?" he sputtered. "No such texts exist in the archives." He was beyond displeased that there was yet another person that had more information than he did.

Joquil coughed, an internal debate warring within him.

"What aren't you telling us, Master?" Helena demanded, her voice layered.

Joquil deflated, his eyes sliding away from hers as he stared at the floor. "When I was younger, a Keeper who was traveling through the Forsaken Territories found my village."

Helena went entirely still as she processed his words. Joquil was from one of the lost tribes. There was a sharp intake of breath from behind her as one of the others deciphered his words as well, but no one spoke.

"When they found me playing in the back of my father's market stall, the Keeper stopped in the middle of his conversation with one of the tribe elders to study me. He stepped over and grasped my arm, his touch burning me like a brand." Joquil's usually honeyed voice was hoarse as he continued, "I will never forget the way his eyes went out of focus, or the peculiar milky-white hue they turned as they bore into my own. When he spoke, his voice cut like a knife."

Joquil's hands were trembling as they ran over his face. "I still remember his words:

'The Vessel comes. You must help her bear the Crown of Embers if she has any hope of becoming the Queen of Light. When it's time, you must submit, giving in to her power completely.

Your training begins now, young Master, for your prowess will be her guide, and without you she will not find her way. To serve, you must leave the life you know behind. There can be no ties, save the one you have to her.

Your destiny awaits.'"

There was a moment of tense silence before Joquil continued, "I left with him that day, arriving in Tigaera to begin my apprenticeship with the retired Circle members. My family saw it as a great honor to be discovered by the Keeper; there were no tears when they said goodbye. It is simply not the way of those born to the twilight."

"You are from the Forest of Whispers," Timmins said, recognizing the phrase.

"A Night Stalker!" Darrin whispered in shock.

Joquil looked up, amber eyes burning as he solemnly confirmed, "Yes."

As the admission left his lips, he held himself stiffly, as if braced for a blow. He was a Master in all four of the five Branches of magic available to him; a rare and considerable accomplishment throughout all of Elysia. There were perhaps only a handful of others that could say the same. The amount of power he could command was astounding, and yet, this confession stripped him of it all. To see him brought so low, all of his quiet dignity laying in tatters at his feet, made Helena's heart ache and her anger at his omission ebb.

"Why keep it from us?" Helena asked gently.

His laugh was short and brittle. "Never would one of the Forsaken be allowed to enter into the service of a Circle. We are savages not fit to be near any of the Chosen, let alone the Kiri."

Each bitter word landed like an arrow through Helena's heart.

"The only way to serve, the only way to fulfill my destiny, was to hide my past. And so I buried it." His eyes burned with defiant pride. Even after all they had been through together, a part of him still expected to be cast aside with the admission.

Helena was startled by the tear that rolled down her cheek. Joquil's story was unexpected to say the least. Although, discovering that he was one of the Night Stalkers explained much. His penchant for silence and his ability to quietly fade into the background were two of the most notable.

Speaking over the emotionally charged silence Von asked dryly, "All right, so you are one of the Stalkers, what does that have to do with the Stormbringer's challenge?"

Joquil blinked, not expecting the revelation of his lifelong secret to be brushed aside so quickly. Sitting a little straighter he answered, "When I traveled with the Keeper, he told me many things. One night during our journey, we received word about a new Stormbringer ascending. The Keeper explained how the title was earned and told me that a time would come when I would witness it for myself. I had forgotten all about it until we stood before him." As he said the last he looked again toward Helena, remorse shining in the depths of his eyes.

That explains what happened in the hall then, Helena thought with a sigh. "Do you remember what he told you of the challenge?"

Joquil nodded, his panic flaring again. "I do."

"And?" Von drawled.

Joquil lifted a brow, matching Von's bland tone perfectly, "Do you recall the maelstrom just off the coast?"

"No… I must have missed it," Von replied, deadpan.

Helena shot him a look, but he stared unblinkingly at the Master.

Kragen and Darrin snickered, both enjoying someone else being at the end of one of Von's barbed statements, had Ronan been there he would have joined them.

Joquil's eyes narrowed but the left side of his lip began to curl in amusement. His shoulders relaxed and he crossed his arms mirroring Von's stance. "Your lack of observation is impressive. I had higher hopes for the Commander of the Daejaran mercenaries."

Von smirked and Joquil grinned. Helena frowned, her eyes zipping between the two men. *What in the Mother...* she thought, and then it clicked. By treating him as if he had not just shared his most closely guarded secret, Von had shown Joquil that nothing had changed. Helena snorted with disbelief, *Men*.

"Okay, now that whatever that was is out of the way..." Helena started.

Joquil cleared his throat, "Right. The maelstrom is the answer."

Helena blinked and looked at the others thinking she'd missed something. "Remind me of the question."

"In order to defeat the reigning Stormbringer, and to beat Aegaeon's Challenge, the one who declared the challenge must summon a storm from the depths of the maelstrom. The cyclone that you saw when we arrived, that was created by Anduin when he ascended."

"His power has kept it going all this time?" Timmins asked.

"Yes."

Helena could feel her skin leeching of all color but forced herself not to give in to her panic. "So we must both draw a cyclone from the depths of Aegaeon's maelstrom?"

"He said that it's a death match," Darrin pointed out.

Joquil's face was grave as he confirmed, "The winner is only declared when their storm overpowers the other. The loser is always swallowed by the storm."

"Oh."

Adrenaline sent her pulse roaring in her ears. Feeling her rising panic, Von sent waves of calm and support through their bond.

In theory it seemed simple: call forth a storm more powerful than the other. But having felt the magic pulsing through the air, Helena knew it would require considerable skill to manipulate and then control the forces already at play. She had enough trouble controlling her own power on a good day and now she was supposed to handle someone else's? Not only that, she was supposed to use it to murder them? Here she was trying to stop people from dying and she'd just inadvertently walked right onto another kind of killing field. The thought was so absurd she wanted to laugh.

Kragen's booming laugh startled her out of her thoughts.

"Oh, not you too," she moaned, thinking back to Ronan's earlier laughter.

Kragen shrugged. "I just couldn't help but think *Battle of the Storms* seems a much more fitting name than *Aegaeon's Challenge*. At the very least it's more straightforward when it comes to what's expected."

Helena's lips quirked. At least one of them didn't appear worried about tomorrow's outcome.

"Aegaeon was the first master of Air and Water. He is the one that created the maelstrom," Joquil informed them.

Timmins gave him a startled look, before sighing deeply. Miranda would have been highly amused to see that she was not the only cause of those sighs.

Helena lifted her brow, smirking. "See. When you know what it means, it's abundantly clear."

Kragen grinned. "You really think you would have pieced it all together with only that information?"

She shrugged. "Maybe not, but if I could, why would I need you lot?" His knowing smile grew, causing her to add, "In any event, I still would have figured it out before you!"

Kragen winked and the other men laughed.

There was a loud crash as the door flew open, smashing into the wall.

"Helena!" Ronan roared, rushing inside.

"*Mother's tits!*" Von swore, releasing the power he'd already pulled up and had aimed at the door.

Earlier joking aside, they were all still very much on edge.

"I-I know what the challenge entails," he panted, out of breath from his full sprint back to her.

"So do I," she informed him.

His rush of words stopped as he stared at her, mouth agape. "How?"

Helena's eyes slid toward Joquil, but the guarded look he wore halted her words. She would tell Ronan what they'd learned, but not while the wounds were still raw.

"My Circle is cleverer than they appear."

"Do you think you'll be able to do it?"

Helena was unsure which of the men had asked the question. Each of them were staring at her intently as they waited for her answer. Except for Von, he alone seemed entirely confident in her ability.

She opened her mouth to respond, but stopped, faltering as she recalled the roiling mass of water and the endless black hole it encircled. Could she? Helena wasn't so sure. At least, not entirely on her own. The night before she had performed powerful magic, but it was only after she'd woven the threads of their individual power together that she was able to make the earth open up and swallow the acidfall.

Helena forced herself to stand tall before them, pushing all of her fear and doubt away. There was only one answer she could give them, so she did.

"Yes."

Whether it was true or not remained to be seen.

CHAPTER 13

They strategized for a while longer, agreeing that Joquil would be their key to soliciting help from the rest of the Night Stalkers, given his inside knowledge. Assuming, of course, they made it through tomorrow unscathed. That much finalized, the others left to find their own rooms and get ready for the evening's festivities. They'd spoken much longer than she'd thought, leaving her with barely enough time to bathe and get dressed before they were expected downstairs. In fact, Helena was certain they were already late.

She finished brushing her hair and looked longingly at the bed. The last thing she wanted to do the night before facing-off against Anduin was go to another party. Especially considering how the last one had ended. Unfortunately, Helena the woman's wishes lost out to Helena the Kiri's duties almost every time. Tonight was no exception.

She sighed, trying to work out the tightness in her shoulders. Knowing what was expected of her tomorrow had her stomach in knots. There was very little, if anything, that she was enjoying about her current predicament. She was here to forge alliances and remind the Storm Forged that they were part of the Chosen. Somehow, destroying their leader didn't seem to be the best way to go about creating that partnership. It went against everything she believed in and was fighting for in the first place.

Hearing the door to the bathing chamber open, Helena made to turn toward her Mate when she felt him at her back. Von swept her tangle of curls aside and brushed a lingering kiss on the base of her neck. His fingers trailed softly down the side of it before continuing their journey down her shoulder.

Helena shivered, eyes falling closed as she leaned into him. *"You're starting something we don't have time to finish, Mate,"* she protested weakly, loving the feel of him against her. She craved his touch, which was nothing new, but there was something infinitely more desperate about her current need for him. Ever since she'd gotten him back, they'd been thrown into Rowena's chaos and barely had a chance to enjoy being reunited.

She missed him. Missed the quiet moments when they would curl up together whispering in the darkness, and the way she could surprise him into laughter. But more than anything, Helena missed the feel of him sliding inside her and the way he'd hold her close as she fell apart beneath him. She wanted those moments with him more than she wanted her next breath.

Being with her Mate was easy. It didn't require effort or complicated decisions like everything else in her life. She was exhausted and overwhelmed by the emotional weight she'd been carrying these last few months. When she was with Von, all she had to do was let go. Right now, Helena was desperate to let everything go.

"That doesn't mean I can't take advantage of the time we do have," he whispered hotly against her skin before biting down on the muscle between her neck and shoulder.

Helena sucked in a breath and arched into Von as he wrapped his other arm around her, pressing his palm flat against her belly. His heat surrounded her and all thoughts of responsibility and politics fled, leaving only Von in their wake.

He continued trailing kisses along the skin exposed by her dress, his fingers working their way down her body. She could feel his fingers resting just above the growing ache between her legs and let out a soft groan. The hand at her shoulder moved across her chest, his hand palming and kneading her breast.

"V-von," she stuttered in weak protest.

"Helena," he murmured in her ear before lightly licking the outer shell.

She shivered, his gentle assault making her need for him all-consuming. The fingers splayed over her belly began to flex and slowly gather her skirt. The air felt cool as it kissed the skin of her legs. He worked quickly, until the skirt was bunched about her waist and his warm fingers were pressed directly against her.

Helena had the distant realization that he was using his power to keep her skirt up, but then he began to stroke along her center and there were no conscious thoughts, only need. How he could do this to her, steal her focus and become the center of her world, even on the eve of battle, amazed her. Then again, if these stolen moments were the last they'd have, was there a better way to spend them?

"Von," she moaned again, arm lifting to wrap around his head and hold him closer; her hips moving desperately in response to his teasing fingers. He was stroking the skin between her legs lightly, never quite hitting the spot that ached to feel him.

The hand at her breast dipped down under the dress, his fingers plucking and twisting her pert nipple. The sensation set off little fireworks behind her eyes and a gasp left her parted lips.

"I love how responsive you are, *Mira*," he said.

"O-only for you," she panted.

She could feel his answering grin, even though she could not see it.

"Do you want me to touch you here," he asked pressing a slick finger down her center, "or here?" With that he slid his fingers further down and up inside of her.

Helena gasped and arched into him. "Wh-why not both?"

"Good answer," he chuckled, beginning to work her in earnest.

Her need began to spiral tight inside of her, an arrow flying toward its target.

There was a loud knock at the door and a voice called, "The Stormbringer requests your presence downstairs, Kiri."

Helena's eyes flew open and she tried to squirm away, with a strangled, "Be right there!"

But Von held her tight, growling, "You're not going anywhere until you come for me, Helena."

"O-oh," she moaned, torn between not wanting to be caught and her body's need.

"Now, Helena," he demanded, fingers hitting the perfect tempo.

She shattered around him, body clamping down on the fingers that were still moving inside of her.

"That's it. I want all of it."

"V-von," she whispered brokenly as her climax continued.

Another knock sounded at the door. "Kiri?"

Spent and languid, Helena forced her eyes open. "I'll be right down; I just need a few more minutes."

"Very well, Kiri. I'll let the Stormbringer know you are on your way," the muffled voice replied before the sound of receding footsteps met her ears.

Helena twisted in Von's arms, her heart still pounding in her chest.

He grinned at her wickedly, taking in her flushed state with satisfaction shining in his gray eyes. "And you said we didn't have time."

"It appears I was wrong," she said breathlessly.

Still grinning, he lifted his fingers to his lips, his eyes never leaving hers. "Mmm," he murmured as he licked them.

Helena blushed, the erotic sight enough to make her ready for him again. She ran nervous fingers down her unbound hair while simultaneously trying to smooth out her now-rumpled dress.

Von gave her one last, knowing grin before declaring, "All right, now we can go downstairs."

"Hopefully it's not too obvious what made us late. Or was that your intention?" she half-heartedly accused.

"Oh, it was."

Her eyes flew to his. Von shrugged, entirely unapologetic. "You looked tense. Now you don't." He smirked and she felt it throughout her body. "I couldn't let you go in there looking like you were worried about tomorrow. That's practically rule number one. Your opponent should never see you doubting yourself. It gives them an advantage and that is the last thing you ever want."

She studied him for a moment. There was definitely a special kind of logic he was using, but her brain was still too fuzzy for her to pinpoint the flaws in it. Besides, she had to admit she appreciated the results.

"I suppose I can't argue with that. I certainly feel less tense," she admitted before adding wryly, "actually, I'm not even sure I remember my name."

His answering chuckle followed her the entire way downstairs.

HELENA HAD BEEN ANTICIPATING an opulent affair in line with the kind of events thrown at the Palace. She could not have been more wrong. The Storm Forged were not an extravagant people. The room was filled with their crowing laughs and the clinking of glasses as they drank deeply, but there were no special adornments or displays of magic. The large stone hall with its wall of windows overlooking the sea, was exactly the same as it had been when they were in there earlier. The only differences were the vibrant splash of color added by the sun as it completed its descent and the additional tables which had been brought in to hold the food and people. Overall the atmosphere was merry but completely relaxed.

Spotting the Circle, Helena and Von went to join them. "Not what you were expecting?" he asked in a subdued tone as he walked beside her.

"Not in the least. With all his talk of ceremony and tradition, I had expected something a bit more..." she trailed off.

"Stuffy?" he provided.

Helena laughed, that was exactly what she had expected: austere expressions, barbed threats hidden behind saccharine smiles, and a lot of posturing. Instead the atmosphere was warm and inviting, and the people around her couldn't care less about who she was and why she was there. After their welcome this morning, it was a drastic change to say the least.

"Well, you won't hear me complain about the difference," she replied.

"Nor I," he agreed just as they reached the others.

"Now this is my kind of gathering," Ronan commented, his words echoing their sentiments and making Helena chuckle.

"And mine," Kragen agreed, slapping him on the back. The two men grinned at each other before sauntering over to a nearby table laden with ale.

The two men were completely oblivious to the female heads which turned to stare at them in their wake. Helena couldn't fault the women for noticing that they were attractive, well-built warriors. When those same eyes began to ogle Von, however, Helena found herself feeling less understanding. She frowned and forced herself to look away before she caused a scene.

As she did, Helena caught Serena glaring menacingly at one particularly obvious group of admirers. The women had hailed Ronan and Kragen, waylaying them before they made it back to their friends, and were now flirting shamelessly. Kragen was eating up the attention, flexing at the request of a couple women. Ronan looked more uncomfortable, shrugging off one dark-haired woman's wandering hands.

Feeling her friend's stare, Serena met her eyes before grinning sheepishly. "Just because he's not mine, doesn't mean I'm not allowed to feel protective."

"Mmhmm," Helena murmured, wondering if she should intervene on Ronan's behalf when he excused himself from the group and joined Timmins and Joquil on the other side of the hall.

Nial walked over then and Serena's entire face lit up. While the blonde beauty still felt a little possessive of her ex-lover, she was very much in love and committed to the younger Holbrooke. Helena couldn't fault her for that. Mated or not, she was also fiercely protective of those she counted as hers.

Needing to touch Von, she wove her fingers through his.

"Feeling a little territorial yourself?" he asked, not missing the way she had scowled when female eyes turned his way.

Helena bared her teeth in a feral smile that made him laugh. He pulled her toward him, brushing his lips against her forehead. *"Have you already forgotten what happened upstairs?"*

She blushed, her insides going liquid at the memory. When she looked up at him her aqua eyes were shining. *"Why do you think I am feeling the need to gnash my teeth and snarl 'Mine!'?"*

Von brushed a stray curl from her face, his expression tender. *"If it makes you feel better, I share the urge."*

It did. They shared a heated look, all others forgotten.

"I wouldn't mind more parties like this," Darrin remarked, breaking their moment.

Helena found herself in silent agreement. There was something beautiful in the simplicity of the gathering. At the Palace, the parties were a celebration of the Mother's magic; here it was a celebration of life.

"There's nothing stopping us from having our own gatherings like this," she replied.

"Except for a raging psychopath currently on the loose and slaughtering your people," Darrin pointed out.

With his words, all of Von's work to distract her was undone and the full burden of her responsibility returned. Helena frowned, "You know exactly how to kill a mood. Have I ever mentioned that?"

Darrin gave her a sidelong glance, assessing how much of her words were temper versus truth. "If by 'kill a mood' you mean remind you that we're surrounded by danger and cannot afford to lower our guard, then what you're really saying is I'm good at my job and I thank you for noticing. I did vow to shield you from harm, Helena. Not throw you headlong into it."

"Where in your job description does it say you get to be a smug bastard?" Helena asked archly.

Darrin burst out laughing. "Ah, Hellion. You didn't like admitting you were wrong when we were children and it would seem you like it even less now."

"I'll have you know that I am almost never wrong. You on the other hand…"

"Pfft," he sputtered, "as if there's anyone here that would buy that."

Von lifted his brow but didn't comment. He was used to their antics and knew better than to insert himself in the middle.

Effie just shook her head in amusement, hiding her laughter behind her hand. Sensing that the friendly insults weren't far away from devolving completely, she pointed her head in the direction of the couples dancing. "Care to dance?"

Darrin was torn, enjoying the almost normal moment with his best friend, but also looking forward to the idea of having a beautiful woman in his arms. It was no surprise which of the two won out. With barely a backward glance, Darrin escorted Effie to the center of the room.

Effie spun around and the look on Darrin's face as he watched her was a look Helena recognized. It was the same one Von wore when she'd catch him staring at her. Helena's heart ached as the reality of what was before her took shape.

"He's falling for her," Helena said softly.

"Well, the boy isn't entirely stupid."

Helena's lips lifted in a smile but fell just as quickly. "They can never be together, not while he serves in the Circle."

Von's voice grew serious, "I know and so does he, Helena. He knows where his duty lies."

"But does she?" Helena asked sadly, her voice barely more than a whisper as she noted the joy on Effie's face as Darrin twirled her in his arms again and again. "I don't want to be the reason he has to break her heart, Von. It isn't fair to either of them."

"He knew what he was agreeing to when he made his vows, Helena. All of us do. There are reasons for the rules."

"Now you sound like Timmins," she muttered.

"Hey!" he protested. "Now *you're* just being mean. I am not saying I will enjoy watching this play out as it must, but there can be no hesitation, Helena. If he gets put in a situation where he has to choose between saving her or you, how is he supposed to make that decision? As the Shield, the duty to serve his Kiri must come before everything."

Helena snorted. "As if rules ever stopped anyone from doing anything they knew in their heart to be right. If he loves her, Von, then he will always choose her. Any other vow will be meaningless. I would never fault him for that."

"That is not what it means to serve."

"No, that is what it means to be human."

Von was silent. She was right.

"I would release him from his vows, if he asked me."

"He will never ask."

"Then maybe, when this is over, I will find a way to change the rules so he doesn't have to."

Von stared at her in stunned silence.

"What?"

Von shook his head. "You continue to amaze me, *Mira.*"

"It's the right thing to do. No one should have to deny themselves the chance for love or finding their Mate, just because they also serve. That cannot be what the Mother truly intends for her children."

"Perhaps not," Von agreed.

After a moment of silence where they watched the other couple dance, Helena added, "How hard can it be, really? I mean, I am the one in charge after all. Don't people have to do what I say?"

Von's laughter caused many curious stares to turn their way. "I love how you remember that whenever it's convenient, but you forget it when it truly matters."

Helena shrugged. "As long as everyone else remembers."

They grew silent again, the sounds of laughter and music swelling around them.

After a few heartbeats she spoke again. "It's a stupid rule, and stupid rules should be broken if they cannot be changed."

"As one who has broken every rule ever set in front of him, I must wholeheartedly agree."

"I knew I could count on you."

"Always." He reinforced the promise so that it echoed through their bond.

CHAPTER 14

It was still early, but Helena was already standing on the beach, the sound of the crashing waves and the echoing caw of gulls her only companions. When she'd awoken that morning, the salty tang of the sea was permeating her room, even though no windows had been open, and she'd felt the need to go down and become familiar with the element she'd be trying to control only a few hours later.

The wind still raged, although the Stormbringer's keep sheltered her from the worst of it. She hadn't gone far from the gates, just over to the small beach off of the main entrance. Most were still asleep, so she'd only had to endure a few curious glances, and one barely concealed yawn, as she'd made her way.

At the time, it'd seemed entirely reasonable to introduce herself to the sea but now that she was standing here she felt incredibly foolish. The problem was that she didn't know exactly what she was trying to do. She'd woken with a nameless need to be outside, and so she'd followed it. Now that she was here, she was at a bit of a loss.

She'd already given up trying to control her hair. Every time she'd tie it back the wind would pull it free so that it'd whip around her. As it was, she could barely keep the cloak she'd brought clasped about her shoulders. Helena removed her boots and walked further out on the soft sand until it became wet beneath her feet. It was chilly, but bearable. She forced herself to take the final two steps until the waves began lapping at her feet. She shivered but did not move away.

Yesterday, when they'd been greeted by the storm, and the man that controlled it, there was a sense of threat in the water and air. Not today. The way that the wind was teasing her felt curious and playful. She could feel none of Anduin in it; this was the Mother's magic, wild and free.

Closing her eyes, Helena opened herself up to the power surrounding her. She let her magic bubble up and flow out of her. The reaction was subtle but instantaneous. The wind whipped up, and the waves began to crash with increasing frequency. It was a greeting; the elements here recognized her.

In her own way, Helena recognized them as well. Even though she was standing in the Emerald Ocean, she could feel the icy current of the Mother's Tears. The river nearly bisected Elysia, flowing from Vyruul until it fed the ocean at the southern tip of Daejara. That wasn't the only reason why she recognized the feel of it though. When they'd traveled through Bael, the Mother's Tears had been her source of water for nourishment as well as bathing. She'd been immersed in this water once before.

Helena was feeling fanciful. She imagined that the water she'd drank months before had become a part of her, and that even now its residual energy lived within her. She laughed at her silliness and opened her eyes.

Her power was radiating out of her in glowing waves of energy. She was sure no one else who saw her would see what she could see and was glad for it. Helena caused enough of a stir as it was, no need to add to the gossip fodder. She watched as tendrils of the iridescent power swam through the water and spun through the air. Her power was weaving itself into the elements around them. Each individual strand pulsed in time to her heartbeat.

It was breathtaking.

As her magic moved through the elements, she could feel them accept her presence amongst them. The wind continued to play, twisting around her body and making the loose strands of her hair dance in the breeze. Tentatively, Helena used her power to push the wind out and away from her. Not forcefully; it was a tickle not a shove. She could feel the air around her shiver before it assented to her request and flowed away from her. The sea, in response to the air, grew still. Its churning waves died down until the water was placid and calm around her. There was a sense of expectation, as if they were waiting to see what she would do next. She felt for all the world as if she was playing hide and seek with children.

Not wanting to disappoint them, Helena answered the unspoken request. She called the air back to her, using it to form a massive ball. If not for the swirl of her power within it, she would have looked as if she was holding nothing. Pushing the air out toward the water, she added her energy and strength to the ball. Where the ball met the water, it pushed it aside, dividing the ocean and creating a little path for her to walk through. The water was not high here, perhaps only to her knees, but as she walked forward, she could see the ocean straining against the invisible barrier of air she used to reinforce the divide. Helena had the distinct impression the water was trembling with laughter, loving her antics.

With a startled laugh, she stepped back onto the beach and released her hold on the water and air, letting them return to their natural state. They wasted no time coming back to her, it was like a game of chase; they were not ready for her to leave. Helena laughed again, feeling the joy in the elements around her.

Any doubts she still had vanished, disappearing with the wind. Helena knew these elements and they knew her. More than that, they'd already recognized her authority. Whatever she had to ask of them today, they would grant her. They'd just proven it.

She was going to win.

IT WAS ONLY a couple hours later, but the playfulness from the morning was nowhere to be found. Helena stood on the dock she'd arrived at yesterday, although this time she stood alone. Anduin was also standing alone, although he was on a dock some hundred yards away from her. Before each of them, the maelstrom churned, its inky depths howling with fury.

The Circle and those that traveled with her stood beside the Storm Forged on the rocky cliffs a safe distance away. Apparently, it was just as dangerous to be an observer as a participant in Aegaeon's Challenge given how often a challenger would lose control of their storm.

As if he could feel her looking for him, Von called to her through the bond. *"Are you ready, Mira?"*

"As ready as I can be."

"He is a fool to underestimate you."

Helena considered his words before responding, *"I do not get the impression that he does."*

"What makes you say that?"

"The way he responded to Starshine, and the look in his eyes when we mentioned the prophecy. He wanted to discount it as childish stories, but I sensed the fear in him. I think it is desperation that makes him cling to his beliefs. He is afraid of the alternative."

"I'm not sure if that makes him smart or foolish."

Helena's answering laugh flowed through their bond. *"A man can be both wise and foolish, one does not preclude the other. It is hope for peace that makes him want to bury his head in the sand... or should I say sea?"*

"Both are sure ways to die," Von replied, his own amusement in the words.

"I think we just proved my point with our own silliness."

Growing serious Von said, *"Be careful, Mira. Anduin intends to fight to the death, he does not realize you will try to save him. A man that desperate to deny the truth will not go down easily."*

"I know."

"If you have need of me, I am here."

His words were a balm. Feeling him through the bond and knowing that he was close even if they were not touching, filled her with a sense of calm. She might be standing by herself, but she was not alone.

One of the Storm Forged's priests had briefed her on the challenge. He hadn't told her much more than she'd learned from Joquil the day before, but he'd let her know that the challenge would start once lightning cracked across the sky and would not stop until only one of them was still standing. Shivering, Helena turned her eyes upward, waiting for the sign that the challenge had begun.

She did not have to wait long. The crack of lightning flared bright, illuminating everything around them. As soon as the flash receded, the sky went dark; black clouds rolling in out of nowhere. The sea responded to the shift. The water surged, causing the dock to quake beneath her feet. *Anduin* she realized. He'd already begun and she was still standing here admiring the sky.

Her hair was flying wildly around her in the wind while icy rain pelted her from every direction, but she ignored it. Blocking out everything but the sea, Helena summoned her power as she had that morning. She distantly felt her body react as she released it but was solely focused on the shimmering tendrils that began to weave themselves into the air and sea.

From her place on the dock she could see down into the center of the maelstrom. She funneled her power toward it, feeling the slightest resistance before the water gave way, allowing her power to become part of the massive spiral. As it did, the glowing threads of her magic swirled down and into the center of the maelstrom. They crackled like electricity as the twisting fury of the water helped it gather strength.

While Helena was focused on the maelstrom and building her storm from its depths, Anduin had moved straight toward his cyclone. What had already been an impressive blend of wind and water was now a towering beast that had flashes of lightning shooting out of it. She could see him only peripherally, but his hands were outstretched above him, moving like he was shaping the spinning mass between them. She knew it was only a matter of time before he sent it straight toward her.

The wind and rain continued to beat at her, and she felt herself rocking like a tree in a storm as she withstood the attack. It was time to pull her own tempest from the maelstrom. She started to raise her arms, willing the water to follow. The maelstrom fought back, the intensity of its current unwilling to surrender to her will. Helena pushed more of her power into the churning water. There was a stutter in the spiraling water, as if her power had struck it like a blow, knocking it off course. It was all the opening she needed.

Helena pulled, her teeth baring down until she tasted blood. A twisting ball of water began to form in the center of the maelstrom, growing in strength and size very quickly. In order to overtake Anduin's, Helena knew that it would have to be so much more than an ordinary cyclone, so she continued to feed the storm. She used her power to pull more water from the eye of the maelstrom, while pushing the air to keep it spinning. It was only a matter of a few heartbeats before two cyclones spun on the horizon.

Anduin's storm was a deep pulsing black, the bright flickers of lightning making the water seem to glow the same color as his eyes. Helena's was a smoky gray, the water spinning so fast that its foam diluted the color of the water until it appeared almost entirely white. In size they were evenly matched, but Anduin's seemed deadlier as it began to shoot across the water straight toward her.

Helena threw her hand out, and her storm responded, lurching to intercept the attack. Her sparkling eyes flicked to where Anduin stood, and even with the distance between them she could make out the fierce smile on his face. He was enjoying himself.

Helena had to admit, so was she. Her heart was pounding within her, but the way her power merged with the intensity of the storm was like nothing she'd ever experienced. She felt wholly alive. There was raw power here, and an unmatched ferocity in the elements that was now pulsing through her. Under different circumstances, she might even say she was having fun.

That was when the dueling storms collided. Thunder roared, and the dock trembled but did not break. Helena lurched back, her body reeling from the impact. Anduin fared worse. He was thrown backwards, swept off his feet by the force. She was vibrating like the plucked string of an instrument, the tangle of wind, water and power becoming a tangible barrier pushing against her very fragile body.

Helena couldn't remember ever being quite this aware of her mortality before. Even with the full force of her power unleashed, giving her almost limitless strength, her human body was not immune to the power of the elements that surrounded her. If she lost control, they'd tear her apart.

As Anduin pushed to his feet, she watched his eyes blaze white-hot before his tower of black water flung itself into hers. What her cyclone lacked in speed, it more than made up for in strength. It didn't falter under the repeated blows.

Helena was starting to realize his strategy. He would continue to ram at her storm, and through it her power, weakening both to the point he could blast through and obliterate them. She would not survive the instantaneous loss of control. That kind of attack on her power would be the equivalent of a hammer shattering her mind, thereby severing her body's connection to her innermost self. It was a brilliant strategy, although utterly merciless.

Her initial reaction was to continue to reinforce the storm, but she wouldn't be able to keep that up indefinitely. Eventually Anduin would find a way through. Instead, Helena took a cue she'd learned from Anderson many years ago.

When she'd first learned how to ride a horse, Anderson had warned her that she would eventually fall off. In order to protect herself, he'd taught her that when that day came, she would need to become as limp as her rag doll, so that her body would absorb and not fight the impact. He said it could be the difference between whether or not she survived the fall.

Helena was about to test his theory with these storms. Instead of fighting against the attack, she would release a bit of her hold on it, allowing Anduin's to slip through. Once the storms were fully integrated she would tighten her hold again, trapping his storm within hers. To defeat him, she would then have to use her power to force his into submission. She just hoped he didn't sense the trap.

She would need to time this perfectly. He could not sense the change in resistance, until it was too late for him to pull back. Taking a deep breath, Helena began to pull small tendrils of power back into herself. By the time Anduin struck again, Helena's hold on the cyclone was quite loose and his storm blew a hole through hers.

Even from this distance she could hear the startled gasps and fierce cheers from the crowd. Anduin let out his own battle cry, sensing victory was within his grasp.

Helena waited for two long heartbeats, not wanting to move too quickly. Just as Anduin's storm had the power to destroy her, so too could her storm end him. But unlike Anduin, that was not her goal.

She needed to nullify his power. That was going to require her to absorb it completely. She would have to act fast, once he realized he was caged, he would throw everything he had at trying to escape her hold.

Helena took one last breath just as the second half of Anduin's storm made contact with the far edge of hers. She pumped every bit of power she still had back into the storm, strengthening it to the point that the water nearest to the cyclone began to push away, creating angry waves that moved toward the crowd.

"No!" Anduin screamed, finally realizing what Helena had done, but not ready to give up.

As she predicted, his power lashed out at her. Helena bore down, bearing the attack. Seeing the glowing blue ribbons of Anduin's power spiraling through the water, Helena pushed her own shining strands toward them, willing the power to merge. Where the threads of power touched, lightning sparked and booms of thunder split the sky. With what felt like a shudder, the strands combined, fusing into one glowing beam. Helena had taken full control of both storms.

Anduin dropped to his knees, defeated.

The violence of the storm threatened to overwhelm her, but Helena pushed the water back down into the sea. At the same time, she used the air to send the rain and clouds out and away from the cyclone so that they would stop feeding the storm. Both elements resisted at first, seeming to relish their dance across the ocean, but eventually, layers of the storm were stripped away, floating out across the sky or sliding back into the sea.

With shaking limbs, Helena began to draw her power back into herself, slowly releasing her hold on the cyclone entirely. When she was done, her cyclone, now much diminished in size, was left lazily spinning beside the maelstrom.

Anduin lifted his head, eyes glowing as he stared at her in awe. Helena shrugged sheepishly, before her knees buckled and she staggered. The euphoria she'd felt controlling the storm left along with her hold on it, and all she felt now was a bone-deep weariness.

She made to move toward the beach and the crowd, but her legs didn't want to carry her. They didn't have to. Von was already there, picking her up and spinning her around.

"You did it!"

The rest of her Circle was not far behind, whooping and laughing in celebration.

"Helena Stormbringer!" Darrin crowed, grinning at her.

With a shaky smile, Helena waved away their cheers before burying her face in Von's neck and closing her eyes. She had passed out before he made it off the dock.

CHAPTER 15

*H*elena stretched and rubbed a bit of sleep from her eyes. She'd slept through the night and well into the next day and now her body felt equal parts heavy and weak, almost like she'd spent the night drinking instead of sleeping.

Apparently, there are side effects to playing with storms, she thought with a grimace.

Swinging her feet over the side of the bed, she padded softly to the side table that held a cup of magic-heated tea and a neatly folded letter.

She eyed the note curiously but moved for the tea first. Wasn't Timmins always telling her that establishing priorities was an important part of ruling? Helena was certain tea constituted a priority. The warm liquid did much to ease the sluggishness she was feeling. She sent a thanks to Von for including the healing brew in the drink and lifted the heavy cream parchment.

It was addressed to "The Stormbringer."

"Hmm," she murmured, before taking another sip and setting her cup down.

She unfolded the note and scanned it quickly. The words were simple but formal.

Greetings Stormbringer,

I wish to speak with you at your first convenience. I am awaiting you in my study.

~ A

Helena ran a finger over the boldly penned words. The nib had been pressed down hard, leaving deep indents in the paper. She did not need magic to feel the conflict in his looping letters. This was not a man used to making requests, even writing one made him uncomfortable. Helena smirked at that; she had a habit of making strong men uncomfortable.

Not wanting to further delay their trip to the next tribe, Helena quickly finished her tea and got dressed in her traveling clothes. Von walked in just as she laced the last of her boots. Seeing the scrap of paper sitting on the table, he picked it up and scanned the contents.

"Want company?"

Helena shook her head, smiling at his annoyed expression. "Anduin poses no threat."

"Backup is never a bad idea."

"You just want to know what he has to say."

He shrugged, but his lips lifted in the ghost of a grin.

She made for the door. "I'm not the one that needs a babysitter. If you'd like to make yourself truly useful, go ensure the others are ready to leave as soon as I'm finished."

He grasped her arm as she moved past, tugging her back toward him.

At her questioning look he murmured, "You forgot something." He leaned over and pressed a kiss to her lips.

The kiss ended as quickly as it began, but even still Helena felt her insides turn to liquid. She blinked up at him a few times before stepping back. "What was I doing?"

Von laughed. "You're off to salvage what you can of a man's bruised ego."

"Is it Firesday already?" she deadpanned, indicating that such was a normal occurrence.

"Minx," he growled affectionately, before slapping her on the ass and sending her on her way.

She blew him a kiss over her shoulder and left the room. Helena strode toward the central hall, keeping an eye out for one of the Storm Forged. Since she had not received any sort of tour, Helena had absolutely no clue where Anduin's study was located. She was hoping to run into someone that wouldn't mind pointing her in the right direction.

The lack of people about was surprising. Yesterday, the keep had been a flurry of activity, but today it was a ghost town. The silence was unnerving. After fifteen minutes of wandering aimlessly, Helena finally spotted a turquoise-haired woman.

"Excuse me!" Helena called. "Hey!" she shouted in exasperation when the woman pretended to ignore her and continued to scurry down the hall. Helena had wasted enough time; she wasn't about to miss this opportunity. Silently apologizing for what she was about to do, Helena summoned a wall of Air directly in the woman's path.

The woman bounced off it with a startled cry, providing Helena with just enough time to catch up to her. She spun around ready to launch into a verbal attack but realized it was Helena and quickly cast her eyes down.

Summoning her sweetest voice, Helena said, "Sorry for that, I was just hoping you'd be so kind as to give me directions to Anduin's study. He's waiting for me, and I don't want to keep him."

The woman refused to meet her eyes and rubbed her nose before pointing back down the hallway they'd just traveled. "Take a right and follow it all the way down." She didn't even wait for a response before she scurried off.

Helena watched her retreating back before shaking her head and walking away. *What is with everyone today?*

She moved quickly down the arched halls and knew she'd reached the Stormbringer's room when she saw the stunning relief carved into the door. It was a seascape, with men and women brilliantly disguised within the shapes of the rolling waves, almost as if they were made from the water. Wishing she had more time to study the beautiful scene, she allowed herself only a moment to run her fingers over the shape of one woman whose hair curled into tufts of wind. At her touch the image came to life. The tangy scent of the sea and the roar of waves greeted her. She would have sworn she could hear laughter, but the door swung open pulling her attention away from the scene and toward the man standing in the doorway.

Anduin's glowing eyes flashed as he took in the sight of her. "Stormbringer."

Helena just barely resisted the urge to laugh; the sound of the title on his lips was forced and sullen.

"I have no wish for another title, Anduin. These are your people, more so than they will ever be mine."

His eyes widened in surprise, but he remained silent.

"I only want what I asked for: assistance. Those were the terms of our bargain."

"Even so, Kiri, that is not the way of the Storm Forged. You won the challenge, the title is rightfully yours."

Helena rolled her eyes, tired of jumping through political hoops. "Fine, then as your rightful leader, I am telling you that the Storm Forged will be assisting the Chosen in this battle."

Anduin's lips flattened, but he inclined his head. "As you wish."

She sighed. "Anduin. Look at me."

He met her gaze.

"We cannot defeat Rowena without your help. Her victory will be the end of us all. If you would like the Storm Forged to be able to continue on with their way of life, this is the only way."

Fear and anger raged in his eyes like a storm about to break. "She wouldn't dare threaten the Storm Forged."

Laying a gentle hand on his arm Helena replied, "She already has. Will you let her threat go unanswered?"

Anduin straightened his shoulders, pride making him stand tall. "Never."

Helena nodded. "So it's settled. The Storm Forged will ally themselves with the Chosen. Not just because of our bargain, but because they are defending their home and way of life."

She could feel the reaction her words caused. Anduin's answering smile was not forced.

"I have others I need to meet, but I will send word once we're ready."

As she made to leave, Anduin called her name. "Helena."

She glanced over her shoulder, startled only because it was the first time he'd refrained from using a title. "Yes?"

"What happens after?"

Her brows furrowed. "After what?"

"After we defeat her."

The confusion cleared. Anduin wanted to know what would happen to the Storm Forged, or more specifically, to him. She gave him a wide smile. "I already told you. I do not want your title. I have my hands full with one realm as it is; I have no need of another. The Ebon Isle is yours, Anduin."

She watched his shoulders rise as he took a deep breath. When he let it out, it was as if a massive weight had fallen away. He gave her a grateful smile. "Thank you, Kiri."

With a wink she called, "Until next time, Stormbringer."

HELENA WASN'T sure where the others had gone off to but she should have known better than to worry. It would have been impossible to miss the crowd of people and creatures milling about near the docks. Starshine's white fur would have been enough of a beacon on its own. Feeling her mistress, Starshine let out a roar of greeting. Those nearest to the Talyrian jumped, not yet seeing Helena in the distance.

Seeing Starshine made Helena yearn to feel the wind in her hair. Unable to fly, Helena took the only option available to her and set off at a run.

"I think we've caused enough chaos here for the time being."

Darrin turned toward her as she closed the distance between them. "These days you seem to bring chaos with you wherever you go."

Helena frowned. "Not true."

He raised a brow. "It is most definitely true."

"You seem to have forgotten that I'm not a six-year-old girl any longer. I'm strong enough that I can kick your ass, with my fists or with my magic. Do you require a demonstration?"

Titters of laughter met Ronan's murmured, "I can vouch for that."

Darrin tutted. "My my my, aren't you quick to threaten violence these days. How quickly a minor victory goes to your head."

Helena sputtered, ready to defend her honor but Von wrapped an arm around her waist, whispering, "Ignore him."

The urge to stick her tongue out at Darrin was strong. She turned from him instead. "Gladly."

Darrin laughed at her, and Helena was just about to zap him with a little lightning when Timmins drawled, "If you two are quite done…"

"He started it," she muttered defensively, feeling chastised even though she hadn't actually done anything.

"Of course he did," Timmins agreed, making the others laugh.

Joquil stepped forward, and Miranda handed him one of the unused Kaelpas stones. His warm amber eyes met hers. "Are you ready to go, Kiri?"

"Are you?"

It was a loaded question. This would be the first time he'd return to his childhood home in almost thirty years. Who knew what, or who, would be waiting for him.

Joquil nodded, "As much as I can be."

The Circle moved in close, getting into position. Helena looked around, partially to ensure that everyone was accounted for, but also to get one final look at her cyclone which was spinning just off the horizon. She was leaving the Ebon Isle in capable hands, but a part of her would remain behind to stand guard.

"Then let's—"

Before she could finish, the familiar feeling of being turned inside out was upon her. When she was able to open her eyes again they were surrounded by a new kind of sea.

"Welcome to the Forest of Whispers, Kiri."

CHAPTER 16

The forest was both beautiful and ancient. Everywhere Helena looked, she was surrounded by life. Trees towered above them, all but obscuring the sky. Their trunks were as wide as three or four grown men standing shoulder-to-shoulder. She ran a hand along the rough edges of bark, feeling a spark of energy in response to the touch.

Helena opened her mouth to ask Joquil where exactly they were, but the hiss of a blade being drawn had her on full alert. Between one heartbeat and the next, she'd shielded the group and called her power; it hummed beneath her skin ready to be unleashed.

"What—" Effie started, but Helena shook her head and held a finger to her lips. The rest of the group were more attuned to battle and didn't need to ask. They had already slipped into position around her, drawing weapons and summoning their power.

"If they wanted you dead, they would not have let you hear them," Joquil murmured. "That was a warning."

"Friendly folks, are they? Is this how they welcome all visitors?" Helena asked neutrally, eyes still scanning the woods for a sign of where someone might be hiding.

Starshine crouched and began to growl, her bared teeth glistening in the dim sunlight.

"Easy girl," Helena cautioned.

The Daejaran pack took up Starshine's call, angry snarls filling the silence.

Memories of the last time Starshine and she walked in the woods came to mind. Apparently, Ronan also recalled the caebris attack, because when she hazarded a glance at him, his steady ice-blue eyes were locked onto her. She wasn't certain if the look was supposed to be a warning, or if he was checking to make sure she remembered that some beasts were adept at hiding in plain sight. Either way, the result was the same. They were on the lookout for something their eyes could not see. He gave her a slow nod and they both went back to searching for the threat the animals could already sense.

Helena loosened her hold on her power, her senses coming alive with the added magic. The trees were pulsing with magic of their own, which would explain the energy she felt when she touched them, but so far nothing else was revealed.

A blade was flung from above. Helena would have missed it until it smacked into the shield, if not for her magic-enhanced vision. She used air to push the dagger off course, causing it to bury itself in the ground just beside her.

"You say you're visitors and yet you've arrived with an army." The female voice also came to them from above.

"We do not mean you any harm," Helena shouted.

"I have no reason to trust you."

Helena wanted to point out that neither did they, especially given that they were not the ones throwing knives. Leaving her shield up, Helena released her power and motioned for the others to do the same.

Her friends scowled, not appreciating the request, but knowing better than to undermine it. Their weapons were just tools anyway. Helena knew that if they truly needed to defend themselves, any of the men and women around her would be able to wield their magic with deadly precision. And for those that did not have magic, they would need only seconds to attack. The ones with magic would buy them that time. All in all, the move was more of a show than anything.

"No one invited you," a second voice hissed.

Helena tilted her head up, only barely able to make out the hazy edges of a woman perched high in the tree nearest to her.

"Intruders," another voice cried. Others took up the cry and soon the forest was filled with jeering calls.

"Do not listen to their lies!"

"Slit their throats before they take another step."

Helena bristled at the menace she heard in the voices. Lifting a brow, she glanced at Joquil. His face was puzzled, as if this greeting was unexpected to him as well.

"We've had others visit recently. They too showed up without invitation. We do not care to repeat the experience," the first voice said.

There was a barely audible oomph to her right. Helena twisted in time to see Von's elbow lowering and Joquil giving him a narrow-eyed glare.

"Was that necessary?"

"What's the point in having a native as your guide if they aren't going to establish safe entry?"

It was a fair question. Von turned his smoky stare back toward Joquil who nervously cleared his throat before calling out, "I am one of you! My father is Demond Mascura of the Mascura tribe."

"More lies," the second voice hissed.

"Demond has no son," the first voice countered.

"Not anymore, perhaps. His son Joquil was taken from him by a Keeper twenty-eight years ago in order to fulfill his destiny. I have returned."

"A likely story."

"He speaks the truth," Miranda said.

"Why come back now?" The voice was cautious, as if it wasn't sure why it was asking the question but could not help but ask it anyway.

"We have need of the Night Stalkers' expertise to defeat an enemy that threatens all of Elysia."

"Pretty words, but the Night Stalkers are not for sale."

"That's not what I heard," Darrin muttered.

"Mother's tits, Darrin! Could you not keep your damned mouth shut for once?" Helena snapped with exasperation.

The others, even Effie, glared at him. Darrin colored, but did not respond.

Wind whipped through the trees making the leaves rattle like thousands of whispers. One-by-one they somersaulted gracefully from the sky, cloaked in shadows like falling clouds. As they rose from the ground, they took shape, releasing the hold on their camouflage. Helena's people were surrounded.

The woman closest to Helena appeared to be the leader. Her mass of black hair was a tangle of curls and braids. She had swirls of black paint obscuring most of her face. It only made her leaf-green eyes stand out in harsh relief. Her body was covered in leather and weapons, but Helena had the impression they were only window dressing. She was the true weapon. Helena felt a kind of kinship with her in that moment because so was she.

"You are not a daughter of the Forest," the woman commented, studying Helena in kind.

"I am the Mother's daughter," she replied.

"One of the Chosen," a voice from behind her spat.

"The Duskfall tribe is dead because of *their* kind!" another voice shouted.

Helena went still at that. *"What does she mean?"*

Von was slow to respond. *"I'm not sure, but I am getting the impression that someone may have beaten us here."*

"Rowena." Helena's disgust for the woman filled the word.

Von dipped his chin in agreement but did not take his eyes off a man spinning twin daggers in his hands. They glowed a sickly green that could only mean one thing: poison.

"The Kiri and her people have not harmed, nor do they have any reason to harm, any of the Forest tribes," Miranda said, holding up her hands as she took a tentative step toward Helena.

"And yet they call us the Forsaken. Those forgotten by the rest of Elysia, left to fend for themselves." The people encircling them shifted warily, their weapons visibly leveled on each of the Chosen.

"I would not be here if I thought that way," Helena countered.

"It is true!" Nial spoke up, startling both Helena and Von. "The Kiri has already lifted the ban on my people. She seeks to unite Elysia, not continue to divide it."

"We have come to seek your help," Timmins added.

"What could the Mother's spoiled children want from us?" For all that the words were an insult, they were truly curious.

"It is as he said. We are here to ask for your help. I believe we share a common enemy."

Helena spoke calmly. These people were looking for any reason to attack; they had probably intended to attack first but had been surprised by Joquil's revelation. Helena had no doubt he was the only reason the Night Stalkers had stayed their hands.

"We have nothing in common," the man standing before Von said, twisting and spitting at his feet.

Von grinned, malice and danger rolling off him in waves. "Do that again."

Ronan and Serena stepped forward, their expressions each holding the promise of violence.

The man glowered, his black paint smeared down the better part of his face and giving the impression he was still cloaked in darkness.

"Ryder, enough," their leader said. The man bit off a curse but stepped back.

"Not the time," Helena told Von. She felt his desire to return the man's insult, but he remained quiet.

"Reyna, this woman arrives unannounced and with an army at her back, mere days after the attack on Duskfall, and yet you let her live?" The question came from behind them.

"I think I know who may have attacked your people. If you were to take us to the site, I would be able to confirm it." Helena's words caused the others to go still.

"It is a tainted, unholy place. We will not go back there," Reyna said in a cold, hard voice.

"I can help with that, as well," Helena offered.

There were murmurs as her words were repeated through the crowd.

Reyna tilted her head, staring at Helena as she considered the offer. "You can help the spirits find peace?"

"I can try."

Silence greeted her response. After another long, measured look, Reyna said, "Very well, let us see what you can do. Ryder, stay here and stand guard with your men. The rest of you, with me."

Ryder looked like he wanted to protest, but only grunted his assent before calling swirling shadows around his body and disappearing back into the trees. A handful of men followed suit, each one seamlessly blending into the shadows of the forest.

Helena found herself wondering how the Night Stalkers were able to do that, and if she would also be able to cloak herself that way.

"Jealous?" Von asked, catching the trail of her thoughts.

Helena smiled. *"Maybe just a little."*

Von's expression didn't change, but she could feel his amusement. *"All that power and yet you still want more."*

"What? It's a useful trick."

"Coming?" Reyna asked, already a good distance away.

Helena nodded and quickly caught up while Von's silent laughter and the others followed close behind her.

SOMETHING WAS DEFINITELY WRONG HERE. Given the animals' whines, they were clearly in agreement with her assessment. They'd been walking for a few hours and with each step the sounds of the forest grew quieter. The air felt thick and oppressive, and Helena's senses were screaming for her to run back in the other direction. She'd even looked up, multiple times, to check and see if the sun had disappeared, but it was still there.

"Do you feel that?" she asked.

"Aye."

The strained tone of Von's voice had Helena pausing to look at him. There was something wild about the look in his eyes, his nostrils flaring as if he could smell something in the air. Helena sniffed delicately, trying to see if she could sense anything, but all she detected was the rich scent of pine. That wasn't to say there wasn't anything there. Von had told her once that the reason he'd been able to defeat so many enemies was that he could sense and counter their magic before they even realized he was upon them. He'd never been a fan of what he could not see or touch, but it'd never stopped him from using it to his advantage.

"What's wrong?"

Von shook his head. *"I'm not sure, but it feels familiar. I would bet my life that we've felt this magic before."*

"If it's Rowena that should not be a surprise."

He hesitated, considering. *"It does not feel like Rowena. Her corruption grates at my senses, and even though I can feel the wrongness in the land, this is different. It feels more sinister. As if death itself is here."*

Helena shuddered.

Reyna halted a few steps ahead of them, her face grim. "This is what remains of the Duskfall village."

Helena glanced around, still seeing only trees. Joquil brushed shaking fingers against her arm, before mutely pointing up. Helena tilted her head back, gasping at the village hidden in the treetops. There was an entire city spanned in the trees above them. At least, there had been.

Huge circular houses were interconnected by spiraling stairways and roped bridges. The wooden structures looked almost untouched in places, and completely demolished in others. It almost made it worse, to see the beauty of what once was beside the horror of what was left.

Parts of the houses were still smoking, as if the fire had only just gone out. Huge holes allowed her to peer into the skeletons of the houses. It was heartbreaking to see the evidence of life; like the soft pink of a child's blanket abandoned beside a half-torn doll. There had been happiness here, but now all she could feel was the joy someone had taken in destroying it. For that was what Helena felt as she looked at the charred remains: joy in destruction and pleasure in others' pain. Rowena had definitely been here.

"Where are the bodies?" she asked in a hollow voice. Because of course there would be bodies, there was always a row of corpses to greet them when they'd come across a village Rowena's Shadows had destroyed.

"There are none."

Heads spun toward Reyna in surprise.

"What do you mean?" Von asked.

"No bodies and no survivors. The Duskfall tribe is gone."

"But you mentioned spirits," Timmins said, horror at her words bleaching the color from his skin.

Reyna closed her eyes, as if pained. "Can you not feel the death here? Just because there were no bodies, does not mean there was no death or suffering. The agony of it still haunts this place."

Helena's blood went cold. If what Reyna said was true, then Rowena had come in and turned an entire village into more of her creatures. Those that had died had probably been the village's defenders, the strongest of the men and women. Once the rest of the tribe, likely elders and children, had come face-to-face with the abominations and seen what they were capable of, it would not have taken long for Rowena to convince them that joining her would be a better option. The Duskfall tribe could not have known what they agreed to, or they would have chosen death.

She swallowed back her revulsion, her own eyes falling closed as the ghost of screams met her ears. This place was indeed haunted. But it was not just the people that had suffered. The trees they'd lived in and drawn power from still held an imprint of the attack. It was a wound that could not heal, not while the forest still held onto all of the pain and fear.

It was too much, she couldn't stand it one second longer. Without a word, Helena let her magic free. She felt it flow out of her and over the land. Pushing it out until it wrapped around each tree branch and all that was left of the village. Then, like a sponge, she began to absorb the corruption into the web created by her magic. Even with her eyes closed, she could see the oily black remains of the power used here, the power that still infected the land. Helena trembled as her power came into contact with the worst of the tainted essence, but she did not stop.

Where the corruption did not want to let go, she demanded. When it tried to get around her tendrils of magic, she snared it and pulled it out anyway. She coaxed. She tricked. She was relentless.

By the time she was done drawing the last of it out, Helena was shaky and sweating. She was also left with a problem. Helena could not simply release her hold on this kind of toxic power; it still had the potential to destroy. She would have to nullify it completely, but the only way to do that was to purify it with her own. That would require her to lower her innermost shields and let the heart of her power come into contact with the writhing mass of corruption.

"Helena, no," Von demanded, completely in tune with her thoughts.

"It's the only way," she replied, her voice spectral and echoing throughout the forest.

"It's too dangerous," he insisted aloud, for the benefit of the others.

Ignoring him, Helena lowered her inner barriers, pushing her essence out. The corrupted echo of power she still held onto shrieked and tried to pull away from the light that was radiating out of her body. Helena held firm. Her power slammed into the mass. Everywhere it made contact, the corruption shrank and recoiled, until all that was left was a speck of darkness that finally winked out.

When Helena opened her eyes, they still glowed with her power. The village was still destroyed, a testament to the people that had lived there, but the land had been healed. It was at peace. But she was not finished yet. There was still one last thing she must do. Helena opened her hands, revealing a small pile of glittering dust in her palms.

There were gasps as the others realized what she held. Not only had she pulled out the corruption, she'd also gathered the souls of those that had died. Helena blew softly, the soul dust blowing up and away from her like a sparkling cloud. It flew high, up and over the trees until it made contact with the sky. The sky flared brightly where it came into contact with the motes, and instead of the light fading completely, a star twinkled in its wake.

"May the spirits of the fallen watch over and guide your people," Helena said in the harmonious voice of her power.

Reyna and the Night Stalkers were on their knees, mouths gaping in awe. Reyna's eyes were wet with tears, smearing the black whirls on her skin. "Th-thank you, Kiri. Whatever you need, the people of the Forest are yours."

The Chosen had remained standing, and yet their expressions were no less awestruck. Feeling raw and over-exposed, Helena walked away from the others, needing time to find her way back to herself.

Von followed. She could feel him at her back, quietly trailing her as she headed deeper into the forest. When she could carry herself no further, her knees buckled and she fell to the floor. She gagged, her body heaving as it purged the remnants of the contaminated magic. For all that she'd destroyed it, some of its taint had still been absorbed into her body and now her magic was forcing it out.

Helena sat back on her heels, a shaking hand wiping at her mouth. Von rubbed her back and brushed a warm hand over her clammy skin.

"Are you all right?" he asked gruffly.

Helena shrugged. There were no words to explain what it had felt like to come into contact with that much corruption. No words to tell him how much it had hurt, both physically and emotionally, or about the bruises that it had left on her heart. Nor could she express what it had been like to hold the fragments of those tortured souls in the palm of her hand. It was beautiful. It was horrifying. It was more than any one person should bear.

She looked up at him with pleading aqua eyes. Nameless emotions swam in his own as he looked at her, assessing the damage and all that she could not say. In silence he wrapped his arms around her, holding her trembling body tight against his own. Von used his strength to provide the comfort his words could not. He held her until she felt strong enough to stand. And then, together, they returned to the others.

CHAPTER 17

Helena did not recall much about the walk back to Reyna's village. Like Duskfall, it too was practically a city hidden in the trees. For their quadruped companions, who didn't think much about such things, there were a series of nearby dens where they could make themselves comfortable. Starshine, as usual, took to the sky to find her own sleeping arrangements.

In order to get access to the treetop village of Penumbra, Reyna pressed on a nondescript knot of wood causing golden light to spill forth as a hidden door fell open. Just beyond the door a staircase spiraled up and into the massive trunk of the tree. From what Helena had gathered, it was not the sole means of entrance to the city, but all others were known only to those that called it home.

Once they'd returned to the village, the runners were able to use the Kaelpas stones to bring the remainder of their people from the Ebon Isle to the Forest of Whispers. To say they were worried would have been an understatement. Unfortunately, there hadn't been an opportunity to send anyone back before then, especially in the midst of a potential ambush.

Before she'd wandered off, Reyna had mentioned that dinner would be served in something they affectionately referred to as the crow's nest. It was a communal structure located in the middle of

Penumbra where all the villagers took their meals. As it was the only building that was enclosed by windows on all sides, providing a fully panoramic view of the forest, Reyna said they'd have no trouble finding their way when the bell rang.

There was not much in the way of additional space, at least not for housing forty unexpected people, so Helena found herself sharing rather cramped quarters with Von, Ronan, Darrin, Nial, Serena, and Effie. How the seven of them managed to end up together, Helena could only guess. Perhaps it was the similarity in their ages, or the tangle of shared relationships and history among them. More likely, it was the Mother having a bit of a joke at their expense. While there was no outward hostility amongst any of them, there was an undeniable underlying tension.

Ronan had it the worst. He'd handled Serena and Nial's budding relationship with more grace than she ever would have expected from one who'd shared that kind of intimacy with her. There was no doubt that he certainly handled it better than she would have. The image of Von from her trial, thrusting into another woman while grinning wickedly up at her, was still one she could not manage to unsee, at least not completely. The thought alone was enough to set her blood boiling with jealous anger. How Ronan could manage to stay pleasant around his ex-lover and her new one eluded Helena. But while he was tolerant, it didn't mean he cared to be slapped in the face with their relationship more than was absolutely necessary. Some heartaches were not easily mended, and there was only so much his pride could stand. He'd taken one look at Serena and Nial setting up their joint bedroll and dropped his pack on the floor with a muttered, "I'll be back later."

Shortly thereafter, Effie and Serena had wandered off looking for a place to clean up. Still unsettled from the day's events, Von had wanted to explore their surroundings and establish a watch rotation. Nial had gone with him, still enjoying the freedom his newly healed legs granted, which left Darrin and Helena alone for the first time in weeks.

Helena was slowly unpacking what she needed for the evening when Darrin sat down beside her.

"I'm sorry," he groaned, scrubbing his hands over his face. At the raise of her eyebrow, he elaborated, "For earlier. With my comments. You know how I get…"

Helena sighed. That she did. Darrin's mouth ran without the consent of his brain more often than not. It always had. All things considered, his muttered comment was a non-event, but it could have been the difference between an alliance and an attack. For that reason, she could not simply let it go.

Her voice was weary when she spoke, "There is so much at stake, Darrin. We cannot risk offending potential allies because of hearsay. Where did you even hear such rumors about the Night Stalkers anyway?"

Darrin shrugged uncomfortably, his eyes not meeting hers as he answered, "You know how gossip is. A soldier knows a guy, who knows a guy, who met a Night Stalker once…"

Helena's stare was weighted, but she did not chastise him further. She was not his mother, for all that he still acted like a child.

"Can you at least try to keep your comments to yourself? If only when we are around any that aren't part of the Circle? I value your opinions—" Darrin opened his mouth as if he would disagree, but Helena spoke over him, "even when you see fit to constantly contradict and undermine me. I know that your concern for me stems from love."

His green eyes were warm as he smiled wryly. "It does."

"As does mine," Helena said, squeezing his arm before returning to unpacking.

Darrin took a deep breath. "I know, Hellion. That has never changed."

They shared a smile, their years of friendship apparent in the knowing gazes. It was because of that friendship she broached the other subject between them. "So, when are you going to tell a certain blonde about your feelings for her?"

Darrin went crimson. He protested immediately, sputtering, "There is no blonde. That is, I have no feelings one way or the other about any woman. I took a vow!"

Helena rolled her eyes. "Don't forget who you're talking to, Shield.

I can feel the lie through the Jaka." She scratched at her side where her tattoo faintly buzzed to prove the point. "Not to mention one need only look at you to see it on your face. You are falling for her."

It was not a question.

Darrin's shoulders slumped. "I have tried to fight it. I know that nothing will come of it." He looked so hopeless that her heart ached.

"What if it could?"

His eyes shot to hers. "What are you saying?"

Helena shrugged. "I'm just asking what it would mean to you if you could act on your feelings."

"I have no wish to leave the Circle!" he said with panic.

"Who said anything about that?" she asked, genuinely confused.

"But there is no other way…" he trailed off.

She smirked at him, the impish girl she'd once been evident in the expression. "What's the point of being in charge if you cannot make your own rules?" The question was an echo of one she'd already posed to Von.

Darrin's grin grew as her meaning became clear. "Are you saying—"

"Do not lose hope."

He jumped up, lifting her in his arms and spinning her around. "Hellion… you do not know how happy you've just made me."

She laughed, a pure joyous sound. He set her down, a hand on each of her shoulders. "Helena, truly. Thank you. Just the chance to have something real with her… it is more than I dared hope for."

His hands moved to her cheeks and he pressed a happy, smacking kiss to her forehead before clambering for the door. "I have a need to get clean all of a sudden!" he called.

"But not before you get dirty," she said under her breath, unable to resist.

Popping his head back through the door, he asked: "Did you say something?"

"No!" she lied, smiling brightly.

With a cheery wave, he was off.

Helena had barely retied her pack when Ronan walked back in.

Glancing around he asked, "Where'd everyone go?"

Helena filled him in quickly as she settled on her bedroll and contemplated taking a short nap before dinner. So much had happened in the span of a few days that the extra sleep felt almost like a luxury.

Ronan sat down in a leather armchair, his elbows resting on his knees. He looked around the room, visibly flinching when his eyes found the area Serena and Nial had claimed.

"How are you holding up?" she asked.

His icy eyes moved back to hers and she was struck by how handsome he was. Helena had always thought Ronan was good-looking in a rugged, could probably kill you with his bare hands, kind of way. But without the scar marring the perfect symmetry of his face, Helena could see that he was actually devastatingly handsome. For her part, she greatly preferred inky hair and smoldering silver eyes but that didn't mean she couldn't appreciate his masculine beauty.

The question made his brows dip. "Is it obvious?"

Helena shook her head. "No. Not to the others. You do a good job of hiding it."

He raked a hand through his hair, tugging at the braided strands. Then, like water bursting through a dam, words poured out of him on a tortured groan, "I know she is his, but a part of me cannot help but look at her and think '*mine.*'"

"I know what it is like to lose the one your soul has claimed."

They shared a look only those who were intimately familiar with heartache would recognize.

Her own experience aside, Helena still didn't need to imagine the kind of emotional hell Ronan was going through. Now that her power was continuing to evolve and grow with Von back, she could actually feel snippets of what those connected to her through her Jaka were feeling. It was how she knew Darrin was trying to lie to her. The Jaka granted a sense of knowing or intuition that was often accompanied by a slight burn or tingle beneath her skin. The awareness was nothing like what she shared with Von, as it was only the barest hint of emotion or thought, but it was enough.

Ronan hung his head. "That's the twist isn't it? It's not my soul, but my heart. The damned fool does not want to admit defeat, even though it knows the truth."

"That is the way of hope."

"If what I've been feeling is even a hint of what you went through while he was gone… you're a damned sight stronger than anyone ever gave you credit for."

Helena laughed in surprise. "The last thing I ever felt was strong. Most days I could hardly recognize myself as broken as I felt, but I had friends that did not allow me to break completely. They held me together when it felt like nothing could."

Sad blue eyes met hers, forcing her to admit, "I would not have made it without you pushing me forward."

He smiled at that. "It is no less than you would do for me."

"And here we are." They chuckled.

As the laughter faded, he said, "It gets easier as the days pass. Sometimes it just sneaks up on me. A look or gesture and it's as if nothing has changed, and then I remember." His eyes shuttered and he pulled his emotions back inside, the warrior once more. "Anyway, it will pass." He slapped his hands on his knees, pushing himself out of the chair.

Helena knew better than to mention that there would be another. For one who had loved as wholly as Ronan, it was very likely there never would be. Unless he was lucky enough to find his mate, as Serena had. She would not give him empty platitudes. They were too close for that.

"You once told me that she was your strength, but that is not true, Ronan. Your true strength is in your ability to love and your loyalty to those who are fortunate enough to earn it. Serena was lucky enough to experience both. You loved her so much, you wanted nothing but her happiness. It was why you were able to let her go. It may never feel that way, but you are a better man because of it."

Ronan had already turned away from her, and his body hunched at her words as if they had inflicted a wound but also cradled him. He looked back at her over her shoulder, a sheen in his eyes.

For Ronan, she would pretend that she did not notice the streak of wetness down his smooth cheek. Helena's hand was braced over her Jaka, a silent reminder that she did not forget what his symbol meant, or how its presence there would always connect them.

When he smiled at her, it was a beautifully broken thing. "One lesson I have learned from your Mate, is that a warrior never knows if his next battle will be the last. Life is a gift from the Mother. I will not begrudge anyone their right to happiness during the handful of days the Mother grants them."

"You have a poet's soul, Ronan."

He gave her a disgusted look. "You're lucky no one heard you say such a hateful thing." Then he winked.

Helena sighed and shook her head. She closed her eyes, thanking the Mother for sending her a wonderful friend like Ronan, and asking her to please heal his broken heart. Before she could make good on her wish for a nap there was a light tapping on the door.

Serena strode in with an apologetic smile.

Helena sat up and just stared at the door with an incredulous expression. "Is there a queue out there or something?"

Serena blinked in confusion. "What?"

Helena pointed. "Out there, are people lined up waiting their turn to speak to me? Is there a sign on the wall saying I'm giving out free advice? I only ask because the timing today has been impeccable. It's as if you all planned this."

Serena threw her head back and laughed. "I suppose it could certainly seem that way. Alas, I am merely here to summon you to dinner."

"I didn't hear a bell."

"The mysterious one," Serena paused and made a gesture with her hand to indicate the swirling make-up of the Night Stalkers' leader.

"Reyna?" Helena asked.

"Sure."

Helena snorted. "Aren't you supposed to be observant? I seem to remember something about attention to detail being a highly valued skill for mercenaries and warriors alike."

Serena shrugged. "I forgot a name, bite me. You figured out who I was talking about through my reference to said details."

"Because wiggling fingers in front of your face is a clear detail. I think that speaks more to my skills at deduction than your description."

Unimpressed with Helena's logic, Serena's violet eyes narrowed and she continued, "Anyway, as I was saying. *Reyna* ran into Effie and me on our way back. She let us know food was already being set out. She also said it doesn't last long and we might want to hustle if we prefer our food hot."

With a groan, Helena pushed herself off the bedroll and into a standing position. "Lead the way," she sighed with resignation. Looks like she wouldn't be getting a nap after all.

"Are you sure you trust me to get us there? I may have forgotten some key details and may lead you straight off a bridge."

"If that's the case then you're the one that will have to explain what happened to Von and Ronan. As the ones that trained you, I can't see them reacting very well to the attempted murder of their favorite female."

"Pfft. You sure think highly of yourself. I've known them years longer than you."

"Yes, but they like me better."

The women laughed, their teasing a welcome respite from the intensity of the day.

"Are you feeling a bit better?" Serena asked seriously, weaving her arm through Helena's.

"A bit, although I don't think any of us will rest easy until this is over."

The blonde woman nodded as she said, "That is always the way of war. And yet somehow, we will still sleep, and dream, and live."

Helena smiled, her cheeks flushing as she thought back to Von and their stolen moments together. "Yes, even in times of war, we must also find time to live."

Giving Helena an appraising look, Serena whistled. "From the way you say live, I gather you mean fu—"

"Shhhhh," Helena interjected, slapping a hand over her friend's mouth as the curious gaze of one of the Night Stalkers passed over them. Once they were clear of the man, Helena dropped her hand and added under her breath, "You weren't wrong."

Serena blinked comically and after a moment of surprised silence let out a bark of laughter. The two women walked into the crow's nest laughing hysterically, no longer caring who was looking at them.

THE CROW'S nest was loud, and by loud Helena did not mean just a little noisy. It was positively deafening. Something about a group of people who prided themselves on moving about undetected being responsible for this kind of racket amused Helena greatly. But her smile began to waver as she realized it was because the Night Stalkers felt safe here. Even after what had happened in Duskfall, these people felt untouchable. If she'd learned only one thing in the past year it was that nowhere was truly safe. Not with Rowena and her ghastly minions intent on wreaking havoc.

Von's warm hand curled around hers beneath the table. It was a small gesture but helped anchor her back to the present. She gave him a thankful smile and pushed her plate away. For the most part the meal had been uneventful, but the food was good and the mood relaxed. Actually, maybe not completely relaxed. There was a sense of anticipation buzzing throughout the room, the voices holding an expectant edge. Every now and then she'd catch a sidelong glance from someone who had heard what she'd done in Duskfall. Who was she kidding, everyone in the room knew what had happened.

There was no scraping of the chair against the floor to signal that Reyna was about to stand, but Helena didn't need a signal to realize something was about to happen. The room fell silent instantly. The immediate shift in sound made her head feel as if it was suddenly filled with cotton. She had the urge to clap her hands, or drop something on the floor, anything to prove that her ears still functioned.

Kragen's eyes met hers from across the table. After a cursory glance he lifted his brows as though asking if she needed something.

Her expression must have broadcasted her absurd thoughts. Bemused, Helena shook her head, returning her attention to Reyna.

"For centuries the Night Stalkers have called the Forest of Whispers home. There are few among us that have ever left the beauty of the Forest, fewer still that leave never to return."

The hush in the room was absolute. Everyone was focused on Reyna as she continued, "Our people are born from the first shadows of nightfall. From the time we can walk, we already know how to wrap ourselves in a cloak of darkness to conceal us from our enemies. Our greatest gift is our ability to move through the trees, remaining unseen and unheard until it is time to strike. Many call us assassins because of the secretive nature of our work. What they do not realize is that we are the guardians; the protectors of the Forest and her secrets."

There were a few cheers and Reyna's lips lifted in the slightest semblance of a smile. "In order for us to fulfill our duty, the time has come for us to leave our home. It must be done if we want to keep it safe. This time, it is not enough to remain amongst the trees and wait for our enemies to come to us. This time, we must bring the fight to them. We will fight as one, with the Chosen as our allies, until our enemy has been destroyed."

The roar of approval was immediate. Helena had expected more of a resistance, especially after Reyna's mention that few had ever left the Forest.

Pulling out a small glimmering piece of metal from beneath her shirt, Reyna held it up so that it could catch the light. Gasps filled the room. Helena looked to Joquil, hoping he might have an explanation for the crowd's reaction. His amber eyes were wide and his mouth had fallen open in shock. Feeling the weight of her stare, he turned and whispered, "I always thought it was a myth."

"Long has my family passed this down, each generation gifting it to the eldest daughter when she comes of age. With it comes the reminder to not use it lightly, for it can only ever be used once. Never has one of my line had need to call on the aid of the Watchers. Until now." Reyna raised her voice, speaking over the shocked whispers, "I do not make this choice lightly. Let there be no doubt among you what our failure will mean. There is a fate worse than death, as we have learned from our brothers and sisters in Duskfall. We will take no chances."

The room fell silent again, until a man called out, "A worthy cause indeed!"

"Aye!"

Reyna lifted a hand to halt the cheering of the crowd. "Knowing what is on the line, and that I cannot guarantee you a safe return, I will not force any of you into this decision. There is still time before the battle will begin. It is up to you if you will join me. I will not think less of any that wish to remain." With a final look at the glittering necklace, Reyna let it fall back against her chest and then strode quickly from the room.

Helena peered at the men and women sitting beside her. "What just happened?"

"The stuff of legend," Joquil answered in a hushed voice. "Reyna is going to call in the Watchers' promise."

With a lift of her brow that clearly expressed how little he'd enlightened her, Joquil flushed and continued. "There is a story that the Night Stalkers pass down from generation to generation. When the first of the Night Stalkers began to settle in the Forest, they were faced with the Watchers, who did not want their land polluted by humans. With nowhere left to go after being cast out of Chosen lands, the Night Stalkers vowed their allegiance to the Watchers, promising to be the guardians of the Forest. The Watchers laughed, as they were its true defenders, but they were intrigued by these small men who thought they would be able to protect the Forest, and so they agreed to let them stay."

Joquil cleared his throat, uncomfortable with the attention of the others. "Years passed without any issue, until a new tribe tried to settle in the Forest. The Watchers gave them a choice: make the same vow as the others or leave. The tribe refused and set about burning the Forest down. In the years that they'd been citizens of the Forest, the Night Stalkers learned from the Watchers how to become part of it. They discovered the skill of shadow weaving. Now they put it to use, hiding atop the trees and spying on their would-be attackers. Armed with information, the Night Stalkers and Watchers were able to defeat the tribe."

Joquil was all but vibrating with pride as he spoke about his ancestors, his excitement that the story was true impossible to hide. "As thanks to the humans, who ensured their victory since they were small enough to move about unseen and unheard where the Watchers could not, they made a promise. It was represented by a token, the golden acorn. If ever there was a time of great need, when the Night Stalkers were threatened by an enemy they could not defeat on their own, the Watchers would come to their aid."

The members of the Circle were quiet, until Darrin finally asked. "But what *are* the Watchers?"

Joquil's voice was barely more than a breath. "The oldest denizens of the Forest: the trees themselves."

Helena wasn't sure how one was supposed to respond to that kind of revelation. So she let out a soft, "Oh."

Joquil nodded. "And now you understand."

Helena wasn't sure she did, not entirely, but she was starting to. They'd just gained an ally more powerful than she'd ever thought possible. Not only would they be fighting beside the full force of the Night Stalkers, but the Forest itself would be at their side.

FAR AWAY IN a much smaller room, a man knelt before the shimmering surface of an ancient mirror.

"The Circle is still intact," an icy voice accused.

"Yes, my Queen."

"Why?"

The word hit him like the blow of a lash. The man barely restrained himself from flinching. "The usurper had a stash of Kaelpas stones that allowed her and her party to move about more quickly than anticipated. I was unable to locate her, because I did not have one within their initial ranks."

"And now?"

The man lifted his head and grinned. "And now I do."

There was a thaw in the room, and he would have said his Queen was pleased if he didn't know her better. One didn't become her lover by failing to correctly interpret her moods. Rather, one did not *remain* her lover. The latter was a much more difficult feat to achieve.

"Good. Then there will be no more mistakes."

"No, my Queen," he promised.

"My patience is wearing thin, Thomas. Break the Circle, or I will have no choice but to break you."

Her hazy visage faded from the mirror until all he could see were his own coal eyes staring back at him from a grizzled face. He watched as his lips lifted in a sadistic smile, despite her threat. It was hardly the worst thing she'd ever said to him.

"It will be done."

CHAPTER 18

"I need more time!" Helena growled in frustration, her fingers squeezing the bridge of her nose in an attempt to stave off her growing headache. She wasn't sure any longer if this was a strategy meeting or an intervention.

"Time is one thing you can no longer afford," Darrin protested. "You saw what she did to their village. Rowena is still ten steps ahead of you! We need to move. Now."

Helena shot him a venomous look. "We are making the time. This is important, Shield."

"You already have the Storm Forged and the Night Stalkers, not to mention their Watchers. And this is on top of the Chosen forces that already swore their allegiance."

Helena glared at him. "What part of this is important do you not understand?"

"How big of an army do you need?" he asked in exasperation.

"As big as possible," she ground out.

The two stared at each other in silence, neither party wanting to look away first.

"Helena," he tried again in a softer, pleading voice.

"She is taking control of entire villages, Darrin. If you think our army is big, hers is still twice the size, if not larger. We. Need. Allies."

Darrin hung his head in defeat. He recognized that stubborn set of her jaw from a childhood filled with such arguments.

Von's hand lifted to squeeze her shoulder, his indication that he had something to add. "Do you need to make the request personally?"

Helena looked at him in surprise. Von did not often go against her, especially not in front of the others. "What do you mean?"

"You both make solid arguments. We need allies, but we have to move as quickly as possible if we hope to gain the upper hand—"

Helena cut him off, "I'm going as fast as I can. We've already cut out weeks of travel by using the Kaelpas stones. How much faster do you want me to go?"

Von lifted his brows, waiting for her to finish. "I'm not arguing that. I'm merely pointing out that perhaps if we split up, we could make these last two visits in the time it has taken us to visit one. That would give us much-needed time, but still provide you with your allies. So my question for you stands, does it have to be you?"

Helena frowned, considering the question.

"Kiri," Timmins began. Lifting her eyes, Helena focused on her Advisor. He was leaning on a bookcase just beside Miranda and Kragen. "As the Advisor, I could go in your stead. Any of the Circle could. Since it is known that the Circle is bound to you, it would not be unexpected, or even seen as an insult, if we made the request on your behalf."

"I don't know," she murmured. Something about not being there felt wrong.

"For what it is worth, I do not think the Talyrians would tolerate more than you and Von anyway. At least not for an initial visit to their lands. The rest of us could easily represent you in the Broken Vale." Ronan's voice was measured, as if he knew his reasoning would not necessarily be welcome.

"He's right," Von added through the bond. Helena wanted to snarl at him but refrained. She felt cornered.

"It just feels wrong somehow," she said, echoing her earlier thoughts aloud. She took the time to meet each of their eyes, hoping she could express through her gaze what she was failing to explain with her words. While she saw understanding reflected back at her, it was the urgency she felt through her Jaka that truly resonated. The attack on the Night Stalkers hit them harder than she had realized.

Helena's shoulders slumped. She could force them to do it her way, but what would she really gain? She already trusted these men with her life, this task should be easy by comparison. "I just don't want to give them any reason to doubt the importance or sincerity of my request."

"We won't let them," Joquil assured her. Danger glittered in his amber eyes. He took the attack on Duskfall personally. Now that he did not have to hide his ancestry, it was clear he still felt deep ties to the people of the Forest.

With a sigh she relented completely. "What are you proposing?"

"Essentially the plan would not change. Reyna is providing us with one of her Night Stalkers that has ties to the Broken Vale. With their assistance, we will use the Kaelpas stones and seek an audience. Meanwhile, you and Von will travel with Starshine to Talyria. You should be able to make the trip in a couple of days. We will regroup in Etillion in five days' time and meet with our allies to discuss a full assault on Vyruul."

Von looked amused as Ronan spoke. Usually, he was the one laying out the battle plans. "It is unlikely we will find Rowena in Vyruul."

Ronan's answering smile was fierce. "Perhaps not, but Greyspire is. She will not react well to losing her ancestral home."

"You hope to force her hand and make her come out of hiding before she is ready."

Ronan nodded. "What better way to smoke the rat out?"

The other men murmured their approval.

The plan was sound, if simple, but Helena could not shake the feeling that it wouldn't be so straightforward. Rowena had proven that time and again. Instead of saying so, Helena remained silent. They could worry about the details once they knew what resources they truly had. Any plans made before then were likely to be changed anyway.

"I know you do not like the idea of splitting up, Mira. But we will be safe with the Talyrians."

"It's not us I'm worried about."

"Ronan will not let any harm come to your Circle."

Helena frowned at him. *"And who will protect him? With each meeting there has been an obstacle none of us anticipated: Rowena's general, the challenge, the ambush. It has taken our combined strength and my power to see us through, and this time we will be sending them off without it."*

Von wrapped his arm around her and held her close. *"They have fought and won many battles without you, Mira. They are more prepared than you give them credit for."*

Her frown deepened, but she did not argue further. She knew what he said was true, but that didn't make him right. Rowena wasn't just another enemy.

"Fine." She sighed with resignation. "I suppose we should get some sleep then. There's long days ahead for all of us."

ONLY REYNA WAS awake to see them off. Since they were flying rather than traveling via Kaelpas stone, they needed to make an early start of it. She had led them to a small clearing, just outside of the Penumbra camp. It was still protected by the forest, but a break in the trees would allow them to take flight. The sky was clear but dark; the last of the stars still twinkling above them.

"Thank you again, Kiri. What you did for my people…"

Helena held up a hand to stop her. "If either of us should be saying thank you, it is I. Your help in the days to come will be invaluable."

The women smiled at each other, kindred spirits despite a lifetime of different experiences.

Reyna held out her leather clad arm. "Safe travels until we meet again, Kiri."

"Mother's blessings, Reyna," Helena replied, grasping the proffered arm with her hand.

They shared another smile before stepping away from each other. Turning, Helena watched as Von double-checked the bags they'd strapped to Starshine. The Talyrian Queen tolerated the inspection, but only just. From the snicker behind her, Helena knew that Reyna noticed as well.

Von turned toward her with a smile. "Ready?"

Helena nodded and closed the distance between them. Starshine's luminous turquoise eye swiveled as it watched her approach. The Talyrian stood perfectly still while Helena ran a hand along the length of her neck. Starshine lifted her wings as a rumbling purr started deep in her throat.

"I've missed you too, girl," Helena murmured, pressing her forehead into the velvety fur.

"Sneaking off in the middle of the night?" a loud voice called from the edge of the clearing.

Helena and Von turned toward the voice, neither surprised to see Ronan and the rest of the Circle standing there. Ronan was grinning smugly; this was his doing then.

Von shrugged and called out, "We were trying to give you assholes a bit of much-needed beauty sleep."

There were some chuckles as the men moved closer.

"Sleep is overrated. Besides, I'm too pretty by half these days and we couldn't let you go without a proper send off," Ronan said.

Helena laughed as she said, "In that case, you might as well get over here."

Darrin reached her first. He was smiling but his green eyes were tinged with sadness as he pulled her in for a tight hug. "It is only for a few days, everything will be fine. You'll see that this was the right call."

Helena made a face causing him to laugh and roll his eyes.

"Be safe, Hellion."

"You as well, Shield. That's an order," she replied in a thick voice, trying to swallow back the emotion that was threatening to spill forth. Nothing about saying goodbye to these men was sitting right with her.

With a tug of her braid and a wink, Darrin moved aside for Kragen. Her Sword picked her up and spun her around, causing her to sputter with laughter.

"See you soon, Hellion," he rumbled.

She pressed a hand to his cheek. "Stay safe, Kragen."

He grinned, setting her down gently before stepping to the side.

Timmins came next. He reached formally for her hand, moving to bow and press a kiss to the back of it.

"I think we are far past the days of such ceremony, Advisor."

With a laugh, Timmins pulled her in for a quick hug. He rested his head atop hers as he promised, "We will not fail you, Kiri."

"I do not doubt it, Timmins."

His smile was forced as he nodded and turned away, making room for her Master to step forward. Joquil's amber eyes seemed to glow in the darkness. They shared a soft smile and hugged each other tight. "Remember what I've taught you," he whispered.

"As if I could forget."

Joquil chuckled and made to step back, but Helena stopped him, gripping his hand. "Thank you for being brave."

His brows furrowed as he tried to make sense of her words.

"It took much for you to tell us of your past. It is because of you we found such powerful allies. Thank you for trusting me with your secret."

Joquil smiled in surprise and ducked his head. He nodded once more before walking away.

Ronan was the last to come forth. He stared at her for a long moment, his blue eyes dark with emotion. Helena let out a shaky breath as he wrapped his strong arms around her.

"I do not like saying goodbye to you," she admitted in a watery voice.

"Nor I," he replied gruffly.

"Keep them safe for me, Ronan."

"With my dying breath," he promised.

"All right, that's enough of that," Von said, giving Ronan's shoulder a sharp shove.

"You're just afraid she's enjoying my embrace more than yours."

"Actually, I can feel the revulsion your touch causes and am trying to spare her."

The men snickered, grasping hands and pulling each other in for a quick hug.

"Be safe, bastard."

"You as well, brother."

The friends slapped each other on the back and stepped apart.

"Tell the others…" Helena trailed off; what was there to say? But the men nodded anyway, understanding the intent even if there wasn't a clear message.

It was time. Helena let out one last long breath and turned toward Starshine, blindly pulling herself up. Von vaulted up behind her, wrapping his arms around her waist as he settled in.

"Let's go, girl."

With a wave they were off, springing up into the starry sky.

Helena felt tears stinging her eyes as the trees below them disappeared. Whether it was due to the wind, or the pieces of her heart that remained behind, she wasn't sure. One thing was certain, however. The farther away they got from her Circle, the greater her sense of foreboding. Something was coming. She just hoped they would be ready.

CHAPTER 19

They flew for hours, the world below them nothing more than a sea of clouds. The gentle rocking of Starshine's body as she beat her wings was hypnotic, and more than once Helena found herself nodding off. If not for Von's arms banded about her, she was certain she would have toppled off the Talyrian's back entirely.

Shortly after they'd taken off, Helena had created an aural shield, which blocked out most of the roaring wind and allowed her and Von to speak without shouting at each other. Even though they could have relied on their bond to communicate, it was nice to be able to speak freely.

Starshine dipped suddenly, angling her massive body down toward the ground.

"Oh!" Helena gasped, clenching Starshine's mane to remain upright.

"I guess it's time for a rest," Von commented wryly as he tightened his hold on her.

"Apparently so."

"I wouldn't mind a break. I could do with a stretch and something to eat."

Helena nodded her agreement, even though she felt conflicted about stopping so soon. Her desire to make it to Talyria as quickly as possible was urging her to keep going. The trip would take another full day's ride at least. She sighed, knowing there was no point in asking Starshine to continue on for a bit longer. There was absolutely no way she could win an argument with a Talyrian. Create a raging storm out of thin air, absolutely. Make fire rain down from the sky, easy. Change a Talyrian's mind once they've settled on a decision, no fucking way.

As the land below them began to take shape, Helena just kept telling herself that there was little harm to be had in resting for a while. She wasn't sure where exactly they were, but given the shimmering pools streaking across large patches of green, Helena would guess somewhere in Sylverlands.

Starshine continued her dive, beginning to spiral in large swooping circles as she neared the ground. Probably to ensure the area was safe, although that was just Helena's guess. Not exactly like she could ask. When they landed, Helena could feel the diluted reverberation of the trembling earth from where she was still perched atop Starshine. She waited for the tremors to settle before sliding down. Von had already dismounted and was waiting to catch her. His hands were warm where they pressed into her waist.

She smiled up at him in wordless thanks and accepted the soft kiss he pressed against her lips with an appreciative moan. He nipped at her bottom lip playfully, his eyes going silver as he grinned at her.

"Alone at last."

"Was that your plan all along?" she teased.

"No," he admitted aloud, "but it should have been. It's a definite side benefit regardless."

"Mmm, definitely," she agreed, kissing him again. Before they could get carried away, Starshine snorted, silvery plumes of smoke wafting around them.

Helena giggled, her cheeks flushing as if they had been caught doing something inappropriate. Turning toward her feline companion, Helena asked, "Need something?"

Starshine sat down hard, as if to say, I just wanted to remind you that I'm right here. Helena couldn't help but laugh. As she was turning back to Von to comment she overheard the tail end of his bitter mutterings.

"…ck blocked by a Talyrian…"

"What was that?" she snickered.

He shot the feline a darkly annoyed glance. "Nothing."

The stare-down between the two was intense, both wanting to assert their dominance over the other. Helena tried hard to fight the laughter that bubbled up and failed miserably. She only laughed harder when it was Von who looked away first. The sounds of his bitter cursing filled the air. With a satisfied huff, Starshine shook out her mane before standing back up and stretching. As she stretched, her gleaming claws were on full display, which Helena was certain was no coincidence. It was just another way for Starshine to show Von why she was the superior creature.

"I suppose we should find some water?" Helena intervened once her laughter had finally died off.

Von just grunted.

Shoulders shaking with amusement, Helena said, "Come on you two."

As Von came abreast of the Talyrian he muttered, "She is *my* Mate, you know."

Starshine huffed again, not even sparing him a glance.

"Doesn't seem like she thinks much of your title," Helena commented.

"Don't start."

Helena grinned, but let it go.

The trio headed off in the direction of the lakes they had noted during their descent. The nearest of them couldn't have been too far off, but it was hard to tell without the aid of true landmarks. The land was flat and open as far as the eye could see and there were no houses or anything to suggest that the area was inhabited. There were a few scattered trees, but nothing like the dense forest they had occupied only that morning.

All-in-all it was a pleasant walk. The sun was warm, but not overbearing, as it beamed down between fluffy white clouds. The lake was further than they'd originally thought, and all three kept a cautious eye on the horizon, just in case anyone mistook their approach as a threat. But there was no one, and they made their way entirely unchallenged.

She knew they were close when the sounds of water hitting the shore met her ears. It was only another fifteen minutes before they saw the silvery sheen of the lake's reflection. Starshine loped ahead, sniffing at the water before eagerly dipping her head down and lapping it up.

When Von and Helena reached her, she threw her head up and thousands of miniature droplets flew through the air, each shimmering in the sunlight as they fell back down. Helena held out a palm, letting the droplets fall into her hand. She turned toward Von, ready to toss the tiny handful of water at him, but her hands fell when she took in the ashen sight of him. He was staring straight ahead, utterly transfixed. His mouth had fallen slack, and she could tell from the vacant look in his eyes that he was a million miles away. It was then she realized what had happened. Just as Miranda had predicted, his memories of the mist had snared him once more.

Apparently the tiny drops of water falling in the air had been just similar enough to the effect of the mist that it had caught him off guard. Helena moved quickly. She grabbed him, shaking him hard, hoping the movement would be enough to pull his focus. It wasn't.

"Von!" she shouted, echoing the cry through their bond. *"Von!"*

Silence.

Beside her, Starshine began to growl menacingly, as if sensing danger.

"Keep watch girl," Helena murmured, trusting the Talyrian to guard them while she focused solely on her Mate.

Placing a hand on either side of his face, Helena closed her eyes and used her power to send a psychic tendril into his mind. She navigated carefully, searching for any sign of Von's presence. When she didn't sense him, she peeled back another layer continuing on until she found herself just outside of his innermost barriers. She had been here once before, when she had helped him finally breakthrough the *Bellamorte's* hold and face his captors.

As she had the last time, Helena placed a metaphorical hand against the barrier, letting it identify her and give her permission to move past. She filled the touch with all of her love and concern for Von. The barrier rippled pleasantly against her senses, similar to a cool breeze on a warm day. Recognizing her, the barrier grew transparent until it gave way completely. Helena found herself standing within the core of Von's mind.

Images surrounded her. *Memories*, she realized. There were ghostly images of Von and Nial playing as children. There was Ronan, snarling as he slammed his fiery ax into an enemy that was about to strike Von. And there she was, smiling shyly up at him as they spoke in the Palace garden.

Helena wanted to walk through all of the memories, learning everything about the man she loved as she relived his past through them. But they were not her memories to explore, and so she resisted. Instead, Helena wandered through them, careful not to touch or disturb any of the wispy fragments. She wasn't certain what effect her interruption would cause and she didn't want to accidentally cause further harm.

Focusing on the feel of him, strong and steady through their bond, Helena used that as her guide. It did not take long for her to find him, but she was unprepared for what she found.

This was no pale memory. Whatever was happening to the shuddering body sitting and rocking on the ground was real. Her heart wrenched painfully in her chest when she heard his rasping moan.

"No more." He was curled into a ball, his hands drawn up over his head and clenched into tight fists. "No more," he groaned again. His voice was raw, as though he had been screaming for hours without end.

While she may have only been a projection of herself, Helena found herself shaking. Not knowing what else to do, she crouched beside him, holding her hand just above his head, not quite making contact.

"Von," she whispered, not wanting to startle him.

There was no response, no indication that he knew she was there at all. Helena let her hand close the gap between them, touching him as gently as possible. When she made contact, light flared brightly obscuring everything around her and forcing her to close her eyes. As the light faded, and her eyes were finally able to flutter open, she wished they'd stayed closed. Swallowing back a scream, Helena staggered to her feet.

VON'S NIGHTMARE RAGED ON. All around him, the bodies of those he loved were chained and bloody. They were lined up, one after the other, a grisly exhibit of human misery. Strips of skin were torn and hanging down where the whip had sliced through to the bone. He gagged, but made himself swallow back his revulsion, forcing himself not to give in to the emotional torture. Instead, he made himself focus on the need for vengeance which was screaming for him to repay each sadistic blow in kind.

But he couldn't move. He, too, was chained. Von struggled against the bonds, more wild animal than man as he worked to get free. He needed to get out of here. To get them all away from this hellhole of a dungeon. Von gnashed his teeth, biting back a scream as the enchanted metal began to sear through his skin. Unable to bear it any longer, he gave in to the roar of pain that clawed its way out of his throat.

There was a bright flash of light, almost as if a door had been opened. He threw his head to the side, squeezing his eyes shut before the light blinded him.

Then he heard the whimper.

"Von."

His eyes flew open.

"Helena?"

"V-Von," came the hopeful but broken reply. From the restored darkness at the end of the room, Helena limped out of the shadows. She was wearing what only the most optimistic would call a white gown. It was so liberally coated in blood that it was more crimson than white. He could see bits of her bone peering out from some of the gaping wounds. Her skin looked purple because of all the bruises, and her face was swollen almost beyond recognition. Whoever had done this to her had taken their time. If the others were an exhibit, she was the masterpiece.

"What did she do to you?" he snarled, lurching forward until his chains went taut. Von roared, going absolutely mad when he could not get to her.

"It's a lie."

Von blinked, the voice in his mind momentarily pulling him out of the nightmare.

"Do not believe the mist."

The mist… Von went entirely still. Was he still lost in the mist? But no, Helena had saved him. And now she was standing right there, beaten almost within an inch of her life. This was some new fresh hell that they were trapped in. This was real… wasn't it?

"Let me show you," the voice insisted.

Von hesitated, equally afraid and desperate to believe the voice. The doubt was enough to break the nightmare's hold. The world swam in and out of focus, the dark dungeon superimposed over a field of green and silver.

He blinked again, and the dungeon settled back into place. The moans of his brother snagging his attention.

"No!" the voice demanded.

Von felt his face twisting away from the writhing body. Startled that his body was moving against his will, he fought the movement.

"Really?" the voice snapped in exasperation. *"You will fight against me, but not the hallucination?"*

That gave him pause. There was only one person who would dare to use that tone with him, especially when he was in this state. Any that knew him well, or even those that knew of his history on the battlefield would recognize the bloodlust that consumed him. It would not abate until he was the last one standing. To interfere with that was a death wish.

"Helena?" He said her name out loud, confused that she could be speaking in his mind when she was collapsed in a heap at his feet.

"Von, you need to resist it. You have to see the lie to break its hold."

He glanced around, not sure how he was supposed to do that.

He thought he heard a sigh, but before he could respond further, his body began to tingle. Every ache and throb was soon replaced with soothing warmth. He recognized that warmth. It was the feeling he'd associated with Helena ever since he'd healed her after her trial, and in doing so, initiated their bond.

"See the lie."

Von looked around, staring at the nearest body. It was Serena, only it wasn't. There was a fuzziness to the outline of her body that became more apparent the longer he stared. He'd been so overwhelmed by the injuries that he'd been unable to look past them and note the other details. Ronan, or rather what he had believed to be Ronan, was tied up beside her and quietly weeping. Ronan would never weep. Not like that. He would be roaring and fighting, just as Von had been, at least until he passed out or his captors knocked him out.

"That's it."

Glancing down where Helena's body was supposed to be, he noted the color of the eyes that were cracked open, staring at the ceiling. If Helena had been tortured, her eyes would have burned with the iridescence of her power as she fought back. No one who caught her would have lived long enough to cause that level of damage to her body.

Helena's warmth grew in intensity, until he felt like he was on fire. He looked at himself, running his hands over his body to ensure that he wasn't. Then he realized what he'd just done and did a double take. His arms were no longer cast in irons. Glancing up, he noticed that the bodies and dungeon were gone.

He was free.

VON WAS NOW LYING PEACEFULLY beside her. When she'd touched him, she'd been sucked into his nightmare. It had taken her awhile to separate herself from the gruesome images that were playing out in front of her. She'd been trapped in Von's body, experiencing everything as he did. It was when she'd seen herself stumbling toward him that she remembered why she was there and was able to help him fight against the hallucination. Knowing now the kind of assault his mind had been under when he'd been trapped within for so many months, Helena could not believe he was still sane.

She stroked a hand along the length of his back, willing him to return to consciousness. They were still within the innermost barrier of his mind and she would not leave him until she knew that he was safely free of the *Bellamorte*.

Remembering the dark smudges she'd seen the first time she'd treated him, Helena cast her awareness out. At first, all she sensed were the wisps of his memories, which still swirled around them, but then she felt it. The sense of something that didn't belong. Focusing on it, she moved away from the resting form of her Mate. Helena wandered through the corridors of his mind until she came to the very center. There she found a flickering ball of light. It was so beautiful she couldn't decide whether she wanted to cry, or laugh, or grasp it carefully in her hand and cradle it against her chest.

The longer she stared at the ball of light, the happier she became. Sensing her happiness, it grew brighter, spinning about almost playfully. As it spun, Helena finally saw what she had been searching for. Pressed against the perfect brightness of his soul, for that's certainly what Helena had found, there was the tiniest smear. No wonder she had missed it before. It was so miniscule that it had been disguised, but now that she knew what to look for, it could no longer hide.

Helena moved closer, calling her power into the tip of her finger. She could not afford to do something careless like toss a bolt of power at it. One wrong move and her power could destroy more than just the mote. Helena shuddered, not wanting to think overlong on that possibility.

Holding her finger out, she stroked the side of the ball, pulling away the mote of darkness. Von's essence rippled where it had come into contact with her hand. It seemed to want her to keep touching it, moving with her as she pulled her hand away. The reaction was reminiscent of a cat that arched its back to encourage further pettings. The thought made Helena smile.

Looking down at her hand, Helena found the smudge still clinging to her finger. With a shake of her head, she made a small o with her lips and blew, infusing her breath with magic. When it touched the mote, instead of sending it flying into the air, it obliterated it completely. Helena smiled, satisfied that she had been able to get rid of the final lingering piece.

Her work here was done, but it was hard to leave. The sense of peace and joy she felt standing beside the beautiful orb was like nothing she'd ever experienced. That was when the orb began to glow a bright, molten gold. It was the same color as Von's eyes when their power merged.

"Oh," she gasped, her hand moving up to her chest where a sudden heat flared. It continued to grow and swell within her until she could feel it in every part of her body. Helena watched in awe as the orb pulsed in time with her heartbeat.

She stood in silence, filled with a happiness so absolute it eclipsed all else. This was a special kind of magic that had nothing to do with the elements and everything to do with love.

Helena may never know what the final step had been, her whisper of a touch or the small blast of air filled with her power, but she knew without a doubt that their bond was now complete.

CHAPTER 20

When Helena opened her eyes, she was still standing in front of Von with her hands pressed against his cheeks. Hours must have passed while they had been in his mind, the sun was now a burnt-orange ball, half-hidden by the horizon.

Starshine let out a low whine, which sounded very much like a question.

"We're safe," Helena answered with a whisper, her eyes never leaving Von's face.

Appeased, Starshine moved away to give the couple a bit of privacy. Despite the added distance, she was no less of a guard.

Helena ran her thumbs along the dark slashes of Von's brows, willing him to open his eyes. She repeated the soft stokes until she noticed his eyelids begin to flutter. When his eyes finally opened they were molten gold. Helena's heart began to pound. They stared, twin looks of wonder on each of their faces.

Nothing was overtly different, but something had clearly changed. Their bond was still there, a steady presence burning brightly inside of them. It was just more: more intense, more vibrant, more focused.

Without a word Von slammed his lips down on hers, kissing her fiercely. They were so in tune with one another, that she could feel Von's reaction to her touch as if it was her own. The added awareness created an intensity to their kisses that had her desperate for him after only a few heartbeats.

Her urgency was his. Von moved his lips from hers, kissing down her neck as his hands began to make quick work of her travel clothes, removing only what was needed. They were still in the open, but Helena didn't care. All she wanted was to feel physically what she was already feeling in her heart; the sense of fullness and completion that would come once he slid inside her.

"Helena," he groaned in her mind, his lips never ceasing their teasing. *"I—"*

"I feel it too." She wrapped her arms around his head and back, holding his mouth against her body. *"Please don't stop."*

He didn't. His hands roamed her body, equal parts possessive and reverent. Where her skin was exposed, goosebumps were left in his wake. She shivered, needing more. Before it was even a conscious thought, he was already there, touching her exactly as she needed. It was not just instinct driving their movements; it was absolute knowing. Each touch carried certainty, as though they were reenacting something they'd done a thousand times before. But there was nothing repetitive about the experience. It felt like the first time.

Helena was not conscious of the moment they moved to the ground. Her senses were too overwhelmed by the emotions spiraling within her, his as well as hers.

Von broke away, and her eyes fluttered open, knowing that he needed her to look at him. His hair was tousled, and his eyes heavy-lidded. Dark stubble coated his jaw and his lips were swollen from their hungry kisses. Helena licked her lips, desire pounding through her at the sight of him poised above her.

His hand moved down, spreading her before he entered her in one hard thrust, his eyes never once straying from hers.

Helena gasped, coming apart from just that single motion. But Von wasn't done with her. He continued to move inside her, each thrust causing her climax to extend.

She was panting incoherent fragments of words as he relentlessly loved her. Each drive of his hips set off another explosion of sensation and Helena started to feel like entire universes were being created and destroyed within her. Finally, just as she was certain she would pass out, Von came, growling her name. Helena joined him, the feeling of him throbbing inside her setting off one last tidal wave that surpassed every other.

"I love you."

It was a struggle, but Helena forced her eyes to open. Her body was beyond spent, and the urge to fall asleep was almost impossible to fight.

"I love you more," she teased, her voice hoarse from her cries.

He smirked at her, even as he brushed stray strands of hair from her face. "With an orgasm like that I don't doubt it."

Helena didn't even have the energy to deny it. With a yawn and the lift of a shoulder she asked, "Can you blame me? I'm not sure if it was one continuous one, or hundreds of them back-to-back."

With a satisfied smile, he bent down and pressed a kiss to her forehead. "Rest now so we can try it again."

Between one chuckle and the next she fell asleep in his arms.

WHEN SHE WOKE, they were still curled up in the sweet-smelling grass, although Von had made a point to refasten her clothes while she'd slept. It was full night now, and the sky was blanketed with stars.

"Sleep well?" Von asked, his voice a low rumble.

"Mmm," she murmured, lifting her arms above her head in a sinuous stretch. When she relaxed, she noted Von's appreciative leer.

Completely unapologetic, he grinned when he caught her gaze. "Beautiful."

Helena opened her mouth to respond, and then noticed something that had her quickly sitting up. Startled, Von's body tensed and he immediately began to scan the area for danger. "What is it?"

"Your eyes!"

Confused, he looked back at her. "What about them?"

Helena shook her head, unable to explain.

"Here," she said, scrambling up and pulling him with her. "Look," she demanded, pointing into the glassy reflection of the lake. The stars above provided more than enough illumination for them to see their own shimmering reflections.

Peering into the water, it did not take more than a second for Von to notice what she had. Around each of his pupils was a thin iridescent band, just like in hers.

"I guess we match now," he said after a moment of stunned silence.

Helena smiled. "I guess we do."

"Do you think that means…" Von trailed off, not completing the question.

"That our power has merged?" Helena asked for him.

He nodded, his brows lowering as he contemplated what that could mean.

Helena shrugged. "I'm not sure. Shall we test it?"

"How?"

Helena bit down on her lip as she considered. "What's something I can do that you can't?"

He lifted a brow. "Really? Can we set the bar a little lower, please?"

"Okay, fair point," she laughed. "Um… I guess just try something and we'll see what happens."

He agreed with a nod and took a few steps away from her. Focusing intently on where Starshine dozed across the lake, Von took a deep breath and vanished. Almost instantly he reappeared beside a grumpy Starshine who did not appreciate the unexpected company. So their assumption had been right, at least to an extent. Blinking was something he'd already been able to do, but never across a distance that great before. His power had definitely received a boost as a result of their completed bond.

Helena watched as Starshine sniffed at Von. He stood still, uncertain about what the Talyrian was doing. She looked confused as well, twisting her head from Von to Helena and back again, before dipping down to sniff him once more.

He gave Helena a baffled glance. *"Should I be concerned?"*

"I have no idea," Helena admitted with a shrug.

Von looked back at Starshine who was now pressing her face into him. Tentatively, Von lifted a hand and began to stroke her gleaming fur. Helena let out a snort of laughter when Starshine's purrs were audible even where she was standing.

"I guess that answers that."

Starshine had always tolerated Von, but she had never made any overt signs of affection before. Up until now, those had been exclusively reserved for Helena. Starshine must be sensing Helena's essence in Von. She could only assume this was another unanticipated side effect of their completed bond.

"Do you think this means she'll let me ride her without you now?" Von asked as he ran his hand along the length of Starshine's muzzle. Starshine twisted her head away, playfully swiping at Von with her paw. It was her way of letting him know he'd erred when he'd stopped scratching behind her ears. Von jumped back with a startled shout, narrowly avoiding sharp black claws. Unfortunately, what was playful for a Talyrian was still potentially deadly to a human, especially when said paw was the size of a dinner plate.

"Definitely not," Helena snickered.

"Mother's tits! I don't think I'd trust her even if she did."

"She really is quite easy to understand once you learn her tells."

"It's no wonder. Only a fool would chance repeating a mistake with her."

Helena's laughter rang out, filling the night with her joyful melody.

CHAPTER 21

Seeing Talyria for the first time was something Helena knew she would never forget. The air was thick with power. She felt it as soon as they flew across the border. It didn't feel like magic, at least not in the way she understood it; this was ancient and much more primal. She wondered if it was what had kept Talyria separated from the rest of Elysia for centuries; if that ancient energy was, in fact, a powerful barrier that kept everyone else out. Knowing that she was one of the first to see the land of the Talyrians was a privilege she would never take for granted.

The setting sun painted the sky in bright oranges and rosy pinks, and thick red clouds obscured all but the highest mountain peaks. These were not the sloping, snow-capped mountains of Vyruul, but rather sheer-faced cliffs that towered high above the ground. From her vantage point, she started to notice cave-like openings scattered across the cliffs. They were often accompanied by small stretches of rock that could act as landing areas.

As they flew deeper into the heart of Talyria, Starshine dipped beneath the clouds, and the land below came into view. There were a few massive waterfalls that surged off of the cliffs, turning into deep pools that broke up the otherwise reddish-brown land. The pools of water were so clear, Helena could see fish darting below the surface.

They were sprayed by the water as they flew past, and what didn't hit them hung in the air like tiny prisms. Helena risked a glance over her shoulder, grinning when she saw that Von's look of delight was a mirror of her own. If the Ebon Isle was a reminder of the deadly power of the elements, Talyria was a testament to their unending beauty. It was paradise.

They were more than an hour inland before Helena caught her first glimpse at another Talyrian. Massive feline heads tracked their movements, letting out roars of greeting as their queen flew past. A few leapt off the cliffs, joining them in flight. Soon the sky was full of beating wings in a variety of colors. Some were dark like Starshine's, while others were so light they appeared to be smoke moving across the sky.

By the changing angle of Starshine's body, Helena knew that they were about to land in an opening that had emerged between two of the flat-topped mountains. Just as they were about to touch down, Helena noticed two balls of fur rolling and playing in the dusty red earth. She let out a small gasp of wonder; they were baby Talyrians.

One of the cubs was an inky black, its glowing violet eyes narrowing as it prepared to pounce. The other was milky-white with amber eyes and small patches of orange covering its tiny body. The black one leapt, jet-black wings flaring out on either side, holding it airborne for an instant before its paws made contact with its target. The white and orange cub tried to dodge the attack, but wasn't fast enough, and ended up rolling backwards.

It jumped up, shaking off the dust and snarling its challenge at the black one. Helena was certain the little one thought the sound was quite fierce, but the snarl sounded more like a squeak and Helena could not contain her giggle. The cubs were about as ferocious as stuffed toys, but she knew better than to ever say so aloud. Especially with two protective mamas standing watch just behind them. She wondered if she had a chance of snuggling one of them.

Starshine landed, and two Talyrian males immediately approached her. Both of the males were bigger in size than Starshine, but there was no doubt she was the alpha here. The silver one reached her first, rumbling a greeting before bowing his head. The other was the black of a midnight sky. Without the glittering sapphire of its eyes, which were utterly focused on his Queen, he could have easily been mistaken for a rippling shadow. A mistake his enemy would likely never survive to repeat. This one did not bow, but stalked toward her until they were all but touching. There was a growl and he bared razor-sharp teeth. Starshine didn't flinch.

The midnight Talyrian growled again, a sound that had the hair on the back of Helena's neck standing on end. Starshine opened her mouth and roared, plumes of smokes flaring up around her. With a huff, the male sat down, its wings shaking out in what seemed like annoyance.

"What in the Mother's name is going on?" Helena asked.

"Isn't it obvious? The midnight one is letting her know he's displeased with how long she's been gone, and in reply Starshine told him to fuck off."

Helena was only mildly surprised that Von had translated the situation so easily. After replaying the last few seconds with his assessment in place she had to agree it held the definite ring of truth.

"Apparently males of all species like to tell their queens what to do," Helena commented dryly.

Von snickered, *"Only the smart ones."*

"See, that is where we disagree."

Starshine finally sat back, allowing Von and Helena to slide down. The glowing gazes of the nearby Talyrians followed them warily; they must have been the first humans they'd ever seen. Helena could not fault their caution.

The cubs were already being carried away from the strangers. *I guess I won't be playing with the babies anytime soon,* Helena thought a bit dejectedly, watching as they dangled from their mothers' jaws.

Following her train of thought, Von rubbed his hand along her back. When she looked over at him he smiled sympathetically. *"Don't take it personally. How comfortable would we be letting a Talyrian play with one of our young?"*

"I know but..." Helena stopped midsentence when she heard the

whine slip into her psychic tone. She gave Von a rueful smile. *"You wanted to play with them too, didn't you?"*

"There's a reason I'm not allowed near the Daejaran litters anymore."

"Oh?"

"The mamas didn't appreciate having to track their pups down. Usually in my room."

Helena chuckled. *"How do people ever mistake you for a fearsome warrior?"*

Von gave her a dark look paired with a wicked grin.

"Let's just hope none of the cubs go missing while we're here. I have a feeling you might be the first suspect."

Their mirth flowed through the bond, but they focused back on the massive felines before them. Knowing the Talyrians would react to any display of weakness, Helena held her chin up and strode purposefully to Starshine's side. She didn't allow herself to so much as blink while the darker of the two males sniffed her. It was not a threatening act, but it was certainly intimidating.

Beside her Starshine let out a warning growl. She did not need Von to translate this time; Starshine had just declared Helena as hers. By association, that meant that she had just declared Helena as *Pride*. There was a confused whine from the silver male, but Starshine's warning had only made the black one more curious.

"And we thought the Talyrians would be the easiest of the tribes to convince..."

"He just wants to make sure you are not a threat. He's protecting the ones he loves."

"Does he have to be so thorough?" she asked, her voice terse as his sniffed between her legs.

Von let out his own warning growl. Apparently Starshine wasn't the only one that felt the need to claim her. Helena sighed.

Curious about the two-legged creature that would attempt to intimidate him, the black Talyrian shifted focus to her Mate. He unfurled his wings until they were fully extended and blocked out everything but him and his glowing sapphire eyes. Helena stiffened, knowing this was a challenge.

Von crossed his arms and lifted his chin, never once looking away from the sapphire gaze. The Talyrian lowered his head until it was level with Von's. The two males stared at each other silently. After a long moment, the Talyrian opened his mouth and bellowed. Von's hair and cloak blew back, but otherwise he stood still. The Talyrian blinked, surprised that the other male had not cowered.

"Are you done?" Von asked in a slightly bored tone. The tone, if not the words, were clear. The Talyrian huffed. There was a calculating cast to his gaze now, as if a decision was being reached.

Finally, he nudged Von, rubbing him with his head and marking him with his scent. Starshine let out a rumble of approval.

"Looks like I'm not the only one who's been claimed. What will Karma do when you come home with your own Talyrian?"

Von shook his head. *"I'm not sure he's going to have much of a say in the matter."*

Helena wasn't certain any of them did.

Moving slowly, Von extended his hand, stroking the velvety fur of his Talyrian's neck.

"What will you call him?"

Von considered the question for a moment. *"If Starshine was named for the color of her fur, then there's really only one name for him."*

"Midnight," they said together.

"Welcome to the family, Midnight," Helena said aloud.

Midnight did not reply, he was too busy purring as Von scratched him behind the ears.

THE CHOSEN SERIES

Their time in Talyria passed quickly. After the initial meeting, they'd been taken deeper into the heart of the encampment located between the two mountains. There was a central valley with its own pool of water surrounded by a series of caves and tunnels where the Talyrians made their homes. Starshine's cave was the furthest back, whether as a show of respect, or because it was the best protected, Helena wasn't certain. The caves were massive and had clearly been created by the Chosen who had once been welcome here. Soft light glowed, reflecting golden light all along the ebony walls. There were also smaller rooms, more proportioned in size to something one of the Chosen would be comfortable with. Von and Helena had shared one such room in Starshine's cave.

The morning after their arrival, Starshine left the cave early. Catching a glimpse of the brilliant white fur streaking past her room, Helena started to follow her but stopped dead when Starshine turned. With one warning growl the Talyrian made it clear that Helena was not welcome at whatever meeting was about to take place.

Without being present it was impossible to know what transpired, but given their situation, it seemed most likely that Starshine was calling the Talyrians to war. When she did not see the Talyrian Queen for the rest of the day, Helena figured Starshine was spending time with the family she'd had to leave behind when she came to Tigaera. Or perhaps it wasn't her entire family but just one midnight fellow in particular. Either way, Helena couldn't blame the girl.

But now, with the sun just beginning to break through the clouds, it was time to meet the rest of the Circle in Etillion. When they'd left the others, they'd agreed to meet again in five days, and they'd been in Talyria for two, which meant they were already a couple hours behind schedule if they wanted to make it to Etillion by nightfall. Talyrians were fast, but they were not Kaelpas stones.

Helena stepped out of the cave and was stunned by the number of Talyrians that greeted her. At most, she'd come into contact with perhaps fifteen Talyrians in the past few days, and sadly not one of them was a snuggly cub. Now, however, there were well over forty gathered and preparing for flight. Some would surely stay behind to protect the young, but otherwise, they had a greater aerial force than she'd imagined.

Standing in the front of them all was Starshine. She looked more than a little majestic when surrounded by the others. As she made to walk over toward the Talyrian Queen, something unexpected happened.

Starshine tipped her head back and roared, a blast of flame lighting up the early morning sky. As one, every Talyrian responded in kind, their roars deafening. As the roars tapered off, they dropped low, baring their necks in the universal sign of submission. But it was not to Starshine that they made this display; it was to Helena.

Helena trembled, her throat thick with emotion as she watched the beautiful and proud creatures pledge themselves, and their lives, to her. And then Von was there, stepping past her and moving to stand beside Midnight.

"Von," she whispered, her voice quavering as she realized what he was going to do.

His gaze held hers as he joined the Talyrians, dropping to his knee and bowing his head.

"My power, my life, and my love are yours, Mira."

"That's all?" she asked, teasing because anything else would have her in tears. In the end, her levity didn't matter. When Von replied, his words leveled her.

"It's all that I am."

"It is more than I deserve."

His eyes went dark with the same emotion that filled her.

Too overwhelmed to speak, Helena placed her hand over her heart and dipped her head, bowing until she was almost bent in half. It was the Chosen's sign of deepest respect and reverence, one often used in the Mother's temples. As Kiri, there were none that she should ever have to bow to, but it was the only way she could think of to express how deeply their act had touched her.

There was another roar, and the Talyrians stood, moving to stand closer to her. Helena spent the next hour greeting and thanking each of them for their service. After she'd met the last of the Talyrians, Helena moved back to Starshine.

This time, Von would not be riding with her. Midnight had made it clear that he alone would have the privilege of carrying her Mate. Helena felt her heart stutter and then slam against her ribs as she caught sight of Von seated atop the great beast. It was like looking at a painting of her ancestors in the Palace. The sky was a blaze of fiery color while the two warriors were wrapped in darkness. The symbolism was not lost on her.

Von had dressed for battle, his ebony armor glinting in the sun's rays. Below him, Midnight's wings were raised as he prepared to leap into the air. Individually, each male was a force to be reckoned with. Together, they were the promise of a quick and painful death. Helena couldn't help but wonder how many would die with the image of Von astride Midnight being the last thing they ever saw.

Blinking she forced herself to turn away. Using a small burst of Air, Helena quickly got into position on Starshine.

"All right, girl. Let's go meet our friends."

With a final roar, Starshine leapt into the air. Behind her, Helena could hear the echoing roars of the Pride as they followed suit. Helena looked back over her shoulder seeing the sky fill with flapping wings. As Talyria grew smaller, Helena's heart grew heavy. This might be the last time any of them would see their home. The unwelcome thought settled tight and heavy in the bottom of her stomach.

Turning back around, she let out her own battle cry followed by a fiercely whispered promise, "I'm coming for you, you fucking bitch. Too many have already been lost because of your greed. You may have struck the first blow, but mine will be the last."

Helena's words were lost to the wind, but she hoped they found Rowena wherever she was hiding.

CHAPTER 22

*H*elena knew they must be in Etillion even without being able to see the massive wall that notoriously divided it from Endoshan. In the months after the twin territories divided, the wall was erected as a physical reminder of the separation. Flying from Talyria meant that they came into the realm from the Northeast and as such, were on the opposite side of the landmark. Even so, the hills that they'd been riding over had given way to flat land that had become pockmarked with buildings in the last hour or so.

Taking shape on the horizon was a much larger structure that she assumed was the embassy. Helena could just make out the silver tree on the forest green flags flying from each of the building's towers. As a Chosen territory, there was no capital as such. Just the sprawling building that housed the ambassador and her family. The additional bedrooms were for visiting Chosen.

There was comfort in seeing the familiar image, although it did little to ease the tension sitting in her neck and shoulders. While Helena clearly remembered the Etillion scholars that she'd met, she never had caught their names. She grimaced, already anticipating the potentially awkward greeting. Hopefully the others were already here, and Timmins could fill her in before she made an ass out of herself.

Being able to make use of the Kaelpas stones, they should have already arrived, assuming everything had gone according to their plan. She was eager to see her friends and hear about their time in the Broken Vale.

As they descended, Helena scanned the ground for some sign of her people, expecting they'd be on the lookout for her and Von's arrival, but there was none. No one was waiting to greet them. In fact, given the shouts of alarm, it did not seem like anyone was expecting them at all. Helena frowned, her spike of concern shooting like an arrow through her bond.

"They could just be delayed."

The unflappably calm sound of his voice did what nothing else could. Helena let out a breath she was unaware she'd been holding. *"We are already later than we'd planned. I had thought they would have made it by now."*

"As did I, but it is too soon for alarm."

Helena worried at her lower lip, but finally nodded. They still had a handful of hours left in the day. Technically no one was late. Yet.

Using her power to project her voice, she called out to the Etillions standing guard, "I am Kiri Helena Solene. I request the hospitality of my Etillion brothers and sisters."

A woman came running from the front door, waving her arms and shouting up at guards, "Stand down! Let them pass!" Her short brown hair and face were familiar. This was the woman that had come to the Palace.

They landed, the Talyrians spreading out until they all but surrounded the building. Helena could certainly appreciate the guards' hesitation to lower their weapons. Nothing about being surrounded by them felt safe. At least, until you saw them as allies and not a threat.

Helena and Von dismounted, walking quickly to reach the woman who they'd first met in Tigaera.

"Thank the Mother that you're here, Kiri. I did not expect you to arrive so soon!" The woman looked around, as if searching for others. "You did not bring your army?"

It was Helena's turn to look confused. "What do you mean?"

"Aren't you here because of Endoshan?"

"No," Helena said slowly. "What's happened to Endoshan?"

The woman's face went pale, she obviously did not relish the idea of breaking the news. "It has fallen, Kiri. Rowena's army marched through not two days past." Her voice broke as she added, "There were no survivors."

Helena felt like she was going to be sick, it was the Forest all over again. She had not been overly fond of the Endoshan heir, with his intense frowns and barbed comments, but he and the Endoshans were still her people.

"Etillion has been on guard ever since, expecting that we'd be her obvious next stop, but we've seen no sign of her army. It's as if they've entirely disappeared. We sent word to you at the Palace, but I gather you were not there to receive it."

There was a moment of stunned silence before Helena shook her head and replied. "No. I've been traveling throughout Elysia to gather allies. Etillion was to become our base. The rest of our party was supposed to meet us here today so that we could begin preparing for our own assault of Vyruul."

She did not think it was possible, but the woman's face became graver. "You are the first people we've seen since the messenger brought news of Endoshan."

Von frowned, sharing a concerned look with Helena.

To think, when they'd landed Helena's first concern was a forgotten name. The slip deserved to be rectified but there was little time to beat around the bush, so she opted for the direct approach. "I'm so sorry, but I can't seem to remember your name."

"There's no need to apologize, Kiri. There was little time for introductions when we last met. I'm Amara."

Helena smiled gratefully. "Amara, is there anyone here, another scholar perhaps, who is familiar with the Broken Vale?"

Amara frowned. "The Forsaken territory? Why, do you think that's where Rowena is?"

Shaking her head, Helena clarified, "It's where the rest of my

Circle is. I need to get word to them about Endoshan. I thought they would beat us here since they have use of the Kaelpas stones, but something must have delayed them."

Amara looked momentarily impressed, but did not hesitate to answer, "We can ask Xander. He's traveled often as part of his studies. If anyone here would be familiar with such a place, it would be him."

Amara made to move into the stone building and Helena turned before she followed, speaking to Starshine, "Stand guard. Let me know when the others arrive."

Starshine dipped her head in acknowledgement of the order.

Sharing one last worried look with Von, the couple followed Amara into the Embassy.

XANDER, it turned out, was the long-haired man that had accompanied Amara to the Palace. Amara had taken them straight to where he was busy flipping through heavy leather-bound tomes.

He looked up in surprise when they'd entered the study, his gaze suggesting he did not appreciate the interruption. When he realized who it was that interrupted him, he'd done a double take before dropping the book he'd been holding.

"K-Kiri! You made it. Thank the Mother."

Amara was quick to shake her head and cut off his effusive thanks. "They only just heard of Endoshan when they arrived. We need to send word to the Circle in the Broken Vale."

Xander's eyebrows dropped in a frown. "What in the Mother's name is the Circle doing with the Forsaken?"

Helena couldn't help her amusement at the censorious cast of his voice. Von's arms crossed and he lifted a brow as the younger man continued.

"Has everyone forgotten that we're in the middle of a war? A war that they asked *us* to help resolve?"

Amara's cheeks went red and she cleared her throat in warning.

Xander blinked, as he remembered who he was speaking to. He had the grace to look embarrassed, but he did not look away.

"Apologies, Kiri. It's been a stressful few days, well weeks really, ever since the attack at the Palace."

She shook her head, dismissing his apology. "It's been a trying time for us all. No need to apologize."

Von was feeling less forgiving, and just continued to stare although he remained quiet. The lack of words did not make his message any less clear.

Xander, looking flustered, began to shuffle the papers on his desk.

"I think you're making him nervous."

"Good."

"And that's helpful how exactly?" she asked in exasperation.

Relenting, Von lowered his arms and turned the force of his gaze from Xander, back to her.

"Can you help us get a message to the Circle in the Broken Vale?"

Xander's eyes grew distant. "It could be possible to get a message to a specific individual, regardless of the place. Do you have something that belongs to one of them?"

Helena took a mental inventory, working through the list of all that she had packed to take with her to Talyria. Just as she was about the shake her head, she remembered Effie had tucked a heavy cloak in her bag. "It could be cold that far North," she'd said when Helena went to protest the addition. It looked like Effie's foresight might be what saved them all.

"I have a cloak."

"Perfect," Xander murmured. "We will need to borrow it."

Helena nodded her agreement.

"The birds should be able to track the individual through their scent."

"Isn't it a little far for them to pick-up the trail?" Von asked dubiously.

"These are no ordinary birds," Xander said with no little bit of pride.

Von snorted in disbelief. Xander's chest puffed out as his mouth fell open. Helena had no doubt he was about to launch into an extensive defense of his birds. Having no patience, or time, for male posturing, she interjected before Xander could.

"Go grab your birds, please. I will prepare a message and gather the cloak."

Xander shot a parting look at Von who rolled his eyes.

"You can't really believe this is going to work."

"What other choice do we have?"

Von shook his head and turned toward the open window behind him. There were a few long moments of silence as the trio waited for Xander to return.

"Helena!" Von shouted suddenly, just as Starshine bellowed a warning.

Rushing to his side at the window, Helena looked where Von was pointing. It was a little hard to see at first, but she could easily spot the human shape once her eyes adjusted to the dim light. Wasting no time, Helena ran for the door, flying through the halls like the hounds of hell were at her heels. Von and Amara were mere seconds behind her as she stumbled back outside. She didn't stop until she was standing just beside a man she vaguely recognized as one of their runners. The man was covered in dirt and smears of what looked like blood.

Her heart seized at the sight. She already knew what he was about to tell her.

"Kiri?" he rasped.

Dropping to her knees, Helena took his hand and held it tightly in hers. "Yes."

"Thank the Mother I found you," the man said before breaking into wet coughs. Helena ran her palm over his chest, doing what she could to numb his pain. As she opened herself to perform the healing, she found the gaping wound in his back; he'd been stabbed.

"Where are the others?" Helena asked through a tight throat.

His one-word reply was inaudible so she dipped her head, all but pressing her ear to his lips. He repeated himself just as his eyes rolled back into his head and he fell unconscious. Her face bleached of color as she looked back up at the others.

"What'd he say?" Von demanded.

"Attack."

Above them the sky ripped in two as a bolt of lightning shot down. A storm began to rage around them, but it had nothing on the one raging inside of her.

FOREST OF WHISPERS
FIVE DAYS EARLIER

Ronan watched Helena and Von disappear into the sky, a ripple of unease running along his spine. He'd felt that same warning tingle countless times before. Normally it preceded an attack or battle, but glancing around, there was nothing to indicate any enemies were lurking in the shadows.

"May the Mother watch over you both," he whispered.

The men standing on either side of him shifted, preparing to head back. He was the last to turn away and was startled to see that Reyna had also remained behind.

"You are close to them," she stated after her intense green eyes scanned his face.

Ronan nodded once, wondering what it was that she'd read there. Her expression was hard to decipher beneath the black swirls of paint.

"Not used to being left behind?" she guessed.

Ronan lifted his right shoulder in a shrug. "The last time the Circle was parted was hard on all of us. Some memories do not easily fade."

Her eyes softened. "No, they do not."

The only sound as they walked was the soft crunch of dried leaves beneath their feet. After a long pause she asked, "Are you worried for their safety?"

Ronan's eyes narrowed as he examined the unease that still ate at him. "No," he finally answered. "I do not believe it is their safety that concerns me. Helena is more than capable of handling whatever comes their way and Von would die before he let something happen to his Mate. Nor do I doubt the Talyrians will come to their aid if necessary."

"Your Kiri is quite powerful," Reyna said after a long pause.

Ronan gave her a sidelong glance. "Aye. She is."

"Is it love for her that has you worried then?"

Ronan let out a loud bark of laughter at the absurdity of the question. The subtle pink tinge on Reyna's cheeks had the last of his laughter fading. "No, not like that anyway."

"Oh."

Ronan spared her another curious glance as he moved to lift a branch out of their path. He was struggling to make sense of the Night Stalker's line of questioning. Reyna ducked below the branch and continued without looking back. "What has you worried then, Chosen?"

Ronan let out a frustrated sigh, raking his hands through his unbound hair. The problem was that he had no clue what was causing the itchy feeling just beneath his skin. "Something is coming," he finally answered.

"That is not news," she stated, eying him over her shoulder as he closed the distance between them. "It is why you sought our assistance in the first place."

He scowled at her. "It's not the threat of battle." And it wasn't. Battle made his blood sing, it was why he'd never questioned following Von when he'd went mercenary. "What I'm feeling is different. Darker somehow. I cannot explain it."

Reyna's hand burned where it made contact with his arm. He lifted a brow in question, surprised by the touch. Reyna looked equally confused and slowly moved her hand off his arm. "Do not ignore whatever it is that is trying to warn you." Her voice was low and urgent, her green eyes glittering with intensity.

Ronan nodded once. "I won't."

The Night Stalker let out a slow breath as her village came back into view. "I would go with you now, if I could. But my people aren't ready for the battle to come. We need more time."

"I know."

Reyna gave him one last inscrutable look. "Do not die, Chosen. I would like to see you again." With that she turned and walked away.

"What the fuck docs that mean?" he asked himself, rubbing a hand along the back of his neck.

THE CHOSEN WERE ALREADY PACKED and ready to go by the time he returned. Serena and Effie were talking in low voices when he joined them. Sensing his presence, Serena spun around looking furious.

"You didn't think we would also appreciate getting to see them off?"

"You were sleeping."

"So?"

Ronan threw up his hands, not ready to walk through a verbal minefield. "I wasn't the only one that didn't wake you up, why am I the one getting the lecture?"

"Because you know better."

"Oh, for fuck's sake."

Effie was trying to smother a smile, which only infuriated him further.

He stuck a finger in her face. "You gonna give me shit too?"

She pressed her lips together and quickly shook her head, her blue eyes twinkling with suppressed laughter.

"That's a fucking first."

Serena's eyes widened at the hint of his temper. "What crawled up your ass?"

Not about to get into another circular conversation regarding what had him on edge he just shook his head.

"Seriously, Ronan. Is everything okay?" The anger had left her face and Serena was looking at him with concerned violet eyes.

Ronan rubbed at his eyes before pinching the bridge of his nose, squeezing hard to relieve some of the extra tension. When he spoke, he sounded tired but steady, "It's just a feeling I can't shake. Nothing to worry about."

The women studied him but did not push him further.

Surprised they let it go so easily, Ronan glanced at each of them. Both women were standing with the alert stillness of warriors awaiting orders. It was then that Ronan realized they had heard all that he hadn't said. Effie because of her natural insight and Serena because of her years of training and fighting beside him. She'd seen what happened when they ignored his 'feelings' in the past and did not care to repeat that experience ever again. He was glad for it. If there was anyone he trusted to watch his back when Von was gone, it was certainly her.

The knowledge steadied him further. Taking the first easy breath since he'd woken that morning, he gave them each a grateful smile before turning to address the others that had gathered behind him.

Ronan cleared his throat, easily silencing the murmuring voices of the gathered crowd. If the men in the Circle minded that he was speaking for them they did not let on. Of all of them, he was the one most used to speaking to large groups. His sheer size and the carrying boom of his voice made him a natural at it.

"Chosen, it's time to leave. We've been lucky so far, no doubt because of our Kiri's power, but that does not mean our luck will continue. As we move through the Broken Vale, be alert, be watchful, but most importantly, be respectful. We do not know which of our actions may cause offense and we cannot risk a misunderstanding."

The men and women nodded solemnly. Even the wolves seemed to bob their heads in agreement. It was clear that they all understood the seriousness of the task that laid ahead of them.

"Gather with your groups, runners be ready to follow shortly."

The crowd dispersed as they moved into position. The men of the

Circle were already waiting for him, along with Miranda, Effie, Serena, Nial and their runner. They'd gotten lucky when they learned that one of the Night Stalkers had been to the Vale before, and that she was going to help the first group make the trip.

The group took hands, bunching in tight. Ronan took the hand of their runner. As he did, a cold tingle ran in a straight line along the back of his neck, almost as if a finger was brushing against it. He shuddered and twisted his head to catch a look at the woman whose hand he was holding. Her face blurred, the swirls of her make-up slithering like snakes across her face. He blinked rapidly, about to shout out a warning as the woman's green eyes went coal black and her lips twisted into a sinister sneer.

Before he could do anything, she activated the Kaelpas stone and made the jump to the Vale.

WHEN THEY LANDED, Ronan fought the wave of sickness that always accompanied the jump, looking for the runner. She was already gone, which meant that they were stranded here; wherever here was. It was not a place he recognized. There was only fine sand as far as the eye could see.

Ronan roared, the others jumping in surprise at the sound.

"What is it?" Effie asked, reaching for him with concern.

Beside her, Miranda stared just past his shoulder in growing horror. "I have Seen this," she murmured.

Effie spun back toward her grandmother. "What did you See?"

Even Timmins, who usually wore a look of thinly veiled contempt when he looked at the Keeper was staring at her intently as they awaited her answer.

"Darkness and bloodshed," she whispered.

Ronan shielded and reached for his axes, but they had been stored. He settled for clenched fists, ready to swing at the first sign of attack.

"What do you mean?" Timmins demanded. His voice held none of the disbelief it usually did when speaking to the Keeper.

Miranda blinked, appearing to return from wherever her thoughts had wandered. When she spoke, she seemed apologetic. "It is only images, nothing specific."

"Whatever warning your vision could provide may be all the upper-hand we need to change the outcome," Kragen said softly.

Some of the color was beginning to return to her face as she spoke. "There is a mountain, surrounded by a forest of trees. A rock breaks from the mountain and flies away. When the rock comes to rest, it is alone in a sea of sand. Darkness rolls in on every side until the rock drowns in it. When light returns all that remains is a ring of blood."

"Not a ring. A Circle," Effie corrected.

Miranda's midnight eyes flew to her granddaughter, who seemed startled that she'd even spoken. Her cornflower blue eyes were wide and her hands had flown up to cover her mouth.

Haunted by her words, Ronan shuddered. If what the Keeper saw was indeed a warning, it seemed that not all of them would be walking away from whatever came with the darkness. At least not entirely unscathed. He glanced around at the others, wondering if they'd reached the same conclusion.

Each of the men looked grim but determined. Nial wrapped his arm around Serena, who looked shaken.

"So what now?" Darrin asked, his eyes ping-ponging between the Keeper and her granddaughter, as if they held more answers.

The group looked around, finally taking in their surroundings. Not that there was much to see. In every direction it was the same. Sand. Sand on the ground and sand whirling through the air carried by gusts of wind. Above them, the sun beat down, its heat punishing.

"Do you think she brought us to the Vale after all?" Serena asked.

"From everything I was able to find, that must be where we are. It's a broken realm, its buildings predominantly in ruins after the great uprising."

"So where are all the people?" It was Darrin who asked the question, but they'd all been wondering the same thing.

"Underground," Joquil answered.

Ronan's brow lifted in disbelief.

"It's true," Nial said. "After the uprising, none of the buildings were fit for habitation. Instead of rebuilding, believing the spirits of their ancestors would haunt anything built on the land where they'd be killed, they used their power to create a network of caverns and tunnels below ground."

Kragen cursed softly. "How are we supposed to find an entrance to these magical tunnels?"

Nial shrugged. "I don't think we are. They are referred to as the lost tribes for a reason."

"Are they really lost if they know where they are and we are the ones that can't seem to find them?" Darrin mused aloud.

The group chuckled, the philosophical question seeming out of place given the circumstances.

Ronan sighed, lifting his hand to cover his eyes as he squinted into the distance. "I'm sure Helena would have a plan to find them, but I cannot pretend to know it. Let us hope that our presence here disturbed some sort of alarm and they come to us. I cannot think of another way to find help."

"Do you think that the Night Stalkers are behind this betrayal?" Kragen asked, purposefully avoiding Joquil's gaze.

"No," Ronan said without hesitation. "This was another of Rowena's spies. They must have stayed behind after the attack on Duskfall, waiting for an opportunity like this one. No one knows where we are save the runner. It is doubtful help is on the way."

"Should we seek shelter then?" Kragen asked. "It does not seem like a good idea to simply wait here if we are indeed about to be attacked."

Ronan frowned as he considered Miranda's warning and their situation. "Do you think the darkness was literal? Does the threat come with the night?"

Miranda shrugged. "I don't know. It's possible."

He looked up, trying to discern the time based on the sun's position in the sky. "At most we have eight hours before nightfall. We may not find anything in that time, but if there's a chance we should probably take it. If for no other reason than to not be sitting ducks, remaining in the exact place the traitor left us."

The group nodded their agreement.

"So which direction do we go?" Serena asked.

"Fuck if I know," Ronan replied. "Your guess is as good as mine."

"Let's head west," Effie said, surprising the others with her suggestion. It was rare for her to take charge.

"Why west?" Darrin asked.

"Doesn't the Vale share a border with the Forest? Perhaps we are not too far away and can get back there. Or at least close enough that their scouts will see us."

Darrin's eyes shone with approval at her reasoning. Even Ronan had to admit he was impressed; he hadn't even considered the possibility. "It's as good of a reason as any, and probably better than most. If there's a chance we could get word to the Night Stalkers, we should definitely take it."

The others were quick to agree.

"All right," Ronan decided, "to the West it is. Stay alert everyone, we may be out in the open, but that means our enemies will be as well. Keep your shields up, but do not use your power more than you have to. We want to be ready when the strike comes, because there is no doubt one is coming."

CHAPTER 24

Ronan was wrong. When the attack came, no one saw it coming.

They had trudged through the sand for hours, no closer to finding shelter for the effort. They'd finally ended up making camp for the night right there in the open. Two days passed with more of the same. Then, on the fourth day, just as the sun begun to set, clouds filled the sky. Around them sand whipped up into the air, making it impossible to see much of anything.

Their only warning was one long keening cry before a ball of fire flew through the sky and landed at their feet. Suddenly the air cleared and Ronan could make out the black wave of Rowena's army coming at them. It was twelve against twelve hundred, but it would have to be enough. There had been no way to get word to Helena, no one would be coming to save them.

There was no time for words of inspiration. The sound of weapons being drawn rang around him while the four wolves, Karma and Shepa among them, growled and crouched ready for battle. Ronan's eyes caught Serena's, both were wide with panic but when they met a feeling of calm washed through him. He saw the same peace spread across her face.

The first of the Shadows were already running for them. Nial was murmuring, summoning his considerable power to create a shield around them all. Where the Shadows made impact with the smoky barrier it sizzled, and the Shadows flew back with howls of pain. The magic ate at their skin like acid, not stopping until it reached bone.

But they continued to swarm, undaunted. It was only a matter of time before they got through the barrier. Soon Timmins and Joquil were adding their power to reinforce the barrier. Their goal to try to whittle through the numbers as much as possible before they had to start their own attack. The backlash of power through the barrier was not enough to kill the Shadows, but it was strong enough to eat through limbs, which made many of the abominations less of a threat.

Sweat was dripping down Nial's face as he tried to keep the barrier up. Each blow against its surface reverberated through him and it was taking a toll. At least an hour had passed without any sign of relent. Ronan saw the moment Nial knew he'd have to let it go; the burden was becoming more than he could physically withstand. Ronan nodded at Nial, letting him know that it was okay; they were ready to take up the fight.

Ronan moved into position, and the others followed suit around him. There was no hesitation, no sign of fear. He knew this dance well. Whatever the outcome, he was born for battle. The only way he'd stop fighting was if they killed him, and if that was to be the case, he'd take down as many of the walking corpses as he could before he fell.

Ahead of him, standing on a sand dune was Rowena. She was decked out entirely in black, her dress shining like scales of armor. Her crown was twisted spikes of metal, looking more like a weapon than an ornamental headpiece. Ice filled his veins as she smiled down at him. He knew, despite the distance, that her smile was for him alone. The certainty on her face had his own lips pulling back in a snarl. Let her believe she would win this. It would make their victory that much sweeter.

Rowena made a gesture and one of the men standing beside her peeled away from the others to join the fray. But Ronan didn't have time to be distracted by where he went.

When Nial dropped the barrier, Ronan threw his head back and screamed, pouring his rage into the sound. The others joined him, their voices becoming a bloodthirsty chorus.

The battle had begun.

Ronan soon lost sight of the others. Time lost all meaning. Nothing existed but him and the swing of his axes. Each blow was reinforced with his power, and every strike was true. He knew he was leaving a pile of bodies in his wake, but there was no end to the enemies. His only focus was to clear a path to the she-bitch waiting for him atop the hill.

That was when her general struck. Just as at the Palace, this one had corrupted power. A ball of purple-black flame grew in his hand. He threw it, aiming for Ronan. Grabbing the Shadow that was standing beside him, Ronan tossed the creature in front of him before ducking and rolling to the side. When he stood, he twisted back to see the Shadow who had become a pillar of purple flames. The flames made quick work of the body but were not extinguished once the body had been consumed. Instead they continued to burn, snaking slowly toward him.

Ronan continued to throw as many bodies between himself and the flames as possible. Soon the air was thick with pale purple smoke and there were a number of purple fires raging within the crush of bodies. At least the fire also destroyed the Shadows. It had helped take down a number of them so that Ronan could move about a bit more freely.

"Use the flames!" he shouted.

Darrin had caught up to him and nodded his understanding, ducking and ramming his shoulder into the body of the Shadow that was running at him. The Shadow flipped over him and fell on his back into the fire.

The distraction of watching the other man nearly cost him. Ronan did not see the fist that flew toward his face. He took the blow, his vision going dark as stars burst behind his eyes. Using instinct, Ronan lashed out, listening for the grunt that accompanied his ax's impact to determine how to position his body for the next strike. He was rewarded with the gurgle of blood and the thud of a body. Blinking a few more times his vision finally cleared, although he was not entirely certain what it was he was now seeing.

Outside the swarm of Shadows tall dark shapes were beginning to form. It looked like trees, but that didn't make any sense. There had been nothing but sand for days.

There was a shout behind him. Recognizing the voice, Ronan spun. As Serena's face came into view he saw that it was not a shout of warning but excitement. She noticed the gathering shapes as well but knew what they were. He was too far away to hear her words but could make out well enough what her lips were saying.

It looked like she'd said, "Watchers."

Understanding dawned. If the Watchers were here, that meant the Night Stalkers had found them. They must have been close to the border after all. He was going to make a point to give Effie a proper kiss once this was over. Assuming he lived to see the end of it. That girl had probably saved their lives with her suggestion to head west.

The horizon began to fill with shadowy shapes until it looked like the forest was descending on them. There was a shriek of outrage as Rowena took notice. He watched her face twist in anger before she called forth one of her other four generals.

"Not feeling so good now that it's a fair fight, do you, you stupid bitch?" he murmured gleefully. With a renewed sense of purpose, Ronan moved to intercept him before he could add his twisted magic to the fray.

It was full night now, but they had not stopped. The battle had been raging for hours. Darrin could feel his body growing tired but pressed on. He was not sure how much longer he would last, but they had not lost anyone so far, and Darrin did not intend to let that change. He kept his eye on Effie, knowing that she did not have power to aid her as the others did. So far, that had not done much to hamper his girl.

She fought like an alley cat, using her small size to her advantage. She would move and twist faster than the Shadows could anticipate, dancing out of the way of their attacks and striking from behind them. He could not help the surge of pride he felt watching her take down the hulking creatures.

The wolves were coated in black blood, the pack responsible for taking down at least a hundred of the monsters on their own. They fought together, going for the throat or distracting their target so another could attack. It was hard to tell if they'd sustained any injuries, but it appeared as if at least one of them was limping slightly. Even so, it did not slow them down at all.

Joquil, Timmins, Miranda and Nial were grouped together, using their power to take down as many of the Shadows as possible. Balls of Fire would hit a Shadow to be followed by one of Water to try to stop the flames from growing out of control. So far, the Water did not seem to do anything against the purple flames that Rowena's general kept launching. Miranda was using Air to keep the pale purple smoke away from them. Darrin's lungs were still burning from the one breath he accidentally inhaled.

Kragen and Serena were relentless, their blades both dripping with blood. Ronan's had been as well, but Darrin had lost sight of him shortly after his tip about the fire. That had been about the time that the Night Stalkers had arrived. The extra numbers quickly changed the tide. The blurred figures were like nothing Darrin had ever seen. They would appear behind their target, using their weapons and sometimes just their hands to rip off the heads of the creatures and then toss them into the smoking fire, before quickly blurring and moving onto another. It was impossible to anticipate where they would strike next.

The Watchers were just as incredible. Darrin wasn't even sure what he was seeing was real when the first of the colossal tree-men moved into range. He was absolutely massive, each of his movements deliberate and slow. That did not mean they were not powerful. With each lumbering step, the Watcher crushed dozens of their enemies. Darrin had the impression of trees swaying in a storm but did not have the time to spend thinking about it. He'd barely had time to crane his head back and try to find the gnarled face etched into the upper trunk of the tree. Darrin had to force himself to look away; he'd study them later. Once they'd won this battle.

As he continued to fight, Darrin saw more of the Watchers come into focus. They would stoop down, using their branches to pick up and fling a handful of Shadows into the crowd. Often the maneuver would kill a Shadow on impact, their necks snapping with the force. More often, Rowena's minions would pick themselves up and rush back into the fray. Still, the Watcher's had greatly culled her force.

A high-pitched scream pulled Darrin out of his thoughts. He spun, making quick work of the two stumbling Shadows in front of him. Both looked more corpse than human, and it was not hard to remove their heads from their bodies. Once they'd fallen he saw what made Effie scream.

Ronan was battling one of the generals. It was hard to tell Rowena's men apart unless they were using their power, but this one had long stringy hair. Its lips were twisted in some gruesome semblance of a smile and it was lifting its hand as it called on its power. There was a chittering sound coming from its gaping mouth that could have been a taunt or laughter. Darrin was too far away to tell but the sound had Ronan launching himself in the air, throwing his axes one after the other. The general stumbled as the axes made contact. One neatly shearing off an arm, while the other buried itself in its chest.

The general snarled, using its remaining arm to pull the ax free and toss it to the ground. Deep black blood spurted from the wounds, but the general did not falter. Still holding onto his power, the general released it down into the sand. That was when Darrin realized which general this one must be. Earth.

When Ronan landed, he began to sink into the mass of quicksand the Earth general had created. He sank fast, his body more than half obscured by the pit of burbling sand. Darrin started to run, intent on saving him before he was completely submerged.

Darrin was full-on sprinting, his heart thundering in his chest. He wasn't going to make it. He was just too far away.

Beside Ronan, shadows rippled and peeled away. In their place,

Reyna took shape. Her face was hidden behind the swirls of her make-up but that did nothing to obscure the look of murderous rage in her glittering green eyes. She dropped to her knees, using her considerable strength to pull Ronan out of the sand. At the same time, she flung her other arm out. Her dagger burying itself in the general's neck. It was not enough to kill him, but it did knock him down.

With a shriek of outrage, Reyna began to stand, digging her heels into the sand and using the counterbalance to help her pull Ronan free. For a moment it did not appear that she would be successful, his body weight combined with the force of the quicksand more than a match for her. But with another shriek, she tugged again. There was a loud, wet sucking sound and Ronan surged upward before promptly falling onto the sand beside her.

They were both panting, but there was no time for them to catch their breath. As one, they stood and raced for the general, who was already struggling back to his feet. Ronan grabbed his ax as he ran toward the man, using his momentum to swing it into the general's neck. The slice was so clean, it almost appeared as if the blow did not land. The general was still blinking when his head began to slide off of his neck and fall to the floor.

Rowena screamed in outrage as her general fell, and with a swirl of her black cloak she fled the battle. Darrin grinned, knowing that her retreat meant the battle would be theirs. Focusing back on the chaos around him, he began to work his way toward Effie. If he hadn't been looking for her, he never would have seen the swirling ball of purple fire as it left the Fire general's hand heading straight toward her.

"No!" Darrin screamed, rushing toward Effie, intent on pushing her out of harm's way. Darrin ran faster than he'd ever moved before, feeling his power give him an inhuman burst of speed. Effie's eyes went wide and he could see them fill with fear as she watched the fireball race toward her.

It was over in a heartbeat, but it felt as though time had slowed completely. He was aware of each frame as it occurred. The blink of her beautiful blue eyes and the way her lashes tangled together when they closed. The petal pink of her lips as her mouth opened on a scream. The heavy thud of her body as it made contact with the ground.

But more than anything, Darrin was aware of the burst of pain as the fireball hit his back and then consumed him. The corrupted flames made quick work of his shield and armor until nothing stood between them and his skin. The pain was absolute.

Darrin stared into Effie's eyes, wanting the image of the woman he'd fallen in love with be the last thing he ever saw as his knees buckled and hit the ground.

A look of confusion, and then horror, crossed Effie's face as she realized what had happened. "Darrin!" she screamed, scrambling on her hands and knees toward him.

He could see the purple flames licking up his chest and arms. It would not be long before they covered him completely. It was impossible to think, let alone form words, but somehow he did. With what he wanted to say, it was too important not to.

"Effie," he gasped.

"Nonononono!" Effie screamed over and over, tears streaming down her face. She searched for something to extinguish the flames but found nothing except the skirt of her travel dress. Even as she tore the fabric using it to beat at the fire, Darrin knew it was futile. The shadow flames had melted armor on impact, there was little that a piece of cloth could do against it. As predicted, the flimsy fabric easily caught fire, forcing Effie to drop it with a strangled cry.

"I love you." The words were barely audible as they left his mouth. Darrin only knew she'd heard him because her face twisted in pain and she repeated them brokenly as she sobbed.

It was all he needed to let go. As his eyes fell closed, Effie's face blurred and faded away. With it went the pain. In his last coherent moment, Darrin was overcome with peace as he saw the familiar face of his best friend take shape within his mind.

Helena, he thought with a mix of relief and surprise. *At least I am not dying alone.*

CHAPTER 25

It was Effie's scream that pulled Ronan's attention away from the still twitching body of Rowena's general. As he turned toward the sound, he saw the pyre of purple flames she was kneeling beside.

"What the hell does she think she's doing?" he muttered darkly, wondering why she was letting her hand hover so close to the deadly flames. That was when he realized Darrin was missing.

Since the battle had started, hell, since they'd left Tigaera a few weeks ago, he'd barely strayed from her side. He may have been Helena's Shield in name and by vow, but he'd clearly extended that duty to Effie. So why wasn't he the one pulling her out of harm's way now?

The answer came to him as he watched the small woman's body begin to shake with the force of her sobs. It wasn't the flames she was trying to touch; it was what was concealed within them.

"Mother be merciful," he said, taking off at a dead run.

"Where do you think—" Reyna started to shout as she efficiently beheaded another of the Shadows, but he didn't have time to explain.

He covered the distance easily, despite the protesting ache of his body from hours of endless fighting.

"Effie," he said softly, watching her begin to rock back and forth.

She didn't hear him.

Ronan glanced around, ensuring that they would remain safe for the moment, before squatting down beside her. "Come on, *Mira*. Let's get you somewhere safe." The Chosen's term of endearment also had no effect. It wasn't until he touched her shoulder that she looked up, hissing at him like a feral cat. Her eyes were crazed and unseeing.

"Shhh, Effie. It's me."

Effie blinked, her eyes returning to normal as she recognized the man in front of her.

"R-Ronan," she sobbed, launching herself at him.

She may have been small, but her momentum almost knocked him on his ass. He caught and held her with a muffled oomph.

"Da-Darrin," she started.

"Shhh," he whispered, tucking her head into his chest so that she could not look back at the body, or what was left of it.

"We can't leave him here," she hiccupped.

Ronan frowned. Darrin wasn't going anywhere. There was nothing he knew of that would extinguish the flames. The Water the others had summoned to try just that didn't even slow the purple blaze down. Perhaps Helena would have been able to do something, but she wasn't here. And by the time she got here... well, there'd be nothing left to bury.

"I'll take care of it," he promised.

Effie looked up at him from where she was cradled in his arms. She looked like a broken doll, her face smeared with dirt and streaked with tears. The sadness in her big blue eyes made his heart ache. "Thank you," she whispered.

They were the last words Effie said for quite some time. It was as if, with that last task assured, she could retreat into the safety of her thoughts to mourn the future she'd never have. Ronan easily picked her up and carried her through the fray. It would have been a comical sight, the way he had to duck and weave around those that were engaged in battle, if so much wasn't on the line.

He carried her to her grandmother, knowing that Miranda would be able to take over from there. He opened his mouth to explain, but by the look in those ancient midnight eyes, he saw he didn't have to. She already knew. The Keeper had probably known it was going to happen days, or maybe even years, before it did. What a burden that must have been.

As he set Effie down, Ronan pressed a swift kiss to her forehead. "Stay strong, little bird. He would not want to see this break you."

The words breathed new life into her, and Effie looked up nodding her understanding.

It wasn't until he turned to run back to the others that he realized what Darrin's death truly meant. The Circle was broken.

Helena had made him promise he would protect them, and he'd let her down. She was never going to forgive him.

EVEN WITH THE appearance of the Night Stalkers, and the rest of the Chosen who'd shown up shortly thereafter once the runners had been able to reestablish their relay, they fought for several more hours. Eventually though, either due to the Mother's grace or sheer dumb luck, they were able to dispatch the remaining Shadows.

Still, it was by no means quick or easy. They were already exhausted and still very much outnumbered. But by the time the sun began to rise, the body count was high but the Chosen were the last ones standing.

No one saw what happened to Rowena or her four remaining generals. Ronan assumed that they must have fled once they saw Darrin fall. He had a feeling that had been what she was after. Ronan wouldn't rest until they he watched the woman breathe her last. Just because she was out of sight, did not mean she was gone.

The battle might be over, but his work here wasn't finished. He tried not to groan as he forced himself forward. He had a promise to keep.

Around him, others worked through what was left of the bodies checking to make sure there were no survivors. They were also carrying off their dead so that they could be given a proper burial. It was grim work, but important.

Reyna caught his eye and gave him a smile so brief he half-thought he imagined it. He still wasn't sure what to make of the Night Stalker, but he did owe her a heartfelt thank you at some point. If it hadn't been for her, none of them would be alive right now.

He walked deliberately, stepping carefully around the shadowy purple flames and dead bodies. As the fight had continued through the night, the purple glow had illuminated the battlefield with its eerie light. Now that the sun was beginning to shine, the glow was almost black.

The fire had a sentience he couldn't explain. It burned through whatever it touched, moving on in search of a new target once its fuel had been consumed. Judging by the fact that the entire landscape was not a blazing purple inferno, it would seem that if the flames did not find a new fuel source they died out on their own. Nothing else they tried had been able to, but to be fair, they'd also had their hands full with the mindless corpses that were trying to kill them.

Ronan sighed as he returned to the spot he'd found Effie and Darrin. He'd lost men before, good men, but this was different. In the months they'd spent searching for Von, the younger man had become part of his family. This loss cut deep. He could only imagine how much worse it would be for Helena. Especially when Darrin had been the last link to her past. A wave of sadness and guilt washed over him at the thought of having to tell her what had happened.

Kneeling, he took a deep breath. There was nothing left except ash. It would have to be enough. He began to scoop the still-smoking pile into one of his travel sacks and was proud when his hands only trembled slightly as they came into contact of what remained of his friend.

Before he stood, Ronan closed his eyes and offered a prayer to the Mother, asking her to welcome her son home. He was not a devout man by any stretch of the imagination. He'd seen entirely too much death and hatefulness in the world to believe that there was really a deity out there watching over them. If the Mother did exist, how could she allow such tragedies to occur? But as he gently lifted the now full bag in his hands, he desperately needed to believe.

Ronan turned back toward the hill where they'd set up a sort of camp and his breath left him with a whoosh. The lone figure standing sentinel was unexpected. He blinked quickly to ensure she was not some kind of mirage. She wasn't. When his eyes reopened, Helena was still there.

The weight of the bag grew heavier with each step as Ronan closed the distance between them, his eyes never once leaving hers. As he neared her, he could see that Von was standing just to the side of her, ready if she needed him. In his own way, Ronan wanted to lend her his strength as well. So he did it in the only way he could, by bearing witness to the full weight of her pain. He let it wash over him, hoping that by sharing it he could ease some of the burden. Ronan had thought Effie had been grief-stricken, but it was nothing compared to the tortured expression in Helena's aqua eyes.

She stood stiffly, holding herself so tightly that her knuckles were white. It looked like she was physically trying to hold herself together, probably to keep herself from completely falling apart. Ronan swallowed down a wave of emotion as he finally reached her. It wasn't until he was standing just in front of her that she looked down at what he was offering her.

Her face and eyes were dry, but Ronan knew that she was dying inside. He could feel it as surely as if he was standing next to her. Her nostrils flared as her eyes flew back up to his. He watched her struggle to catch her breath as she reached out to accept the bag. A part of him wanted to keep it in hopes that it would spare her, but he knew it was far too late for that. There was no escaping this pain.

Helena took the bag from him and curled herself protectively around it, resting her cheek against the top. She stayed there a long time, just holding what was left of her friend close to her. All the while her lips were moving silently, almost like she was praying, or perhaps whispering words meant for him alone. It wasn't until she was done that he saw the first of her tears or took notice of the rain.

HELENA DIDN'T NEED anyone to tell her what had happened. She'd felt it the instant they'd arrived in the Broken Vale. The pain that exploded through her Jaka was enough to have her fall to her knees and clutch at her side. Its intensity was overwhelming; she could hardly focus enough to make sense of what the pain meant. As she struggled to breathe through the waves of fiery pain, she was finally able to gather herself enough to follow the pain to its source. The emptiness that greeted her there rendered her completely numb. The loss was too much for her brain to process.

Ever since Ronan had given her the Jaka, she'd felt the connection to each of the men that comprised her Circle. She'd grown used to the unique feeling of each individual strand, recognizing the nuances that separated each of them without having to try. It was how she knew with utter certainty that one was missing, and who it was.

"Helena, what is it?" Von shouted, the frantic cast of his voice alerting her to the fact that this wasn't the first time he'd asked.

She looked up at him from where she'd curled up on the ground. "Darrin."

The hollow tone of her voice told him everything. His eyes went dark, and he let out a long breath. "What do you need?"

Helena pushed herself to her feet. "We need to find the others. They might still need our help."

A conflicted look crossed his face. Von knew that she was barely holding on, she knew he could feel it through their bond. He'd also witnessed her rage and grief over losing the man who raised her only weeks ago. There was no way he would believe that she was unaffected by the loss of the man she'd grown up with, no matter what sort of brave face she tried to present. But there was a time and a place to grieve, and this was not it. She knew Von reached the same conclusion when he held out a hand to help her stand up.

There was a soft cough. The runner was staring awkwardly at the ground, waiting for them to take notice of him and the Etillions that had travelled with them.

"Do you know where they are?" she asked in the same hollowed out voice.

The man nodded.

"Take me there."

There was no indication that a battle still raged. The sun was just starting to light up the sky, and the world around them was quiet. They did not have to walk far, just over the crest of a sand dune. Helena's stomach rolled at the sight that greeted her, but she did not let herself look away. This was her fault. She should never have left them to face this alone. Her presence could have made all the difference. It could have been what kept Darrin alive.

"You cannot take on that burden, Mira. This is not your fault."

"You don't know that."

"I do," Von countered firmly. *"Rowena was always going to strike, and there cannot be a battle without casualties. We always knew this would end in bloodshed, in death."*

"But not his." The admission was too much. Her psychic voice broke and she shook her head, indicating that she did not want to speak further. Not even to him.

The chaos before them was hard to make sense of. There were bodies everywhere, randomly interspersed with dark purple flames. Helena did not have to try hard to feel the corruption wafting up from them. Her eyes flew over the scene, looking for someone she recognized. A familiar red head snagged her attention, pulling all of her focus. She watched as Ronan walked through the bodies, looking as though he was searching for something. After a few more steps, he stopped and dropped to the ground. His hands seemed to fumble as they pulled open a travel-worn bag.

Helena's heart squeezed painfully and it hurt to breathe as she watched him carefully begin to scoop what could only be ash into the bag. The seconds dragged as she watched him fill it before slowly standing back up. He saw her instantly, his eyes focused intently on her face. The protective way he carried the bag made her want to sob, but she knew if she started, she wouldn't be able to stop. So instead, she made herself take a breath in time with each of his steps. Right foot, in.

Left foot, out. Right foot, in. Left foot, out. There was room for nothing else.

When he reached her he didn't speak, but his thoughts were written across his face. She watched as he debated handing the bag over and could tell he wanted to spare her. Her heart thanked him for that kindness, even though she couldn't say so.

His eyes bore into hers, begging her to forgive him for causing her more pain with this action. She wished she could comfort him, but as soon as the bag made contact with her hands, there wasn't room to worry about any life except the extinguished one she now carried.

It was lighter than she would have thought, knowing that it contained the man who'd towered over her when he hugged her. She'd always felt so safe in his arms. She wanted, needed, him to feel that now. She clutched the bag close to her chest, holding onto him with all the strength she still possessed.

Resting her cheek on the top of the bag, the way he used to do with her head, she whispered, "Goodbye dearest friend. I am so sorry that I wasn't here to save you. I never thought there would be a day I would have to face without you. I know that we didn't always see eye to eye on, well, hardly anything. But I know that you always wanted what was best for me. I will always love you, Darrin. I am so sorry that you will never have the life that you deserved. I will make sure Effie wants for nothing. You do not need to worry about her, or any of us. Rest now. We will handle it from here."

Closing her eyes, she took a shuddering breath, no longer able to keep the tears at bay. When the drops began to fall down her cheeks, she wasn't sure if it was from the tears, or the rain that poured from the sky.

CHAPTER 26

$\mathcal{V}$on had helped keep the others at bay until she was ready to face them. And by ready, she meant numb. There was too much going on for the world to stop and let her process the death of her best friend. In some twisted way, the threat of Rowena's next attack allowed her to shift her focus and compartmentalize her grief. She had a feeling that when the loss truly hit her, she would be completely useless.

Helena stepped out of the makeshift tent and headed toward the familiar faces of her friends. It was actually a minor miracle she found them so easily. There were people scattered everywhere. Chosen, Night Stalkers, Watchers, Etillions, Talyrians, Daejaran wolves; it was a motley crew and a lot to take in.

They'd created a temporary camp of sorts. A place for them to care for the injured, get a few hours of much-needed sleep and perhaps eat, if their stomach could handle it. Once those necessities were seen to, they would regroup in a more appropriate location. Not that Helena knew where that was these days. Rowena had already proven with her attacks that nowhere would remain safe for long.

That was why the animals were currently patrolling the perimeter of the camp. Under other circumstances, she would have been amused by the uneasy truce between the wolves and Talyrians. Or the Talyrians and anyone, really. If the Chosen had been shocked by the appearance of Starshine, they were at a complete loss when they saw Midnight prowling at her side.

Of the Talyrians that had flown to Etillion, only Starshine and Midnight had made the trip to the Vale with them. She'd had to leave the rest behind because the remaining charge of the Kaelpas stone was not enough to transport them as well as the Etillions. Besides, the need to travel immediately outweighed all else.

Most of Reyna's Watchers had returned to the Forest, although a few had stayed behind. Helena had not gotten a very good look at any of the hulking tree men, although she was curious how they communicated with the Night Stalkers. Could they even speak? Perhaps Reyna would fill her in before she had to test it out.

There were also the fifteen Etillions that had come with them to the Vale. The plan had been to see what they were up against and hopefully use additional runners to bring more assistance if needed, but since the fighting was already over by the time they'd arrived, it was a moot point. They, along with the thirty or so remaining Chosen who had initially left with them from Tigaera, plus Reyna's two hundred some odd Night Stalkers, currently comprised their group.

What those numbers really meant was that Helena was surrounded by a lot of unfamiliar faces and she was more than a little uneasy about it. They'd had too many traitors among them as it was; friend and stranger alike. The reminder that she knew little, if anything, about the people she was surrounded by left her restless and feeling like she was being watched.

Helena began to walk faster, no longer content with her solitude. As she made her way toward Von and the rest of her Circle, she noticed Amara speaking to Serena and Kragen, while Xander seemed to be interrogating Reyna. Ronan was standing a bit off to the side speaking with Von and Nial. Timmins and Joquil were listening to a solemn Miranda, and Effie was nowhere to be seen.

Do not look for him, she ordered as soon as her eyes began to search for the familiar golden head. Helena shifted her focus to the ground and headed in the direction of Von. He reached for her hand as soon as she made it to his side. The touch helped steady her frayed nerves.

"Helena," Ronan started.

"You have nothing to apologize for," she said, surprising him.

"I should have—"

"No," she said firmly, but softly. She wasn't ready to talk about it, and she certainly didn't want anyone else carrying the guilt of this death. That burden was hers alone. If she had been here, she could have stopped it.

His eyes softened and he nodded, moving as if to walk away. She stopped him with a hand on his arm. "I do not blame you, and I am ordering you to not blame yourself."

Ronan's eyebrows shot up in surprise. "How, exactly, do you intend to enforce that?"

"You're an honorable man, Ronan. Don't let me down."

"Tricksy female."

Her lips lifted in the barest hint of a smile. Ronan reached out and pulled her into his arms, holding her tightly for one long moment before letting her go and backing away.

Sensing the tidal wave of emotion threatening to overwhelm her, Von stepped forward and redirected the conversation. "Have we decided what our next steps will be?"

"No, not beyond the immediate needs. We will honor the dead, but I would like to take Darrin," her voice quavered as she said his name, "home with us. The Palace is big enough to house all of our new allies, perhaps we should start by gathering there and planning our next steps once everyone is assembled."

Von and Ronan exchanged a look. They weren't thrilled with the idea of creating an easy target for Rowena, but they also understood Helena's rationale.

"What if we gather in Daejara?" Von offered by way of compromise.

"Why would we do that? The Palace is more central."

"But also more obvious."

Helena mulled it over before nodding her agreement. "Fine. We will tell the others to join us there in a few days' time. That will allow us to send word to those that are not already with us."

"How do we avoid sending anything that can be intercepted?" Ronan asked.

Nial cleared his throat, "Leave that to me."

Von lifted a questioning brow.

"I discovered something in a few of the books Timmins lent me. Secrecy should not be a problem."

"All right, if that's settled, then all we need to worry about for the moment is saying goodbye."

Helena was tired of saying goodbye. It felt like she was doing it more and more frequently. They'd been lucky, all things considered, and had only suffered a few losses. Unfortunately, that did not lessen the weight or impact of them. One was too many in that regard.

"Kiri," Reyna's low voice interjected.

"Yes?"

"Due to the fire, there is not much that remains of the fallen. It makes it impossible for us to lay them to rest properly. Do you think…" she cleared her throat, "would you mind, doing for them what you did for those in Duskfall?"

The hesitancy of the strong woman's voice swayed her more than anything else could. Reyna did not want to ask this favor when Helena was so clearly distraught, but her desire to do what was right for her people, both the living and the dead, pushed her to anyway. It was not that Helena would have denied the request, or even that she had not been planning on doing so anyway, but the simple fact that Reyna felt she'd had to ask in the first place. It was a reminder, a call to duty. As the Mother's Vessel, she could not get lost in her own grief. She had to put the needs of the others before her own. At least until this was over.

"Of course."

Relief washed over the other woman's face. "Thank you, Kiri."

Helena took a deep, centering breath before turning to face the wreckage. Calling on her power, Helena called to the spirits of the fallen. All of them. The Shadows had once been Chosen too. She would not leave them here.

As in Duskfall, shimmering dust began to rise up from the ground. The people around her had gone silent, watching her work with varying degrees of awe and reverence. By the time she had finished, thousands of new stars were twinkling in the sky, visible despite the presence of the sun.

Feeling empty and heartbroken, Helena sent a single thought to Von. *"Let's go home."*

CHAPTER 27

hen Effie found her, she was sitting in Anderson's garden, watching the clouds move across the sky. The bag filled with Darrin's ashes sat in her lap.

"H-hi," Effie said in a voice hoarse with disuse. No one had heard her say a word since she'd spoken to Ronan on the battlefield.

Helena took in the girl's dark circles and red-rimmed eyes with a healer's assessing gaze. "Are you ready?"

Effie gave Helena a look. "Can you ever really be ready for something like this?"

"No, I guess not." Standing, she handed the bag out toward Effie. "Here, you should be the one to do it."

Effie's eyes went wide. "Me?"

Helena's smile was kind, even though it wobbled slightly. "You were his choice, Effie. The honor is yours."

Effie's nose went red and her eyes filled with tears. "But his loyalty was always to you first, Helena."

"No one is questioning his loyalty. He was sworn into my service, but he died to protect *you*."

Her lips quavered, and she looked up at Helena with lost blue eyes. "Why? Why did he do that Helena? I am no one. He had a duty, he was part of the Circle. He should have let me—"

Helena cut her off. "Because he loved you, Effie. In his eyes, taking care of you was his only duty. You were everything. Do not dishonor his death by discounting his reasoning."

Effie sniffed back her tears. "How can you even stand to look at me? Don't you hate me for being the reason he is gone?"

"Hate you?" Helena looked shocked by the question. "Effie, Darrin was my best friend. I was thrilled he'd had someone to love and love him in return. Even if it was for too short a time. I will never hold that against you."

The blonde woman still looked uncertain.

"Let me ask you this. Would you have done the same for him?"

"Of course! But—"

"No, there are no buts, Effie. It is what anyone would do for the one that they love."

Effie closed her eyes, more tears rolling down her cheeks. She took one long shuddering breath and then opened them. "Let's do it together," she said.

Helena's heart twisted in her chest, but she bit down on her lip, keeping her emotions in check. "Okay."

The women turned to face the center of garden, each holding one of the looping strands of leather that held the bag closed.

"What should we say?" Effie whispered.

"You don't have to say anything," Helena murmured.

They shared one last look and flung open the bag, tossing the ashes out over the garden. As they did, a gentle gust of wind came, carrying the ashes up toward the sky.

Effie let out a small gasp of surprise as she watched the twirling ashes fly away.

"Welcome home," Helena whispered, her heart feeling as though it was being clenched in a vice.

There was one more gust of wind, its breeze warm and fragrant with the scent of flowers. Helena could have sworn it caressed her cheek, wiping away her tears. Her eyes fluttered closed and she had to focus on breathing before she could speak again. "I'll miss you."

The two women stayed there, staring at the sky for a long while.

Eventually, Helena left Effie alone so that she could say the rest of her goodbyes in private.

THE PALACE WAS QUIET, but it was the quiet of peace, not sadness. Despite everything that had happened in the last handful of weeks, there was a sense of calm that resonated throughout the massive structure. Whether it was because it had been imbued with some residual power of those that built it, or because it held its own kind of magic, Helena wasn't sure. She just knew that it felt easier to breathe when she was surrounded by the safety of its walls.

"Kiri," Alina called.

Helena acknowledged her with a soft smile.

"They are waiting for you in the Chambers."

"Thanks, Alina," she said before sighing. More meetings. She was sorely tired of the politics and strategy. She knew it was necessary, but one would think being in charge meant you got to spend more time doing what you wanted to do. Sadly, that was hardly ever the case. Her childhood self would have been gutted to learn it.

Helena took the spiraling staircase a step at a time, walking slowly even though the men were waiting for her. She wanted to stretch out her last remaining moments of peace as long as possible.

When she stepped in the room, five sets of eyes were staring at her with mixed degrees of concern. She felt Von's phantom caress and struggled not to lean into it. He smirked at her from where he was leaning against the wall.

Kragen and Joquil were already seated at the table, and Ronan was pacing at the far end of the room. Timmins set down the papers he'd been holding.

"Where would you like to start?" she asked without preamble, shutting the door behind her.

"Well the most pressing order of business is what you want to do about the Circle."

"Ronan will take Darrin's place."

Ronan's head snapped around toward her. "What?"

Helena blinked in surprise, looking at the others. "Is that really a question? Is there any doubt that he is the best choice?"

Von was grinning as he asked, "All in favor?"

The four other men all lifted their hands.

Ronan looked shocked. Helena's smile faltered. "You do not have to, Ronan. I know that it is a lot to ask."

Ronan shook his head. "No, it is not that, Helena. I just, I didn't think…" he trailed off, looking at his feet. "You honor me."

Von tossed a book at Ronan's head. Ronan ducked, narrowly dodging the attack. "What was that for?"

"Stop being stupid. There is no one else I would trust more to keep her safe."

"Nor I," Helena murmured with a smile.

Von scowled at her. *"Hey now."*

"I thought that the 'besides you' was implied."

"It better have been."

Helena rolled her eyes.

"Do I take the vow now?" Ronan asked, looking sheepish.

Timmins placed a hand on his shoulder. "There is time for us to do it properly. I will get everything in order so that we can hold the ceremony tonight."

"So what else is there to discuss?" Helena asked.

"The Daejaran ambassador is dead."

"How?" Helena asked. "Rowena?"

Timmins quickly shook his head. "No, not as far as we can tell. It appears to be natural causes. I was thinking that Nial would make a good replacement."

Helena's eyes shifted to Von's, checking to see if he had any objection.

"He will not want to stay behind or be separated from Serena."

"He would not have to be. It is more a position in name, a go between for us and the people of Daejara. Other than yourself, he seems uniquely qualified."

Von nodded his agreement.

"Speaking of Serena," Timmins continued, "She and Nial have placed a formal request for their mating bond to be recognized."

Helena's eyes moved to Ronan, but he was lost in his thoughts.

"They want to have a wedding now?" Kragen asked in disbelief. "Have they forgotten we're sort of in the middle of things?"

It was Ronan who spoke next. "What better time? If Darrin's death has taught us anything it is that tomorrow is not a guarantee. You cannot blame them for wanting to take advantage of the time they do have together, while it's still a possibility."

The room was quiet as they processed his words.

"Of course, if that is what they wish, we will make time to do it right. We can hold the ceremony once we are in Daejara so that both their families can be present."

Von smiled at Helena's suggestion. "My parents will be thrilled."

Helena returned his grin, happy that they would have the chance to celebrate something for once. It was an unexpected and very welcome change.

"Is there anything else?" she asked again.

Timmins glanced at his notes. "Nial has sent word to our allies. They should be joining us in Daejara by week's end. That gives us time to hold the mating ceremony before their arrival."

Just like that, Helena's stress and worry returned in full force. "Can the Holbrooke Estate really hold all those people?" she asked.

Von shook his head. "Not within the Estate itself, but there is more than enough land and abandoned houses that can be utilized. The Estate will house the representatives of each realm, but their forces will need to remain in their own camps until we move out."

She closed her eyes. "Where do we even start? Rowena could be anywhere."

"We will draw her out, make her come to us. It is our turn to start calling the shots," Ronan said with utter confidence.

"Do you know how we intend to do that?"

"Not yet. But we will."

His fierceness and determination were contagious. She could feel the steadying effect it had on the others.

"We will be ready to head out tomorrow," Timmins said.

Helena nodded. She wished they could spend more time here, but she understood why they couldn't. At least they had the night to spend with each other. She would take a page from Nial and Serena's book and make sure to use it wisely. It could very well be the last time they were all together.

"It was done?" Rowena's icy voice snapped.

"Aye, my Queen. The Circle has been broken, as promised."

"You are certain?"

"I watched her Shield fall myself. There is no doubt."

"Excellent," Rowena replied, her voice sounding almost warm. "Then we can move ahead with phase two."

"It has already been set in motion, my Queen."

"Come here, Thomas. I think you have earned a reward."

Thomas stood and swiftly closed the distance between them. Rowena smiled at him as he walked up the stone steps to the top of the dais where her throne sat. Her dress was the color of darkness and rustled like dead leaves as she stood. He reached for her, but before he could touch her, Rowena lifted up a hand and summoned her power.

"My dear, *I* am not the reward."

Thomas' dark eyes clouded with confusion. "My Queen?"

Rowena's laugh was cold and brittle. "The impostor was not the only one whose Circle was broken. And that simply cannot stand."

Thomas' eyes widened. "Rowena, no! Please. I've done everything you asked. I've only ever wanted to serve you."

Her hands were already glowing with corrupted power as she smiled. "And you shall, darling. Eternally." When she was done, his once coal-black eyes were now milky-white and snaking with dark lines.

CHAPTER 28

$\mathcal{H}$elena had never seen Ronan look so nervous. Actually, Helena had never seen him nervous period. He'd taken special care with his appearance that evening, which for a warrior turned mercenary was saying something.

His red hair had been left down, hanging in cinnamon waves past his shoulders. It was a cross between a lion's mane and a halo, which was fitting, all things considered. He'd even left his leather garb behind, opting for a fitted pair of black trousers with a matching jacket and silky lavender shirt.

"Did you help him dress tonight?" Helena asked, recognizing the style immediately.

"I may have made a few suggestions."

Helena lips twitched in amusement. Poor Ronan. There was no hope he'd escape the notice of any woman dressed like that. Even without the scar bisecting his face, his towering presence and aura of fierce brutality usually kept them at bay. But not tonight. The snug black fabric clung to his muscular build, making him a present any woman would be happy to unwrap. They'd gladly risk his temper in the hopes they could see what came with it.

"You can stop gawking at him any time now."

Helena snickered and sent an appreciative look her Mate's way. *"Jealous, my love?"*

"Please."

She laughed and pressed a lingering kiss against his sculpted lips. *"You have nothing to worry about."*

His eyes were warm and slightly hooded as they met hers. *"I know."* He ran a phantom hand along the length of her back causing her to shiver and flush. It was his turn to grin.

Helena blinked, breaking the seductive spell he'd woven around her, and shifted her focus back to the other men in the room. Her smile widened as she realized they'd all incorporated varying shades of purple into their outfits, in honor of her. She was actually the only one in the room not wearing purple. Alina had worked her own special brand of magic, as usual. Helena had tried to protest, saying there wasn't time for such extravagance, but Alina wouldn't budge.

"Is this not a special occasion?" she'd demanded. Helena couldn't argue that it wasn't. It was incredibly rare to replace anyone in the Circle, especially after less than a year of formal service. It was not something that was done lightly.

Relenting, Helena had allowed Alina to have her way and instead of the traditional purple, Alina had chosen gold. There was nothing special about the cut or shape of the dress. It was fitted from chest to hips before flaring down to the ground. What made it special was how, the dress seemed to shine no matter where she was standing. Helena had become a beacon of light.

The pièce de résistance was actually the crown Alina had placed upon her head. It, too, was golden, but a molten, fiery gold. When she turned, the crown would flash, creating the illusion of sparks flying off of the metal. Alina had given her a crown of embers. It was a warning wrapped in decoration.

"Shall we get started?" Timmins asked.

"Mother yes," Ronan said gruffly, his nerves getting the better of him.

Helena pressed her lips together, trying hard not to laugh.

"Do you remember the words we went over earlier?" Timmins asked Ronan in a low voice.

Ronan glowered at him. "Just because I'm from Daejara doesn't mean I'm a simpleton. I can remember a damn vow."

Von snickered, his hand lifting to cover his mouth. He'd said nearly the same thing when Timmins had prepared him for his own ceremony.

Timmins didn't bat an eye. It was hardly the first time he'd caused one of the Circle to snap at him. It certainly wouldn't be the last. "Then if you are ready, we will begin."

Ronan nodded, moving to stand beside Helena.

Timmins began the ceremony with an invocation of the Mother. "Mother, please recognize the vows that are made here today. Bless them with your acceptance to further strengthen the bonds between your Vessel and her Circle."

With that, each of the men repeated the vows they'd already made to her. As her Mate, Von went first. Followed by Timmins, Joquil and then Kragen. After Kragen's rumbling voice quieted, Ronan's clear blue eyes looked into hers. He remained silent, staring down at her.

"Are you sure this is what you want?" he asked quietly, for her alone.

"Are you?" Helena asked, suddenly worried that he felt forced into the decision.

"There are better men than me to be shackled to for a lifetime."

Helena's worry faded completely. She grinned up at him. "Be that as it may, there is no one else I would rather have watching over me."

His serious gaze searched her face awhile longer before he finally nodded. "Be it on your head then when I fuck it up."

The men laughed.

"You wouldn't be the first," she promised, which only caused them to laugh harder.

Ronan grinned, looking more himself than he had since she'd walked into the room. "In that case," he said kneeling, "let's get this over with." Despite his teasing, he was utterly serious when he spoke the words that would bind them together. "I vow to uphold and obey your beliefs and take them as my own. I will be your shield, protecting your life and light from any that would seek to destroy it. I will spend the rest of my days in service to you and your will, until such a time as the Mother reclaims me or the blade of war strikes me."

Helena's grin wavered as an image of a bowed golden head uttering those same words was superimposed over Ronan's form. She closed her eyes, savoring the reminder even though it hurt. When her eyes opened, Ronan was looking up at her, understanding shining in his eyes.

Pressing her hand to his cheek, Helena made her own vow. She'd improvised the first time she'd made a vow to her Circle; tonight was no different. "I will strive to be worthy of the gift of your service, to remain out of harm's way whenever possible so as to not needlessly place your life in danger."

Ronan smirked at that, knowing it was an impossible promise under the circumstances.

"I vow to never take your service for granted, nor will I ask you to give up more than I am willing to give. May your strength be my shield, and my light your compass, in the days and years to come. Rise, Shield."

Ronan stood, looking equal parts humbled and honored. Helena lifted the chalice, finishing the words of the ceremony. As she did, she made a point to look each man in the eyes, "Blood of my blood these five shall be, my voice, my light, my shield, my sword, and my soul. I take them unto me, as my own, to cherish and protect as I would myself, until such a time as the Mother reclaims me."

She drank deep, adding a final silent request as she did. *Mother watch over these men. I have lost so much already. Please…*

She handed the cup to Von, who took a drink and passed it on. So it went, until all had drank and the cup was empty. Remembering the first time they'd taken the vows, Helena looked around with a smirk. "So now what?"

Ronan looked around at the others. "I don't know about you, but I could use a drink."

"That's as good a plan as any."

There was laughter and murmurs of agreement throughout the

room. Timmins pulled open the door and called for one of the nearby guards.

"Bring some refreshments please."

"And lager! Lots of lager!" Ronan shouted.

Helena threw back her head and laughed. At least this time when she wiped away a tear, it was one of laughter.

EPILOGUE

*H*ours had passed as the group welcomed their newest member officially into the fold, while also remembering the one they'd lost. Helena cherished every second of it. It was a moment of joy in the midst of all the chaos.

Somewhere along the way, Serena, Nial and Miranda had all joined them. They'd tried to get Effie to come as well, but she wasn't quite ready for company.

"Mother's tits! What time is it?" Ronan slurred from the chair he was slouched in.

Von, not in a much better condition, glanced out the window, which was covered, trying to discern the time by the color of the night sky. "Looks like it must be near morning."

Helena traded amused glances with Serena and shook her head. "I think that means it's time to get you to bed."

"What?" Ronan roared, "The party is just getting started."

Von winked at her salaciously, before asking in his own suggestive slur, "Bedtime issit?"

"Boyo, in the shape you're in, you're no good to anyone," Kragen commented dryly. He'd drank every bit as deeply as the others but seemed almost entirely unaffected. If not for the subtle shine in his eyes, Helena would have thought he was completely sober.

Von sneered, "Am too."

"Impressive comeback, darling," Helena snickered.

Von opened his mouth, ready to continue proving his abilities, but Helena put her hand over his mouth and shook her head. Von licked her.

There was a discrete tap on the door. Helena was busy wiping her hand on her dress and laughing at her very drunk Mate. She did not immediately notice Alina waiting for their attention.

Still laughing, Helena asked, "What is it, Alina?"

Alina's face was bleached of color, and she wasn't smiling despite the jovial atmosphere of the room. "A letter just arrived for you, Kiri."

"A letter? At this hour?" Helena asked, already walking toward her.

Alina held the black envelope out with a trembling hand.

All amusement fled. She recognized that seal.

"Rowena."

Everyone went deadly silent, instantly sobered by the name.

Von pushed himself up and stood beside her. His eyes were glassy, but focused.

"Open it," he said in a dangerous voice.

Helena was already ahead of him. The thick black envelope was open, and she pulled out the silvery parchment it had contained. There was nothing on the folded piece of paper to indicate what it would entail.

Her heart was pounding as she unfolded it. *What would it be this time? More taunts?*

"We request the honor of your presence for a masquerade ball in celebration of the Solstice," she read aloud. The words were scrawled with precision, obviously written en mass. Below them, in a more feminine and bold hand, it read:

Feel free to bring what's left of your Circle.

Helena crumpled the paper in her fist, already vibrating with anger.

Having been reading over her shoulder, Joquil's amber eyes were wide with fear when he said, "It's a trap, Kiri. You cannot mean to take her up on her invitation."

"Why not?"

"Helena, be serious," Timmins snapped, as he took the ball from her fist and smoothed it out for the others to see. "You know you cannot walk into her trap like that."

"We can make it a trap of our own. The party is not for two weeks. There's time."

"Hellion," Kragen rumbled, "the likelihood we'd be able to manipulate her in her own home is beyond slim."

She turned to face Ronan and Von, waiting for their protests. They had none.

"If this is what you wish to do, we will find a way," Ronan said, his voice steady and eyes clear.

Timmins sputtered, and Joquil and Kragen spun on the Daejarans.

Helena silenced their protests with a shout, "Stop! Let Rowena think she has the upper hand. It only benefits us because it makes her careless."

"Kiri," Timmins tried again.

"No. I am done letting her underestimate me. I am not some bunny that cannot defend myself." She paused, unsheathing her lethal black claws and watching them glimmer in the flickering firelight. "She doesn't realize what she's welcoming into her den with this invitation. Let's take the opportunity to remind her what it means to be the Mother's true Vessel."

As Helena reflected on all Rowena had taken from her, the flames throughout the room began to grow and dance wildly, the wind outside howling and shaking the windows with its intensity.

In a voice filled with deadly promise, Helena lifted her iridescent gaze, "But while the Mother might be merciful, I won't be."

THE CHOSEN: BOOK 4
QUEEN OF LIGHT
MEG ANNE

"Look at how a single candle can both defy and define the darkness."
— Anne Frank

"The scariest monsters are the ones that lurk within our souls..."
— Edgar Allan Poe

CHAPTER 1

Three towering figures stood facing each other in a loose semi-circle. The ruby red of their robes was the only discernible color in the darkness. From afar the color seemed like a bloody smear against the inky black of the cave's wall. Up close, the splash of color only served to emphasize the seemingly empty space within the recessed area of their hoods.

There was no outward sign that the figures were aware of the storm raging just beyond the cave's entrance. They were unmoving even as a flash of lightning filled the cavern with its blinding glare while an answering crash of thunder echoed along its length.

"The pieces are almost in place."

"It won't be long now."

"She is finally ready to become who she was always meant to be."

"Our salvation."

"Perhaps."

Two of the figures twisted their heads to face the one standing between them.

"But it has been foretold."

"It is but one of two paths."

The leftmost figure's robe rippled, as if the person within was fidgeting restlessly.

"For all that we See, we cannot Know."
"Not until it has come to pass."
"There is always a choice."

The figure in the center dipped its head in a nod. *"And so you understand."*

The wind howled as the storm raged on.

"We will wait."
"And bear witness."
"Where is the Vessel now?"

The central figure's shoulders shook with what might have been laughter. Without waiting to see if the others would follow, he turned and began to make his way deeper into the catacombs.

"She celebrates life before she must greet death."

"SWEET MOTHER, YES!" Helena screamed as Von drove into her with one final, toe-curling thrust.

Von's eyes glittered with wicked satisfaction as he leaned down to kiss her before rolling onto his side and pulling her limp body against his. "We should just stay locked in here tonight and skip the dog and pony show."

Helena let out a snort of amusement as she twisted her head to look at her Mate. "That dog and pony show is your brother's mating ceremony."

"Yes, but I much prefer our *mating* ceremonies." There was no mistaking his innuendo or the sexual promise shining in his silvery gaze.

Despite barely being able to keep her eyes open, Helena's blood quickened at his words. "You're trying to kill me," she finally declared.

"But what a way to go."

They chuckled together, sharing another brief kiss. Von moved to lie on his back, and Helena followed him, curling into his side and resting her head over the still thundering beat of his heart. With her fingers lazily tracing the scrolling lines of his Jaka, she sighed and said, "I should probably go down to check on things. There's not much time left before the guests start to arrive."

Von grunted, holding her tighter.

Knowing better than to try to protest, Helena let her sleepy eyes take in the room. Last time she'd stayed at the Holbrooke Estate, they'd set her up in one of their guest rooms. This time she was sharing Von's childhood room, and it amused her to see the evidence of the boy he'd once been still littered around the chamber.

"So how many women know about your penchant for drawing?" she teased.

Von raised a brow. "My what?"

Helena gestured toward the crudely sketched portrait of what she assumed was a Daejaran wolf.

Von followed her hand before bursting into surprised laughter. "Oh, that. Nial made it for me. When he was four."

"And here I was thinking I finally found something you were terrible at." Helena's words were playful, and her smile grew at the thought of the proud little boy showing his big brother what he'd drawn.

He scoffed. "If I *had* drawn it… hell, if it was just a bunch of stick figures holding swords, and I told you I'd made it especially for you, you'd do the same thing."

"What's your point?"

"That the value is not in the skill."

"Obviously."

Von peered at her curiously. "You wanted to take it, didn't you? When you thought I had drawn it?"

"Maybe."

His chest rumbled with his laughter. "Do you want me to draw you a picture, *Mira*?"

"Only if you use stick figures."

They laughed again.

"And what did you mean *my women*?" he asked once their laughter had faded. "Just how many do you think have been in my room?"

Helena's cheeks grew warm. "Well, I mean… clearly you have a past. You don't learn how to do *that* without experience."

"Helena, look at me." His warm voice grew serious. He didn't continue speaking until her eyes met his. "You are the only woman I've ever allowed into my room, at least in any kind of romantic capacity."

The pleasure and relief that filled her at his admission almost surprised her. "But surely you had conquests…"

"Aye, but never here." At her confused expression, he elaborated. "It saves you from enduring a series of uncomfortable conversations. Not to mention it's a lot harder to leave once you've finished when it's your room."

Helena shook her head with mock disapproval. "Quite the lover even then."

Von gave her a wry smile. "Love had nothing to do with it, and there was never a reason to stay."

"Never?"

"Not until you."

Helena could feel the sincerity of his words filling her through their bond. "Lucky me," she murmured, moving to kiss him.

"No, Helena. Lucky me," he corrected, brushing a stray curl behind her ear before closing the distance between their lips.

Before their tender kisses could go any further, a knock sounded at the door.

"Your brother is looking for you," Ronan called from the other side.

"He probably needs advice about what to do after the ceremony," Von muttered dryly, making no move to get up.

Helena gave him a saccharine smile. "If you've seen the way Serena looks at him when she thinks no one's watching, you'd know he doesn't need any help in that regard."

"How could you possibly know that?"

"It's the same way I look at you."

Von's fingers wove into her hair as he pulled her down for a searing kiss. Ronan had to knock three more times before the lovers finally made it out of their bed to greet him.

"About damn time," he said without any heat. Ronan's blue eyes were twinkling with amusement as Von punched his shoulder by way of greeting.

"Fucker," he said beneath his breath as he walked past the newest member of her Circle.

"Bastard," Ronan returned, saluting Von's retreating back.

"Heard that."

"Mcant you to."

"See you down there," Helena told Von, staying behind. She wanted a moment alone with Ronan before the ceremony.

"Don't take too long. You know I can only handle my mother in small doses without you as my buffer."

Helena's answering laugh followed Von down the hall. "Poor Margo."

Ronan lifted an inquiring brow.

"Seeing both of her son's happy and whole is proving to be too much for her. She can't seem to go more than ten minutes without bursting into tears. Von is finding it… trying."

"Only a woman cries because she's too happy."

"Careful, Shield."

"What? It's true."

"I'm starting to think Von didn't hit you hard enough."

Ronan snickered. "He's just lucky I stopped punching back."

"Because you know you'd have to deal with me."

Ronan's answering smile was warm. "Can you think of a better reason?"

Weaving her arm through his, they started walking. Helena considered his question for a moment before replying, "No. Self-preservation is a powerful motivator."

"Indeed, it is." They walked a bit further in companionable silence before Ronan sighed and said, "Just ask. I know you want to."

Not even pretending to misunderstand him, she blurted out, "Are you sure you're okay with this?" Helena had hoped she'd be able to read his feelings through the Jaka, but all she could sense was a tangle of conflicted emotions. Her eyes searched his face, looking for physical signs of how he was doing, but it was a neutral mask. "If this is going to be too much for you, I can find some errand to send you on."

"And leave you unprotected? Not a chance." His words were gruff, but he raised his hand to place it over hers and squeezed. He appreciated her offer, even though he would never take her up on it.

"I am hardly unprotected, and I know several men who would take great offense at the implication."

"Maybe if they'd stop losing all their sparring matches with me, I'd have a little more faith in their abilities."

Helena laughed, remembering how the remaining men in her Circle had all found a reason to take her aside and complain about Ronan's morning practices throughout the course of the week. She knew his words were a cover, Ronan didn't doubt Von's ability to protect her for an instant.

"Are you sure?" she asked again in a softer voice.

Ronan was silent for a long stretch. When he finally spoke, his voice was so soft she barely heard him. "It's time."

Time to really let go. Time to say goodbye. Time to move on. Yes, it was time.

"Then let's go."

THERE WASN'T enough space in the Holbrooke's home to fit all Nial and Serena's guests, so they'd decided to hold the ceremony outside. Even if that hadn't been the case, and had it been her decision to make, Helena would have decided the same. It was beautiful being among the trees and mountainside. The roaring sound of the crashing ocean waves was a perfect soundtrack as the sun began its descent through the sky.

Further decoration was unnecessary, given the vibrant beauty of their natural surroundings, but a small pavilion had been erected and swathed in fresh flowers. The scent of roses and jasmine wafted in the mild breeze.

Ronan had left her once she'd made it outside, citing a need to check on his men. Helena scanned the yard, looking for someone that appeared to be in charge. Technically it should have been her, seeing as how the ceremony was her idea, but frankly she was tired of making decisions and gladly passed all decision making on to the couple. It was their day, after all.

Helena's thoughts began to wander, and she closed her eyes only to find Rowena's icy stare waiting for her. She shuddered and shoved the thought away, forcing herself to take a deep, centering breath. The Circle and their new allies would deal with her soon enough. Today was not a day for worrying about such things. It was a day for celebration, probably the last they'd have until the war was over. Today she would focus on love and life; two of the Mother's most precious gifts.

She sent a caress down the bond, wanting her Mate to know that she was thinking of him. An answering ripple of warmth greeted her, washing away the chill her thoughts of Rowena had caused.

Helena looked back at the pavilion, watching the fragile flower petals flutter in the breeze. In a few short hours, she'd be standing there, speaking the words that formally commemorated what two souls had already acknowledged. It would have been nice to be able to stand on the sidelines and simply be a guest for once. But that was not who she was, or who she was meant to be. Not anymore.

Perhaps it never really was.

"Mira?" Von asked, sensing her disappointment.

"It's nothing."

She felt his curiosity as if it was a tickle up her spine, but he did not question her further.

"Isn't it perfect?" Serena asked, joining her.

"That it is," Helena answered with a smile. "Aren't you supposed to be hidden away until the ceremony starts?"

"Alina just finished helping me get ready and I couldn't stand being cooped up any longer. That woman is truly gifted. I've never felt so feminine in my entire life." Serena laughed as she said the words, the warrior in her appreciating the irony. For years she'd had to pretend that she wasn't soft so that the men around her would take her seriously. Today she could set that instinct aside and embrace the purely female part of herself. Still chuckling, Serena asked, "Isn't this dress divine?" She performed a small twirl, holding her arms out to let her simple lilac gown billow around her.

Helena's smile grew, completely understanding the sentiment. She was no stranger to Alina's ministrations, or her miracles. "You look beautiful," Helena agreed, but it was not because of the dress or her upswept curls that had been held back with a garland of flowers. Serena was glowing with the intensity of her joy. She was a woman in love; one who had been lucky enough to find her mate. It was a rare and beautiful gift that none of the Chosen would take for granted.

"Thank you!" Serena beamed brightly before her lips twisted in a grimace. "I'm just ready to get this over with."

"Don't say that," Helena urged, placing a hand on her friend's arm. "Cherish every second of today."

Serena's jaw clenched and her violet eyes hardened. She heard the words that Helena did not say: they were on borrowed time. Rowena could strike at any minute, although given her less than subtle invitation, it appeared that she was in the process of setting the stage for her next salvo.

The blonde woman took Helena's hand in hers and squeezed, hard. "You're right. It's just my nerves speaking."

"I think that's normal," Helena replied, remembering the way her stomach had felt like it was somersaulting within her the day she and Von made their vows.

"You're probably right."

"Aren't I always?"

"Hardly."

They shared a look before bursting into laughter.

"Now that's what I like to see," Nial said from behind them.

They moved to make room for him, Serena peering at him almost shyly as he took in the sight of her.

"Beautiful," he murmured, his storm-gray eyes shining with a possessive intensity Helena instantly recognized.

Knowing that neither of them remembered she was still standing there, Helena quietly stepped away, giving the couple a few stolen moments of solitude before their ceremony began. She smiled softly as she watched the way that they fussed over the other, their tender caresses and heated looks making her long for something she couldn't name.

CHAPTER 2

A few of their new allies had arrived in Daejara early. Rather than have them remain segregated in their various camps, the Circle had made the call to include them in the festivities. There really was no better way to cement a new partnership than with a raging party and copious amounts of alcohol. It was clear that help was definitely required in that regard.

Helena winced at the reminder. Anduin and his Storm Forged had been the first to arrive. She'd barely closed the door behind the Stormbringer when Reyna and the Night Stalkers began to knock. To say their initial meeting had been uneasy was an understatement. The two leaders had taken one look at each other standing in the Holbrooke's hallway and any trace of warmth they'd had when greeting Helena drained away. Their distrust was palpable. Even Kragen's ever-present grin vanished when he noticed Reyna's hand move to the dagger sheathed at her hip.

To be fair, the move had not been entirely uncalled for. One of Anduin's party had made a snide comment about how it was a surprise to see that the Night Stalkers were let out of their cages during the day. Helena's own hand had itched to slap the self-satisfied smile off the man's face while around him others shuffled uncomfortably. If not for

Timmins stepping in, Helena wasn't sure they would have avoided the two groups coming to blows.

Helena let her eyes find Reyna in the crowd, noting the stiff way she was perched on her seat. She sighed. It seemed that not much had changed in the last four days.

Following her gaze, Von's lips twitched up in the ghost of a smile. *"Lucky for us, Reyna chose to wear a dress without weapon sheaths."*

Helena fought the urge to laugh. *"If you believe that then you aren't half the master strategist you think you are."*

"All right, fine. At least the Storm Forged are seated well away from the Night Stalkers."

"That much is true. It's almost like someone had the foresight to do that on purpose."

"Who can we thank for that?"

Helena bit back a grin that would have seemed entirely out of place to those not participating in the current conversation—namely everyone else. *"I'm not sure, but when you find him, can you give him a big kiss from me?"*

"Hey now," Von said, his eyes catching and holding hers from where he stood, just to the left of the pavilion, *"those kisses belong to me."* The iridescent rings around his pupils seemed to glow in what was left of the sunlight.

Seeing the physical evidence of their connection made her heart swell with primal satisfaction. It wasn't just her kisses that belonged to him. It was her very essence. They were soul-bound, tied together in a way that only death could ever rip apart.

Helena winked at him. *"You can collect them later."*

"Count on it."

Returning to their initial conversation, Helena said, *"I can't believe I thought getting the Forsaken to agree to join us would be the hard part. I didn't even stop to consider how we were going to convince everyone to work together."*

"Hopefully tonight's party will be the first step in bridging that gap."

"From your lips to the Mother's ears..."

"From my lips to—"

"Shhh!" Helena cut him off, already feeling the telling heat of a blush rising to her cheeks. Now was definitely not the time to think about that. Not with so many eyes on her.

Guests slowly began to take their seats, their mingled voices swelling like a wave about to crash. Helena stood beneath the pavilion, smiling in greeting as familiar and unfamiliar faces alike caught her eye.

Von and Nial's parents were seated in the first row with Margo already dabbing at her eyes. Helena could feel Von's mental eye-roll at the sight, which only made her smile grow. Just beside the couple, filling out the row, were the rest of the Circle. Despite being impeccably dressed and on their best behavior, her men looked entirely out of place amid the other guests. It wasn't just the sheer size of them, although Kragen and Ronan were clearly blocking the view of everyone sitting behind them. More than one guest had sat down only to immediately begin craning their neck around the towering wall of pure muscle in an attempt to get a better view. Not one of them had been successful. Finally, they'd simply given up entirely and left the seats directly behind her Sword and Shield empty.

No, it was not their size. It was less obvious and more intangible than that, like an aura of violence that was never quite abated even during times of peace. There was just something about them, especially when all together, that made it impossible to forget who they were and what they were capable of. Not that Helena ever worried, they were hers after all, but given the sidelong glances thrown their way, others were certainly aware of the not-so-subtle threat. Smart of them to remain on guard, really. Even now.

Kragen caught her looking at him and gave her a wide grin, his dark eyes crinkling with his amusement. He seemed to know exactly what she was thinking and reveled in the suspicious stares. Upon further inspection, it appeared that all of her Circle did. They were proud of the fact that they made others nervous. That was why, even though they were not doing anything to provoke or encourage the stares, they were doing absolutely nothing to mitigate them either. Not even Timmins, who was usually too well-behaved to give in to such a blatant display of male ego.

Helena snickered. Timmins thought he had them all fooled, but these past couple of days he'd been running around in a near panic when he could not find the sacred text he'd brought from Tigaera. It contained the ceremonial words required to bind two souls during a formal mating ceremony within its ancient pages. He'd finally snapped when Helena had shrugged and said she'd wing it.

"One does not 'wing' the Mother's sacred words!"

"Maybe you don't…"

He scowled at her. "Helena, this is the most hallowed of ceremonies. We need that book."

"Timmins, calm down. You're looking apoplectic."

He huffed and snapped his lips closed.

Helena placed a hand on his shoulder. "Timmins," she started in her most soothing voice, "I've been improvising for the last year and the Mother hasn't struck me down yet. Tomorrow will be no different. In the end, they are just words. It is the intention of the two being bound that matters."

Timmins looked no more convinced, but the fight left him. "If you say so, Kiri."

"I do."

Timmins let out a long-suffering sigh. "Better you than me."

Helena punched him lightly on the shoulder. "That's the spirit."

He scowled and rubbed his shoulder. "You spend entirely too much time in the company of your Mate and Shield."

Helena was smiling with the memory of her Advisor. Few, if any, saw him in those rare moments of uncertainty. Helena secretly cherished them. Knowing that not even he had the answer or solution to every situation made her feel infinitely better about the fact that neither did she. Perfection was an impossible task, even for the Mother's Vessel.

Ronan was the personification of male disinterest. His arms were crossed and he was leaning back in his chair with his long legs sprawled out before him. Helena didn't buy it for a second, but she was likely the only one. If it wasn't for their connection, she too would be unaware of the undercurrent of tension simmering beneath that aloof countenance.

Sensing her eyes on him, he shifted his gaze up from his leather boots toward her. Helena raised a brow in silent question. Ronan's lips lifted in the ghost of a smile, understanding that she was repeating her offer from earlier, and he discretely shifted his chin in the barest of shakes. *No.*

With a small nod of understanding, Helena turned her focus at last to Joquil. Her Master had returned to his long-drawn-out silences since arriving in Daejara, but something had changed since revealing his secret. While quiet, he did not keep to the sidelines, as if ready to flee at a moment's notice. There was a new determination that glimmered in his amber eyes. *He's no longer afraid of being cast aside,* Helena realized. He finally felt accepted. Seeing the almost easy way he interacted with Reyna's people, Helena thought that being amongst his countrymen had something to do with that as well.

Helena made a mental note to speak with Reyna about the ways of the Night Stalkers. Perhaps there were some traditions she could bring back to Tigaera that would help her Master feel more at home.

The subtle strains of the music shifted, letting the guests know that the ceremony was about to begin. Helena pulled her wandering thoughts back, refocusing on the task that lay before her. By the smug cast of Timmins smile, Helena was certain he was mocking her. She could almost hear his taunting, *"Not so sure about winging it now are you?"* She barely restrained herself from sticking her tongue out at him.

The music continued to build as the guests of honor took their respective places. Margo's happy sniffling could just be heard over the lilting melody. In deference to the Great Mother, and as a symbol that they had been blessed, the couple wore her color. Nial looked devastatingly handsome in his fitted suit of pale purple as he stood beside his brother at the bottom of the pavilion. Helena could not recall a time she'd seen the younger Holbrooke look quite so blissfully happy.

Toward the back of the crowd, Serena stood with her arms woven through each of her parents'. The long length of her lilac dress rippled in the soft breeze, causing it to flutter behind her like a banner. Her head was tilted down as her father whispered something into her ear. From the quick grin and shake of Serena's head, Helena thought she knew what he had asked her.

As Serena's violet eyes lifted back up they met and held her mate's. She did not look away, did not so much as blink, as the trio made their way down the aisle. Neither did Nial. In that moment, Helena wasn't sure if it was Serena's graceful steps or the force of Nial's will that carried her down the aisle. With his back to her, Helena could not see his face, but there was no disputing that he was impatient for her to reach him. Nial could not stand still. He kept shifting his weight, like he was about to step forward and then had to fight against the urge to lift his foot. A small, private smile played about Serena's lips. Maybe she could also sense his desire to rush toward her. Or maybe it was just the knowing smile always shared between two lovers.

The music reached its crescendo just as Serena and her parents arrived at the base of the pavilion. A hush settled over the crowd as Serena's father lifted her hand from his arm and placed it in Nial's outstretched palm. The two stood there, gazing at each other, utterly oblivious to everything else around them. Helena waited as long as she could before softly clearing her throat to get their attention.

Nial and Serena wore matching blushes as they spun toward her.

"Sorry," Serena mouthed, while the guests chuckled.

"I'm not," Nial added, loud enough for the guests to hear. Their laughter turned to approving hoots and hollers.

"Perhaps we should get started before our two lovebirds sneak away." The cheering continued for a few moments longer before finally settling down.

"Nial, Serena," Helena began, looking at each of them as she said their names, "we are gathered here today under the ever-watchful eye of the Mother so that you may publicly declare what your souls already recognize. Today, you will take the vows that will bind your souls together."

At that, Nial looked down at Serena with a look so full of love and devotion, Helena felt tears prick her eyes. Feeling the tide of emotion rise within her, Von ran a phantom hand along the length of her back, infusing the caress with his strength. She shot him a grateful look and continued.

"From the time we are children, each of us learn that somewhere in this world the other half of our soul is waiting for us to find it. It does not take us much longer to realize how rare a gift it is to actually do so. When any of the Chosen find their true mate, it is a cause for all of us to celebrate, which is why we gather to bear witness to such a joyful occasion."

Helena paused to address Nial and Serena. "Did you two prepare your own vows?"

"We did," Nial affirmed as Serena nodded beside him.

Addressing the crowd again, Helena raised her voice. "Now they shall share the words in their hearts."

Nial took each of Serena's hands in his. "Serena, the first time I laid eyes on you I knew. It felt like all of the air left my lungs, and there was a moment when I forgot how to breathe because I was so lost in you. I do not love you just because you are strong, or beautiful, or that you know how to set me in my place, even though you are all those things. You are my equal. The part of me that had been missing my whole life even though I never realized how empty I had been until you were there to fill the void. I was told many times that I was not a whole man because I could not walk. But I can say with complete sincerity that I was not a whole man, because I had not yet found you."

A lone tear caught the sun as it shimmered against Serena's lashes before sliding down her cheek. Nial paused to brush it away.

"Serena, loving you has made me a better man. I do not know if I will ever be worthy of the gift you are to me, but I shall spend whatever time the Mother grants us endeavoring to be."

Serena's breath caught on a sob, and her lower lip trembled as Nial's words washed over her. "You are," she whispered to him, before swallowing back her emotions. Nial's thumbs brushed the back of her hands as she composed herself.

"Nial, it is no secret that I have been twice blessed by the Mother. I never thought to ask her for my mate, because I had been loved so completely that I never had a reason to want for more."

Ronan sat straighter in his chair, his red braid and blue eyes shining bright in the afternoon sun.

"At first, I fought my feelings for you, even as I sought every opportunity to spend more time with you. I was terrified of what it said about me that I had already known love, and still I could feel the depth of emotion that I did for a man I had known for only a handful of days. It wasn't long before I realized that what is between us is not something as simple as love. It is completion."

Nial's eyes darkened, his own breath catching.

"The Mother loves to test us. She gave me her greatest gift, but it was up to me to recognize it and to accept it. It was the only way to truly earn her gift, to earn you." Serena's voice had gone husky with the depth of her emotions. "And so, I had to walk away from the life I had built in order to run toward one I never even knew I wanted. I do not say this to suggest that loving you is a burden, only to say that I would sacrifice anything to be with you. Whatever the price, I will pay it. My place, my future, my life is with you. For as many days as the Mother gives us, I am yours."

Nial's hands moved to cup her cheeks as he brought his lips down against hers. There were a few heartfelt sighs as members of the audience secretly wished to experience that kind of love, even as others snickered and whistled suggestively.

"Pssst," Helena stage-whispered. "We're not quite done here."

The couple pulled apart with a chuckle and turned toward her once more.

"I have no desire to draw this out longer than necessary."

"Thank the Mother," Nial fervently swore.

The crowd laughed appreciatively while Helena shook her head with mock disapproval. Once everyone had settled, Helena continued, "Since you are of the Mother, and it is her grace that brought you together, we celebrate being her Chosen with the offering of a gift." There was an air of hushed anticipation as the crowd refocused on the couple, eager to see what the mating gifts would be.

This was always the most anticipated part of any Chosen mating ceremony. It was, in fact, the single most defining moment. It had seemed silly to Helena as a child that giving someone a present held so much more importance than declaring your love and acceptance of them. She had finally begun to understand the importance of the act once her mother explained it to her, but it wasn't until she actually received Von's gift that she truly understood it.

The traditional gift giving was similar to what happened during the Kiri's search for her Mate, at least in terms of the meaning behind the act. For a Kiri, tradition mandated that each of her suitors present a gift as part of their declaration of intent, and she took it to show that she was recognizing their suit. For the rest of the Chosen, gifts were exchanged to symbolize the actual moment when two mates fully accepted the bond, and each other.

Using their power, a combination potentially as singular as a fingerprint, the gifts were unique to the individuals being joined. They would create the most meaningful, and usually spectacular, present that they were able. Something that highlighted their individuality, as well as the person they were offering it to. In a mating ceremony, that exchange of such a personal and unique gift was symbolic of the sharing of one's self. No two gifts would, or in fact could, ever be the same.

The only difference in Helena's case was that, as Kiri, she was not required to create or provide a gift. As the Mother's hand-selected representative, she *was* the gift. Or that was what tradition said anyway. Now that she was reflecting on it, Helena was a bit dismayed to realize that she had never taken the time to make a mating gift for Von. Knowing what the magnolia had come to mean to her, that she refused to travel without it no matter where they were going, Helena made a silent pledge to remedy the situation as soon as possible. It was the least she could do for the man she loved.

Helena looked over the couple, toward her Mate. He was already looking at her, his eyes warm as he too remembered that moment on the dais. It was the first time she'd publicly declared that he was hers. Something that had taken all of five minutes for her to do after meeting him, although in truth, she had known the first time those gray eyes bore into hers.

His smile was soft and gently mocking as he said along their bond, *"If I would have actually thought I had a chance with you, I would have tried a little harder to give you something special."*

"I wouldn't change a thing. It's my most precious possession... well, after you."

She saw laughter sparkling in his eyes. *"Helena, it's just a flower. Hardly anything to write home about."*

"It's not just a flower," she insisted, offended at the implication. *"It proved that even when you thought it was just for show, you took the time to ensure that your gift would be something meaningful to me in particular. For a mercenary, it was an especially tender gift. It alluded to your true nature, even as you tried so hard to hide it, proved you were thoughtful and kind, that you could be gentle. When I saw that pristine white bloom cradled in your scarred hand, I saw the hands that would cradle and protect me. It will never just be a flower, Von. It was,"* she paused to correct herself, *"it is a promise. A promise about the kind of Mate you will be and the sort of life we will have together."*

His eyes had darkened with emotion as she spoke, the iridescent rings shining in sharp contrast against the stormy gray. She watched as he swallowed, seeming to be at a loss for words.

"If I had known that you were out there waiting for me, I would have left everything behind and walked to the ends of the world to find you."

"Had I known, I would have met you halfway, if only to shorten the journey."

They shared a long look, their love on clear display had anyone bothered to spare them a glance. Fortunately, everyone else was too busy watching Nial and Serena. The crowd was too eager to see what they had created for each other to notice the secret moment between their Kiri and her Mate.

Von finally dragged his eyes away from hers as his brother turned toward him. Nial's hands shook slightly as he held one out for his brother to place a wrapped item into.

Removing the slightly crinkled paper, Nial turned back to Serena. The item in his hand sparkled as it caught the light. It was small, barely taking up the full space of his open palm. Helena's vantage point allowed her to see what many others could not. Nial had crafted a figure with remarkable detail. Without having to be told, Helena knew it was Serena as she appeared to him. The small woman was gorgeous and fierce, her eyes glittering with challenge, even as she grinned with wicked amusement.

Nial ran his finger gently along the back of the figurine. The small figure shivered and came alive with a yawn and stretch. Serena gasped in wonder as the figure began to move on her own, her delicate golden curls fluttering on an invisible breeze, while the small mouth twisted with a war cry.

As if conjured by air, another figure appeared, this one a winged and fanged creature of legend. It could only be one of the Macabruls. Each one of its black scales glittered like jewels as it let out a silent roar. The tiny Serena wasted no time, launching itself into the air in a flying spin, using a sword that glowed with ruby flames to make quick work of the beast. As the sword made contact with the long serpentine neck, the Macabrul disappeared in a cloud of glittering smoke. The figurine landed in a crouch, before standing back up and brushing a few lingering pieces of dust off her silver armor.

Serena held out her hand and the tiny warrior fearlessly stalked toward the new territory. Sensing that she was home, the little figure dropped her sword and let out a big yawn before promptly curling up in a ball and falling asleep.

Serena looked up with wide-eyes, unable to speak.

Nial was one of the few true magic masters, there was no question of his ability. He had brought together each of the four Branches he commanded to create life out of nothing. And not just any life, a representation of his mate and her various accomplishments.

It was stunning in its detail and mastery. There were few, if any, who would be capable of ever crafting it's like.

Serena curled her hand protectively over the figure, letting out a watery laugh as the figure began to snore.

"It's beautiful," she whispered.

Nial shrugged, looking pleased and embarrassed. "It's you."

Serena appeared nervous as she called forth a Daejaran warrior who was standing just off to the side.

The man carried a large object that had been covered with a white sheet. At Serena's nod, the man gently set down the item on a table that had been set up for the purpose and pulled away the sheet.

"So that I may protect you even if we are apart," Serena whispered, as Nial's mouth fell open.

Serena was not a master of four Branches as her mate was, but she was skilled in her own right. A warrior first and foremost, Serena had created a suit of armor. It was not a traditional chest plate of leather and metal. Helena recognized the color immediately, it was the deep stormy blue of his eyes. Nial would be easy to spot amongst a crowd, probably part of Serena's intention.

"A small punch of power, if you wouldn't mind, Kiri," Serena requested.

Helena raised an eyebrow in surprise but called up her power. A ball of dancing flame quickly took shape in her palm. At Serena's nod, Helena released the fireball, launching it at the armor. As it made impact, the plate began to glow a deep and pulsing violet. There was an audible hiss and the fire disintegrated, leaving the armor entirely unharmed.

The crowd let out startled gasps and then burst into roaring applause.

"I know that our duties will not always allow us to stand together, but at least when you wear that, I will not have to overly worry about your safety."

Nial looked between his new armor and his mate, clearly moved by her words and her gift. "You honor me," he whispered.

Sensing their need to be together, Helena moved into action. "Now that that's out of the way, let's finish this up. The Mother brought you together, it will be up to the two of you to ensure that you cherish her gift and help it thrive. From this day forth, your souls will forever be one."

The crowd exploded in cheers.

Leaning forward, Helena whispered, "Now you can kiss her."

With a roguish grin she knew too well, Nial bent down and claimed Serena's lips in another searing kiss. Helena looked away, her eyes moving toward her Mate.

As far as ceremonies went, it was very different from what she and Von had shared. Even still, Helena would not change a thing. From the heat in his silvery gaze, Helena knew that her Mate felt the same.

"I love you."

Von's eyes softened and his smile grew. *"And I you."*

Using magic to enhance her voice, Helena spoke over the roar of the crowd. "Now for the part you've really been waiting for! Let's eat!"

Nial and Serena were impervious as their guests made their way to the tables overlooking the cliffs and the raging ocean below, still too busy taking their fill of each other.

CHAPTER 3

Ronan stared into the bottom of his mug, surprised to see that it was already empty.

"I do not get the impression that you are celebrating."

Ronan looked up into eyes the color of forest leaves. "Reyna."

She dipped her head in greeting and gestured again toward his cup. "Do you want another?"

"Need and want are two very different things."

"So, this is definitely not a celebration."

Ronan's lips twisted in a mocking smile. "There are days you think a wound has fully healed only to find that you have simply grown accustomed to the pain."

Reyna's eyes glittered with understanding. Gesturing toward the empty seat next to him she asked, "May I?"

"By all means."

Reyna swept her skirt to the side and gracefully lowered herself into the chair. The movement was so smooth Ronan was reminded of the way shadows slid across a forest floor.

He eyed the dark-haired woman beside him. Her hair was still a wild mix of braids and long curls, but her face was wiped clean of the Night Stalkers' iconic face paint. In its absence her skin glowed, complementing the golden flecks in her eyes. Ronan would say that she appeared more feminine, but that wasn't strictly true. Reyna had never appeared anything but feminine to begin with. It was more a sense of being tamed, although one only need look in her eyes to see the wildness was barely leashed. She was a feral creature, more suited to the starlit shadows of the forest than the glittering decadence of a ballroom. Ronan let his eyes wander along her body, appreciating the way her dress showcased her curves, even as he wished she was wearing her black leather instead.

Reyna coughed pointedly.

Ronan was slow to pull his eyes up, only grinning when she shook her head at him. He shrugged, not bothering to apologize for getting caught.

"There are many men who have felt the sharp edge of my blade for daring to look at me that way." Despite the threat, amusement laced her voice.

"Lucky for me, you don't have it on you."

The words had barely left his mouth when the shadows around them rippled and Reyna's hand, now gripping a golden dagger, was at his throat. "Don't be so sure about that."

Ronan lifted a brow, but otherwise showed no reaction. "Point taken."

Reyna smirked and vanished her dagger. "Now, about that drink." With a slight lift of her chin, Reyna was able to get the attention of a server. The boy scurried over, using Air to keep his tray of drinks stable while he dodged the partygoers. Reyna plucked two glasses off the tray and dismissed the boy with a brief, but warm, smile.

She was already taking a sip from her glass as she held the other out to Ronan. He couldn't help but appreciate her sense of priorities. Apparently, he was not the only one who needed something to dull the edges tonight.

Ronan had just begun to drink deeply from his glass when Reyna said, "You were the lover she referred to."

Ronan began to choke on his ale, barely getting his mug on the table as he coughed up the amber liquid. "You don't pull any punches, do you?"

Reyna lifted one shoulder. "What's the point? I am just stating the obvious. Your relationship wasn't a secret, was it?"

Despite wishing someone else was at the receiving end of her interrogation, Ronan had to admire her no-nonsense approach to conversation. At least you would always know where you stood with the lady.

Ronan wasn't sure which question to answer, so he remained silent.

"The Night Stalkers do not have such a narrow view of mates."

Ronan raised a brow, waiting for her to continue.

"It is foolish to believe that there is only one person in the world that you are supposed to love."

"The possibly of a mate does not impede your ability to love another," Ronan stated flatly. The irony of his statement was not lost on either of them. He was clearly proof.

"That's not what I meant." Reyna took another deep gulp, her glass now more than half empty. "It is only that we are constantly evolving. The person that was right for me ten years ago, is not the person that will fulfill me now."

"Your true mate grows with you. They are the piece that completes you." It was Ronan's turn to drink deeply. Setting his empty mug down, he added, "Although it is said that you will not find your mate until you are ready to accept them."

"Is that not true of all lovers?"

"You're missing the point."

"Am I?"

Ronan sighed with exasperation. How could he possibly explain something he'd never experienced? Instead of admitting defeat he went on the offensive. Scrubbing a hand down his face, he groaned. "Woman, you are exhausting."

Reyna's laugh was deep and throaty. He felt it move over him like the gentlest of caresses. His body was quick to respond. Ronan looked at his lap in surprise. That was unexpected.

She shifted in her seat, placing her hand lightly on his arm. "I did not mean to insult your beliefs, Shield. I was just trying, perhaps in a misguided way, to let you know that you are not doomed to be alone just because she was not your mate. You may have lost the one you thought was your forever, but that doesn't mean there is not another, or even many, that will bring you happiness again." Reyna's eyes had turned a bright, glowing emerald as she spoke.

Ronan's mouth went dry.

"You will find her, when you're ready."

The words, so softly spoken, settled something that had been loose within him. Ronan wasn't sure he was ready, but for the first time, he wanted to be.

"Thank you," he said, his deep voice barely a whisper.

Reyna offered him a small smile and settled back into her seat. The loss of contact chilled him, and Ronan found that he wasn't quite ready to let the conversation, or the company, go just yet.

"So why are you drinking tonight?"

The warmth left Reyna's eyes, leaving them almost black. Her smile turned sarcastic as she replied, "Can't you tell? Preservation, same as you."

Ronan's brows dropped low over his eyes. "What do you mean?"

"If one more ignorant bastard makes a comment about me or my people, I will gut them. I do not want to risk your Kiri's wrath by killing one of her people."

Anger rose swift and sure, warming him with the intensity of its heat. "One of the Chosen dared insult you?"

Reyna's expression softened, the hard line of her mouth curling upwards. "No, not one of the Chosen."

"The Storm Forged?" Reyna nodded, causing Ronan's frown to deepen. "I'll take care of it."

Reyna's brows lifted in surprise. "If I recall correctly, I am not the one you are supposed to be protecting, Shield."

Ronan snarled. "You are Helena's friend. I protect what is hers."

Reyna stared at him thoughtfully, her face an inscrutable mask. After a long moment, she finally said, "Then I will gladly accept the help."

The urge to protect and defend raged within him, but now was neither the time nor the place. Seeking a return to levity, Ronan asked, "Out of curiosity, whose preservation? Yours or theirs?"

Reyna's smile was so filled with the threat of violence that Ronan already knew the answer.

"Fair enough," he said with a chuckle, grabbing two glasses of ale as another server walked by. "Here's to preservation."

"I'll drink to that!" Reyna clinked her glass with his, eagerly tipping it back.

Ronan watched in stunned amazement as the Night Stalker drank, and drank. The way her throat worked as she swallowed threatened to distract him. Realizing she was going to drain the whole glass, Ronan quickly followed suit. She slammed her glass down on the table only seconds before he did.

"Now what?" Her eyes glowed with challenge and perhaps the smallest amount of inebriation.

"Now we dance."

Reyna sputtered. "What?"

Ronan was already standing and holding a hand out for her to grab. "It is a party."

"Do you even know how to dance?" she asked, uncertainly placing her hand in his.

Ronan's answer was a confident smile. "Only one way to find out."

"If you step on my toes..." Reyna threatened half-heartedly, seeming distracted by Ronan's roguish grin.

Feeling devious, Ronan leaned down and whispered in her ear, "If I step on your toes, you can take it out on me any way you want to." With that he made his way to the dance floor, pulling a dumbstruck Reyna behind him.

HELENA WATCHED Reyna trailing behind Ronan with amusement.

"What's that face for?" Von asked.

"I'm just trying to recall the last time Ronan looked so relaxed."

Von turned his silvery gaze on his best friend before laughing softly. "That's not relaxed, *Mira*. That's determined. Your Shield is on a mission."

Helena studied Ronan a bit more closely, noting the calculating look in his eye as well as his single-minded focus on the dark-haired Night Stalker. "Does the name of his mission start with an R?"

Von's dimple flashed, letting her know that she had arrived at the correct answer.

Ronan dancing wasn't a sight Helena thought she would ever encounter. Like everything else he did, his moves were testosterone laden and aggressive. There was no other way to classify the way he rolled his hips up and into his partner. Reyna's shock was short lived as she began to move her hips and shoulders to the beat, giving Ronan a run for his money. For each seductive move he made, she made another in kind. Both tried to remain unaffected, but it was clear from the heated looks they sent one another that neither was immune.

"I'm not entirely sure who is pursuing who."

"Does it have to be one or the other?"

Helena shook her head. "I'm just curious which one is going to try to take credit for the win."

Von let out a bark of laughter. "That is the kind of argument that leads to the bedroom and is never entirely resolved."

"So, they're both winners."

"Exactly."

Von and Helena shared a long, heated look, memories of their own time in the bedroom passing between them.

"How much longer do we need to stay down here?" Von asked, brushing a kiss against her lips.

"A while yet, I'm afraid," she answered, regret heavy in her voice.

Von scowled. "My little brother is grown and yet he continues to annoy me."

"You can't blame him. It's your position as my Mate that requires your presence more so than yours as his brother."

He gave her a scorching look. "I shall try to suffer in silence, my love."

Helena laughed in his face. "You're about as likely to remain silent as Darrin is to walk through that door."

"You wound me," he said as he wrapped his arms around her waist and pulled her back to his chest.

"That doesn't feel like a wound to me."

"The longer it's neglected, the more that it aches."

Helena knew that she had started it, but she was not prepared for the effect his words had on her. "Mother's tits," she gasped, pressing into him.

Von leaned forward, under the guise of adjusting her necklace, and pressed a trail of kisses along her neck and shoulder. "You're the one that won't let us leave," he reminded her with a final nip at her ear.

Helena blinked a few times, trying to pull herself out of her Mate's seductive web.

Von chuckled, stepping away from her. "So, what else is required of us tonight?"

Helena gave him a blank look, letting his words echo about her mind as she tried to make sense of them. "What?"

"What else do we need to take care of before we can go to bed," he repeated, his smile making it clear that sleep was the last thing on his mind.

Helena racked her brain, trying to remember what specific duties she still had to perform. After the ceremony, they had made their way to the tables that had been set up for dinner. The meal had been relatively informal, with plates being passed around the table for guests to take what they wanted before passing it on. After the guests had finished eating, there was a round of increasingly inappropriate toasts, one of which Helena had made. Then about twenty minutes ago, the musicians had started up again, opening the dance floor for the rowdy guests. As far as she could recall, there was nothing left for her to officially do.

"Now that I think on it, I guess we're technically done. Although it's frowned upon to leave before the newly mated couple."

"Who would dare tell you when you are allowed to leave?"

Helena gave him a pointed look.

Von sighed, but his disappointment was short lived. When he began to smile, Helena knew that he was up to something. With a mischievous lift of his brow, he stepped away from her and started making his way toward his brother, who was currently spinning Serena around the dance floor.

"What are you doing?"

"What every good brother should."

"Von…"

He winked at her over his shoulder but did not slow down. Nial gave his brother a wide grin as he approached, his smile faltering only slightly as Von grabbed his arm and pulled him to the side before whispering in his ear.

Nial laughed and nodded, eagerly returning to his curious mate. In a similar fashion, Nial bent down and whispered something that caused Serena's eyes to go dreamy. She nodded, looking up at him from under her lashes. With barely a glance at the rest of their guests, Nial and Serena slipped away.

"There," Von said, returning to her side. "Can we go now?"

Helena's mouth fell open. "You did not just send your brother to bed on his mating night."

"I told him it was bad form to keep his mate waiting." There was nothing but smug satisfaction in his voice.

"You are terrible," she informed him, unable to keep her laughter in check long enough to maintain her pretense of chastisement.

"No, my love. Simply a man of action."

Just as Helena was about to agree, Margo walked over to them.

"Your brother ran off without dancing with his mother!"

Von stared at her with frustrated amusement. "I suppose that means you're looking for a stand in?"

"But of course!"

Von held out his arm, letting his mother weave her own arm through it before he led her to the dance floor.

"So close," he said mournfully through the bond.

"We have all night, my love."

"From your lips…" he said, repeating her words from earlier.

Helena's laugh was muffled by the sweeping strains of the music as Von began to dance with his mother. It was with joy, and perhaps a small bit of wistfulness, that she stayed there to watch them, knowing as she did that their window for such simple pleasures was swiftly closing.

CHAPTER 4

GREYSPIRE

"The scouts have returned."

"And?" Rowena didn't bother to turn around and address the man directly.

"They remain in hiding. There has been no sign of the Kiri or her Circle."

"Incompetent fools," she hissed, letting her pointed nails rake across the glass as she looked over her shoulder.

There was a discernible wince on the handsome face, but it passed quickly. It was only the sound, and not her displeasure, that caused the reaction. Rowena could tell because there was no sign of fear in the golden eyes that boldly stared back into hers. There hadn't been since the day she had met him standing defiantly at the door of his stone palace. *This one believes he is my equal. Brave*, Rowena decided, impressed despite herself. Although she would never tell him that. It had been years since anyone mistakenly believed the same, but he would learn. Eventually. They always did. No one was her equal.

Not even the Endoshan heir.

When given the choice to join her or die, the same choice she had offered each of the Chosen she had come across, Kai-Soren surprised her by being the first to willingly accept... albeit for a price. For months Rowena and her army had marched across Elysia, taking by force what he freely offered. She could have Endoshan, but only if he stood at her side. An alliance, he said, to be forged by marriage. An easy enough promise to make, and not one she had any intention of keeping. But he didn't need to know that. Not yet.

Kai-Soren had already proven to be a useful ally. For all their power, there was much his Endoshans could do that her Shadows could not. Most notably, the Endoshans could move amongst the Chosen unnoticed. Rumors were beautiful things, both powerful and effective. It was easy enough to convince the others that Endoshan had been lost. One bloodied runner had been enough to convince the Etillions, and from there, they had handled the rest. Just like that, an entire territory was under her control with no more effort than a simple, "I accept."

Rowena couldn't wait to see that aqua-eyed impostor's face when she saw she didn't control the Chosen as completely as she believed. As it did every time she thought of that little bitch sitting on her throne, Rowena's anger multiplied. She turned to face Kai-Soren fully. The window had frozen where her hand had been, small fissures appearing in the glass as it began to shatter beneath the assault. He didn't even spare the cracking glass a glance, his eyes remaining steadily leveled on her.

"I am displeased."

"I can see that."

A cold smile made her lips tilt up. "Would you like to see what happened to the last man who displeased me?"

There was a flicker in the golden eyes. She had struck a nerve. *Good. He is learning already.*

"How may I remedy the situation, my lady?"

Rowena tilted her head, considering her answer. After a long-drawn-out silence, she shrugged. "It is no matter. The bitch will come to us."

Kai-Soren bowed his head. "As you say."

"We will be ready when she arrives." It was an order, not a question.

"Yes, my lady. They will not leave alive."

"I cannot think of a more pleasing betrothal gift."

The smile that twisted his lips matched hers for depravity. "Nor I."

MEANWHILE, IN DAEJARA

THE MORNING after Nial and Serena's ceremony found her in yet another crowded room, although this time there was a decided lack of smiling faces. Helena's eyes moved from face to face, trying to gauge the level of unease. She grimaced. Getting these stubborn fools to agree to work together was going to be no small feat.

Overnight, the last of her allies had arrived in Daejara. At least those that were still alive. She frowned with the memory of Endoshan. There was little love lost between her and the Endoshan heir, that much was true, but she would not wish Rowena's brand of justice on anyone.

Sitting uncomfortably in the room were the representatives for the Night Stalkers, the Storm Forged, the Daejarans, the Calderans, the Etillions, and the Sylvanese. The only allies not accounted for were the Talyrians, and that was more for logistical reasons than anything. Although, if she was being honest, Helena would feel more confident if Starshine and her teeth were close at hand. The threat of a Talyrian bite worked almost better than anything else to keep others in line. Helena flexed her hands, the tips of her black claws making a brief appearance. They would have to do. She smirked at the thought of acting as the Talyrian enforcer. She had a feeling Starshine would have been equal parts proud and amused.

Each territory had been allowed no more than three representatives to be present. Always the exception, the Circle was fully accounted for. Sitting beside her Mate, representing Daejara, were Nial, Serena, and Effie. The latter was a ghost of her former self. Helena had been shocked when Effie insisted on being the third as she'd barely left her room since they had buried Darrin. Helena wished she'd had more time to spend offering comfort to the woman so clearly consumed by mourning. There was little she would refuse the petite blonde; she would give anything to help keep her busy and distracted.

The Calderans were next. Tinka and Khouman were present, along with a new female with bright red braids liberally streaked with gray. She was as small as Tinka and as fierce-looking as Khouman. Helena would guess that she was the one calling the shots for Calderan.

Beside them were the Etillions. Helena recognized Amara and Xander from her brief and unfortunately memorable trip to Etillion. With them was a younger man who looked like he might be related to Amara. A brother or cousin perhaps. He was struggling to keep from staring at the cerulean-skinned woman seated beside him.

Helena couldn't blame him. The Storm Forged were certainly alluring with their tinged skin and colorful hair. Anduin sat between two turquoise-haired women whom Helena did not recognize. She mentally applauded his efforts at diplomacy by not bringing the troublemakers who had been causing problems with the Night Stalkers.

On the other side of the Storm Forged sat the Sylvanese. The trio looked familiar, but she could not say with certainty which she had met before, if any. They were another group that she would guess were all related in some capacity.

Rounding out the table were Reyna and her Night Stalkers. She sat beside Ronan with Ryder and another dark-haired man. All three of them appeared battle-ready, their swirls of paint and fitted leathers a clear, and not very subtle, message.

The room was warm, and Helena regretted asking Margo to light the hearth in the massive stone chamber. She had thought that the amber glow would help create a welcoming atmosphere, but the dribble of sweat she felt roll down her back mocked her. *So much for atmosphere.* Calling on Air, Helena wrapped the cool current around herself.

She was just about ready to call the room to order when a quick knock rapped on the door. Not waiting for permission, the door opened to reveal Miranda.

"Kiri, I request permission to attend on behalf of the Keepers."

At the mention of the notorious historians and secret-keepers, the room fell silent.

"Permission granted." Helena could see no reason to exclude her, and Miranda had already proven herself an asset. If she wanted to use her title to gain access to this meeting so be it, Helena would take all the help she could get.

Effie went to make space beside her at the table, but Timmins had already stood and offered his seat to the Keeper. Miranda gave Timmins a smile of thanks and lowered herself into his vacated seat.

"She just needs to fuck him already and put the poor bastard out of his misery."

"Who says she hasn't?" Helena replied, watching her Mate's head swivel to better study her Advisor and the Keeper. There had always been a palpable energy between those two, but it seemed more pronounced now. Solidified perhaps. Helena lifted a brow, something had certainly changed between them, and she was almost certain they'd finally acted on the sexual tension they'd been fighting since they'd first met.

"Shall we get started?" Helena asked.

There were a few murmurs of assent, but the group otherwise remained silent.

"Shortly after I returned home from the Vale I received an invitation. One I plan to accept." Helena lifted a hand to silence the protests that were already rising. "Before you say anything, yes, I am aware that it is a trap. However, there is no better time or way for us to infiltrate her defenses and strike."

"She will be expecting you to, Kiri. You cannot think she won't," Khouman said.

Helena nodded her agreement. "She will lay her trap well, but she will be expecting the Kiri."

Her words were met with looks of confusion.

Helena elaborated, "She does not know that I can alter my appearance. I have been working with Joquil on ways to extend that power to others."

"You expect to sneak in without suspicion," Anduin said, admiration coloring his voice.

Helena shrugged. "It wouldn't be the first time."

"What do you need from us?" Reyna asked.

"A distraction."

"How big?" Ronan asked with a dangerous grin.

Helena smiled at him before addressing the others. "I want to strike before she can. We need to do as much damage as quickly as possible."

Kragen rubbed his hands together gleefully.

"In the confusion of the attack, I want her and her generals separated from the chaos so that they cannot assist. It should give us time to take out the bulk of her army."

"A Talyrian strike?" Von asked, already picturing how they could maximize the casualties.

"She won't expect it," Helena replied as she considered the suggestion.

There were nods of agreement around the table.

"You cannot expect to go in alone," Reyna pointed out.

"I was hoping some of the Night Stalkers could join me. Your people are the most adept at subterfuge and close-range combat."

The Night Stalkers' answering grin would have been chilling if they had not been mirrors of her own.

"Rowena will not stay idle," one of the Sylvanese warned.

"Which is why the rest of you will need to be ready. Ronan, Von, can you work with the others to create a plan? When Rowena realizes what is happening, she will not hesitate. The full force of our army will need to be prepared for that eventuality."

The men nodded.

"My people can provide cover until we are ready to reveal ourselves, Kiri," Anduin offered.

"I am certain you will live up to your name, Stormbringer."

He dipped his head in agreement.

"Do you remember the layout of Greyspire?" Ronan asked Von.

Her Mate's eyes went hazy. "Enough."

Helena's lips tilted in a frown as she recalled his capture. The tendril of Von's unease she felt snaking through their bond did little to dilute her rage at the reminder.

"Do you really think she does not expect you to try to strike, Kiri?" Amara asked, looking worried.

Helena's eyes went iridescent. "Rowena underestimates me. She forgets that as the Mother's Vessel I am more than a figurehead. I am the Mother's wrath every bit as much as I am Her love. It is time to show her my claws."

There was a ripple of panic throughout the room as her words affected them. To some degree, they had all witnessed her power, but none had seen her fully unleash it with the intent to destroy.

"Sometimes to cleanse, first you must burn," Miranda reminded them in her midnight voice.

"Then let the world burn," Von said, his voice steel.

"There are many kinds of storms," Anduin added, bloodlust making his pupils flare.

"We are yours to command, Kiri. Wherever you lead us, we are with you," Serena said. The rest of the group murmured their agreement.

Helena smiled gratefully at her friends, new and old.

"When do we leave?" Joquil asked.

"Three days."

If anyone thought it wasn't enough time, they didn't say so.

CHAPTER 5

'When attempting transformational magic, it is essential
the weaver knows the most minute details of their
subject. The better the understanding, the more
authentic the transformation. Any discrepancy could
be the tell that gives away the magic. Detail is
everything in transformational magic.'

Helena slammed the musty tome closed with a frustrated sigh. She was not readily finding the answers she needed, and they were out of time. So much of what she knew about her power came from intuition. She thought of what she wanted and her power responded. True, it wasn't always perfect, but it was instinct and therefore so much simpler than trying to make sense of half-hocked attempts to explain what she was supposed to think and feel. Magic was emotional for her. Not scientific. Trying to force it like this had left her frustrated, not to mention unsuccessful, for days.

It was imperative that she find a way to hide the small group of Night Stalkers and Chosen who would join her inside Rowena's party. But there was the rub. She was not the only one that had to take on a new form. For each person that joined her, she needed to create a new identity that made sense amongst the other partygoers. Someone who would not cause others to look at them askance. That sounded easy in theory, but how could she turn someone into another person she had never met? It was one thing to create something entirely new, but the need to blend in severely tempered any creative license.

Shapeshifting was tied to detail and an intimate knowledge of what you were trying to transform into. The problem was Helena didn't know who she was supposed to make these people become. They needed to be unremarkable and easily overlooked. Faces in a crowd that were easily forgotten as curious eyes looked on and toward something more interesting.

Helena rubbed her forehead, closing her eyes in an attempt to alleviate her pounding headache.

She heard the library door open but didn't bother turning around.

"I seem to find you as I left you, Kiri."

"Then perhaps you have returned too soon, Keeper," Helena replied, her voice low and laced with tension.

Miranda's hand perched momentarily on Helena's shoulder, a display of comfort or perhaps understanding. The older woman moved around the ancient table, taking a seat across from her.

"Perhaps you are thinking about this the wrong way."

Helena opened an eye to glare blearily at her. "Spare me your riddles and speak plainly."

Gesturing toward the bevy of open and unopened books that littered the table, Miranda asked, "Must they be transformed? Is there not another way to hide amongst a crowd? Deceit does not always have to be in the details, but their absence."

Helena continued to glare, even as the words worked their way around her brain. There was a truth to them that she could not quite ascertain. It was as if the answer was hidden just out of reach. A fact which only increased her ire. Something in her face must have given that away because Miranda had the grace to dip her head and murmur an apology.

"I do not pretend to know the answer, Kiri. I am not half as gifted as you. It is just, sometimes thinking of a problem from a new angle can present the solution we could not initially find."

Helena could not help but agree. "That is certainly true, Keeper."

"I find that talking through the situation with another can sometimes present other avenues to explore."

"Are you offering your services, Keeper?" Helena asked with a wry smile.

Miranda's midnight eyes glittered, but her smile was nothing less than respectful as she replied, "Always, Kiri."

"How many times must I insist that you call me Helena?"

"You are my Kiri, first and foremost. When speaking of matters of politics and war, it is only appropriate to address you such. When we speak as two equals then you can be Helena."

"Is that not what we are right now?"

Miranda's smile was kind but tinged with sadness. "I'm afraid not, Kiri. Not when we discuss such important things."

"Not even if I consider you my equal?" Helena pressed.

The Keeper reached out a hand and laid it gently on hers. "It would seem I am not the only one with trouble remembering her lessons."

Helena's smile was puzzled. "I'm afraid I don't follow, although I am more than certain you must be correct. There is much I seem to forget, as Joquil and Timmins so often take pleasure in reminding me. Would you care to enlighten me on which lesson it would seem I have forgotten this time?"

"Dearest Kiri, only the most important one."

Helena's brows dropped in a deeper frown.

Taking pity on her, Miranda laughed and sat back in her chair. "Only this: None are your equal."

Her words had the air of prophecy even though she had not taken on any of the physical traits often associated with the Sight.

Helena sat up straighter in her chair. "Not even my Mate?"

Miranda shook her head slightly, a small smile still playing about her lips. "Not even he that completes you. You alone are the Mother's Vessel. That is a power no other can match, and so they will seek to thwart it for their own gain."

"You are speaking of the prophecy, aren't you? The one warning of my corruption?"

Miranda shrugged. "It is one of many warnings, although I was not being specific."

A niggling voice had Helena asking, "What do you know that you are not saying, Keeper?"

Miranda's eyes lost their amusement as a newfound respect entered their glittering midnight depths. "The Sight is not perfect. There is always room for misinterpretation, as you are aware."

Helena nodded.

Looking away and into the dusty stacks of books that sat on the library shelves that surrounded them, Miranda remained quiet for a long moment. As she watched and waited for an answer, Helena was reminded of one who rifled through the pages of an old book, as if seeking a specific passage.

When Miranda spoke again, it was not the words of prophecy, but yet another warning. "Do not underestimate the Corruptor. She values that which you have and will seek to use it against you and what you hold most dear. Even now she spins her web, knowing that her prey will find it irresistible."

A heavy sense of foreboding settled in the pit of Helena's stomach. There was nothing the woman said that she did not already know, and yet… the sense of inevitability was exhausting. There was no getting around Rowena or her traps. Helena did not know what she planned, only that she did. It was hard to be prepared for the unknown, but given her opponent, she had to try. It could be the difference between victory or the bitterest defeat.

"Do not despair, Kiri. The future is not yet written. There are many pieces to move and choices to make."

"It is not despair I feel, Keeper."

Miranda's answering smile was full of pride. "Good. Then all is certainly not lost."

The words did little to bolster her.

"Helena," Miranda said more softly.

Surprised to hear her name after the Keeper's earlier comment, Helena looked at her in confusion.

"Do not be afraid of what lies in the darkness, only of getting lost in it. Your strength lies in being able to navigate both darkness and light. Make sure you keep sight of your compass, so that you may find your way back." With that, Miranda abruptly stood. "I should take my leave so that you may return to your studies. Remember what I said, Kiri."

There wasn't a chance for Helena to question her further. Miranda left as quickly as she had arrived, although her words lingered long after she did.

Helena let out a few choice curses before warily muttering, "Which words would you like me to remember, Keeper? You leave me with many."

Eying the stack of books she'd been studying, Helena decided to focus on the first bits of advice: approach her problem from a different angle and talk it through with someone else.

"Mate?"

Von's voice, when it found her, was tinged with concern as he responded to the despondency in her own. *"Mira?"*

"How do you conceal something in plain sight?"

She felt the swift shift of emotions as he processed the question and considered his answer. *"Cloaking it?"*

"You mean invisibility?"

"That is the easiest way."

"But not always practical for people that must move about a room."

"Ahh..." he replied, understanding the purpose of her question more fully.

"If I cannot transform my party to appear as expected partygoers, how can I make them fit in? What is both seen and unseen?"

"Scenery?" Von replied flippantly.

"Your wit is limitless," she said dryly. But his answer did spark an idea. Scenery was in fact something that was both seen and unseen. It was noticed and summarily dismissed. If she would not be

transforming the others, perhaps there was a way for her to make them blend into the background. *"Is blurring a thing?"* she asked, her excitement working its way into her mental voice.

"I do not think that I have heard of it," he admitted.

"But it is not impossible?"

"What you are speaking of, on the level on which you are speaking, would require not just a spell cast upon individuals but an entire group of people."

"Like when I can use my emotions to control the emotions of others?"

"Well... yes. However, in this case you would be convincing a room of people not *to look closely at something, instead of influencing them unknowingly with your emotions."*

"Purposeful intention rather than emotional ripples. Interesting," she replied, already making notes on the piece of paper that had until now only been used for errant doodles. *"This just might work."*

"Happy to help," he teased, sensing that her focus was no longer on their conversation.

Morning gave way to afternoon as Helena's plan took shape on the paper beside her. When she was finished, the room was dark and her hand was cramped, but she knew what she was going to do.

Helena's smile was triumphant and fierce as she spoke to the darkness. "You are not the only one that plots, Corruptor. You should be more careful what you wish for; your invitation has just given us the opening we needed."

CHAPTER 6

The sound of drills rang through the courtyard. All signs of the mating ceremony had been removed and in its place a training ground had been erected. If it was not for the cliffs just off to the side and the soft call of the gulls as they flew above the crashing waves, Helena would not have realized she was standing in the exact same spot as she had only days prior.

It was the last day before they would make their way to Vyruul and whatever secrets awaited them there. Ronan and Von had agreed that given the different ways of fighting each of the groups employed, it was important that their army could recognize friend from foe on the battlefield. More than that, they needed to be able to combine their skills and work together.

Even now, a few days into the training, it was still more contest than collaborative effort. Helena winced at Ronan's roar. "Again! Are you deaf or just stupid? How many times do I need to say this? Expand your cover to those around you so that they can sneak up on their opponent as well. You keep jumping ahead and end up leaving them with their asses flapping in the breeze."

"Better your ass than your dick," Kragen commented in a bland tone.

"True, although your ass is a bigger target," Von replied mildly.

Nial barely covered his snicker with a cough as Serena glared at the three of them.

"It's not our fault," a dark-skinned girl of no more than seventeen whined. "Their thrice-cursed wind keeps blowing away our cover."

The nearest of the Storm Forged scowled at her. "Perhaps your little shadows are not strong enough if a breeze can knock them off course."

Green fire blazed in the girl's eyes as she rounded on the man. "Would you like to put it to the test, stormy bastard?"

"Smoke-stained bitch."

Ronan moved fast, his arm already extended so that his palm loudly smacked the chest of the Storm Forged who launched himself at the young Night Stalker. Reyna grabbed the girl from the back of her cloak and pulled hard, catching her before she could wrap the familiar cloak of darkness around her body and attack. The girl stumbled back a few steps while the Storm Forged rubbed at his chest. Both mumbled apologies but continued to glower at each other.

"We're doomed."

Von's chuckle met her like a warm caress on a chilly night. She tingled as it wrapped itself around her.

"We're not. They will learn that they despise the enemy more than each other when the time comes."

"Can that time come now?"

Von ran a hand along the length of her braid, tugging slightly when he got to the bottom. *"Perhaps they simply require some inspiration."*

Helena worried at her bottom lip as she thought on his words. *What sort of inspiration would suffice? Surely not another speech. Words didn't seem to have a lasting effect on them.*

Von carefully extracted her bottom lip from her teeth, using his thumb to stroke it. *"You distract me when you do that."*

She looked up at him through her lashes, smiling cheekily at the hunger burning in his eyes. *"And you distract me when you look at me like that, so stop it."*

"You first."

Helena stuck her tongue out at him.

"Not helping..."

Helena bit back a smile as she moved away from her Mate and toward her Shield. For what she had in mind, it didn't seem right to act without informing the Commander of her intention. She waited for him to finish correcting the maneuver of another group and waved him over.

Ronan had pulled his hair into a knot on the top of his head. Loose tendrils were stuck to his cheeks and neck, giving the appearance of bright streaks of blood across his tanned skin. Helena shuddered, focusing on his eyes to rid herself of the image.

He wiped sweat off his forehead with the back of his arm as he greeted her. "Hellion."

"I have an idea."

Ronan raised a brow. "Can it wait until after practice? Today is our last chance to get this right."

She glared at him. "It's about practice, you ass."

He winked at her. "Oh, well. In that case, do tell."

Helena rose up on her toes and whispered her plan into his ear. He looked at her in surprise before he said, "Mother's tits, that's devious and fucking brilliant. Why didn't I think of that before?"

She shrugged.

"By all means, go for it." He grinned with anticipation as he gestured for her to proceed.

"Should we give them warning first?" she asked as she considered how they might react.

Ronan folded his arms. "Part of being the army is being ready at all times. They cannot expect the enemy to politely tap them on the shoulder and say 'how-do' before they attack. Practice should be no different if they are to actually learn from it."

Helena couldn't help but agree with his assessment. You were never really ready for a battle until you were already in the thick of it and even then, ready wasn't exactly the word she would use.

"Here goes nothing. Let us hope they rise to the occasion. And that nobody dies," she added as an afterthought.

"That's all we can ever hope for." Ronan chuckled.

"True," she agreed before unleashing unholy hell amongst the lot of them.

By the time Helena was done, what had once been a brilliantly beautiful afternoon in Daejara was now under siege by thick roiling clouds and huge cracks of lightning. The storm was furious, but that was not the major concern at the moment.

Running at their army from every direction were dozens of skeletal Shadows. Their vacant snaking eyes and gaping mouths just as gruesome as the real thing. Since coming up with her plan for Rowena's party, Helena had been practicing casting mass illusions. Given the terrified sobs of the cowering girl before her, she would have to say she was getting better.

There was certainly nothing fake about the screams that met her ears as Helena and her Circle moved away from the chaos her magic had created. If the troops wanted to get out of this in one piece, they would have to work together. There'd be no help from any of their leaders.

Helena would have loved to say that the group came together seamlessly, but that was not remotely the case. All of Ronan's drills may as well have been instructions on etiquette at a tea party for all the effect they seemed to have. Before her, the Storm Forged, Night Stalkers and Chosen fought like three separate entities, which they technically were. The problem was that the conflicting styles were actively working against each other instead of complimenting each other.

The goal was for the Storm Forged to control the weather, using it to help conceal the Night Stalkers and the various groups of Chosen to help them evade notice. The Night Stalkers were supposed to extend their shadow cover to further assist the Chosen while they snuck up and attacked. But none of those things were happening.

The Chosen seemed to have entirely forgotten that there was a plan. They made absolutely no attempts to maneuver within the confines of Night Stalkers' or Storm Forged's concealments. Instead, they were running full out at the beasts, hurling their weapons or balls of power at the Shadows, and generally making beautiful targets for the Shadows to easily dispatch. Not that anyone was actually harmed. As part of her spell, Helena wove in a stun effect that held the person immobile if the Shadow made what would have been a killing blow, rendering them incapable of continuing the drill.

When more than half of the army was frozen in place, Helena let out a disgusted scream. "Enough!" With a flick of her wrist, the illusions vanished, but she held onto the storm, letting it rage above them as if contained by an invisible barrier while she retained the immobilization, wanting the lesson to sink in along with their failure.

"Is this a game to you?" she hissed, her voice echoing with the effects of her storm.

The people blanched. No one had ever seen her anger directed at them like this before.

Her Circle moved into place behind her, and Helena knew without looking that their expressions of displeasure were likely mirrors of her own. Anduin and Reyna moved to stand with her without hesitation, showing with the movement that they recognized and yielded to her authority, both leaders in sync for the first time since their arrival in Daejara.

One of the men that had not been hit by a Shadow snickered, thinking that her words were not meant for him. Helena lashed out, using Air to create a hand that gripped him at his ankle and pulled, causing him to fall hard on his ass. Those around him were too stunned to laugh.

"Is your pride worth more than your life? Than the lives of those around you? Are you so naïve that you truly believe your way is the right and only way to defeat our enemy?"

Her words rang about the field, the silence and humiliation of the troops absolute. For all their attempts, not one of them had brought down a single Shadow.

"No, Kiri," a girl whispered, her voice carrying in the silence.

"Are you sure? Because based on what I just saw, not one of you gives a damn who wins this war. Should we give up now and save ourselves the effort?"

"No, Kiri," more voices called out, growing stronger with their conviction.

"Prove it," she roared, releasing her hold on the storm and the people giving them only a heartbeat to stand as the Shadows flared back into being.

This time the groups worked together, and while it was not perfect, it was a start.

"This will be a lesson they won't soon forget," Reyna murmured thoughtfully as she watched yet another of her Night Stalkers get stunned.

"I wanted to make a point."

"Oh, you did," Anduin said. "One with a very sharp edge."

"Death would be the best they can hope for if they don't learn this lesson," Ronan added.

"If Rowena wins, death would be a mercy."

Helena's words caused Reyna to visibly shudder. "I will continue to work with the Night Stalkers. They will not disappoint you again."

"And I with the Storm Forged."

It took over an hour for the group to best half of Helena's Shadows. Even then more than half of the group had been stunned. Feeling merciless, Helena merely snapped and shouted, "Again!"

After three more attempts, the groups were finally working together, able to coordinate their attacks to best subdue and attack the Shadows without suffering any casualties. It took them less than an hour to finally take down all twenty-five of the illusions.

When they were done, Helena's army panted and shook with exhaustion. She had a feeling that no one would complain about what a demanding Commander her Shield was again. She'd just proven she was far worse. Hopefully, they'd all live long enough to complain about it.

"Or thank you for it," Von added, picking up on her thoughts.

She looked at him over her shoulder and smiled slightly. *"Somehow I doubt anyone ever remembers that part."*

"As the one who is usually in your position, I can confirm the accuracy of the statement. However, you do not need them to thank you for being demanding in your training. Or right about its necessity. Take comfort in each and every heart that still beats at the end of the war."

Helena nodded, her smile grim. *"I will."*

Ronan moved to her side with a whistle as they watched the troops disperse for showers and a hot meal. "I think you just put me out of a job."

She snickered. "Hardly. The last thing I want to do is wake up at ungodly hours of the morning to have people run drills."

Ronan laughed, but the amusement faded from his voice when he spoke. "You've just proven that you can prepare them in ways I never even thought of. They learned more from you today than they have from me in days of practice."

"They would have failed if not for those days of practice."

"They did fail," Ronan pointed out.

"Only because they refused to follow your commands. Once they did, they were successful."

Ronan was silent while he considered her words. "I suppose you're right."

"Of course, I am."

He raised an eyebrow but grinned when he saw that she was laughing.

"Perhaps you can just stop by every now and then and put them in their place?"

"Isn't that what I always do?" she teased.

Ronan let out a loud bark of laughter that had the rest of the Circle looking toward them. "I'll be damned. You totally do."

She winked at him, leaning over to whisper conspiratorially, "Don't tell Von, but I learned it from you."

"I heard that."

"Of course, you did. But he needed the compliment more than you did."

She felt Von's mental shrug. *"I'm not worried, Mira. If you learned it from him, it's only because he learned it from me."*

Helena shook her head, his twisted male logic making her laugh. *"It's always a competition with you two."*

"Oh, it's no competition."

She rolled her eyes, amused despite herself. *"If you say so."*

"Do you think we're ready?" Reyna asked, her husky voice uncharacteristically subdued.

Helena shifted focus, turning to look fully at the other woman. "As ready as we can be given the time constraints that we're under."

Reyna frowned but nodded. "We still have a few days before the party."

"True, but we will be trying to move into place undetected. Many of us will be separated. There will not be time to practice all together like this again."

"No, but that does not mean they cannot continue to run their Commander's drills on their own." Her gaze flit to Ronan for confirmation.

"Only if it is safe to do so. We cannot risk detection," he replied.

Reyna nodded her agreement.

"The Storm Forged can help with that. I will ensure it," Anduin offered.

Reyna looked up at him in surprise. "We will be glad of the assistance," she replied.

Anduin held out a hand. "I apologize that our people got off on the wrong foot. I hope that there is still a chance for friendship between us."

Reyna was slower to offer her hand, but she took his and nodded. "As do I, Stormbringer."

With that Anduin walked away, leaving Helena, Reyna, Ronan, and Von still standing in the clearing.

"Well, well, Hellion. It looks like you are a miracle worker after all," Ronan said.

"After everything she's done, *that's* the miracle?" Von asked.

"You know better than anyone the harm that years of prejudice can cause. They are almost impossible to bridge."

Von nodded. "Aye, I do."

"All Helena had to do was whip everyone's ass and prove that they were ignorant fools, and now they want to make nice."

"Is that what I did?"

"What would you call it?" Ronan challenged.

"I…" she paused, shrugging. "Practice?"

Her friends laughed.

"Whatever you want to call it, it was an important first step toward victory. We knew that we could not defeat Rowena on our own. Now you have an army that is willing to work together. If nothing else, I'll drink to that," Ronan said, as they began slowly walking back toward the house.

"And I," Von agreed.

Helena smiled, feeling more relieved than she had in months. "I suppose you're right. That is worth celebrating."

"Care to repeat that?" Ronan asked, holding up a hand to his ear.

Helena punched him in the shoulder. "If you missed it, it was your fault you weren't paying attention."

Reyna snickered.

"Hey now, don't go taking her side."

"Who said I was on your side to begin with?" Reyna asked, arching her brow.

Ronan gave her a dark look and shook his head. "You think you know a girl."

Reyna wove her arm through his, pulling him in the direction of the kitchens. "Come now, let me mend your wounded ego with a glass of ale."

"It's like you know me," Ronan said, placing a hand to his heart.

"Or the quickest way to earn a man's forgiveness, at the very least."

"I can think of better ways," Ronan said with a wink.

They continued to bicker playfully as they walked. Von and Helena watched them in silence, turning to one another once they were alone.

"Do you really think it will help?" she asked, finally letting the fear and doubt she'd been trying to hide show to the only person who would understand.

Von placed both of his hands on her shoulders. "I do, *Mira*. A group that bands together will always be stronger than one that does not." He took her hand and lifted it so that it was in front of her face. Wiggling her fingers, he said, "A hand can cause harm like this, but it does much more damage when it strikes like this." As he said it, he balled her hand into a fist. "You have taught them to strike as one. They will be more powerful because of it."

"Then let us hope they remember that when the time comes."

"They will," Von said confidently.

"How can you be so sure?"

His eyes glowed as he said, "You reminded them what their failure meant. They had to watch, over and over, as their friends fell in battle. It will haunt them."

"I didn't mean—"

He cut her off. "It was an important lesson, Helena. One you should never feel guilty for. You saved lives today."

She took a deep breath, letting his words soothe the part of her that could still hear the cries of fear. Some of their party were seasoned warriors, but many in their ranks had never seen a battle firsthand. Not at this scale. They had been safely tucked away living in relative peace their entire lives. Ronan's lessons had not sunk in, because they had not fully understood the importance of what he was trying to teach them.

Now they did.

When she thought of it that way, she much preferred that she was the one causing the nightmares rather than Rowena. Because at least if it was her, they were all still alive.

CHAPTER 7

"*It begins.*"

The three robed figures stood at the edge of a cliff overlooking the twisted stone that made up Greyspire. Their hoods were lowered as they stared down at the snow-covered fortress. Wind whipped at their cloaks, revealing the snaking navy runes that pulsed and moved along their skin.

"*It is yet another step down a long and arduous path.*"

"*The outcome will be telling.*"

"*She cannot go back now.*"

"*She never could.*"

"*The choice was made long before she entered this world.*"

The central figure lifted a skeletal arm and pointed in the direction of the forest. "*The Vessel is near.*"

The men on either side tilted their faces up, the pits of their eyes staring vacantly up into the glittering night sky.

"*So much power.*"

"*It tastes so sweet.*"

"*Pure.*"

"*For now.*"

They lowered their chins and turned their faces to look in the direction of the forest, as if they could see the woman of whom they spoke. Perhaps they could.

"The darkness swells around her."

"A storm about to strike."

"Ready to devour us all."

"She sits at its heart."

As one, they took a step back from the cliff, moving out of sight. Before they faded into the cavern at their backs, the central figure stopped and sniffed the air.

"Our daughter will be joining us soon."

The others turned, the gesture sharp, indicating surprise at the announcement.

"You are certain?"

"There is no doubt."

"That is joyous news indeed."

"Shall we stay awhile longer to greet her?"

"No. This is not the place for it."

The men nodded, and the trio disappeared into the inky darkness.

"THAT'S THE LAST OF THEM," Von said.

Helena eyed the newest arrivals, wincing in sympathy as some immediately hunched over and began to empty out the contents of their stomachs. Travel by Kaelpas stone was certainly not for everyone, and the first time was especially difficult.

"Have we heard word from the others that they are also in place?"

Von dipped his chin. "Aye."

Helena took a deep breath, letting the wintery pine scent fill her lungs and settle her. The weather here was so different from Daejara. Usually a trip like this would take weeks, so a person had time to adjust to the change in temperature, but only moments ago she had been in Daejara's much more temperate clime.

She shivered at the frostbitten air. "I forgot how cold it was here."

"You were a bit preoccupied last time."

Her lips quirked up. "To say the least."

Von frowned as he stared at the castle. "I do not like that you are going back in there without me."

Helena's heart twisted in her chest. She didn't like it either, but she needed him handling things out here. Their bond gave her a direct line of communication to what was happening outside and would allow her to signal them when it was time to strike. There was no one else who could relay the message for her.

The castle was still, there was no hint that a party was already underway inside.

"Tell me again that this will work," she pleaded, using the bond so that no one else would hear her uncertainty. Right now they needed her to be fearless, even though that was the last thing she was feeling.

Von ran a hand along her back, moving it to wrap around her hips and pull her back to him. He rested his cheek along the top of her head. *"I cannot promise we will not fail. No one can. But if we are to fail, we will take down every last one of them on our way."*

"Your pep talk could use some work."

He chuckled. *"Would you rather I lied?"*

"No," she said honestly, sighing.

"We are as ready as we can be."

Helena nodded, her expression grim. She was not afraid to face Rowena, the heartless bitch certainly had it coming. She'd taken enough from Helena. First Von, then Anderson, and finally Darrin. The time to repay her cruelty was more than overdue. It was the thought of having to say goodbye to more people she loved that had her stomach twisted in knots.

Her mind ran through the plan one final time. Everyone knew their roles. She'd split up the Circle so that at least one or two members were paired and overseeing a portion of the army. Reyna, Ryder, and seven others in her contingent would be joining Helena, along with Kragen. No one in the Circle was willing to budge on that point. They would not send their Kiri into Rowena's trap without at least one of them by her side. With Von needed outside and Ronan leading the main charge, her Sword was the obvious choice.

Von would be stationed on the nearby cliffs with Starshine and the rest of the Talyrian pride awaiting Helena's signal. Ronan's melee force would be hiding in plain sight, Anduin and Reyna's people concealing them with a combination of their unique abilities. The sheer number of people Anduin and Reyna's forces were concealing was beyond impressive. Ronan, Nial, Serena, Effie, and the rest of the Chosen and Forsaken fighting force had already begun to move into place so they would be ready when Von took to the skies. Helena knew where everyone was situated, but even still, she could not make out any sign of them amongst the snowy banks leading up to the castle.

Timmins and Joquil would be staying in the forest and heading up the ranged team. They would remain hidden until the battle began, supporting the fighters with their magic to help pick off any of the outlying threats. Miranda and the Etillions were with them, their skills more suited to ranged attacks than hand-to-hand combat.

"Everyone seems to be in place, I guess that means it's time for me to do the same."

Von remained silent behind her, his concern and love washing over her in a soothing wave. She curled into his embrace, laying her head on his shoulder and feeling his heart beat in time with hers. The world fell away. The Talyrians' snarls, the nervous chatter, the call of the birds. For a series of heartbeats, the only people in that forest were her and her Mate. There were no words to say, the bond making speech unnecessary. Hope. Fear. Love. It was all there swelling around them.

Helena forced herself to step away, knowing she had to be the one to make the first move. Von would never willingly walk away from her. Not after everything they'd been through. His eyes bore into hers, flaring gold as the intensity of his emotion took over.

"I'll be waiting for you in the sky, my love."

"Don't have too much fun without me, Mate."

"I could never." He smiled, but it didn't reach his eyes.

Helena leaned forward and pressed a fast kiss to his stubbled cheek. Tears made her eyes blur, so she spun away and all but ran toward the spot where Reyna was waiting for her. As she passed Midnight, she stopped and looked the massive cat dead in the eye.

"If you let anything happen to him while you're up there, I will geld you myself."

The Talyrian snarled at her and backed away.

Her eyes moved to Starshine. "Keep them safe for me, beautiful girl. If all goes well, I'll be joining you soon."

Starshine pressed into her, the peaty smell of fire and smoke filling her nose as the velvety fur rubbed against her skin.

"Let's go," she said thickly, not pausing to wait and see if she was followed, and not sure why leaving them felt so much like saying goodbye.

The others fell in line behind her, moving away from those that were staying behind. When they were a good distance away and not yet in sight of the castle, Helena called her power up. It rose quickly, greeting her like an old friend.

Illusion magic was a complicated blend of Spirit, Water, and Air. The power that rose felt like being submerged in a warm pool of water. She let it flow along her skin, feeling the subtle changes of her body as the transformation took place. Once it was complete, she pushed it out, watching as it washed over the rest of the party. *Smoke and mirrors*, she thought. She could see the bodies standing before her, but her eyes felt the pull to look away. Strong magic indeed, if even she was affected by its lure.

With a little bit of effort, she was able to fight the pull and focus on her friends. There was nothing specific that had changed about them, although it did appear as though their faces were slightly blurred and their dark attire was hazy at the edges, as if their bodies were trying to blend in with the forest around them. With one final pulse of magic, Helena made subtle changes to their clothing, turning their leather armor into more appropriate party wear.

Pleased with the results, she nodded and turned her attention back to herself. While none of them would be attending the party as themselves, the role she had to play required that she stand out a bit more than the others, which meant that she needed to take slightly more effort on her appearance.

As she released a breath, Helena ran her hands along her body, feeling her fighting leathers transform into a satin dress the color of midnight. It hugged her body, swishing as she moved. The top was a fitted corset, the bodice staying tight until just below her hips, where it flared out in black waves to the floor. To enhance the air of mystery, she added a netted veil that attached to a small feathered headpiece and obscured her face. She knew that they would receive masks once they were inside, but she didn't want to take any chances that someone would be able to see through the illusion and recognize her.

When she was done, she could feel nine sets of eyes on her. She looked up, wondering if something was amiss with her disguise.

"Von is going to kill me," Kragen declared.

Reyna whistled. "If discretion is your plan, you've chosen the wrong dress. I have never had a preference for women, but you're giving me ideas."

Helena laughed, color rising to her cheeks at the comments. "Let us hope no one feels the need to get too handsy."

"We will be nearby ready to relieve anyone of the offending limbs if they try, Kiri," Reyna promised.

Helena moved into position in front of them, the constriction of her dress making her usually long strides slow, while the hidden slits gave teasing glimpses of creamy skin as she walked. The flash of light against the dark material made her think of moonlight shining through the clouds.

Kragen looked up to the night sky, his calloused hand running over his bald head. "He might as well kill me now and get it over with."

Helena spared him a glance over her shoulder. "Don't forget who you serve, Sword. You have more to fear from me than him."

"That's what you think. When it comes to protecting you, he is more fearsome by half."

Helena smiled. He wasn't wrong.

"All right everyone, it's time to enter the viper's nest. Keep your eyes open and stay close to your partner. No one goes anywhere alone."

The others moved into position around her, and as one, they made their way up the path to the castle doors.

CHAPTER 8

The shadow of Greyspire loomed over them, casting them in total darkness as they stood before the massive door. Helena lifted a hand to knock, but there wasn't a chance before it swung open on silent hinges.

Helena peered inside, expecting the foyer to be well-lit considering they were supposed to be some of only hundreds of guests that were in attendance, but she was wrong. There were only a few candelabras placed randomly throughout the room, their flickering reflections casting pools of light on the black stone floor. She shuddered, feeling like she was walking into a cave. Or a tomb.

"Lovely," Reyna murmured, her voice pitched low so that only Helena could hear it.

Remembering that she was not alone helped strengthen her resolve. She moved deeper into the chamber, barely recognizing it from her brief time here before.

Just as she started to wonder where they were supposed to go, a pale-faced boy appeared before them. His hair was almost as pale as his skin, giving him the appearance of a ghost. He kept his eyes downcast, not speaking, merely waiting for them all to gather in the entryway before motioning for them to follow. He led them slowly, seeming to float down the winding halls like a miniature specter as they made their way to the ballroom.

"Mother's tits, he's a creepy little fucker," Kragen said. She heard one of the others muffle their amusement. She didn't disagree.

Helena began to hear the haunting strains of music as they got closer. Fear danced up her spine at the sound. The sounds were harsh and sharp, a cacophonous melody that had the hairs lifting on her arms. This was not a joyous occasion but some macabre imitation of one. Helena let her eyes fall briefly closed. Everything was a distraction, all with the intention of ensnaring her so Rowena could strike. She could not allow herself to react. She let out a breath and opened her eyes.

The boy had stopped just outside of two blood-red doors. They were the only sign of color since entering the castle and Helena did not think that was a coincidence. There was no life here, only death and bloodshed. With a gentle shove, the boy pushed the doors, open spilling light and more music into the hall.

Helena flinched at the noise. The music sounded more like wailing cats than anything she would want to dance to. She risked a glance to her left, sharing a look with Kragen before stepping into the ballroom.

Nothing would have prepared her for the sight that greeted her. The ballroom was full of swaying bodies, with lavish masks and headdresses obscuring their identities. Helena was shocked by the sheer number of people in attendance. She had assumed there would be a significant number, but nothing close to the amount of people that were present. *Who are they? Where had they come from?*

Helena grabbed a random mask and took a moment to scan the room, trying to get her bearings. The monochromatic theme from the rest of the castle was echoed throughout, although splashes of deep violet and red did adorn a few of the guests' outfits and broke up the black. Each person had a unique mask that seemed to resemble a creature, although no one remained still long enough for Helena to identify any of them with certainty. A couple moved past her, giving Helena a brief glimpse of feathers and fangs. Macabruls perhaps, although why anyone would want to be one of those dastardly beasts, she could only hazard a guess.

Those that were not dancing stood along the sides of the room talking or engaging in other more intimate displays of affection. The public demonstrations were unlike anything she'd witnessed before. *Where am I?*

Helena's eyes lifted, noting the massive black crystal chandelier hanging in the center of the room, where it glittered like the darkest of night stars. Just beyond the sparkling monstrosity, sitting on a throne of twisted metal was a woman swathed in black. *Rowena.*

Her mask completely concealed her hair, its twisting horns adorned with ropes of expensive jewels. Icy eyes were all but invisible behind the lace and leather masterpiece. Her lips were an unsmiling ruby slash against pale skin. She stood suddenly, moving to stand at the center of the dais. Her dress rippled as it fell to the floor, it looked like liquid night, reflecting the candlelight that blazed about the room.

A man approached her, his mask similar in shape, although much less extravagant than Rowena's, the horns curling down and back instead of up and out. If one could show submission via headpiece, that was certainly the way. He lifted a feathered cloak from her shoulders, the feathers having created an elaborate fan behind her masked head before they began to lay flat against the rest of the cloth.

Without the cloak, her shoulders and neck were bare, save for the egg-sized pendant that hung above her breasts. Helena's breath caught. It was a pendant, so like hers, but it was white with snaking black lines. She shuddered, the similarity between it and the Shadows' eyes certainly no coincidence.

Rowena lifted her arms and the music came to a sudden stop. Helena and her friends moved to the sides of the room, trying to blend in with the others.

"What a perfect evening for a celebration. I can think of no better time to share my joyous news with you."

Helena stiffened. Whatever brought Rowena joy could hardly be considered a good thing.

The man had set down her cloak while she spoke and had just returned to stand beside her.

"Vyruul is pleased to welcome its newest citizens. Endoshan has proven itself to be as wise as it is mighty when it sought to combine its legacy with ours."

There were a few sporadic cheers throughout the room.

Endoshan? But they are all dead... aren't they? Helena reached for Kragen's hand, squeezing hard to convey her confused disbelief.

That was when the man spoke and fury pure and potent began to boil in her blood.

"Endoshan is singularly blessed to have you agree to join hands with us, not only in partnership, but in marriage."

Helena recognized his smug voice. It was the Endoshan heir. *What have you done?* She wanted to scream, but there was no point. The evidence was irrefutable. Rather than fight, he'd tied the fate of himself and his people to Rowena. Classic power move. The idiot clearly had no idea who he'd just tied himself to. Rowena was more likely to rip his head off than share one iota of her power with him.

"The papers were signed this morning. The deed is done!"

The crowd cheered again.

Helena began to shake with the power of her fury. What a mockery! This was no love-match. This was the desperate attempt of a man who didn't want to be second to a woman. *If he only knew...*

"Let us go into this new era together as equals. Vyruul, meet your King, my Consort, Kai-Soren!"

Behind her, Kragen snarled.

"What should we do, Kiri?" Reyna asked.

"Nothing yet," Helena grit out behind clenched teeth.

"Is this what she wanted you to see?" one of the Night Stalkers asked quietly.

Helena gave a quick nod. "It is probably just the first of many blows she hoped to land."

They shifted uneasily behind her, everyone aware that Endoshan's betrayal was indeed a massive blow. *If they surrendered to Rowena, are there others?* Helena tried to keep her thoughts from spiraling. Now was not the time to go down that particular rabbit hole.

"We have work to do," she said, pulling everyone's focus back to their mission.

With a subtle nod, pairs began to break off from the group. Their mission was to see what they could learn. If they found any of Rowena's Generals, they were to alert Helena immediately so that they could try to neutralize them. In a matter of seconds, Kragen and Helena were alone.

"Shall we dance?" he asked in a mild tone.

Helena gave a stiff nod. Dancing was the last thing she felt like doing. It would be almost impossible to fake the enthusiasm required to blend in with the others. But she would do it, because she had to. It was the only inconspicuous way to get closer to Rowena.

Her part of the plan was deceptively simple. Stay close to Rowena without getting caught while the others find and isolate the Generals. Each team would work on quickly dispatching their General, utilizing the Night Stalkers unique ability to sneak up on their targets. Helena wasn't certain how Rowena would react if they were successful, namely if she would be able to feel when one of her men was snuffed out. It was why the goal was to identify first. If they could coordinate an attack on at least four of the Generals at once, it would cripple Rowena's most powerful warriors and give them a complete advantage, even if Rowena immediately reacted. Assuming she could tell, Helena would be nearby to strike. If she didn't, the pairs were to locate the final General and take him out.

Once the Generals were handled, Helena would send the signal to Von to begin the attack outside. Without her Generals, Rowena would be thrown into chaos once the attack started, allowing the Chosen army to make a—hopefully—massive dent in Rowena's numbers.

That was, of course, assuming everything went perfectly. Helena was an optimist, but she wasn't naïve. Not anymore. She had Rowena to thank for that. It was a gift she actually appreciated. Which was why there was a contingency plan. One she fervently hoped they wouldn't need.

"Just don't step on my feet," she muttered as she took his hand and let him pull her into the crowd of bodies on the dance floor.

He scoffed. "Clearly you've never seen me dance, K—" he stopped before he uttered her title, shooting her an apologetic glance.

Helena thought back. "No, I don't think I ever have."

Kragen grinned down before grasping her wrist and executing a complex spin. Helena stared at him with wide eyes as they came back together.

"Just a different type of footwork," he said by way of explanation.

"And set to music," she pointed out.

He flashed her another grin and they fell silent, both turning their focus back to the present. Her eyes moved about the room, checking to see if any of the others had found their targets. A disappointed shake of Ryder's head left her frowning. It didn't appear that luck was on their side. Not one of the Generals seemed to be in attendance.

Where is she hiding them?

Kragen and Helena had finally gotten close to the dais. Rowena and Kai-Soren were speaking in hushed tones, their heads dipped in toward the other. Helena silently wished that the horns of their masks caught and tangled. She would have loved to see them try to work themselves free.

Minutes began to pass swiftly, making Helena grow anxious. So much rode on their ability to locate the Generals. Kragen and Helena danced to two more songs, before Helena finally pulled him off to the side near a table of refreshments. Not that she had any intention of imbibing anything Rowena had on offer.

Noting her maneuver, Reyna and Ryder closed in.

"If we can't go to them, we need to make them come to us. It's time for Plan B."

Reyna and Ryder nodded, before slipping back into the crowd to warn the others.

"Are you sure about this?" Kragen asked, a touch of concern coloring his voice.

Helena nodded, her eyes going iridescent. There was only one surefire way she could think of to draw those creepy bastards out.

Von is going to kill me once he finds out about this, she thought just as mayhem erupted in the ballroom.

CHAPTER 9

This time when Helena released her magic, it was not so quick to rise. She could feel it there, but it responded more like honey dripping off a spoon than water falling from a cliff. It was clear that she was starting to feel the strain of using so much power so quickly. Usually when she channeled this much magic, it was in short bursts, but she'd already been holding on to ten different illusions for well over an hour, and she was about to add two more.

Helena narrowed her eyes, zeroing in on the feather and fanged couple she'd noted when they first arrived. *They'll do.* She bit down hard on her lip to use the pain as a focus. It gave her the push she needed. Her magic shot out, the illusion falling over the couple like a shimmering curtain. It was a moment before anyone realized what she'd done, but a few startled shouts had heads turning quickly enough.

"My Queen, I see her!"

"It's the Kiri and her Mate!"

"Grab her!"

"Bar the doors, do not let them get away!"

The last insistent shout was none other than Rowena herself.

A mob formed and rushed at the confused couple who was furiously protesting the attention. "M-My Queen," the woman wailed, her arms lifted as if to protect her face from the clawed hands that sought to grab her.

The man beside her tried to squirm away, thinking only to protect himself.

"This won't do," Helena murmured, and Kragen grunted in agreement.

Helena needed the crowd to believe that this couple was, in fact, her and her Mate. She needed the doubles to play along just long enough that Rowena's Generals would come running for Reyna's people to intercept.

Not knowing what else to do, Helena attempted something that she had never consciously tried before. She turned her glittering eyes to the woman who was her twin. With every heartbeat, she pushed her will toward the woman. *You are the Kiri. That woman is your enemy. You do not fear her.* The false Helena's aqua eyes glazed over, and her expression and posture calmed.

"I do not fear you!" she shouted.

The crowd hissed at her.

"Because you are nothing more than a vapid little girl."

Rowena's statement was met by the crowd's cruel laughter. Fake Helena scowled.

"Is that really what I look like when I'm annoyed?" Helena asked Kragen in a low voice, momentarily distracted by her mirror-image.

Kragen chuckled but did not deign to answer the question. "Focus."

Helena took a deep breath and turned her attention onto the absolutely worthless excuse of a Mate who was frantically clawing at the door. *She is your Mate. It is your duty to protect her. Her life means more to you than your own.* This one was harder to convince. The man fought against her persuasion, his selfishness helping him resist the compulsion. *If she dies, you're next.* That did it. Suddenly, Von's twin spun around, roaring at the crowd.

"If you so much as touch her, I will have your heads!"

Helena fought a giggle. It was a Von thing to say, but somehow, he never looked quite so constipated when he was threatening people. It was as if the words were so foreign the man wasn't entirely sure of their meaning. She was willing to bet he'd never actually threatened anyone in his life. Or had to wield a weapon.

Helena sighed. She had chosen her targets on convenience, not talent. Given what she had to work with, and the fact that none of these people actually knew her or her Mate, her doubles were still effective. Even so, she made a mental note to check for temperament the next time she needed a realistic impersonator. These two would never get past a single member of her Circle.

Rowena lifted both her hands, her lips lifting in a smile too cold to be anything but threatening. "Perhaps we got off on the wrong foot. The Kiri and her Mate are my guests."

More snide laughter met the words, and Helena felt her eyes narrow with suspicion as she eyed the people around her. The crowd already knew what Rowena had planned, and they were eager to witness it.

Rowena continued to speak in a deceptively conversational tone, "Although I am surprised you didn't bring the rest of your Circle. They do seem to follow you like dogs after a bitch in heat."

Kragen growled low in his throat, his hands clenched into fists at his sides. Helena brushed her fingers along his arm, not needing her Jaka to feel the violence radiating off him. A shudder raced down his arm at the contact, his temper not easily calmed even with the silent reminder from his Kiri.

The fake Kiri smiled sweetly, not phased at all by the slight. *Good girl,* Helena thought, sending another suggestion her way. When the double spoke, it was with Helena's words. "Thankfully when they feel like a cuddle, I don't have to swallow the vomit induced by their stench. You should really consider putting your beasts down, they just don't look at all healthy. I mean, how can they be when they serve you? Oh right, they don't have a choice. I guess when the only people that willingly serve you are mindless corpses you have to make do."

The smile fell from Rowena's crimson lips long before fake Helena finished speaking. From where she stood, Helena could see a vein begin to pulse in Rowena's temple. The moment stretched on, but Rowena finally broke the silence with a tinkling laugh that sounded more like shards of glass hitting the floor than anything resembling true amusement.

"I think my pets have more than proven their use to me. If your Shield were still alive, he'd certainly agree, don't you think?"

The barb struck true. Helena's control slipped, her fury rolling off her in a tidal wave of power that caused those standing near her to falter and the floor to quake.

Heads spun toward where Helena and Kragen were standing with shock.

"Fuck," Kragen muttered, instinctively reaching for a weapon that wasn't there.

Helena regained control quickly, prompting her double to pull attention back toward her.

"Don't you dare speak of him unless you'd like me to return the favor with another of your pawns!"

The ruse worked. The crowd believed that the double had purposefully targeted that area of the room with "her" power, and the real Kiri and Kragen remained undiscovered. Sweat dripped down Helena's spine, her emotions not entirely settled. Darrin's death was an emotional wound that had yet to fully heal, if it ever would. Having Rowena so callously refer to it was a blow she could not protect herself against. That still did not mean she could allow herself to be swayed off course so easily.

"Perhaps it's time to begin tonight's entertainment."

Both Helena and her double's brows lowered over suspicious eyes. Whatever Rowena thought entertaining was surely anything but.

"Brace yourself," Kragen said.

"You as well," she replied.

For their part, the doubles remained silent while the crowd broke out into excited chatter that did little to reassure Helena.

"Do you think Reyna has found them yet?" Kragen whispered, eager to get away from the overzealous crowd.

Helena shook her head; there was no way to know until the Night Stalker found a way back into the room.

The sound of a door opening pulled everyone's attention to the dais. Two servants clad entirely in black brought in a child that was visibly trembling.

"Is that—" Kragen started to ask.

"That bitch," she seethed before he could finish the question. It was the child that had shown them into the ballroom. Helena knew then that Rowena had purposely given the boy that duty so that Helena would recognize him in this moment.

"Bring him to me," Rowena purred.

Helena and Kragen watched with wide, horror-filled eyes as the sobbing child was dragged to a slightly elevated platform just beside Rowena.

"Let me show you what my so-called corpses do for me," Rowena taunted, her colorless eyes staring down Helena's twin.

There wasn't time to draw in a breath before Rowena unleashed her power, the tainted Spirit magic twisting from her hand straight into the chest of the little boy. His back arched on a soundless cry as Rowena's mouth fell open and she began to feed off his essence. There was no other way to describe it. Within seconds of her power hitting him, the boy began to emit a dull white glow that Rowena quickly inhaled. The more of the glow that Rowena took in, the slower the boy's movements became until all he could manage were a few sluggish twitches of his fingers.

Nausea had Helena's stomach roiling. This was too far. No matter the plan, Helena could not stand by and watch while an innocent child was being tortured.

Rowena's head tilted back with a sexual moan of pleasure, and Helena snapped, losing hold of her disguise entirely. Shocked gasps filled the room at the sudden appearance of a second Kiri. Rowena's head flew back up, annoyance at the interruption clear in her sneer. Kai-Soren whispered something in her ear that had Rowena's head turning toward where they were standing.

"Helena," Kragen warned.

Power surged through Helena, her rage adding to her strength despite how much she'd already pushed herself. With minimal effort, Von and Helena doubles began to appear throughout the room. There were four new sets of imposters between one heartbeat and the next, and several others by the time she was done.

Rowena's eyes wildly scanned the room, trying to determine which of them was the real threat. "Kill them all!" she finally screamed.

Helena didn't waste any time. *"Now!"* she shouted to Von through the bond. Their window to gain the upper hand was rapidly closing, if they had any hope of salvaging this mission, they had to act now, Generals or not.

If he was surprised to hear the fear and fury in her psychic voice, he didn't comment on it. *"Get back to me, Mate,"* he ordered.

The doors flew open and Shadows began to pour into the ballroom, intermingling with the other partygoers. Helena didn't waste breath coordinating with Kragen. They'd already discussed their plan ad nauseam, and they'd fought together enough that they were already on the same page. Their first priority was to get out in one piece, but on the way, they were going to take out as many of their enemies as they could.

Throughout the ballroom, guests lunged at the various doubles, many of whom had no clue what was happening. Helena hadn't had a chance to establish any sort of enhanced connection like she had with the first duo. They tried to defend themselves against friends and family members that no longer recognized them, all while proclaiming their innocence.

Helena held no sympathy as she watched the first couple fall. Everyone in the room had stood by and watched as an innocent child had his life-essence drained from his body. They could all burn.

Not wanting to pull too much attention to themselves and the strength of their combined power, Kragen and Helena used a combination of fists and magic to clear a path as they moved toward the double doors in the back of the room. They worked together to make quick work of people who were clearly not fighters, their physical attacks rarely landing while the ones that did lacked any real power. Those that chose to rely on their magic lobbed colorful orbs that bounced off Kragen and Helena's shields only to fly back toward the attackers. Based on the complete lack of offensive and defensive skills, magical and otherwise, it was clear Rowena intended to use these people purely as fodder.

Helena spun to dodge another clumsy blow when she noticed the first of Rowena's Generals enter the room. Seeing where her eyes were focused, Kragen gave her a quick nod and used his bare hands to snap the neck of the person she'd just dodged. The lifeless body crumpled, but neither spared it a final glance as they stepped over it and toward the next person. Less of the partygoers were daring to approach the duo, sensing that they were the least easy of the targets.

Brawls were still taking place throughout the ballroom, all while the haunting music continued to play.

"I guess fighting can be set to music after all," Helena commented dryly, launching a ball of Fire at the closest Shadow.

Kragen grinned, picking up one of the candelabras to swing it into the face of another.

Helena's Shadow became a pillar of fire, its arms swinging wildly as it tried to extinguish the flames. It was a futile gesture. Her magical flames made quick work of the rotting flesh, but still the creature tried to save itself. Helena used Air to shove the burning Shadow into two others, knocking all three of them over in a pile of smoke and flame.

They were more than halfway to the door, still surrounded by hundreds of Rowena's guests. For her part, Rowena was throwing bolts of power into the crowd, not caring who they hit. Helena shook her head in disgust. The woman's callous disregard for life never ceased to amaze her. She valued nothing but power, everything else was simply a means to an end. Even the lives of her children.

Helena quickly scanned the room, her eyes searching for any sign of the Night Stalkers. Reyna and her people had to be close, especially with one of their targets finally in sight. Using him as her guide, Helena turned her focus back toward the General, who was busy launching acidic orbs toward the nearest of the doubles. Whatever the orbs made contact with immediately began to erode. As a result, there were massive smoking holes in the nearby floor and walls—not to mention the bodies—that were hit.

She called her power to her, preparing to neutralize him, when the air just beside the General seemed to ripple. If she'd have blinked, she would have missed the sight of Reyna's golden dagger cleanly slicing through his neck. The General blinked in shock before falling to the ground.

Reyna looked up, her face an impassive mask as her eyes found Helena's across the room. She shook her head, indicating that they had not found any of the others. Helena jerked her head toward the door, wordlessly communicating that it was time to go. Reyna turned into a blur as she complied.

So far they'd been lucky, and none of their group had been caught by Rowena's people, but they were pushing that luck each time they used their power. With one of Rowena's Generals removed, they'd gotten what they'd come for, at least to some degree.

Voices began to cry out as the battle raged on inside the ballroom.

"Greyspire is under attack!"

"The castle is ablaze, My Queen!"

"We are surrounded!"

Behind them, Rowena let out a blood curdling scream as she realized what had happened.

"It's time to go!" Helena shouted, gripping Kragen's arm as they set off at a dead run. "We need to get to the others."

They made for the door, hurdling over corpses and through the gaps in their race for the exit. Kragen used his bulk to smash into any obstacles, not allowing anyone or anything to slow them down. Helena followed close at his heels, sparing only a second to check behind her. What happened next felt like it happened in slow motion.

From her place on the dais, Rowena's eyes spotted the fleeing Helena. Her lips twisted in a snarl, and she threw an orb of pulsing black light at Helena. Helena tried to dodge but could not entirely escape the ball of corrupted power. She flew back, her body slamming into something hard. There was a loud crack and the feeling of liquid warmth rushing down her neck before the world turned black.

CHAPTER 10

"*Now!*" Even though Von had been waiting for the command, the sound of her panicked voice had adrenaline flooding his veins. The need to protect overwhelmed him, but he couldn't afford to distract her from whatever she was dealing with inside, so he did his best to rein it in.

"Get back to me, Mate!" He purposely used the tone he'd used with his men, the one that did not allow room for argument. He also gave the same order he'd have given any in his command: complete the mission and get back. It was a default mode that allowed him to focus on what he had to do, and not the mind-numbing fear he felt at the fact she had willingly walked back into that prison without him.

That was also the reason he'd used the title. It was a not-so-subtle reminder of her vow to him. She had promised him a life. Together. And he damn well intended to collect on that promise.

"Let's go!" he called in a loud whisper, knowing the Talyrians would hear him without problem.

He felt Midnight's muscles bunch and shift beneath him as the beast readied himself for flight. In less time than it took to draw in a breath, the Talyrian launched his powerful body into the air, his dark wings momentarily blocking the moon and throwing them all into darkness. They covered the distance from the cliffs to the castle quickly, Starshine's bright body acting as the beacon the others were waiting for as she flew close beside him.

The Talyrians were deadly predators, especially at night. The sound of their flapping wings almost entirely silent as they cut through the sky. Despite their size, and various coloring, their prey wouldn't know they were under attack until they felt the fiery breath of the Talyrian as it was upon them.

He loved his Daejaran Wolf, but there was nothing quite like flying through the sky on the back of such a powerful being. Between himself and Midnight, Von knew without a doubt that the Talyrian was the deadlier of them, and even his power paled in comparison to the Talyrian Queen. The fact that there were eight other Talyrians flying behind him filled him with confidence. The Shadows may have them beat in sheer numbers, but the Talyrians more than made up for that in raw power. It was a balanced fight at last.

They completed their circuit, the rest of the army now braced for what came next. Von channeled his rage, letting out a battle cry he knew would leave him hoarse for days after. Answering cries met his ears as the Chosen launched their attack. He recognized Ronan's deep growl, and even Effie's high-pitched shriek. All of them had lost something to this power-crazed bitch. It was time to return the favor.

The Talyrians roared, the combined sound so loud the windows of the castle rattled and shattered under the assault. Their fierce challenge was met instantly as bodies began to pour out of the castle.

Von stiffened in surprise. Even from his perch on Midnight, he could tell that those were not Shadows. The men moved with a precision that the Shadows' stumbling lurch, despite its speed, made impossible. Each new wave moved into position behind the front line, creating a wall that encircled the castle. For their part, Ronan's men remained cloaked by the Night Stalkers' and Storm Forged's combined efforts.

He nudged the Talyrian, signaling that he wanted to get closer. Midnight swooped down, breathing fire along the outer wall of the castle, causing it to go up in flames. The orange light cast an eerie glow on the field, but also helped Von notice what he'd missed.

Von hissed, outrage lifting his lip in a silent snarl. Endoshans. Their unique fighting leathers and curved blades were the only proof he needed of their betrayal. He wished for Helena's abilities then, wanting to rain down fire upon the backstabbing traitors. Sensing his desire, Midnight roared before aiming a jet of flame toward the closest of the Endoshans.

That was all Ronan's men needed. The Endoshans shouted in surprise as the Forsaken released their hold on their magic and thousands of the Chosen took shape before them. It was not long before the sounds of war met his ears.

The screams of the Endoshans were silenced only by the roar of the Talyrians and their resulting death. Nothing had prepared them for this battle. Outmanned and outnumbered, the Endoshans refused to retreat even as waves of their brothers were lost to Talyrian flame. They were warriors; casualties were expected. The Endoshans regrouped, pressing together as they faced off with the Chosen army.

One of the Endoshan's silver blades sliced through a Storm Forged's armor. The woman fell to her knees, screaming in agony. *Poison.* Von had heard tales of a lethal poison the Endoshan warriors used on their blades but had never felt its sting. The woman's cries faded away as she slumped on the ground, dead.

"Ronan!" Von warned, just in time for his friend to dodge another of the deadly blades. Ronan jumped up, lifting his knee and slamming his booted foot into the other man's wrist, shattering the bone and knocking the blade away. The man dropped to his knees, his limp arm cradled against his chest as he stared up into the face of death. Whatever he saw in Ronan's eyes caused his shoulders to slump in defeat moments before Ronan's blade swooped down to finish the kill.

Von continued to watch the battle from above, his eyes scanning the field but rarely straying from the castle doors for longer than a few seconds at a time. *Where are you?* He did not send the thought, but the longer he went without seeing Helena safe and whole, the greater his panic. The only thing keeping him sane was the fact that he could still feel their bond pulsing between them.

There was a loud crash and Midnight reared back, causing Von to slip down his back. He gripped the Talyrian tighter with his thighs and buried a fist deeper into the silky mane.

"Easy boy," he murmured, twisting his head to see what had caused the noise. As he watched more of Greyspire's outer buildings fell victim to the inferno, although it wasn't clear whose fire had started it.

From his vantage point, Von could see Timmins' group working to push the blaze away from them and toward the swarm of Shadows that were beginning to pour onto the field. It was hard to keep track of everyone after that, the bodies below him starting to all blend together under the dirt and blood.

A sharp tug along the bond left him gasping.

"Helena!"

There was no answer, only an endless stretch of silence.

His vision swam, and the metallic taste of blood began to fill his mouth. Von lifted a hand, surprised to find that his head was intact. Given the intensity of the pain, he thought it had been completely bashed in. Understanding dawned and his blood ran cold, terror clearing his mind of everything around him except for his connection to her.

"Answer me, Mate."

Still nothing.

Circling above a battlefield while on the back of a flying dragon-cat that was spouting jets of fire was hardly the time or place to try this, but he didn't care. Von closed his eyes, focusing on the golden tether that bound him to his Mate. Helena had explained how she had once found him while he'd been lost to the *Bella Morte* by following the strand until it led her to him. He was certain that his approach was not nearly as refined as hers, but by focusing on his visual representation of their bond, he instinctively understood what she had meant. It was similar to sending her a thought, except it was his awareness and not just his words that he directed to her.

He could feel the moment his consciousness left his physical body. There was a sense of weightlessness followed by the feeling of trying to force himself through a barrier of hot honey. It was not entirely unpleasant, but it required an intense focus to push himself through to the other side.

The first thing he felt was the pain. It was as if a white-hot blade had been driven straight through his skull.

"Mira!"

"V-von?" a tired, young-sounding Helena asked.

"Helena. Can you feel me?"

"Mmm," she murmured. He recognized the sound as the same one she'd make when rolling over to burrow deeper into his arms in the morning.

"Stay with me, Helena. You can't rest right now."

"Why? I'm so sleepy."

Von scrambled to make sense of her words under the weight of the pain. He was no healer, but if he had to guess, it was like her conscious mind was protecting itself by diving deeper into herself.

"Darling, you have to fight now."

That got her attention. There was a sizzle of awareness and then a sharp cry of pain.

"It hurts!" Her voice was more aware, but no less childlike. He needed to reach the Vessel.

"The Chosen are depending on you. They need their Kiri, and I need my Mate."

He could feel her struggling to awareness, and when she flinched away from the pain. *"It's too much."*

"What do you need?" But even as he asked, he knew. She needed to heal herself. Whatever injury she'd sustained was keeping her from knowing how to access her power and do it herself.

Von took a deep breath, hoping what he was about to do wasn't going to kill them both. He was only partially aware of his physical body and was mildly surprised he hadn't already fallen off Midnight. Focusing on the center of his power, he began to draw as much of it to the surface as he could. The process was similar to pouring water into an empty glass and trying to fill it all the way to the top without losing a drop, except that the glass could expand and so you are also trying to keep it from popping. It was a bizarre juggling act he'd rarely had an opportunity to perfect. So much of how he used his power had to do with short bursts of energy.

He continued to draw on his power until he felt full almost to the point of bursting. Then, with a quick prayer to the Mother, he sent it straight into Helena's injured body. There was no reaction at first, and Von began to worry he'd done something wrong. Her body was absorbing the power but didn't seem to be able to do anything with it.

Helena's sharp gasp let him know she was at least conscious again. Connected as they were, he could feel her sit up, their mental connect still secure although a bit foggy.

"Thank you."

"Whatever you need, Mira. You don't even have to ask."

His mouth, or was that hers, felt bone dry. *"Just a bit more."* Her voice was thin and brittle.

As she began to pull even more of his power into her, he realized why she hadn't been able to immediately heal herself in the first place. She had drained herself almost completely. Von could hardly comprehend the amount of magic she had used trying to keep the various illusions in place on top of whatever else she'd had to do inside. With the depth of her reservoir, his magic was probably akin to a drop in the ocean.

The pain continued to recede as she repaired whatever damage had been done. There was a blinding flash of light before Kragen's face came into view. Von drew back, confused to see him until he realized he was seeing through Helena's eyes.

"Thank the Mother," Kragen swore, checking over his shoulder before looking back down with concern. "Do you need me to carry you?"

Helena shook her head and pushed up onto her feet. "No, Von took care of it."

"Von?" Kragen's brows lowered, and he began to inspect the back of her head.

Helena slapped his hands away. "I'm fine. He gave me the power I needed to heal myself."

"Thank you again, Mate. That was an unexpectedly close call."

"I gave you an order."

He felt her amusement at his gruff reminder. *"We're on our way out now. Reyna and the Night Stalkers should already be outside."*

"I will have Starshine ready for you."

The flicker of amusement he'd felt at Kragen's reaction to her seemingly absurd explanation was quick to fade. Helena had put herself in a position where she'd been too weak to defend herself, and he hadn't been there to protect her. Everything in him that recognized Helena as his raged against the realization. He should have been there with her. She should never have put the safety of so many others above herself. She should have known better. She should have listened to him…

Von's lips lifted at the last one. Helena always listened to him, she just chose to ignore him and do what she wanted to do in the first place more than half the time. It was part of what he loved about her. She was as strong-willed, perhaps even stronger, than he was. Unfortunately, that did little to comfort him, knowing just how close to danger she'd been.

If Rowena had captured her during that moment of weakness, there was nothing that would have stopped him from walking in there and handing himself over just so that he could be with her. He was far too intimately aware of Rowena's brand of torture. He couldn't stand by knowing what she was doing to his Mate. Not if there was a way he could save her. With both of them under Rowena's control, there was very little hope for the rest of the Chosen.

Von shuddered. They'd come close, far too close, to losing everything.

CHAPTER 11

Ronan had lost track of how long he'd been fighting. Time held no meaning in battle, every second stretching out into hours. Thanks to Von's warning, they were mostly able to dodge the poisoned Endoshan blades, although there had been more near misses than he'd care to admit.

He'd like to say he'd been surprised to see the Endoshan force face off against them, but he'd seen more than one man turn traitor to save their own ass. Unfortunately, all the training he'd drilled into his Kiri's army had been focused on fighting the brainless Shadows, not free-thinking men with poisoned blades. There was little time to worry about whether the lessons translated now. They were going to live or die on their own prowess.

Ronan was also thankful for the ranged team at their back. Between the Talyrians and Timmins' team, the heavy influx of fighters was seriously pared down by the time they ever reached him and his men at the front lines. They'd also been using their combined powers to keep the heavy smoke from the various fires out of the main battlefield. A handy trick, too bad it benefited the enemy as much as it did them.

Another Endoshan lunged toward him, and Ronan dodged the blow, using his momentum to spin around the man and shove him into one of his buddies with a well-placed kick to the back. One of Reyna's Night Stalkers finished the kill before moving on.

A sharp pain had Ronan spinning to the right in time to see a Shadow lunging for him. The walking corpses had joined the battle shortly after the courtyard went up in flames. He could only assume that was around the time Rowena realized they were there. Hopefully Helena and Reyna had made it out safely. He hadn't seen either woman since they'd parted ways in the forest. In the chaos, he hadn't had much of a chance to keep track of anyone.

Ronan continued to swing his blade, leaving a path of bodies in his wake. If ever there was something he was good at, it was killing people. A streak of black had his head twisting as his body braced for an attack that didn't come. Instead of facing a blow, Ronan's eyes landed on one of Rowena's Generals. The man had the same pale skin and stringy hair as the others, so it was impossible to tell if it was one of the same ones they'd fought in the Vale. At least until the bastard began to use whatever hell-cursed power Rowena's corruption had caused. That was the only way to really tell the fuckers apart.

The General lifted a pale hand, small gusts of wind lifting the oily strands of his hair. Ronan was already making his way over to him, knowing how fatal they could be once they got going. Rowena's man saw him and grinned, using a skeletal finger to beckon him closer. Ronan's brows lowered, and his lips curled in a menacing smile.

Game.

Fucking.

On.

He had already been a self-contained tornado of activity, his weapon swinging almost without pause, but after that taunt Ronan was unleashed. He used his shoulders, weapon, and fists to mow over anyone standing in his way, littering the ground with corpses and clearing the distance between them in a matter of moments. Just as Ronan's ax was about to swing true, the General laughed and vanished.

Snarling, Ronan spun around to see where he'd gone. *Slippery fucker must control Air.* That was going to make things more difficult.

The General was a good distance away, waving at Ronan before lifting his hand and circling his wrist. The dirt around him began to lift in the air, spinning around him faster and faster until it obscured him completely. The dust storm swelled in size, standing at least two times taller than Ronan himself, before the General released it by pushing it into a group of Chosen. The men and women flew back, flying through the air before falling down, some impaled on pieces of debris while others were killed by the force of their impact with the ground.

Ronan saw red as a murderous rage filled him. Pulling on every ounce of his power, Ronan launched himself into the air, lifting his ax above his head. The General watched him move through the sky. Winking, he vanished once more, half a second before Ronan's blade would have made contact with his face.

His weapon landed first, missing its mark. Ronan was next, landing in a crouched position that spared his body the effects of the impact. With a grunt he stood, pulling his weapon out of the earth, where it had gotten buried halfway up its hilt. Had the General still been standing there, he would have been rent in two.

There was nothing fun about the game of cat and mouse the Air General was playing with him. Ronan's frustration grew, his blood surging through his body as his heart pounded like a drum. This was more than just war now; it was personal.

The General laughed as he watched Ronan make his way toward him for the third time. However, this time he did not wait until the Shield was close before he blinked away. Ronan slammed his fist into one of the few wooden outer buildings that was still intact. The wood cracked, snapping in half and falling into the center of the building. The straw roof teetered at the loss of support before sliding down after it.

If he was going to capture the man, he needed to be smarter. Ronan stood still, letting his eyes follow the General's progress as he created more of his dust storms. There was no discernable pattern, the General moved freely, wanting only to create as much destruction as possible. The mass of bodies had definitely dwindled since the fighting had begun. There were no more groups of people, only small, scattered clusters. Expect for one.

The Chosen's ranged team was still fully intact, having remained separate from the bulk of the fighting. If the General continued as he had been, they would likely be one of his next targets. Ronan zeroed in on the group. Miranda was standing closest to the edge, her face scrunched in concentration as she cast spell after spell. Ronan moved into her line of sight, trying to get her attention without alerting the General of his intention.

Using his blade and a nearby fire, Ronan aimed a beam of light toward the Keeper. Miranda flinched, her eyes squinting as she searched for the source of the light. Her eyes widened with surprise when she found Ronan standing still and staring up at her.

Once they had established eye contact, Ronan very purposefully turned his head toward the direction of the General and then back toward her. She followed his gaze, nodding in understanding when her eyes returned to him. Ronan didn't wait, trusting her to act on the knowledge.

Miranda didn't disappoint. She shouted something unintelligible to the others. Not long after, the group directed their attacks toward the General. Bolts of fire and lighting began to rain upon him, even as he blinked his way across the field. Finally catching on to their targeted attack, the General gave them a sinister smile and vanished.

Ronan used the distraction to conceal his race to the bottom of the ledge. He was just about to ascend when a glint of silver caught his eye. He crouched down, finding a discarded Endoshan blade. Ronan grinned, carefully picking it up. *Perfect.*

When he scaled the top of the ledge, the General had already beat him there. He'd created a wall of Air that held all the others within its center. He spared only a second to look at those held within. Inside, Timmins raged, his face nearly purple from his screams. The Advisor was throwing his fists against the invisible barrier as if he could break it down with the sheer force of his will. Joquil stood beside him, his eyes narrowed in concentration and his lips moving fast as he tried to counteract the powerful magic. But the thing that had captured his attention was what the General was doing to Miranda.

The Keeper was held up in the Air as if strung up by a rope, her hands clawing at her throat as the General called the breath out of her lungs. Miranda's feet flailed as she gasped and struggled to breathe. He was suffocating her with his magic. Ronan's blood ran cold. *Not again.*

The General's back was turned, so Ronan lunged, his borrowed blade ready to strike just as Miranda's eyes rolled back in her head and her struggling ceased.

"No!" Ronan roared, blindly swinging the poisoned blade. He didn't care where he hit the bastard, only that he cut through the skin. The poison would do the rest.

The blade sliced through the decayed-looking skin of the General's shoulder down to the bone, narrowly missing his neck. The pungent smell of rotting flesh met Ronan's nose as the General's arm swung limply at his side. Ronan had already recovered from the first attack and was prepared to strike again, even though he knew the poison had already entered the bloodstream. It was just a matter of time before the General met his final death.

But he didn't.

Miranda's body dropped to the ground, looking like a pile of discarded rags as the General turned his full attention onto Ronan. With another gaping grin, the General lifted his skeletal hand and shot the full force of his power into Ronan.

His lungs were on fire. Ronan gasped for breath, the blade dropping, forgotten from his hands as he struggled to breathe. He felt his booted feet begin to leave the ground, his toes scrambling for purchase. There was no relief. Dark spots began to dance in the corners of his vision.

Nonsensical thoughts began to flash in his mind, even as he continued to gasp like a fish out of water. Until there was only one.

Not like this. Mother's tits, it couldn't end like this.

CHAPTER 12

Kragen and Helena stumbled outside, the night sky painted a burnt orange due to the reflection of the flames. Helena's eyes immediately began to scan the horizon; she did not have to wait long to find what she was looking for.

Von was at her side almost instantly, using his power to blink off Midnight's back and over to her. His arms were around her, pulling her body against his before she had time to open her mouth.

"If you ever do anything that stupid again, I'll—"

"You'll what?" she teased, feeling more worn out than she cared to admit. Despite the influx of Von's power, she'd drained herself much more deeply than she had thought. It would likely take her a few days to fully recover.

"Think of something," he muttered gruffly, pressing a kiss to her forehead. She knew that it was his fear talking, she could feel it like a jagged edge scratching their bond. She had scared him, and he didn't quite know what to do with the feeling.

"I'm okay," she said aloud, for both men's benefit. "I promise."

Kragen was still looking at her with worried eyes, despite the number of assurances she'd given him.

Starshine landed beside Midnight and huffed, drawing Helena's attention over to her. As she turned her head, a figure climbing up the side of the cliff had her heart lurching in her chest. He was heading right toward the ranged group.

"Not so fast," Helena growled, her fatigue forgotten as the need to defend took over. "Let's finish this," she said to the others, squeezing her Mate's hand a final time before walking over to her Talyrian and climbing up.

Kragen gave a wave and took off at a run to join their people in battle.

Von was right behind Helena, vaulting up on Midnight in one fluid motion.

Starshine took flight, covering the distance quickly. As they closed in, the shock of red hair became clear, and Helena's eyes grew wide as she realized her mistake. The figure who had crested the ledge wasn't the threat, the skeletal man facing him was. Horror filled her as she watched Ronan levitate off the ground, a weapon slipping from his fingers as his feet swung helplessly.

Not again. She would not lose another of her Circle to these evil bastards.

Helena opened her mouth on a scream of absolute rage, the sky echoing her fury with jagged bolts of lightning and the answering crack of thunder. It sounded like the world was being split in two as Starshine and Helena streaked toward her Shield.

She drew on her power, preparing to unleash it on the General, but Starshine beat her to the kill. With a mighty roar, the Talyrian Queen swooped low, her jaws snapping closed over the General's head. She never stopped, flying a few feet away before landing and spitting out the General's head with a hiss. She pawed at her face, wiping away the smears of black blood that coated her otherwise pristine fur.

Helena scrambled off the Talyrian's back, rushing over to her friends. A distraught Timmins was on his hands and knees, Joquil next to him, trying to pull him up. Her Shield had fallen when the General's hold on him was released. Von had already dismounted and was beside the very pale Ronan, trying to help him sit up, but he was having none of it and was slapping her Mate's hands away with a scowl.

As relieved as she was to see that they were all well, her heart felt heavy as she knelt beside Miranda's corpse. Even in death, the Keeper looked younger than she did. Helena closed her eyes, swallowing back the tears that threatened to spill over.

"Mother, welcome your daughter with open arms," she whispered, before standing and facing the others.

"This ends now."

ROWENA PACED beside her new husband, her hands twitching with agitation. That little upstart had tricked her. A full-fledged war was currently underway in her courtyard. That was unacceptable.

"I thought your warriors were supposed to be unstoppable!" she snapped.

"Flesh is not immune to fire, My Queen. The Talyrians were an unexpected obstacle."

"They are no less immune to your blades. Perhaps you should try using them."

Kai-Soren's lips folded in a flat line, displeasure barely concealed in his golden eyes.

"I see just as many Chosen corpses," he pointed out.

Rowena's eyes narrowed, her eyes blazing with blue fire. "I lost another General tonight. No amount of lives will justify that death."

"You have four others in your service."

She opened her mouth to point out the obvious and stopped herself. The less he knew, the better.

"There's one now," Kai-Soren said, gesturing toward the courtyard. Her General was blinking around, setting off dust storms that were clearing the battlefield of fighting men, if not of their resulting corpses.

A small smile reached her lips. At least someone was finding success this night. The fewer people left to fight for her enemy, the better.

"You would do well to release the others. They will finish this."

"And risk losing all of them?"

"They are your most powerful weapon, My Queen. They should be fighting."

Rowena weighed the risk against her desire to win. "Perhaps just one more," she decided, signaling for the General she referred to as Pestilence to come over. He reached her side, bringing with him the scent of decayed earth.

"Slaughter them," she ordered.

The man dipped his head and moved to join the battle. His gait was slow and measured, the vegetation beneath his feet withering with each step. Her General opened his mouth, preparing to blow into the faces of nearby Chosen.

A blur of red streaked across the sky, another Talyrian whelp shooting a stream of fire from its snout. He was heading straight for Pestilence.

"No!" Rowena cried, calling on her power. A jet of purple light burst from her fingers, hitting the Talyrian in its side and throwing it off course before its fire could reach her General.

There was a surge of euphoria as the Talyrian's power began to fill her. Rowena's lips curved in a sexual smile, and she fed more of her power into the transfer she'd unknowingly established. As creatures of Spirit, the connection was ten times stronger than what she experienced when creating her Shadows.

The Talyrian's blue eyes began to glow with lavender fire before black lines began to snake across their luminous surface.

Another burst of color came barreling toward her, a Talyrian trying to protect its pride mate. Rowena lifted her other hand, a twin jet of purple power colliding with the newcomer until its eyes also began to change.

"You are mine!" Rowena shouted, draining them both until the change was complete. The flow of power ceased, and Rowena was just about to send her newest pets back into the sky to fight their kin when an invisible blow struck her in the chest.

The breath left her lungs, and she stumbled with a low moan. Suddenly weak, Rowena struggled to stand. She called on her reserve of power, shock quickly replaced by fury to find it almost empty. A loss of power at that scale could mean only one thing. Another of her Generals was gone.

Rowena's head snapped up, her skin colorless and clammy. "It's time to go."

"But, My Queen—"

"Now."

Kai-Soren looked like he wanted to argue further, but he kept silent, moving instead to help her stand. It was a testament to how weak she felt that she allowed it. They needed to get away and regroup. There was no victory to be found here.

It pained her to walk away from her home, but by morning, Greyspire would be a ruin. There was nothing left for her here. There was a hidden network of caves not too far away. Rowena would take what was left of her people and go to ground. She looked over her shoulder, the smoldering flames glittering in her Talyrians' eyes.

A secret smile curved her lips. Perhaps today hadn't been a complete loss after all.

CHAPTER 13

"I swear I saw some of the Shadows running away!" Serena insisted.

"They were probably chasing after their puppet master," Kragen said.

Serena refused to be dismissed. "No, you aren't hearing me. They were attacking some of the Storm Forged, and then they just stopped. They've never fled from a fight before."

The group around her fell silent as they digested the news and what the change of behavior could mean. Helena listened with only half an ear, more interested in watching Greyspire burn. By anyone's standard, the attack had been a success. Anyone's standard but hers. They had few casualties, had taken out two of the enemy's biggest weapons, and crippled her to the point that she fled. But it still wasn't enough. She was still alive.

Joquil broke the silence first, his amber eyes glowing with interest, "Helena's hunch was right. Rowena's power *is* tied to her Generals. She must be using their power to bolster her own."

"And when you removed two of them, she suffered a major loss of power," Von continued, picking up the thread of his thought.

"Don't you see what this means?" Nial asked with excitement. "She can be beat, Helena. If we take out the rest of her Generals before she has a chance to make any more, she will be defenseless against you."

"I don't know about defenseless," Joquil cautioned. "She was still a Damaskiri in her own right, which does require significant power."

"All that means is that she can access Spirit," Serena interjected. "Helena is a master of all five Branches. Rowena doesn't stand a chance against her."

Helena knew they wanted her to be excited by the news, but she couldn't muster the energy. Because of her obsession with breaking Helena's Circle, she'd had a feeling that Rowena would fall without her Generals. Their entire plan had been based upon that premise. The problem was they'd had their chance and failed.

Realizing that she wasn't as thrilled by their discovery as they were, the group fell quiet again.

"Kiri?"

Helena turned her attention back to them. Despite the obvious signs of battle, most were bright-eyed and energized from what they had deemed a victory. At the moment, all Helena felt was bone-deep weariness. She was too drained from the excessive use of power to feel anything else. Timmins was the only other person present who seemed withdrawn. Helena knew that he was struggling to process Miranda's death. It couldn't be easy watching someone you cared about murdered in front of your eyes while you were helpless to stop it.

Von moved closer to her, sensing that she needed the support, both physically and emotionally.

"Thank you."

His fingers wove through hers in response.

"So, what now?" Nial asked, wrapping his arm around his mate.

Helena's mind went blank. She had no clue what to do now. All she had planned for was getting into the castle and launching the surprise assault on Greyspire. She hadn't anticipated an after. Where did they even start when they didn't know where Rowena had gone?

"We should go after her and press our advantage," Serena said.

"Where would we go?" Helena asked.

Serena shifted her weight, at a loss. Her point made, Helena sighed.

"We regroup and get ready for the next battle," Von spoke up, answering the question for her.

Ronan nodded. "Our people have earned a warm meal and rest, at the very least."

"We also need to bury our dead," Timmins said, his voice rusty. Helena did not know if it was from disuse or from the screaming.

A weight settled over them as they thought about the lost Keeper.

"Where is Effie?" Helena asked, voicing the question that was on each of their minds.

"She is still with the others," Ronan answered. "Shall I bring her to you?"

She closed her eyes and nodded, not relishing the task of having to let Effie know about her grandmother. Even that small physical act was a chore. She needed to sleep, but the chance of that happening anytime soon was highly unlikely.

After that, there didn't seem to be much left to say. The battle was over, at least for now. Their enemy had escaped, leaving no trace of her whereabouts behind. There was nothing left for them here.

Even though the future was unclear, the next step seemed fairly obvious.

"Let's go home."

To say that she was angry would have been the understatement of the century. The numbness she'd felt immediately preceding the battle had long since passed and the truth had set in, sending Helena into a full-blown rage.

Rowena had gotten away. Again. The pale-faced harpy slunk away in the middle of battle rather than face her directly. Helena choked on her fury, the weight of it in her chest threatening to consume her.

Her hands were clenched into fists, the tips of her black talons sliding out to bite into the tender skin of her palms. It was hard to maintain control with her emotions at war within her. The others declared their mission a victory, their enemy forced to retreat. Helena couldn't quite see it that way. They'd only eliminated two of their five primary targets. The others were still out there, and now they'd lost the element of surprise, which had been their only true advantage.

Helena had never admitted it out loud, but she'd secretly been hoping that last night would be the end of it. Her plan may not have been fool-proof, but it had been sound. If they had only found the Generals before Rowena caught on to them. *If only…*

The words echoed through her mind, ruthless with their taunting promise. She had been so close, and her victory had been stolen from her. All because Rowena had found a way to escape while she had been distracted by saving her people. Now they were back to square one, with absolutely no idea where the harlot had slipped off to.

She sighed. Presented with the same set of options, Helena would have made the same decisions. Every. Single. Time. Ronan and her Circle's lives would always come before going after Rowena. Perhaps that made her weak and predictable, but she would never sacrifice one for the other.

A frisson of awareness brushed against her senses, alerting her to her Mate's presence long before she acknowledged him. Von's hands settled on her shoulders, the warmth of his touch doing little to ease the turmoil inside of her.

"You have to be kinder to yourself, *Mira*."

"She got away."

"But not without sustaining a major blow. She would not have felt the need to run if she hadn't been scared, Helena."

Helena's jaw flexed, her next words gritted out between clenched teeth. "They got Miranda." She felt the loss of the Keeper deeply. The woman's wisdom and guidance had been invaluable. More than that, she had genuinely liked her. They had not been close, not like she and Darrin, but there had been true kinship there. Miranda had been her friend.

"We all know the risk of battle, Helena. And if anyone can know the time and place of their death, the Keeper was certainly among them."

"How is Effie?" she asked, changing the subject.

Von let out a long breath. "She is… unwell."

Helena's eyes fell closed, the guilt of inflicting more pain on the poor woman because of this war was yet another burden she would carry with her. "I should go see her."

Von's fingers dug into her shoulders. "I would advise against that. At least for the moment."

"Why? What's wrong?" Helena asked, twisting out of his grasp to face him.

He weighed his words carefully before speaking. "She has no one left; it is a hard reality to face."

"She has us," Helena snapped. "Perhaps she needs to be reminded that she is not alone."

"Ronan tried…"

"And?"

"Effie attacked him."

Helena's brows lifted. "Oh."

Von shrugged before stating matter-of-factly, "She is not ready for comfort. She needs to work through the pain before she can start to heal."

"Then let me provide a target."

"Helena," he protested as she moved past him.

"It might as well be me, Von. It is no less than I deserve. She cannot do or say any worse than I am already doing to myself."

His eyes were sad as they met hers. "You are too hard on yourself, my love."

His words were meant to soothe and yet they only enraged her further. He couldn't possibly understand the extent of what she was feeling right now. Helena swallowed back her emotions, trying to explain. "It is my plan that led to her death. If anyone deserves that girl's anger, it is I."

"You did not kill her!" Von swore, slamming his fist into the table, causing it to topple over and crash to the floor.

"Not directly, but my choices did!" Helena raged, flinging the door open.

"When are you going to learn what it means to lead?" he snarled.

The words hurt. Helena looked back over her shoulder, the fingers that held onto the door turning white from the force with which she held it. "When did you stop caring about other people's lives?"

Von's eyes went wide, his mouth falling open. She did not wait for him to speak, not trusting either of them to refrain from saying something that would only cause more damage. They had never fought before, not like this. She knew that it was only love and concern for her that had him speaking as he did. But he did not truly understand what it was like for her. He was able to separate his emotions from battle, she could not. To her, each life was a splinter shoved deep into her heart. Each and every one a scratch that drew blood until she felt like she was slowly bleeding to death.

She stormed through the halls, her temper fueling her momentum. It did not take long to locate Effie; the sounds of furniture being thrown against the wall more than enough of an indication that she was heading in the right direction.

Helena didn't bother knocking before opening the door and walking into the room. Her eyes performed a cursory inspection, noting the shards of wood with interest. The amount of destruction present was impressive for such a small woman. She had even managed to overturn the bed.

"Stupid. Mindless. Waste!" Effie screamed, each word punctuated by a picture being slammed against the side of an armoire that had seen better days.

"Is that how you greet all of your friends, or am I special?" Helena asked in a deceptively neutral tone.

Effie looked up, startled to find she was no longer alone. Her eyes were red-rimmed, deep purple circles beneath them. She had clearly not slept. Or bathed. Her long blonde curls hung in limp and dirty clumps about her shoulders. Her skin streaked with dirt and what looked like blood. All the joy and quiet peace that Helena had begun to associate with Effie was gone; snuffed out like a candle that had reached the end of its wick.

"Kiri," she said formally, her voice hoarse. Effie dropped the picture, the crash sounding too loud in the now painfully quiet room.

Her chin dipped, her hands fluttering to her sides where they continued to twitch restlessly.

"When did I stop being Helena?"

Effie looked up, her blue eyes shining brightly. "I apologize, Kiri. I do not think I am fit for company."

Helena gave the room a pointed glance. "I see that, and yet here I am."

"What do you want?" the girl snapped, before slapping a hand over her mouth. "Apologies, Kiri. I did warn you—"

Helena waved away the apology. "There's no need, I understand."

Effie pressed her lips together, looking like she wanted to argue the point.

Helena's answering laugh was entirely without humor. "You don't think I understand what it's like to lose the final member of one's family? Is your memory that short?"

Tears filled Effie's eyes, the fight leaving her in one watery breath. "Darrin was hard enough, but now I-I have n-nothing left," she whispered brokenly.

Helena moved closer to the grieving girl, her own heart breaking at the sight. This was her fault. "That's not true," Helena murmured, fighting her own tears as she wrapped her arms around Effie's trembling body.

Effie sobbed into Helena's chest, her stream of words entirely unintelligible. Each wave of grief struck Helena like a blow. She had done this, and there was nothing she could do to fix it. It was a long while before Effie's tears abated. She was still shaking as she pushed out of Helena's embrace.

"If I find her before you do, I'm going to kill her myself!" Effie vowed, her low voice no less menacing despite its lack of volume.

"I think you've earned that right," Helena said, as Effie stepped back, wiping at her eyes. "I just wish we knew where to look."

As if the words were a trigger, Effie's body went rigid, her eyes rolling back into her head. Effie's body began to spasm, the tremors so violent that Helena feared for the woman's safety.

"Effie!" Helena shouted, jumping forward to grab her before she hurt herself. "Help!" Helena screamed, sending the plea down the bond and out loud for any that would hear her.

The shaking continued for what felt like hours but may have only been a minute. Effie groaned, her knees sagging. Helena caught her weight and eased her to the ground mere seconds before Effie began to vomit. Helena held the dirty strands of hair out of her face and rubbed her heaving back soothingly.

"What happened?" Von demanded, his weapon drawn and ready for battle. Seeing Effie cradled in Helena's arms as she continued to empty the contents of her stomach, he dropped his weapon and moved inside the room. "Is she okay?"

Helena shrugged, too shocked to reply. One moment they'd been talking; the next Effie had fallen into a seizure the likes of which she'd never seen.

"I saw her," Effie gasped.

"Saw who?" Helena asked in confusion, looking around the room as Effie sat up.

"Rowena."

"What! Where?" Von demanded, just as Ronan and Joquil reached the door.

"Is she hurt?" Ronan demanded, eyeing the trembling Effie.

Von silenced him with a look.

"No, Helena." Effie licked her lips and grimaced. "I *Saw* her."

Understanding dawned and Helena's eyes went wide. She shot a startled look to her Mate, whose own expression was a mix of shock and awe. Apparently, Miranda's legacy hadn't ended with her death after all.

Effie was a Keeper.

The low murmur of voices continued as Helena helped Effie into a chair. The rest of the Circle had been summoned so that they could be present when Effie described her vision.

"Are we sure she's a Keeper? Miranda never did *that* when she had a vision," Kragen asked in a low voice.

"Did you ever see Miranda while she was in the throes of a vision?" Joquil asked, just as quietly.

"Well, no, but don't you think she would have said something?"

"Why? What reason would she have to share that with us?"

Kragen shrugged, his dark eyes considering as they moved back to Effie.

For her part, Effie hadn't spoken further since delivering the news that had shocked them all. At the moment, she was staring at a fixed point on the table, not meeting any of their eyes. Her body was curled in on itself as if she was trying to become as small as possible.

"Effie," Helena said in a soft voice. "Can you tell us what you Saw?"

"I—" she paused to lick her lips. "I'll try."

"Take your time," Ronan said, placing his hand on her shoulder. She flinched, the contact too much for her battered senses. Ronan dropped his hand with a muffled apology.

Effie's eyes lifted, scanning the room before settling on Timmins. His face was pale and drawn, but he gave her an encouraging nod. She took a deep breath and gave a jerky nod of her own. "I was in a dungeon, I think."

"What makes you think it was a dungeon?" Von asked. His voice was calm and measured, the question a prompt not a means of interrogation.

"There were bars," Effie said, her eyes taking a faraway cast.

"What else do you see?"

"A man," she replied in a dreamlike tone.

"What is he wearing?" Helena asked.

"Black with…" her brow furrowed as she searched for the word, "straps?"

"Sounds like an Endoshan," Ronan said softly. The others murmured their agreement.

"Where is Rowena in your vision?" Von asked, trying to direct her focus.

Effie whimpered. "She's mad at the man. She has him gripped by the throat and is saying something. She's so angry."

"Is there anyone else there?" Von asked.

Effie was silent for a few beats. "Yes."

"Do you recognize them?"

She shook her head.

"Can you describe them?"

"Children," she whispered, her body trembling with the word. Whatever she was seeing terrified her.

Helena's eyes shot to Kragen. "She's draining more of them."

Kragen's face was grim. "That's what it sounds like."

Renewed anger surged through Helena at the thought. Now Effie wasn't the only one who was shaking, although it was outrage and not fear that had Helena on edge.

"Is there anything else?" Von asked.

Effie shook her head.

"Thank you, Effie."

She slumped in her chair, completely worn out from the events of the afternoon.

"Perhaps you should lie down and rest for a while," Helena suggested. "Would you like that?"

Effie nodded.

"She can use my room. It's closest," Timmins offered, stepping forward to assist Effie.

She gave him what barely passed for a smile, leaning on him heavily as they left the room.

"So, what does it mean?" Ronan asked once they were alone.

Kragen was the first to speak. "They are in Endoshan, clearly."

"You think?" Helena asked, not certain it was that obvious.

It was Von who answered. "They are allies, it's a logical step."

"But an obvious one," she pointed out.

"It may be obvious, but it does not make it untrue," Joquil said. "Let's think about this logically. You said that Effie entered into the vision *after* you mentioned needing to know where Rowena was located." Joquil waited for her confirmation before he continued, "The first thing she saw was an Endoshan man. That answers the question, doesn't it?"

Helena frowned. That seemed far too simple an explanation. "I don't think that's how visions work. Miranda mentioned more than once that visions aren't straightforward."

Von lifted his hands and shrugged. "It gives us a direction at least, which is more than we have now."

"How do we even know what she saw is occurring now? Maybe it's where Rowena is *going* to be? Or if it is where she is now, how do we know she'll still be there by the time we arrive?" Helena felt like she was the only one not ready to spring into action.

"We don't," Joquil said, "but I can't help but refer back to the sequence of events. It was your words that triggered the vision. One can only assume the vision was an answer to a question."

"But I didn't ask a question," Helena pointed out.

Joquil gave her a look, clearly not appreciating her distinction. "A need then. The vision responded to your need to know where she was. You did not say where she is *going* to be, you said where she *is*."

Helena frowned, still not totally convinced. She looked around the room at their faces. *Why are they all so determined to believe this is the answer?*

Kragen spoke up next. "Rowena was severely weakened during the attack. It makes sense that she would need to go somewhere relatively close to seek out a new source of energy. Endoshan fits that description."

Helena sighed and nodded. That much at least was true.

"We need to find her before she has time to recover fully," Von said.

Helena nodded again. "I know."

"This is our best option," he said.

"This is our only option," Ronan countered.

That's when the answer to her earlier question came to her. Her men needed a purpose. They could not stand sitting still spinning their wheels while their enemy was still out there. Like Von had said, if nothing else, this at least gave them something to do. Worst case scenario she wasn't there, and they were back where they started. But if she was... they could strike while she was still weak.

"Even if she's not there, Kiri," Kragen said, "those children might be. We have to save them."

That sealed it for her. Fruitless endeavor or not, Kragen was right. For the children alone, the trip would be worth it. "Fine," Helena said on a sigh. "Endoshan it is."

"When do you want to be ready to leave?" Ronan asked, already standing.

"Soon," Helena said wearily. "Before nightfall."

They had barely been back in Tigaera for a day, and already they were talking about leaving again. Many of them hadn't even had a chance to sleep since their return, herself included, and she was feeling the strain.

"I'll make sure the others are ready," Ronan promised before leaving. Joquil and Kragen followed him, leaving Von and Helena alone.

He stood next to her, just out of reach, and suddenly the distance felt entirely too far.

"Can you just hold me, and we'll pretend neither of us said anything heinous?"

"There's no need to pretend, *Mira.* You may have had a point."

Helena shook her head. "I was wrong, and you didn't deserve that. Least of all from me."

"You won't even accept my letting you off the hook without putting up a fight," he muttered. His lips quirked up as he reached for her, wrapping his arms around her and kissing the top of her head.

Helena let out a watery laugh.

Von's voice grew serious. "I'm sorry if my words were insensitive or callous."

"Me too. I didn't mean it when I said that you didn't care about others." She wrapped her arms around his waist and held him tight, burying her face in his neck and breathing in the spicy scent of him.

He tilted her chin up so that her eyes met his. "If I was hard on you, it was only because it hurts me to watch you beat yourself up. I can protect you from any enemy except yourself."

"I know," she whispered, her lower lip trembling.

He kissed her then, his lips sealing over hers, taking away the pain, anger, and grief that had been spiraling within her and making her feel off balance.

"I love you, Mira. Always."

"I love you, too."

They pulled apart, Helena feeling steady for the first time since leaving Greyspire.

"What can I do to help ease the burden?" he asked, brushing a stray curl from her cheek.

"You already did it."

He brushed his lips against hers again before looking down to ask, "This is probably a bad time to yell at you for putting yourself at risk, isn't it?"

Helena let out a snort of laughter. "Probably."

He sighed. "I thought so. As long as you know that we will talk about it." For all that his voice was light, she knew he was serious.

Helena nodded. She had made a mistake allowing herself to drain her power so completely at the ball. To be caught damn near defenseless when in the den of her enemy was a rookie mistake. One that she was lucky to have survived.

"Can we get through all of this first? Then I promise I will let you snarl at me as much as you want, and I won't complain once."

Von threw his head back and laughed.

She shoved at his chest playfully. "I know that I scared you. I'm sorry for that. I will try to be more careful."

The smile fell from his lips and his eyes went molten. "Don't you understand? It's self-preservation that makes me want to tuck you away and fight your battles for you. You are more precious to me than anything in this world, Helena. When I say that you are Mine, I do not simply mean my mate. You are my purpose. Without you, I am lost."

"Von," she whispered, the floor feeling like it just dropped from under her. But she did understand, because it was the same for her. She had already had to live in a world without him, and she'd be damned if she ever had to suffer it again.

The need to be close overwhelmed them, and he swept her up in his arms, her legs wrapping around his waist. Everything else could wait, for now the only thing that mattered was the man that held her heart in the palm of his hand.

THERE WAS a light knock on the door.

"Come in!" Helena called, hurriedly folding a few additional shirts to stuff into her pack.

"Is this a bad time?" Effie asked, her voice much more controlled than the last time they'd spoken.

Helena looked up with a frazzled smile. "Not if you don't mind talking while I pack."

"Do you want some help?"

"No, I think I've got it. How are you feeling?"

"Better." Effie searched the room for a seat, but there were clothes scattered about everywhere. "Where's Alina?"

"I gave her the night off. Packing is keeping my hands busy, which is a welcome thing at the moment."

Effie nodded her understanding. "I always thought chores were an excellent distraction."

Helena made a face that had the other woman laughing.

"I didn't say I enjoyed them."

"Fair enough," Helena said, watching as Effie finally decided to perch on the edge of her bed. She looked like she would flee at the first loud noise, she was also entirely dwarfed by the massive bed; her feet not even able to touch the ground.

Effie was looking much better than earlier, although the bath probably had a lot to do with it. Color had returned to her skin, and her hair no longer looked or smelled like the contents of a rubbish bin.

Helena dropped her pack so that she could give her full attention to her friend. "Have there been any other side effects?"

Effie shook her head, her eyes focused on her feet, which were swinging back and forth.

Despite her silence, Helena could tell something was definitely weighing on her. "Do you want to talk about it?"

When she spoke, she floored Helena with her words. "I don't know how to be special."

"Effie—" she protested, but the other woman shook her head and kept talking.

"No, it's okay. I was raised ungifted, I knew that it made me different, and after a while, I came to terms with the fact that I would never have any magic of my own. But now..." Effie's big eyes lifted and met hers. Helena was overcome by the sense of utter helplessness she found there. "I don't even know who I am anymore. Everything I thought I knew... everything that was true... it's gone."

"I know what that feels like."

Effie tilted her head, looking very much like an inquisitive bird. "With all due respect, Kiri. I don't think you do."

Helena's eyes searched hers, wanting to argue, but biting back the words.

"You thought that you were ungifted, but you were never surrounded by those that had magic. You were loved and cared for your whole life. All I ever wanted was to be special enough that my parents would love me. Or to have enough magic that I could live with my grandmother. I was obsessed with it for years before I finally came to terms with the fact that I could never be more than I was."

She didn't look angry as she spoke, only resigned. Helena wasn't sure which was worse.

"You have to understand, Helena. I was nothing. Worse than nothing, for even the servants usually had some ounce of magic, and there wasn't even a single drop in me. I had to fight every day to prove that I wasn't a worthless piece of shit."

Helena flinched. She'd never heard such harsh words from Effie.

"I had to learn how to be invisible, how to do what so many others could do without trying. And now…" she lifted her hands in a helpless shrug, "now I have this gift that I don't understand and I don't want. I would give anything to give it back if it meant she could return." Tears filled Effie's eyes, and she blinked furiously, trying to force them away.

"I'm so sorry, Effie," Helena whispered, knowing the words were useless. They wouldn't make anything better.

Effie wiped away a few stray tears. "It's okay."

"Is there anything I can do to help?"

"I want to come with you."

Helena froze, the words catching her off guard. "Are you sure?"

Effie's jaw clenched, and her hands curled into fists. "I have every right to be there."

"Of course you do. It's just… if you need time—"

"No. Not more crying. Tears don't change anything, only actions do. I want to act."

Helena found herself nodding in agreement. She knew exactly how Effie felt.

"It was my vision that helped you make this decision; I want to see it through."

"Okay."

"Good." Effie let out a breath then, her shoulders sagging. She had been prepared to fight the issue.

"Effie?"

"Yes?"

"For what it's worth, you've never been anything less than amazing to me."

Effie's lower lip trembled. "No one has ever said anything like that to me before."

"I have always admired your quiet strength. In fact, I was jealous of just how sure of yourself you were. I haven't felt that confident or capable a day in my life, and certainly not once since I found out I was Kiri."

Effie gaped at her in surprise.

Helena shrugged. "We all carry our scars, Effie. Just because you can't see them, doesn't mean they aren't there."

"I'll try to remember that."

"It will get easier as you learn how to use your new gifts. Try to remember that it's not something that you have to do on your own. We are all here to help you adjust, however we can."

"Thank you, Helena."

They shared a smile, Effie pushing herself off of the bed and back to her feet. "I guess I should go repack as well. Thanks for letting me come with you, and for listening."

"Anytime."

Effie was almost out the door when she stopped and looked back. "I guess you do understand, after all." With a final shy smile, Effie shut the door behind her.

Helena stared at the closed door for a long time without moving. There was a lot hidden in the words that Effie hadn't said. Secret pains and doubts that still haunted her. Helena would never have guessed that there was so much hidden beneath the surface; Effie hid her past well.

If Helena had learned anything leading up to her trial, it was that one's unspoken fears were the biggest obstacles. There was nothing harder to face than your own demons forged from self-doubt. She just hoped that Effie would remember what she said, and not suffer in silence.

"Mother, stay close to her," Helena whispered, turning back to her clothes. "She is going to need you in the days to come."

CHAPTER 15

*E*ndoshan was not what Helena expected. After her brief visit to Etillion, and knowing that at one time it had been the sister city to Endoshan, she'd expected it to be nearly the same. To an extent perhaps it was, but the differences far outweighed the similarities. Instead of Etillion's rolling green hills, there were wide stretches of dark, swampy water, and there were lush trees with thick ropey vines that hung between them. The heat was oppressive. The air like a living thing around them; a thick barrier that made each movement sluggish.

Even though it bordered Vyruul, it may as well be across the entire realm. There was not a speck of ice in sight. Helena doubted snow was something few, if any, Endoshans had experienced until they'd arrived at Vyruul the first time.

There was a low buzzing and then a loud crack as Ronan slapped his neck. He moved his hand away and inspected it with a grimace. "Bugs should not be allowed to be as big as one's hand. It's disgusting." He shook his hand to fling away the offending insect.

"Gross," Serena muttered, jumping out of the way.

Helena was inclined to agree. Endoshan had the distinct aura of a predator. Something that was hiding in the distance, tracking your movement and preparing to strike. She shuddered. Generally, she was a fan of wildlife, but these were no snuggly creatures. The wildlife here was like nothing she'd experienced growing up in Tigaera. Sure, they had bugs and even a wild wolf or two, but their insects were little harmless ones. Nothing on the scale of the massive buzzing creatures they'd discovered upon their arrival. She was stepping carefully, not wanting to be surprised with a stinger in the eye.

"Are you certain we're in the right place?" she asked Amara. The Etillions were the only ones who had been to Endoshan before, although not since the wall had been erected and Endoshan had effectively closed its borders against them.

Amara nodded. "It's been a few years since our last scouting mission, but the keep should be just around the next bend."

A light breeze stirred the branches of the trees and the resulting whisper of the leaves made the hair along her arms stand on end. Helena risked a glance over her shoulder, more certain than ever that their movements were being tracked.

Helena clutched the small bag of Kaelpas stones tighter in her hand. Never had she had this kind of reaction to a place before. A sense of danger lingered in the air, not like the taint they'd found in the Forest of Whispers, but a wrongness nonetheless. She wanted to go home. They could track Rowena a different way.

Von reached for her hand, squeezing it reassuringly. "You all right, *Mira?*"

She went to nod and stopped herself. The truth was, she wasn't. She just didn't understand what her instinct was trying to tell her. "Stay on guard," she answered instead.

Von studied her face before giving a slow nod. He made a low whistling sound that drew Ronan and Serena up short, along with the Daejarans standing nearest to them. Ronan met Von's eyes and gave a short nod of his own. The sound had been a warning, some signal they had set up long ago so that they could communicate efficiently and without giving anything away.

Von kept his fingers threaded through hers, and Helena was grateful for the contact. No one else seemed to be having the same kind of reaction that she was having, other than mild discomfort because of the heat or a general dislike of the bugs. Whatever she sensed was affecting her alone. *Lovely.*

Helena drew on her power to amplify her senses, realizing the only way she was going to figure out what she was sensing, without it sneaking up and catching them off guard, was to actively search for it. She cast her awareness out, using her magically enhanced eyes to study the world around her. The trees and creatures of the swamp came into sharper focus, the colors of their life essence creating a vivid rainbow that would have been beautiful, if the feeling of otherness wasn't also more apparent.

The trees glowed a deep earthy green, while the bugs appeared as floating specks of lavender, and there, beneath the surface of the water, something was a deep, pulsing red. Despite the size of the shape beneath the surface, Helena sensed nothing that had triggered alarm bells. She continued to search around her, seeing the warm glow of her comrades, especially the beautiful strands that linked her to her Circle.

Her brow furrowed, nothing so far felt out of place. It was not until her final sweep that she finally noticed something amiss. Amongst all of the color, there was a yawning chasm of empty black. Helena stumbled, the void causing her body to break out into a cold sweat. *What was it?*

Even as everything inside of her urged her to stay away, Helena forced herself to start moving toward it.

Worried voices called after her, surprised to see her break rank without so much as a word.

"Helena?"

"Kiri?"

She didn't know how to explain what was happening, so she didn't even try.

And then the one voice she could never ignore called to her. *"Mira?"*

"I need to see this."

"See what?"

"I don't know."

"You aren't going anywhere alone, Helena. We don't know what's out there."

She knew better than to argue after what happened in Greyspire, and truth be told, she didn't want to face this on her own. She just knew that whatever it was, she was going to wish she had never found it. She already wished she had never stepped foot in this Mother-forsaken realm.

Von said something to the others, but she barely heard him. She was wholly focused on the void. Reaching it was going to require crossing the swamp, and she was not equipped with anything other than her power to reach the other side. Not wanting to waste time trying to find a vessel that they could commandeer, Helena used the trick she had learned while visiting the Storm Forged and urged the water to part for her.

There were a few startled gasps behind her as the army witnessed the act. The water was nowhere near as deep as the ocean, and it did not take long for two walls of water to form on either side of her, both towering high over her head. From the corner of her eye, she could see glowing blue orbs that must have been fish playfully swimming in the still churning water.

Helena took the first tentative step, her heart somewhere in the vicinity of her throat. There was a squelching sound as the thick mud clung to her boot. It took more effort than she would have thought to cross the distance, the mud trying to suck her down into its depths. Despite the slow crossing, Von remained right beside her.

Soon, all she could hear was the sound of her racing heart as they finally reached the other side of the water and the raised bit of land where the source of the void seemed to reside. With each step that carried her to the edge of the darkness, she could feel a quiet voice whimpering in the recesses of her mind. *No. I don't want to do this. Please, don't make me do this.*

She was less than two steps away from the void when she saw something that would have had her falling to her knees if Von hadn't been there to catch her. Bones. Thousands of small, child-sized bones.

There were no words. Helena gaped at Von, who was staring at the mass grave in disgust, his jaw continuously clenching and unclenching.

Rowena had done a number of terrible things, but this might have been the worst, if for no other reason than the sheer number of innocent children that she would have had to murder to leave behind that many bones. This was clearly what she had been busy doing with the children of Endoshan. What wasn't clear was whether her new husband knew about it. The remote nature of the mass grave gave the impression that it was a secret, but given the sheer number of bones, someone had to have helped her. It was the only plausible way to cover up a genocide of this magnitude.

"Can you at least put their souls to rest?" Von asked.

The words caught Helena off guard, forcing her to a truth she had not had time to fully process. It was a sense of emptiness that had led her to this place, and a void by its very nature was an absence. It was difficult, but Helena forced herself to discount the piles of bones that were visible as far as she could see. She tried to focus instead on what else might be hidden beyond normal sight.

Helena sucked in a breath as realization dawned. "There are no souls here," she murmured.

Von looked at her sharply. "In the Forest, even when Rowena had destroyed the Night Stalker village, the souls of those that were slain were still present. Why would it be different here?"

"Because of how she murdered them." Helena's voice was hollow.

Von turned to fully face her. "What do you mean?"

Helena swallowed, letting the hold of her power drop, not wanting to feel any more than she absolutely had to. She felt raw and battered, each new revelation bringing with it a surge of powerful emotions that were slowly destroying her. It was like she was under attack from the inside out, and she was entirely incapable of protecting herself from further assault. There was only one defense against the kind of atrocity she was facing, and it was something that the Mother's Vessel would never know: an utter lack of empathy. Only someone truly soulless would be immune.

Soulless.

Helena's eyes moved to Von. "She did not simply kill them. She stole their lives."

Von's eyes narrowed, not understanding the distinction.

"We have always known that Rowena twisted her power, using her Spirit magic to steal the wills and bodies of those that serve her. What we had not allowed ourselves to consider, was that it was more than just their wills she was stealing. Rowena creates her Shadows by taking control of their souls. It is how she gained so much power."

Von looked pale. "I don't… I'm not sure I understand."

Helena didn't blame him. It was too horrific a thought. "You have witnessed Rowena try to transform one into a Shadow."

He nodded, having nearly been a victim himself.

"When she makes that connection, she is taking a part of their essence into herself, creating her own twisted bond. It is what allows her to assert her will over them. They are her puppets, because they are quite literally tied to her. She does not drain them completely, since the body cannot survive without its soul. She needs them to stay alive just enough that they can serve her."

She could tell by the glint in his eye that Von was starting to understand. "Children cannot fight, so they have no use to her."

Helena nodded. "And so she consumes every drop."

"This…" Von started, his voice breaking, "this is the source of her power?"

She desperately wished that she could deny it, but the proof was literally at their feet. "Whatever she has done to so pervert her magic, has allowed her to eat the souls of her victims. That kind of life force must be potent. It has exponentially strengthened whatever gifts she was born with."

"So why isn't she affected when the Shadows die the same way she is when the Generals do?"

It was a good question, and one she already guessed the answer to. "She has taken all but a drop of what remains in her Shadows. They are already a part of her; their loss is no more than a snip of hair falling to the ground. It is a different relationship with the Generals."

"You've lost me again," Von admitted, looking frustrated that he was slower to make the connections that she had.

Helena grew thoughtful, trying to think of an easier way to explain. "The Vessel required a Mate, one strong enough to help her withstand the strength of her power so that it did not consume her."

Von nodded.

"Rowena stole power. More power than she was ever supposed to have. She is not strong enough to contain it on her own, and she does not have a Mate to help her carry the burden."

"So she uses her Generals as a way to keep and control the power," Von stated.

"Exactly. It is why they are so strong."

"When she loses a General, she loses a significant amount of the power she amassed from the Shadows," Von finished, finally understanding.

Helena nodded, looking back out over the scattered bones. "And it is why she was in such a hurry to recoup it."

Von fell silent.

The kind of selfishness that would allow someone to kill without mercy was almost beyond comprehension. These were children. Hundreds and possibly thousands of lives filled with potential that would never be fulfilled. *How could the Mother let this happen? Where is the justice?*

Helena realized she must have asked the questions out loud when Von responded.

"You are the Mother's justice. Let's find her, Helena. Let's find her and make her pay for what she has done."

Helena turned her back on the bones, not wanting to watch as they slowly sank down into the black earth. There was no life left here. Whatever Rowena had done had caused the earth itself to recoil from the taint. Helena pumped her magic back into the land, even as she began to walk away. It sucked greedily, using her power to repair the damage. By the time they had returned to their friends, the water had reclaimed the path, and Helena knew without looking that the void was gone.

It was going to take a lot more than that for her to say the same. The proof of what they were facing, the level to which Rowena would stoop to win, could no longer be ignored. There was only one way this war would end, and it was the same way it started.

Death.

CHAPTER 16

Although they had reunited with the others, Helena remained apart from the group, not ready to relive what she had seen just yet. She left it up to Von to fill them in on the discovery, and to answer the questions such a revelation would necessitate. Knowing that the images would haunt both her waking and nighttime hours was bad enough, but the thought of having to say it aloud and bring those images to life made her want to vomit.

"Are you all right, Kiri?" Reyna asked.

Helena jumped, not having heard her approach. It was a good reminder that she could not afford to become lost in her thoughts right now. She considered lying, but after eyeing the Night Stalker's leader, she decided to go with the truth. "No." She sighed. "Not even a little bit."

"It sounds horrible. So many…" Reyna trailed off, the swirls of paint doing little to hide her pained expression.

Helena's eyes fell closed, and she swallowed, taking a few seconds to let her stomach settle before she responded. "You would think, with as much death as I've seen in the last few months, that it wouldn't affect me like this. But they were only children, Reyna. They didn't deserve this; hell, not even the worst kind of criminal deserves it. Especially not what she's done to them," Helena paused, her shaking hand reaching out and grasping Reyna's. "There won't even be any peace for them. She didn't just take their futures, Reyna. She stole their afterlife. Without souls, they can never return to the Mother."

Reyna's dark green eyes shuttered, but she returned Helena's squeeze with one of her own.

The raw emotions were making her vulnerable, leading Helena to a confession she would not have otherwise made to any but her Mate. "I don't know how to set my emotions aside and lead them right now," she whispered, referring to the army at her back. "All I want to do is curl up and cry over the waste she's made of those lives." Helena's voice was ragged by the time she was done speaking. She sucked in a quick breath and turned to face Reyna directly. "How do you deal with it?"

Reyna's brows shot up in surprised. "You think that it's a lack of emotion that helps me lead?"

Helena nodded. "In order to make rational decisions you have to set them aside, don't you?"

"That sounds like something a man told you."

The memories of Timmins and Joquil helping her prepare for her trial came to mind, and Helena almost smiled at how accurate an assessment it was. In her case, it had been two men.

Reyna laughed bitterly. "Maybe that is true for some rulers, but I would argue the opposite. It is the things we have the strongest reactions to that shows us what our path must be."

Some of the tension in Helena's chest loosened. Learning that a ruler as strong as Reyna let her emotions influence her decisions was a relief. Moreover, there was comfort, and a sense of solidarity, in knowing that she was not the only one who did so. Helena squeezed Reyna's hand once more, this time as a silent thank you, before letting it go. She finally felt steady enough to continue the journey without borrowing someone else's strength.

The Endoshan Keep came into view a couple of seconds later. It looked abandoned, but not because it was in ruins. This was no crumbling castle. Everything still looked pristine, as if everyone finished with their chores and simply got up and left. It was also entirely too quiet, the usual noises of people going about their day absent.

"You don't think we'll find her there, do you?" Reyna asked, watching Helena's face as she took in their surroundings.

Helena shook her head, her eyes not straying from the keep. "No, I don't."

"And yet, you brought your army here anyway." It wasn't a question, but it sounded like one.

"In the end, it matters not if she is here. The choice led us to something we needed to see. If that is all we get from the excursion, it was still an important piece of the puzzle to collect."

Reyna nodded her agreement. "The girl's vision led you here for a reason. Perhaps it just wasn't the one you had thought."

The two women walked in silence a bit longer before coming to a full stop. The rest of the Circle caught up to them a few moments later, their collective faces grim as they studied the keep.

"It's too quiet for an army to be housed within," Kragen said, echoing Helena's earlier assessment.

"That doesn't mean someone isn't tucked away inside," Ronan pointed out.

"It would have to be a fairly small group," Helena mused.

"You think we will find more than one person inside?" Von asked.

Helena shrugged. "Rowena would never go somewhere alone. Especially now. At the very least, she is going to keep her Generals close." She shot Reyna a look.

The Night Stalker looked amused watching Helena carefully walk the line between her beliefs and her Circle's expectations regarding what they would find inside. Studied more carefully, Helena had not actually answered Von's question. She supplied a truth, yes, but it was one that allowed the others to hear what they wanted. Reyna winked at Helena before schooling her face back into a neutral mask.

"What do you want to do, Kiri?" Joquil asked, putting the decision in her hands.

"We're already here. We may as well go inside and see what there is to find."

Von and Ronan split up the troops, selecting a small contingent of men to come inside with them. If Rowena was inside, they didn't want to be caught off-guard. Although, had Helena really believed the Corruptor was here, she would have stormed the damn keep with her whole army, not a mere handful of men. No matter how talented they were.

Effie forced her way forward, her eyes leveled on Helena. "I'm coming with you."

Timmins opened his mouth to protest, but Helena silenced him with a look. "As you wish, Effie. Just stay close."

Without further ceremony, Helena and the others made their way to the door.

SHE COULD HEAR the sound of their footsteps as their boots scratched against the stone floors. There was no other noise to counteract the rustling echo off of the walls. Endoshan Keep was utterly empty. At least, so far.

"Effie, does this look familiar?" Von asked.

The blonde shook her head, her curls swinging wildly. "No. Everything was darker in my vision, and I don't remember seeing any windows. I was underground, perhaps?"

The group looked around the expansive first floor for some sign of a stairwell.

"Over here!" Joquil called.

Helena and the others spun in a circle trying to find him.

"Where are you?" she shouted.

Joquil's head popped out from behind what looked like the center of a stone wall.

Effie screamed, her hand over her heart as if she was trying to keep it from flying out of her chest. "Mother's tits!"

"That shouldn't be possible, right?" Ronan asked in a low voice.

"Definitely not," Kragen replied.

Joquil shifted and suddenly his body was in full view. He was grinning. "Apologies, there's a hidden walkway here. Just walk straight toward me and then look to your left, you'll see what I mean."

There were some dubious eyebrows, but the group took a few tentative steps toward him.

"Oh, this is fun!" Kragen said, seeing what Joquil had meant. "Helena, we definitely need one of these at the Palace."

A few paces behind the others, it took her a bit longer to understand what they were talking about. Once she did, she certainly understood the appeal.

From a distance, Joquil appeared to be standing in front of a solid stone wall. Once you were standing next to him, however, it was clearly an optical illusion. There was another, identical, half-wall directly in front of the other. This allowed for a hidden hallway to be put in plain view. A great place to hide and eavesdrop if nothing else. Helena wondered how many other secret passageways existed in the keep, and if there were, in fact, some in the Palace.

The passage was only large enough for them to walk single file, so Joquil took the lead while one of the Daejarans took the rear. Von insisted on walking in front of Helena, which she couldn't say she overly minded. It gave her a nice view.

Ever since they completed the bond, it had become easier to catch snippets of her Mate's thoughts. Von had clearly just picked up on hers because he asked, *"Like what you see, Mira?"*

"Always."

"Aren't you the one always reminding me we have to stay focused?"

"We could die in the next twenty seconds. If I'm about to return to the Mother, I want to know I spent my last few moments on Her earth wisely."

She could see his shoulders shaking with laughter. *"Fair point well made, as always. Ogle away."*

"As if I needed your permission."

"I'm going to remember you said that."

The distraction was a welcome reprieve from the darkness that surrounded them. Every little sliver of light was the difference between holding on to hope or falling into despair. Helena would selfishly take what happiness she could, for as long as she could. Rowena didn't get to steal that from her, like she had with so much else. The day that they stopped holding on to hope, to the light, was the day that Rowena won. Helena would rather die than let that happen. These stolen moments were the proof that it wasn't over yet.

The hallway dipped, bringing them down a moldy smelling ramp and into a smaller chamber. They filtered into the room, one by one, each of them spreading out to allow the others to step inside. There was little light here, and what small bit was available was from a few flickering candles that were suspended from the walls.

Effie's gasp was the only confirmation Helena needed that this was the place from her vision. The room was long but narrow, a row of cages along the back half of the room. Cages that were occupied. There were about ten children chained in half as many cages. They seemed to be drugged, their small heads dangling down to their chests, and none of them reacting to the appearance of the others in the room.

Helena's rage was swift and absolute. Not waiting for anyone else, she pushed ahead, her hand already outstretched with the intention of breaking open each of the cages.

"Helena, wait," Timmins cautioned softly.

She spun around, her teeth bared in a snarl. "You dare stop me, Advisor?" She had made the transition from Helena to Vessel so quickly, the sound of her harmonious voice surprised even her. It was low and throaty, and there was no mistaking the threat beneath her question.

Timmins held his hands up. "I mean no offense, Kiri. It's just, the children appear to be in stasis. There might be some kind of alarm you could trigger if you touch them."

"Good," she growled, her teeth feeling too large for her mouth. "Let them know I am here. Let them face me." She could feel the black claws pushing their way out of her hands, the predator inside her primed to fight.

Timmins nodded, backing slowly away from her.

Helena reached the first cage, her magic-enhanced claws tearing the door from the cage with a loud crash.

"Who needs an alarm?" Ronan asked.

She was careful to sheath the claws as she reached to brush limp brown hair off the child's face. It was a little girl, her features pinched with fear, even in her unconscious state. There were deep shadows beneath her eyes, and her skin looked waxy. She was clearly unwell. Helena eyed the chains, trying to determine the best way to release the girl, without her getting hurt.

There was an audible click and a hidden door opened, an Endoshan man Helena recognized storming into the room.

Effie whimpered, her skin bone-white. "It's happening," she whispered.

The Chosen went on high alert, knowing that Rowena had been in Effie's vision.

"What do you think you're—" the man's eyes went wide, recognition cutting his tirade short. "Kiri?"

Helena's iridescent eyes were narrowed into twin slits as she stalked toward him. "Where is your queen?" she demanded.

"I don't know, Kiri."

"Liar!" she screamed, throwing her arm up as a bolt of purple power blasted from her palm and into his chest. The Endoshan went flying back into the wall, crumpling to the floor.

"I-I swear, Kiri. I have not seen her since Kai left with her."

"Get up!"

The man struggled to push himself back into a standing position.

"We know about your little boneyard," Helena said, her voice low and menacing.

He gulped audibly. "I tried to reason with him, but he said it was the only way to ensure Endoshan's future."

Helena closed the distance between them, her steps slow and measured. "Is your future more meaningful than theirs?" she asked once they were almost nose to nose, gesturing toward the children in the cages.

"N-no, Kiri."

"So why do you get to live when you've sentenced them to death?"

"I-I haven't, Kiri." The man was crying now, tears falling freely from his golden eyes.

"How do we release them?" she asked, giving him a final opportunity to save himself.

"I don't know," he moaned. "Please, believe me."

"If you do not want to answer for her crimes, it would serve you well to tell me what you know."

"N-nothing, I swear!"

Her power was already coiled and ready to strike. Helena saw nothing but the man's eyes as she warned him, "I will give you until the count of three."

"K-Kiri," he begged.

"One."

"I don't know!"

"Two."

Whatever he saw in her face had him trying to run. Helena's hand snapped out, closing around his throat and holding him in place. His fate was sealed.

"Three," she whispered.

Helena unleashed her power, the full force of it moving through her arm and slamming into his body where they were connected. He gasped, his eyes bulging. One second, he was there; the next, he was gone. It was over as quickly as it began.

She stepped back, looking at her now empty hand. It was coated in a fine red dust. All that remained of him was the dust, which now covered everything between her and the wall she'd held him against. Her power had completely vaporized him. The bloodlust was beginning to fade, and what she'd just done was starting to seep into her awareness.

Helena turned toward the others, her breaths coming in shallow pants. They stared at her in stunned silence, Effie's hand pressed to her mouth. The fact that they didn't know how to approach her right now only increased the sense of alienation she was feeling. *What have I done?*

Reyna was the first to speak, not having the same sense of hesitation as the others. "Are you all right, Kiri?"

She wordlessly shook her head. Helena honestly didn't know what she was. She had never killed another person unprovoked before. She had fought during battles, protecting those she loved and destroying Rowena's Shadows without a second thought, but this had been different. There was no conscious thought, no decision to act. She just did.

Von approached her slowly. *"Mira, look at me."*

She lifted her eyes to his.

"You were well within your right to enact justice for those children."

She sucked in another breath, feeling lightheaded.

"Just focus on me."

Helena nodded to indicate she was trying.

"You did nothing wrong."

"I killed him." Even her psychic voice was trembling.

"You are the Mother's justice. Your actions are her own."

"I am the Mother's justice," she repeated slowly, her voice hollow.

"She was displeased, and She acted through Her Vessel," Timmins chimed in, his voice measured.

The rest of her Circle nodded their agreement, none of them looking at her with anything close to judgment. It was concern for her that had stayed their action, not disgust at what she had done. Their acceptance did more than anything else could.

Helena nodded, her breathing starting to slow. She looked down, shuddering as she realized she was still coated in what was left of the Endoshan.

"Let me help," Joquil murmured, stepping toward her. He waited for Helena's nod before saying, "Close your eyes."

She obeyed, and he moved his open palm over her, a gentle breeze stirring up the strands of hair that had escaped from her braid.

"You can open them," he murmured.

When Helena looked down, she was clean again. All trace of the red dust was gone.

"Thank you," she breathed.

"Of course, Kiri." Joquil stepped back, and Helena turned toward the cages.

The rage that had settled with the Endoshan's death lifted its head again at the sight of the children. Helena forced herself to breathe, pushing the anger down. It had no place here since it would not help the children be any less caged.

Helena walked back toward them, focusing on a sense of icy calm rather than fiery rage. She ran her fingers along the cool steel bars, walking the length of the cage doors that remained. The bars froze beneath the contact. Once she reached the end, she turned and released a breath, the bars snapping and falling to the ground.

Without being asked, the rest of the Chosen moved forward, using their various powers or simply their brute strength to snap the chains that held the children. The small bodies sagged, but the Chosen caught them before they fell, carefully lifting them and carrying them out. From there the children were gently laid out on the floor until each one looked like they might only be sleeping.

"Can you wake them?" Reyna asked.

"Of course she can," Ronan said, winking at Helena.

She gave him a small smile, appreciating the show of support. "It really depends what she's done to them," Helena admitted.

"A bigger concern is what we're going to do with them once they are awake," Timmins said.

He had a point. They couldn't very well take the children with them.

"We'll send them to the Palace," Helena decided on the spot. "We will raise them in Tigaera. If the Endoshans did not think they were worth keeping, they do not deserve to have them back."

There were murmurs of approval.

One of Ronan's men stepped forward. "If you will lend me a stone, Kiri, I can make sure they arrive safely and are well cared for."

"Thank you, Geralt."

The dark-haired man nodded. "It is the least we can do for them."

That much settled, Helena knelt next to the nearest child. It was the same one she'd first discovered. Helena placed her hand gently on the girl's forehead, her eyes fluttering closed as she used her power to seek out the source of the unnatural sleep.

Helena half expected that Rowena had kept the children drugged with *Bella Morte* as she had with Von, but there wasn't a trace of the hallucinogen in her body. *Thank the Mother for small miracles.*

Losing track of time and awareness of her physical body, Helena sent her power out, searching for any sign of interference. It took a couple of passes until she realized it was not a physical issue.

Her eyes opened and she sighed. It was deceptively simple, but no less evil for its simplicity. Rowena had used some of her Spirit to force the children into this state. All it took was a compulsion telling the children to go to sleep, and they had been helpless to fight the urge. Without Rowena here to remove the order, they could not wake on their own.

Not wanting the poor things to be terrified upon waking, Helena crafted her own finely woven compulsion. Bright purple tendrils began to flow out of Helena and wrap themselves around each of the sleeping bodies. She reinforced each tendril with some of her healing magic so that they would wake feeling rested and without any lingering side effects of the obvious drain Rowena had already performed.

Once she was certain the magic had taken hold, Helena said, "You are safe. It's time to wake up now."

The glowing tendrils, which had formed a tightly woven net around each of them, sank into the children until the strands disappeared entirely.

With a rather undignified yawn, the little girl beside Helena stretched and opened her eyes. "Is it time for breakfast?" she asked with a sweet lisp.

"Just about, dear one," Helena replied, brushing the soft hair off her forehead.

The girl scrunched her upturned nose. "Why are you crying? Did something bad happen?"

Helena brushed at her eyes. "It's nothing you need to worry about right now, darling."

Around her, the others began to wake up, the children curiously, but fearlessly, inspecting the grown-ups around them. Helena knew, had it not been for her magic, they would be much more suspicious of the strangers, especially had they remembered what had happened to them.

Von helped her stand, and Helena hid her face in his neck. At least this time her tears were from relief.

She'd finally arrived in time to save someone.

CHAPTER 17

"Are we returning to Tigaera as well?"

The children had been sent to the Palace almost immediately. Without having searched the rest of the keep, no one felt comfortable with the idea of letting them remain there any longer than strictly necessary.

After a thorough search, they were able to determine that the rest of the keep was, in fact, abandoned. The man Helena had killed, the one whose name she didn't even know, had been the only one that remained. Probably to keep an eye on Rowena's pets.

Not sure of their next steps, the Circle gathered in the kitchen. The others, minus Effie who stayed behind, had been sent back to fill in the rest of the army on what had transpired.

"Without a clear destination, where else would we go?" Helena asked, in reply to Kragen's question.

"We could see if asking about Rowena triggers another vision," Ronan said, his eyes shooting over to Effie apologetically.

Effie licked her lips, her eyes darting between Helena and Ronan. "But I was wrong before. I don't know what I'm doing."

"No one blames you, Effie. Look at what we were able to accomplish today because your vision led us here," Ronan said.

"But I was wrong," she insisted.

Timmins was studying Effie carefully. "Your vision is simply a series of images that require your interpretation to decipher their message. Without training, it's understandable that you might infer the wrong meaning."

"It's a shitty time to try to learn," Effie huffed.

Helena's lips twitched up; she liked this side of her. Their sweet flower had grown thorns.

The ghost of a smile made a brief appearance on Timmins' face. "We just need to learn what the images mean to you. Perhaps there were subtle details you missed because you didn't know to look for them."

"What do you mean?" Effie asked, her brows lowering in confusion.

"Well," Timmins paused, choosing his words with care. "Your vision was triggered by a question. The series of images chosen to answer the question are unique to you. They could only be things that held some sort of personal significance or meaning since you cannot See what you do not already know. There'd be no way for you to accurately explain or discern its significance. So, therefore the images must be intimately tied to you and your understanding of them."

Helena could see where he was coming from, but she didn't fully agree with his assessment. "Miranda told me that visions are never straightforward. I doubt we can take them at face value."

"How would we explain that Effie knew to come to Endoshan then?" Von asked.

"Maybe it's not just the images themselves, but their relationship to each other?" Joquil asked.

"Technically Effie didn't know. You were the ones that made the connection to the man she described and Endoshan," Helena reminded them.

The others fell silent. It was hard to solve a puzzle when you couldn't see the pieces.

"Effie, I want you to try something for me, if you wouldn't mind," Von said.

She nodded, biting down on her bottom lip hard enough Helena was worried she might draw blood.

"Close your eyes and try to picture what you Saw."

Effie's eyes widened, but she nodded again and followed his direction.

"Can you see it?"

"Yes," she whispered.

"What are you looking at?"

"The man."

"Had you seen him before?"

"I'm not sure."

"What is it about him that stands out?"

"His leathers. I recognized them." Her eyes popped open. "Joquil was right, it must be association."

"That's great, Effie," Von smiled warmly. "Try again, and this time I want you to focus on the moment when Rowena appears."

Effie swallowed and closed her eyes. After a moment she whispered, "Okay."

"Why do you think the vision is showing you Rowena?"

Her brows furrowed, not understanding the question. "Because it *is* Rowena."

"Is it?"

"It's her," Effie said emphatically.

"Describe her to me."

Effie sighed. "Blonde hair, cold blue eyes, her hand is wrapped around the man's throat as she yells at him."

Helena shivered, not liking how close the description was to her own actions.

"What else?" Von prompted.

"She has a crown…"

"What kind of crown?"

Effie's eyes scrunched in confusion. "Light? No, that's not right. It looks like it's glowing. It's casting light… it's fire?" Effie opened her eyes, looking at the others. "Why would Rowena be wearing a crown like that? Helena is the one who's supposed to wear the Crown of Embers."

Helena flinched at the words, every eye in the room focusing on her.

"She wants the crown?" Kragen offered.

Timmins shook his head. "It's not just the crown she wants. She wants Helena's power."

The others continued to throw out suggestions, but Helena had her own suspicion. "Effie?"

Wide cornflower blue eyes met hers. "Yes?"

"Was there," Helena swallowed, "was there a mirror in your vision?"

"A mirror?"

Helena nodded.

Effie closed her eyes, going silent for a few seconds before she responded. "Yes." She opened her eyes. "What does that mean?"

Helena's shoulders dropped. "It means that it was never Rowena that you Saw. It was always me."

Quiet filled the room as her words sunk in.

"But why? That would mean the vision wasn't triggered by your question at all."

Helena shrugged. "It was stranger that we thought it had been. Miranda never mentioned any of her visions working that way. I think it was purely coincidence that you happened to inherit your power in that moment."

Effie frowned.

"I am the mirror," Helena said matter-of-factly. "You saw my crown on her head, because it was a warning of what would happen when we got here. Of who I would become. She brings out the worst in me, the parts of me that are most like her. It's what she's always wanted."

"No, that's not possible. You are the Vessel."

"And she is the Corruptor. Every move she's made has been with the hope of making me snap. It's why she went after my Mate." Helena shuddered. "She has no idea how close she was to succeeding."

"Helena," Von started, his eyes turning gold.

She stopped him with the lift of her hand. "When Darrin first told me who I was, he reminded me that like calls to like, of what it would mean if I became corrupted. If Rowena is successful, think of what she could accomplish with me on her side."

"But you'd never join her," Effie protested.

"Not unless pushed past all reason," Von said.

"Fuck me," Ronan whispered. "This has all been a trap. Everything."

Helena nodded. "She's been a step ahead of us this whole time."

"She is toying with you," Kragen growled.

"She wants to break me so that I will destroy the Chosen."

"What sense does that make? Who would be left to rule?" Effie asked.

Dread pooled in Helena's stomach as she replied, "Those that she's already corrupted. It would be the start of the Shadow Years. Literally. And I would be the ultimate puppet."

Von moved into her line of sight, forcing her to meet his gaze. "That is *never* going to happen."

"Of course it fucking isn't!" Ronan shouted. "Helena, you can't possibly think she's going to win."

"Look at what happened today," she whispered. "She got to me."

"Who wouldn't be affected by what she had done to those children?" Ronan asked.

Helena shrugged helplessly. "Who else could have done what I did, because of their reaction?"

There was no answer to that, because there was no one else. Only Helena, in her capacity as the Vessel, could have mete out that kind of punishment.

"But it was the Mother's justice," Timmins insisted.

"Unless it wasn't."

Helena felt like her mind was spinning in a million different directions. There was still something they were missing. A piece of the puzzle that they didn't have that was keeping them from being able to see a truth just out of their reach.

Von grasped her face in his hands. "There is nothing, *nothing*," he repeated, "that could ever bring you to the darkness."

"You're wrong."

"You are nothing but light, Helena. You are *my* light."

Tears started to fill her eyes at the certainty in his voice. She may be confused, but there was not a trace of doubt in her Mate.

"Do you hear me?" he asked, his forehead dropping to hers.

"Yes," she said for his ears alone.

"I will keep reminding you until you believe in yourself as much as I do."

"I do not deserve your faith in me. I do not deserve you."

"Yes, you do. Otherwise the Mother would have never brought us together."

"Perhaps this is the game," Ronan said thoughtfully, breaking her from the spell Von had wrapped around her. "Maybe she wants you to be crippled by doubt so that you are too afraid to do what must be done."

Helena could neither agree nor disagree with his assessment. They had grossly underestimated the woman.

The simple fact was, when it came to Rowena, anything was possible.

Helena paced, her earlier revelations keeping her from being able to find any solace in sleep. All of it was a terrifying montage that haunted her waking hours. Who needed nightmares when their reality was one already?

She had come to her garden to walk amongst the simplest form of beauty, needing to see something pure and untainted. Especially now when she could hardly stand to look upon her own reflection. The truth was, she felt unclean. Rowena may not have actually corrupted her, but it felt like it.

When they'd gotten home, Helena had scrubbed her skin until she felt raw, and still it had done nothing to remove the sense of vile filth that surrounded her. This was not a superficial grime that could be removed with ease. It was a dirty smear that defiled her very soul. She may never feel clean again.

"What are you doing out here alone?" Von asked, stepping away from the tree she had once caused to burst with life. It had been in a state of eternal bloom ever since. The memory felt like it belonged to someone else. Helena wished that her foibles were still only minor inconveniences. Mistakes now could lead, and quite frankly had already led, to innocent people being killed.

Helena shrugged, not having a simple answer for her Mate.

He walked toward her, his eyes glittering in the pale moonlight. His fingers brushed against her flowers, until he grasped one and plucked it from its bush. He offered it to her silently.

She accepted his gift, holding the blossom up to her nose to sniff its heady fragrance.

"Beautiful," she sighed, returning her attention to him.

"Yes, you are," Von agreed, brushing his thumb along her jaw and leaning down to kiss her.

"You have a habit of giving me flowers," she murmured once he pulled away.

"They make you smile."

"Mother knows I could certainly use something to smile about right about now." Von gestured toward the flower, making her laugh. "Touché."

"That's better."

Helena rested her head against his shoulder, curling into his body and welcoming the warmth that surrounded her as he held her close. "I'm scared," she whispered.

"I know."

Of course he did. Given their bond, he likely felt her emotions as if they were his own. "I'm trying to be strong."

He tipped her chin up. "You are strong."

"I don't feel like it. How did she weave that web so carefully? How did she know I'd go there?"

Von loosed a breath and looked over her head and into the night as he contemplated her question. "From a tactical standpoint, it makes sense that you would go to investigate Endoshan after learning of their betrayal. She had to assume at some point you would find your way there, and so she left a surprise for you to stumble across along your way. I wouldn't be surprised if there were a few other similar presents scattered along Elysia for you to discover. Even if you don't find them all, you'd be certain to come across at least one of them."

Helena nodded thoughtfully. "I just hate that she was right. She seems to know me better than I know her."

"She sees your compassion as a weakness to exploit. What she doesn't understand is that she's wrong."

"Is she? It worked, didn't it?"

"You lose sight of your wins so easily."

Helena lifted her shoulder in a shrug. "It was a draw at best. She still proved her point."

"So did you."

She tilted her head to stare up at him. "How can your belief in me be so unwavering?"

"I know your soul," Von said simply, holding his hand just above her heart. "If our situations were reversed, would you doubt me?"

"Not for a second."

"There you go."

"But—"

He placed a finger against her lips. "Maybe the question you should be asking is why are you so quick to question yourself? We are the same, you and I; two halves of a whole. If you would not doubt me, there's no reason you should doubt yourself."

She smiled under his finger before nipping at it.

"Light always shines brightest in the dark," he said before claiming her mouth in a heated kiss.

Helena melted into him, loving the way they fit together in every sense of the word.

"Your pep talks have gotten better," she teased.

"I've had a great mentor."

She chuckled. "I love you."

"And I you."

Snuggling back into him, she asked, "So what should I do now, Oh Wise One?"

"You seek out the darkness and you shine."

"When you put it that way, it sounds so easy."

Von's laughter rumbled beneath her, and as always, Helena found peace in the arms of the man who could see her even when she lost sight of herself.

CHAPTER 18

It had been three days, and Helena was no closer to figuring out where to go next. The more time they gave Rowena to scheme, the worse it was going to be once they found her. They needed to act. Now.

"I don't see any way around it," Helena said on a defeated sigh, "we need to go to Bael and seek out the Triumvirate."

Ronan let out a low growl, and Helena peered up at him with tired eyes. Her Shield had not forgotten what happened the last time they had come face-to-face with the powerful trio. Even Von, who had only heard about it after the fact, looked darkly unhappy.

"Look, I don't like it any more than you do. But we're lost here, and I don't see any of you coming up with better ideas. Best case scenario, they point us in the right direction. Worst case, we're in the exact same position we are now."

"It might be good for Effie to meet some of the other Keepers. She could probably use some of their guidance right about now," Timmins said thoughtfully.

Helena clung to the words. "See, exactly! Even more of a reason to go to the Keepers."

"What does Effie have to say about this?" Kragen asked.

"I haven't exactly mentioned it to her yet," Helena admitted. "If she'd rather not come, I'm not going to force her to. It's got to be her choice."

The others nodded their agreement.

"So it's settled."

"Helena," Joquil interjected.

She turned toward her Master. "Yes?"

"Do you know where exactly to find the Keepers?"

Helena's face fell. She did not. There was only one among them who did, and she was dead. "Mother's tits, I can't catch a break," she swore, drawing some amused looks from her Circle.

"I might have an idea," Ronan said.

She turned to him hopefully.

"The Forest of Whispers borders Bael, perhaps Reyna and the Night Stalkers know where to start."

"Good call. I much prefer that option to the one I had."

"Which was?" he asked, his lips already curling up in a smirk.

"Wandering around Bael aimlessly until we found them."

"I should have known," Ronan replied. "You always do seem to prefer the direct approach."

Helena rolled her eyes. He was really starting to turn into the older brother she never wanted. Never wanted, but dearly loved.

There were a few chuckles as the others began to stand, sensing that the meeting was coming to a close.

"It's more likely that they would have found us," Timmins muttered as he pushed his chair in, the heavy wood scraping across the stone floor.

Helena was inclined to agree, especially given their history of sneaking up on her. "Well, either way."

He gave her a small smile and made his way toward the door. "I'll go find Effie and let her know what we are planning."

"Thank you."

The men filtered out until only Von was left. He tugged on her braid, leaning over to kiss her once before heading out. "I think a couple of the Talyrians should come with us."

That reminded her of something she'd been meaning to ask him.

"Speaking of Talyrians… does Starshine seem to be acting strange to you?"

Von stopped and lifted a brow. "You mean more than usual?"

Helena bit her lip. "I don't know what it is, but she seems more… restless? Agitated? I'm not sure, just more something since we've returned from Vyruul."

"Perhaps having her pride in that kind of danger upset her."

"Mmm, perhaps," she murmured.

"You think it's something else?"

Helena shrugged. "The pride has been in hiding. No one has been allowed to see them, not even me. Starshine actually growled at me when I tried to visit them yesterday."

Von tried not to laugh at the childlike offense his Mate had clearly taken to the rebuff.

"Do you think one of the pride has been injured and that's why she doesn't want anyone around? She's protecting them?"

It was Von's turn to shrug. "She's a Queen, it seems like something she would do. Hell, it's something that *you* would do. Perhaps you should try again. If one of them is harmed, Starshine may not want to leave them."

Helena frowned. The thought of something happening to one of those beautiful creatures had her stomach churning. She should have paid closer attention, but she'd been distracted by Miranda's death and then Effie's vision. There hadn't been any free time to spend with the Talyrian Queen, which was why she hadn't had a chance to go see her before yesterday. Helena intended to remedy that oversight and try again with a bit more insistence today.

"Good idea, I'll go down there now."

"Want me to come with you?" he offered.

"No, I don't think so. I want to give them as few reasons as possible to turn me away. Another human might tip the scales against me."

He nodded. "Let me know if you need me."

"I always need you." She smiled.

His eyes glowed with silver fire. "Likewise, my love."

With a wink, he was gone, and Helena went to make good on her promise.

LEAVES CRACKLED underneath her boots as Helena made her way into the series of caves the Talyrians had claimed as their own. It was only a short hike away from the Palace, the main entry just off a bubbling brook that wound its way through her gardens and into a small knot of trees. Prior to her travels, Helena would have considered the trees a forest in their own right, but after experiencing the Forest of Whispers, and even Bael, she knew the description did not ring true.

She purposely made as much noise as possible, not wanting the Talyrians to feel as though she was sneaking up on them. Given that their hearing was likely far superior to her own, she did not think it was necessary, but she didn't want to take any chances.

From the moody swipe of Starshine's tail when Helena approached the cave entrance, it would seem she had made the right decision.

"Hello, my beautiful girl."

Starshine snorted, plumes of smoke rising from her snout.

"Is that any way to greet your friend?" Helena asked, keeping her voice light. She held up her empty hands to signal her intention.

Starshine's turquoise eyes tracked the movement. The only sign of the creature's unease was the nervous flick of her tail.

Helena noted the twitch, but carried on anyway. She took two tentative steps forward, her back stiffening as Starshine bared her teeth and began to growl low in her throat. Knowing she was treading on dangerous ground, Helena stopped entirely.

"Is it all humans that you are mad at, or is it just me?"

Starshine whined and pawed the air, her massive claws sheathed but still deadly.

Helena wasn't sure how to interpret that answer.

"Did something happen to one of the pride?" she asked in a soft voice.

From the drop of Starshine's head at the question, Helena could only infer that she was correct.

"Are they injured? Would you like me to help?"

Starshine huffed, a low angry sound.

Helena swallowed. The Talyrian had never done anything to threaten her before, and while the actions Starshine made were mildly aggressive, Helena did not think they were aimed at her specifically.

"Did... did someone not survive the attack?" she asked in a horrified whisper, for it was the only thing she could think of that would provoke this kind of hostility.

Starshine opened her mouth and roared. Heat blasted against Helena as Starshine's breath rushed over her, causing her cloak and hair to fly back.

Helena's hands were shaking as she held them up again. "I'm so sorry," she whispered brokenly, closing the distance between them and wrapping her arms around Starshine's neck.

The Talyrian tolerated the embrace, but her velvety body was practically vibrating with tension.

"I didn't know. I'm so sorry, girl."

Starshine let out another huff that sounded more like a whimper.

"We will make her pay for this, you have my promise."

At her words, Starshine seemed to relax, finally pressing some of her weight against Helena's body.

Helena pulled away slightly, wanting to be able to look into the Talyrian's eyes as she spoke. "That is part of why I came to visit. We are trying to track that evil bitch and her minions down. I know that you are in mourning, but I would like for you to come with us."

There was nothing to signal what Starshine thought of her words until the massive head dipped in what would have passed for a nod on a human.

Relief filled her, and Helena allowed herself a sharp smile. "I cannot promise you that I will let you repay her kindness in kind."

Starshine's eyes narrowed and she snarled softly.

"You can have anyone else, my beautiful girl. But Rowena's death belongs to me."

The words were infused with her power, her body making the small transformations that tied her so closely to the creature beside her.

Starshine inspected Helena, appreciating the signs of the predator she saw before her.

There was another huff, and Helena knew that the Talyrian had agreed. With that settled, all they needed now was to find her.

Then they could both take their revenge.

CHAPTER 19

"I'm sorry that this was the best we were able to do, Kiri," Reyna said as they ducked beneath a low vine.

Helena laughed. "There's no reason to apologize, Reyna. This is still better than what I would have been able to accomplish."

The Night Stalkers had been familiar with Bael, but only to a certain extent. Large parts of the jungle were off limits to them, keeping them out with very powerful magical barriers. They knew only of the Keeper's Catacombs in theory, having a rough idea of where they might be located given the presence of the barriers. Even still, their guess was a better starting point than what Helena would have been able to offer as it got them straight into the heart of the jungle, thereby saving days of travel on foot.

If the others were tired of bouncing around Elysia in search of Rowena, they gave no indication. If anything, her army seemed more determined than ever.

Ronan moved into place beside her, his handsome face grim as he studied their surroundings.

"Need something?" she asked.

Ronan's eyes cut to hers. "Not specifically, but being here again has me on edge."

Helena couldn't help but notice that Reyna was staring resolutely ahead, completely ignoring the exchange.

"Did I miss something?" Helena asked Von.

"You didn't hear?" Von asked in surprise.

"Considering my question, I think you can safely surmise the answer."

She felt his chuckle as if he was standing right behind her. *"When Reyna learned what happened with the Air General, she ran up to him and slapped him across the face."*

"Wait... what?" Helena stopped dead in her place, her mouth hanging open in shock. *"How in the Mother's name did I miss that?"*

"It happened while you were dealing with other things. I just thought you knew."

"Why did she slap him?"

Von sounded darkly amused as he replied, *"I think her words were something to the effect of 'I didn't risk my life saving you once so that you could go ahead and hand it over at the next opportunity.'"*

"That sounds reasonable," Helena said, her lips turning up in a smile. *"I wish I could have been there to see it."*

"It was fairly memorable, to say the least. I don't think anyone has ever dared to put Ronan in his place like that before."

"What did Ronan have to say about it?"

"Well, at first he sort of glared at her—"

"As Ronan is prone to do."

Von laughed, and the feeling of his mirth filled her with warmth. *"Exactly. But instead of laying into her, as he would have anyone else, he just apologized and watched her storm off."*

"How very interesting."

"Don't you go and start meddling. Those two need to work out whatever is between them on their own."

"I never meddle."

Von's silence was as damning as anything he could have possibly said.

"I don't!" she insisted.

Realizing that Ronan and Reyna had stopped a few feet away while waiting for her to catch up, she rushed forward. "Sorry, distracted."

"Clearly," Ronan said, his jaw clenched. "Do try to pay more attention, Helena. Need I remind you what happened last time you went for a walk here?"

"I don't like your tone," she informed him primly, not appreciating his insinuation on top of the one Von had just given her.

"I don't care."

Helena huffed, ready to remind him who served who when Reyna spun toward her Shield.

"Don't you have something better to do?" she snapped, her eyes like glittering emeralds.

"Something more important than keeping my Kiri safe? No, I don't. I'm the Shield, that's literally my number one priority."

Reyna let out a cold laugh. "Oh, is that what you were doing? It sounded more like you were trying to bully her."

Ronan's blue eyes went wide. "What the hell would you know about it, Night Stalker?"

"As the only other one of us that rules, I would assume a hell of a lot more than you."

"Keep your eyes open," Ronan snapped, his jaw clenched as he turned and walked back to the others.

There was a long moment of silence until Helena finally broke it by asking, "So, you and Ronan, huh?"

Reyna shot wide eyes at Helena before wisps of shadow began to roll up her neck, almost like she was trying to conceal herself behind them. It was an interesting way to blush.

"Listen, you two are adults. I'm less concerned about what you do together and more worried about how it affects him. Ronan is one of the most selflessly loyal men I have ever known. If all you are interested in is toying with him, then you should leave it alone."

"Toying with him?" Reyna repeated. "Not that it's any of your business—"

"He's my Shield, his well-being is very much my business. As much as I like you Night Stalker, if you hurt him, you will have to answer to me."

Reyna's mouth was still open like she wanted to say something, but she closed it when she realized Helena's eyes had turned into sparkling iridescence.

"Fair enough."

Helena nodded, and the two continued to walk in silence.

"You wouldn't call that meddling?" Von asked.

"It was a warning."

"Ronan is perfectly capable of taking care of himself."

"I just watched him piece himself together after the last woman broke his heart. I'm not going to stand idly by and watch it happen again."

"I don't think Reyna's the type of woman who would be that careless, knowing who he belongs to."

"Nor do I, but sometimes a reminder can be useful in resetting one's priorities."

She could hear Von's laugh from somewhere behind her. *"So was it a warning or a reminder?"*

"Why can't it be both?"

"Ronan is lucky to have such a fierce protector."

"He would do the same for me."

"Given that I am the one who would be on the other side of the threats, I am not entirely sure how to feel about that."

Helena smirked. *"You planning on doing something that requires threats?"*

"Not at the moment, but you never know. Forever is a long time; I'm bound to do something stupid eventually."

"Noted. I'll ask Ronan to keep his eyes peeled, just in case he sees an opportunity to give you a good reminder."

"Mother save me. Knowing Ronan, he's going to start coming up with reasons to crawl up my ass and then use protecting you as an excuse to get away with it."

They were both snickering when they came upon a wide clearing that was surrounded on three sides by a burbling stream. Helena glanced toward the sky, or what little of it she could see.

"We should probably set up camp here for the night. We'll send scouts ahead to see if they can find the first of the barriers so we know how close we are come morning."

There were a few shouts of agreement as others set to work.

Dinner had been a quiet affair. A large part of it probably had to do with their diminished size, but Helena knew it also had something to do with the fact that they were all on high alert. Once again, she was traveling with only a select few of her guard plus a small retinue of Reyna's Night Stalkers. Anduin and the Storm Forged had remained behind with the rest of the army at the Palace, ready to call them back if Rowena struck there, or to join Helena if she called for him.

The entire group was scattered around a fire, having just finished off a rabbit and vegetable stew that Effie had prepared for them. How she'd managed to make something so delicious with limited resources was beyond impressive.

"It was amazing, Effie!" Helena said, using a bit of magic to clean the dish before returning the bowl and spoon to her pack.

The rest of them gave satisfied murmurs of agreement.

"Thank you," she beamed. "It was nice to have a familiar task to focus on for a while."

Effie was just settling into place beside Helena when a startled shout had everyone jumping up.

"Sorry everyone! False alarm," a red-faced Daejaran said. "It was just a spider. Caught the little fucker climbing up my neck and I over reacted. You can all stand down."

Helena let out a relieved laugh, glad that she hadn't been the one to have an eight-legged friend crawling all over her. Turning to Effie, to see if she shared in the amusement, Helena let out a startled cry of her own.

897

Effie's blue eyes had rolled back into her head, and she had already started convulsing.

Helena rolled her onto her side and did what she could to keep her from hurting herself.

"What should we do?" Reyna asked.

"I don't think there's anything we can do," Helena murmured, wincing in sympathy as her friend was lost to her vision.

"She just has to ride it out," Timmins added.

Helena discretely wiped away the drool that had started to run from Effie's mouth, her skin feeling like ice beneath her fingers. She had no idea how long the vision lasted, it felt like hours as her friend's body spasmed although it was probably less than a minute in total.

Once she began to still, and it was just small twinges in her arms and legs, Effie's eyes fluttered open. The whites of her eyes were bloodshot, and a small trail of blood was dripping out of her mouth from where she must have bit down on her cheek.

"Do you think you can sit up?" Helena asked in a low voice.

Effie groaned.

"It's okay; take all the time you need. There's no rush."

Effie's pupils were fully dilated, only the barest trace of blue ringing around the swollen black pupils. She still didn't seem to be entirely present.

Looking at her with a healer's curiosity, Helena pressed the palm of her hand into Effie's forehead. Perhaps she could help speed up her friend's recovery by easing the pain the vision had caused.

Helena closed her eyes and pushed a small tendril of power into the newest Keeper.

"Helena, wait!"

She wasn't sure whose voice it was, perhaps it was many, but it didn't matter. As soon as Helena's power flowed into Effie's body, the damage was already done.

Instead of Helena being able to seek out and sever the final ties of the vision, the vision sank its claws into her, sucking her down into its final haunting scenes.

At first, Helena wasn't sure what was happening. The world had become entirely muted, everything cast in shades of gray. It wasn't until she realized that she was no longer kneeling in the clearing that she understood where she was.

"Effie?" she called, but no noise left her mouth. It seemed that she could only bear witness to the events unfolding before her, not interact with them.

Helena looked around, trying to make sense of what was happening. There was nothing she immediately recognized about her surroundings. It looked like she was sitting in the center of a massive web, each shimmering tendril trembling as if caught in the middle of a storm. She could not see far enough to determine what had anchored the web, it seemed to span out as far as she could see in every direction.

An ice-blue spider appeared and began to make its way carefully across the shaking web. It chittered, seeming excited by what it had trapped. Nervous, Helena tried to move out of the center of the web, not wanting to be there when the spider inevitably reached the center.

The more she tried to free herself from the sticky strings, the more hopelessly entangled she became, until eventually, she was fully encased in the silky strands. It wasn't until the ghostly twilight of the world went dark and she was completely encased in darkness that Helena began to scream.

IT WAS the sound of her screams the sent him running, his pants only hastily half-laced. Von had stepped away to water some plants, certain that the others could keep his Mate safe in the handful of seconds he would be out of sight. He was already plotting Ronan's murder for allowing whatever it was to put that level of fear in her voice.

"You have one fucking job, you bastard," he muttered darkly. Logically, he knew Ronan was not to blame for whatever was happening, but having a target to direct his anger toward was infinitely better than the alternative.

He blinked his way back, not paying attention to anything other than where the trees were, since he didn't think it would feel too good randomly appearing right in the middle of one. It took him all of three seconds to make the journey back to their camp, his heart somewhere in the vicinity of his throat the entire time.

When he burst through the last of the vines, he saw Effie curled into the fetal position, Timmins whispering in her ear, and Helena curled into Ronan's arms, her entire body shaking.

"Somebody tell me what the fuck is going on, right the fuck now," he ordered, his voice filled with deadly menace. Anyone that knew him, knew better than to ignore the threat barely concealed within the words. He was on the edge of reason, a heartbeat away from grabbing his weapon and asking questions later.

Surprisingly, it was Reyna who answered.

"Helena was trying to help Effie. Another of her visions was triggered, and it looked like she was finally past the worst of it when Helena touched her. The vision must have pulled your Mate in, one second she was in control of her body, the next she was slumped over the Keeper."

Von's eyes narrowed, not liking that his enemy was something he could not battle. He moved through the others to Helena, carefully pulling her from Ronan's grasp and lifting her in his arms. Her scream had terrified him more than he'd like to admit, and right now, feeling her against him was as much for him as it was for her.

"I'm right here, Mira," he told her. *"You're safe."*

Her tremors began to subside almost immediately. She pulled away, looking sheepish. "I'm not entirely certain what happened."

"It looks like you were drawn into Effie's vision," Ronan said, his voice even although his eyes were wild.

"That's what it felt like," she agreed, her voice not quite steady.

"Is that normal?" Von asked, seeking out Timmins, who usually had the answers for this kind of thing.

Timmins shrugged. "When it comes to the Keepers, there's very little that is known."

Von frowned. "Are you all right?" he asked Helena, who still seemed paler than he would have liked.

She nodded. "I think so. I couldn't even tell you what it was that had me so scared. I just knew that if I stayed there one more second it would have been the end of me." She shuddered, her tongue darting out to lick her lips.

"I felt it too," Effie croaked. Their heads all turned toward her.

"Did you See what I did?" Helena asked.

Effie shrugged. "I wasn't aware of you at all, so I don't know."

"Can you tell the rest of us what you Saw?" Timmins asked.

Effie swayed where she sat. "I can try."

"If you need awhile to recover..." Helena started.

She shook her head. "It's all right. I'd rather get this over with."

"Was it like before?" Kragen asked.

At the same time, Ronan asked, "Did you see Rowena again?"

Effie shook her head. "No. It wasn't like before. I didn't See any people this time."

"If you didn't See people, then what did you See?" Helena asked.

Effie's eyes narrowed as she searched for the words to describe her vision. "It felt more abstract this time. It wasn't as if I was watching a scene as it was happening, like with Rowena and the Endoshan. This time, it was like the images were all a metaphor." She stopped, looking confused. "I'm sorry, I'm not sure how to explain it."

"It's okay, dear. Why don't you just start by telling us what the images were," Timmins said with a kind smile.

Effie nodded, still looking the worse for wear. "At first there was smoke, the kind that you see just after a fire goes out. It was thick and gray; everything was gray."

Von found his eyes moving to Helena, who was silently nodding along with Effie's words.

"After the smoke cleared, all I could see was a web. It was beautiful and so elaborate. Each strand was unique, both in color and in its substance. I found myself wanting to pluck one, knowing that it would show me who or what the strand represented, but I couldn't. At first each strand twinkled with its own separate life, but then the longer I stared, the more they blended until I could no longer tell where one began and another ended." The words were coming out in a rush, and Effie had to pause to catch her breath.

Helena moved out of his arms and sat beside Effie, her hand reaching out to hold the other woman's in a show of solidarity.

Effie smiled at her gratefully before continuing. "Something changed then. It felt like the air contracted, becoming almost heavier. There was chanting, but I couldn't tell if it was one voice or many. The words were coming too fast for me to be able to make any sense of them. That was when I noticed that something was trapped in the center of the web. It thrashed wildly, trying to escape, but only managed to get itself more helplessly tangled in the strands."

Helena let out a gasp. "It was me."

All eyes turned toward her. Helena put her hand up to her mouth and shook her head. "I'm sorry, Effie. Please continue."

Effie blinked, seeming confused by the interruption, but she nodded after a moment and finished her recounting. "Once the victim was fully cocooned in the strands, a spider appeared. It was the palest blue, almost the color of snow, and it had odd markings along its head and body. It was excited by its catch and was eagerly making its way to the middle of the web to see what it had caught. That's where it ended."

Some of the color was starting to return to Effie's face now that she had completed her tale, but while she was looking more normal, Helena was deathly white.

"What did you mean 'It was me'?" Von asked, his arms crossed over his chest.

Helena looked up at him with worried aqua eyes. "When I tried to heal Effie, my power must have latched onto hers. I saw the last moments of the vision, but from a different vantage. I," Helena faltered, taking a shaky breath. Effie squeezed her hand, her eyes shining with understanding. Helena's words sounded forced as she continued, "I was in the center of the web. I tried to break free, but I couldn't. Then I saw the spider, it was beautiful and deadly. I knew if it reached me, I was dead. I started struggling harder, and all of a sudden the world went completely dark. That's when... that's when I started screaming."

Von felt icy fingers move along his spine. He did not pretend to understand he knew what the vision was supposed to represent, but it was clear that Helena and Rowena both played a part. And based on the two retellings of the vision, it certainly did not appear that things were about to go in their favor.

"What do you think it means?" Joquil asked, flames dancing in his eyes as he stared at the women from across the fire.

Helena and Effie shared a glance. Helena shrugged, and Effie opened her mouth to answer. "I think the web represents a trap, one that it takes many people to create."

"The trap must be for me," Helena said.

"Given that you were in the center of it, I'm inclined to agree," Timmins murmured.

"Isn't that too obvious?" Von protested, desperate to find a different explanation.

"What would you say that means?" Kragen asked, and not unkindly.

Von shrugged. "I don't know, maybe Helena is at the center because she is the one who sets the trap."

Ronan's worried eyes found his. "Why then is she the one that was caught in it? And why would someone else be the spider?"

"The spider was Rowena," Helena said, her voice stronger and more sure than it had been until now.

Von thought so too. The coloring the two women described sounded very much like the cold eyes that had found him in most of his nightmares.

The group fell silent, no one sure what to think.

"Do you think it was a warning?" Effie asked hopefully. "Something sent to me now so we could be on guard and avoid it?"

"Aren't we on guard already?" Helena asked with a humorless laugh.

"If the vision is of the future, then the events have not yet passed and can therefore be changed," Timmins said.

Helena looked up at him. "So you're an expert on prophecy now?"

Timmins's cheeks went pink, but he did not respond.

Helena groaned. "I'm sorry. I do not mean to be so surly, it's just… if the vision is the future, then that means I'm destined to be caught in that web. Which feels like it means I'm destined to fail."

"There is always more than one way to interpret a vision, Kiri."

The spectral voice spoke in his mind and had his hand reaching for his weapon. The sound of surprised gasps and weapons being drawn met his ears as Von looked for the source of the voice that had spoken in his mind.

"I told you our new daughter would come to us."

"Her power is strong and yet still untested."

"She needs to learn how to properly harness her gift."

"It will come with time."

As the voices continued to speak, three robed figures entered the clearing. Von would like to say it was a relief to see them, but he'd be lying. On the bright side, they no longer had to spend the next few days wandering around aimlessly because their mission had just been accomplished. At least, in a manner of speaking.

They may not have found the Keepers, but the Keepers had just found them.

CHAPTER 20

Her Circle remained on guard as Helena pushed herself up to stand on shaky legs. "Good evening, Triumvirate. To what do we owe this unexpected visit?" she asked, erring on the side of formality.

"You were the one that sought us out, were you not?"

"Why then the surprise when you found us?"

As always, Helena could not tell which of the three figures were speaking to her. Thankfully, their hoods remained firmly in place, and she did not have to worry about staring into their sightless eyes. Or rather, the place where their eyes had once been.

"Well, to be frank. Technically we did not find you. Therein lies the element of surprise."

There were a few snickers of amusement, but the others soon lapsed back to silence.

Helena sighed, realizing she would not get very far with sarcasm and these men. "We were seeking your aid, yes."

"And here we are."

"You seem troubled, Kiri."

"I am," Helena admitted. "The events of the last few weeks are weighing on me heavily."

"You speak of our daughter's death."

Helena nodded. "In part." She couldn't help wondering if they used the term daughter literally, although given that they had already used the label twice referring to two different individuals, she thought it unlikely.

"It was foretold."

"No one can escape the hour of their passing."

"It is as much a part of life as breathing."

"Even so, it was a devastating loss."

"To return to the Mother is a blessing, Kiri."

"You of all people should know that."

Helena bristled. "Death is never easy on those that are left behind."

"Perhaps."

It was disorienting trying to have a conversation with three separate entities that spoke as though they were one. The voices filled her mind with absolutely no indication of where they were coming from. Helena did her best to look at and speak to all of them, although perhaps focusing on the center figure would have been enough. He did seem to be their leader.

Effie rose to stand at her side. "Are you here for me?" she demanded. Her chin was tilted up, an act that portrayed defiant strength, although her small frame continued to tremble.

The three heads swiveled in perfect synchronicity to look at her. *"One could argue daughter, that you are here for us."*

"Stop calling me that," Effie said through gritted teeth. "The only parents I had are long dead."

Helena placed a hand on Effie's arm. The movement was a reminder of support, not a call to be silent. Effie censored herself anyway, taking a deep breath.

"Can you help us?" Helena asked, pulling their unnerving attention back to her.

"It is not our place to interfere, only to act as witnesses."

"And guides," Helena reminded them.

The central figure shrugged. *"When it suits us."*

"And staving off the potential genocide of the Chosen doesn't suit you?" Helena's eyes were narrowed in dangerous slits.

"You misunderstand, Kiri. We see many paths, all of which hang off a number of various choices to be made by many individuals."

"To tip the balance could disrupt everything and cause the worst possible outcome."

"We cannot interfere."

Helena huffed. It was sound logic, but it didn't make her feel any better at the moment.

"So how do you know when to step in?" Effie asked, her head tilted like a curious cat.

"When it is the only option."

"And now?" Von asked. "Is it the only option now?"

There was a subtle shake of their heads. *"No."*

"There are still choices that must be made."

"But what of my visions?" Effie asked. "Do they not show us what will come to pass?"

"Our gifts are not always supposed to be shared, daughter."

"The misinterpretation of a single one could be treacherous."

"It takes years before one knows how to interpret them with any measure of accuracy."

Helena watched Effie's back straighten at their words, her spine going rigid and her shoulders lifting until they were up around her ears. She was clearly worried about damage she may have caused bringing them to Endoshan.

"I didn't know," she whispered mournfully.

That is enough of that, Helena thought, having no desire for the woman to beat herself up over something that was hardly her fault. "Well, the fact of the matter is that the vision was not just shared, it was also experienced by another. Namely, me. You might as well lend your insights before I make a categorically terrible decision based off what was Seen. You know what my failure means."

Without being able to see their expressions, Helena could not truly know what reaction her words had caused, but there was an unmistakable aura of annoyance rolling off of the trio.

"Very well, Kiri."

"It seems that you leave us with no choice."

Helena could feel Von's mirth, and she shot him a startled glance. *"What is there to possibly be laughing at right now?"* she asked through their bond.

"It seems you found the answer on how to force their hand."

"I did?"

Von's eyes glowed with his amusement. *"Unintentional meddling."*

Helena scowled, rolling her eyes and dismissing him.

"Come here, daughter."

Effie's trembling increased, and she clasped her hands in front of her to try to disguise her nerves.

"You have nothing to fear from us."

"To begin, we must See what you Saw."

"I could just tell you," she offered. "You know, from here."

Ronan placed his hand on her shoulder. Effie looked up at him with scared blue eyes.

"Your retelling will be inaccurate."

"No detail is too small."

"The only way to truly Know is to experience."

Helena could feel the 'I told you so' ready to spring from Timmins lips even from where she was standing.

"It's all right, Effie. We're all right here. We won't let anything bad happen to you," Helena promised.

Ronan reinforced her words with a nod of his own. Ever since Darrin's death, Effie had found comfort in her Shield's imposing presence. It was likely a side effect of what they'd experienced together on the battlefield when Darrin died before their eyes. Either way, Helena couldn't fault her. She knew all too well how important it was to have a safe harbor when one felt like they were drowning. Ronan had been that for her as well while Von had been imprisoned.

Effie swallowed and walked over to the hooded figures. Helena knew it was one of the hardest things she'd had to do. Nothing about the trio was particularly reassuring.

"What do I need to do?" she asked.

"Just close your eyes."

Helena was grateful that the Triumvirate was still choosing to speak in a manner that allowed them all to listen. She was intimately aware of the fact that they could be selective about who they allowed to hear their psychic voices.

Helena could feel the tension emanating from her Circle, without needing to access their strengthened connection through her Jaka. She could feel it, because it was an extension of her own.

The figure in the middle lifted his arm, his tattooed hand with its shifting blue markings revealed as the long sleeves of his robe fell back. He placed his hand on the center of Effie's forehead, very similar to what Helena had done when she'd intended to heal her.

Effie inhaled audibly, and then her head fell back. Her arms dangled uselessly at her sides and her knees buckled, but she did not fall. For all that he was only touching her head, the Keeper seemed to have a firm grasp on her.

There were several tense heartbeats as the Triumvirate did whatever it was they needed to do. Helena knew it was over when Effie sucked in a deep breath, sounding like it was the first she'd had since they'd started. The Keeper released her, and she stumbled forward. He caught her by the shoulders before she could knock him over, setting her unceremoniously back on her feet.

"Was that it?" Effie rasped, eager to move back to the others.

The Triumvirate nodded, and she did nothing to disguise her hurried retreat to the safety of her friends.

"So what does it mean?" Helena asked, bracing herself for the blow.

"Why ask when you already know, Kiri?"

Of all the things for them to say, that was not what she was expecting. True, she had a feeling she knew, but she was desperately hoping she'd been wrong.

"But I don't know. Not for sure. Miranda always warned me visions were never straightforward." Helena was starting to feel like that was her new mantra, she was holding on to the belief that the words were true.

"They rarely are, but that does not mean that you do not already have everything you need to guide you to the correct answer."

"I need you!" she shouted, her annoyance at their intentional opaqueness and the strain of everything else coming to a head.

"Look within yourself for the answer, Kiri."

"We can offer no further help here."

"Mother's tits!" Helena shouted, throwing her hands into the air. Someone had better start giving her a straight answer soon or she was going to start flinging fireballs and to the hell with them all.

"Helena might have what she needs, but I don't," Effie said, her voice no less strong for its softness.

The Triumvirate were silent as they contemplated her words.

"We cannot risk revealing our secrets to you while you remain with them."

"What the hell is that supposed to mean?" Helena raged.

"It is as we already said."

"We cannot interfere."

"Our daughter's ties to you are too strong."

"She would not be able to resist sharing what she learned."

"And in doing so, she could do more harm than good."

"I can keep a fucking secret!" Effie blurted out, surprising them all with her vehemence. "It was my thrice-damned vision, I deserve to know what it means."

"And you will."

"Should you come with us."

That stopped them all short.

"Come with you?" Effie repeated dumbstruck. She looked around at the others, her face draining of color.

"It's the only way for you to learn, daughter."

"You know we speak the truth."

Helena swallowed back her protests, knowing that this was a choice Effie needed to make for herself. As much as she desired answers, she would not get in the way of her friend's destiny.

"But I…" Effie started. "What about the war?"

Helena took Effie's hand, pulling her attention. "There are many ways to fight. Not all of them involve a battlefield."

"If I'm gone, I cannot help you. I won't be able to avenge them," she whispered, her voice wavering with unshed tears.

"Who's to say that's not exactly where you're supposed to be? The Mother has plans for us all, Effie. Maybe that is where you have to go to finish the fight."

Effie wanted to protest, but she could not deny the ring of truth in Helena's words. "Is that what you would choose, Helena?"

Helena shook her head, not wanting to sway her in either direction.

"Please," Effie begged.

"Isn't that the choice I already made? It wasn't long ago someone came to fetch me."

The reference to Darrin seemed to bring a sense of peace. All trace of sadness and doubt vanished, and Effie nodded resolutely. "You're right. If this is the path set before me, I should follow it. I do not want to risk your lives with my ignorance. We've already had a taste of what that is like."

"Effie," Helena said, shaking her head.

"No, it's all right." She turned toward the Triumvirate. "I will go with you. But I would like to spend the night with my friends to say goodbye, if that's all right. Can you come for me in the morning?"

"Yes."

"We could see her off," Helena offered. "If you tell us where to bring her."

"The Catacombs are not for your eyes, Kiri."

"They are the sacred place of the Keepers."

"Only those with the gift have ever stepped foot within."

Helena wanted to throw her title in their faces and demand that they let her go, but she knew it was futile. Her fight was elsewhere.

"Can we not visit?" Ronan asked.

"This goodbye will not be forever."

"Our daughter will let you know when she is ready to see you again."

"Your messages will always find their way to her."

Feeling somewhat better at the news, Helena loosed a shaky breath.

"Until tomorrow then," Effie said, surprising the rest of them with her dismissal.

The Triumvirate did not respond, they merely turned and disappeared back into the forest from whence they'd came.

CHAPTER 21

"Well, shit," Ronan said.

"I think that sums it up nicely," Von said dryly.

"What the fuck are we supposed to do with that? Not only are they refusing to explain what the vision means, they're also taking away the source of the vision, so we have absolutely no fucking idea what lies ahead," Ronan sputtered.

"How's that any different from where we were before?" Helena asked, amused at her Shield's unexpected rant. She knew why she was upset, but she hadn't expected him to feel the same.

"Well, it's not, but… they were supposed to help us, damn it!" Ronan was fuming.

Helena couldn't help herself, her shoulders began to shake with barely suppressed laughter.

"You're laughing?" he asked as the rest of the group joined in. "How can you laugh at a time like this?" Seeing that they had no intention of stopping any time soon, he threw his hands up in the air. "This is a load of steaming wolf shit and you know it!"

"I'm sorry," Helena hiccupped, wiping a tear from her eye. "It's not that I disagree, it's just this is all par for the course, wouldn't you say? Of course the people that can decipher the vision refuse to tell us what it means. These are the same men," Helena paused, wondering for the first time if the Triumvirate were in fact all male. That was a mystery for another day. Waving away the thought, she continued, "That like to give me warnings by terrorizing me."

"I'm sorry, Kiri. I had hoped given what's at stake that they would be more forthcoming," Timmins said on a sigh.

"It's not your fault," she said.

During all of this, Effie remained quiet.

"I'm sorry," Helena said, instantly sobering. "It's not too late to change your mind. If you'd rather not go with them—"

"No. They're right. I'm no use to anybody until I learn how to understand these visions. Besides, it can't possibly be normal for them to affect me as they do. Perhaps they can help me fight the side effects."

Helena pressed her lips together. "You have a home with us any time you desire. You might be a Keeper, Effie, but you will always be one of us."

Effie's lower lip quavered but she fought back her tears. "Thank you, Helena. I will hold you to that."

That much settled, Kragen directed them back to the matter at hand. "So what do you think they meant, you 'have everything you need to guide you to the correct answer'?"

"Precisely that, I'd gather," Timmins said, rubbing his eyes.

Kragen rolled his. "Thanks for that illuminating contribution, Advisor. As always, your insights prove invaluable."

Timmins shrugged. "Not every nugget is going to be perfection. Sometimes one can only work with what's in front of them."

Helena groaned. "They clearly believe that I do not require any outside input to arrive at the correct conclusion. That means that I just need to decipher the clues based on what I already know to be true."

"So how long do you think this is going to take? Ten, twenty minutes?" Ronan drawled, his lips curling into a sarcastic smile.

If only she felt that confident in her ability to rationalize everything out. The only reason she'd been able to connect the dots on Effie's previous vision is because it'd come to pass first, and they'd been able to work backwards. There was no way that particular approach was going to help them again this time.

"At least," Helena replied, wrinkling her nose at him. "Prick."

Ronan gave her a mocking bow. "I live to serve, Kiri."

Helena snorted. "A little more serving and a little less sarcasm, if you will."

Her Shield winked. "What reason could you possibly have to keep me around if I turned so predictable? It's not like you require a second Advisor!"

The other Circle members laughed as Timmins began to clap in long, drawn-out movements. "Your wit sir, is legendary."

The conversation was rapidly devolving, and Helena knew that if she didn't step in fast, they'd lose the thread entirely. "All right, all right. You can tease Timmins later. Right now we have a vision to interpret."

Effie shuffled forward, her hands nervously playing with the front of her dress. "Perhaps I should go pack my things. From what they said, I don't want to unduly influence your assessment."

Helena frowned. "Don't you think that they would have insisted on your going with them immediately, if they were truly worried about it?"

The blonde woman's face brightened considerably. "You're right! Carry on then."

One by one the group settled into place around the campfire. In another time or place, Helena could have simply been regaling them with ghost stories. She yearned for such a day and such simple pleasures.

Von sat directly across from her, his blade brother on one side and his blood brother on the other. Serena sat on the floor between Nial's legs, while Reyna and Ryder chose spots next to Ronan, who lifted a brow at the choice but provided no further comment. Kragen, Timmins, and Joquil took the spots beside Nial, filling in that side of the semi-circle and leaving the rest of the group to sit beside the Night Stalkers. Starshine, who had been off hunting for her dinner, chose that moment to stalk quietly into their camp and take a seat behind her Mate.

Von lifted a hand to rub her in greeting, but she bared her fangs at him. "Or not," he muttered, his hand falling back to his side.

Some things never change. Even in times of chaos, people were just people. It was an uplifting thought. Helena's eyes moved over the group, her heart feeling full. They were faced with the biggest threat the Chosen had to deal with, and yet they still found a way to hold on to their humanity. Her eyes fell on Ronan; they teased. On Reyna; they flirted. On the newly mated Nial and Serena; they loved. The Mother's Chosen were not as fragile as they appeared. For all that their lives could be taken in less time than it took to draw a full breath, so too could they live. It was a beautiful thing, this ability to adapt and endure.

Feeling inspired, Helena turned to Effie, who was standing beside her. "Shall we try this again?"

"What would you like me to do?"

"Well let's talk it out, starting with what we think we know."

"The spider obviously represents Rowena," Von said, not wasting any time.

Helena nodded. "I'm inclined to agree. It's my feeling that the color of spider matched the same cold color of her eyes. And only Rowena would get that much pleasure out of trapping someone."

"That was my thought as well," Effie said.

"Very well, I think we can accept that as fact and move forward."

Unfortunately, that was the first and only fact on which they agreed. The group talked well into the night, each minute detail of the vision hashed out with no further understanding of what it represented.

"But the web is clearly a trap left by the spider, who in this case we all agree is Rowena!" Joquil shouted in exasperation.

"If each strand is a separate individual, those must indicate the Chosen. Rowena's followers lack that kind of diversity," Timmins said as he paced around the fire.

"The Chosen would never agree to be part of such a scheme!" Effie insisted.

"Who says they have a choice? Rowena is a gifted manipulator," Von said.

On and on it went, until she couldn't take it anymore. The longer Helena listened to the other's talk, the more certain she became that she alone would find the answer. For all that her friends were her resources, the truth of the vision lied within her.

"Enough," Helena said wearily. "We've come up with several possible solutions, none of which feel quite right. I'm sure we're on to something, but we may as well get some sleep and try again with fresh perspectives in the morning."

Her words had a sobering effect as the group remembered what the morning would bring.

"She's right," Von said, pushing himself to a standing position. "We aren't getting anywhere; we might as well call it a night."

There were a few murmurs of agreement as people began to make their way to their tents. Effie remained behind.

"I'll wait for you inside," Von said, gesturing to the tent they would share.

"I'll be right there," Helena said with a thankful smile.

"I'm sorry I couldn't be more helpful, Helena. I really wanted to be the one that gave you what you needed to defeat that evil bitch." For all her venom, Effie still reminded Helena of a kitten that had just discovered its claws. The thought made her smile.

"Who's to say that you haven't? Just because you couldn't solve the riddle doesn't mean that you haven't given me the answer."

Effie looked down as she considered the words. "I hope so."

"One way or another, I will find my answer, and I hope," Helena said, her hand reaching out to touch Effie's arm, "that you find yours as well."

One side of Effie's mouth lifted in a wry smile. "Who can say? With the way those three communicate, you never know what you're going to end up with."

Helena laughed. "How very, very true."

When Helena had fallen silent, Effie met her eyes head on and said, "I guess this is it then."

"We will have time in the morning—"

"You and I both know that they will arrive for me long before you wake. They gave me tonight, but they did not promise me the morning," Effie said, cutting her off.

She was right. Helena sighed. "Did you not want to say goodbye to the others?"

Effie shook her head. "I've said enough goodbyes for now. I have no intention of saying it again anytime soon."

Helena tilted her head. "It isn't really goodbye, you know. We'll see each other again."

Effie nodded, her eyes already starting to take on some of the ancient wisdom that her grandmother's had held. "Eventually."

"You take care of yourself, Effie. If you have need of anything, all you have to do is call." Helena held out one of her last fully charged Kaelpas stones. "You will always have a place in my court."

Effie took the stone, clasping it to her chest. "Thank you for being my friend, Helena. You were the first I ever really had."

The words struck her like a blow, and she reached out, pulling Effie in for a hug. "I'm going to miss you."

"And I you."

"Farewell, Effie."

"Send her straight to hell," Effie replied, stepping out of her arms.

Helena nodded, her expression serious. "I intend to."

Effie stared at her a moment longer before turning and walking into the tent she was sharing with Reyna.

When the morning came, she was gone.

CHAPTER 22

Rowena stood looking out over what should by rights be her Queendom. The harsh winds of Vyruul were whipping her hair out of its binding, but it was the only part of her that reacted to the extreme cold of her surroundings. The heat of her rage had long since cooled. Now it was as if she was forged from the ice itself. There was little that would cause her pristine façade to crack.

"My Queen?" Kai-Soren called.

"What do you want?" Rowena asked without turning to face him. They'd been married less than a week and already he'd disappointed her.

"The men are growing restless. When can we return home?"

"Home?" she scoffed. "What home? Greyspire is in ruins, no thanks to you and your 'men,' or did you already forget?"

Kai-Soren waited a moment before replying. "There's still the keep at Endoshan—"

"The Mother will strike me dead before I go crawling into that pile of stones you call a keep."

She could feel his wounded pride from where she stood. Men were so easily broken.

"Well perhaps the men could return so that they at least have a roof over their heads and warmth instead of freezing to death in this cave."

"You seek out comfort over the safety of your Queen? You'd leave me here unprotected?" Her voice grew colder with each word she spoke until the wind soon seemed balmy by comparison.

"Rowena, I—"

"How dare you address me so informally," she snapped, finally spinning around. The full power of her ire was unleashed on him, and for the first time since she'd known him, he looked truly unnerved.

His golden eyes were wide, the whites clearly visible on both top and bottom. He caught himself and quickly schooled his face into an impassive mask. "Apologies, My Queen. It will not happen again."

Rowena sighed, wishing she could use a small bit of compulsion magic to make him less insufferable. Alas, she could not give up the charade entirely. Not yet, but as soon as she could… Rowena's eyes narrowed in malicious glee. Her darling husband Kai-Soren was living on borrowed time, and it tickled her to no end that he was completely clueless.

"You know that we must remain here until I find acceptable replacements for the two that were lost. I cannot let that sniveling impostor discover me until then."

"How do you expect to find anyone while we hide in a cave?" he asked, causing her to grit her teeth.

"I'm working on it."

His eyes shuttered; his faith in her ability to lead was dwindling more each day. He thought her weak for hiding, but she was not sitting idle. As always, she was thinking four and five steps ahead of everyone. How else would she have been able to fool so many into believing she was dead? Things were set in motion long before she ever knew she'd end up here. It was only a matter of time.

Rowena turned back toward Elysia, dismissing him without a word. She was the rightful ruler of the Chosen. One way or another, she'd reclaim her throne.

There was never any doubt about how this was going to end.

*S*HE *WALKED AMONGST THE TWILIGHT, the stars illuminating the path before her with their brilliance. On either side, trees stretched up into the sky, obscuring what lay beyond them. All she could see was the path before her and the stars in the sky watching over her, lighting her way.*

She walked alone, but felt no sense of fear. It was safe here; there was nothing but peace in the starlight. She continued to wander until the road began to curve, opening up on the shore of a beach. The stars continued to shine down, the water reflecting their light back up at them. Everything was awash in shades of blue, giving the secluded beach an air of ethereality.

Seeing nothing else, she walked across the powder soft sand toward the shore. Once she reached the edge, she let her bare toes dip into the water, not caring that the bottom of her gown grew wet. She tilted her head up toward the sky, feeling her hair brush against her back. It tickled, causing her to smile and close her eyes, wanting to memorize the feeling of total peace.

She had no idea how she got here, no clue where she was, and yet she did not want to leave.

"To remain means you must also leave behind. Could you really do that?"

Opening her eyes, she saw the figure of a woman take shape beside her.

"Miranda?" she asked. It was not surprise she felt at seeing the Keeper, merely wonder.

"Hello, Kiri."

Helena smiled. There was no accurate way to describe her joy at finding the friend she thought she had lost.

"Is this where you live now?" Helena asked, looking around for some sign of a dwelling.

Miranda's answering smile was kind. "No. I am just visiting, as are you."

A breeze picked up, causing her to shiver for the first time. Helena cast a glance up at the sky, feeling like some of the stars were starting to dim. The first tendril of concern snaked up her spine.

Miranda held out a hand. "Walk with me a ways."

Helena took her hand and the two women began to walk along the shore.

"Your mind is heavy," Miranda said.

The thoughts and worries that she had forgotten while admiring the stars started to come back, reminding her of what waited. "Yes," she sighed. "I don't know what to do, or how I am supposed to defeat her."

"Yes you do."

Helena frowned.

"Look," Miranda whispered, her arms lifting until they were fully extended on either side of her. Helena let out a startled gasp. The beach had disappeared, giving way to a meadow. The sun was shining overhead and flowers were dancing in the breeze. She blinked, but the image remained intact.

"How did you do that?" Helena asked.

Miranda smiled. "You do not need to look far for your answer, Helena."

Helena opened her mouth, questions ready to fall from her lips, but Miranda stopped her. "The Mother has given you everything you need."

With that, the Keeper lifted a hand and ran it along her cheek and the meadow disappeared.

Helena bolted upright, her heart still thundering as she pulled her consciousness from the grips of the dream. It took her a moment to remember where she was. Seeing the familiar purple of her bed, she let out a deep breath. She was home. She was safe.

Von grunted and rolled toward her, his arms trying to pull her closer, but Helena disentangled herself and pushed out of the bed to pad across the cool floor.

Why did I dream about Miranda? Is she trying to tell me something? For all that she was awake, Helena still felt like her brain was a bit foggy from sleep. Before Darrin had come to her and told her of her destiny, Helena had never put much stock into dreams having any sort of relevance. After all, they were just the images one's mind assigned to things that they had experienced during the day and were remembering on some unconscious level. Weren't they?

Now that she had firsthand knowledge of visions and prophecy, Helena wasn't so sure. Miranda's presence in her dreams had to mean something. It couldn't just be coincidence, not with everything else that had been going on recently.

Helena was absently aware that she had started pacing. Her mind was trying to tell her something. Something that had to do with Miranda. If only she could figure out what.

Frustrated, she sighed, stopping in her tracks. She wasn't getting anywhere, and the longer she was awake, the faster she lost the threads of her dream, which meant if there were clues hidden there, she was quickly losing access to them.

"Oh blast it!" she cursed under her breath, grabbing a lilac robe from the chair where she'd discarded it earlier. She belted the robe loosely and headed for the door. There was no way she was going to fall back asleep now, so she might as well try to get some work done.

If she couldn't recall the specifics of the dream, maybe going to the last place she'd spent time with Miranda might trigger something. It was as good a plan as any this early in the morning. Especially since she couldn't exactly run the idea by others since the rest of her Circle were still abed. She might as well make use of the quiet time to see if she couldn't get any farther deciphering that vision.

Helena moved quickly through the halls of the Palace, not stopping to appreciate any of the small touches that usually captivated her attention. It was completely quiet, something that rarely happened given the number of people running around at any given minute, but for once, it was calm. Dim lights danced in their orbs to light the way for anyone that might need to move around while it was still dark out. It was just enough to see by, and she made her way to the library in record time.

She pushed open the heavy door and stepped into the dark room. There was no natural light in here, so the room was pitch black except for where a sliver of light fell in from the doorway. Helena used her power to softly illuminate the room and then closed the door behind her. The table she'd spent so much time at when trying to find a spell to fool Rowena sat untouched. Helena smiled, Alina must have refused to let anyone put the books away in case Helena had need of them.

Looking down, her eyes ran over the titles while her fingers brushed against the leather-bound tomes. There was something lovely about all the scrolling text and faded colors. So much knowledge hidden within the dusty pages, painstakingly preserved by one who thought it important enough to pass on. If only answers were that easy to find. Helena wished there was a way for her to simply ask her question aloud and have the exact book she needed be pulled out and opened to the page where the answer lay. How easy that would make things.

She lowered herself into the comfortable armchair and pulled her robe more tightly around her. She let her head fall back against its cushioned surface while her mind returned to the last time she was here.

What was it Miranda had told her? Something about trying to think about the problem from a different angle. All right, fine. All this time they'd assumed that the web was Rowena's given that she was the spider. *But what if it wasn't? Whose else could it be? What else could it represent?*

Helena lost track of time as she contemplated the answers to these questions.

According to Effie, the strands of the web had all been different. It reminded Helena a bit of the time she'd been in Bael, her power making her see the colorful strands of power within each of her Circle.

"Maybe the web is a trap created by many," Helena mused, following that train of thought. "Or one so elaborate that it requires significant power to complete it."

Helena's fingers brushed against one of the books, the glittering gold of its title barely visible in the soft light. *The Power of Illusions.* Her finger traced the gilded letters. It wasn't until she was on the second looping o that something snapped into place. Helena sat up.

"Illusions."

That last time she'd been in here, she'd been trying to discover how to create an illusion powerful enough to hide the Night Stalkers in plain sight.

"Is that what you were trying to help me remember?" she asked, not sure who she was talking to. Helena began talking her way through possible answers. "The illusion of a web. No, it's not that literal. Okay… so something that makes it look like I am trapped. Something big enough and believable enough that Rowena buys it."

Excitement had her jumping from the chair. She knew that she was on the right track now. After a few more minutes of mulling over the details, she actually laughed out loud; the answer was so obvious. "The trap is not for me! It's for Rowena! Something to draw her out so that this final battle can be on our terms!"

Helena could feel the truth in her words, and relief filled her. That was what the vision had been showing them. Finally, they had an answer about what to do, but as quickly as her excitement came, it fled.

Helena slumped back into the chair. She'd managed to solve the puzzle, but now she had a bigger problem. What illusion could she possibly cast that would be enticing enough for Rowena to crawl out of hiding?

"You want to do what?" Ronan asked incredulously.

"I want to lay a trap."

"Right, I heard that part," Ronan said. "Where you lost me is the bit about how you are planning to use yourself as bait."

Helena folded her arms. "What part about it are you struggling with?"

"The part where your life is in danger!" he snapped, looking at Von. "Are you just going to sit there or are you going to help me talk some sense into your Mate?"

Von did not look much happier than Ronan, although he'd already resigned himself to her decision. After all, he could appreciate the brilliance of the strategy, even as he hated what it would require.

"You cannot ask us to stand aside while you practically hand yourself over to that she-bitch."

Helena knew that it was fear that made him speak to her like she was incapable of protecting herself, but even still, the insinuation stung. "You don't actually get a say in this, you do realize that, don't you?"

Ronan glowered at her.

Turning to address the others Helena added, "None of you have to help me, but this is what I need to do. Every time we've fought her until now it's been on her terms. That has to stop. We cannot possibly win while Rowena has the upper hand. This is our only way to change that."

None of her men looked happy, but they could not disagree with the assessment.

"How do you plan to lure her?" Joquil asked.

Helena pressed her lips together. This is where things got a little murky. She had the rough sketch of a plan, but not a fully realized idea. She was hoping that they would help fill in those gaps, but given their state of mind, they might be more inclined to use the holes to argue against her.

"I want to create an illusion."

Timmins frowned. "How do you plan on casting an illusion grand enough to reach her where she is?"

"Well, I want it to be big enough that news reaches her wherever she is hiding."

"So this is not just an illusion for Rowena, this is something that will affect anyone who sees it?" Von clarified.

Helena nodded. "I think that's the only way it will work."

"Something on that scale is going to require substantial power, perhaps even more than you are capable of accessing alone," Joquil said, his brows low over his worried amber eyes.

"I think it's safe to say it definitely will require more power than I possess."

"Even with our bond?" Von asked, his eyes darkening.

Helena nodded.

"So you use the Jaka and pull from the rest of the Circle," Kragen said with a shrug.

"It won't be enough."

The silence spoke volumes. They were finally starting to realize the scope of what she was talking about.

"So where do you plan on getting access to that kind of power?"

"I'm not entirely sure yet, but I know that there is a way."

"All right," Ronan interjected, "so let's say you get the power source figured out. What kind of illusion are you talking about?"

Helena took a deep breath, shifting uncomfortably in her chair. "Rowena's gift in Endoshan was meant to be a trigger. She doesn't know yet that we've already found it, so I want her to think it worked. The one thing we have always been able to count on with Rowena is her pride. She thinks that she is infallible. If she believes that I fell for her trap and turned, she will come running to collect her prize."

While she'd been speaking, Helena had been staring resolutely down at the table, but once she was done, she looked back up. Von's eyes were the first to find hers.

"You're going to pretend that you have turned." His voice was quiet thunder.

Helena nodded slowly.

"And you plan on being convincing enough that Rowena isn't the only one that falls for it?"

"Yes."

"What kind of destruction are you talking?" Kragen asked, his face serious.

Helena lifted her eyes to him. "Absolute."

"Mother's tits," Ronan swore. "Can you actually do that?"

"I think so. I've already been shown what my corruption looks like," Helena paused to let out a humorless laugh. "Trust me, it's not a sight you easily forget."

"Your trial," Timmins whispered, remembering her description of what had transpired there.

"What happens when she comes for you?" Von asked. He was no

longer sitting at the table but had stood and was holding himself stiffly. He looked like he had a very loose grasp on his control.

Helena forced herself to stand.

"Helena, what happens when she comes for you?" he repeated, his voice deadly soft. He'd never spoken to her that way before, it was a tone he reserved exclusively for those he had at the tip of his sword.

She pushed her shoulders back and tilted her chin up, refusing to be intimidated.

"Answer the question," he growled.

"She takes me."

The room erupted. Before she could move, Von had blinked and had destroyed the table by landing on top of it. Splinters were still falling around them. The others had barely pushed out of their chairs in time, but even they had rounded on her.

"Absolutely not," Von snarled, his nose pressed against hers.

"She has to believe she's won."

"No. Fucking. Way." He enunciated each word slowly, his eyes pure gold.

"She has—"

"No!" he shouted. "You want to do this fine, but she does not lay a hand on you."

Helena forced herself to breathe and not react to his temper. Von was terrified. She could feel the tidal wave of emotion surging through her. He had been Rowena's prisoner once, and the thought of Helena being put in a similar situation was causing him to unravel. The only way to defuse him was to help him calm down.

"We will not give her time to actually harm me," Helena insisted, forcing her voice to stay steady as she mentally added *or not very much*. This wouldn't work without proof. Rowena would need to be certain of her victory before letting her guard down long enough for them to strike.

Von tilted his head, looking like an inquisitive Talyrian. "Explain."

"While Rowena is distracted by me, the rest of you will attack. We need to finish off the Generals so that while Rowena and I are alone, I can finally end her."

Von's eyes searched hers and he started to shake his head. "I don't like it. There's something you aren't saying."

She could feel him probing at her mind, and so she reinforced every mental barrier she had. It was the first time she'd ever actively tried to keep him out. From the wounded look in his eyes, Von knew what she was doing.

"This is the only way."

Her Circle was silent, the five men each processing her words.

"Are you sure?" Kragen asked.

"As sure as I can be."

"How much can we tell the others?" Joquil asked.

"As little as possible," Helena said with a wince. Sometimes to save a friend, you have to play the enemy. In her case, it might not be enough to simply play. Helena shut down that line of thinking, not ready to contemplate all of the ways this could go wrong.

Timmins' brows pulled together in a frown. "It will not be easy to keep this from everyone."

"They can know we set a trap, but not what it is. I think it's safer for everyone that way."

"I will start working with Kragen and the others on a strategy," Ronan said. It was as close as she was going to get at a peace offering right now.

Helena nodded.

"Joquil and I will see what we can find about helping you acquire the additional power that you will need," Timmins offered.

"Thank you."

The four of them left, leaving Von and her alone.

"You're really going to do this?" he asked.

"I have to."

"This will not be an easy part for you to play," he said levelly.

"I know."

"There are some who will never fully trust you again."

"I know," she said again, her voice trembling slightly.

Von let out a deep breath, his shoulders falling. Running a hand through his hair, he shook his head. "She'll never believe you've turned if I'm still unharmed."

Helena swallowed. She hadn't considered that.

"You're going to have to use me."

Helena began to shake her head. "No. I don't want you anywhere near this."

Von shrugged. "We all have our parts to play. You committed us to this path, and according to you, there's no other way but through. So we will walk down it. Together."

"Von," she whispered, knowing he was right and hating what it meant.

"It will be the thing that convinces the others." He gave her a grim but determined smile. "In this case, *Mira*. I think you have to ask yourself, what would Rowena do?"

Helena frowned. The kind of game he was talking about was a dangerous one indeed. "With as much power as I think will be running through me, there's no guarantee…" she trailed off, not able to say the words out loud. *"The damage could be permanent. You could be seriously hurt."*

Von closed the distance between them, pulling her into his arms and resting his head on top of hers. "So could you, *Mira*. It is the risk we take whenever we step onto the battlefield."

The adrenaline that had been running through her ever since she woke up that morning had finally started to ebb, leaving her exhausted. She knew this plan was risky, but she also knew it was their only option. She had been okay with the idea of getting hurt herself if it meant saving the others, but the thought of Von suffering at her hands made her ill.

"I don't know if I can do it," she said into his chest. "The chance of losing control…"

Von pressed a finger to her lips, his eyes so filled with love that her heart ached. "I've told you before, I trust you with my life, Helena. Now's my chance to prove it."

CHAPTER 23

Von watched Helena retreat further into herself. Her aqua eyes stared unseeing out the window and her arms were wrapped protectively around her middle. As the days passed and they struggled to find the answers she needed, she grew more despondent and withdrawn. He knew that the thought of having to deceive the people she loved was weighing on her, and the longer she had to put it off, the more time she had to think about all of the things that could go wrong.

He was in awe of her power. The fact that she had the capability of creating an illusion on that grand a scale was hard for him to comprehend. He recalled the nightmarish day when they'd received Rowena's box, and the rush of power he'd experienced as Helena channeled her resulting rage through him to siphon it off. At the time, he'd thought she must have finally reached the limit of what she could control.

Von shook his head at his foolishness. He now realized that was only a teardrop in the ocean compared to the amount she would have to manipulate and maintain for what she was about to attempt.

He'd tried to talk her through it, but words were empty. It wasn't like he had any sort of firsthand knowledge about what she was going through. Hand him a sword and point him in the right direction and he'd figure it out as he went, but this… this was a whole different battlefield.

Von sighed, his lips drawn in a flat line. All he knew for sure was that watching her go through this, and being helpless to do anything, was driving him mad. He'd already worn out three training dummies and four new recruits trying to find an outlet for the pent-up frustration. Ronan had banned him from the practice ring after he'd knocked a Daejaran trainee unconscious with a single blow, which meant that now, even that small bit of relief had been taken from him.

He let his eyes trail along his Mate, noting the pensive crease between her arched brows and the way her lips tilted in a frown. Even now, she still managed to take his breath away.

There was a mistaken belief amongst the Chosen that the Mother's Vessel was perfect. Those were the ones that did not truly see her; the ones that did not understand her. For Von, it was obvious, but then, she was his other half. Helena's true power stemmed from her flaws. She may not be perfect in the general sense of the term, but he wouldn't have wanted her if she had been. How could someone who had never truly experienced life and all of its messiness ever fully understand one such as him? But Helena did, and it was because she was no stranger to grief, or humility, or anger. Things someone can only ever learn by experiencing firsthand the pain of mistakes and heartache. She was wholly alive, and she had been made for him; a gift he still thanked the Mother for daily, even though he still didn't quite believe he deserved it. And because she was his, he would do anything to save her. Even if it meant sacrificing himself.

What good was life when your reason for living was gone?

Von pushed off of the wall and started to walk toward her, wanting to smooth away the worried crease between her eyes. Before he could reach her, a knock sounded on the door, drawing everyone's attention as it opened without waiting for permission.

His brother tipped his dark head inside.

"Nial?" Von asked, concern already coloring his voice and making it come out sharper than usual. Something must have happened if his brother risked interrupting their meeting. Not that anything much had been happening, but Nial didn't know that. "What's going on?"

"Sorry for the intrusion." Nial was vibrating with tension. It was as if his body was simultaneously trying to come closer and run away, and as a result, he was locked in a perpetual sway as his muscles tried to handle the conflicting orders.

"There's no need to apologize," Helena said, hiding her worried thoughts behind a mask of polite formality. She was getting very skilled at playing the diplomat.

Feeling his eyes on her, Helena looked over and gave him a small smile.

Nial stepped further into the room, his scholar robes rumpled and stained. It would seem they were not the only ones that had been pouring through the archives.

"Did you find something?" he asked his brother, recognizing the excitement shining in his eyes.

Nial nodded. "I think so. It's just a hunch, mind you, but I think it could work."

"Spit it out," Ronan growled, crossing his arms and bringing a booted foot up against the wall.

Timmins gave him a dark look, but didn't waste breath telling him to get his dirty feet off the wall. Poor, proper Timmins. Still offended by the most minor offenses.

"There was something you said that triggered a memory, but I couldn't remember the exact reference out of context, so it took me a few days to locate it." The words poured out of Nial in a rush.

"What did you find, Nial?" Helena asked, her impatience tempered by amusement.

"You mentioned that you needed access to more than just your own power, and I remembered that sometimes for really complex magic, multiple sources are required to anchor it. That's when I remembered the Storm Forged's cyclone."

Von lifted a brow, not sure where his brother was going with this information. "The cyclone is the remnant of the Stormbringer's rise to power. What does that have to do with anchoring a spell?"

Nial shot him an exasperated look. "I'm getting to that."

"Perhaps you should hurry up," Kragen suggested.

"Do you want to hear this or not?" Nial snapped, before realizing who he was speaking to. Color moved up his neck as he dropped his eyes, and his voice. "Apologies, Sword."

"It would seem the only one keeping us from hearing the news is you, boy-o," Joquil commented, his amber eyes glowing with laughter.

Nial sighed. "The Stormbringer's cyclone would die out without constant reinforcement. To channel that much power regularly would drain him almost completely. Yet clearly, that's not the case or he wouldn't be here. The only reason that's possible is because the rest of the Storm Forged help anchor the magic. It is fed by all of them and yet none feel the drain."

"Do we know how it's done?" Helena asked, her aqua eyes bright. Von could feel her hope like a warm blast of sunshine along their bond.

Nial shook his head. "No, but with Anduin here, that's not the issue. If he could talk us through it, I should be able to find a way to replicate it for your use."

"What if he does not want to share Storm Forged secrets?" Timmins asked.

"He won't have a choice," Von said, the hint of a snarl creeping into his voice.

"What are we waiting for?" Helena asked. "Someone go find Anduin."

Kragen jumped up. "On it," he said.

"Thank you, Nial," Helena said, giving Von's brother a tight hug.

"Where's my hug?" Von teased.

"Bring me more information like that and you can have all of them."

Von smirked. *"You never complained about my less-than-scholarly nature before now, Mira."*

Her cheeks heated, and she shook her head at him.

He winked, happy to see her smiling again.

"Good work, brother," Von said, giving Nial a one-armed hug.

Nial glowed at the praise. "As I said, it's just a theory, but—"

"There's no need to be modest. It was a brilliant discovery. One that could very well allow us to seize control of this war. Accept the thanks you're due," Von ordered.

Nial nodded, his quiet pride making his eyes shine.

Von squeezed his shoulder, stepping back to reclaim his place by the hearth. The heavy tension that had been in the room only moments before was gone, replaced by the sweet feeling of relief tinged with hope. His bookish little brother might have just brought them the final piece of this devilish puzzle, and none of them were more thankful than he.

HELENA GOT the feeling that the Storm Forged did not like to be in enclosed spaces for longer than necessary. Anduin had taken the spot closest to the window, and even though he'd only been in the room a handful of minutes at best, he kept casting distracted glances out the window every chance he got.

"Looking for something?" she finally asked.

"I am not usually this far from the sea. I find it unsettling," he admitted, turning his eyes on her.

"For all its beauty, the Palace definitely lacks a view of the ocean," Helena acknowledged.

Anduin smiled, but it did not reach his eyes. "I am surprised that you are seeking out my aid instead of that Night Stalker you so favor."

Helena frowned at the unnecessary vitriol she heard in his voice. There was no need for it when they were all working toward the same goal. "I had not realized you were lacking my attention. I shall endeavor to do better at stroking your ego."

The Stormbringer laughed, the sound reminding her of waves crashing against the sand. "I had not meant offense, only that it is usually her counsel you seek. How may I assist you, Kiri?" The question was directed at her, but his eyes were looking at each of her Circle in kind.

Nial had joined them around the newly repaired table, leaving only

Helena and Anduin standing. Helena could feel their intense focus behind her, but she kept her eyes on the Stormbringer.

"Your cyclone," she stated, causing his brow to lift in surprise. "Can you explain to me how the rest of the Storm Forged help anchor it?"

Anduin studied her, his glowing sapphire eyes searching for something in her expression. "How do you know about that?"

Nial cleared his throat, but Helena spoke before the Stormbringer could look away. "It is common knowledge that the storm would fade without constant tending."

Anduin smiled, but it was a cold, brittle thing. "No, it's not."

Helena rolled her eyes. "It only makes sense that you alone are not responsible for doing so, or you would not be able to stay away from the Ebon Isle for so long. Besides, the drain on you would be considerable. You would be too weak for much more than sitting upon your throne."

His smile fell, and Anduin turned away, his back facing all of them.

"I need to know how the Storm Forged accomplish this, Anduin. It is not a request."

Anduin sighed. "The knowledge of the giving is a sacred thing amongst the Storm Forged. In the wrong hands, it could be perverted… no longer a gift, but a curse."

"All power can be corrupted in the wrong hands," Helena said pointedly.

The Stormbringer nodded, his colorful hair rippling like water. "I will tell you, because I trust you, Helena. You have shown mercy where many others would not."

"Thank you," she said, the relief at his words giving her voice a breathless quality. Entirely too much hinged upon his compliance, and their alliance was still tenuous at best.

Anduin turned back to the room. "Generally, the giving requires a connection, something that links the intention of the one lending their power and the one who will wield it. A joint purpose, if you will. For the Storm Forged, our connection is obvious." Anduin paused, his eyes meeting each of the Circle's, as if trying to convince them of the importance of his words. "It is not enough to trust, the giver's conviction must be absolute, otherwise the power will not be contained once it leaves its source. It will return to the world unrealized."

"Conviction?" Nial asked, looking up from the notes he was furiously scribbling.

"In its purpose. The goal of the magic," Anduin further clarified when he realized the others were not following. "The gift of power must have an end goal; it is what keeps the gift contained."

Helena felt her back stiffen, worry that what she needed would require that she give up the entirety of her plan and thereby condemning it to failure.

"Is it enough that the givers all believed that their gift is going to be used to create a trap? Or would they need to know the specifics of the trap?" Von asked, feeling the tension coiling inside of her. He was careful not to look directly at her, but she could sense his quiet support like a hand brushing down her spine.

Anduin considered the questions. "Knowing the purpose of the trap would be enough. The stronger the belief, the stronger the power. Too many details would muddy the purity of the gift."

"So knowing it was a trap for Rowena that they were helping to build would be ideal?" Helena asked, seeking clarification.

Anduin nodded, and Helena's body relaxed.

"So how does the giving occur?" Nial asked, using Anduin's unfamiliar term.

Anduin closed his eyes, his pulse fluttering wildly in his throat. This was the part that he did not want to reveal, the part that could be twisted and bent until it broke entirely.

"I wouldn't be asking if it wasn't crucial," Helena said softly.

"I know." Anduin opened his eyes. "For us, it is always part of a celebration. We gift our power directly to the Stormbringer, so that it may be gathered and released into the storm itself."

"Forgive my ignorance," Nial interjected, "but how does one gift their power?"

"I am sure there are many ways it could be done, but we use water to aid the transfer." Anduin smiled. "Stick with what you know, right?"

There were a few coughs of laughter, but the room fell silent quickly. "The way I was taught was simple, hold the cup of water in your hands and send your intention into it. When the Stormbringer drinks from the cup, they consume the raw bit of power until they are ready to release it."

"And you're sure this is not simply ceremonial?" Timmins asked, his lips in a dubious frown.

"As one who has partaken of the gifts, I can assure you it is very real," Anduin said, his voice reminding her of the angry churn of the sea.

Helena glanced at the others to see if they had already picked up on their next problem. While Anduin had provided a rather simple answer, it was not going to be as easy as drinking some magically enhanced water. The sheer amount that she needed would preclude it, let alone the fact that she would not be able to contain it long enough to travel far.

"Does it have to be consumed?" Helena asked.

"How else would the power transfer occur?" Anduin asked.

"Would blood work?" Nial asked, surprising them all.

"Blood?" Helena squeaked, the thought of consuming others' blood making her lightheaded.

Nial was biting down on his lip as he sketched something out. He spoke slowly, working his thoughts out on paper before saying them aloud. "If we used blood for the transfer, it could contain and hold the power just as water does. It's a small but potent vessel."

"There can be great power in the blood. It could act as an amplifier," Joquil murmured thoughtfully.

"Uh, guys," Helena said, "I'm not comfortable with the idea of drinking blood."

Nial's eyes widened at the words and he burst out laughing. "Mother no, not drink it. Add yours to it."

Helena took her first full breath since Anduin had joined them.

Joquil and Timmins seemed to understand what Nial was implying, but all Helena understood was that she would not have to drink anyone's blood. She could have wept with her relief.

"Explain," Von said.

"Well, as the Stormbringer stated, the act of tying one's will to the power in order to use it is essential. Rather than having Helena trying to contain that much power inside of her body, she could add a drop of her blood into the rest of gifted drops, and thereby claim them. It would limit the amount of time she had to hold the power so that she could wait until she was ready to release it."

"If it's that easy to take control of the power, what's to stop it from transferring to someone else after they add their blood to the mix?" Ronan asked.

"It goes back to intention," Nial said with a smile.

Ronan looked ready to throttle him. Thankfully, Timmins interjected. "The gift is intended for Helena's use. The power is limited to her and her alone. No one else would be able to lay claim to it."

Nial nodded as if it was obvious.

Helena looked at Anduin. "Do you think it could work?"

"In theory," Anduin shrugged, "I do not see why not. However, it has not been tested. There is always a chance it does not."

Only a chance, but it was the only option available to them. "We will need to make sure that the others understand what we are asking of them. It has to be a choice, freely given." Helena did not want anyone to feel forced to participate.

"Is there anything else we need to know?" Nial asked Anduin, who shook his head. "All right, I will gather what we need. Can the rest of you help collect the," he risked a glance at Helena and chose his words with care, "gifts?"

Her Circle nodded.

"I can help," Helena said, feeling that this was something she should be a part of.

"You have other things to attend to," Von reminded her.

"He's right, Kiri," Joquil added. "You need to be ready to act as soon as we are finished."

Helena sighed. "Fine."

Anduin brushed his hand against her arm. "The Storm Forged will help explain to the rest of the Chosen what to do. When the time comes, we will add our gifts as well."

"Anduin," Helena started, moved that he would offer so freely.

The Stormbringer shrugged. "As you said, we are in this together. Anything we can do to assist, you need only ask." With a small nod, he made his way for the door, the men of her Circle standing to follow.

Von hesitated at the door, looking at her with eyes that saw too much. "It won't be long now," he said.

Helena nodded. "I know."

"You are ready for this, *Mira*."

As always, his faith in her filled her with resolve. "Now to go rid some folks of their blood." Von made a face. "I've been doing it for years and never thought to simply ask for it?"

Helena let out a sharp bark of laughter at the crude joke. He gave her wink, her laughter clearly his intention. He gave her one final roguish grin and walked out, leaving her shaking her head and smiling behind him.

Mother how she loved him.

CHAPTER 24

In less than twenty-four hours, her Circle, along with Anduin's Storm Forged, had managed to collect the blood gifts from the entire Chosen army. Helena had barely been able to contain her tears of astonished gratitude. She had never dared to hope so many would be willing to contribute. Parting with blood was no small ask, and it was rarely required in Chosen spells since their power came from within. However, there were a few records that detailed its powers of amplification as well as its ability to be used as a tracking mechanism. Once acquired, the blood could be used to turn one's power against them. To gift it blindly said much about their trust in her.

Once again, Helena found herself back in the Circle's Chambers. Something about Anduin's reference to a ceremony had stuck with Nial, so Timmins suggested that the Circle, both literal and honorary, wait until the other gifts had been collected before offering their own. This would allow those closest to her to present their offering directly. Helena would be the last to add her blood and would not do so until she was ready to initiate the illusion.

Despite the gravity of their undertaking, the group had worked hard to make this a festive gathering. While it was an unspoken understanding, they knew this might be the last time they were all together, and each of them wanted this memory to hold close in case of the worst.

"There are too many of us crammed in here," Helena laughed, accepting a goblet of wine from Alina.

Alina scanned the crowded room and nodded her agreement. "Indeed, I can hardly hear myself think over the noise. Should I send some people away?" she asked.

Helena shook her head. "No, definitely not. We might just need to move this party outside."

Overhearing her, Ronan shouted his approval. "Mother's tits, yes! It's hot as fucking balls in here."

Helena lifted her brow at the colorful description.

Ronan gave her a one-sided grin and shrugged. "If you had your own set, you'd know what I mean."

Helena took a sip of her wine before giving him a wicked smile. "What makes you think I haven't?"

Her Shield laughed. "Just because you hold your Mate's balls in your knapsack doesn't mean you know what it's like..." Ronan trailed off at her amused expression. "When did you have balls?" he asked, truly astounded.

"When I posed as Micha."

"That's right!" he said, laughing as he shook his head. "I'd forgotten. But still, borrowing a set and actually living with them are two different things."

Helena just laughed at the absurdity of their conversation. "You can keep your knee knockers, Shield. I have no interest in them."

Ronan snorted with laughter, clinking his glass with her own. "Shall we reconvene under the stars then?"

Helena nodded, loving the idea of having the Mother bear witness to their impromptu ceremony.

Ronan let out a long ear-piercing whistle. The room fell silent enough for him to shout, "Outside you scoundrels!" That was all it took for the room to empty and the laughing, tipsy lot to make their way outside.

Helena found herself at the end of the line, smiling softly as she watched them wind their way through the halls. Their laughter bounced off the walls and filled the Palace with easy joy. No one was thinking about what tomorrow would bring. No one except her.

Seeing her lingering behind, Von waited for her to catch up. He didn't have to say anything, she could feel his concern brushing against her and see its echo in his somber gray eyes. The eyes that had always looked straight to the heart of her. Helena never could hide what she was thinking from him.

"I'm fine," she promised, giving him a quick kiss once she reached him at the top of the spiraling stairs. "Just enjoying this while it lasts."

Von rested his arms on the banister beside her. "Aye. It's nice to be home with everyone like this, even if it's temporary."

Home. The word brought a smile to her lips. She had never really thought of the Palace as home. To some extent, that would always be the cottage she had shared with her mother. The Palace was just the place where her things were. For Helena, home was not a building as much as the people that were housed within it. If by home, Von meant spending time with the ones she loved, then she was inclined to agree. It was nice.

On the heels of that thought was a reminder of the people that were missing: Anderson, Darrin, Miranda, and Effie. Those she loved that were no longer able to sit around and drink themselves silly as they toasted to a future they wished would come to be. Her smile turned wistful as she studied her Mate's chiseled profile.

His face was serious despite the smile, as if his thoughts were as heavy as hers. She ran her finger along his nose, causing him to laugh and glance over at her.

She stared at him, her eyes lovingly memorizing every line and angle of his face. The dark slash of his brows, the perfect line of his nose, and sharp edge of his cheekbones. She ran her fingers along the scruff at his jaw, loving the way it scratched her fingers before they made their way into the feather soft strands of his inky black hair.

Von nuzzled into the caress, pressing his lips into the palm of her hand.

"I love you," she whispered when his eyes met hers again.

His eyes darkened, and his hand lifted to brush her cheek. Helena let her eyes fall closed as she leaned into the touch. "I love you, Helena." His voice was deep and warm, wrapping itself around her.

She felt the whisper of a touch on her nose, it was the only warning before his lips dipped down to meet hers. The kiss was achingly gentle, like the sealing of a promise. She pressed against him, eager to deepen it, but he kept it sweet and slow.

"There's no need to rush," he whispered through their bond, his lips continuing to tease her. *"We have our whole lives for this."*

Helena was about to protest, but he stopped her before she could with a hand that tangled in her hair, lightly tugging her back.

"You promised me forever," he said against her lips. Helena's eyes fluttered open to find his tinged with gold and boring into hers. "I refuse to act like tonight will be our last."

Desire and love spiraled through her at the tender rebuke. What had she ever done to be worthy of such a Mate?

Von nipped at her bottom lip before pulling away to gift her one of his most seductive smiles. "I intend to hold you to your promise, Mate."

"As well you should," she whispered, her voice husky. She was leaning forward to claim another kiss when Ronan called loudly from the bottom of the stairs.

"Save that for later, you two. We should probably get on with this before too many of us get too deep in our cups. I can't imagine the alcohol will do much for your magicking."

Helena stepped away with a scowl. She knew he was right, but that didn't make her need any less.

"One day, Ronan," Von called, taking Helena's hand in his as they began their descent, "you're going to find a woman, and I will be able to return the favor with no shortage of enjoyment."

Ronan shrugged, his arms crossed. "Good luck with that, brother."

Once Von was beside him, he leaned close and said in a low growl. "May your balls forever be blue, you smug bastard."

Ronan threw his head back and laughed, the sound rolling through the room and bouncing off the high ceiling.

"What is with you two and your obsession with balls tonight?" Helena asked, shaking her head.

Von raised a brow in confusion. "What do you mean?"

"Ask him, he started it," she said, stepping away from the still laughing Shield and out into the gardens below.

HELENA NEVER WOULD HAVE KNOWN that the party was unplanned. By the time she reached the garden, tables and chairs were set up with sparkling centerpieces and laden with food. There was also a small platform in the middle of the set-up where Helena assumed she would be standing as people stepped forward with their offering.

Overhead, the sky was filled with stars. She tipped her head back, breathing in the fragrant scent of night-blooming flowers and just basking in the glow of the moonlight. It was a beautiful evening. One made for dancing or sneaking off into the dark corners of the garden with a lover, definitely not one for bloodletting, although that was what it was about to be used for. She sighed and opened her eyes, making her way to the platform. Maybe one night soon she could dance beneath the stars, but tonight was not that night.

Helena took her place, and her friends' animated voices grew quiet as they took note of her. She cleared her throat awkwardly, not sure what to say. She hadn't planned to make a speech tonight, although it was starting to look like it was about to happen anyway.

"I, uh…" she trailed off and shrugged at their polite laughter. "I have no clue what I'm supposed to say right now. Thank you seems too small a phrase to express the depth of my gratitude for your continued sacrifices."

Helena paused to take a breath and settle her nerves, her eyes seeking out each person individually. In the back were her Circle, their strength and combined power making them a considerable force, even at rest. She gave each of them a smile before looking on to Reyna and her favored guards. Next was Anduin and the two women who joined him for most diplomatic events. Then Serena and Nial, representing

Daejara; Alina and her brother, the selected representatives of Tigaera; the Etillions, Amara and Xander; the Caedarans, Tinka and Khouman. It looked like everyone was here. Or maybe not.

With a mighty roar, a bright jet of orange flame, Starshine flew through the sky and landed in the back of the group. The floor rocked with the force of her landing, and a few of the guests stumbled into each other. It would seem that a certain Talyrian had not appreciated being left out of this gathering.

Helena snickered. "Always one for the dramatic entrance," she teased.

Starshine opened her mouth and let out a smoky huff, pale gray smoke twisting up into the sky as her mouth closed. If the sound had a translation, Helena was certain she had just been told to shut up.

Settled once more, the Chosen returned their attention to their Kiri.

"I never wanted this war, but Rowena took that choice away from me when she began slaughtering hundreds of our brothers and sisters. She must be stopped."

There were cheers of approval as her friends lifted their glasses in salute to her words.

"This ends tomorrow. Come dawn I will leave you to set the trap that will bring her straight to me. Your gifts tonight will make that possible."

More raucous cheers rang out at her words. Helena gave them a fierce smile, one filled with bloodlust and promise.

"There is only one way this will end, my friends, and that is with the Corruptor's death. Some sins cannot be forgiven or overlooked. While the Mother is merciful, she will not stand for the slaughter of her Chosen. The time has come for justice."

Starshine tipped her head back and roared into the night sky, the cries of the Chosen deafening as they joined her.

"In the days to come, hold firm to your faith in the Mother, and in me. The only way through this is united. To justice!" Helena shouted, holding up her glass.

"To justice!" they shouted in unison.

Helena drank deep, draining her glass completely. Even without the

Jaka, she could feel the love and approval radiating from those standing before her. More than anything, Helena wanted to be worthy of it, of them. These people were her family, they were her home, and she would die to protect them.

Nial was the first to step forward, an orb of swirling crimson held in his outstretched hand.

He gave her a lopsided grin. "I went ahead and consolidated the other gifts for you. I had the feeling you might appreciate not having to deal with it in its organic form."

Helena grinned. "Whatever gave you that impression?"

He winked. "Call it instinct."

"Thank you, Nial." Her heart clenched at the sweetness of his gesture.

He placed the orb in her hand and she was surprised by its warmth. The orb was smooth, like glass, while the swirls of red rose and crashed like the sea inside.

Nial nodded, holding out his hand as he slashed his palm with a silver dagger she had not noticed until then. He squeezed his fist together, his eyes focusing intently on the orb she now held cupped in her palms. Two drops of blood dripped onto the surface of the orb, which absorbed it instantly, leaving no trace of the dark liquid on its surface.

Helena shivered, the hair on her arms standing on end as the offering merged with its predecessors. This was potent magic indeed. Her eyes lifted, but Nial was already holding out the now clean blade to the next person.

One by one they came to her. First the Chosen delegates, then the Forsaken, with her Circle going last. Just as Kragen was to hand the blade to Ronan, Starshine snarled, stalking her way to Helena's platform.

Ronan raised a brow, unsure of the Talyrian's intent. "Are you next?" he asked.

Starshine huffed and nudged him to the side.

Ronan backed away with wide eyes. "Are you seeing this?" he asked Von in a loud whisper.

Von, who had slightly more experience with the Talyrian Queen than the others, merely chuckled. "Just don't get in her way and you'll be fine," he promised.

The platform gave Helena enough height that she was able to meet Starshine's gaze head on. The Talyrian dipped her head, using a fang to slash at the thick pad of her paw. The blood welled quickly and Helena held out the orb, her heart aching at the beading red that left a trail behind it on the snow-white fur.

Beyond all others, Helena had never anticipated this. "Thank you," she whispered, emotion causing her voice to break.

Starshine huffed again and then held out her paw to Von. It took a moment for clarity, but he finally realized she was demanding that he heal the wound.

"Me?" he asked as he took the paw in his hand.

Starshine bared her teeth like she was just about at her limit of dealing with silly humans when Von held his hand above her paw and closed his eyes. The bright blue of his healing magic moved into Starshine's paw, closing the gash and wiping away all traces of blood.

Von dropped her paw, and Starshine nudged his shoulder with her snout.

Helena snickered. Starshine had practically just called Von a good boy in front of the rest of them.

Ronan was still shaking his head in disbelief as he moved into place. "I don't know how you handle being around more than one of them."

Helena shrugged. "We're kindred."

Ronan's eyes shone bright as he looked into hers. "Yes, we are."

Helena smiled at the way he twisted the words, which allowed her to miss the flash of the blade as he sunk it into his flesh. Even still, she grimaced. She could feel the sting of the cut for each of the men in her Circle, and it resonated a bit more as they went down the line.

"'Tis but a flesh wound," he said with a wink. "I've had worse on the practice field, Hellion. No need to get your panties in a bunch."

"You should go take a long walk off a short cliff," she said with a shit-eating grin of her own.

He reached out with his uninjured hand and gave her arm a squeeze. "A drop of blood is nothing, Helena. If needed, I would lay down my life for you."

Helena swallowed, her laughter dying at the serious blue eyes that stared into hers. "And I for you, Ronan."

"But not today," he said, his teeth flashing in a smile. "Today, we live."

Helena nodded, still blinking back the tears his words had caused. "Today, we live," she agreed.

Ronan stepped away, leaving only her Mate.

Von looked up at her and grinned. "And so we meet again."

"At least no one is booing you this time."

"I'm sure I could remedy that if you'd like to reenact the first time we met?" His words were so earnest that laughter bubbled forth.

"As much as I would love to relive the moment our souls found each other, they just started tolerating you a few weeks ago. No need to get them riled up again."

Von laughed. "Fair enough, *Mira*."

Between one heartbeat and the next, Von had cut his palm and pressed it down into the orb. He closed his hand around it, keeping it cupped in between their hands.

"Von," she warned since he had already given more than just a drop or two.

He did not look away from her. "Everything that I am is yours."

It was a vow he had made to her before, and Helena opened her mouth to reply as lightning flashed in the sky. There were a few shocked gasps as thunder followed, so loud that it sounded like the sky had split in two. Even though she did not look away from her Mate, she could see the rest of the guests look up toward the sky.

"It would seem the Mother has spoken," he said with a wry smile, lifting his hand from the orb.

"Apparently," Helena replied, her body thrumming from the contact with the orb. As his hand lifted, she looked down. The swirls of color were moving so fast they blurred, but that did nothing to hide the effect Von's blood had. After he had added his offering to the mix, the crimson had changed into a bright, luminescent gold.

"You sure know how to give a girl a gift," she murmured, staring at the orb in awe.

"You told me you were tired of flowers," he said.

Helena's eyes cut to his. "Never," she insisted.

He tilted his chin up, and Helena leaned down, meeting him halfway for a soft kiss. His hands went to her waist, and he lifted her off the platform and back onto the ground.

"What are we supposed to do now?" she asked.

Von shrugged, his grin so filled with mischief that her heart began to race with excitement. "Whatever the fuck we want."

"Oh, I'll drink to that," Helena said.

And so they did.

CHAPTER 25

Helena woke the next morning with only a small headache from the previous night's festivities. All in all, it could have been much worse. At least she had memories of laughter and dancing—which she was happy to note did occur after all—to offset the minor ache. She rose before the sun, spending those quiet moments brushing the hair from Von's face and kissing him sweetly awake.

"Good morning, handsome."

"Good morning, my love," he grumbled sleepily.

"If we want to leave before the others wake up, we need to get up now," she whispered as she ran her fingers along the curve of his spine.

Von grunted, his word quota for the morning already met. He wrapped his arm around her and pulled her body until it was flush against his.

Helena chuckled, appreciating the sentiment even though she knew she couldn't indulge in it. "I'll leave without you, if you'd rather sleep."

That got his attention. Von opened one bleary eye. "You'll do no such thing."

Helena nodded. "Indeed, I will."

Von sighed and rolled over onto his back with a groan. Helena openly ogled him, appreciating the way the sheet rode low on his hips.

How easy it would be to forget the task at hand and spend the morning in bed with her Mate. Helena forced her eyes away from the chiseled V at his hips. The temptation would be damn near impossible to resist if she didn't try to maintain some semblance of self-control.

"Five more minutes," he pleaded, his arm thrown across his eyes.

She smiled at the petulant cast of his voice and lifted his arm, waiting patiently until he looked at her.

"Now," she said firmly, following the word by sliding out of bed.

"Oh, that's just mean," Von growled as Helena made her way across the room stark naked.

"Consider it an incentive."

Von's eyes were predatory as he sat up, one arm propped behind him. "How so?"

Helena looked over her shoulder, her chestnut curls sliding across her back as she looked up at him through her lashes. "If you catch me before I get dressed, you can have your way with me."

Von was launching himself over the foot of the bed before Helena had finished the sentence, slamming her into the wall with his lips claiming hers in a breathless kiss. He pulled away to look down at her with an unapologetically smug smile. "Challenge accepted."

Helena melted into him, his proximity making her lose track of just exactly what she had been trying to do. There was nothing sweet or gentle about the way his body pressed against her. Von slid his hands down her sides, stopping mid-thigh to grasp her legs and pull them up around his waist.

At Helena's gasp, he pulled back with a chuckle. Nipping her lip before moving his head back toward her ear. "You did promise anything," he growled.

Her head fell back against the wall. "By all means..." her voice trailed off, further coherent words impossible.

He anchored her against the wall with his hips, the throbbing length of him pressed tightly against her aching core while he used his phantom hands to tease her body. "I like this game," he murmured, coming up from another breath-stealing kiss.

Helena's eyelids felt heavy as she forced them open to look at him. "Mmm," she murmured.

"We should play it every morning," he said, sliding his velvety length along her center.

"Oh," she groaned, pressing her hips against him to increase the pressure.

She heard his snicker of approval before his hips swiveled and he drove straight into her.

"Oh!" she gasped again, clenching around every pulsing inch of him.

"Look at me," he demanded as he drove into her.

It was damn near impossible, but she made her eyes focus on his face. There was no need for words. The look in his eyes told her everything he wanted her to know, while the bond reinforced it with its loving heat.

Their frenzied lovemaking was over as quickly as it began, each thrust causing sparks to burst behind her eyelids until she finally lost herself to the ecstasy of his touch. He came with a growl, his teeth biting down into her neck as he spent himself inside her. They stayed there, their hearts thundering in their chests as they held onto each other.

"Now you can go get ready," he told her, letting her body slide down his until her feet touched the floor.

Helena was proud of herself when her knees only buckled once. "I don't know who you think you're giving permission," she informed him primly. "If I hadn't wanted you, I wouldn't have given you the opportunity."

Von's eyes were pure molten silver when he replied, "Oh darling, if you think I was going to let you walk away without reminding you who you belong to, you've forgotten who I am."

Helena turned to face him completely. "Who says *you* were reminding *me*?" With a wink, she spun back around and headed into the bathroom to enjoy the last handful of moments she had left before leaving to face the darkest part of her soul.

LESS THAN AN HOUR LATER, Helena was standing on the top of a hill at the westernmost border of Tigaera. There was nothing particularly special about the area, other than being wedged between the Palace and Endoshan. Helena could have cast her illusion anywhere, the location didn't matter so much as the results, but she felt it would be most believable the closer she was to Rowena's hidden cemetery.

The sun had just started its rise, and the sky was a brilliant wash of red and orange. It looked as if the sky was on fire, and Helena took that as a good sign, considering what she was about to do.

She heard the rustle of Von's clothes as he stepped closer to her, laying each of his hands on her shoulders. Her eyes fell closed, savoring the warmth of his touch. He brushed a kiss to the base of her neck and then, without a word, he walked away to give her the space she needed to concentrate.

There was no more putting it off with strategy meetings, or last-minute ceremonies, or lovemaking. The time had come. Helena pulled the golden orb from the hidden pocket in her cloak, the hair of her arms standing on end at the contact.

The orb pulsed with latent power that called to her, hungry for its release. The pool of her power rippled in response like the flow of the tide feeling the pull of the moon. Helena called on her rage, summoning every pain-filled memory to the front of her mind. She shuddered, her body transforming in response to the swift rise of fury. The tips of her fingers became deadly black claws, and even her teeth felt as though they had lengthened. She didn't give herself time to think before she slashed at her arm with one of the Talyrian claws. Blood rose swiftly, splashing from the gash in her arm and coating the orb.

As soon as her blood made contact, the orb began to glow, shifting from gold to a blinding white. She lifted the orb up, blood still running down her arms and dripping to the ground, before letting go of it entirely. As the orb began to fall, she closed her eyes, shifting her focus as she dove straight into the depths of her power. Helena had never gone that deep that fast, and the rise of power was heady. She could feel her physical body sway, but she did not stop, pushing herself down even deeper.

Distantly, she heard the shattering of glass. That was her cue. Pulling every ounce of power to the surface, Helena opened her eyes and screamed. She screamed for pointless deaths, futures that would never be, and for all the Chosen who had been suffering for so long that their screams had long gone silent with their belief that no one could hear them, or worse, that no one cared. It was the pain of her people that fueled her, and she made herself feel every ugly piece of it.

Birds burst from the trees as thunder began to roll overhead. The sky filled with thick black clouds from which drops of blood began to fall, coating the land in its deep crimson. The earth shook under the assault, the transformation already underway.

Helena did not have to concentrate overly hard on what she wanted. All it took was the echo of three spectral voices in her head for the vision from her trial to bring every gory detail into pristine focus.

'You have a choice before you.'

'See the cost of your choice.'

Blood continued to fall from the sky, while the pieces of ash blowing up from the ground further obscured the air. The trees, once vibrant and alive, were now charred skeletons, many of them still on fire. The unearthly wind continued to whip up piles of ash, flinging them into the air until they fluttered like ghostly butterflies. In the face of such destruction, it was almost impossible to see past her hand, but Helena didn't need to see. She already knew what she would find. The ground was no longer rolling green hills, instead it was endless piles of corpses. She refused to look down, not wanting to be greeted by the faces of the dead. Seeing them once was enough.

She felt his approach before she heard it, and by the time he'd reached her, she was already facing him. Helena watched him fight to keep his face neutral, but she could see her reflection in his eyes. She was a wild thing, more creature than human. Her hair was flying around her while embers flickered at the tips, giving her a fiery halo.

Her eyes were not the iridescent color of her power but pits of ebony with shimmering echoes of flame in their depths.

Helena licked her lips, tasting blood and ash. "The eyes can see what the heart knows to be false." She thought she had whispered the words, but they echoed from every direction as if they had been spoken by a legion.

"Then I shall close my eyes, so I see only what is true," Von said.

Helena felt herself waver, and blinked a few times before shoving every emotion besides pain and grief into a deeply recessed part of her heart.

"It is time to break the tether." Again, her words swirled around them while thunder continued to growl in the sky.

Von swallowed but gave no other outward sign of fear. Instead, her beautiful warrior faced her head on and spoke in a controlled voice, "Do your worst and know that I love you."

If she allowed herself to focus on their bond, she might have felt the flutter of panic when she cast the final, darkest part of the spell. As with before, all it took was a memory of voices.

'Without the tether, you will fracture.'

'Eternally lost to the darkness.'

For Rowena to truly fall for Helena's deception, her bond to Von must appear severed. Von had already known what had to happen when he pulled her aside. His strategist's mind had seen the play before she ever did. Mostly because it was not something she would ever willingly consider. Once triggered, it would enable them to each experience the one thing with the potential to destroy them both. There was no telling how they would react.

But this was war, and there was no other choice. Everything about the illusion had to be unfailingly convincing. The Kiri and her Mate must truly believe the bond was gone. That required them to actually *feel* like their bond was gone.

There was no explosion of power this time, just a gasp as Von crumpled to his knees before a loud, keening cry was torn from his throat. "Helena," he rasped, his eyes staring up at her in horror.

She was merciless, focusing only on what she needed the power to do and not the whimpering voice in the back of her mind pleading with her to end this and find another way.

There was no determining how much time had passed when Von finally labored to his feet, his body trembling. When his eyes met hers, they were not the silvery gray that she adored, but a milky white snaking with black.

The illusion had been cast, and the magic was so powerful that by the time Helena was done, even her heart could no longer tell what was true.

CHAPTER 26

$\mathcal{R}$onan swore under his breath as he stormed down the stairs and walked out to the armory.

"Rough morning?" Reyna asked in a deceptively sweet voice as he rounded the corner. She began to walk beside him, matching his ground-eating stride with ease.

Ronan scowled at her. "They left without us."

Reyna lifted a brow. "And that surprised you?"

He glared. "Obviously."

Her brows veed over her eyes and she stopped him with a touch. "She gave us a time and a place to meet her. You had to realize Helena was going to go ahead of us."

Ronan bit back a slew of harsh words. He'd been so damn preoccupied he hadn't realized it, and it chafed to no end that Helena and Von had left him behind. He was her Shield damn it. His place was at her side, more so now than ever.

"Whatever," he muttered, slamming into someone rushing the other way. "Get out of my way," Ronan snarled. The poor boy who had been carrying armor whimpered and scurried away.

"You're making children piss themselves now."

"Children, grown men… what's the difference?"

"Really, Ronan?" The disappointment in her voice was undeniable.

959

Ronan stopped again, running a hand along his face. "I'm just on edge."

"We all are. You're not the only one heading into this battle."

He turned to face her, his eyes blazing with blue fire. "Yes, but there's never been this much at stake before. I've fought for Daejara, I've fought because I've been paid to do it, but never have I been more scared of what happens if I lose."

"It sounds like it's the first time you truly cared about the outcome," Reyna commented softly.

He was about to protest, but she was right. Daejara had been his home, and he'd believed in Von when he'd joined him, but Ronan had never stopped to worry about what tomorrow would bring. If he died in battle, at least he'd go out in a blaze of glory. Now, however, it wasn't even the thought of his death that had his heart filled with dread. Death would be a mercy if they lost.

Determination had him gritting his teeth. He couldn't guarantee that no one would die today, but he'd make damn sure that those corrupted pieces of shit would have to go through him before snuffing out the life of another person that had become his family.

"Chosen!" he shouted, causing everyone in the room to freeze mid-act. "Fall out. We leave in ten to meet your Kiri and join the fight for our way of life!"

The room burst into excited cheers and men and women rushed to finish their preparations.

"Spoken like a man who has something to prove," Reyna said, her eyes looking much softer than they had only moments before.

"Spoken like a man who has something to protect," he corrected. "It is not our lives she wants, it is our souls. Rowena seeks to destroy all that holds any value to the Chosen. Her victory is not simply the end of us, it is the end of everything. Is that not worth fighting against? Mother's tits, Reyna. Is that not worth dying to prevent?"

Reyna was quiet, and Ronan could see the flutter of her pulse at her throat. She was not unaffected by his words, although her face remained impassive.

"Oh the hell with it," she muttered a second before pressing her hands to his cheeks and pulling his face down to hers. When her lips touched his, his heart stuttered. He was frozen for only a heartbeat before his arms slid around her and pulled her lithe body against his.

The kiss was a force of nature, violence and passion colliding as they said with their lips all the things they had not had a chance to express with words.

Reyna pulled back first, panting hard. "You will live today, Shield," she said fiercely, her forest green eyes burning into his. "I'm not done with you yet."

"Yes, ma'am," he whispered, his lips tilting up in a one-sided grin.

Reyna nodded matter-of-factly and disentangled herself from his embrace.

Flickering shadows danced around her body as she walked away, and Ronan found himself staring after her in wonder. Yes, they definitely had some unfinished business.

RONAN STARED at the decimated land before him, his eyes wide with shock.

"Well, it will certainly grab Rowena's attention," Kragen said, his expression a twin of Ronan's.

"That's one way to put it. Have you seen any sign of Helena or Von?"

"Negative," Kragen replied, shifting to face him. "The others are growing restless. They had not anticipated their gifts were going to be used to create… this."

Ronan spared a glance at the people who stood as far from the blood and ash covered land as possible. He didn't blame them. Everything about this place was grating against his senses. The mounds of corpses were especially revolting.

"I almost can't believe Helena was capable of creating this," Kragen muttered.

Ronan had no trouble believing it. He remembered watching her as her power sparked out of control. This was what it looked like when that power was not tempered by her love.

"We should make sure that the Chosen remember this is only a trick meant for Rowena. We cannot afford to have them lose faith in Helena."

Kragen nodded. "It is one thing to be told and another to come face-to-face with the results of said trick. There are likely many that are reconsidering their presence here."

"It was what she intended, since she needs word to get back to Rowena."

Kragen sighed. "I know. I will ensure that the message is reinforced so that it is only a few lost instead of an entire army."

A disturbance in one of the mounds caught his attention, and Ronan squinted, trying to make sense of what he was seeing. One of the corpses was pushing itself up. Wait. That wasn't a corpse. He would have recognized that sword anywhere. He'd helped forge it. That alone was enough for him to recognize the figure that slowly approached them.

"Mother be merciful," Ronan whispered, watching what had once been the brother of his heart take slow shuffling steps toward them. "Helena, what have you done?" Even as he knew this had to be part of the illusion, seeing Von's eyes snaking with the telltale black lines was too much.

Ronan lurched, half running half falling as he raced toward his best friend. "Von!" he shouted, hoping that he would reply and prove that this was only a trick.

The man that had once been Von opened his mouth on an endless scream. That was when Ronan noticed the figure standing in one of the crumbling defense towers in the distance. Her hair billowed around her like she stood at the center of a storm, the ends smoldering embers.

His stomach rolled, and he swallowed hard to avoid being unmanned entirely. It was too much. That couldn't be the woman he'd bound his life to.

Even from this distance, Ronan could tell that soulless black eyes were staring directly at him. He saw her mouth open, although he was too far to hear the words or read her lips. It didn't matter. As soon as Von lunged for him, he knew what she had ordered. It had been one, unmistakable word: attack.

"Let me in on the game, brother," Ronan begged as soon as Von was within hearing distance. "Are we putting on a show for the others?"

Ronan watched in horror as the man who had been more than a brother to him came after him, holding nothing back as he began to fight, not as a warrior but as a Shadow. At first, Ronan clung to the belief that this was all part of the elaborate scheme, and his moves were entirely defensive, but as soon as Von bit into the side of his arm and pulled back with a piece of flesh, Ronan knew they were doomed.

It may have started off as an illusion, but somewhere along the way, Helena had been lost to the darkness. It was the only explanation.

He pushed Von, or what was left of him, away with a snarl and eased himself into a fighting stance. The one thing he still had going for him was that he had fought Von hundreds of times, he knew without conscious thought how and where his friend would strike. For all that Von had lost his mind, his instincts were still intact.

"All right, you bastard. Let's dance."

The next time Von lunged, Ronan pounced, and the two men met in the air before falling to the ground in a tangle of limbs. They fought brutally, holding nothing back as they traded blows. That was nothing new, they'd always pushed each other to the limits, knowing it was necessary to keep them primed for battle. The only difference this time was it wasn't in the name of practice.

This time, the battle was real.

CHAPTER 27

Rowena stared at the trembling messenger in disbelief. A bubble of something that must be happiness rose in her chest, but the feeling was so foreign, Rowena didn't recognize it. "Say that again," she demanded.

"It is as I said, My Queen. The prophecy has been fulfilled. Even now, the Mother's Vessel is in Endoshan commanding her own army of Shadows into attacking the Chosen army. As one falls, she turns them, using the dead to create a new army."

Rowena fell back in her makeshift throne, her fingers lifting to her lips as a breathless laugh bubbled up. She had won. Her fingers traced her lips, feeling them lift in an unfamiliar smile.

"Bring me my husband," she ordered.

The messenger bowed and swiftly exited the cavern she had claimed as her throne room.

It was done. She had won. Rowena knew it was only a matter of time, but now that it was here… her thoughts continued to chase each other, each one bringing with it a buoyant joy she hadn't experienced since the birth of her twins. Back when the sniveling traitors meant something to her.

"My Queen?" Kai-Soren called as he walked in.

"Have you heard?"

"I have, My Queen." There was a bland sense of disinterest in his voice that confused her, but she was too elated to care.

"Ready the men. We leave for Endoshan before nightfall. It is time to go meet my finest creation."

His dark slash of a brow lifted. "Your creation, My Queen?"

Rowena's smile hung frozen on her lips. "You doubt me?"

"Never, My Queen. I simply do not understand."

That Rowena easily believed. Her smile grew, although now it was tinged with a familiar icy cruelty. "It would seem my pet has discovered my gift. Her acceptance is a most welcome sign."

Kai-Soren shook his head. "I do not follow."

Rowena sighed. He was really taking the fun out of this for her. "You don't need to. All that should matter to you is the Vessel has been shattered. She is ours to use as we please. Don't you know what this means? Elysia and the Chosen are mine."

Her husband looked like he wished to say something more, but apparently he had finally learned his lesson because he simply gave her an empty smile and bowed. "Very good, My Queen. I will make sure the men are ready for our departure."

His lack of excitement didn't matter. He wouldn't be around much longer anyway. Not now that she had what she needed. Once she claimed what was rightfully hers, Kai-Soren would be nothing more than an unpleasant afterthought.

ROWENA HAD to admit she was impressed. She knew that the Vessel would be helpless to resist the pull of her little present, but she hadn't quite expected this. There was no denying that her newest ally was a powerful one, and much more valuable than a full team of Generals. With the kind of power the Vessel was putting off, the need for Generals was obsolete.

Rowena felt a flicker of relief. Considering she had never gotten around to replacing the last two, that was welcome news.

The mounds of corpses made it hard to traverse easily across the land, and the sky continued to rain down blood and ash. The slaughter was absolute. Rowena had thought the messenger said that the Chosen were being turned before they died, but it would appear the Vessel had gotten tired of building her own army. No matter, between the two of them, there were more than enough Shadows already.

She smiled in delight. "If it wasn't already obvious, let us reinforce our victory with a bit more destruction, shall we?" Rowena whistled, calling for the two Talyrians she had managed to turn the last time she had faced off with the Chosen.

Mother of Shadows indeed. Not only did she have the two beasts, she now owned the Vessel as well. The Mother may have spat upon her when she withheld her greatest gift, but it didn't matter anymore because Rowena had fought for, and taken, all that should have belonged to her by right. This victory proved that none were her equal. The Chosen would be obliterated, the entire race replaced by a people of her creation. She would be revered and worshiped for the rest of time.

Rowena could feel the air shift behind her as the wings of the beasts pushed through the blood and ash. Even with the limited light, their bodies cast shadows on the ground below. A figure standing in the middle of the carnage twisted, finally taking notice of Rowena and the army at her back.

Her smile grew as recognition dawned. It was the Mate, or what had once been the Mate. Rowena laughed, it would appear the Vessel had finished what she had started. She still had not seen any sign of her once opponent, but any vestige of doubt that might have remained about the truth of the messenger's words fled at the sight of the twisted figure before her.

She did not require any further proof that Helena's corruption was absolute. That didn't mean she didn't want to drive the point home to completely shatter what was left of the broken army that still hoped to oppose her.

"Destroy him," Rowena commanded, her voice a gleeful purr. Rowena pointed toward Von, and the Shadow Talyrians wasted no time hesitating, purple jets of Shadow Fire spouting from their mouths as they careened toward their target.

Surely no other victory had ever tasted so sweet.

CHAPTER 28

Helena's hands were braced on the stone blocks that made up the watchtower. She watched the figures below with no more interest than one gave to an ant. The sense that she was forgetting something important continued to gnaw at her. It had started when the red-headed one grappled with her new pet, but she'd grown tired of watching and had called on her power to encase him in stone.

Her pet had been furious that she'd denied him the kill, but the act had released some of the pressure that had been building in her chest as the fight between them had carried on.

Shortly after, dozens of others had peeled away from the massive crowd gathered at the furthest edge of the field. Her pet had snarled and made like he was going to attack, and soon that nagging feeling rose again until Helena froze those men as well. And then the next. And the next, until finally everyone that remained had been encased in stone. It had taken no more than a thought and each body was a statue, frozen in a moment of time. As coated in blood and ash as they were, it was impossible to tell that they were no longer animated with life.

It didn't matter. Nothing did. All she cared about was that the pressure in her chest eased once they were unable to act further.

Helena had no memory of how she got here or how long she'd been standing as still as one of her statues. She knew not what she waited for, only that she was, in fact, waiting. Time held no meaning. The sky remained a roiling mass of black clouds and lightning as blood fell from the sky. Day or night, it made no difference. The sky cast no true light, only an endless darkness.

She tipped her face back, opening her mouth to gulp the warm liquid, tasting the power and fury that drove the storm, and wanting to claim a part of it for herself. She could feel the magic roll through her, her body warming in response to its call.

A jet of color in the black of the sky caught her eye, and Helena's head twisted toward the movement. Streaks of red and orange were growing larger as they arced through the sky. There was something familiar about the shape of them and the way they moved. Her head tilted as she struggled to remember the name for the flying creatures.

That was when she noticed them swoop low, diving straight for her pet.

The pressure in her chest that had dimmed with the statues, increased until she was gasping for breath. At the same time, she watched the creatures, now shooting purple flames from their mouths, creating a ring of fire her pet could not escape. Helena's fury rose until she could hear her blood roaring in her ears. Two things happened simultaneously, making it impossible to tell which act triggered the other.

The tensioning in her chest broke and a snarling word was torn from her mouth as her body came undone. The word boomed across the sky, wrapping her inside of it as she was remade.

"MINE!"

The figures of stone began to crack, and the black clouds peeled back from the sky, revealing a blood-red moon.

Her body was no longer her own. Helena's back stretched and arched as her battle cry echoed on. Her limbs lengthened, growing thick and corded with muscle until it was too hard to stand on only two feet. She fell forward, noticing the glistening black claws that scratched deep divots into the gray stone, as white fur that sparkled like diamonds began to sprout from her skin.

A weight at her back caused her to shake in an attempt to dislodge it, but as she shook, she felt the weight move with her. Wanting to ease the tension, she rolled her shoulders and saw out of the corner of her eye as she did, a massive golden wing tipped with shiny black talons unfurl.

There was no conscious thought, no sense of self or understanding. Only instinct and one truth that rang louder than everything else.

Mine.

Those foul beasts wanted what was hers, and she wasn't about to let them have it.

Helena roared, pushing herself up until all four of her feet were balanced precariously on the edge of stone. There were shouts below and then the sound of roars filled the sky, filling her chest with the need to answer the call. Tipping her head back she roared, blinding white fire flowing from her mouth to light up the sky.

She was not aware of what happened beneath her, other than the statues were frozen no longer. Now freed, they joined in her cries, adding their voices to the chorus.

She jumped from the ledge, trusting her wings to catch the air. This was no graceful dive, but a mix of physics and haphazard gliding. Her body may know what it wanted to do, but it did not mean she possessed any semblance of talent in this new, powerful form.

Luckily, she did not need to worry about landing. Helena made contact with the larger of the two creatures, her claws sinking into its decaying flesh as easily as parting butter. She held tight as her mouth opened on a furious roar before sinking her teeth into its neck and ripping back. The beast's head was torn from its body and its wings beat once, twice, before stuttering and falling limp. She released her hold on the body as it began to tumble, not ready to go down with it.

Her wings were still outstretched, and she beat them hard to try to regain some height. The other creature turned its lavender eyes toward her, the snaking lines almost hypnotic. *Wrong,* she thought. This beast had once been majestic, but now it was tainted.

It opened its mouth, ready to spew more of its purple fire at her, but she lashed out with a claw, raking it across its eyes. The blow was so strong, it knocked the creature from the sky. She followed it down, not wanting to give her prey a chance to escape.

It tried to correct its descent, its wings pumping furiously, but she caught the sinuous length with her claws and pulled back, hearing a snap and then a furious roar. The wing tore from its body with no more effort than plucking a feather from a bird. It sped toward the ground, tumbling as it fell through the sky.

Helena felt her body stretch as it tried to close the distance between them. There was another roar, and a spout of hot flame before another beast, a white one with black wings and bright turquoise eyes, intercepted the orange body, savagely tearing it apart, flinging the broken pieces away before covering the broken body in cleansing flame.

Helena landed as best she could, her new legs stumbling under the impact. Her fury at the kill being stolen from her was replaced with respect as the other creature calmly stalked toward her. Helena felt the need to curl her tail between her legs. She did not want this one's anger. She feared it but did not understand why.

She held perfectly still as a turquoise eye inspected her, feeling as though she was holding her breath the entire time. The feline was much larger than she was, although Helena knew that she was more than a match for her if it came down to a fight. She could feel the power rippling through her body even in this new form.

But it was not a fight the creature was interested in. After one long sniff, the other cat nuzzled against her and began to lick at her fur, cleaning away the remnants of blood and gore. Helena felt her chest vibrate with pleasure. Where she had once felt only fury and possessive anger, now she felt a tidal wave of love.

The remaining remnants of the illusion fell away, showing the truth that had been concealed by its darkness. What was left of it exploded in a shower of light. The land was green and whole once more, and the only bodies that remained were wholly alive.

Helena blinked, memories returning to her in a rush. She staggered under the weight of what had happened, shocked that she had lost enough of herself to the illusion that she hadn't understood what was happening.

Von, entirely unharmed, ran over to the two Talyrian females, his hands raised.

"Helena?" he asked, his voice rusty. "Are you in there?"

She padded forward, eying her tiny two-legged Mate. Before she could pounce on him and claim him as hers in front of the others, a sharp wail had her hackles rising.

"NO! You stupid bitch, I have already won! You belong to me! You all belong to me!"

Helena snarled at the woman standing on the other side of the hill. *Rowena.*

This was not the time for claiming after all. There was still work to be done. She was the Mother's Vessel; the Mother's vengeance; and now more than ever, the Mother's teeth and claws. It was time to fight.

VON HAD no recollection of what had happened after Helena had cast the final piece of the illusion. He had felt like he was suffocating, the pain of their bond being ripped away more devastatingly painful than he'd ever anticipated. It was like he blacked out, everything about him ceasing to be until just moments ago when he rose from a crouched position on the floor. He'd been surrounded by purple flames, but there had been a gap just large enough for him to launch himself through where the flames had not yet met.

He had seen the glowing iridescent eyes of the second white Talyrian and recognized his Mate instantly. Even in this form, she called to him.

The bond had returned in full force, but the messages it was sending were a chaotic jumble. He wasn't sure if it was Helena's new form, or if it was simply Helena herself. Needing to see for himself that she was okay, he'd ran toward the two Talyrians, slowing down once he was close enough to catch their attention.

Helena's Talyrian gaze zeroed in on him, and he froze in place as a flood of energy zinged through him. He didn't know what had changed, only that she had somehow tapped into even more power than she'd ever held before. Is that what had allowed the change? Or was it merely leftover power from the Chosen's offerings? There were too many questions and no time to get answers.

A woman's angry cry had them looking past Helena's shoulder to the top of a hill. Rowena's fists were clenched in her skirt and her face was twisted in an angry mask. She was furious at their betrayal.

Von smiled, his eyes glittering with malice while his Mate snarled, her Talyrian body posed for attack.

Rowena shouted more orders, but the words were unintelligible from this distance. Three dark figures moved into view, and Von zeroed in on his target. In order to end this once and for all, those three had to go down.

He heard the sound of hundreds of footsteps and glanced over his shoulder to see a confused army come into view. Ronan was at the head, Kragen and Reyna on either side of him. Ronan's blue eyes were troubled and cautious. The others looked equally uncertain.

Helena had warned him that the others might fall victim to the illusion, but he hadn't actually believed her. Since he himself had no recollection of what had happened, he just hoped nothing unforgivable had transpired.

"Von?" Ronan asked.

Von looked around, making sure he was still standing alone. "Who else would I be?"

"Thank the Mother," Ronan said, rushing forward to wrap Von in a bone-crushing hug.

Von grunted but returned the harsh back slaps with a few of his own. "I take it there was some doubt for a while?"

"Just long enough to make me shit myself," Ronan muttered darkly.

Von wanted to laugh, but the fear was still too fresh in his friend's eyes.

"I'm sorry that we scared you. You understand it had to happen, don't you?"

Ronan nodded, but the shadows lingered in his eyes. "Now is not the time for apologies. I'm just glad you are okay."

The Circle fell into place behind him, their eyes rounded as they took in the sight of their Kiri.

"Do you think it's permanent?" Joquil asked in a hushed tone.

"Nothing like this has ever happened before," Timmins replied. "I can only hope for all our sakes that it's not."

"It's not," Von said firmly. There was no doubt in his mind Helena would return to herself once this was over, if not before. There was no telling how long the transformation would last, but he figured it would end once the excess power ran itself out.

There was another cry, and Rowena's Shadows began to swarm the field while her Generals wasted no time wreaking havoc.

Von's brows lowered, and he pulled his sword from its scabbard, running a hand along its length to set it on fire. "Let's finish this," he roared, holding up his sword and rushing head long into the frenzied mob.

The final battle was at hand.

CHAPTER 29

The three Generals split up, one moving straight through the center of the crowd, while the other two moved to each side. It was an unspoken agreement that the Chosen's leaders would divide their main forces to counter the major threats, while the bulk of the army led by Timmins and Joquil would handle the Shadows.

Ronan and Reyna's Night Stalkers peeled toward the left, heading toward a decaying figure that had flies buzzing about him and a trail of dead grass in his wake.

Kragen and the Storm Forged went right, moving to intercept a General that had called forth the water from a nearby stream and was sending wave after wave toward the Chosen gathered nearby.

For his part, Von followed the Talyrians who were chasing down a General whose affinity appeared to be Fire. More of the purple Shadow Fire danced in his hands. The Talyrians could fly far faster than he could run, even while using his power, so Von gave up the chase when he spied Kai-Soren spinning twin daggers in his palms.

Von's mouth stretched into a sinister smile, he would do just as nicely. "Seems you chose the wrong side, Heir."

"I did what was best for my people, Daejaran. Something I think you'd understand."

"Turning on your people to save your own ass? No, I don't think we have anything in common."

Kai-Soren's golden eyes narrowed at the dig. "That only makes this easier." He flung one of the daggers, the silver metal glinting as it spun through the air. Von's blade cut out to his side, knocking the dagger uselessly to the ground. Four more daggers followed in rapid succession, and Von maneuvered his blade just as fast, none of the poisoned daggers meeting their mark.

"That all you got?" Von taunted, pleased to see Kai-Soren's left eye begin to twitch.

"Daejaran scum!" he spat, lunging toward Von.

Anticipating a hidden blade, Von dodged the attack, twirling to the side so that his flaming sword slid across the Endoshan heir's back, the sharp edge of the blade cutting through leather and skin, while Kai-Soren's hair went up in flame. Von smirked, enjoying himself far too much. He'd disliked the heir ever since their first meeting when he'd flung ignorant insult after insult at Von.

For all the prestige laid at the Endoshan warrior's feet, Von was underwhelmed by the skill of their heir. *He probably lets the poison do the work for him.* Von snorted with derision. No true leader should be outmatched by the rest of their people. It's one thing to surround yourself by those strong where you are not, it's another thing entirely to be utterly incompetent. Something wasn't adding up.

Kai-Soren's blows were half-hearted at best, and Von was able to dodge and disarm him easily.

"Stop playing with me and end it," the heir hissed, staring up at Von from where he'd landed on his back after Von had swept his legs out from under him.

Von gave him a long considering look. "Can't stand to deal with the mess you've made of things? Where's that infamous Endoshan honor now?"

Kai-Soren looked away, and it was all the answer Von needed.

"You've failed your people. You are not worthy to lead them."

"End it, Daejaran!"

"With pleasure," Von hissed, using his blade to slit the filthy traitor's throat.

Von was not his Mate. When presented with an opportunity to show mercy, it did not come naturally to him to take that route. Besides, there were less honorable ways to die than on a battlefield during a war. The only mercy Von would show was not telling what was left of his people that their heir had begged for his death like a coward.

It would have to be good enough, and it was still more than he deserved.

HELENA FLEW at the head of the pride, Starshine on her right and Midnight on her left. She could feel the heat of the Talyrian flames as they took out wave after wave of the Shadow army. With each skeletal body that was lost to the flames, she felt an answering call of satisfaction.

She focused solely on the man in black whose hands were playing with purple licks of Fire. If given the chance, he would unleash that corrupted Fire on her people, and it would not stop until it ran out of things to consume. They could not give him that chance.

Starshine roared and the Talyrians broke rank, confusing the Fire General as he could no longer anticipate where the attack would come from. They played with him like a cat with a mouse, one Talyrian swooping in low while another shot off a jet of flame. He dodged the attacks, jumping out of the way of one with barely enough time to dodge the other. He was their puppet on a string.

The General grew tired of the game quickly. He started to lob balls of purple flames up into the sky. For every Talyrian he knocked off course in their attempt to dodge the flame, another one took its place.

Starshine circled the General, swatting at him with extended claws. He raised his arms, trying to protect his face from the deadly tips but was only successful in providing easier access to his skin. Her claws raked against him, thick lines of black ichor beginning to show everywhere Starshine made contact. The General cried out in pain and rage, a ball of Shadow Fire growing in the palm of his hand.

Game time was over.

Helena swooped down, her Talyrian fangs bared as she growled low in her throat. She watched the General's empty eyes staring up at her as her mouth opened and ripped the arm from its socket. Next was Midnight, his teeth raking the flesh clean off the other arm before snapping it in two. With the threat of Shadow Fire neutralized, the General was unable to do more than spin in an impotent circle. Starshine was last, the Talyrian Queen ripping out his throat and completing the kill.

From her place on the hill, Rowena screeched in outrage, more of her power lost. It was nowhere near enough to avenge the unfortunate deaths of the two Talyrians that had fallen to Rowena's twisted power, but it was a damned good start.

The pride flew across the sky, their howls of victory interrupted only by jets of flame as they laid waste to more of the Shadow fiends below.

One down, two to go.

VON SPUN, looking for his next target. Ronan and Reyna looked like they had their hands full with the decaying General, but before he could get to them, a wave knocked him over. His skin stung everywhere the water touched him, and Von hissed in pain. He looked down to see his skin erupt in blisters. Steam rose from the water before it was absorbed back into the earth, which quickly turned to mud.

The decision made for him, Von made his way toward Kragen instead, blinking across the muddy ground instead of fighting against it.

The Water General was keeping the Chosen busy dodging his waves, but the Storm Forged were giving as good as they got. While the Chosen worked on the group of Shadows that were attacking, the Storm Forged worked to take control of the water. Every time it looked like they would be successful, a new wave would appear behind them and break their concentration, causing them to start over.

When it came to controlling Water, there was only one person that outmatched the Stormbringer, and she was currently flying through the sky with the rest of the Talyrians, but at the moment, Anduin seemed anything but in control.

"Stormbringer," Von greeted when he appeared beside him.

Anduin's eyes were pinched and he had broken out into a sweat. "This is the first time water has felt like it was fighting against me. There is something, unclean, about it."

Von nodded, not surprised to hear that the element the General was commanding was tainted. It was the nature of Rowena's Generals.

"What do you need?" Von asked.

"A distraction. Something that will let us take control of the water and cleanse it before returning it to the earth. In its current form, the damage it's doing to the land and its potential to harm those that come into contact with it is…" Anduin shrugged, at a loss for words. "It's bad," he said finally.

Von nodded. A distraction he could do. "Regroup and wait for my signal."

The Stormbringer nodded, looking relieved that someone else was taking control.

Kragen was wiping black ichor from his blade when he looked up at Von. "Slimy little fuckers," he said by way of greeting.

Von laughed and nodded. "That they are, brother."

"I wouldn't mind so much if it wasn't for the smell," Kragen continued conversationally, decapitating another Shadow with his blade as if this was a normal occurrence. Perhaps these days it was.

Seeing as how they did emit the distinct aroma of rotting vegetation and feces, Von wasn't about to disagree.

"Do you remember that one time during training, where the recruit tripped over his own boot and went flying into Ronan?" Von asked.

Kragen gave a snicker of laughter. "I can hardly forget, especially after Ronan bashed the kid upside his head and sent him spinning, but is this really the time to dredge up our fondest memories?" Kragen punctuated the question by driving the tip of his sword into the chest of another Shadow before pulling it out and gutting him.

"We're going to recreate it."

Kragen paused only long enough to look at Von and ask, "You want to trip over your boot and into me? Now?"

"No, dumbass, I want you to launch me into the General so I can knock him over and distract him long enough for Anduin to gain control of the water."

Understanding flickered in Kragen's dark eyes. "You don't want him to see you coming."

"Exactly."

Kragen grinned, his eyes crinkling with unconcealed delight. "Don't take this the wrong way, but I am damned sure I am going to enjoy this far more than you. Brace yourself."

Von was by no means a small man, but Kragen still towered above him. With less effort than he would have liked, Kragen grabbed Von by the back of his shirt and hauled him up into the air. Von could feel the tingle of power as Kragen reinforced his throw with Air. Within seconds, Von was flying, his arms spindling out of control as he flew like an arrow straight toward the General. By the time the bastard noticed him catapulting toward him, the General could do nothing except fall under Von's weight.

There was a loud grunt and crack. After a quick mental check, he was certain that no major injuries were sustained, at least on his part. The General tried to push Von off him, but Von continued to shift and move, keeping the General pinned beneath his weight.

After a moment of the wrestling, Von realized it was absolutely stupid to wait for a distraction when he was in such a prime position. He hoisted himself up just enough to pull one of the daggers he'd knicked from Kai-Soren and drove it into the side of the General's neck. Black ichor spewed from the wound as he drew the blade back out.

"Nighty night," he crooned as the General gasped before wet gurgles of ichor bubbled from his mouth.

Von was enjoying himself entirely too much. Such was the way of the bloodlust.

Kragen stood above him, staring down with such a downcast look that Von was concerned. "What's wrong?"

"Can't you save some for the rest of us?" Kragen winked, and Von shook his head.

"Help me up, Sword, and I'll see what I can do for you."

Kragen grasped Von's forearm and pulled him up with ease. Together the two men turned to face the Storm Forged, who were using the last of the corrupted water to capture and drown the Shadows nearest to them.

"Remind me not to piss that guy off," Kragen said in a low voice.

There was a scream, and the world began to shake.

"Brother," Von said, "the Stormbringer is the least of our worries."

RONAN GRUNTED as the razor-sharp nails of the Shadow scored his skin. They'd been ambushed by the cadavers as soon as they'd gotten within reach of the General.

Reyna took one look at the blight that spread out in a ring wherever he stood and ripped her necklace off. Ronan gave her a baffled look but did not have time to wonder what in the Mother's name she was doing.

A jet of Talyrian fire helped take care of a few Shadows, giving Ronan a chance to breathe and re-center himself. He'd lost track of the battle raging around him, focusing only on the opponents before him and clearing a path to take down another of Rowena's Generals.

Reyna was muttering something under her breath, and Ronan gave her another look.

"What are you doing?"

The Night Stalker blinked up at him. "Summoning the Watchers."

It was Ronan's turn to blink. "I thought that they had fulfilled their promise in the Vale."

Reyna shrugged. "It's all in how you look at it, I suppose. What matters now is that they're here." She gestured toward the horizon where the trees seemed to shift and stretch.

"But—"

She slapped him on the shoulder. "Save your deep thinking for later, Shield. We have enemies to kill."

Ronan shook his head, amazed at how fast the trees had transformed. He recognized the lumbering tree men from the brief time he'd seen them during the Battle of the Vale, but he'd forgotten just how impressive they were. The trees moved slowly, but their massive size more than made up for it by helping them cover the distance quickly; their method of execution by stomping was probably the greatest thing Ronan had ever seen.

Second greatest thing, he corrected instantly, seeing two golden Talyrian wings carry Helena across the sky toward the hill Rowena cowered upon. He still did not understand where the ability to transform had come from, but he was endlessly thankful for it. If Helena was moving toward Rowena, it meant that there must only be one General left.

Ronan sprang back into action, hacking at the Shadows without end. Soon there was nothing between Ronan and the last of the Generals. The man opened his mouth and blew. Ronan watched as a thick green cloud flew from his mouth.

Reyna hissed, moving from somewhere behind Ronan to his side before he could comprehend the movement. She shoved him down, throwing her body on top of his.

"Do you have no regard for your life?" she raged.

"What?"

Reyna scowled, looking as furious as she had when she'd slapped the shit out of him. Once he got over the shock of it, he'd been rather impressed. No one had ever left such a perfect handprint on him for any amount of time, let alone the three hours hers took to even begin to fade.

"He was trying to poison you, or are you too stupid to notice?" Reyna snapped, pulling him back to the present.

Ronan pushed her off, rolling until he was above her. Reyna

squirmed beneath him, and Ronan gave her a look that had her going still.

"Thank you," he said dryly, before looking around to see where the General had moved to.

What he saw next had him jumping to his feet.

In the minute he'd been pushed to the ground, the world had gone to shit. Or part of it had. Everything that had come into contact with the General's plague cloud had withered and died. That included two of the Watchers that had been the closest. The ground was littered with Night Stalkers and Chosen alike, the rotting tree men standing over their bodies like morbid sentinels.

Reyna looked at the bodies of the dead, her own body vibrating with fury until wisps of shadow were floating away from her.

"Reyna," Ronan cautioned, seeing the General turn his attention back to them.

But she was already gone. Shadow-stepping to a place just behind the General, Reyna's daggers flashed as she slid the sharp surface along his neck. She was fast, but so was he. The General had time to puff out one final breath of toxic air. Ronan watched Reyna's eyes go wide, the whites showing as she fought against the General's grasp.

"No!" he roared, fear turning his blood to ice.

Reyna vanished, staggering when she reappeared beside him. Ronan looked at the once flawless face that twisted and sagged on one side, one of her forest green eyes now a milky white.

"Ronan?" she asked, her fear making her voice child-like.

Years of bearing witness to fatal injuries were all that helped him school his face. His expression gave nothing away. Scars meant little to him, he'd had his fair share for years before Helena had taken them away. He ran his hand along the uninjured side of her face, his fingers weaving into her hair to hold her still while he pressed a gentle kiss to the unmarred part of her forehead.

"Ronan?" she asked again, her fingers biting into his arms hard enough to bruise.

Before he could try to murmur nonsensical words of comfort, a scream of inhuman pain filled the air and the ground began to quake.

CHAPTER 30

Helena stretched her wings as she glided through the air, loving the feel of her powerful Talyrian form. The battle raged on below, her Chosen laying waste to the Shadow army. She watched from the sky as her friends took out Rowena's Generals, one after the other, and she itched to join them in battle. They were close, so close, to her finally being able to go after Rowena. She felt like a dog on a chain. The beast in her was eager to be unleashed, and the anticipation of being free was causing her blood to roar in her ears. Until the last one fell, she didn't want to risk getting too close. For all of the perks that came with being a Talyrian, she was also a much larger target.

While removed from the bulk of the fighting, Rowena was by no means idle. She was busy shouting orders and trying to replace her fallen Shadows by picking off the Chosen closest to her. A few had fallen from her efforts, but between the Talyrian fire and the speed with which the Generals were being taken out, Rowena could not balance out her losses. It was a fact that brought Helena no end of pleasure. For once they had finally taken, and managed to keep, the upper hand.

After sustaining the loss of two more Generals, the Corruptor was looking decidedly worse for wear. Her hair was falling around her face in limp strands and her pale complexion was a mottled red. She was furious and desperate, a dangerous combination.

Helena knew the moment Rowena decided to change her strategy. She abruptly stopped targeting the Chosen and scrambled her way to the top of another small hill, zeroing in on Helena. Unsure what to expect, Helena swooped down low, which proved to be a costly mistake.

Rowena's mouth fell open in a cruel smile when she saw Helena coming back into range. With a high-pitched scream, she unleashed a jet of corrupted Spirit aimed straight for Helena. Helena was able to easily dodge the first jet, but soon bolt after bolt was being flung her way. She ducked and wove, but it was soon impossible to navigate the sky as it became filled by the evil purple bolts. All Helena could rely on was instinct as she tried to avoid them, but eventually she chose to bank right when she should have dropped down. It was a move that allowed her to avoid one of the glowing jets only to end up flying headfirst into another. Seeing her error, Helena tried to jerk back, using her wings to pull her up, but it was too late.

Searing pain radiated from her chest, and Helena let out a surprised roar as she began to fall from the sky. As she fell, she heard Von echo her cry, his voice a blend of shock and pain as the blow reverberated through their bond. It wasn't just the physical pain they felt, it was the huge drain of power Helena experienced as a result of the leeching shadow bolt. *That thieving bitch just stole my power,* Helena thought with an angry snarl.

Rowena cackled manically, the injection of power more than enough to regenerate her depleted power stores.

Helena tried to beat her wings, but it was as if she'd lost the ability to control them. She continued to tumble through the sky, feeling her body fighting against the transformation back to human as she did. She started to feel true fear as the ground loomed closer. A fall from this height would mean only one thing unless she could find a way to cushion the landing. As she flipped through the air, she caught sight of Von's inky black hair as he raced across the ground.

"Helena!" he roared, his voice frantic.

The feeling of transition was disorientating. She was no longer full Talyrian, but not quite human either. Her golden wings had retracted, and her massive paws were already turning back into pale hands with glinting black claws. Her beautiful fur was gone, replaced by her fighting gear. While in the feline form, some of her senses had sharpened, almost like when she tapped into the sensory enhancement provided by her power, although not quite as potent. Her ability to tap into her rippling pool of power was also impossible in the Talyrian form. As a being made of magic, she supposed it made a certain kind of sense that she couldn't also manipulate it past the abilities already accessible in that form.

In a last-ditch effort, Helena tried to call her power up, but the partial shift was still cutting off her access. She sucked in a breath, at a loss for what to do. For it to end now… like this. The Mother couldn't possibly intend for it to end this way. She opened her mouth to vent her impotent rage the only way she could.

Instead of screaming, she gasped as her body was caught and then… bounced. Stunned, Helena froze, her hands splayed on something malleable and cool. She slowly twisted her neck, looking around her in wonder. A bubble of Air and Water held her suspended in the sky, slowing her descent as she floated the final feet to the ground.

"Mother keep you, Stormbringer," she groaned, dizzy with the relief she felt at Anduin's quick thinking.

She landed, and the bubble burst, releasing some of the wild power that was unique to the Vale. She was back on her feet only a heartbeat before Von reached her. His arms were around her, pulling her trembling, fully human body against him.

"I thought…" he stopped, unable to even utter the words. She didn't need them, the thundering beat of his heart and the icy terror blasting through their bond said more than enough.

"Me too," she whispered.

That was all there was time to say. This was still a battlefield, and Rowena was still very much alive. Fortunately for them all, so was she.

Helena stepped away from her Mate, feeling mostly centered, although a part of her still felt like it was trapped in an endless free fall.

She turned her attention to Rowena, whose malicious smile slipped slightly at the sight of an uninjured Helena.

"Why won't you die?" she screeched, pulling back her arm, ready to release another bolt.

Helena felt a sinister smile of her own stretch across her face. "The feeling is entirely mutual."

The sounds of battle raged on. The earth shook and Rowena doubled over with an inhuman wail. "No!" she cried.

There were only a few feet separating them now, and Helena could read every flicker of emotion that crossed Rowena's face. Helena knew there was only one thing that had the ability to cause the heartless bitch's eyes to widen like that. The last General had fallen. For the first time, Rowena looked truly afraid.

Perfect, the feral part of Helena purred.

Rowena licked her lips, her eyes wide as she cast them about her. "You can't beat me." Helena knew that she meant for the words to sound threatening, but her quavering voice did little to pull it off.

Helena lifted a brow. "Watch me."

WITH THE LAST of the Generals gone, only the Shadows and a handful of the most loyal Endoshans remained. As each General fell, more and more of the Shadows seemed to be breaking free from Rowena's mental hold. The loss of power was affecting her ability to contain them. Even now, more packs of the monsters fled from the battle.

Let them run, Ronan thought with a snarl. He would hunt every last one of them down until Elysia was freed from their taint.

He gently pushed Reyna back, his eyes scanning the field for any sign of his friends. His eyes found Serena's blonde head first. She was hacking away at one of the ambling Shadows, while her mate blasted another beast with Fire. Kragen and the Storm Forged were just past them on the left, using swirling waves of Water to topple Shadows and slowly drown them. Timmins and Joquil were working together to help get the fallen off of the field and out of harm's way. That only left Von and Helena unaccounted for.

The last time he saw her, Helena had been flapping massive golden wings and flying through the air between Starshine and Midnight. He looked toward the sky but did not see her. Ronan frowned.

"What is it?" Reyna asked, her husky voice coming out on a hiss of pain.

Ronan shook his head. It was too soon to say.

A familiar mop of hair caught his eyes at the bottom of a hill. Ronan breathed a sigh of relief. If Von was there, Helena must be nearby. There is no way he'd let her out of his sight once she was grounded.

He lifted his eyes up just in time to watch Helena slap away Rowena's arm.

It felt like the world stopped spinning, the moment suspended in time. At first there was nothing, and then a giant pulse of power knocked him off of his feet. He hit the ground with a grunt, Reyna landing in a sprawl beside him. Ronan shielded his eyes as blinding light shot from Helena's body, making it impossible for him to see what was happening.

"Mother's tits!" he shouted, surprise ripping the words from his chest without conscious thought.

Once the light faded, Ronan pushed himself up, holding out a hand to help pull Reyna back up. The Night Stalker eyed his hand as if debating whether she was going to accept the help.

"Take it," he growled.

For once she didn't argue. Her mismatched eyes blinked up at him, her thick lashes tangling at the tips. "Thank you," she murmured.

"You're welcome," he said more curtly than he intended. Ronan was torn between wanting to pick her up and take her somewhere safe, and wanting to run over to see if Helena was okay.

In the end, the choice was made for him. By the time he pulled his eyes away from Reyna, all that was left to do was watch in awe as one by one Shadows that had been frozen mid attack began to fall. As they hit the floor, their bodies exploded in a shower of dust until nothing but the floating black powder remained.

The Chosen had won.

Rowena's glacial blue eyes continued to flicker from side to side, her lips bracketing when she didn't find what she was looking for.

"You have something that belongs to me. I want it back," Helena snarled.

"No," Rowena hissed. "The power is mine. ELYSIA IS MINE!"

Helena borrowed a trick from Von and blinked until she was standing just behind the disheveled blonde. "You'll have to kill me first," she whispered in Rowena's ear.

Rowena's breath hitched, and she spun around, a bolt of power fizzling out as Helena slammed a palm into her arm to knock it away. Rowena's skin began to sizzle where Helena's hand pressed into it, and Rowena began to shriek in rage and pain.

Instinct guiding her, Helena wrapped her hand around the other woman's arm and held tighter. It was the first time they'd ever made any kind of physical contact, and Helena didn't think it was a coincidence. The longer she held on, the more disorientated she became. Rowena struggled against her, but Helena refused to let go even when she felt her own palm begin to blister from the searing heat.

Helena's eyes rolled back in her head, and she let out her own gasp of pain. All see could see was a yawning black chasm. There was nothing but endless darkness; a void that wanted her to sink beneath its weight. It pressed against her, making it hard to breathe. Her chest felt like it was being crushed in a vise, and her lungs were soon starving for air. She sucked in a breath that felt more like swallowing living flame.

Distantly, she thought she heard someone bellow her name, but she was frozen, poised on the edge of a cliff. If she let go, she would fall. Not just down on her knees in the dirt, but down into a never-ending pit. All she could do was hold on, hold tighter, as she clung to life. It was the only way to fight against the feeling of nothingness and despair.

For that's what the darkness was, Helena realized. It was the culmination of every terrible moment of her life played on an eternal loop. This was what it meant to be truly hopeless. It was then that Helena knew she was looking into Rowena's soul. Or rather, her lack of a soul. Whatever twisted things she'd done with her magic had taken the worst kind of toll. No wonder she needed so many Shadows and the Generals to empower her. She had nothing left. She was empty; a husk. There was only a void where what had made her human once resided. It made her more of a monster than her Shadows could ever be.

Helena grit her teeth, unwilling to ever go back to that place. The illusion of corruption had been more than enough for her. She had no intention of ever experiencing that again. Helena focused on Von. It was her love for him that brought her back from the brink once, she knew that he would be the one to help her break the spell again. She couldn't access their bond from this place, but the harder she focused, the easier it was to breathe. Soon she could feel him, like a warm and steady presence that surrounded her. Helena took her first full breath just as a speck of golden light found its way into the darkness.

Rowena continued to scream and thrash as the ground rolled beneath their feet. The sky broke in two as lightning snaked across the sky. A blinding white light burst from Helena as Rowena fell to her knees, her screams of pain drowned out by the roar of thunder.

The golden light grew brighter. The darkness began to roll back, repelled by the light. It slunk away, fading until it was less than the size of a pin, before vanishing completely.

Helena sagged, her hand falling away from Rowena's charred skin.

Rowena was curling into a ball, her body shaking. "What did you do? What did you do to me?" she screamed.

What was left of Rowena was ancient and ghastly. She was utterly ravaged. Her hair had fallen almost completely out, only a few stringy clumps remaining on her bloody scalp. Her body had sunken in on itself, making her look more corpse than living being, and her skin, where it still remained, was oozing. Even her eyes had changed, the colorless orbs crying tears of blood.

"Mother's tits!" The cry sounded behind her, but Helena didn't dare look away from Rowena.

"Nothing less than you deserve." Helena's voice was quiet, but there was no missing the menace in it. There would be no mercy here. The Mother's justice was upon them.

All that was left of the color in Rowena's face drained away. There was no way out of this, and she knew it. Helena didn't let the sight of Rowena's frail and shaking body sway her. She bent down until her nose was a mere breath away from Rowena's.

"This is what happens when you try to take what is mine." The words reverberated with the harmonious voice of her power.

Helena punched her Talyrian claw-tipped hand through Rowena's chest, listening to the wet crunch of her bones with satisfaction. She fisted it around the thumping muscle and jerked back until Rowena's still beating heart was laying in the palm of her hand.

There was a gurgle and bright red blood began to drip from Rowena's mouth.

"Elysia will never be yours," Helena spat, watching the rest of the life drain from Rowena's eyes. Her fist closed around Rowena's heart, crushing it into a fine red dust.

There was a final whistle of breath, but any words she wanted to say died with her.

The Corruptor was dead.

CHAPTER 31

"*L*ong live the Vessel!"

"Mother bless the Kiri!"

Helena smiled as she lifted her chalice to yet another toast. Beneath the table, Von wove his fingers between hers.

"That smile is as fake as the purple flames in the hearth."

Helena shuddered at the reminder. The Chosen had wanted to throw a feast to formally commemorate their victory over the Corruptor. It was a mandatory holiday, all able bodied people joining in the celebration at the Palace or holding their own, smaller parties at home. To that end, the ballroom had been decorated in shades of purple in her honor, but the smoldering purple flames left her tensing in her seat every time they caught her eye. She couldn't help but be reminded of the insidious shadow flames.

She loosed a breath before giving Von a smile that was more a baring of teeth than anything. *"It's not their fault."*

"Eleven hours of celebrating is taxing on the best of us."

Helena smirked. *"You'd never know it by looking at them."*

Von's eyes darkened as his expression grew somber. He brushed his thumb along the back of her hand. *"How are you feeling, Mira?"*

"Do you really need to ask?" Helena asked with a wry lift of her brow.

"You know I don't, but I figured it was politer to let you deny it if you weren't ready to talk."

Helena sighed. It wasn't the time or the place to get into the tangle of emotions she'd been wading through since the battle at Endoshan. *"I will be,"* she answered, negating the need to lie.

It was hard to relax or dance when a part of her was terrified that Rowena would walk through the door at any moment. She'd literally ripped the bitch's heart out, and yet she was afraid it was too good to be true. The woman had haunted her for months, it wasn't something she could let go of easily.

The excited cheers of her people drew her attention back to the dance floor. For the last hour, they'd been competing with demonstrations of their talents, each act a tribute to Helena's first year of reign. Of course, the only moment they seemed to want to recreate was that final bloody battle. It was… too soon.

Helena gripped Von's hand as another shudder wracked her body.

No one knew what Helena had experienced while facing down Rowena's darkness, or even when she came face-to-face with her own during the illusion. Helena didn't have the words to describe it, and the Circle had been too kind to ask more than once. She didn't doubt they had filled in the blanks on their own. That would have to be good enough. No one else needed the nightmares.

Kragen and Joquil were the de facto judges of the competition, Helena adamantly refused to participate, although only the Circle knew that. She watched as the two men crowned the trio who had done an interpretive dance of Helena taking down the Shadow Talyrians. She clapped politely alongside her Mate until the music resumed and the floor filled with dancing bodies.

"Care to dance?"

Helena was about to refuse, but resisted the urge. At least if she was pressed against him, she wouldn't have to be pretending to enjoy herself.

Von stood, pulling her behind him as they joined the others. There were cheers when the Chosen noticed their Kiri dancing alongside them. Von spun her in a slow circle before pulling her body close to his. They swayed slowly, completely ignoring the music's fast-paced tempo. Helena rested her head on Von's shoulder, her mind emptying of everything except the heat of his hands against the small of her back.

"I'm proud of you, Helena."

She pulled her head back to look up at him, her brows scrunching together.

"There are very few people that could face the darkest parts of themselves and walk away whole."

"Who says I did?"

"Me."

The unwavering conviction in his voice did her in. Her lower lip quavered.

Von dipped his head, stealing a kiss and her breath in one fell swoop. *"None of that, beautiful."*

The raucous cheering at their display of affection had Helena pulling back with a laugh, her cheeks tinged pink. Von winked, letting her know that had been his intention. Helena shook her head, before snuggling close once more.

"If I am unscathed, it is only because of you." Helena paused, taking a steadying breath before allowing herself to admit, *"There was a moment on that balcony when I couldn't have cared less what happened below, and then I saw those two Talyrians barreling toward you and it was like I snapped back. Not all of me, not right away, but the pieces that knew you were Mine."*

Von ran a hand along her back, his heart beating steadily beneath her ear. *"It was enough."*

"You were *enough. You are what keeps me whole. They might be cheering my name, but none of this would have been possible without you."*

Von's eyes glittered suspiciously, and he bent down for another kiss. His teeth grazed her lip as he went to deepen the kiss, but a not-so-discreet cough at her shoulder had them pulling away.

"I believe this dance belongs to me," Ronan said with a smug smile.

Von grunted, his arms tightening around her.

Ronan rolled his eyes. "You have your whole life to fondle my Kiri. Back off and let me dance with her."

Von flashed his teeth in a grin, giving Helena one last kiss before stepping away.

"Are you sure baiting him is a good idea? He's got a lot of free time on his hands these days," Helena asked, stepping into Ronan's arms.

Ronan snickered. "It's how he knows that I love him. Besides, the fucker bit me. He can deal with it."

Helena's head fell back as she laughed, a deep rolling belly laugh. By the time she caught her breath, Ronan was smiling at her.

"It's good to see you laughing again, Hellion."

The nickname had a breath catch in her throat.

"Since he isn't here to tell you, let me say it on his behalf. Your Shield—past, present, and future—are incredibly proud of you."

Helena swallowed back her emotion, opting for a more light-hearted response. "Speaking on behalf of my future Shield as well? Are you planning on being replaced?"

Ronan sputtered. "Replaced? Not even death can rip the title from me, Helena. This life and the next, you're stuck with me."

The tear fell down her cheek before she could try to blink it away. "Well, fuck Ronan. You had to go and make me cry, didn't you?"

Ronan's smile was soft as he pulled her close, shielding her teary eyes from the rest of the room. He dropped his head to whisper in her ear, "It's how you know I love you too."

HELENA STOOD at her window watching the festivities wage on. It had been two weeks since they returned to Tigaera victorious, and the jubilant cries of the Chosen had not stopped since.

Von's arm snaked about her waist, pulling Helena back against his chest.

"What reason could you possibly have to leave our bed?" he asked in a sleepy grumble as he pressed a kiss to her shoulder.

Helena smiled and gestured wordlessly to the dancing bodies below.

"Did they wake you? We can sic Ronan and Kragen on them if you want them to shut up."

Laughter bubbled up at the mental image that caused. "No, no. It's nothing like that." Helena's words faltered, and she shrugged, still smiling as she watched.

The truth was she hadn't been able to sleep for more than an hour or two at a time since they'd come home. Von would keep her awake for hours with his lovemaking until she finally passed out in a sweaty and satiated heap beside him, but inevitably, she would wake up when the same restless energy ate at her.

Von's hand found her hips and tugged her around until she was facing him. Brushing a thick curl from her face, he asked, "What's bothering you, my love?"

Helena shrugged, feeling foolish. Rowena was dead, they were alive. There was simply no explanation for her to feel anything less than ecstatic. But a part of her felt empty. For the first time since her arrival here almost a year ago, there was nothing for her to do.

Even her new friends were returning home when it became clear they could not justify their absences any longer. Anduin and his Storm Forged had left for the Vale a few days ago, with the Daejaran contingent not far behind them. The Caederans and Etillions left yesterday, promising that they would keep in better contact so that nothing like this could ever happen again. Only Reyna and a few of her Night Stalkers remained as guests at the Palace, but Helena thought that had more to do with a certain blue-eyed Daejaran than anything else.

Von laughed, picking up on the nameless emotions. "Can it be that my beautiful Mate is bored?"

She shook her head, intending to disagree but stopped short. Was she? What sense did that make?

In the immediate aftermath of Endoshan, Helena had felt only bone-deep satisfaction. Within a couple of days, the feeling had been replaced with a growing restlessness. She had tried to find an answer about what exactly had transpired when her skin had connected with Rowena's, but the best Timmins had been able to offer was a guess. It was his belief that in Rowena's desperation for power, she sacrificed part of her soul each time she used the corrupted Spirit magic. Eventually, there was nothing left but the void of the corruption within her and when it came into contact with the purity of Helena's completed soul, it shattered. Whether that was true, the Mother only knew, but it was as good an answer as they were going to get.

Either way, the result had been the same. The Shadows fell without Rowena's power to animate them, and without the strength of her Generals to protect her, Rowena was nothing more than a human woman. She was no match at all for the Mother's Vessel. Her death had been swift and total.

Helena frowned. Was that what was bothering her? That it had been over too quickly? After months of build-up, of single-minded focus and purpose, Rowena was dead. What was she supposed to do now?

Von's understanding smile let Helena know that she'd asked the question out loud.

"Whatever the fuck you want," he whispered, pressing a hot kiss to her mouth and making the breath leave her in a whoosh.

She chuckled as he grinned down at her. "Yes, but no one needs me anymore. I've never had a chance to do something just because I've wanted to."

Von frowned, his brows dipping low over his gray eyes. "I need you."

Helena pressed her palm to his scruffy cheek. "I need you too, my love. But that's not what I meant."

She'd grown used to the adventure and its accompanying race of adrenaline through her blood. The thought of only having her days filled with the monotonous tedium of being a political figurehead, even if her nights would be filled by her Mate, left her rather uninspired.

"Darling, no one is saying you have to keep yourself locked away in the Palace."

Interest piqued, she asked in an excited rush, "What are you thinking?"

Von grinned. "You've only seen a sliver of the land that you rule. You have new friends and allies that we can visit or we could go and meet the rest of your people. If that's not to your liking, I'm sure the pride will want to spend time with their newest member."

Helena's smile grew, her heart thumping excitedly at the thought of all the possible adventures that might still be ahead of them.

He ran his nose along hers, pressing a kiss to her cheek before whispering in her ear. "You made me a promise, Mate. Time for just the two of us once the war was over."

Helena's eyes flitted to the unmade bed and then the magically locked door. "What have we been doing these last two weeks?"

"You've been running off to spend time with your friends before they return home, answering Timmins's endless questions so that he could make the appropriate notes for the archives, holding court over your subjects, not to mention the time you spent helping Ronan train the new recruits," Von listed. "By the time I get you to myself, everyone else has all but exhausted you with their demands, but that ends now. You and I are going away."

Her pulse raced at his words. "We are?"

His eyes were molten when they met hers. "We are. Now pack." He slapped her ass once, and Helena's knees locked at the flood of heat that pooled between her legs as a result.

Von's nostrils flared, and his eyes darkened with arousal. "Hold that thought. I want us gone before anyone tries to distract you."

Her smile grew. "We aren't telling them we're leaving?"

Her Mate shook his head. "We'll leave them a note so they don't worry, but for the next few weeks, *Mira*, the only title you'll answer to is Mate, and your only responsibility will be to please me," he whispered, dipping his head for another scorching kiss before stepping away and quickly tossing some clothes in his pack.

Helena licked her lips, her mind going foggy. A different kind of restless heat wound its way through her body. One thing she definitely was not feeling right now was bored.

He lifted a brow when she didn't move. "You coming?"

"Not yet, but I intend to be shortly," she answered in a sexual purr as she slid past him, her pebbled nipples rubbing against his bare chest.

"Fuck it," Von said, grasping her around the legs and tossing her over his shoulder as he carried her back to their bed. "Ten minutes longer won't make a difference."

"Only ten minutes?" she pouted.

He slid his hands up her legs, pulling them wide to make room for him.

"You're insatiable," he murmured, running a calloused finger along her slick fold.

"It's your fault."

Von grinned. "Damn straight."

He slid his body up hers, stopping to kiss and nibble along the way.

"Please," she begged, pressing her hips against his to try to ease the pulsing ache at her center. "I need you."

"I will always need you," he whispered hotly, sliding home in one, hard thrust.

Helena shattered beneath him, wave after wave of her climax flooding through her body, and through their bond.

Von grit his teeth, furiously pumping into her as her inner muscles fluttered against his velvety length. Between her body, and the feeling of her orgasm through their bond, he was coming inside her with a shout only a few heartbeats later.

She wrapped her arms around his back, peppering kisses across the top of his Jaka. "You said ten minutes, we have at least five more."

Von snickered, still hot and thick inside of her. "Utterly insatiable," he growled, but it wasn't a complaint. He began to move again, long slow thrusts that had her toes curling and her back arching up and off the bed. Time lost all meaning as they worshiped each other with their bodies.

Ten minutes had come and gone a hundred times over before they finally made their way out of bed, and then out of the Palace. The future might be uncertain, but with her Mate at her side, there was absolutely no way she'd ever be bored.

RONAN LET the note fall to the floor with a disgusted snort.

"I can't believe they just left the rest of us here."

"You can't?" Reyna asked with an amused lift of her once again perfect brow. Helena had made a point to personally heal Reyna, removing all traces of the General's corruption. Ronan almost missed the scars. Scars were proof that you had fought and won. Reyna was a powerful woman; she would have borne her scars with pride.

His lips twisted in a wry grin. "All right, so maybe it's not that hard to believe."

Von and Helena had left a note saying only that they were going to be out of touch for a few weeks and that Ronan was in charge in their place. They didn't even leave a way for Ronan to reach them if something came up.

"I think she's earned her rest," Ronan finally said. No one in the Circle had spoken about the fact that Helena had come face first with the darkest parts of her soul, or that she had nearly succumbed to it. They also hadn't brought up her transformation, at least not in front of her. Whether it was a skill Helena still had access to, no one was certain. The popular belief was that the leftover power gifted to her by the rest of the Chosen had allowed her body to make the transition in response to her need to defend her Mate. It was just one more thing, in an already long list, that made Helena the most impressive Kiri the Chosen had ever seen.

Reyna murmured her agreement and made to stand as a knock sounded on the door. They shared a curious look as Ronan went to open the door.

Alina stood there, wringing her hands nervously. "A letter has arrived; it's addressed to the Kiri."

Ronan frowned, holding out his hand. "I'll take it."

Alina looked relieved as she handed it to him before bobbing a curtsey and scurrying away.

The thick green velum was expensive, and the scrawling text on the front was unfamiliar.

Without waiting, Ronan peeled back the seal and quickly read the text, his amusement fading with each new sentence.

Reyna read over his shoulder, her expression a twin to his own.

"We've been summoned," Ronan said.

"What do you think it means?" Reyna asked, already walking with him as they went to find the remaining Circle members.

Ronan shrugged. "Effie wouldn't have sent it if she didn't need our help. It can't possibly be good."

"That's what I was afraid of," Reyna said with a sigh.

Ronan lifted his brow. "You don't have to come, Night Stalker. This is Circle business."

Reyna scowled at him. "As if I would let you wander around Bael unprotected."

"Worried about me?" he asked with a smug, purely masculine smile.

Reyna rolled her eyes, calling over her shoulder as she walked away, "I already told you, Shield. I'm not done with you yet."

Ronan's smile grew as he watched Reyna's swaying hips. After a moment, he shook his head, pulling himself out of his reverie. Following her, he let out a low whistle before muttering under his breath. "Mother's tits, this is going to be fun."

EPILOGUE

The Triumvirate stood overlooking their favorite cliff, their faces tilted up toward the stars.

"The pieces are finally in place."

"Is she ready?"

"The first step has already been made."

Their cloaks billowed around them as the wind swept up.

"There is much she must learn."

"We will teach her."

"She is stubborn and unfocused."

"She doesn't trust us."

"It doesn't matter; she is where she was destined to be."

"The rest will soon fall into place."

The scrape of a boot against a rock had the three figures twisting toward the mouth of the cave.

"What are you doing out here?" an annoyed voice snapped.

"Daughter." As always, it was impossible to tell which of the three figures was speaking.

Effie grit her teeth, her blonde hair flying around her in the breeze. "I told you to stop calling me that. I am *not* your daughter."

The central figure shrugged. *"And yet here you are."*

"Because you promised you'd teach me," she shouted, frustration and grief twisting her face. It had been weeks since she'd joined the Keepers and she was no closer to understanding her visions or fighting off the horrible side effects. All she felt was more desperately alone than ever.

"Then perhaps it's time we begin."

NOTE FROM MEG

Thank you so much for taking the time to read Von and Helena's journey! These were the first books I ever wrote (and published) and it constantly amazes me that something that came to me in a dream turned out to be so much more than I ever anticipated. And it's all because of readers like you.

Every author will tell you that they look back at their early works and cringe because of how much they have learned and grown since those stories were published. I'm no different, but that doesn't change how deeply I love these characters or this world. I find it endlessly humbling when others tell me they feel the same. The Chosen will always be special to me. I don't think this is a world I will ever leave completely.

Until next time, happy reading!

♥ Meg Anne

If you enjoyed this book, please consider writing a short review and posting it on Amazon, Bookbub, Goodreads and/or anywhere else you share your love of books. Reviews are very helpful to other readers and are greatly appreciated by authors. (Especially this one!)

Want to know when I have a new release or get exclusive access to my newest works? Join my mailing list:

MegAnneWrites.com/Newsletter

ALSO BY MEG ANNE

FANTASY ROMANCE

THE CHOSEN UNIVERSE

THE CHOSEN

MOTHER OF SHADOWS

REIGN OF ASH

CROWN OF EMBERS

QUEEN OF LIGHT

THE KEEPERS

THE DREAMER – A KEEPERS STORY

THE KEEPER'S LEGACY

THE KEEPER'S RETRIBUTION

THE KEEPER'S VOW

PARANORMAL & URBAN FANTASY ROMANCE

THE GYPSY'S CURSE

CO-WRITTEN WITH JESSICA WAYNE

VISIONS OF DEATH

VISIONS OF VENGEANCE

VISIONS OF TRIUMPH

CURSED HEARTS: THE COMPLETE COLLECTION

THE GRIMM BROTHERHOOD

CO-WRITTEN WITH KEL CARPENTER

REAPER'S BLOOD

Reaping Havoc

Reaper Reborn

Undercover Magic

Hint of Danger

Face of Danger

World of Danger* *Pre-order*

Anthologies

The Monster Ball Year 2

**contains Undercover Magic prequel novella, Shade of Danger, which takes place after events in The Keeper's Vow*

ABOUT THE AUTHOR

Meg Anne has always had stories running on a loop in her head. They started off as daydreams about how the evil queen (aka Mom) had her slaving away doing chores; and more recently shifted into creating backgrounds about the people stuck beside her during rush hour. The stories have always been there; they were just waiting for her to tell them.

Like any true SoCal native, Meg enjoys staying inside curled up with a good book and her cat Henry . . . or maybe that's just her. You can convince Meg to buy just about anything if it's covered in glitter or rhinestones, or make her laugh by sharing your favorite bad joke. She also accepts bribes in the form of baked goods and Mexican food.

Meg loves to write about sassy heroines and the men that love them. She is best known for her adult fantasy romance series The Chosen, which can be found on Amazon.

9 781951 738907